51 STO SAP

HIS ONE-MAN OMNIBUS OF THRILL AND ADVENTURE

H&S

HODDER AND STOUGHTON

LTD · LONDON

British Library Cataloguing-in-Publication Data
A catalogue record for this book is available from
the British Library

H. C. McNeile

Herman Cyril McNeile was born on 28th September 1888, in Bodmin, England. His father, Malcolm McNeile was a captain in the Royal Navy, but at the time of Cyril's birth, was the governor of Bodmin Naval Prison.

McNeile attended a prep school in Eastbourne before his secondary education at Cheltenham College. He then enrolled at the Royal Military Academy, Woolwich, where he began his training for the armed forces. By 1914 he had reached the rank of captain and travelled to France as part of the British Expeditionary Service to fight in the First World War.

McNeile's writing career began in 1915 when the Daily Mail serialised *Reminiscences of Sergeant Michael Cassidy*. He wrote under the pseudonym "Sapper" due to British Army personnel being barred from publishing under their real names. "Sapper" was a fitting pen name because it echoed the nickname of "Sappers" given to the Royal Engineers of which McNeile was part.

He continued to write throughout the war, publishing the short story collections *Sergeant Michael Cassidy, R.E.* (1915), *The Lieutenant and Others* (1915), Men, *Women, and Guns* (1916), *No Man's Land* (1917), and *The Human Touch* (1918). During this period he saw action at Ypres and the Battle of the Somme. He was also awarded the Military Cross and was mentioned in despatches.

McNeile's most famous creation was that of Bull—Dog Drummond in 1920. Drummond was an ex-army captain with a thirst for adventure and defeating bad guys. This character went on to appear in ten full-length novels by McNeile and several further works by Gerard Fairlie. He was also adapted into a series of Hollywood films.

McNeile died in 1937 of cancer, possibly caused by inhalation of gas during the war. He had a funeral with full military honours at Woking crematorium.

INTRODUCTION

IT is an easy matter, comparatively, to write an introduction for the other fellow's book. Such phrases
as—"lucid style," "gripping interest," "not a dull
moment from cover to cover," etc., flow easily from the
pen. The trouble is that any such expressions concerning one's own work would lead, quite rightly, to expul-
sion from one's club, and immediate prosecution for
endeavouring to obtain money under false pretences.

So what is the alternative? To say that the contents
of the volume furnish one more proof, if another be
needed, that under no circumstances should the author
ever be allowed to write again, might well result in
slightly strained relations. And though that would not
be the case when introducing one's own work, I feel
that the publishers might justifiably feel a little annoyed.
It is, after all, tantamount to saying that they should
be put under restraint as well as myself.

I will, therefore, try to steer a middle course in asking
you to believe that the man at the piano has tried to do
his best. And so, if from the following pages my
readers get an occasional thrill, an occasional laugh,
or even an occasional tear, it must serve as my excuse
for collecting these stories together in one volume.

LIST OF STORIES

	PAGE
Out of the Blue	9
The Film that was Never Shown	24
A Funny Little Man	41
Uncle James's Golf Match	58
Mark Danver's Sin	78
The Missing Line	96
Stubby	117
Bulton's Revenge	136
Coincidence	152
The Porterhouse Steak	171
The Old Dining-Room	190
When Greek meets Greek	206
Jimmy Lethbridge's Temptation	227
The Man who could not get Drunk	247
The Saving Clause	266
The Rubber Strap	282
Rout of the Oliver Samuelsons	300
Cynthia Delmorton's Mistake	321
The Eleventh Hour	339
Three of a Kind	354
The Finger of Fate	375
The Diamond Hair-slide	395
The Black Monk	414
The Hidden Witness	438

PAGE

Will You Walk Into My Parlour ? 457
A Hopeless Case 476
The Undoing of Mrs. Cransby 492
A Question of Mud 510
That Bullet Hole has a History 528
Fer de Lance 546
The Man in Ratcatcher 563
The House by the Headland 585
The Man who would not Play Cards . . . 603
A Question of Personality. 623
The Unbroken Line 646
The Real Test 665
"Good Hunting, Old Chap" 684
The Man with His Hand in His Pocket. . . 702
A Payment on Account 721
The Message 744
Two Photographs 761
A Matter of Voice 778
A Native Superstition 796
Blackmail 816
Mrs. Peter Skeffington's Revenge . . . 832
Marie 851
The King of Hearts. 869
The Other Side of the Wall 889
The Haunting of Jack Burnham 906
The Professor's Christmas Party . . . 928
The Impassive Footman 947

BASIL PENDER looked thoughtfully round his sitting-room. Everything was just as usual—the prints, the photographs in their silver frames on the piano, the books in the corner: they were all just as they had been for the last five years. To-morrow night also there would be no change. The same prints, the same books, the same ceaseless rumble of London traffic coming through the open window.

To-morrow night it was true he would not be there himself. It was unfortunate but unavoidable. He would have liked to have spent the first few hours after he had murdered Sinclair in the surroundings where he had so often murdered him in spirit. But it was impossible.

It was something at any rate to have been able to begin his scheme in this familiar atmosphere. It augured well for success. No undue hurry: nothing precipitate—just the quiet, orderly, working out of a carefully considered plan. And the first move in the game had already been taken.

Such a simple little move—and yet very important. It was in details of that sort where brain came in. Who would possibly attach any significance whatever to the fact that he had removed one of his two cars from the garage where he habitually kept them both, and placed it in another, where he was quite unknown? What had such a simple fact to do with murder?

He smiled gently, as he helped himself to a whisky and soda. He was thinking of the conversation he had been listening to at the club only that very evening. Cresswell, of the police, had been holding forth on crime; and an intolerable bore he was. And yet there had been a certain amount of truth in what he had said.

Undoubtedly the motive in a case of murder is the first thing for which the police look. No one but a madman commits murder without a motive. Passion, hatred, money—once the motive is established, it generally points with an unerring finger at someone. That was why Pender had left the club arm in arm with Sinclair, and walked with him part of the way to his house in Brook Street. A very normal proceeding on the part of one of Sinclair's best friends.

He'd been devilish clever about it. No one knew, no one had even the ghost of a suspicion of the deadly, black-hearted hatred he felt for the man he had just left. The world thought they were friends: even Sinclair himself thought so—damned fool that he was. It would come as a slight shock to him to-morrow when he realized the truth.

But no one else would ever know it. And in case his plan, thought out and perfected in every little detail since he had heard that Sinclair was going down alone to his empty house in Kent—just in case it miscarried, the question of motive would never indicate him with unerring finger. He was safe on that point.

Not that the matter was ever likely to arise in this case. Before people begin talking about motive it must look as if the cause of death was murder. And he had no intention of allowing Sinclair's death to look like murder. It was to be accidental: a shocking, ghastly accident. He pictured himself hurrying back from

Scotland when he heard the terrible news: comforting Enid—Sinclair's wife.

Widow, rather—not wife: Sinclair's widow. Just his card to start with: his card and a little message of tender sympathy for her in her great sorrow. Perhaps some flowers. And then after a week or so he would see her for a few minutes, and let her realize how his heart bled for her. Nothing precipitate, of course, he was far too old a stager with women for that. But in six months perhaps—or maybe a year—the time would be ripe.

Basil Pender's white teeth bared in a sudden ungovernable snarl. What waste of time! Six weeks, six minutes were too long to wait. How dared that swine Sinclair come between him and Enid? How dared he make her his wife?

The sweat glistened on his forehead, and he shook his fists in the air. Then with a great effort he controlled himself: this was a frame of mind in which he had forbidden himself to indulge. It destroyed the power of clear thought, and clear thought was essential for success. After all, the perpetration of a murder was very much like a game of chess. Move followed move, and provided no mistake was made the result was mate. And there would be no mistake in this case.

Nerve, brain, and money: given those three attributes and the thing was easy. But it was interesting— devilish interesting. The whole thing had a fascination about it which he would hardly have believed possible. Once again his thoughts drifted back to Cresswell: what was it he had been saying? He could see him now with a fat cigar between his lips, lying back in his chair and emphasizing his points with a podgy finger.

"It's those unexpected, unlooked for, unallowed for,

isolated facts against which no criminal can guard, however skilfully he lays his plans. He may think that he has allowed for everything—taken into account every possible contingency, then suddenly—out of the blue —comes one disconnected event, and the whole carefully-thought-out scheme goes wrong."

Well, of course, there was something in that. But the same might be said of anything in life: not only crime. And in this case he had reduced the risk of anything unexpected happening to a minimum. There was nothing difficult about his scheme, in fact, it was extraordinarily simple. It amused him now to recall the complicated plans he had evolved in the past for killing Sinclair. For years he had hated him: from the days they were at school together he had hated him. And then, to cap everything, he had married Enid. It was that which had definitely suggested murder to his mind.

At first he had hardly treated the matter seriously. Idly he had thought out different schemes—schemes of all sorts and descriptions which had, however, one common factor. Each one of them ended in the same way—with Sinclair's death. And gradually the matter had insisted upon being taken seriously. He found himself thinking of it at all hours of the day. If he woke in the night the picture of Sinclair with Enid by his side would come to him out of the darkness.

But it is one thing to think of murder: to do it is altogether different. Murderers who get caught suffer an unpleasant fate, and Pender had no intention whatever of being hanged. And since in all his schemes the risk of his suffering that fate had been pronounced, they had remained just schemes. And then suddenly three days ago had come the idea. He had been dining with the Sinclairs, and the conversation had turned on White Lodge, their house in Kent. It had been in the hands of the builders; new bathrooms put in, fresh papers, all sorts of improvements. And now it was empty; the workmen had gone; the keys had been returned to Sinclair.

"A darned good job they have made of it, too," his host had said. "I've got to go down there on Thursday to get a gun of mine which I forgot to bring up with me. Why don't you come down with me, Basil? I know Enid can't: she's got some show on that day. We could take down some sandwiches, and feed in the hall; and we'll test the new broadcasting set."

It had been some power outside his own that had made him answer as he did. At that moment the devilish idea had not come to him; he was only conscious of a strong desire to make some excuse to avoid spending a day alone with Sinclair. If Enid had been going it would have been different.

"Thanks very much," he had remarked, "but I shall probably be starting for Scotland on Thursday."

No more had been said: he usually did go to Scotland about that time: there was nothing strange or unusual in the fact. But when he returned to his rooms the idea had been born. He had not been going to Scotland on Thursday, but he had said so—said so in front of Enid. And Sinclair was going to White Lodge on Thursday—an empty house. He knew White Lodge well; he had stayed there in the past. It was a desolate sort of place, half a mile from the road and surrounded by trees. Enid had wanted her husband to sell it, but it had a sentimental attraction for him, and he had compromised by having it completely done up. And suddenly there had recurred to his mind a remark he had heard her make when she first saw the house.

"It looks the sort of place where anything might happen—murder or ghosts."

Murder! Strange that she should have said that.

Almost prophetic. Murder! For a moment or two he had recoiled from the thought: this was different to the fantastic schemes he had so often planned out in the past. This was the real thing: he knew that with a sort of blinding certainty even before he began to think out details. Well—what if it was? Step by step he had worked it out—discarding here, building up there. And after a while he became almost staggered with the simplicity of the thing. Surely murder must be a more complicated matter than this?

Coolly and logically he had examined every move, and could find no fault. And now once more on Wednesday night he strove to discover a flaw. It was not too late yet: he had done nothing incriminating so far. He had merely removed one of his two cars to a strange garage, and mentioned at the club that he was off to Scotland next morning. It was perfectly easy to return the car to its usual home and change his mind about Scotland.

And the other two things—the tiny phial filled with a colourless liquid, and the four short straps now reposing in the locked drawer of his desk. There was nothing suspicious about them. No question of poison —nothing so crude as that. Poison lingers in the system, and chemists ask questions if you ask them for poison. But a strong sleeping draught is quite a normal affair; and straps of all sorts and conditions are useful for motoring.

No; there was no flaw. And with a smile of satisfaction Pender turned out the light in his sitting-room and went to bed.

It was to his permanent garage that he repaired in the morning, and five minutes later he drove away in his touring Sunbeam. He left it in Waterloo Place, and getting into a taxi he gave the address of the second garage.

"Just starting for Scotland," he informed the manager, and having settled his bill he drove round to his rooms for luggage. It was early yet for much traffic, and half an hour saw him not far from his destination —Hitchin. And in Hitchin, strange and peculiar magneto trouble occurred—due doubtless to the use of a screwdriver in skilful hands on that delicate piece of mechanism. So pronounced was the trouble, however, that it became necessary to invoke the assistance of a local garage. And with becoming gravity Pender listened to the diagnosis.

"I see," he said, when the mechanic had finished. "Possibly some hours, you say. Then I think that I will go out and call on friends and return later. I might even stay the night with them. That will give you plenty of time to make a good job of it."

With which remark he left the garage, and made his way to the station where he took a first-class return ticket to London. The excellent train service was one of the reasons which had made him decide on Hitchin. It was not too close into London, but the journey did not take long. And it was essential that he should be at the White House before lunch-time.

He ran over the car time-table as he sat in his corner seat. He would take the Sunbeam from Waterloo Place, and motor down to White Lodge in it. He knew the exact spot where he would leave it—not too near the house, not too far away. A deserted spot where the chances of the car being seen were remote. And even if it was seen, who would pay any attention?

Then after it was over he would return to London, and leave it in St. James's Square. Not Waterloo Place again; the man in charge there might recognize him. And then back to Hitchin by train. It would depend on the time whether he telephoned to his usual garage from there, or from some place farther north.

"Completely forgot the Sunbeam; send a man round to St. James's Square for it."

That would be the message; further proof that he was on his way to Scotland. But he couldn't have done it if both cars had been at the same place. It looks silly to get one car to start with and then go back a few minutes later to get the other.

Brain—that was it; that was the whole secret. Just like chess, only a thousand times more fascinating.

It was just half-past eleven as he drove past the Oval. He had an hour's run before him, and it struck him that he could not have timed it better. Sinclair was dining at Ranelagh that evening, so he wouldn't be remaining too late at White Lodge. And anyway the sooner the thing was done the better. It would enable him to get farther on the Great North Road before calling up his garage.

He left the car in the place he had decided on. Not a soul was in sight; for the last two miles he had seen no one. The house was a hundred yards away, almost hidden in the trees, and he strolled towards it quite openly.

There was a possibility that Enid might have altered her mind at the last moment, or that Sinclair had brought someone else down with him. If so, he was not committed to anything; therein lay the beauty—the simplicity of the scheme. He had merely changed his mind about Scotland, and having nothing better to do had run down to see the improvements at White Lodge as Sinclair had suggested.

At the front door stood Sinclair's car, and as Pender stepped on to the drive Sinclair himself appeared.

"Hullo! old man," he cried. "I thought you were on the road to Scotland."

"Changed my mind at the last moment," said Pender easily, "so I thought I'd come down and see the house."

"But where's your car?"

"I stupidly missed the turn out of the village, and got on to the track leading through the copse. It's up there now."

"Well, it's quite safe there, anyway. Let's have some lunch, and then I'll show you round."

"All alone?" asked Pender.

"Yes, Enid couldn't come."

He was rummaging in the car for sandwiches, and Pender turned away quickly. So it was the end after all, and at the moment he did not want Sinclair to see his face.

"Come on in. There is enough grub here for a regiment, and I'll search round and get another glass."

He led the way to the gun-room, leaving his flask on the table. Then he went out, and Pender heard him wandering round the back premises. Now that the actual time had come he felt as cool as ice: it was all so simple and easy. From his pocket he took the little phial, and taking out the stopper he emptied the contents into the flask. Then slipping the empty phial back in his pocket he strolled over to the window.

"This is about the only room in the house they haven't touched," said Sinclair, as he came in with a glass a few moments later. "I left everything as it was in here —guns and all. Say when."

"I won't have any whisky, thanks. Just a little of that Perrier."

"Well, I've got a thirst on me like the devil," said the other, mixing himself a drink. "Get on with the sandwiches."

Sinclair drained his glass with a sigh of relief, and proceeded to mix himself another.

"They really have made a very good job of it. The extra bathrooms make the whole difference."

"Excellent," said Pender.   "I shall look forward to having a go at your pheasants later on."

His eyes, narrowed and expectant, had seen the sudden half-drunken lurch given by Sinclair.

"Good Lord, Pender," he cried, "I feel damned funny."

"Take another drink.   It may be the heat or something."

"I feel—absolutely—blotto.   It can't be anything—anything—matter—whisky."

He looked stupidly across the table, and then his eyes closed and his head fell forward.   With a gigantic effort he rose to his feet, only to fall back in his chair again.   Sinclair slept.

With a faint smile Pender got up: the thing was done.   There were one or two small points now to be attended to, but the main thing was done, and more successfully and easily than he had ever dared to hope.

First he took from his pocket a pair of wash-leather gloves, and picking up his glass he dried it carefully with a clean pocket handkerchief.   Then leaving the room he returned it to its proper place in the pantry.   Next he took up the flask, and Sinclair's tumbler, and emptied the contents of both down the sink, afterwards replacing them on the table beside the unconscious man.   To give the impression that the flask had been emptied would make the accident seem more credible.   Just a little too much to drink: just enough to make Sinclair a trifle careless. . . .

Then from his pocket he removed four straps, and still retaining his gloves he fastened Sinclair's hands and feet to the arms and legs of the chair in which he was sprawling.   He wasn't quite sure how long it would be before Sinclair recovered from the effect of the sleeping draught, and the binding process must be done before that happened.

And now remained only the final thing. From the glass-fronted cupboard in the corner he took a double-barrelled gun, and into one of the barrels he slipped a cartridge. Sinclair still slept.

For a moment or two Pender hesitated. It would be so easy to do it now. And it would be safer. Everything had gone so wonderfully that it seemed like tempting Fate to delay. There sat the man he hated, unconscious, and at his mercy. He had only to press the trigger and the thing would be done. But where would be the satisfaction in that? He wanted Sinclair to understand—to realize what was going to happen to him. He wanted revenge, and to kill an unconscious man was no revenge. He wanted to see terror dawn in those keen blue eyes: above all, he wanted to speak about Enid.

Half an hour passed and Sinclair still lolled forward in his chair, while Pender sat opposite him—waiting. And then suddenly the sleeper awoke and stared dazedly across the table.

"Where am I?" he muttered foolishly. "What's happened?"

"You are at White Lodge, Sinclair," said Pender quietly. "And I gave you a little drug to send you to sleep which seems to have acted admirably."

"But why am I bound like this?" He was struggling against the fog in his brain.

"Because, before I kill you, I want to have a talk with you, Sinclair. And I adopted that method to ensure your keeping still."

Sinclair blinked foolishly. Kill! What the devil was Pender talking about? Kill! Was he mad? Were they both mad?

"Doubtless you feel a little surprised, Sinclair. You wonder if you are still dreaming. But I can assure you that you are not: you are very much awake."

"Is this some damned silly jest, Pender?" His mind was clearing rapidly. "If so, it's gone far enough. And what the devil is that gun doing on the table?"

"We will come to the gun in due course, my friend." Pender leaned across the table, and his teeth showed in a sudden snarl. "You swine; I can hardly believe that I've got you at last."

Sinclair said nothing; full realization of his position had come to him. Of course the man had gone off his head; he was alone—bound and powerless—with a homicidal maniac.

"Please don't think that I'm mad, Sinclair," continued Pender, as if divining his thoughts. "I can assure you that I've never been saner in my life. This is merely the logical outcome of the intense hatred I've felt for you for years. It started at school, Sinclair. Do you remember on one occasion thrashing me till I was almost unconscious?"

"Because you came for me with a knife," answered the other quietly.

"I don't care why—but the fact remains that you thrashed me. That started it, Sinclair; I swore then that some day I'd get my own back."

"In spite of the fact that you shook hands the next day," said Sinclair scornfully. "You rotten Dago."

"So you always called me—all you fellows." Pender's voice shook with ungovernable rage. "Do you suppose I could help having South American blood in me? Anyway, the rotten Dago has got the upper hand now."

He controlled himself and went on quietly.

"As I say, that started it, Sinclair. And all through school it was the same. It was Sinclair, Captain of the Eleven; Sinclair, Captain of the Fifteen; Sinclair, Senior Prefect. And it was Sinclair who in his kindly benevolence accorded his divine protection to the rotten

Dago. Do you think I liked you for it, you swine? I loathed you all the more. There's no good straining at those straps. They're new and strong."

"You entrancing exhibition of beastliness," roared Sinclair. "Do you mean to tell me that after all these years—after having dined in my house, and eaten my salt—you propose to kill me, because I did better than you at school?"

"Good heavens, no! I was merely starting at the beginning. I don't deny that frequently I have felt like murdering you. At country houses sometimes when it's been Sinclair who was shooting so wonderfully— and Sinclair who played polo so marvellously—and Sinclair this, and Sinclair that—I could have killed you willingly. But I don't think I should ever have done it but for one thing—Enid."

Sinclair sat very still; he understood at last. And though no sign of it showed on his face, fear was clutching at his heart. No maniac this, but a dangerous, revengeful man.

"Did you know I asked her to marry me, Sinclair? Of course you do. And she refused. But she might have accepted me in time if you hadn't come on the scene. Always you; always you. She is the only woman in the world, Sinclair, whom I have ever wished to make my wife. And she is yours."

"So that is why you propose to murder me," said Sinclair. "A nice method of disposing of a husband, but as a means of endearing yourself to the widow— a trifle crude."

He was talking for time—trying desperately to think.

"And do you really imagine, Sinclair, that I shall let Enid discover the truth? You must have a very poor opinion of my intelligence. Your death will be entirely accidental, and when I hear about it in Scotland I shall hurry back to attend the—er—obsequies. I am on my way to Scotland now, you know."

"You fool," said Sinclair harshly. "They'll catch you for a certainty, and you'll hang."

"I think not," answered Pender. "I have devoted what brains I possess to this problem, and I venture to think—not unsuccessfully. You've no idea how fascinating it is—planning a murder. I won't weary you with the precautions I have taken to cover my tracks, but you can see for yourself two or three little things I have done in this room. My glass removed, for instance; a second glass would certainly give rise to comment. Your flask emptied, serving the double purpose of removing all traces of the drug and giving the impression that you had drunk a little too much. It will help to account for the accident that is shortly going to happen, Sinclair. A strange accident for such a careful shot as you—but these things will happen."

Sinclair moistened his lips.

"Cut fooling, Pender. This thing has gone far enough."

"I can promise you it is going considerably farther," sneered the other. "Right through to the end, in fact. That gun is loaded, and in a moment or two now I shall put the muzzle under your chin and blow your damned face off. An accident in cleaning will be the verdict, Sinclair, and I'll attend your funeral even as I attended your wedding. And then in time maybe Enid will do what she would have done if you hadn't come on the scene—marry me."

"You devil." The veins stood out like whipcord on Sinclair's forehead as he strained and tugged at the straps. And then of a sudden he sat very still: Pender had picked up the gun in his gloved hands. The end was very near, and with his head thrown back and a look of utter contempt in his eyes he waited for it.

"The straps will be off when they find you, Sinclair: the gun on the floor at your feet. No unexpected, unlooked-for event out of the blue, such as that fool Cresswell talked about, to save you: nothing to incriminate me."

The hatred in his eyes was maniacal: the cool scorn on the other's face seemed to drive him to a frenzy.

"You can sneer," screamed Pender, "but you won't when the muzzle is an inch from your chin and my finger is on the trigger. This is the position, Sinclair —just as I am now, only it will be your chin, not mine."

He sat there, the gun between his knees, his chin almost resting on the muzzle.

"Just like this," he repeated softly.

"Hullo!"

It came from the hall—a man's cheerful hail, and Pender gave a violent start.

"Hullo! Hullo!"

Then a pause.

"2 L O calling."

But there was no one to listen to the prominent politician's speech on the Near East which continued cheerfully for the next half-hour.

For Sinclair—well, Sinclair had fainted for the first time in his life.

And Pender—well, Pender had had his finger—that carefully gloved finger—near the trigger when he gave that violent start. And his chin had been almost resting on the muzzle.

In fact, it was only by his clothes that a few hours later he was officially identified as Pender.

II   THE FILM THAT WAS NEVER SHOWN

I

THE Trade Show was just over. The leading man and the leading lady, having watched themselves for two hours on the screen, had appeared before the audience in the flesh. The producer had come on to the stage and bowed. And finally the man who had expended well over forty thousand pounds on the production came on and bowed also.

At each separate rise of the curtain renewed applause broke out from the audience. There was no doubt that "Loaded Dice," in spite of its somewhat melodramatic name, was something distinctly out of the ordinary. Hardly a dissentient voice was to be heard amongst the hundreds of critical spectators who had been invited to the Alhambra to see the first public exhibition. Actors, authors, film-stars, and—most critical of all—other producers agreed that "Loaded Dice" was an exceptionally fine film, brilliantly acted and lavishly staged.

Carlton Bellairs, the leading man and a London actor-manager of note, had fully sustained his great reputation in a strong emotional part; Sylvaine Lankester, the leading lady, had supported him with her usual consummate ability. And quite up to their standard had been John Drage, who was the third of the principals.

The action of the film had revolved round these three. Not for one moment had the interest flagged through the whole six reels. A few side issues had been introduced principally for the purpose of showing some wonderful photographs of Italian and Egyptian scenery; but only a few. The film required no padding. Right from the start it led steadily and inexorably to the final clash between the two men for the possession of the girl. One knew it was coming, and yet—so good was the story—one never wanted to get on quicker; to skip, as one might say in book parlance.

And when it finally came it held one breathless, principally because of the marvellous acting. To write it may render it banal; its very essential lay in the unspoken horror and tragedy of the scene. Carlton Bellairs, of course, was acting the part of the hero, Hubert Malden, and Sylvaine played the girl, Mary Maxwell. John Drage, the other principal, was in popular phraseology the villain, Edward Latford. And the final scene took place in Mary's villa at Florence. She was seated with Hubert Malden on a sofa in the drawing-room, thinking that at long last their troubles were over. Edward Latford had, as they thought, been finally disposed of, and she had just promised to marry Hubert.

And after a while he had risen and pressed the bell for the butler to bring tea. They were secure; they were in love; everything was wonderful. And in that mood they waited for the tea, while we who looked on, keyed up with excitement, waited, too. At last the door opened; doubtless the butler bringing tea. The happy couple on the sofa moved decorously apart, and even as they did so a shadow was thrown on the wall—a shadow which they could not see but which we could. It was the shadow of an arm outstretched a little, and a revolver was in the hand. Slowly the shadow moved forward until the body appeared, and then finally the man himself. Still the pair on the sofa waited in blissful ignorance; only we knew that it was not the butler, but Edward Latford. And on his face there blazed a look of fanatical hate.

Suddenly he swung round the door, and they saw

him. For a moment they held the position, and we had time to see the superb acting of all three. Speechless horror by the girl; a momentary indecision by the hero before he flung himself at the villain; blazing fury by the villain. Then the villain fired, and the hero pitched forward on his face. The scene faded out, and then showed again to let us see that the villain had turned his revolver on his own head and committed suicide.

Such, in brief, was the climax up to which a very remarkable film led. I have no intention of telling any more of the story; when "Loaded Dice" is released in due course the public may see it for themselves. But it has been necessary to give this one scene, in order to make clear the extraordinary statement which was made to me that evening by a wild-eyed man in a little restaurant in Soho. I still cannot make up my mind as to whether his story was the truth or not, though some day, if I am in Italy with time to spare, I may test it. Certain it is that this man knew all that there was to be known of the inside of the film business; that he had either acted himself, or, at any rate, worked in some capacity in a studio admits of no doubt. I know sufficient of the game myself to feel assured of that. But whether he was what he said he was, or whether he was partially demented and had imagined it, I know not. Those who are interested can read on and judge for themselves.

The audience was thinning out when I first saw him. Little knots of people stood about discussing the film, and in the centre of one group stood Sylvaine Lankester, receiving the congratulations she richly deserved.

"Magnificent, my dear," said one woman, and a general murmur of assent followed—a murmur which was broken by a harsh, discordant laugh, which made everyone swing round hurriedly. It was a man whom I had noticed as I left my stall, a man with blazing eyes. His clothes were somewhat shabby, and I had wondered casually when I first saw him how he had got in to the Trade Show. But now he stood on the edge of the group which surrounded Sylvaine Lankester, and stared at her mockingly.

"Magnificent!" he sneered. "Why, you were rotten. Rotten, I tell you, Sylvaine Lankester. What did you want to register fear for—fear and horror—as Edward Latford came round the door? Blank, I know, blank ammunition was in the revolver. And the fool producer told you to show fear. But supposing it hadn't been blank, Sylvaine Lankester? Supposing that film had been the truth, what then?"

Instinctively the girl recoiled from him, and someone in the group muttered: "He's mad; the man's mad."

But even if he heard he took no heed; his eyes were still fixed on the actress who had played the part of Mary Maxwell.

"You wouldn't have shown fear then, Sylvaine Lankester—not if you were such a woman as Mary. You would have shown a steady courage, a supreme indifference, a blazing contempt."

"Extremely interesting," drawled a man standing by. "And may one ask how you happen to know all this?"

"Because that is what Mary Maxwell *did* show," answered the stranger quietly. "Courage, indifference, contempt—but not fear. A thousand times no; not fear."

Without another word he turned and walked away, leaving the people in the group staring after him open-mouthed. What on earth had he meant—"That is what Mary Maxwell *did* show"? And then in a moment or two, with a few significant shrugs of their shoulders, they dismissed the matter from their minds. Obviously a lunatic, was the general comment, and lunatics are not very interesting. But I, who had heard it all, was not so sure. To me it had seemed as if there was a ring of sincerity underlying the wild words—a ring of truth. And on the spur of the moment I hurried after him. I overtook him outside the Empire, and touched him on the shoulder. He swung round and stared at me with eyes full of hostility, and for a moment I regretted my hasty impulse.

"What do you want?" he snapped. "I don't know you."

His collar was frayed, his coat was ragged, but there was an indefinable something about his face, now that I saw him close to, which made me determined to go on with it in spite of his uncompromising attitude. The difficulty lay in what line to take with him. I felt that the barest hint of charity would freeze him up like an oyster; there was a strange fierce pride in those sombre eyes of his. And then I had a sudden inspiration.

"I'm an author of sorts," I said quietly, "and I was in the Alhambra a few minutes ago. I heard what you said to Miss Lankester, and I think, if I may say so, that you were wrong. No woman would show anything but fear in such circumstances."

For a moment he stared at me with a faint, half-contemptuous smile on his lips.

"You think so?" he remarked. "Well, it's you who are wrong—just as Sylvaine Lankester was wrong. And if you care to supply me with a little dinner to-night—I regret that on threepence-halfpenny I cannot offer to act as host myself—I will prove to you that you are wrong."

"Certainly," I answered at once. "I shall be delighted if you'll dine with me. Shall we say eight o'clock at Bordini's Restaurant in Greek Street?"

"Would it inconvenience you greatly to make it a little earlier?" he said. "Since yesterday at midday I'm afraid I haven't had very much to eat."

"Good Lord! My dear fellow," I cried, aghast, "any time you like. Shall we say seven—or six-thirty?"

"Six-thirty," he answered promptly. "Bordini's! I know it."

With a quick nod he was gone, leaving me staring after him a little foolishly. Was the man a fraud, or had he really got some strange story hidden in his mind? I strolled towards the club, still wondering.

II

Promptly at six-thirty I turned through the swing doors of the restaurant to find him sitting at one of the tables inside. I suggested a cocktail, which he refused, and under my breath I cursed myself for a fool. One does not offer cocktails to men who haven't fed for thirty hours or more. Instead I ordered dinner at once, with a pint of the Chianti for which Bordini's is famous. And then for the next half-hour I watched one of the most pathetic sights in the world—a gentleman who is starving, with food before him. For the man was a gentleman all right—his hands alone were sufficient to prove it. And he was trying to eat as a gentleman eats, while all the time hunger—stark hunger—was gnawing at him. And I wondered what he'd had even so recently as midday the day before.

But at last he finished, and with another flagon of Chianti between us, and a cigarette alight in his mouth, he leaned back in his chair and stared at me with a gleam of mocking humour in his eyes.

"And now I suppose I must pay for my dinner," he remarked.

"Damn it!" I said, a little stiffly, "it was you who suggested it. If you look at it that way, please consider the matter ended and we'll go."

"Forgive me!" He leaned across the table. "I'm a sarcastic brute, though I wasn't once. But there are some people, my friend, for whom nothing ever seems to go right in this world. Maybe it's their own fault—maybe it isn't. Incidentally, the cause doesn't make much odds—it's the effect that counts."

He broke off abruptly. "How did you like that film to-day?"

"Very much," I answered. "Very much indeed."

He nodded thoughtfully. "I wrote it."

"You did what?" I said, staring at him in surprise.

"I wrote it. I wrote the scenario, and I played in the original film."

"But surely," I cried, "that was an original production this afternoon? It was announced as such."

"Parts of it were original; parts of it had never been done before. But parts of it had; I suppose half of it had—quite half. And that half I have seen once on the screen. There's just one copy of it in existence to-day."

"But do these people who produced 'Loaded Dice' know about it?" I asked.

"I don't know if they do or not," he answered. "And it doesn't make much odds, because it will never be shown."

"What part did you play?" I asked.

"Hubert Malden," he remarked quietly. "The part taken by Carlton Bellairs this afternoon."

I preserved a discreet silence. I could hardly see this lean, cadaverous, down-at-heels man in the character as it had been created for me by Bellairs.

"Yes—I played the part of Hubert Malden," he continued, after a while. "But that's the end of the story. I'll begin at the beginning."

He refilled his glass and lit another cigarette.

"I don't know if you're interested in the film business. I am, or rather"—and he smiled faintly—"I was. Right from the very start the immense possibilities of the moving picture impressed me. Even in those days when the standard consisted of a one-reel play which gave you a headache to look at, I had visualized in my own mind something of the perfection which you can see to-day. And I went into the show heart and soul. I acted a bit, and I did a certain amount of producing—you'll remember that this was in the days before a producer, if he knew his job, could command almost any salary he liked to ask—and in my spare time I wrote one or two scenarios. I didn't attach myself to any particular company; I was just a free-lance. And though I say it myself, my name was fairly well known in the industry. What that name is doesn't make much odds; it's forgotten to-day."

He paused a moment to press out his cigarette.

"One day in London the agent of a certain Italian firm approached me with an offer to produce their new film for them in Italy. They wanted an English producer, as the film was an English film and most of the artistes were English also. They offered me what in those days was quite a considerable sum; to-day a producer would laugh in your face if you mentioned such a figure. However, it was good enough for me, and I accepted. I read the scenario going out to Italy, and was ready to begin work as soon as I arrived. It was just an ordinary straightforward English story, the adaptation of a novel—and I've only mentioned it because I said I'd start at the beginning. That film was the beginning of my acquaintance with—well, shall we call her Mary Maxwell? She was one of the English actresses engaged by the firm, and I fell in love with her the first moment I saw her."

Again he smiled faintly as he looked at me.

"I'm not going to bore you with lover's rhapsodies," he continued. "I'm only going to say that she was then, and has remained ever since, the loveliest girl I have ever seen. She made one catch one's breath with the wonder of her, and she was utterly and absolutely unspoiled. She was so immeasurably more lovely than Sylvaine Lankester that any comparison even would be ludicrous. And somewhat naturally I was not the only man who had noticed the fact. Love has a knack of quickening up one's powers of observation, and I hadn't been in that studio for two days before I realized that one of the Italian actors in the cast—Paolo Cimetti by name—was in love with her, too. A film studio, as you probably know, is a fairly free-and-easy place, and sometimes for hours on end actors and actresses will be sitting about doing nothing, while other scenes in which they do not appear are being taken. Only the producer is busy the whole time, and often it was as much as I could do to concentrate on my job, when I knew that Mary and the Italian were not in the studio where I could see them. I used to imagine things; I used to grow almost mad with jealousy; once I let down a complete scene because my mind was wandering.

"Not that I had the slightest right to be jealous; beyond talking to her as a producer I had hardly said two words to Mary since I had arrived. As far as I knew I was less than nothing to her; but men in the condition I was in are not over-logical. Certain it was that she gave the Italian not the slightest encouragement—at any rate in public, though his attitude to her very soon became obvious to everybody. He followed her about like a dog; he brought her flowers and chocolates, and his eyes used to be on her whereever she was. God! how I hated that man, though I did my best not to show it. But he knew—right from the beginning he knew—and he hated me just as bitterly.

"And then one day came the first flare-up between him and me. He was a good actor—a very good actor—and he was fully aware of the fact. In addition, he was playing lead—by the way, I don't think I mentioned that Mary was also playing lead. And he was fully aware of that fact also. On this particular occasion we were doing a close-up of him alone. In a corner of the studio was Mary talking to someone, and in the middle of the shot her laugh rang out suddenly. And Cimetti looked across at her. It was an unpardonable thing to do, and he knew it, even before I stopped the camera.

"'Again, please,' I said. 'And kindly pay attention.'

"He said nothing; there was nothing he could say, but for the first time in my life I realized the meaning of the phrase to have murder in one's eyes. There was murder in Cimetti's eyes as he looked at me.

"And then very soon afterwards matters came to a head. What took me upstairs past the dressing-rooms I don't know, but as I rounded a corner I saw Mary struggling in Cimetti's arms. They were standing in the passage outside her room, and he was trying to kiss her whilst she was pushing him away with both her hands. It was enough for me; I hit him on the point of the jaw with every atom of strength I could put into it. He crashed like a log, hitting his head against the wall as he fell. And then—well, my friend,

it's difficult to say how these things happen—I found
Mary in my arms, and this time she didn't struggle.
Instead she gave me her lips—her wonderful mouth
—to kiss."

He said the words almost under his breath, and
then for a while sat motionless, staring across the little
restaurant thick with the blue haze of tobacco smoke.
In his eyes was a look of dumb, hopeless longing; he
was back in the past with his memories. For the moment I was forgotten; nothing lived, nothing counted
with the man opposite save the touch of a woman's
lips on his.

"What is it that Goethe says somewhere?" he continued after a while. " 'There are many echoes, but
few voices.' There's only been one voice in my life,
and that voice there was no misunderstanding. My
love for that girl dwarfed everything else, and when
I found that it was the same with her the whole world
just changed. You're a stranger to me, and I don't
really know why I'm telling you all this, except that
you've given me a dinner. I don't know whether
you've ever been in love, and—what is far more wonderful—been loved as I was. But if you have, then
you will know that I do not exaggerate when I say
that no Heaven of imagination can give anything quite
so marvellous if it lasts, and no Hell anything quite
so agonizing if it ceases. Time heals the wound a
little but it's always there, my friend, it's always there."

Thoughtfully he lit another cigarette.

"However, I'm not here to bore you with a dissertation on love. Let us go back for a moment to where
I was standing in the passage with Mary in my arms.
Cimetti was forgotten, and then some movement on
his part reminded us of his presence. I looked down
and saw him, and for a second my heart stood still.
He was crouching back against the wall, with every

tooth in his head bared in a snarl, and a long stiletto half-pulled from his pocket. But it was his eyes that fascinated me. They were gleaming with such a frenzy of diabolical hatred that for a moment I thought the man was a maniac. And then, even as he saw me looking at him over Mary's shoulder, the madness faded and was replaced by an expressionless mask. So quickly did he control himself that, when I came to think about it afterwards, I wondered if I hadn't made a mistake. Some trick of the light, perhaps, in the passage. He stood up, muttered a word or two of apology to Mary, and walked away. And she shuddered in my arms.

" 'He frightens me,' she whispered, and I soothed her and comforted her till she forgot him.

"And now I must get on. You're wondering, maybe, where the film you saw this afternoon comes in. Well—it comes in very soon. I told you, didn't I? that I had written the scenario of 'Loaded Dice,' and I had taken it with me to Italy to polish it up and round off one or two edges. And one night I read it to Mary. She was immensely struck with it—as you saw for yourself to-day, it made a good film—and she at once suggested to me that I should offer the scenario to the firm we were then working with. Further, she suggested that she and I should play joint lead if the directors agreed. And then we sat together seeing visions and dreaming dreams of the future. How we would stagger the film industry with our consummate acting; how we should leave this small firm we were with and go over to America where the big money lies; above all, how we would get married. We'd do it before we took the Egyptian part of the film, we decided. It wouldn't mean long to wait; the present production was nearly over. Another six weeks, perhaps two months, would see us through all the Italian interiors of 'Loaded Dice,' and then—marriage. Of course, I need hardly tell you that no film is taken in the actual order in which it is shown. All the scenes of any one place are taken at the same time, and later when the film is finally joined together, they are put into the proper sequence.

"So we dreamed that night, and next day we could scarcely believe our eyes when it seemed as if all the dreams were coming true. The firm jumped at the scenario, and bought it from me on the spot. At first they wanted me to produce it, but Mary pleaded and argued. She was insistent that I should play lead with her, and when the directors discovered that we were engaged they agreed with true Southern gallantry. I'd played lead before, of course, with English companies.

"There was an American producer—quite a well-known man—in Rome at the time, and they engaged him in my place. And then we came to the question of casting the various parts. First and foremost came Edward Latford—the part taken by John Drage to-day. Unanimously they decided on Cimetti, and Mary and I looked at one another. We didn't want him in the cast at all, but there was no possible way of dispensing with him. He was under contract—the firm would have had to pay his salary in any case, and he was a first-class actor. To the directors the choice was obvious, so obvious that to protest against it would have been an impossibility. For, after all, what could we have said? That we didn't like him! Likes and dislikes are as common in the film world as elsewhere —perhaps commoner. And to do the man justice I had to admit to myself that I had no fault to find with his behaviour since Mary and I had become engaged. He had been consistently polite and courteous, and had been one of the first to congratulate me on my good fortune. And so the wheel of fate took another relentless turn towards the inevitable end."

He rested his elbows on the table and stared at me with sombre eyes.

"I suppose you've guessed that end already," he went on, slowly. "Sometimes now, when I look back on the weeks that followed, I nearly go mad. When I realize that all through those wonderful days every beat of the clock was just one second nearer the end, my brain seems almost bursting. If only one could have known: if only one could have had some premonition of what was to happen. And yet perhaps it was better so. It could have done no good: it would have only made my Mary miserable and unhappy had she been frightened with vague fears of impending danger. Because by the very nature of the thing it was inevitable: you see, *it was a part of the film itself.* And so I who wrote the film am responsible for killing the woman I loved."

His hands were clenching and unclenching, and the sweat was glistening on his forehead.

"I killed her, man—I killed her; just as surely, just as inevitably, as that devil Cimetti who actually fired the shot. Listen carefully—for there's not much more to tell.

"You remember the scene, don't you—the climax of the film—where Hubert Malden and Mary Maxwell, having rung the bell for the butler, sit waiting on the sofa and then Edward Latford enters instead: the scene about which I spoke to Sylvaine Lankester this afternoon. It was almost the last scene to be taken before we left and went to Egypt, and though it's so long ago I can recall every detail of that morning.

"Everybody was in the best of spirits—excited over going to Egypt. And as for me—well, you can imagine my feelings. In two days I was going to marry Mary. And as we sat a little apart from the others on the sofa which was to be used in the scene I felt almost dazed with the wonder of it. A carpenter was putting a finishing touch on the door; the photographer was fixing up lights. But at last we were ready and the producer took charge.

"'Now we'll run through this scene,' he began. 'Cimetti—are you ready?' Cimetti, who had just appeared, stepped forward and bowed to Mary. 'You'll open the door slowly,' went on the producer, 'and then you'll stretch out your hand with the revolver in it so that only the shadow is seen by the camera. Try that.'

"Cimetti tried it, and the lights had to be adjusted because there was a double shadow. And all this time Mary and I sat on the sofa, just utterly happy because we were near one another. The actual entrance, you see, was a separate scene into which we didn't come.

"At last we heard the camera turning, and we watched Cimetti come round the door, the revolver in his hand. It was a good entrance, splendid: it couldn't have been done better, and Mary congratulated him. Again he bowed, but for the first time a vague fear shot through me. It seemed to me as if there was a smouldering look in his eyes: as if—— But I hadn't time to worry; it was Mary's turn now and mine. First, Cimetti alone: then Mary and I: then all three of us together in the great scene.

"'You'll get up,' said the producer, 'showing fear and horror. And you,' he said to me, 'make one step forward as if to get in front of her.'

"We tried it once, and it seemed to me as if a mocking smile had shown for a moment on Cimetti's face.

But when that scene was over it was his turn to come and congratulate Mary.

" 'Fine!' said the producer. 'Now for the last one.'

"The cameras were adjusted, the lights were moved, and Cimetti stayed with us, talking.

" 'To-morrow is it—or the next day?' he asked. 'And a honeymoon in Egypt. How delightful—how romantic!'

"The smile glinted again, and once more a dreadful fear shot through me: a presentiment of some awful danger. And yet—what danger could there be? Here—in a film studio, surrounded by people.

"And now the producer was ready, and we ran through the final scene. We faced Cimetti, whose back was towards the camera, and on his lips the smile still lingered.

" 'Hold it like that,' said the producer, 'and when I shout "Now," you will fire, Cimetti, and you,' he said to me, 'pitch forward on your face.'

"And so we ran through it—once, twice, and still Cimetti smiled.

" 'That's bully.' The producer was rubbing his hands together. 'I think, Miss Maxwell,' he went on, 'that as he falls you had better say: "Oh, God!" as you go on your knees beside him. Camera ready? Right: let's get on with it.' "

The man opposite drew a deep breath.

"And that was the end. The next few records are a little blurred in my mind. The camera started and with it the smile faded from Cimetti's face, to be replaced by the same look of diabolical hatred that I had seen that day weeks before when I had knocked him down. Only Mary and I could see it; but I think she knew as well as I did that it was no pretence this time. I think she knew as well as I did that the revolver was loaded.

" 'Great!' I heard the producer's voice as if from a great distance. And then it came. Simultaneous with the 'Now' there was the crack of a revolver. I felt something sear through me: there was a roaring in my ears, and I knew nothing more."

He paused and lit a cigarette with a hand that trembled a little.

"And if the camera-man had not gone on mechanically turning the handle, it would have ended there. I should not have said what I did to Miss Lankester to-day, for my Mary was told to show fear, too. But the photographer, dazed by what had happened, went on winding automatically. And the police took the result.

"I saw it six months later when I came out of hospital—still more dead than alive. And when I saw it I wished that Cimetti's aim had been truer in my case. I saw myself facing him: I saw Mary standing beside me. And then, my friend—for the camera doesn't lie—I saw the scene played as it should have been—not as the producer thought it should have been. It was Mary who tried to step in front of me, even as he fired. And then—she didn't say 'Oh, God!' and fall beside me. No: she faced Cimetti for the half-second in which she lived with contempt, indifference and indomitable courage. Of fear there was no trace—no vestige.

"And that was the way that Mary died. I think he shot her through the heart, and she fell on top of me as I lay at her feet, covering me with her dear arms. Then the devil shot himself."

He fell silent, and I was silent, too: there seemed to be nothing to say.

"I don't think now that I shall be long in joining her," he went on after a while. "My money is gone: I've dropped out of sight in the film world—and I'm not strong. Cimetti's bullet did that for me, though it failed to kill me as I would have wished. And Mary—my Mary is calling me to go to her. She wants our honeymoon in Egypt. I think I should have gone before, but I heard our film—Mary's and mine—had been sold to another company, and I wanted to see it before I met Mary again. You see, I must tell her how they've done it: she'll be interested."

And with that he was gone. It seemed to me as if he had seen someone in the street that he knew, but when I followed him to the door he was walking rapidly towards Shaftesbury Avenue alone. And yet was he alone—or was he talking to someone who walked at his side—someone I could not see? The street-lamps play strange tricks with one's sight, and maybe it was just my imagination.

It was Bordini himself who looked at me significantly as I paid my bill.

"He always leaves like that—quite suddenly," he said. "Just as if someone had passed the door whom he wanted to overtake. And often the street is empty at the time."

And then he tapped his head.

I wonder. Some day, when I have time, I shall make it my business to find out.

III   A FUNNY LITTLE MAN

THAT one may frequently judge a man's character by his outward appearance is true: that one's judgment is frequently wrong is even truer. The man of great bulk with a voice like a bull is found on trial to have the courage of a louse; whilst the pale, slight specimen goes through the test with a will of tempered steel. And people are surprised—why, it is difficult to see. The best-looking apples are often the rottenest inside.

Which preamble is by way of introduction to John Septimus Flynn, fifth clerk in the office of Morgan and Son, who were and still are wholesale people for something or other down in the City. He was called fifth clerk principally to distinguish him from the office-boy, who received two shillings a week less than Septimus. And that difference was a very fair indication of the difference of their respective responsibilities. They both did odd jobs in the office, such as addressing envelopes; they both did odd jobs outside in the errand line. But Septimus, by reason of that extra two shillings a week, was entrusted with any private errands unconnected with the business, which Mr. Morgan or his son might wish carried out during the course of the day. From which it will be seen that John Septimus Flynn's position in the scheme of things was not such as would entitle him to expect an invitation to a Foreign Office reception.

In appearance he had not been smiled on by nature. In fact the third and fourth clerks openly alluded to him as a freak, a description which was unkind and yet not altogether unjustified. Short and undersized in body, he possessed an abnormally large head, which looked the more grotesque owing to his habit of wearing collars at least half an inch too high. His hair was sandy, his complexion muddy, and an addiction to Woodbine cigarettes had stained his fingers to a bright orange. In short, it must be admitted that John Septimus was an unprepossessing young man, who would have been frankly impossible but for one strange asset.

It is doubtful if that asset would ever have been noticed by his fellow clerks—a city office is a prosaic place—but for the fact that one afternoon a great painter who was a great artist as well came in to see Mr. Morgan. It happened that he had to pass the desk where Septimus Flynn was busy addressing envelopes. And Septimus Flynn was not addressing envelopes: he was staring out of the window over the smoky roofs towards the sun, which was setting in a riot of golden glory, splashed with pinky grey. In the distance the silver streak of the Thames shone and glittered with a thousand fires, while a barge, moving slowly down-stream towards the open sea, seemed to be gliding through a lake of liquid light.

For a moment or two the visitor paused by the desk, while the clerk, who should have been addressing envelopes, utterly oblivious of his presence, continued to stare out of the window. Then, in a very quiet, gentle voice, the great painter spoke.

"What are you looking at, my boy?"

And Septimus Flynn, his mind all eternity away, answered:

"God."

Then with a sudden start he came back to reality, and the scarlet mounted in waves to his face. A clerk at the next desk tittered, and in an agony of shame, Septimus turned feverishly to his envelopes. What had he said it for: why had he given away his great and wonderful secret? To be laughed at by these others. . . . To be held up to ridicule. . . .

But there was no laughter on the face of the grave-eyed man who stood by his desk, only a faintly puzzled frown. Not at the somewhat unexpected answer, but at the utterly unexpected change which a second or two had wrought in the answerer. This young man with the stained fingers licking envelopes was merely a rather dreadful nonentity: a few moments before he had been—what?

"Mr. Morgan is waiting to see you, sir."

The voice of the chief clerk at his elbow recalled the painter to the object of his visit, and he turned to follow his guide.

"It's his eyes, of course." So ran his thoughts as he steered his way through desks. "They're the most marvellous things I've ever seen. They're the eyes of a God-given genius."

He found himself shaking hands absent-mindedly with Mr. Morgan—a prosperous individual whose waistcoat measurements were beginning to be the subject of earnest thought on the part of his tailor.

"Good afternoon, Sir John." Mr. Morgan pulled forward a chair. "So glad you've come round."

"Tell me, Mr. Morgan," said the great painter, "what is the name of the funny little man in the office out there with the wonderful eyes?"

Mr. Morgan gazed at him in amazement.

"Wonderful eyes! I haven't an idea. Never noticed anything of that sort myself. Bennett, have we got a clerk with wonderful eyes?"

"I think Sir John means Flynn, sir," said the chief clerk from the door. "He spoke to him coming through the office."

The painter nodded.

"That's the one I mean. Flynn: strange, very strange indeed."

"I've never noticed his eyes," laughed Mr. Morgan. "He's a funny little man, as you said yourself, and he's a damned bad clerk. We use him to run errands."

And with that the subject dropped, though, in the office, it was not forgotten. From then onwards Septimus Flynn was known as the funny little man with the wonderful eyes. At the slightest deviation from duty his seniors waxed sarcastic and alluded to his *beaux yeux*; the office boy contented himself with pointed references to his bally blinkers. And as time went on Flynn grew to hate the man who had unwittingly been the cause of it all, and retired more and more within himself—to the secret which was all that made life worth living.

He hated the office routine—had hated it from the first—but what else was there for him to do? Man cannot live on dreams alone—not even his dreams, where strange haunting thoughts came to him, and he strove to catch them ere they faded and write them down on paper. The room at home—it was little more than a garret—was where he dreamed most often. In the night sometimes they would come to him, floating into his brain almost as if a voice was speaking. And then he would get out of bed, and seize a stub of pencil and a scrap of paper and write until the voice ceased, when he would creep back shivering between the coarse sheets and sleep like a log.

He'd oversleep himself sometimes, and his father would curse. Didn't he go to bed early enough, and if so, why the devil didn't he get up in the morning? Did he want a valet to call him? And the boy didn't dare to say that he had been awake half the night scribbling feverishly on leaves torn from a penny note-book—leaves now locked away in a tin money-box hidden under the bed.

And then there had come that awful night when in some inexplicable way his father had found him out. He hadn't time to do anything: he was caught *in flagrante delicto* burning a candle at 2 a.m. with the precious money-box open by his side.

"So this is why you're late in the morning, is it?" His father, in a towering rage, had stalked into the room while he cowered back trembling. "What's all this drivel you're writing?" He had picked up two or three of the sheets, and broken into derisive laughter

as he read them. "If you paid a little more attention
to your work in the office, and a little less to this twaddle,
you'd be earning a bit more money."

With that he had crammed the lot in his pocket and
left the room with a final Parthian shot:

"They'll do for the fire to-morrow morning."

And that night Septimus Flynn sobbed himself to
sleep.

But he didn't stop writing. As well try and stem
the flow of a mountain torrent as check the thoughts
that came flooding into his brain. And when they came
he felt he must write; it was a physical necessity. He
took more care now: his father had never discovered
him again. But as his father was firmly under the
impression that he was partially mad, and had long
given up all hope of his being anything but the family
idiot, it didn't occur to him that Septimus was less and
less at home. And had he been told that his son might
be seen every evening sitting on the grass in the park
gazing dreamily up at the sky and occasionally scribbling
in a little note-book; had he been aware that the best
part of a month's wages had gone in the purchase of
a really good electric torch which could be used under
the bedclothes and extinguished in an instant, he would
doubtless have regarded the facts as symptoms of
lunacy. But he didn't know and he didn't care—and
Septimus Flynn dreamed on undisturbed. The awful
routine at the office was just a necessary evil to be got
through: a hideous break in all that counted in life.
He was living within himself; nothing and nobody
else mattered.

And so it might have gone on for years, had not
an incident occurred which altered the whole outlook
of Septimus Flynn's life. In view of that extra two
shillings, he was always entrusted, as has been said,
with private errands for Mr. Morgan or his son. And

it so happened that one morning in June, Mrs. Morgan, having a very particular luncheon party at the house in Hampstead, had ordered her spouse to call in on his way to the office at a certain celebrated fruit shop in Piccadilly, and tell them to send up some of their choicest Muscatel grapes. Which order had completely passed out of Mr. Morgan's head until he suddenly recollected it at about twelve o'clock. For a moment he thought of telephoning to the shop; then, realizing the time and knowing the habits of errand-boys, he bethought him of Flynn.

"Go at once," he said when Flynn stood before him, "to Abraham's, in Piccadilly, and buy three pounds of their best Muscatel grapes. Take a taxi. Then go up to my house in Hampstead. Be there with the grapes by one. Here's two pounds, and get a move on."

He arrived, to be exact, at a quarter to one, and, as he ascended the steps to the front door, it suddenly opened and a girl came out. She stopped as she saw Septimus and gave a little exclamation of relief.

"At last! Why are you so dreadfully late? I was just going out to buy some locally."

"Mr. Morgan told me one o'clock, miss," stammered Septimus, handing her the grapes.

"Aren't you from Abraham's?"

"No, miss; I'm one of Mr. Morgan's clerks."

"Oh! I see." The girl smiled slightly. "Daddy forgot, as usual, I suppose." And then her smile grew more kindly as she saw the look on the face of the peculiar little man who was standing first on one foot and then on the other, staring at her. She was used to male adoration, though it was not generally quite so obviously expressed as in this case. And she was also a dear, who hated to hurt anyone's feelings. So she gave Septimus a smile that two or three men would

have crossed England to obtain, and held out her
hand.

"Thank you so much; you've saved me such a horrid
walk."

Then with a little nod she turned away and the door
shut behind her while Septimus stumbled blindly down
the steps into the drive.   His head was buzzing, his
brain was reeling, he was unconscious of where he
went or how.   He got into a tube somewhere, vaguely
conscious that he had heavily bumped an immaculately
dressed young man who swore at him, and then came
a kind of dim recollection that one to two was his lunch-
time—which gave him more than an hour to dream of
this marvellous being whom he had spoken to.   Never
in his wildest imagination had he pictured anything so
wonderfully lovely as this girl.   And seeing that many
men who had known the women of five continents
would have been inclined to concur with his judgment, Septimus Flynn's state of mind was not surprising.

Denise Morgan *was* a gloriously pretty girl.   She
was the apple of old Morgan's eye, who refused her
nothing, and yet she remained quite unspoiled.   She
had not quite made up her mind as to which of two
men it was going to be—Toby Carstairs in the Coldstream, or George Temple, who had a big property
in Shropshire, though she rather tended to Toby.

Certainly he looked a very pleasing specimen of
humanity as he came into the room a few minutes after
Septimus Flynn had gone.

"I'm early, old thing," he remarked as he shook
hands.   "But I was very nearly outed down the road
there.   A thing that looked like a newt was running
round in small circles, muttering horribly, and he butted
me in the stomach."

"I wonder if it was the funny little man who brought

the grapes," said Denise, with a smile. "I think my
appearance rather overcame him."

"By Gad! he's forgiven.   Death no longer threatens
him.   I habitually do it myself after leaving you."

And with that the conversation turned to other topics,
while the thing that looked like a newt was feverishly
scribbling illegible words, in a train that rocked and
swayed towards Piccadilly Circus.

Thus was Septimus Flynn's life altered.   Before that
never-to-be-forgotten day, women and girls had been
to him as men were—other occupants of that material
world which he got away from whenever he could.
Now he escaped more often still, but never alone.
Always there came with him into his land of dreams
a wonderful girl in a white dress, who sat beside him
as he wrote, and who listened with a tender smile while
he read to her.   Sometimes he touched her hand, and
once—but this was when he had been asleep—he had
kissed her. He woke up immediately after, trembling
all over, and it was then that the amazing—the staggering idea was born.   Supposing he could actually read to
her: supposing that that part of his dream came true.
Supposing he could touch her hand: supposing he
could—but even the bare thought of kissing that divine
girl drove him out of bed to sit by the open window
and watch the first grey tints of dawn spreading over
the sky.

It was impossible, of course—and yet was it?   Somehow he felt she would understand.   And as he squeezed
himself into his appalling collar the next morning, there
came to him the dazzling vision of life spent beside her,
a life where they dreamed together of those things which
the others couldn't understand.   Poor, funny little man!

But as with most dreams, it is the practical realization that counts.   And the practical realization of this
one presented slight difficulties.   The first, of which

Septimus was not aware, lay in the fact that the girl had completely forgotten his existence. The second, of which he was fully aware, was that it was one thing to watch this glorious creature drive off in a car at night from her house, when he was hidden in some bushes near by, and quite another to go and speak to her. Besides, there was generally a man with her—a large, good-looking man with lazy blue eyes. He grew to hate this man, with a bitter hatred.

But at last the opportunity came. Morgan and Son was a conservative firm, with whom any traditions or customs died hard. And there was one particular custom which had been inaugurated by Mr. Morgan's father more than fifty years ago. It had started when the difference, both social and financial, between the head of the firm and his clerks was not anything like so pronounced as to-day, and it had continued ever since. It took place on some day in July, and consisted of a state visit of the entire staff, down to and including the office-boy, to Mr. Morgan's house in Hampstead.

It was a ghastly entertainment, but it was just one of those things that had to be. Neither side would have dreamed of dropping the habit: it was a point of honour with Mr. Morgan to ask them—it was a point of honour with the staff to accept. The function was as inexorable as the laws of the Medes and Persians.

Only once had Septimus Flynn been, and then in an agony of shyness he had effaced himself in a corner. Denise had been away from home, and the wretched Septimus had shaken like an aspen leaf before the kindly but somewhat majestic Mrs. Morgan.

But this time it was going to be different: the girl was going to be there. He had been standing by the chief clerk when Mr. Morgan had issued the command invitation, and he had distinctly heard her mentioned.

"Mrs. Morgan and my daughter will be at home on

Saturday, Bennett," he had said. "Let the others know, will you. Hope they'll all be able to come."

Septimus Flynn felt his heart pound madly as he listened: he felt he could have struck the decorous Bennett for his impassive bow as he thanked his employer. Didn't the fool realize that the most wonderful girl in the world was going to be there? But the fool in question was only realizing that a worthy lady whom *he* had once called the most wonderful girl in the world would undoubtedly demand another hat for the occasion. She always did.

For days before the fateful Saturday, Septimus read, and re-read and selected and rejected the written dreams he was going to read to her. He had quite made up his mind what was going to happen: the whole thing was most carefully thought out. He would waylay her quite naturally in the garden somewhere, and, while the others were playing croquet or quoits, he would ask her if she liked poetry. Of course she would say yes. Then he would take her on one side and read to her a few lines; and as she began to understand he would read more until he carried her away, right away with him to his land of dreams. And finally, a little breathless, she would ask him who had written it, and he would tell her, in that great culminating moment. Beyond that Septimus Flynn's imagination failed to carry him. Dimly he visualized countless days where the same thing would happen, but just at the moment it was Saturday only that counted. He couldn't get much beyond that.

It is doubtful if any bride ever dressed for her wedding day with the same care as Septimus expended on his toilet after lunch. A green butterfly tie with a distinctive yellow marking was adjusted with meticulous accuracy in the centre of a three-inch turn-down collar: a Norfolk jacket with a strap round the waist, pale grey trousers, and light brown boots finally formed a picture not easily forgotten. And when to this were added wash-leather gloves, an imitation ebony stick with a bone top, and a bowler with the bow at the back, it will be readily conceded that, as far as outward appearances were concerned, Septimus was leaving nothing to chance. He arrived a little early, and put through the time walking up and down the big avenue that led to the tube station. Once or twice, as he passed a certain tree, behind which he had sometimes stood to watch the girl go out to dinner or a dance, he gave a little smile of amused contentment. That was all over now: after this afternoon that absurd performance would never occur again.

A familiar figure hove in sight walking with a woman. They were coming from the station, and Septimus, descending to earthly levels again, recognized the chief clerk, Mr. Bennett. As he came nearer it was obvious that he was not in the best of tempers: to be exact there had been a slight contretemps over the new hat and Mrs. Bennett had shown a fluency of utterance at the midday meal which had astonished even him.

"Good God! Flynn!" he almost shouted, "what the devil are you doing in that rig? This isn't a fancy dress ball."

At any other time Mrs. Bennett would have backed him up, but the question of the hat still rankled.

"I think you look very nice, Mr. Flynn," she remarked sweetly. "Mr. Bennett seems to imagine he's the only person in England who knows anything about clothes."

She smiled graciously and sailed on, while her husband followed, muttering darkly. And as for Septimus, what did he care? *She* would not bother over such trifles.

He waited for a few minutes after the Bennetts had disappeared: then, with a last final feeling in his pocket to make sure the precious papers were safe, he, too, rang the bell.

The butler opened the door, and stood staring for an appreciable time. Then, with his hand over his mouth and his shoulders shaking, he led the way through the hall to the door that led into the garden.

"Through there," he remarked tersely. "Mrs. Morgan is in the garden."

For a moment or two Septimus stood bewildered, until he saw his hostess in the distance. A voice at his side—it was the office-boy surreptitiously eating chocolates—"Crumps! You don't 'alf look a swell, Sep"—restored his confidence, and he walked across the lawn to Mrs. Morgan. And having left her in a partially dazed condition, he looked round for the girl. At first he couldn't see her: then, suddenly, he did, and the whole world went black. Standing by her side was the large, good-looking man with the lazy blue eyes—the man he hated so much. They were laughing together, and Septimus turned away, with a sick feeling of rage, to be immediately roped in for a game of golf croquet.

"But, my dear old thing," Toby Carstairs was saying between gusts of laughter, "it's incredible. I've never seen such a menagerie in my life. I know the office-boy in the corner is going to be sick in a minute—and now that other apparition——" He stared at Septimus, feverishly hitting a croquet ball. . . . "Why—it's the newt. Once seen, never forgotten. You remember that day, some weeks ago, I told you about the little bird who was running round in small circles and who butted me in the stomach. That's the little blighter himself."

"I think he's in love with me, Toby," laughed the girl. "Poor little man: he's such a funny little fellow, too. It's a shame to laugh at him."

"My dear, how can you help it? Look at his rig. That tie! My sainted aunt!"

"Well, you asked for variety, Toby—and you've got it. After tea you've got to play quoits with the newt, and up till then you can amuse yourself. No you can't . . . you can do a job of work. Mrs. Bennett —-I want to introduce Captain Carstairs—my fiancé— to you."

She heard Toby swear horribly under his breath: then with a little gurgle of laughter she left them to flounder together, while she moved about the garden, the very incarnation of sweet girlhood. Even the office-boy ceased his occupation of gorging sweets as she came near him, and gazed at her open-mouthed.

And so, in due course, she came to Septimus Flynn. The golf croquet was over, and he was sitting by himself still holding his mallet.

"I don't think I thanked you properly for bringing up those grapes," said Denise, with a smile. "It was so good of you."

Septimus dropped his mallet and rose, blushing furiously. It had all seemed so easy before—now . . .

"Not at all," he stuttered. Why couldn't he be easy and natural like that big man?

"Would you like to have another game of croquet?" she asked gently. Somehow or other a great feeling of pity for this funny little man was taking possession of her: he seemed so extraordinarily pathetic.

"N . . . n . . . no, thank you, Miss Morgan," he stammered. "Miss M . . . Morgan, do you like poetry?"

It came out with a rush, like a bullet from a gun— this pent-up and carefully rehearsed opening to a great dream.

The girl looked a little bewildered: it was so extremely sudden, and so very unexpected.

"I love it," she answered. "Why?"

"I was wondering," he went on, with gathering confidence, "if you'd let me read you one or two things I've written."

She sternly suppressed a strong desire to laugh.

"Of course," she said gravely, "I should like to hear them immensely. But I think we'd better put it off till after tea."

With that she had left him to go and talk to one of the others, and Septimus Flynn—the first great obstacle passed—was content. Away from all this chattering crowd: away, above all, from the big man he hated: away—alone with her. It was coming true—his dream —and he felt he could hardly believe it. Half an hour —perhaps an hour—and it would be realized. He stared with unseeing eyes at the people playing croquet, heard with unheeding ears the click of the balls and the casual snatches of conversation around him, immersed utterly in that strange world of his own into which so soon the girl was going to accompany him.

And it was just before tea that Toby Carstairs, having shaken the dust of Mrs. Bennett from his feet, passed close by him, and saw the look on his face. For a moment the soldier hesitated almost as if he had received some shock: then with a little shake of his shoulders he went on towards Denise.

"My God! What a bunch!" he said. "The office-boy has been sick: that woman—oh! that woman—and the newt is mad."

"How do you mean, mad?" said the girl.

"Have you seen the look in his eyes, Denise," and Toby's voice was almost serious. "He's as mad as a hatter."

Which was about as near as one could expect a singularly cheerful soldier's diagnosis of the case to agree with that of a great painter who was also a great artist.

"I don't know whether he's mad or not," answered the girl with a laugh. "But after tea he's going to read me some poetry he's written."

"Good Lord! you haven't been encouraging him, have you?"

"No, he suggested it himself. I should think it ought to be one long scream."

"I'm going to come and listen, too," announced Toby.

"You are not," said the girl. "You'd put the poor little chap completely off his stride. But if you promise to be good, and not laugh, I'll take him to the little summer-house and you can hide somewhere and look on."

And so the dream came true. It was just Fate; no one was to blame for the *dénouement*. But there are times, even now, when Toby Carstairs falls into a deep reverie, and his big fists clench, and into his eyes there steals a look of dreadful pain, such as a man feels who has hurt a child unwittingly. And then his wife comes to him, and puts her arms around his neck, till after a while he shakes himself like a dog, and swears a little and goes out to walk it off. It was just Fate, and yet . . .

Only once have I heard him speak of it, and that was one night after we'd dined together at the club. And it was what he told me then, in short, jerky sentences, that led me to find out from other sources the few scanty pegs on which I have hung the story of Septimus Flynn.

"Denise took him into the summer-house"—Toby bit the end of his cigar—" and I, like the damned fool I was, hid in some bushes close by. You know the way she's got with her, and he—poor little devil—was stammering and stuttering like a board-school child in front of a bishop. He got redder and redder in the face, and that ghastly green tie, with yellow spots, had slipped round to the back of his neck somewhere. Then he fished a bit of paper out of his pocket and started to read. I couldn't hear a word he said—I don't think Denise did either—for I wasn't much farther away from him than she was. . . ."

Toby paused, and drained his brandy at a gulp.

"And then I laughed. . . . There's no excuse, Bill —none: I laughed. If it hadn't ended as it did, I suppose I should say that he was such an irresistibly funny sight that I couldn't help it. I laughed—and he heard me."

Once again Toby Carstairs paused, and I didn't hurry him.

"I'm not a poetic sort of bloke," he went on gravely, "but I didn't need to be that to realize what I'd done. He swung round as if he'd been hit in the face, and he saw me. I tried to pass it off—but he never looked at me again. He just looked at Denise, and she said hurriedly: 'This is my fiancé, Mr. Flynn. Do go on.'

"But it wasn't any good. I don't know what he'd thought before—poor little blighter; but I suppose it suddenly came to him that he was being made a fool of. And he just gave a cry like an animal that has been hurt, and bolted."

Toby took a long breath.

"They brought it in as an accident," he continued after a while. "He went down in front of a train on one of the tubes—that evening. Slipped—according to the onlookers. His father at the inquest said he'd always been a bit queer."

He rose and shook himself.

"Did you ever see any of the stuff he'd written?" I asked curiously.

"No. Though, strangely enough, I believe Sir John Drayton—the painter man—went down to see the father, and tried to get some. But the father had burnt the lot. . . . Tripe, I suppose, of sorts—there's no doubt he was a little bit up the pole. You'd only got to look at his eyes to spot that. . . ."

I wonder: poor, funny little man. . . .

IV   UNCLE   JAMES'S   GOLF   MATCH

I

"UNCLE JAMES should be here soon," said Molly thoughtfully from the other end of the tea-table. "For Heaven's sake be nice to him, Peter."

"When have I ever not been nice to Uncle James?" I demanded. "But I tell you candidly, Molly, that it can't last much longer. He's only fifty-five: he will almost certainly live another forty years. And I can't stand another forty years of Uncle James."

"I'm sure he'll leave us all his money, old boy," she said pleadingly.

"I can't help that," I retorted firmly—at least as firmly as I ever can retort to Molly. "A man can buy money at too great a price. And if he brings another of his abominable inventions with him this time, I shall tell him what I think. He ought to know better at his age."

"I know, Peter," she answered gently. "But it's only for the week-end. . . ."

"Only!" I echoed bitterly. "Thank God for it."

"I must say I do hope he hasn't invented anything else for saving work in the house," she conceded. "Servants are so difficult in these days, and the parlour-maid seems to be settling down at last."

"He should confine his atrocities to his own home," I said. "A man who tries to emulate Heath Robinson in real life ought to be locked up."

Molly sighed. "I know, darling," she murmured. "But think of the money."

And they say that women are idealists. . . .

"Take that last week-end he spent here," I began wrathfully, and then Molly stopped me.

"Don't, dear, don't," she begged. "And that reminds me, they've never sent up yet to repair the kitchen ceiling."

Mind you, if the diabolical contrivances conceived in Uncle James's perverted mind were harmless little things like patent match-boxes or unbreakable sock-suspenders, I wouldn't mind. He is an excellent judge of wine, and has an excellent cellar—two assets which enable one to slur over small idiosyncrasies in their possessor. But—well, take that last week-end.

I feared the worst when he arrived: he was so infernally pleased with himself. He came on Friday, and on Saturday I had to go up to Town, so my knowledge of what happened is only second-hand. I was met at the station by Molly—a rather wild-eyed Molly—who poured out the whole hideous story on the way up to the house. Uncle James had waited till I was well away before he sprang it on her—and even she had tried to be firm when she heard what it was.

"It was a patent labour-saving device for me in the kitchen, Peter," she exclaimed weakly. "Little pulleys and things—and bits of string. I explained everything to Martha—told her he was eccentric, and that we could take it down the instant he went—and she seemed to understand."

She faltered a little and my heart sank.

"It took him two hours to put it up with stepladders, while Martha sat sardonically in a corner. Then he explained to us how it worked. Oh! it was awful."

I took her arm: she was rapidly becoming hysterical.

"Of course, something went wrong. Uncle James says it was the hook coming out of the ceiling—I know the plaster is all over the floor. But whatever it was, the big saucepan of potatoes shot into the corner—Martha's corner—and she couldn't get out of the way in time."

Molly gulped. "She got up with potatoes all over her, and threw them one by one at Uncle James."

"Did she hit him?" I asked eagerly.

"Twice," answered Molly. "Then she left the house."

Well, now that was the last time he stayed with us. Do you wonder that at times I felt I couldn't stand it much longer? Of course, Molly's account of it was a trifle incoherent—possibly even a trifle exaggerated. But the one salient fact remains that his last visit cost us Martha.

A series of loud explosions outside the door recalled me from the bitter past, and Molly got up, looking alarmed.

"Good gracious, what's that?" she cried.

"Probably he has invented a motor-car," I answered grimly, "which goes sideways with the passengers underneath."

"Do you think it's Uncle James?" she asked uneasily, and at that moment the front-door bell rang.

It was Uncle James right enough, and we went out into the hall to greet him.

"Ah! my dear children," he cried as he saw us, "I've arrived."

"Anything wrong with the car?" asked Molly as she kissed him.

"Not going very well," he answered, shaking hands with me. "And now it's stopped altogether. I wish you'd just give me a hand, Peter."

"Certainly." I'm afraid my smile was a trifle

strained. With an ordinary car I can compete: not with Uncle James's. "What's the trouble?"

"Well—I'll just show you the idea," he said cheerfully as he led the way. "I've got a few notions of my own incorporated into the general design—little gadgets, you know. Now, first of all"—he gazed pensively at the dashboard—"we'll try that a little farther open. And, Peter—if you just pull that wire by the steering-pillar she ought to start."

I pulled the wire, and Uncle James tackled the starting-handle. There was an alarming report, and a cloud of white smoke which seemed to please him.

"Ah! spark's all right, anyway," he murmured. "Once more."

This time she back-fired so violently that only the greatest agility on his part saved him from a broken wrist. In view of what was to come, I found myself wishing later that he hadn't been quite so agile.

"Pull harder, Peter," he cried, returning to the assault.

I did: I pulled the whole wire out, and the car promptly started.

"I knew she'd go," he announced complacently. "Just a little patience wanted."

I preserved a discreet silence as we went round to the garage: there are moments when speech is both unwise and tactless. And it was not until we were strolling back to the house, my sin still undiscovered, that I breathed again.

"You must let me run you up to the club-house in mine to-morrow morning, Uncle James," I said lightly. "Course in splendid condition."

"Aren't you going to London to-morrow?" he demanded.

"No. I'm taking a holiday in honour of your visit."

I forbore to tell him that Molly had threatened divorce unless I did.

"What sort of time will suit you?" I went on. "Then I can ring up and let them know about caddies."

Uncle James did not immediately reply, and I noticed he looked a little thoughtful.

"To tell you the truth, Peter," he began slowly, "I wasn't particularly anxious to play golf with you to-morrow morning. The fact is, I wanted—" he hesitated for a moment—"I wanted to practise a bit before I played you again."

"Well—we won't play a serious round, Uncle James," I said mildly. "We might get up there and knock about a bit: have some lunch, don't you know—and play in the afternoon."

Anything to keep him out of the house; those were Molly's instructions.

"Yes," he agreed. "We might do that. And in the afternoon I shall beat you."

"Why, of course. Beat my head off."

"I have cured my slice, Peter," he announced.

"Good," I cried. "You'd have beaten me last time but for that."

"No—not last time. But I shall this."

There was an air of such complete conviction about his tone that I glanced at him in mild surprise. Uncle James may be and is an excellent judge of wine; Uncle James may be and is a public pest with his inventions; but Uncle James cannot be and is not and never will be a golfer. He is not like anything on this earth that I have ever seen when he gets a golf-club in his hands. He is, and I say it advisedly with due regard to the solemnity of making such a claim for any man, the worst golfer in the world.

"I have—er—turned what little ingenuity I possess, Peter, upon a lengthy and scientific consideration of the game of golf." He spoke as a man does who weighs his words with care, and involuntarily we both paused. "I have read many books on the game—by Vardon and Taylor and others—men doubtless well qualified to write on the subject."

I bowed silently: speech was beyond me.

"And it seems to me," he went on, "that they evade the real issue. For instance now, they unite in saying that the essence of golf lies in the swing. But how am I to know that my swing is like theirs?"

"How indeed?" I murmured chokingly.

"Again they reiterate the statement, 'slow back.' But ideas of slowness differ."

"True," I agreed—"very true."

To see Uncle James take his club back reminds one of a man lunging furiously at a wasp.

"Two points of many, you perceive, Peter," he continued, "on which I came to the conclusion that a little ingenuity might be of great assistance. And so, I have —er—perfected, or am in the process of perfecting, a small device, by which the—er—comparative novice like myself can obtain mechanical assistance in carrying out these maxims."

Thank God! Molly joined us at that moment: I was beginning to turn pale. Uncle James encased in pulleys on a Saturday morning on the links was a prospect that made me feel faint. Better a thousand times that the entire domestic staff should resign.

"Is it a very complicated device, Uncle James?" I asked feebly, and I heard Molly catch her breath.

"It takes a little adjustment," he answered. "And I shall require Molly's assistance."

"Uncle James has invented something," I explained, studiously avoiding her eye, "which he thinks will improve his golf."

"What sort of thing?" inquired Molly.

"It's not so much an original invention," he explained, "as a common-sense application of a well-known principle—the principle of elasticity."

I suppose I looked mystified—I certainly felt it—and he beamed at us contentedly. Then he fumbled in his pocket and produced a small parcel.

"It is my firm belief," he continued, as he undid the string, "that with this I shall be able to reduce my handicap to single figures, or even"—he paused for a moment, and his voice shook a little at the thought—"or even to scratch."

At first sight the invention looked like a cross between a young octopus and the tram-lines at the Elephant and Castle. On closer inspection it looked like a nightmare. Streamers of india-rubber flowed in all directions from metal rings, terminating in little clips and loops. Some were short and some were long; some were thick and some were thin—and to each was affixed a label.

"There it is, you see," he remarked proudly, "neat and simple. Merely following first principles, Peter."

"But," I stammered, "how does it work, Uncle James?"

"You must surely follow the main idea," he exclaimed, with the genial toleration of the great brain. "Each of these lengths of rubber fulfils a purpose of its own, and the thickness and length have been calculated to enable them to fulfil that purpose scientifically. For instance—this one."

He indicated a short, stocky little fellow, with a loop at the end.

"Now, Duncan lays great stress on the action of the right elbow during the upward swing. He insists that it should be kept close to the body. By the simple process of attaching this loop round the right elbow—the result is obtained."

"I'm afraid I'm still rather dense," I said dazedly.

"The ring—this metal ring," he explained a little wearily, "is attached to the inside of my coat. From it the rubber goes to my right elbow. These others go elsewhere. Similarly with the remaining rings. Each is securely fastened inside my coat, and from them the rubber cords go to their respective places where they are secured."

"What is the long, thin one, Uncle James?" asked Molly wildly.

"That one?" He examined the label. "To left wrist for follow through. You see it fulfils a dual purpose. It restrains one in the upward swing—and assists one in the downward."

And then, thank heavens! the dressing-bell rang, and we went indoors. My brain was reeling: it was incredible to think that any man could have such a mind. And what made it worse was that Molly seemed to be in a splendid temper. I even heard her congratulate her abominable relative on his cleverness.

"Could anything be better, old boy?" she said, coming into my dressing-room. "He'll be perfectly happy on the links, with you and his india-rubber." She choked slightly.

"Understand me, Molly," I answered coldly. "I go to London to-morrow, and I do not return till Uncle James has left. I shall have a telephone message in the morning. I utterly and absolutely refuse to take your confounded relative up to the links on a Saturday morning, swathed from head to foot in rubber bands."

"But, Peter darling," she began soothingly.

"Go away," I said firmly—"go away. I hate your family."

"But, Peter darling," she continued, "he won't do any harm. He can't play any worse with it on than he does with it off."

"That," I agreed, "is an indubitable fact. But—why, confound it, Molly—it's against the rules. It must be against the rules. It's absolutely immoral."

"I know, dearest," she answered. "But no one will find out—and it keeps him happy. After all, it's better than letting him loose in the house. . . ."

Of course, I gave in finally; I knew I should, I always do with Molly. And after all she was quite right. The infernal machine would be hidden underneath his coat, and no one need know. And he *has* got a lot of money.

II

We got off about ten on Saturday morning—Uncle James and I. Molly had sewn the rings into his coat after dinner the night before under his expert eye; she had then superintended the connecting up in the morning after breakfast. And that completed her share of the performance. She flatly refused to accompany us to the links, on the plea of household duties. She equally flatly refused to speak to me alone, or even to meet my eye. So I placed Uncle James's bag of nineteen clubs in the car and we started.

It was a beautiful day for golf—soft, balmy, and without a breath of wind. Moreover, Uncle James was in a splendid temper.

"I shall do a good round this afternoon, Peter," he affirmed confidently. "Splendid device, this of mine. Tried one or two practice swings while you were getting the car."

"Good," I cried. With the new day had come a certain cheerful optimism, and I let the car out a bit more. "But if I was you, Uncle James, I'd lie low about it. Don't tell anyone, and you might make a bit of money to-morrow."

I could see the pride of the inventor struggling with

the wonderful idea I had suggested.   To actually beat
somebody at golf!   It opened a vista of possibility
almost too marvellous for imagination.

"You see," I continued craftily, "people might be-
little your game if they knew."

I left it at that, and hoped for the best.   There were
quite a number of men about when we arrived at the
club-house, and as Uncle James wanted to try his device,
I fixed up a game for the morning.   Then I showed him
a hole where he could practise approach shots, and left
him.   It was a fatal move on my part: I ought to have
known better.   To leave Uncle James alone on a links
—especially on Saturday morning—is asking for trouble.
I got it.

The first man I saw as I came in after my round was
Colonel Thresher.   He was talking to the secretary,
who was trying to soothe him.

"I'll look into it, Colonel," he said mildly.   "Leave it
to me."

"But I tell you there's a madman on the links,"
roared the irate officer.   "He's dug a hole on the seventeenth fairway big enough to bury a cow in."

My heart sank; it was the seventeenth where I had
left Uncle James.

"The damned man is a menace to public safety,"
fumed the Colonel.   "He hits the ball backwards and
through his legs.   And he's using the most appalling
language.   Here he is, sir—here he is."

I choked and turned round as Uncle James entered.
I could see at a glance that he was no longer in a splendid
temper.   Far from it.

"The lies on this course are atrocious, Peter," he cried
as soon as he saw me—"positively atrocious."

I attempted to intervene—but it was too late.

"And they won't be improved, sir," roared the
Colonel, "by your exhibition of trench digging.   Damn

it—a man falling into some of those holes you've made would break his neck."

"Confound your impertinence, sir," began Uncle James, shaking his fist in his rage. And then he paused suddenly: in mid-air, so to speak. A spasm of pain passed over his face, and a loud twanging noise came from the region of his back. The Colonel started violently, and retreated, while the secretary took two rapid paces to the rear.

"I told you he was mad," muttered the Colonel nervously. "He's got a musical-box in his shirt."

It was that remark that finished it, and removed the last vestige of Uncle James's self-control. To have his latest invention alluded to as a musical-box turned him temporarily into a raving lunatic. And as other members drew near in awestruck silence a torrent of words in a strange tongue poured from his lips. It turned out to be some Indian dialect, of which my relative knew a smattering. Unfortunately, so did the Colonel, and he answered in the same language. I gathered later from an onlooker, who also understood the lingo, that honours were about easy, with the betting slightly on Uncle James. He'd got in first with some of the choicer terms of endearment. And then Uncle still further lost his head. He challenged the Colonel to a game that afternoon for a tenner—a challenge which that warrior immediately accepted with a sardonic laugh.

To everyone else it seemed a most happy termination of the incident: to me it was the last straw. Uncle James had no more chance of beating the Colonel than I should have of beating Abe Mitchell. Not that the Colonel was a good golfer; he wasn't. But he was one of those steady players who can be relied on to go round in two or three over sevens. Which, with Uncle as his opponent, meant a victory for the Colonel by ten and eight.

However, the challenge had been given and accepted: there was nothing for it but to hope for the best. Uncle James had disappeared to wash his hands; the Colonel had been led away, breathing hard, when I suddenly thought of Molly. After all, he was *her* relative.

"Is that you, Molly?" I said over the 'phone. "Well, the worst has occurred. Your uncle has challenged old Colonel Thresher to a game this afternoon—after the combined efforts of most of the members just prevented a free fight in the smoking-room."

I heard her choke gently. Then—"Well, that's all right, Peter."

"It isn't," I fumed. "He's got no more chance of winning than—than—— Don't you understand: Thresher called his invention a musical-box. It came into action as they were abusing one another, and twanged. It's an affair of honour with Uncle James. And if he loses, he'll never forgive us."

"He mustn't lose, Peter." I thought her voice was thoughtful.

"Then I wish to heaven you'd come up and prevent it," I said peevishly.

"I will," she said, and I gasped. "What ball is he using?"

"Silver Kings. Red dots. But look here, Molly, you mustn't . . . It's for a tenner. . . . Are you there?"

She wasn't: she'd rung off. And somewhat pensively I joined Uncle James at the bar. I never quite know with Molly: she is capable of doing most peculiar things.

"I'll teach him, Peter." He greeted me with a scowl. "What did he say—musical-box? The infernal scoundrel."

"What was it that made the noise, Uncle James?" I asked soothingly.

"One of the longer rubbers got caught up in my

braces," he said.   "Incidentally it nipped a bit of my
back. . . .   Bah!   Musical-box.   The villain."

"Is it acting all right?"   I led him towards the dining-room.

"I shall adjust it finally after lunch," he stated.

"You don't think," I hazarded, "that as you haven't
actually perfected it yet, it would perhaps be better to
play without it."

"Certainly not."   He glared sombrely at the back of
his rival, and once again I heard him whisper: "Musical-
box."

Then we sat down to lunch.   It was a silent meal and
I was glad when it was over.   Uncle James—that genial
if eccentric individual—had departed: an infuriated and
revengeful man had taken his place.   And what would
be the result on his disposition when he forked up ten
Bradburys to the Colonel was beyond my mental scope.
He was never at his best on the golf-links: but this
time . . .

He disappeared for a considerable time, after consuming two glasses of our best light port, which he stated
was completely unfit for human consumption, and I
wandered thoughtfully towards the first tee.   There
was no sign of Molly, though I thought I saw the flutter
of something red in the distance, which might have been
her.   And then the professional strolled up.

"Hear there's a tenner on Colonel Thresher's game,"
he said affably.

"There is," I answered grimly.   "Did you see his
opponent playing this morning?"

"I saw the gentleman doing exercises on the seventeenth," he said guardedly.

"That's my uncle, Jenkins," I cried bitterly—"or
rather my wife's uncle.   Can you as a man and a golfer
give me the faintest shadow of hope that the match
won't end on the tenth green?"

"Your uncle, is he," he returned diplomatically. "Peculiar style, sir, hasn't he?"

"Peculiar," I groaned. "He'd earn a fortune on the variety stage. By the way, you haven't seen my wife, have you?"

"Yes, sir. I thought she was playing with you. She's just bought a couple of old remakes."

"What brand, Jenkins?" I asked slowly.

"Red-dot Silver Kings. Seemed very keen on 'em, though she generally uses Dunlops."

I turned away lest he should see my face. I had more or less resigned myself to being cut out of Uncle James's will and to seeing his money go to a home for lost cats; but to be turned out of the club as well for Molly's nefarious scheme was a bit over the odds. What devilry she contemplated I did not know—I didn't even try to guess. But not for nothing had she invested in two remake red dots, and disappeared into the blue.

"Here they are," said Jenkins. "Odd sort of walk your uncle has got, sir."

Now Uncle James has many peculiarities, but I had never noticed anything strange about his pedestrianism. The shock, therefore, was all the greater. To what portion of his anatomy he had attached his infernal machine factory I was in ignorance: but the net result was fierce. He looked like a cross between a king penguin and a trussed fowl suffering from an acute attack of locomotor ataxy. A perfect bevy of members had gathered outside the club-house, and were watching him with awed fascination: his caddy, after one fearful convulsion of laughter, had relapsed into his customary after-luncheon hiccoughs. It was a dreadful spectacle—but worse, far worse, was to come.

The Colonel stalked to the tee in grim silence. His face was a little flushed: in his eyes was the light of battle.

"Ten pounds, you said, sir—I believe."

"I will make it twenty, if you prefer," said Uncle James loftily.

"Certainly," snapped the Colonel, and addressed his ball.

Usually after lunch the Colonel fails to reach the fairway of the first hole. On this occasion, however, the ball flew quite a hundred yards down the middle of the course, and the Colonel stepped magnificently off the tee and proceeded to light a cigar.

The members drew closer as Uncle James advanced, and even the caddy forbore to hiccough. The moment was tense with emotion: it still lives in my memory and ever will.

"Slow back," had said Vardon; "follow through," had ordered Ray. Merciful heavens! they should have seen the result of their teaching. Uncle James achieved the most wonderful wind shot of modern times.

He lifted his driver like a professional weight-lifter, and at about the same velocity. Then, his face grim with determination, he let it down again. To say that he followed through would be to damn with faint praise. The club itself finished twenty yards in front of the Colonel's ball, and Uncle James fell over backwards.

"Very good," said the Colonel. "But the object of the game is to get your ball into the hole—not your club."

"Another driver, boy," said Uncle James magnificently when he was again in a vertical position, and at that moment I felt proud of being related to him. Once more Uncle James lifted his club; once more, under the combined influence of the "to left wrist for follow through" rubber and his inflexible determination, the club descended. And this time he hit the ball. In cricket phraseology point would have got it in the neck. As it was, the Colonel's caddy sprang into the air with a scream of fear, and got it in the stomach, whence the ball rebounded into the tee box.

"Confound it, sir!" roared the Colonel. "That's my boy."

"Precisely, sir," returned Uncle James complacently. "It is therefore my hole."

For a moment I feared for Colonel Thresher's reason. Even Jenkins, a most phlegmatic man, retired rapidly behind the starter's box, and laid his head on a cold stone. In fact, only Uncle James seemed unperturbed. He unwound himself, twanged faintly, and started for the second tee.

"I must adjust my 'right elbow in' grip, Peter," he remarked as I trailed weakly behind him. "It prevents me raising my club with the freedom required for a perfect swing."

"Do you mean to say, sir,"—the Colonel had at last found his voice—"that you intend to claim that hole?"

"I presume that we are playing under the rules of golf." Uncle James regarded him coldly. "And the point is legislated for. Should a player's ball strike his opponent or his opponent's caddy the player wins the hole."

"That doesn't apply to attempted murder off the tee," howled the Colonel.

"You are not in the least degree funny, sir," returned Uncle James still more coldly. "In fact, I find you rather insulting. If you like, and care to forfeit the stakes, we will call the match off."

"I'll be damned if I do," roared the other. "But before you drive next time, sir, I'll take precautions. I came out to play golf, not to be killed by a brass band."

Uncle James turned white, but he controlled himself admirably. Even when he reached the second tee, and the Colonel, seizing his caddy, went to ground in a pot bunker, over the edge of which they both peered fearfully, Uncle retained his dignity.

"Straight down the middle is the line, I suppose," he remarked to his caddy.

"Yus," said the caddy from a range of twenty yards.

But unfortunately Uncle James did not go straight down the middle. It's a very nice five hole is our second: a drive, a full brassie and a mashie on to the green over a little hill. But you must get your drive—otherwise . . . And Uncle was otherwise.

I measured it afterwards. His driver hit the ground exactly eighteen inches behind the ball, travelling with all the force of "to left wrist for follow through." The shaft followed through: the head did not. It remained completely embedded in the turf.

"Have you finished?" demanded the Colonel, emerging from his dugout. Then he pointed an outraged finger at the broken head. "This is a tee, sir, not a timber-yard. Would you be good enough to remove that foreign body before I drive?"

I removed it: I was afraid Uncle would twang again if he stooped. And then the Colonel addressed his ball. From there by easy stages, with a fine-losing hazard off a tree, it travelled out of bounds.

"Stroke and distance, I presume," murmured Uncle. "Boy, another driver."

And then ensued a spectacle which almost shattered my nerves. Uncle James got stuck. He got his club up but he couldn't get it down. Both arms were wrapped round his neck, the club lay over his left shoulder pointing at the ground. And there he remained, saying the most dreadful things, and biting his sleeve.

"Posing for a statue?" asked the Colonel satirically.

"G-r-r-r—" said Uncle, and suddenly something snapped. The club came down like a streak of lightning—there was a sweet, clear click, and even Duncan would have been satisfied with the result.   Probably it was the most exquisite moment of Uncle's life.   Heaven knows how it happened—certainly the performer didn't. But for the first time and—I feel tolerably confident— the last, Uncle James hit a perfect drive.   It was three hundred yards if it was an inch, and the Colonel turned pale.

"That's two I've played," said Uncle calmly.   "You play the odd, sir."

It was then that the fighting spirit awoke in all its intensity in his opponent, and Uncle James followed him from bunker to bunker counting audibly until they came up with his drive.

"I'm playing one off ten," he remarked genially.

"And you'll bally well play it," snapped the Colonel.

Uncle James smiled tolerantly.   "Certainly.   As you please.   Boy, the wry-necked mashie."

But it wasn't the wry-necked mashie's day in.   Whatever Duncan might have thought about Uncle's drive, I don't think he'd have passed the wry-necked mashie. At the best of times it was a fearsome weapon—on this occasion it became diabolical.   Turf and mud flew in all directions—only the ball remained *in statu quo*.

"That's like as we lie," said the Colonel, as Uncle paused for breath.

"Confound you, sir—go away," roared Uncle James, completely losing all vestige of self-control.   And at that moment I saw Molly peering over the hill that guarded the green.

"The laid-back niblick, boy."   Uncle threw the wry-necked mashie into a neighbouring garden—and resumed the attack.

"Fourteen—fifteen—sixteen," boomed the Colonel. "Why not get a spade. . . .   Ah! congratulations. You've hit the ball, even if you have sliced it out of bounds. Perhaps you'd replace some of the turf—or shall I send for a 'ground under repair' notice."

"Your shot, sir," said Uncle thickly.

"Let me see—I'm playing one off six," remarked the Colonel. "And you're out of bounds."

"I may not be." Uncle ground his teeth. "I may have hit a tree and bounced back. G-r-r-r!"

There was a loud tearing noise, and Uncle James started as if an asp had stung him.

"Confound you, sir," howled the Colonel, as he topped his ball, "will you be silent when I'm playing?"

But Uncle James was beyond aid.

"My God, Peter!" he muttered. "I've come undone."

It was only too true: he was twanging all over like a jazz band. Portions of india-rubber were popping out of his garments like worms on a damp green, and every now and then the back of his coat was convulsed by some internal spasm.

"Can't you take it off altogether?" I asked feverishly.

"No. I can't," he snapped. "The beastly thing is sewn in."

We heard the Colonel's voice from the green.

"I have played sixteen," he began——then he stopped with a strangled snort. And as we topped the hill we saw him staring horror-struck at the hole, his lips moving soundlessly.

"That was a lucky shot of yours, Uncle," came Molly's gentle voice from a shelter where she was knitting. "Hit that log and bounced right back into the hole."

And the brazen woman came across the green towards us literally staring me straight in the face.

"How does the game stand, Colonel Thresher?" she asked sweetly.

"The game, madam," he choked. "This isn't a game

—it's an—an epidemic. He's murdered my caddy and dug a grave for him, and supplied the music—and now he's bounced into the hole." He shook his putter in the air and faced Uncle James.

"You have that for a half," said Uncle, dispassionately regarding a twenty-yard putt. Then he looked at the Colonel and frowned. "What are you staring at, confound you, sir?"

But the Colonel was backing away, stealthily, muttering to himself.

"I knew it—I knew it," he said shakingly. "It's a monkey: the damned man's a musical monkey. He's got a tail—he's got two tails. He's got tails all over him. I've got 'em again: must have. What on earth will Maria say?"

"What the devil?" began Uncle James furiously.

"It's all right—quite all right, sir," answered the Colonel. "I'm not very well to-day. Touch of fever. Tails—scores of tails. Completely surrounded by tails. Some long—some short: some with loops—and some without. Great heavens! there's another just popped out of his neck. Must go and see a doctor at once. Never touch the club port again, I swear it. Never ——"

Still muttering, he faded into the distance, leaving Uncle James speechless on the green.

"What the devil is the matter with the fool?" he roared when he had partially recovered his speech.

"I don't think he's very well, Uncle," said Molly chokingly.

"But isn't he going to play any more?" demanded Uncle. "He'd never have holed that putt, and I'd have been two up."

"I know, dear," said Molly, slipping her arm through his and leading him gently from the green. "But I think he's a little upset."

"Of course, if the man's ill," began Uncle doubt-fully.

"He is, Uncle James," I said firmly—"a touch of the sun." I warily dodged two long streamers trailing be-hind him, and took his other arm. "What about going home for tea?"

Uncle brightened.

"That reminds me," he murmured, "I've just per-fected a small device for automatically washing dirty cups and saucers."

"Splendid," I remarked, staring grimly at Molly. "You shall try it this afternoon."

v   MARK DANVER'S SIN

THE letter came to me at breakfast—a bulky one, addressed in an unknown hand. The eagle eye of my hostess's small son had at once spotted the stamp, and an instant demand had gone forth that it should be presented to him in due course. It was a Tonga Island—one of those nice stamps which por-tray strange birds and animals in beautiful colours— and even as I promised he should have it, I was try-ing to think who on earth could be writing to me from such an outlandish spot. The letter had been re-addressed on to me from my club, and after a while, in deference to young Jack's continued demands for the stamp, I gave up the delightful pastime of guess-ing and opened it. There were two enclosures inside: one a heavily sealed envelope addressed to me in a well-known hand, but one that I had not seen for many long years; the other just a covering letter.

It was the envelope I studied first. What could have induced dear old Mark Danver to break the silence of years, and then label his letter "strictly private"?   And what a strange coincidence that it should have reached me in this of all houses!

Then I glanced at the covering letter, and for a moment I felt as if someone had given me a blow in the face.   It was from a firm of lawyers, and was brief and to the point.

"*Dear Sir,*" it ran,—

"*The enclosed was amongst the effects of the late Mr. Mark Danver.   We should be glad if you would acknowledge the receipt in due course.*"

I laid down the letter by my untouched breakfast, and stared out of the window.   Poor old Mark dead —that priceless, cheery soul who had so strangely dropped out of our lives.   In Tonga Island of all places.   For he had known my host and hostess, too, known them before I did.   And now, seated at their table, I had got the news of his death.

I don't know why I said nothing at the time; I think, perhaps, that it was because Mark had been my particular pal, and now from the grave he was speaking to me.   And I wanted to hear what the old chap had to say first.   So I put his letter unopened in my pocket, and I gave young Jack his stamp.   And half an hour later I carried a deck-chair into the shade of a chestnut tree and carefully slit the envelope.   Inside were several sheets of foolscap covered with Mark's writing, and for a moment my eyes grew a little blurred. Then I began to read.

"They tell me, old man, that I haven't very long to go.   The Doctor here, who diagnoses quite well when he's sober and operates quite well when he's drunk, broke it to me this morning.   Incidentally I'd guessed it already, and I can't pretend that I mind

very much.   But since the end is coming fairly soon,
I want to write to you, my oldest pal, and explain
why I have cut myself adrift from you all these last
few years.   And also I want to put on record a confession which will come as a big surprise to you.   In
case anything should happen in the future you will
have it by you, and will know what use to make of
it.   And apart from that, it's going to be a bit of a
comfort to me to put it down on paper, and know that
someone I trust will see it.   One gets a bit cowardly
towards the end—sometimes.   Depends, I suppose, on
the race you've run.   And if there's been a bad foul
it gibbers at you and mocks you.   Especially at night,
when you can't sleep.   I've been sleeping damnably
just lately.

"There will be parts of this confession of mine that
you know already; but I am going to put it down in
full in case it should ever be needed.   I'll tell it to
you, Dick, in the form of a story—my first attempt
at literary work.   But they say that everyone could
write at least one yarn—the yarn of their own life, so
perhaps the fact that it is true will atone for lack of
style.   Anyway—here goes.

"It's just eight years ago this month that I was up
on a shooting trip in Uganda.   And on the way back
through British East Africa, I went down with a bad
dose of fever.   Luckily for me, there was a farm close
by, and my boys carried me there.   That farm belonged to a youngster whom you got to know afterwards—Jack Onslow.   And since you know him I
won't waste time describing him for you.   Just sufficient to say that he was one of the straightest, cleanest
boys that I have ever met; a white man through and
through.   He was there by himself growing coffee,
and he wouldn't hear of my going on until I was absolutely fit.   As a matter of fact I think he was glad

of the companionship; it's lonely work, that sort of
life, as you know.

"So I stopped on with him after I was fit, and day
by day I got to know him and like him better. And
then there came an evening when I asked him why
he didn't get married.

" 'It's not good, Jack,' I said, 'for a man to live
in the wilds alone.' He turned a bit red, and fumbled
in his pocket. Of course, I guessed at once what he
was looking for, but I tried to look suitably surprised
when he handed me a battered leather case.

" 'I'm engaged, old man,' he said, a bit awkwardly.
'There's her photograph. And I'm just trying to get
the place into a real going concern before she comes
out to join me.'

"I took the case and I opened it, and I tell you,
Dick, I was staggered. It was just a coloured photograph of a girl, and for sheer flawless beauty I had
never seen her equal. She was more than beautiful
—she was lovely, with the sweetest expression in her
eyes. And I just sat there holding the portrait in the
circle of the lamplight, drinking her in.

"I hardly heard what Jack was saying, so absorbed
was I in that perfect face. He was rambling on, talking a little disjointedly, a little shyly. His face was
in the shadow, and for a while he talked of the things
that lie deep down in a man—the things which it is
not given often for another man to hear. I don't suppose he evolved a single original idea, but who wants
original ideas? He just told me in a queer, half-jerky
voice of his hopes and plans; of what life was going
to bring him; of what he was going to do. But always
he came back to his girl; it was 'we'—never 'I.'

" 'She's wonderful, Mark,' he said, and he took the
frame out of my hand. 'She's such a marvellous pal.'

" 'Well, frankly, Jack,' I answered, 'I felt nervous

when I saw you producing that frame. I have suffered before from lovers' rhapsodies, and my sole coherent thought was that it's lucky we don't all think alike. But this girl of yours strikes me as being the loveliest thing I've ever seen. You're a lucky devil.'

"He looked at me quietly.

" 'Wait till you see her yourself, Mark. She's a thousand times more lovely than this photograph.' I smiled, and reached for the whisky bottle.

" 'I'll take your word for it, old man,' I said. 'In the meantime, a final night-cap, and I'm turning in.'

"And I remember that night, as I was going to my room, I looked back at the wrong moment. He had his lips pressed to the picture, and I could almost feel the savage intensity of his longing. It is not good for a man to be alone in the Tropics.

"I suppose it was a week later that it happened. I was returning from shooting when the native house-boy met me gibbering like a monkey. He was in the last extremity of terror, but I caught enough to make me start running like a hare towards the bungalow. Outside, the other servants were cowering together like frightened sheep, and I dashed past them up the steps and into the living-room. Seated at the table, quite motionless, with a revolver in his hand and an empty bottle of whisky beside him, was Jack Onslow. In the other hand he clutched a letter, and in front of him was a copy of *The Times*.

"He paid not the slightest attention to me, though once his eyes, with a dreadful glitter in them, stared at me and through me. Then he began to laugh, harshly and discordantly, and my first thought was that he'd gone mad. Such things have happened before in the back of beyond. Then he stopped laughing and stared at me again.

" 'Mark Danver, isn't it?' he croaked. 'Well, sit down, Mr. Mark Danver, and don't dare to move, or I'll plug you as full of lead as a mine. Because I've been telling you lies—packs and packs of rotten damned lies—and you've got to hear the truth. I've told you, haven't I, that there was a girl in England of surpassing beauty? I was engaged to her, Danver, that wonderful girl. I was going to marry her, Danver, and she was going to come out here and live with me. I've shown you her photograph, haven't I?' He stared at me, and his head nodded a little. 'Speak, damn you, speak!'

" 'Yes, Jack, you've shown me her photograph,' I said quietly.

" 'Well, if you look behind you on the wall you can see it a second time.'

"I looked over my shoulder and saw the frame nailed to the wall. He'd been shooting at it with his revolver, and more than one bullet had gone clean through the picture.

" 'That's what it's worth, Mr. Danver. That's all that rotten girl is worth. I've put five shots through her, and there's one left here for me.' He laughed again discordantly, and began muttering to himself: 'A fool there was, and he made his prayer.'

" 'You haven't told me yet, Jack, what's happened,' I said steadily. At all costs I had to calm him sufficiently to get his revolver away from him, and to do that I wanted to get close to him without making him suspicious. Jack Onslow was mad right enough, but only with drink, for he was usually an abstemious boy.

" 'Haven't I told you?' he snarled. 'What a regrettable oversight! Well, I'll tell you now. This wonderful girl of mine has married another man. It's all quite in order; they've put it in *The Times*, and if you come round here you can see the announcement.'

"It was what I was waiting for, and I crossed the room to his side. I didn't look at *The Times*—that could wait; but I caught his right wrist. He wasn't expecting it, and anyway I was a stronger man than he. And the next instant I'd slipped his revolver into my pocket.

"He sprang to his feet, and for a moment or two I thought he was going to strike me. And then, quite suddenly, came the change. After all he was but a boy. He just crumpled up in his chair and, putting his arms on the table, he laid his head on them and sobbed like a little child. No—that is not right, for a child's tears are as a passing shower. And Jack Onslow sobbed as a man sobs, and there is no more dreadful sound in all this world. But I knew the danger was over.

"After a while he grew silent. Only a deep shuddering breath every now and then told me he was conscious: except for that he was motionless in his exhaustion. And my heart bled for the boy.

"I had seen the announcement in *The Times*—scored and scored again by Jack with a thick blue pencil:

" '*Dryden: Barstairs.—On the 5th May, at the Old Parish Church, Okehampton, Herbert Dryden to Joan Barstairs, only daughter of Captain Barstairs, late of Royal Navy.*'

"And I marvelled in my mind that such a girl as she had seemed to me from her picture could do such a thing.

"At length his breathing grew quieter, and he slept. I didn't touch him or disturb him; it was better to let Nature have her way. Through all the dreary months ahead he'd have to suffer; let him sleep now and forget. So I left him there with the letter still clutched in his hand. And when he woke the African night had come down and the lamps were lit.

"He sat up and stared at me dazedly across the table. Memory hadn't come back; he didn't realize what had happened. And then he saw the letter in his hand, and his face went haggard.

" 'I've been asleep, Mark?' he asked.

" 'Yes, old chap,' I said, 'you've been asleep. I want you to eat some dinner now.'

"He shook his head.

" 'It was that whisky,' he said slowly. 'I've been mad. Did I say some terrible things, Mark, about Joan?'

"He steadied his voice well—remarkably well—as he said her name.

" 'Whatever you may have said, Jack,' I said, putting my hand on his shoulder, 'it was only I who heard you. And when a man's lowered a bottle of whisky neat, only a fool pays any attention to what he says.'

"He looked at me, and his eyes were tired.

" ' Dear old Mark,' he said, 'I think you saved my life. It's in here'—he touched his forehead—'like a bad dream—all that happened after you came in. But what I want you to understand, old man, is that it's not her fault. It's not one little bit Joan's fault. It's all in her letter here. You see, this man Dryden had her father in his power. Something about money it was; dear old Barstairs is the biggest fool in the world over money. And he threatened to ruin him and her mother unless she married him.' He shook his fists suddenly in the air, and the sweat glistened on his forehead. 'Great God!' he shouted, 'what a swine that man must be!' Then he pulled himself together again and went on quietly: 'So, you see, she couldn't help it—my little girl. She couldn't see her father

and mother made penniless beggars, could she? S
she sacrificed herself for them.   It's all down here i
the letter.'

" 'Confound it all,' I snapped, 'it seems to me sh
sacrificed you as well.'

"For a moment his shoulder shook and he turne
away.   Then he steadied himself, and I went out o
to the verandah.   I wasn't in the mood to hear an
more excuses about the girl; to me the big traged
was the one at hand—that priceless boy.   And the
I heard his voice again, and looked back into th
room.

"He was standing by the photograph and I thin
he'd forgotten my existence for the moment, or els
he thought I'd gone into the compound.   But as h
took it down from the wall he spoke.

" 'Forgive me, my darling.   I couldn't help it.
was mad.   But I understand.   Joan; I understand
now.'

"And damn it, Dick, I couldn't have spoken at tha
moment if my life had depended on it.

"That's the first part of my confession, old man
You will probably say to yourself that up to now there'
been nothing to confess.   Quite right; but I had t
put it down in detail so that you should know th
terms I was on with Jack Onslow.   He was a pal o
mine—almost as great a pal as you yourself, save tha
he was a younger man.   I want to make that clear
I want to emphasize it, for it has a big bearing on wha
is to come.

"I suppose it was a month later that I left Jack
He was still carrying on, but all the spring had gon
out of his work.   Only once did he allude to the girl
and that was the night before I left.

" 'What's the use, Mark?' he said, with an od

twisted smile. 'I was doing it for her, and now, what's the use?'

"The next day I left him. I was going back to England, and I remember looking back as the road turned for a last view of the farm. Jack was standing on the verandah and he waved his hand once. Then he went inside, and I pictured him sitting at the table staring in front of him with hopeless eyes.

" 'What's the use, Mark; what's the use?'

"His words were echoing in my brain, and as I rode on I made up my mind that when opportunity offered I would seek out Mrs. Dryden and I would paint a picture for her which she would not forget in a hurry. I would tell this girl exactly what the salvation of her father had meant to Jack Onslow. And it was three months later that I arrived in Okehampton with the intention of looking for her.

"Of course, I had no idea where she was living, but since the wedding had taken place there I thought I should be able to get the information I wanted. And I was right; the first person I asked at one of the hotels told me where they lived. Then he looked at me a bit curiously.

" 'Do you know him—Herbert Dryden?'

" 'No,' I said briefly, 'I don't. What sort of a man is he?'

" 'You'll see for yourself,' he answered, and I couldn't get any more out of him. But his tone of voice spoke volumes.

"And as I ate my lunch I reflected that she deserved all she got; my mind was still sore over Jack.

"I'm not going to weary you with a long account of how I got to know Dryden. It was through Brayfield, a major in the Gunners, who was in camp there, as a matter of fact. I'd known him in the past, and he asked me up to dine one guest-night. And Dryden

was there—a thin-lipped, austere-looking man of about
fifty.   His face seemed to be set in a continual sneer,
and his eyes were cold and fishy.   I remember I asked
Brayfield about him, and he shrugged his shoulders.

" 'He's exactly what he looks like,' he remarked.
'Personally, I think he's one of the most horrible swine
I've ever met in my life, and how he ever induced his
wife to marry him is one of those things which are
beyond human comprehension.'

" 'What sort of a girl is she?' I asked carelessly.

" 'Well, I don't think I'm exaggerating,' he answered quietly, 'when I say that she is the sweetest
and most lovely woman I've ever seen in my life.
And,' he finished up savagely, 'he treats her like a
dog.   By the way, you paint, don't you?'

" 'I dabble in it,' I said, rather surprised at the
question.

" 'So does he,' answered Brayfield.   'I'll introduce
you to him after dinner, and he's sure to ask you up
to his house.   And then you can see his wife for
yourself.'

"It fell out as he said.   Dryden, it appeared, was
inordinately proud of his water-colours, and liked nothing better than to show them to an appreciative
audience.   And since I wanted to get to the house I
exaggerated my ability somewhat.

"I went up the next day to lunch.   It was a big
house, standing in rather a lonely position.   The
grounds were well kept and extensive, and it was evident that Dryden had money.   And a woman who
could chuck Jack and marry Dryden for money must
be pretty rotten.   I'm afraid I didn't pay too much
attention to the ruined father stunt; in fact, I had
almost forgotten it.   All I could think of was Jack
sobbing his soul out as the night came down on his
farm in Uganda.

"And then I saw the girl. You know her, Dick, so I won't bore you with trying to describe her. But all I could realize at the moment when I saw her picking some flowers in the garden was that Brayfield had understated the case. She had on a cotton frock—I can remember it as if it were yesterday—and when she saw me she put down her basket and came towards me.

" 'How do you do?' she said, holding out her hand. 'My husband will be here in a moment.'

"I stood there, Dick, like a callow schoolboy gaping at her, and then, moved by some uncontrollable impulse, I blurted out what was in my mind.

" 'Why, in Heaven's name, have you smashed Jack Onslow's life?'

"For a moment I thought she was going to fall. Every vestige of colour left her face and she swayed dizzily. Then she pulled herself together, and I heard her agonized whisper:

" 'Don't mention it before my husband, for God's sake!'

"I heard a step behind me on the gravel, and turned round to find Dryden approaching. By day he looked even more unpleasant than at night, and it was with a feeling almost of repugnance that I took his hand.

" 'I see you have introduced each other,' he remarked suavely. 'Mr. Danver is interested in painting, Joan; and—what should appeal to you more—he has been in Uganda.'

"Every word came out like a drop of iced water, and he was watching her as a cat watches a mouse.

"She was superb.

" 'Indeed!' she said. 'How interesting! It must be a most fascinating country.'

"She led the way towards the house, and we followed. Every hard thought I'd had about her had

vanished—just been blotted out.   I knew that it wasn't
her fault—that Jack had been right.   Knowing her as
you do you'll understand my sudden conversion.   All
I knew and felt for certain was that some damnable
tragedy had taken place, and that this fish-eyed brute
was at the bottom of it.

"I wish I could give you some idea of the devilish
way he treated that wonderful, glorious girl.   At lunch
that day, for instance, he wouldn't keep off the subject of Uganda; asked me if by any chance I knew a
man called Jack Onslow; hoped that he was in the
best of health and spirits; trusted that he would marry
some nice girl soon.   And all the time his eyes were
fixed on his wife—searching her face to see if his shots
had got home.   And I, fool that I was, had added to
her burden by telling her that she'd smashed Jack's
life.

"Not by the quiver of an eyelid did she let her husband see that he'd scored.   She sat there calm-eyed
and disdainful, and I was torn between a desire to
cry: 'Well played, you topping girl,' and a positive
craving to hit the swine in the face.

"She disappeared after lunch, and Dryden bored me
with his rotten paintings.   I escaped as soon as I
could; I felt I couldn't bear the man any longer.   And
I wanted to see the girl again, and tell her that Jack
was all right and that he understood.   But there was
no sign of her about the garden, and with a sick feeling of impotence I walked out over the moors.   I felt
I wanted to get away into the open, and try to get the
taste of Dryden out of my mouth.

"And then quite suddenly and unexpectedly I came
on her.   She was sitting down in a little hollow, and
a terrier was at her feet.   She stared at me as I came
up, and the hopeless misery in her eyes made me
catch my breath.

" 'So I've smashed his life, have I?' she said at length.

"I sat down beside her on the grass.

" 'He's better now, Mrs. Dryden,' I answered gently. 'But I was with him when the news came —and he took it hard. Tell me—why did you do it?'

"And then little by little the whole story came out. She wasn't very clear on the business points involved, but I gathered that it was concerned with a mortgage. Her father had speculated—led on, as she found out later, by Dryden. Then he had mortgaged his house and Dryden had taken it up—only to threaten to foreclose a month or two later. It was utterly impossible to find the money, and Dryden's price for not foreclosing was—her.

"She had told him everything—gone down on her knees to him, but it was useless. He had wanted her for years, and her love for Jack Onslow was nothing to him. He wanted her for his wife, and he was going to have her for his wife. Otherwise utter absolute ruin for her mother and father. That was the choice he gave her.

" 'You heard him at lunch to-day, Mr. Danver,' she said, and her voice was trembling. 'It's always the same. I believe he hates me; hates me because I won't pretend what I can't feel. I know I hate him, and though he forced me to marry him, he can't force me to love him. There will never be anybody in my life but Jack. And if—' the tears were running down her cheeks—'if you see him again, will you tell him so? Tell him that Tim and I come out here and talk about him.' She laid her hand on the dog's head. 'Tim is his dog, you know.'

"I bit at my pipe, Dick, and sat there like a tongue-tied fool.

" 'Don't tell him I'm miserable, because that would make him miserable, too. But don't tell him I'm happy, Mr. Danver, because I couldn't bear him to think I could be happy tied to Herbert.'

" 'But look here, Mrs. Dryden,' I cried, 'why go on like this? A man who could drive such an abominable bargain as your husband has, doesn't deserve the slightest consideration. Write to Jack, and tell him to come home and take you away with him back to Uganda. It would be less wrong than going on as you are.'

"She gave a little pitiful smile.

" 'Three days after we were married, Herbert informed me that he still held the mortgage, and that should I be foolish enough to contemplate leaving his roof the question of foreclosing would again arise. He also stated that he was unalterably opposed to divorce.'

"And then she fell to asking me about Jack: how he was looking; how the farm was doing; all the little intimate details a woman wants to know about her man. Who looked after his clothes—of all things—God bless her. As if I knew.

"And at last, after about an hour, she rose.

" 'Good-bye, Mr. Danver,' she said. 'I think if you don't mind I'd sooner not see you again.'

" 'I'm going to-morrow,' I answered. 'And if I see Jack I'll tell him.'

"She gave a little choking cry and was gone, stumbling over the rough ground, with Tim scampering round her feet. And having watched her out of sight I turned and strode away over the moor. I felt I'd like to hit somebody or something; I felt that life could hold no more wonderful joy than ten minutes alone with Herbert Dryden and a rhinoceros-hide whip. And at that moment, Dick, I saw him.

"Sometimes now I think it was Fate's inexorable

decree; sometimes now I think that it was intended from the beginning of things. And then, at others, I lie sweating in the night and wonder. You know that they brought it in as an accident. You know that he was found with his head crushed in at the bottom of Dead Man's Pool, with his easel and his camp-stool on the edge of the cliff two hundred feet above. You know that at the inquest I gave evidence to the effect that I had seen him stand up with his pencil in his hand as if to take some measurements, and suddenly stumble and disappear into the depths below. And they brought it in as a sudden attack of vertigo.

"It was a lie, Dick; I murdered him. I killed Herbert Dryden that evening at Dead Man's Pool, and I leave the verdict in your hands.

"He saw me coming towards him and he waved his hand.

" 'Having a look round for some local colour?' he cried. 'Well, you won't find a better place to start than this. I've done it half a dozen times and the light is never the same.'

"I stood by his side in silence, watching him work. For an amateur he wasn't at all bad, and had he been anybody else I should have been interested. It was an ideal spot for a sketch, with some wonderful colour effects. Deep down below us lay the sheet of black water—sombre and sunless—with the sinister name earned from tragedies of the past. Once, presumably, an old quarry, now it was disused, and the local people avoided it.

"There were stories told about it: one in particular of a hard-riding, hard-living squire of a bygone day, whose horse had bolted with him and gone over the edge. And it was said that the great shout of 'Gone away' which he gave as he realized that he'd come to

the last fence, and was falling like a stone into the
depths below, could sometimes now be heard echoing
faintly over the moors.

"The top of the quarry lay in a little depression,
so that we were at the bottom of a saucer, so to speak.
And for a while I watched him getting in the wonderful yellow of the broom on the opposite side of the
pool.   He worked in silence, his fishy eyes absorbed
in their task, until suddenly he put down his brush
and looked at me.

" 'So you know Jack Onslow,' he said, with an ugly
smile.   'Tell me about the young swine.'

"It was then that something snapped, Dick; up to
that moment I swear I had no thought of what I was
going to do.   But in my brain I could see only two
pictures—Jack sobbing his soul out across the table,
and this fish-eyed brute gloating in front of me.

"But I didn't do anything rashly; to this day I can
remember how ice-cold and clear my mind felt.

" 'I think it should interest you, Mr. Dryden,' I
remarked, 'to know that one of the last times I saw
Jack Onslow, he was mad drunk on a bottle of whisky.
He had a photograph nailed to the wall of his bungalow, and he was firing at it with his revolver.   And
the photograph was of your wife.'

"I took one quick look round: there was no soul
in sight.   And then I picked up a huge stone lying
at my feet.   There was just time to see the unholy
joy on his face turn to a fearful terror—but no more.
I brought the stone down on his head with all my
force, and he fell over the edge like a log.   I heard
the crash as he hit the rock below, and then he
toppled into the pool.   Finally, I threw the stone far
out into the water, picked up his camp-stool, which
had fallen over, and went straight back and gave the
alarm.

"The result you know; there was no known motive for my killing him; there was never even any suspicion of it. It was an accident—and as such it has remained to this day.

"But now, old Dick, as my own last fence is looming in sight, it haunts me sometimes. Was I justified in doing such a thing? Can anyone ever be justified in doing such a thing? When I can't sleep o' nights, I see those eyes of his staring at me out of the darkness—and they mock me. They seem to say: 'You're coming, too, Mark Danver; you, who dared to judge me.'

"But it wasn't for myself, Dick, that I did it—that much I can say. It was for Jack and that wonderful girl. And when those eyes of his get very bad there's another picture comes to my mind, and the eyes fade away. I see again Jack's farm, with Jack standing on the verandah. On his face is a look of dawning wonder, as he stares at the girl standing beside him. Just once he passes his hand across his eyes, and I hear him whisper: 'Dear heavens! but I'm dreaming.'

"And then she goes to him and her arms are round his neck.

" 'Not dreaming, my darling—it's truth. It's all come right at last.'

"At that I leave it. They must never know, Dick; they must never have an inkling that it was not an accident. But now that I'm going, I've written this to you in case anything ever happens. It's not likely to, so long after, but it might. And if it did—you know.

"The final punishment will lie in other hands, though it's begun already. These last few years have been hell. That's why I've buried myself and cut adrift from you all. You see, I loved her, too, as I never believed I could have loved a woman.   That's another thing they must never know.

"Good-bye, old chap."

For a while I sat staring across the sunlit garden. On the lawn young Jack was being instructed in the rudiments of cricket by his father, while his mother kept wicket. And even more did I marvel at the strangeness of the coincidence that had brought Mark's letter to me in this of all houses.

At last the game was over, and young Jack departed with his nurse. And as they watched him go I saw Jack Onslow turn to the girl at his side. For a moment he looked at her as a man may look at only one woman, and she gave a little happy laugh. Yes—it's all come right at last, dear old Mark—it's all come right.

VI   THE MISSING LINE

"MELODRAMA is a loose phrase." The Actor leaned back in his chair and surveyed his guests thoughtfully. "A farce is a farce all the world over; so is a comedy. So, to a lesser extent, perhaps, is tragedy. But melodrama—well, what is melodrama? Understand me. I am not alluding to gorgeously staged shipwrecks and horse-races at Drury Lane. I want more than that. I want a definition that will include everything that the world calls melodrama."

The Writer splashed some soda-water into his glass.

"Roughly I would give this as a definition," he said. "The presentation of exciting things, which really do not happen in ordinary life, in a sufficiently plausible manner to make them appear convincing.

Gentlemen-burglars, revolvers in the drawing-room—all that sort of thing."

"And yet there *are* gentlemen-burglars," retorted his host. "And a few weeks ago in the papers was the picture of two men lying dead in a street in New York: they had killed one another with revolvers. Because no one has ever flourished a pistol under my nose, does that make a gun-man melodramatic?"

"He might very reasonably be a melodramatic figure on the stage," argued the Doctor.

"Not in a country where gun-men are common," cried the Actor. "The standard must vary. Melodrama in London may be the most natural thing in the world in Italy. And I go further——" He paused and looked at the Writer. "Things that don't happen: that is your criterion, is it? Very well; I will meet you on your own ground. And when I've told you the story of the thing which happened to me —good Lord, it's twenty odd years ago now!—you shall tell me whether you still hold to that definition or not."

With some deliberation he lit a cigar, while the other men settled themselves comfortably in their chairs to listen. The dinner had been perfect; the Actor's cigars were beyond reproach. Moreover, the Actor's powers as a raconteur were well known.

"I don't know where you all were at the time," he began, when his cigar was drawing to his satisfaction. Anyway, it doesn't much matter. Those of you who were at home have probably completely forgotten the affair. It didn't make much of a sensation even at the time; and I don't suppose there are half a dozen people, outside those who were actually in the theatre when it occurred, who would remember anything about it to-day.

I had been in management rather over a year, and,

fortunately for me, very successfully. My first play had run for six months; my second was still playing to good business. But it had reached the point when I realized that definite steps would have to be taken with regard to its successor. I had two or three possibles in my mind, and I was glancing through them one morning to make my final choice, when the telephone rang in my room.

It was Hastings, the well-known literary agent, and he asked me if I could make it convenient to go round and see him without delay. He had a play which he thought might interest me, and he wanted to talk to me about it.

As you probably know, there are agents and agents. But when a man like Hastings, who is quite at the top of the tree, rings you up on a matter of that sort it doesn't do to disregard it. So I went round to see him that morning.

"I telephoned you," he said, as soon as I was seated in his office, "because there are circumstances about the case which are a little unusual. There's the play"—he pushed it across his desk—"and I can tell you the circumstances better than I can write them."

"Before we come to that," I interrupted, "have you read the play?"

"I have," he answered.

"Is it good?"

"Personally I think it is very good—very good indeed. In fact, I may say that it is the best play I have had through my hands for years." And then, with an enigmatic smile, he added: "As far as it goes."

I stared at him.

"What on earth do you mean?" I said. "Isn't it finished?"

"No—it isn't. The curtain of the last act has been

deliberately omitted. But I have it on the author's own word that it is written."

"But what the deuce has he done that for?" I said blankly. "By the way, who is the author?"

I glanced at the script. John Strangeways—a name I'd never heard of.

"That is a pseudonym," said Hastings.

"Do you know who he is?" I demanded.

"I've met him—if that's what you mean. He has been in this office; he has sat in the chair you are sitting in. But beyond that I can't say I know him." He leaned forward across the desk. "I'd better come down to the circumstances I spoke of—or rather the conditions. I may say that they are a little peculiar. In the first place—and this, I think you will agree, is very peculiar—he wants no royalties."

"What an eminently satisfactory man!" I murmured.

"He is, I gather, very wealthy," went on Hastings, "and he is prepared to pay for his caprices. Not only does he require no royalties, but he is prepared to finance the play."

I stared at him even harder.

"That means one of two things," I remarked. "Either the play is no good or the man is a little wanting."

Hastings smiled slightly.

"Neither, I think. There is a third reason—in this case I have no doubt the true one. *Cherchez la femme.* He makes it an absolute condition that Paula Vendon should play the part of the heroine."

"Paula Vendon," I said. "I've heard of her, but —what's she doing now?"

I *had* heard of her in the way one hears of a lot of people on the stage with whom one never comes in contact. Certainly she had never done anything big.

"At the present moment she is playing a small part at the Haymarket," said Hastings.

"Can she act?" I asked.

"To tell you the truth, I really don't know," he answered.

"I thought there was a catch somewhere," I said, fingering the script. "Let's have the other conditions."

"The second of them is similar. A man called Leslie Merrill is to play the part of her lover."

"And what the devil am I to do?" I exclaimed. "The butler——"

Hastings smiled.

"It will be clearer when you've read the script," he answered. "You are to play the husband, which is the biggest part in the cast."

"I've heard often of men financing a play for a woman," I said, "but it's the first occasion to my knowledge when a man has been included. What sort of a fellow is this John Strangeways?"

"He struck me as a hard-headed business man," answered Hastings. "There is a trace of something Southern in him, though not marked, and his real name is as Anglo-Saxon as his *nom de plume.* Moreover, I should think he's got the devil of a temper when roused. However, there are one or two other conditions which I'd better tell you. Under no circumstances is either Miss Vendon or this man Merrill to be told that it was at the author's wish that they were given these two parts. It must come direct from you, as if it was your original idea. And, finally, the finish of the last act will not be given to you until the evening of the first night."

"But that's preposterous," I said, a little angrily. "The finish of the last act must be rehearsed the same as everything else."

"The very thing I pointed out to him," remarked Hastings, lighting a cigarette. "But I am bound to say that he had a very good reason—or, at any rate, as good a reason as one could expect. He tells me that the play is complete—save for one line: a line to be spoken by you. Since the tag is never spoken during rehearsal—he is quite well up in theatrical customs—he argues that that one line is not wanted till the first night. I have, as I told you, read the play myself, and he's quite right. The play is finished— but for a line, and a little action. Anyway, it's an unalterable condition."

"Hang it all, Hastings," I said irritably, "the whole thing strikes me as being the most extraordinary thing I've ever heard of. You're sure the man is quite sane?"

"As sane as you or I. Undoubtedly he is eccentric, but he struck me as a gentleman who can afford to pay for his eccentricity. Candidly, Bourne, I felt just the same as you do about it. At first I was inclined to wash my hands of the whole affair. And then, out of curiosity, I read the play. Well, all I can say is, before you decide anything further, read it yourself."

Whereupon, he handed me the manuscript.

"All right, I will. When am I to meet this strange individual?"

"A condition I was almost forgetting. You will not meet him. Should there be any point which you wish to discuss with him, he would like you to do it through me. In any question of finance I am to act for him. And he particularly desires that no effort should be made to discover his identity."

"Well, I'm damned!" I muttered. "However, I'll read it, and I'll let you know my decision as soon as possible."

With that I shook hands and left him with the play under my arm. To say that I was intrigued would be to express my feelings too lightly: I was downright curious. Any possibility of the thing being some elaborate hoax was ruled out of court by the fact that it was Hastings who was handling it. He was far too big a man to lend himself to any foolish tricks of that sort.

All through lunch at my club I tried to puzzle things out, but I couldn't see a ray of light. And it was only as I was starting to walk home that I suddenly remembered there was an extra *matinée* at the Haymarket that afternoon—my only chance of seeing the unknown's two *protégés* act. It had got as far as that in my mind.

Well, I watched them from the stalls. The girl had a small part which she filled perfectly capably; so had the man. There was nothing to single either of them out in any way, with the possible exception of the girl's looks. She really was astoundingly pretty, with that wonderful English colouring which is unfortunately getting rarer and rarer. But you want something more than wonderful English colouring when you're going to play lead. And I saw nothing that afternoon to lead me to suppose that she had it. Of course, it might be there, lying dormant, ready to come out on a big occasion. On the other hand, it might not. At any rate, I'd seen them; now to read the play.

I had no time that evening before I went down to the theatre, and all through my own show my mind was subconsciously dwelling on the affair. It all seemed so strange, so unaccountable. Some kindly man wishing to do these two a good turn, perhaps, and remain unknown. But why the mystery of the missing line? Why no royalties? Why a hundred things?

At any rate, I was so intrigued that any thought of bed was out of the question until I'd read it. I started at midnight, and an hour later I sat back in my chair if anything more perplexed than ever. In spite of what Hastings had told me, I hadn't been able to rid my mind of the thought that the real reason of the mystery was that the play was bad, and the unknown author was trying to buy me. But as I put the script down I knew that Hastings was right. It was good: thundering good. I don't say that it was a masterpiece, but it was a play which anyone would have thankfully accepted on the spot and asked for more of the same kind. It was dramatic, it was tense, and it had plenty of action. I don't propose to tell you all the plot; it would only bore you. But to make what follows clear I must give you a brief outline of the end of the play—the bit that led up to the missing line. The situation was that the lady's husband, and the man whom the husband had strongly suspected of being on rather more than mere calling terms with his wife, occupied the stage. The real bone of contention, led up to in two acts of good gripping stuff, had occurred the previous night at the end of the second act. It presupposed one of those admirable stage houses which, thank heavens! are beyond the worst nightmare of even a modern jerry-builder—the type of bungalow effect where the bedrooms lead out of the hall. Behold, then, at the finish of the second act, husband returning somewhat unexpectedly to discover wife's bedroom door locked. And coming from the room a man's voice. Now all that was well done. The audience didn't know who was in there. They had seen the lover depart earlier, after scene of renunciation: they had seen the wife go to her bedroom. They had seen her pause in the doorway, stagger a little, and gasp out, "My God! You!" Then she had disappeared. Who was it in the room? Had the lover returned through the window? Was he a dirty dog, after all?

Then husband arrives: hears voice: beats on door. After a perceptible pause the door opens and wife appears. The room is empty; the man, whoever it was, has escaped through the window. Husband accuses her point-blank: mentions the lover by name. Horror upon horror—she does not deny it. Let him think what he will. In fact, not only does she not deny it, she admits it. And then she sinks half-fainting on the floor, while husband, uttering hoarse noises, beats it rapidly for the garden and a little fresh air.

Such was the situation which had to be cleared up in the third act. But before I come to that I must mention one more character—the lady's younger brother. He hadn't come in much, though he had been seen, and his principal claim to notoriety lay in the fact that he had spent quite a considerable portion of his life at His Majesty's expense. It is also gathered that he had just laid himself open to a further sojourn in the same quarters. An undesirable fellow, but adored—as undesirable fellows so often are—by his sister.

You've guessed, of course. He was to be the saviour of the situation. He it was whose voice the husband had heard the preceding night.

"You're a stern man; you're a harsh man," says the lover. "You take no excuse for weakness. It is a fact that I love your wife; but never by word or deed has she been disloyal to you. She was frightened to tell you last night who was in her room. She thought you'd ring for the police. It was her brother who was with her: if you want proof—open that door. She lied to save him."

He stood there pointing at the door, and there the script ended. There was one line more: what was it? What was that line—and what was on the other side of the door?

Lord! you fellows, how I cursed that unknown playwright! What was this line locked up in his mind? I couldn't get away from it. It haunted me. I could think of half a dozen, but none of them were good. Not a single line that I could think of kept up the tension till the curtain dropped. Was it to be a question of "My dear, forgive me, and my unworthy doubts," while the lover steals gently away to the Colonies? Were we to find the brother manacled between large policemen, as a sort of *tableau vivant?* Horrible. The bare thought of it made me shudder.

However, on one point I'd made up my mind. Missing line or no missing line, I was going to do that play next. If the worst came to the worst, and the curtain proved a bad one, I had sufficient faith in myself to think that I could substitute something or other which would prove satisfactory. After all, I had two months at least. And, furthermore, I thought it not unlikely that through Hastings I might be able to persuade the author to waive this particular condition a little nearer the time. There was no hurry about it at the moment.

Accordingly, next day, I again went round to see Hastings. He smiled as I entered his office and said: "I thought you would."

"Would what?" I demanded.

"Take the play. I've got the agreement all ready for you to sign."

I read it through, and, assuredly, it was a strange document. No mention of royalties or American rights or anything of that sort. Everything was mine unconditionally, or rather I should say everything was mine subject to the author's reservations, which I had already heard. But these were emphasized in no uncertain way.

"Should the licensee," ran a clause, "break the above conditions either in letter or in spirit, the agreement shall terminate forthwith. The author or his agent shall be sole arbiters of such infringement."

I kicked at that: it seemed to put me too completely in his hands. But, as Hastings pointed out, a further clause indemnifying me against any financial loss in such an event was a very efficient safeguard.

At any rate, I signed. Not without some misgivings at the last moment, it's true; but I signed. And there I was definitely committed to the production of an unfinished play by an unknown author, with two practically unknown people in two of the principal parts.

The first thing was to get hold of them. The run at the Haymarket was almost over, so I knew they would be free when I wanted them. And I asked them both to come round to see me at my theatre one evening after a *matinée*. They came, obviously a little surprised, and when I told them what I wanted their surprise did not decrease. To play lead with me—well, I don't want to appear unduly conceited—was an immense leg-up for both of them.

"I saw you at the Haymarket," I said, "and it struck me, from every point of view, that you are just what I want in this new play."

She looked at him, and she was even prettier close to than on the stage. And he looked at her, while I looked at them both. Accept—of course they would: with fervent gratitude and joy. And even while they were stammering out their thanks, I realized one thing.

Paula Vendon and Merrill were in love with one another.

It threw a light on the situation: it gave a possible solution. The unknown author was a philanthropist anxious to help these two to get married. And they'd have made a deuced fine couple, for he was a good-looking fellow, was Merrill.

Of course, as a solution, it didn't explain the extraordinary condition as to the missing line, but at any rate it explained the others. And for two or three weeks I let it go at that. I got the cast together, and, having completed the other preliminaries, we went into rehearsal.

First I read them the play. It's strange, isn't it, when one looks back on things by the light of future events, how a man marvels at his blindness? And yet when I came to the end of the second act—the bedroom scene I have told you of—and Paula Vendon, white to the lips, stood up with a stifled scream, nothing untoward struck me. In fact, so incredible can the density of the human brain be, that I thought her agitation was due to my masterly reading. I had carried her away, and if that was so she might really prove an actress.

She said nothing, and after a moment or two she resumed her chair with a little apology. But all through the third act I felt her great eyes fixed on me with an almost uncanny stare, and once, when I glanced at Merrill, he, too, was looking at me with a strange intentness.

I laid down the script and an excited chorus assailed me. "What then? What's the end?"

"Ah, ha!" I laughed, "I'm not going to tell you that. That's the tag—and that's a mystery."

They loved that, of course. We're all of us children; stage people more so than most. And soon the stage was empty save for Paula Vendon and Merrill. I'd noticed them talking earnestly in a corner, and when the others had gone they came up to me.

"Mr. Bourne," said the girl quietly, "who wrote this play?"

"A man who calls himself John Strangeways," I answered.

"That isn't his real name?" she asked.

"No. And I don't know what his real name is."

And then she looked at me as if she would read my very soul.

"Mr. Bourne," she said, "you've got to tell us. What is that missing line? What lies behind that door?"

Instinctively her hand went out to Merrill, and he took it in his own quite naturally.

"My dear," I answered quietly, "you may believe me or not, as you like—but I don't know myself. It is a whim of the author's that that should be kept a secret even from me until—er—until later on."

I think she saw I was speaking the truth, and she turned with a little shiver to Merrill.

"Leslie—I'm frightened. The whole thing is uncanny."

"My dear child——" I began, but Merrill interrupted me.

"Don't think, Mr. Bourne, that it's fanciful imagination. The fact is—" he hesitated a moment before taking the plunge—"the fact is that the play bears the most astounding resemblance to what actually happened to a—to a very dear friend of Miss Vendon."

"My dear fellow," I said, "is there anything unique in that? Most plays, certainly most good plays, must bear a resemblance to what has actually happened to someone. Otherwise they wouldn't be good. And the fact that this bears a resemblance to what happened to a friend of Miss Vendon strikes me as being merely a coincidence."

"That's so," he muttered, but I could see he wasn't convinced. Nor was she. Great heavens! in the light of future events I don't wonder. But who in their wildest imagination could have possibly anticipated those events? Certainly not I, for one.

The next day we went into rehearsal in earnest. Whatever misgivings Paula Vendon may have felt, she gave no further sign of them. She was ambitious— intensely so: and, what was more to the point, I soon saw that she was a fine actress. Merrill, too, was excellent: in fact, everything was going swimmingly. The only fly in my ointment was the absolute refusal on the part of the author to reconsider his condition as to the missing line. I told Hastings that I would swear on my most sacred word of honour not to let another soul know what it was, if only he would tell me. And I was met with an absolutely blank refusal. On the first night, and not till then, would the secret be revealed.

Of course, it was impossible to stop the company from talking. And after a week or two the reporters got to hear of it. This was something new: a first-class stunt. They lay in wait for me: they besieged my dressing-room, and I had to say something. And then paragraphs began to appear something after this fashion:

"Accustomed though we all of us are to the secrecy surrounding forthcoming theatrical productions, Mr. Arthur Bourne has gone a step farther. He assures us that he himself is in complete ignorance of the final curtain of his new play. He tells us, however," etc., etc.

Then there were headlines in the weekly sporting papers:

"What Lies Behind the Closed Door?"

"What is the Missing Line?"

So it went on: a truly gorgeous advertisement. Never has there been such an advertisement before or since. Everybody was talking about it. Men at the club gnashed their teeth with envy: asked me if it was my idea. And quite politely, but very definitely, they flatly refused to believe me when I said it was the truth. The company didn't believe me—and after a time I let it go at that. Advertisement is an excellent thing—and since the world had taken it that way, let it remain so.

And then one day dear old Jimmy Maunders gave me a bit of a jolt. We were lunching together, and, as usual, the conversation came round to the play.

"You really mean, Arthur," he said, "that you have no idea of this curtain?"

"Jimmy," I answered, "there are some men I don't lie to, and you're one of 'em. I haven't the ghost of a notion."

For a moment or two he crumbled his bread, while he stared at me from under his shaggy eyebrows.

"Then all I can say, old man," he said, at length, "is that I hope you won't be let down. If, after all this talking and mystery, the mountain brings forth a mouse, it won't do you any good. And, I tell you, it will have to be something astonishingly big to survive this prolonged period of gestation."

I stared at him.

"By Jove! Jimmy, you're right," I said. "It hadn't struck me that way before. But it wasn't I who started this damned advertisement."

He laughed.

"I dare say not. But most of your friends and all your enemies will think it was."

As I said, it hadn't struck me in that light before. To have a thumping advertisement and then present the public with a thing like a damp squib is not a good thing to do. And I was under no delusions on one point. All the tentative endings which had occurred to me would produce exactly that effect. When I had thought of them vaguely at the beginning, there had been no question of this newspaper stunt. Any of them would have done at a pinch—then: now the thing was completely different. And the more I thought of it, the less I liked it. I used to have nightmares of the door opening slowly before the excited audience to reveal Miss Vendon standing on her head. And then I'd wake in a muck sweat with the jeers and hisses of the whole theatre ringing in my ears.

I redoubled my efforts through Hastings.

"Point out to the author," I said, "the position we're in. He may be eccentric; but he must want his play to succeed. And if, after this advertisement, that final curtain is a frost, the whole thing will be a hopeless failure."

It was useless. Hastings fully saw my point, and did everything he possibly could.

"You can assure Mr. Bourne," was the only answer, "that the more advertisement there is the better I shall be pleased. The final curtain will not be a frost, but will be the strongest point in the play."

And with that I had to rest content. Once or twice I seriously thought of chucking up the whole thing—but I couldn't. I was too involved: things had gone too far. There was nothing for it but to carry on and trust for the best.

The date for production drew nearer and nearer, and but for that one haunting fear I should have been delighted. I knew I had a winner. The company were splendid: Paula had fairly astounded me. Whatever the cause of her first vague fears, she had apparently completely got over them, and she was superb.

In her I saw my future leading lady for as long as she liked, and I told her so. She was delighted, and I watched her passing it on to Merrill in a corner of the stage, and then he said something to her and touched her hand—and they laughed a little as lovers do. A good pair; there would always be a place in the cast for Merrill as well.

It was two days before the dress rehearsal that Hastings came round to see me.

"About that bally door of yours," he began.

"He's told you!" I cried excitedly.

"Not a word," he answered, and my heart sank. "But he wants that door boxed in so that the stage-hands can't see. In fact, he wants a little room made behind the stage set, out of which that door will open."

I stared at him in amazement: the wildest thoughts were passing through my mind. You fellows probably have no idea of the astounding things which some people will submit for staging; I had.

"Good Lord, Hastings!" I said anxiously, "what's the game? Surely he hasn't got some French cabaret ending with Paula waiting for me in a minimum of clothes—or anything of that sort! Because if that's it," I added firmly, "I'll postpone the play. I won't do it; and people can think what they like."

Hastings hurried off, and half an hour later he rang me up.

"It's all right, Bourne," he said. "It's nothing indecent. But he wants Miss Vendon to be in that room three minutes before the end of the play. She is to be dressed in the evening frock she is wearing earlier in the act."

So I sent for the stage carpenter and gave him the necessary instructions. God! what a fool I was! As I said before, a man's blindness can be incredible.

Yet who would have thought. Who *could* have thought?

The dress rehearsal went without a hitch. A few specially invited people waxed enthusiastic, though one or two of them were mildly sarcastic. The line, you see, was still missing.

"So you won't even trust *us?*" said one of them to me after. "It must be the devil of an ending, old man."

And when I told him I didn't know it myself, he smiled politely.

I don't think I've ever spent a more nerve-racking day than the next. Most of the morning papers had allusions to it—and all the evening ones: "Mystery of the Closed Door to be Solved To-night."

The demand for seats had been unprecedented: as you know, a first-night is generally a largely paper house, but there was less paper on this occasion than on any other in my career. Six o'clock came; seven —and I was getting in a fever. No inkling of what the curtain was to be had come.

Hastings rang me up, and I could tell he was uneasy himself; he'd heard nothing. And I cursed him foolishly over the wire.

I went down to the theatre, where the usual first-night fever was in evidence. And there I found Hastings looking very worried.

"Look here, Bourne," he said, "I'm sorry to say I've got bad news for you."

I stood very still.

"You mean the curtain is hopeless?" I said.

"Not quite as bad as that. But the author now states that he will not reveal the curtain until the moment comes. He wishes you to stand facing the door: Merrill with his back to it."

"But," I almost screamed, "what am I to say?"

"He says you'll know at the time.   Above all things you're not to worry.   He is mad keen on a success. I think," he added, in a pitiful attempt to cheer me up, "you can trust him.   I have a feeling he's not going to let you down.   He's not that type of man."

I nodded dully; was ever a man in such a position? A crammed, excited audience; all this damnable advertisement—and I didn't know the answer.

"If that man does let me down, Hastings," I said savagely, "I swear to Heaven I'll never forgive you."

But he was a good fellow and took no offence.

Of course I didn't let the company know; that would have been fatal.   And they played superbly.   I forced that ghastly final fence out of mind as much as I could, and did my best; but at the end of the first act I heard a man's voice from the stalls: "The girl's magnificent, but Bourne's a bit mechanical for him."

Do you wonder?

The second act was a triumph.   We had fifteen curtains—Paula and I, and the girl's eyes were all dewy with happiness and success.

Then came the third.   Lord! you fellows, I could feel the tension on the other side of the house; now the secret which had set London talking was to be revealed.   I played in a sort of daze, and every moment it got nearer—the still-missing line.   Two minutes to go; Paula was there now—behind the door. And then began Merrill's last speech:

"You're a stern man; you're a harsh man."

I was staring at the door; and suddenly my heart began to beat in great sickening thumps.   Dimly I heard Merrill's voice; but the stage was swimming. No—not nervousness: horror.   Stark, unbelievable horror.   From underneath the door a stream was trickling.   And the stream was scarlet.   It oozed gently on till it came to the carpet; and then more came and more. It took fantastic shapes; it went with little rushes—then it stopped. Then on again. It was blood.

"It was her brother who was with her. If you want proof—open that door. She lied to save him."

From a vast distance I heard his voice. And then the door opened. The audience, I was told afterwards, were literally rising in their seats; the moment had come. And to my dying day I shall never forget the terror of it. It swung open—that door; and with it came Paula. A dagger had been plunged up to the hilt in her heart, and she lay there on the stage with a look of pitiful fear in her eyes—eyes already glazed and sightless.

And then came a voice, a harsh, terrible voice.

"Her brother was arrested by the police three days ago."

The missing line was known at last.

The next few minutes are just a blur in my mind. Someone lowered the curtain, and wave after wave of applause came from the other side. And still I stood there speechless. Up it went again; no one had seen anything in the wings, while all the time the stream grew larger and larger.

And then came the climax: Merrill had swung round and seen it, too. Clear above the applause came his agonized shout, and as he knelt down beside the girl a dead silence fell. He lifted her in his arms and as he did so the great red stain showed clear to the people in the dress-circle.

A woman screamed, and at last I found my voice.

"Lower the curtain!" I shouted. And as it went down I called across the footlights: "A doctor, if there is one—at once."

Then I stumbled through the door—that cursed

door—to find Merrill fighting like a madman with some of the stage-hands. He was trying to get at a man in evening clothes who was facing him—also in the grip of scene-shifters.

"'Ere's the swine wot did it, sir," said one of them as he saw me.

"A capital performance, Mr. Bourne," said the stranger politely. "My dear wife scored a veritable triumph."

"Good God, man!" said a voice beside me. "That's the author."

It was Hastings, and his face was as white as his shirt-front.

There isn't much more to tell. Recognizing the man as Paula Vendon's husband, the doorkeeper had let him pass—and it was a stage-hand up above who told me what had happened. He'd seen it all, for there was no roof on the room behind the door. Paula was standing there when he came in, and she shrank back in evident surprise at his sudden appearance. And then, before the horrified gaze of the man, who was powerless to interfere, the devil had whipped out a dagger and stabbed her. He placed her sitting against the door, and held her there till the moment came—and the door opened.

But it was Merrill himself who supplied the missing links.

"It was my fault," he muttered brokenly. "I over-persuaded her. I forced myself to think it was only a strange coincidence—and I made her think it, too. Besides, I never dreamed, I never thought—— Who could have? You see, it was true—this play." He looked at me with sombre eyes. "It happened—all except the finish." For a while he broke down utterly. "It was true that her brother had been taken by the police three days before he caught us, but until to-night I never realized he knew. And there was nothing wrong, Bourne, that I swear. I was in her room, but it was only to make one more attempt to get her to leave what was nothing more than a hell on earth and come away with me. But that brute would never have believed it, so I lied to him. And so did she. We said it was her brother, and he pretended to believe. And he knew all the time. For three years has that devil kept it dark, waiting for his revenge. And now—oh, my little girl, my little girl!"

He staggered blindly from my dressing-room, and I sat on, thinking dully. Reporters were seething outside, but I refused to see them. I felt that I was to blame, and yet, as poor Merrill said, who could have dreamed of such an end? Step by step that devil had led up to it—and then, in the hour of her triumph, he killed her. They found him mad; as far as I know, he's in Broadmoor to-day.

But—and this is the point—assuming that ending, without the actual tragedy, would you have called that play melodrama?

VII   STUBBY

"IT'S not for want of asking," sighed Mrs. Tremayne. "If he's proposed once he must have done it half a dozen times. Mona simply will not give him a definite answer."

"I gather," murmured the Soldier, "that you would like the answer when it does come to be in the affirmative?"

"Naturally," said our hostess. "Ever since they were kiddies it has been our wish, and his people's, too. An understood thing. It's so eminently suitable. The properties adjoin: Desmond is an only child, and so is Mona. The two families are connected in a hundred ways by ties of sentiment and place and everything else. Desmond is standing for this constituency next election, and my old Tom is a leading light in the Conservative Association here. Besides—look at them. Have you ever seen a better-looking pair?"

And making due allowance for maternal pride, one could but agree: they were a magnificent pair. Mona —well, of course, on the subject of Mona Tremayne even I was partially dotty. At the advanced age of sixty, with senile decay coming on apace, I had the greatest difficulty in refraining from proposing to her myself. In fact, only the certainty of her becoming hysterical with laughter restrained me. So I contented myself with being called Uncle Dick—uncle out of deference only to my grey and scanty hairs—and having the top of my head kissed. But what a darling she is!

And I admit that young Brooke was almost worthy of her. Clever, wealthy, a wonderful athlete, and very good-looking, he was essentially what would be described as an excellent match. A little inclined, perhaps, to be sarcastic; a little too intolerant, perhaps, of fools— but withal one of the best. At least so I thought.

Our hostess left us, and the Soldier relit his pipe.

"These settled things, old Dick, have a way of not coming off."

"My dear Bill," I answered, "don't forget we're hopelessly old-fashioned. As far as I can make out, if a man proposes to a girl to-day he just says: 'What about it?' and she says, 'Not a hope.' Then they push off to a night-club and come home with the milk."

"Perhaps," he said. "But that doesn't apply to Miss Mona." He was staring thoughtfully across the lawn. "She's a thoroughbred—that girl."

"So, I think, is young Brooke," I replied.

He didn't speak for a while, and then he said something which surprised me.

"I wonder," he remarked. "I wonder. First-class in the show ring, I admit: a prize-winner every time. But it's a funny thing, Dick, how often one finds a yellow streak in that type when it comes to the test."

He broke off suddenly: Mona was standing behind us.

"You two lazy men have got to come and play tennis," she said smiling. But there was a thoughtful look in her eyes, and I couldn't help wondering if she'd heard.

Certainly it was an idea that would never have occurred to me: in common with a good many other people, I had always looked on Brooke as just about as perfect a specimen of young manhood as it was possible to find. But Bill Saunders was a man of understanding, used to men and the ways of men, and as a judge of character—male characters at any rate—I have yet to meet his superior. And after we'd finished our tennis he reverted to the subject. We were strolling back to the house together, with Mona and young Brooke some way behind.

"I hope the little girl didn't hear what I said about the yellow streak," he remarked. "But I'm open to a small bet of an even shilling that it's there. Not that, in all probability, the fact will ever come out, so your shilling is safe."

"But what makes you think so, Bill?" I demanded.

He shrugged his shoulders.

"My dear old man," he said, "in the course of my long and disreputable career I've run across a good many fellows. And there have been times when an accurate appreciation of character has been of the greatest value to me. And I tell you now that if I knew I was going to find myself in a really tight corner I'd sooner have that sandy-haired boy with the snub nose and the freckles by my side than young Brooke."

"What—Stubby?" I laughed incredulously. "Dear old Stubby! Though I agree that he's an awfully nice boy. But, Bill, no one could take Stubby seriously." And Bill Saunders smiled and said nothing.

It was at school that he got his nickname, and when you met him you realized why. His real name was Jack Stretton, but so universal was the use of the other that frequently a house-party broke up with half the guests in ignorance of what that real name was. Complete strangers called him Stubby, and Stubby grinned all over his freckled face and loved it.

His age was twenty-seven, and he would not have won a prize at a beauty show. Unless, maybe, it had been a prize for eyes only. Cover up the rest of Stubby's face, cover up his short sandy hair, and one stood almost tongue-tied at the beauty of those great brown eyes of his. I've tried it, and I know.

Not that anybody had ever mentioned the fact to him. He would have been reduced to a condition of impotent bashfulness and rage, which would have rendered him speechless. He would probably, in fact, have regarded it as a deadly insult. And yet those brown eyes of his are the most beautiful things I have ever seen in the world.

Like a spaniel's—just full of confidence and trust and love and—what is lacking in a dog—a wonderful glint of humour. That the humour was generally directed against himself was beside the point; perhaps, even, it increased the charm.

For Stubby was one of those dear fellows who invariably did the wrong thing. If, in any conversation, there was a chance of someone putting their foot into it, the only safe thing to do, if Stubby was present, was to muzzle him. Otherwise he would be that someone with unfailing regularity. And yet nobody could ever be angry with him for long.

He would seize a lull in the conversation to discuss the subject of wigs with some aged woman in an obvious brown toupée, and when he was frowned into silence by his hostess, would tactfully extricate himself by saying to the outraged female that he never realized it wasn't her own hair. "So well made, don't you know. By Jove! yes—rather. Corking fit. Have some muffin, won't you?"

Another of his little peculiarities was his usefulness. He was a sort of universal fag.

"Stubby, darling—will you be an angel, and trot back to the house? I've left my parasol in the hall."

And Stubby would trot back half a mile or so, and return beaming with a large golfing umbrella.

At games, or anything in the sport line, he was probably the world's worst rabbit. When Stubby shot, strong men in his vicinity lay prostrate on the ground: when Stubby rode—well, I will not labour the point. He seemed to adopt the sentiment towards his saddle of the gentleman from the backwoods towards a spittoon.

"If you don't take that durned thing away I'll spit in it."

Similarly Stubby.

"If you don't take that durned saddle away I'll sit in it."

But it was at games that his really staggering ineptitude was most apparent. At cricket, if the batsman hit a catch in his direction he would merely pat the wicket in preparation for the next ball. And it is on record that on the one known occasion when he held a catch the umpires conferred together before giving the batsman out, in order to be certain that lunch had not been too much for their eyesight.

It was the same at tennis and golf.   He was hopeless
—incredibly, unbelievably hopeless.   And yet withal he
was a sportsman in the truest sense of the word.   For
the test of true sportsmanship is not the ability with
which a thing is done, but the spirit in which it is done.
And Stubby's spirit was pure gold clean through.

But, as I said to Bill Saunders, no one took him seriously.   He was—and always would be—just Stubby.
If any other man had shown such obvious adoration for
Mona, Brooke might reasonably have felt uneasy.   But
with Stubby it didn't matter.   He knew how things
stood: he knew that it was a sort of tacitly accepted
matter that in the fullness of time Mona would marry
Brooke—in fact, we all assumed it.   And that in itself
was sufficient to prevent his dreaming of anything serious—for Stubby was a loyal soul.

Just as he adored Mona, so in a different way did he
worship Brooke.   It was almost pathetic—his admiration for this man who did everything so supremely well;
admiration untarnished by the slightest trace of jealousy.
Did Brooke do something good playing cricket for the
county it was Stubby who missed no ball in the telling
of it; did Brooke shoot well it was Stubby who faithfully
recorded every right and left.   And having done so he
would then with great solemnity propose to Mona across
the dinner-table.

"Some day, Stubby darling, I shall accept you," said
Mona one evening.   "Are you aware that this is the
forty-ninth time?"

"Fiftieth," said Stubby promptly.   "You've forgotten the one at breakfast last Tuesday week."

Which was fairly indicative of the state of affairs when
Bill Saunders made his shilling bet with me.

I can't say that I thought much more about it: as he
said, it was very improbable that anyone would ever discover the fact, even if he was right.

And then there occurred the Rosenthal incident.

We were having tea out of doors—the Tremaynes, Bill Saunders and I—when the Rosenthals arrived. We knew them both very slightly and they were of the type which causes one to barricade oneself in the most inaccessible attic and refuse to move. But escape was impossible, and with a sort of frozen calm we watched them descend from their car. The man had been something in the City, and was entitled on sight to a residence in the charming old-world town of Jerusalem.

They were new-comers and late-goers; and until that afternoon I never realized the true descriptiveness of the phrase "to descend on people." They descended on us: they didn't just cross the lawn and sit down—they descended. And as they descended from one quarter Stubby ascended from another.

He was in his dirtiest pair of old grey flannel trousers, and in his arms he carried a terrier. It was moaning feebly, and it seemed a queer sort of shape, but it still had enough strength in its poor little broken body to lick his hand. They met at the tea-table, and suddenly I heard Mona give a little gasp. And she was not looking at the dog—she was looking at Stubby. For there was that in his eyes which I had never seen before—blind, black rage.

"Are you aware, sir," he said, "that you ran over my dog one hundred yards down the road, and then failed to stop when I shouted to you, though I saw you look round?"

It was an awkward moment, but worse was to come. As I have said, Stubby was in his oldest clothes, and the mistake was perhaps excusable. To the gentleman who had been something in the City there seemed only one solution. It was most annoying: he could hear his wife breathing heavily at such an unfortunate contretemps. Just as they were calling on one of the leaders of The

County Set, and she with her best pearls on. This common young man: dreadful. . . .

"There, there, my man," he remarked suavely. "How very unfortunate. Here's a fiver for you to—er —buy another dog with."

And once again Mona gave a little gasp.

"You splay-faced swab!" said Stubby slowly and very distinctly. "You horrible parody of a human being! You cross between a bucket-shop proprietor and an Italian waiter—how dare you offer me money? If I had gloves on, you perspiring excrescence, I would make you eat your dirty fiver. Go away—" he laid the dog gently in Mona's lap—"go away from here, and never let me see you again, you—you outrage on decency! If I had a tank I'd passage it backwards and forwards over your beastly person, and howl with joy as you squashed!"

"Good God! my dear—he's mad!"

With agitation written large on their faces, the callers were backing towards their car with Stubby following them step by step. Surely Mr. Tremayne would do something: it was monstrous that they should be insulted by a common young man merely because of a wretched dog: monstrous. And yet Mr. Tremayne seemed more interested in the little brute than in them.

"I am not mad," continued Stubby, still driving them in front of him. "Far from it. And if you'd had the common decency—it's about the only common attribute you lack—to stop when you ran over my dog, I wouldn't have minded so much."

"I'll summons you for assault and battery," howled the man.

He and his wife, white and shaking with rage, were in the car by now.

"I wish you would," said Stubby. "That would finally finish your chance of getting to know anyone

decent. This address will find me for the next fortnight."

The words died away on the City gentleman's lips;
this terrible young man was a member of the house-
party.

"Home," he snarled to the chauffeur. Heavens!
how he'd take it out of the fool later for not being more
careful in his driving.

"Stubby, dear!" said Mrs. Tremayne, as he joined
us after watching the car out of sight. "Weren't you
just a little——"

"I'm sorry," said Stubby quietly. "I couldn't help
it. Oh! my God—look at little Dick!"

He was bending over Mona, and suddenly she looked
up at him. Something wet had splashed on her hand,
and she was a girl of great understanding.

"Let's take him to the stables, Stubby, and see if we
can do anything?"

They went off together, but there was nothing to be
done. Dick would kill no more rats, and they buried
him that evening in a special corner of the garden.
They didn't see me; they were too engrossed in what
they were doing. And when it was all over, they stood
there for a moment or two looking down at the grave.
It was then it happened. She took Stubby in her arms
and kissed him on the lips.

"Stubby, dear," she said, "I just loved you at tea
to-day."

She was gone, leaving Stubby staring after her foolishly. He was swaying a little—like a man partially
dazed. And as he passed me a few moments later, completely unconscious of my presence, he was muttering
to himself:

"Don't be a silly fool, you ass; don't be a silly fool!"

But there was a look on his face that hurt, and for the

first time in my life I felt annoyed with Mona.   I knew
she'd meant it kindly, but it wasn't quite fair to the boy.
And I made up my mind, if I got an opportunity, to
mention it to her.

I found Bill Saunders on the lawn, and he grinned
gently as he saw me.

"A refreshing flow of language," he remarked.   "But
I fear it's going to be a little awkward.   I gather the
Hebraic gentleman is somewhat of a power politically."

"I didn't know Stubby had it in him," I said.

And once again Bill smiled and said nothing.

But it was awkward all right, and the awkwardness
started at dinner.

Desmond had come over, and it soon became obvious
that he was annoyed.

"I say, Stubby," he began, almost as soon as we sat
down, "what is this I hear from Jackson?"   Jackson
was the lodge-keeper.   "He spun me some interminable
yarn about your having insulted that fellow Rosenthal
this afternoon."

For a moment no one spoke; by tacit consent the
subject had not been alluded to again.

"He killed Dick," said Stubby.   "Run over him
with his beastly motor-car.   Never even stopped, and
then offered me a fiver."

Desmond frowned irritably.

"Well, I don't suppose he ran over the dog on purpose.   And if you were in your usual rig I don't
wonder that he offered you money."

"But, great Scott, old man!" cried Stubby, " he's the
most unredeemable swine, so what does it matter?"

"It matters this," answered the other.   "Your little
entertainment this afternoon has in all probability cost
me five or six hundred votes.   I know the fellow is a
swine—but he's got works in Murchester.   And he's
got a lot of interests in Murchester.   And in this con-

stituency the way the Murchester vote goes is very important."

"My dear old man, I *am* sorry!" Stubby was genuinely distressed. "That aspect of the case simply never dawned on me. But surely the fact that I slanged the bounder won't affect you?"

"Oh, Stubby—don't be such an ass!" Desmond Brooke laughed, but his underlying irritation was still obvious. "Everybody round here knows that you and I are friends. Apart from that, the thing was done in this house, and Mr. Tremayne is the head of our association."

He laughed again and pushed away his plate.

"Doesn't matter, old man; don't worry. But next time choose someone less important to give tongue to."

"Would it do any good if I went and apologized?" said Stubby. "I can't say that I want to, but——"

"If you do," broke in Mona calmly, "I will never speak to you again. So that's that. Now let's talk of something else."

That was that all right, but as a conversational effort it did not add to the harmony of the evening. Brooke flushed angrily, and looked sullen; Stubby glanced anxiously from one god to the other. And things did not improve after dinner.

In the billiard-room Desmond Brooke was studiously polite to Mona in such a marked fashion as to make it obvious. And after a while Mona laid down her cue.

"If you're trying to pick a quarrel with me, Desmond," she remarked, "say so straight out. I dislike people beating about the bush."

Only Stubby and I were there, and Desmond returned his own cue to the rack.

"Perhaps it would be as well if we could have a little

private talk," he said.   "I don't think there is anyone
in the gun-room."

He held the door open for her, and Stubby, with
misery in his eyes, watched them disappear.

"What a blithering ass I am," he muttered.   "It's
all my silly fault.   They'll have a row now."

And I, with the memory of what I had seen in the
garden fresh in my mind, marvelled that so much loyalty
could exist in a human being.

There was no doubt about the row.   Five minutes
later the door was flung open, and Desmond, his face
black as thunder, appeared.

"I say, old man——"   Stubby started forward.

"Go to blazes!" snarled the other.   And then he
paused ominously.   "Or rather, since you seem to be
the pattern of all the virtues, go to Mona."

With that he left the billiard-room, and a little later
I heard the front door slam.   Undoubtedly a new experience for Master Desmond; and a very salutary one.

Shortly after he had gone Mona came in from the
gun-room.   Her colour was a little higher, but otherwise there was no sign that anything had occurred.

"We might play three-handed, don't you think?" she
said.   "All against all."

"I say, Mona—what an awful box-up!" cried Stubby.

"Don't be an ass, Stubby dear," she said quietly, and
picked up her cue.

No more was said, and it wasn't until just before we
went to bed that I got a word with her alone.   I felt I
just had to—for Stubby's sake.

"Dear child," I said, "you've had a bit of a row with
Desmond, I know.   And though I'm old and venerable
and suffering from senile decay, I wonder if you'd let
me say one thing to you?"

"Anything you like, Uncle Dick," she answered
gently.

"Well, it's this. The row will blow over in a day or two, but until it does, of your mercy be careful with Stubby."

"What *do* you mean?" she said with a puzzled look on her face.

"In a way he's the cause of the row, isn't he? I mean what he did. Well, don't be too kind to him just because you're angry with Desmond. It would mean nothing to you—I was in the garden to-day when you buried Dick, and I saw you kiss him, and that meant nothing to you. But, my dear, don't forget how he adores you, and I don't want him to suffer."

"You darling," she said. "You darling! Nor do I."

And with that she left the room very quickly.

Strange how utterly blind people are at times. I suppose it is that one gets a preconceived idea in one's head, and there isn't room for anything else. Certainly during the next two months things went on as usual. Desmond came and went, and Stubby came and went, while I emulated the celebrated brook. Desmond was working full time in the constituency: a Very Great Man had come to stay for the week-end and had given as his Very Great and Considered Opinion that there was a big future in front of young Brooke.

"He has brains, money, charm and tact," he remarked, "and with those four assets a man can get anywhere."

And Stubby, who heard him, beamed all over his ugly face and said: "Top-hole. Good old Desmond!"

It seemed certain that with or without the Murchester vote he would get into Parliament at the next election. In fact, the Rosenthal incident was forgotten. On the advice of Mr. Tremayne, Stubby had written him a short note regretting that in the heat of the moment he might have expressed himself a little strongly, and had received a curt line of acknowledgment.   And there it had ended. In fact, everything seemed just as it was before it happened—except for one thing.

I noticed it in a lot of little ways—Brooke's behaviour to Stubby, but it came to a head at a big tennis tournament given by the Tremaynes.   They had four courts and it was a three-day show, with one or two star performers specially invited.   And in it a miracle occurred. Stubby, who received forty every game, much helped by two walk-overs, had reached the final in the handicap singles.   And Desmond Brooke was the other finalist.

The result, of course, was a foregone conclusion. Stubby had no more chance—even with his handicap— of beating Brooke than he would have had of beating Tilden.   But he was so keen, and he was so excited. To reach the final of anything was so inconceivably beyond his wildest dream that he was almost incoherent.

The court was crowded with spectators to see the prospective new member, and—well, dash it all—I know Brooke had the game in his pocket, but even so, he might surely have made some small effort to appear interested.   Not a bit of it; he seemed to go out of his way to make Stubby look a fool.   And he succeeded.

In a story, I suppose, Stubby would have won.   He didn't; I don't think he got a game.   With the sweat dripping off his face he rushed wildly backwards and forwards, while Brooke—who hadn't troubled to take off his sweater—simply played with him.

And after a while people began to laugh, and Brooke began to smile.   In fact, I thought I was the only person looking on who wasn't laughing till I turned round and found Mona behind me.   And she wasn't laughing either.   She didn't say anything, though she saw me right enough.   But when it was over, and Brooke was surrounded by a bevy of admiring people, she went across to Stubby—who was mopping his face in a corner by himself. And by chance I glanced at Brooke, and caught the look on his face as he saw them. It was gone in a moment, but it was the same as it had worn when he snarled at Stubby in the billiard-room on the night of the Rosenthal incident.

It was incredible to think that Brooke was jealous of Stubby, and yet what other solution was there? As I say, the tennis tournament was only the culmination of a whole series of similar things, and for the first time I began to wonder whether the universal assumption with regard to the matrimonial stakes was correct. And I wondered even more ten minutes later. I went over to one of the marquees to get a whisky and soda and I heard voices from the other side of a big palm. It was impossible to avoid listening, and, as I say, I wondered even more.

"Look here, Stubby,"—it was Brooke speaking—"I don't want to be unpleasant. But kindly remember in future that Mona is to all intents and purposes engaged to me. I don't want you making her conspicuous."

"But, good Lord, old man!" cried Stubby aghast. "I wouldn't do such a thing for the world."

"Well, be a little more discreet in future, then," said Brooke, as he left the tent.

The whole accusation was rankly unfair even if Brooke had been actually engaged to the girl. As he wasn't, it was grossly impertinent. But Stubby took it to heart badly. And during the next fortnight I often caught Mona looking at him with a puzzled frown. He used to flee from her presence as if she had an infectious disease.

"Look here, Stubby," she said to him one day, "what on earth is the matter with you? Why are you avoiding me like the pest?"

He flushed all over his face, and began stammering something or other.

"No excuses," she remarked. "I want the truth."

She listened in silence, and when he had finished there was an ominous look in her eyes.

"Thank you, Stubby," she said quietly. "I understand. I'm driving over to Murchester to fetch Desmond now."

"You won't say anything to the old boy," said Stubby, greatly agitated.

She looked at him with a faint smile.

"There are times, Stubby, when I could kiss you, and there are times when I could smack you. I'm not certain which this is."

With that she was gone, and we watched her drive away from the door behind a spanking great bay horse. The Tremaynes had a car, but they stuck to the old-fashioned way as well, for short distances.

"I'm always putting my foot in it," said Stubby miserably. "Now they'll have another row."

"Look here, young fellow," I said, "if you take my advice you'll think a little less of Desmond and a little more of yourself. Brooke is quite capable of taking care of himself."

It was two hours later that a white-faced groom brought the dog-cart back alone. The bay was lathered in sweat, and we rushed out to see what had happened.

"Where's Miss Mona?" cried her father in an agony.

"Miss Mona's all right, sir," cried the man, "it's Mr. Stretton. For Gawd's sake get a doctor! Tim got frightened by a traction engine coming out o' Murchester and bolted for two miles. I couldn't stop him and no more could Miss Mona. Mr. Brooke fell out: I seed him running after us. And we was coming to Bury Hill. Suddenly we sees Mr. Stretton a-walking along the road in front. He looks round and sees us, and he makes a dive at Tim's 'ead. He 'ung on, sir— and he was dragged something cruel. But 'e stopped Tim just at the top of the 'ill. And then—well, the wheel went over 'im, sir—just at the end. I've left 'im there, sir—with Miss Mona. She told me to come on and send a doctor."

Stubby was unconscious when we got there: lying on the grass beside the road with his head on Mona's lap.

"Where's the doctor?" she cried.

"Coming, my darling," said her father. "Are you all right?"

"I'm not even touched," she answered. And then her voice broke. "But oh! Dad—I'm afraid Stubby is done for. And it's all my fault."

And at that moment he opened his eyes.

"Hullo!" he said feebly. Then he seemed to remember. "Are you all right, Mona? Not hurt?"

"Not a bit, Stubby dear, thanks to you." And before us all she went down and kissed him on the mouth.

For a moment a wonderful look came into his eyes; then his mind began to wander.

"All right, old man," he muttered. "Of course I won't make her conspicuous. As if I could—with a face like mine."

He stirred restlessly: only the touch of Mona's hand on his forehead seemed to soothe him. And always his words were of the girl, till the tears were pouring down her face unchecked, and her father cursed childishly at the non-arrival of the doctor.

But he came at last, and made his examination. And when he had finished his face was grave.

"I don't know," he said quietly. "I can't say for certain. But we must get him back to your house in an ambulance at once. Then I can make a closer over-haul."

The chauffeur was sent post haste to Murchester, while we waited there beside the road. And it was while we waited that the doctor told me what he feared— a broken back.

Poor old Stubby! Lying there, muttering out the secrets of his heart—secrets he fondly imagined we'd none of us guessed. And once the girl whispered pitifully—she didn't know I was close behind her—"You've got to pull through, old man—you've got to, for my sake."

And Stubby only muttered on.

But the ambulance arrived at last, and we got him back to the house. It was while the doctor was making his detailed examination that Mona joined me in the garden. And there was a look in her eyes which hurt.

"Dear girl," I said, "don't take it so much to heart. After all, he just did what one would have expected Stubby to do. It's lucky Desmond wasn't hurt when he fell out. By the way, I wonder where he is."

"Fell out, Uncle Dick!" she said slowly. "He didn't fall out. When Tim bolted—he jumped. You look amazed," she continued. "I don't wonder. Even now, though I saw it with my own eyes, it seems incredible. But he jumped."

I said nothing, and after a while she went on.

"Do you remember months ago talking to General Saunders on the lawn. And he said something about Desmond having a yellow streak in him. He didn't mean me to hear—but I did. It didn't make much impression on me at the time: after all, it was only a guess on his part, and I thought that whatever other faults Desmond had in his character cowardice was not one of them. I knew he was intensely selfish; I knew he was mean—I don't allude to money matters. You can't grow up with someone and not spot things like that. I knew he was intensely jealous—and jealous in the worst way. Not jealous because he's in love with a person: but jealous because he's in love with his own position. And if I knew it before, I've known it doubly since that row between Stubby and the Rosenthals. He was furious with me for taking Stubby's side, and he's revenged himself—or tried to—on Stubby since."

She paused and stared across the park.

"But cowardice—I didn't think that." She turned and faced me squarely. "Uncle Dick—I said it was all my fault; it is. There was a moment this afternoon, just as Tim was getting out of hand, when I could have controlled him. I know it. And some devil in me prompted me to look at Desmond's face. And I saw in it stark fear. It staggered me. I·remembered General Saunders' remark, and I didn't pull Tim up. Nothing seemed to matter except to see what Desmond would do. And he jumped. The groom didn't see— Tim had got away properly—and he was leaning over on my other side hauling on the reins. But I saw. He stood up swaying—and then he jumped. And just before he jumped he looked at me. He knows I know."

"Heavens!" I muttered; "it seems impossible."

"As if it mattered what he did," she went on. "Stubby is all that counts—and oh, God!—won't that doctor ever come? It's my fault—don't you see? All my fault." She was clutching my arm. "If I'd stopped Tim this would never have happened."

And then suddenly she grew very still: her father was coming across the lawn towards us.

"It's all right, dear," he cried. "Three ribs: a collar-bone: and some appalling bruises."

She swayed a little, and I put an arm round her to steady her.

"He's asking for you," went on Tom as he joined us.

"Uncle Dick," said Mona quietly. "Will you tell

Dad what I've told you?   But after that I don't want it to go any farther."

Then she went indoors.

He heard me in silence, did Tom Tremayne, with amazement written large on his face.

"A mistake, Dick," he said when I'd finished.   "She must have made a mistake."

But I could see he didn't think so.

"Why, it would break his father's heart."

"I don't see that his father need ever know, Tom."

"What's Mona going to do?"

"The betting is a fiver to a shilling that she's going to marry Stubby," I said.

"Marry Stubby!" gasped Tom.   "Good Lord!"

Ten minutes later we peeped into Stubby's room.

They never even saw us, but on Stubby's ugly face there was an expression of such wonder and joy that old Tom blew his nose loudly as we went downstairs.

"Good boy," he said gruffly.   "Very good boy; I suppose he's proposed and she's said yes."

But he hadn't: Mona told me that afterwards in confidence.   She'd had to propose to him.

And I sent Bill Saunders a shilling postal order the next day.

VIII   BULTON'S REVENGE

THERE were five of us altogether waiting in Mombasa for the boat.   She was late—held up with engine trouble or something, and they expected her in next morning.   And they weren't certain even then if she'd be able to continue her voyage without a further overhaul.   So there was nothing for it but to wait with what patience one could.

It was after dinner, I remember, and hot as blazes. There was Williamson, the coffee man, Scott, of the police, and Ewhurst, a gunner, all sitting in the lounge swearing between drinks. My recollection is that there wasn't much swearing. The fourth man was a tall, rather immaculate-looking fellow with fair hair and a small moustache. His face seemed vaguely familiar to me, but I couldn't put a name to him. He was English obviously, but he wasn't communicative about himself. His voice when he talked had rather a faint, cultivated drawl, but he seemed quite a decent sort. And he was interested in things and native customs. Didn't know the country, it being his first trip down the East Coast, whereas most of us wished we didn't know it quite so well.

It was while Scott was holding forth about ju-ju that I first noticed the sixth man. He had come in quietly and was now glancing at some old illustrated papers. There was no difficulty about placing him; you meet the type all the world over. Hard-bitten, lean, fit as nails—they'll do anything from elephant shooting to running a gambling hell. Some are straight, and some are crooked—but it's as well not to trust even the straightest too far.

Scott finished, and the fair-haired man asked him some question. And quite by chance I happened to be looking at the new-comer's face just as he spoke. As I've said, it was an unmistakable sort of voice, and it appeared to give the stranger a nasty shock. The brand he belonged to can school their expressions better than most, but that voice must have just caught him napping for a moment. Remember the fair-haired man had his back to the stranger, so his face hadn't been seen. It was just the voice and nothing else that did it, and it was all over so quickly that after a moment or two I wondered if it hadn't been my imagination.   With a look of surprised amazement the new-comer glanced up from his paper and stared at the back of the fair-haired man's head.   And then the surprise and the amazement faded, to be replaced by a look of such devilish rage as I have seldom seen on a man's face before or since.   For a second his teeth bared in a wolfish snarl: his fist clenched on the table. Then it was over, and save for me no one had seen it.

Scott was holding forth again, and after a while the stranger got up to ring the bell.   He wanted a drink, and he passed close to Williamson's chair.   And as he gave the order to the waiter, Williamson looked at him as one does at a man, if one's not quite certain if one knows him.

"Surely," began Williamson tentatively.

"You're Williamson, aren't you?" said the stranger. "Thought I recognized you as I came in.   I'm Bulton. Don't you remember I came back through your place two years ago?   You gave me some much-needed grub."

"Of course, I remember!" cried Williamson heartily. "Come and join us."

Bulton nodded and drew up a chair, and the conversation became general again.   But there was one little thing which aroused my curiosity.   There was no trace of recognition on the part of the fair-haired man as far as Bulton was concerned.   Quite obviously he had never met the man before.   Then why had that sudden look of diabolical rage crossed Bulton's face?   Or had it been a trick of the light?   I knew it hadn't, and, as I say, my curiosity was aroused.

It didn't occur to me at the time, though it did later, that it was Bulton who started the topic.   Ewhurst and Scott were talking, it's true, about a native they'd hanged in the back of beyond for a triple murder— but it was Bulton who introduced the wide subject of capital punishment generally. Was it sound, was it a good thing? Above all, did it succeed in its object?

The usual arguments were advanced for and against. It was Scott who was all for its retention, and who argued that the whole idea of punishment was that it should act as a deterrent to others, and not be regarded entirely as a punishment to the culprit. But was death more of a deterrent than, say, imprisonment for life?

Yes, emphatically, argued Scott. Men who have received such sentences may say that it is worse than death—but words are easy. Give them the alternative, and see what their answer would be. Everyone clings to life when it comes to the point.

But, I objected, principally for argument's sake, when it comes to murder, who thinks of the future? In nine cases out of ten blind insensate rage has the would-be murderer in its grip. He is out to kill; he is obsessed with the idea. He never thinks of the punishment that will inevitably be his. So does hanging act as a deterrent? And if it doesn't, isn't it too terrible a punishment?

Scott snorted—but Scott was a policeman. And it was Williamson who drew attention to the mental side of the punishment.

"Surely the actual physical act of killing a man by hanging him is the least important side of the question. The awful thing to my mind would be the three weeks, waiting. Knowing that every time the sun rose, death came one day nearer. The mental side of the punishment is the worse by far. And that can be no deterrent on others, because no one can realize what it means until they're in that position themselves."

Then the fair-haired man ranged himself on Scott's side in no halting language.

"Rank sentimentality," he remarked. "There are crimes of violence and assault which I would punish

by torture rather than mere hanging. Brutal, unpro-
voked murders—and attempts at murder—for which
no mercy should be shown in this world, or the next.
Why, I know a case——" He broke off suddenly.

"Go on," said Bulton quietly, and he was staring at
the fair-haired man.

"It's a case of the most brutal assault on a woman,"
said the fair-haired man. "The cowardly swine tried
to throttle her—left her for dead and bolted. In wish,
in desire, in every way save the actual deed he *did*
murder her. It was only a fluke that she didn't die.
And when she recovered consciousness she was so dis-
traught that she couldn't give any clear description of
her assailant."

"But was there no motive?" asked Ewhurst.

The fair-haired man shrugged his shoulders.

"We could never find one. She had on her pearls
at the time, so it was possibly robbery——"

"And possibly not," said Bulton. "Motives are
difficult things to arrive at sometimes. Strangely
enough I, too, know of a very similar case to the one
you have mentioned. It was told me by a—by a man
I met a year ago. And he was the principal actor in
the drama. He nearly throttled a woman to death,
but in his case one thing was a little different. In his
case it wasn't that she couldn't give any clear description of her assailant, but that she wouldn't. A change
of a solitary letter which makes a considerable difference. In fact it lifts the story from what you, sir, so
aptly describe as a brutal and motiveless assault into
the plane of psychology. Would you care to hear
about it?"

He glanced round the group and Scott nodded.

"Fire right ahead," he said. "And the calling is
on me this time. Waiter—repeat the dose all round."

"I guess the name of the man who told me doesn't

signify," began Bulton. "He was dying of fever when I ran across him, and I stayed with him till he pegged out. I mention that fact because he rambled a bit in his delirium, though he was perfectly lucid most of the time. But when a man rambles you either get gibberish, or very intimate truth. I got the latter, and it kind of made me see the characters of his story in a way I wouldn't have been able to do otherwise. He made 'em live, in a way no mere tale of words and deeds can ever do; got inside 'em and took me with him. And, as I say, his name doesn't signify, but I'll call him Jack for the sake of clearness.

"Before the war he'd been training to become an electrical engineer. Not a particularly bright sort of fellow, I should imagine, but at the same time no fool. Rather a shy, *gauche* boy, and, like so many shy people, he had wonderful ideals. He never expressed them; kept them locked up in his heart. Particularly the ones about women. I guess you'd never believe the extraordinary hallucinations that boy had about the other sex, though wild horses wouldn't have made him confess it. To him they were just something apart— something sacred and holy for a man to guard and cherish and work for. Damned funny, of course— and damned dangerous. For when a fellow like that gets his awakening, it hits him harder than you or me.

"However, that comes a bit later. At the age of twenty-four this boy fell in love. He fell in love as a fellow of that description might be expected to fall in love—madly, desperately, unreasonably. He'd been straight himself all his life, and he set the girl up on a pedestal about twice the height of Nelson in Trafalgar Square. And the higher he set her up, and the more desperately he became in love, the more unconquerable did his shyness become. He'd met her first at a dance—by the way, we might as well call her Ruth

—and he'd asked her for two. Incredible to relate, she gave them to him, and because he didn't dance badly, she'd managed a third. From that moment it became hopeless. Ruth filled his life to the exclusion of everything else, and even interfered considerably with his work. Not that she knew it, of course : to her he was just one of the numerous young men who came and went about the house, and who was incidentally rather duller than most. But though, perhaps, he didn't talk as much as the others, he saw a good deal more. And the first thing he noticed was the extraordinary position occupied in the household by Ruth's younger sister Molly."

Was it my imagination, or did the fair-haired man give the faintest perceptible start?

"Father, mother, Ruth—to say nothing of the servants—rotated round Molly. Her slightest whim was their law; she was fussed over, petted and flattered till it almost amazed him. True, she had been delicate when young; true, she was one of the most lovely girls he had ever seen in his life—lovelier by far than Ruth, even *he* admitted that—but was that any good and sufficient reason for such extreme adulation? Especially since the net result was that it had turned the girl into a being so supremely selfish as to render her hardly human. As her absolute right she accepted every sacrifice they made for her; she sulked for days if her smallest caprices were not instantly obeyed—sulked, that is, provided none of the men she kept dangling after her were about the place; she wasn't such a fool as to sulk then. The best of everything was hers by divine ordinance, and if other people went without, what on earth did it matter to her? And, amazing as it seemed, the most devoted slave of all, the one who appeared blindest to her faults, was her sister Ruth.

"It puzzled Jack considerably. To him there was

absolutely no comparison between the two girls.   Molly
was the prettier, though Ruth was lovely enough for
any man—but there it ended.   To Jack, the elder
sister was so immeasurably the better girl of the two
that he marvelled that the men who thronged the house
didn't see it also.   The family adoration he accepted
as one of those peculiar and inexplicable things which
just happen and must be left at that; but that outsiders
should do the same defeated him.   And the only
person in the household who spotted his feelings was
Molly herself.

"She hated him for it with a bitter, deadly hatred.
She knew that he was the only man who saw through
her; she found, moreover, though only she knew how
hard she tried, that he was the only man who saw her
frequently whom she couldn't make fall in love with
her.   She even went so far as to kiss him once at a
dance—to kiss him on the lips unasked.   And she felt
him stiffen and recoil.   She never forgave that, and
she used to go out of her way to sneer at him and make
him feel awkward.   She left no stone unturned to get
him to cease coming to the house, but for one of the
few times in her life she failed.   You see, he thought
that Ruth was beginning to like him—and he was a
sticker even if he was shy."

Bulton finished his drink and lit a cigarette.

"I expect you wonder when I'm coming to the
point," he went on after a moment.   "But I'm trying
to condense it as much as I can.   To understand that
fellow's story, I guess you've got to get the mentality
of those two girls placed in your mind.   You've got
to see 'em as he made me see 'em when the fever was
on him, and he was back living it all over again.

"Anyway, I'll get on with it.   The unbelievable
thing as far as Jack was concerned happened one night
about three months before he was due to pass his final

examination. He didn't know how it happened—it just did, as such things have happened before. He found, of a sudden, that Ruth was in his arms—that he was kissing her, that—wonder upon wonder—she was kissing him. He felt the glory of her lips on his, the yielding of the whole of her young body against his own. He heard her whisper—'My dear, I love you,' and it seemed to him at that moment that life could hold no more. Of course, they would get married. Father and mother jibbed a bit at first, though since it wasn't Molly it didn't matter quite so much. Nothing would have induced them to allow Molly to marry an obscure electrical engineer; for that matter, nothing would have induced Molly to have contemplated such a ridiculous course of procedure for an instant. But Ruth was different. Ruth—well, after all, Ruth was another proposition. The poor darling couldn't expect to have very many chances, overshadowed as she was by Molly. Only one thing did her father insist on. Jack must go clear away, free from all distraction, until he had passed his final exams. It was only three months, and Jack, who was no fool as I have said, agreed with the wisdom of the course. So he went away and he worked as he'd never worked before. He buried himself in the country, and he slaved for fifteen hours a day. By a supreme effort of will he banished all thoughts of the girl from his mind—at least almost all thoughts. Just occasionally he'd sit and dream of the years to come—the wonderful years. And then he'd go back to volts and amperes and things and cover more paper with uninteresting figures. He passed all right—passed with flying colours, and then he went to see Ruth."

Bulton paused, and there was a strange look in his eyes.

"It was her father who told him what had happened

—told this idealistic boy the incredible thing. And he was a stern man, the father, a bit of a Puritan for all his stupidity over Molly.

" 'I wouldn't tell you before your exam.,' he said to Jack. 'It wouldn't have been fair to put you off. But Ruth is no longer a daughter of mine. I have disowned her.'

"Jack sat there in the study, and he was swallowing hard.

" 'What do you mean?' he stammered at length.

"And then it came out. Of all people in the world, a roller-skating rink instructor! At least she might have chosen a gentleman. Jack knew the fellow; had seen him in a red uniform giving lessons once or twice when he had skated there. Good-looking in a flashy way.

" 'But when were they married?' he blurted out.

"And the elder man's voice was terrible as he answered:

" 'They are not married,' was all he said."

Once again Bulton paused, and I glanced at the fair-haired man. And he was staring at Bulton with a sort of savage intensity.

"It mightn't have hit some fellows quite so hard," went on Bulton after a while. "But you've got to remember what manner of boy Jack was. When he lived it over again in his delirium, when his mind was back in the days that followed, I got to see into his soul. It killed him mentally and morally as surely as a revolver bullet can kill physically. From being an idealistic boy, he turned into a bitter man, cursing women and all their ways. He felt that he'd staked his all and lost, and deliberately he set out to get his own back on the whole sex. Not pretty, I grant you —but when you start monkeying with a man's soul something's going to happen. He had made just one inquiry to substantiate her father's statement and that was to Molly. And Molly, looking very sweet and lovely, had given a pathetic little smile and nodded.

" 'Poor dear Jack,' she had whispered in a choking whisper. 'Poor dear boy.'

"That had settled it; there was no more to be said. He chucked everything, and went abroad. And for five years he lived a life of which the less said the better. But in one way it had its effect; up to a point he forgot. Not quite, mark you—but up to a point. And then came the war.

"Now I'm not going to weary you with what he did during that performance, since he did no more and no less than thousands of others. But there came the moment when he stopped one in the shoulder, and the R.A.M.C., having taken him into their coils, deposited him in a base hospital near Étaples. And there on the first night he saw her; saw the woman he hadn't seen for nine years. For a while he thought it was a fever dream. She had just come on duty, and with a shaded lamp in her hand she was walking slowly between the two ranks of muttering and restless men. And at the foot of his bed she paused and their eyes met. He knew then that it was no dream, but reality.

" 'Jack!' he heard her whisper, and she came and laid her hand on his forehead—a hand that was trembling. And with the concentrated bitterness of nine years' hell in his mind, he cursed her savagely and horribly. He said dreadful things to her—wicked, inexcusable things—and she answered never a word. She just stood there beside his bed looking at him, and in her eyes there was no reproach. Just divine pity and love and a wonderful tenderness. And he, miserable fool that he was, could only see a rink instructor in a red uniform."

The sweat was standing out on Bulton's forehead, and he drained his whisky at a gulp.

"They came over that night—the Bosches. You remember, of course, the big Étaples raid when they got the hospitals. They got the one Jack was in, and when the mess had been cleared away he scrambled madly out of bed and through folds of flapping canvas with sick fear in his heart. For the bomb had burst in her end of the marquee, and everything—rink instructor included—was forgotten. He was a boy again, and she was the girl of his dreams. And, thank God! he got to her before she died.

"At a glance he saw it was hopeless, but she held out her arms to him. And with a great cry he caught her to his heart.

" 'Forgive me, my dear,' he sobbed. 'Forgive those awful things I said. Who am I to judge?'

" 'Forgive me, Jack,' she said gravely. 'I realize now, I have realized for many years, that I had no right to sacrifice you.'

"He looked at her wonderingly.

" 'What do you mean, Ruth?'

" 'Dear lad,' she said, and her voice was growing weaker, 'you don't really think I did it, do you? I hoped you'd come and let me explain. But you didn't and I couldn't find where you'd gone.'

"I think his heart was beating in great sickening thumps just then. I think he stared at her as a man bereft of his senses.

" 'What are you saying?' he muttered. 'My darling—speak to me!'

"But the end was very near, and with a sudden passionate madness he strained her to him.

" 'Stay with me, darling!' he almost shouted, but with a pitiful little smile she shook her head. And with one last supreme effort she raised herself and kissed him on the lips. Then she died.

"They found him wandering about the sand dunes

the next morning, partially demented. They thought
it was shell shock from the effects of the bomb, and
they sent him home. I don't really wonder at their
diagnosis, because he was obsessed with one idea.
And apparently, he often talked aloud about it in his
sleep. It was such a strange idea that I'm not surprised they kept him on for far longer than necessary
in a charming country house, devoted to nerve cases.
He wanted to find a rink instructor in a red uniform
—that was all. But quite enough, in all conscience,
for grave men who talked learnedly about mental aber-
rations and nerve centres and other dull things.

"It was just about armistice time that they let him
go, and in due course he was demobilized. And then,
systematically, he started on his search. He never
gave up hope though he pursued false clue after false
clue. He advertised for six months continuously in
every paper he could think of without avail. And
finally, he ran his quarry to ground not half a mile
from the rink where he had been instructing. He'd
come back there after wandering round the country,
and he was doing a clerk's job in some garage. At
first he was suspicious and uncommunicative—but
finally he was persuaded to talk. And with an occasional smirk of self-complacency on his face he admitted
several things. Naturally, no gentleman speaks of
such matters, but since it was ancient history now,
there seemed to be no harm. Though, of course, it
must go no farther. He remembered the girl well—
a nice little soul; very pretty. Her people left the
place, he believed, when she married. But really there
had been so many in those days.

" 'And her name?' said Jack in a quiet voice.

" 'Well, I always used to call her Molly,' answered
the rink instructor, twirling his moustache.

" 'She had a sister, I believe,' went on Jack.

" 'Yes—an elder sister. But no go in her—you can take it from me. That was where the joke lay —Molly using her cloak whenever she came to me.'

" 'Thank you,' said Jack heavily, rising to go.

" 'Don't mention it,' remarked the other. 'Those were the days, those were. Nothing doing in this line, believe you me. Will you come and have a tiddley?'

"No—he would not have a tiddley. Nor would he take that smirking little swine and batter in his head as he had once battered in a German's during a trench raid. After all, *he* was not the principal culprit. That honour lay elsewhere.

"He thought things over quietly and dispassionately —did Jack. There was no particular hurry—now. At times it seemed almost incredible that such a sacrifice could have been accepted even by a girl like Molly. It was almost too amazing to be conceivable, even taking into consideration the unique position she had occupied in her family. Of course there were still details to fill in, small points which were obscure. It was just within the bounds of possibility that there might be something he didn't know which would palliate this monstrous thing. So he determined to make quite sure; he determined to give her every chance. He went to see her at the palatial country house where she now lived. By the way, did I mention that her husband was a peer of the realm—an earl, to be exact?"

The fair-haired man drew in his breath with a sharp hiss and for the first time, I think, the other men realized that more than just a mere story was being unfolded. I know Williamson was fidgeting in his seat, and Scott had a worried look on his face.

"He was ushered into the great lady's presence by a pompous butler, and she seemed to have a little diffi-

culty in recognizing him, though the knuckles of her
hand on the chair gleamed white as she saw him, and
stark fear showed for a moment in her eyes. At
length, however, she was graciously pleased to recall to
her aristocratic mind this obscure individual from the
past, and all the time he just stood there staring at her
without speaking a word.   And after a while she began
to tremble, and blotches showed on her cheeks through
the make-up.   He knew, and she knew that he knew.
Moreover, the callow boy had gone ; in his place stood
a dangerous man.

" 'Why do you look at me like that, Jack?' she
whispered at length.

" 'Because I want to find out if there lives one redeeming feature in your beastly little soul,' he said
quietly.   'At present it doesn't look like it, but I will
give you every chance.   Why did you let Ruth bear
the blame for your rotten intrigue with that rink instructor?   Why did you always go to his rooms in her
cloak?   And don't try to lie to me.'

"At first she tried to bluster, but not for long.   She
hadn't any excuse, none, save that she was young and
stupid.   The man had fascinated her, and she had
gone to his rooms without thinking of the consequences.

" 'In Ruth's cloak,' put in Jack contemptuously.

"Then she'd got engaged—a wonderful match—to
her present husband.   She'd met him while she was
staying away at a friend's house.   But even while she
was engaged she couldn't give up the rink instructor;
she still went to his rooms.   And one night she was
seen—coming away.   It was to Ruth she had rushed
—it was to Ruth that she poured out the story.   And
it was Ruth who had suggested the way out.   She was
very insistent on that point; she seemed to think it was
some excuse.   And it was helped by the fact that the
kindly persons who carried the story to her father had

thought it was Ruth owing to the cloak. Didn't Jack understand, couldn't he see the awful predicament? Any breath of scandal and her *fiancé* might break off the engagement—would break it off. And how could she have known that Jack would take it as he did?

"'Is that all you have to say?' said Jack as she finished.

"'What are you going to do?' she almost screamed.

"'I'm going to commit every word of it to paper, and send it to your husband,' he replied.

"And then she went mad. She implored, she entreated, she went on her knees to him—until something snapped suddenly in his brain. It seemed to him that this was no woman in front of him—but something loathsome and unclean. All the old hatred he had felt for her as a boy came surging back, and with it the face of Ruth, as she had died in his arms. And I think he must have had his hands on her throat for a minute before he realized the fact."

With great deliberation Bulton lit a cigarette, and his glance never wavered from the fair-haired man's face.

"He didn't quite throttle her; though, as you said, sir, like the man in your case, in every way save the actual deed he did. They found her just breathing half an hour later, and she was unable to give any description of the man who had done it. Couldn't or wouldn't? I leave you to judge. And is that one of the crimes of violence you would punish by torture rather than by mere hanging?"

For a moment or two there was dead silence; there didn't seem to be anything much to say. For the issue had narrowed down to Bulton and the fair-haired man; we were out of the picture. And it was Scott's quick gasp that made me look up.

The fair-haired man was staring over Bulton's head at a woman who was approaching. She was tall and very beautiful—but her face had no soul in it.   It was devoid of expression, like the face of a lovely doll.

"Have you heard anything more about the boat, Henry?" she said languidly, and at the sound of her voice Bulton turned slowly in his chair and looked at her.

And then we knew.   Not necessary to watch the sudden ashen cheeks; not necessary to hear the one choked-out word "Jack!"; not necessary even to see three ugly red scars on the white neck—we knew without that.   And like a drunken man Henry, Earl of Pyrford, lurched across the room, and went out through the open windows into the African night.

IX   COINCIDENCE

I MET her first in Monte Carlo.   She called herself the Comtesse de Gramont, though who the Comte de Gramont was or had been was a matter which was never satisfactorily elucidated.   Certainly if he existed he never appeared on the scene: her invariable companion was a fierce-looking maiden lady of doubtful age who rejoiced in the name of Miss Muggleston.   And with Miss Muggleston we are not concerned.   Beyond stating that she was addicted to Patience and invariably retired early to bed, Miss Muggleston may be dismissed from these pages, with the same completeness as she was, on occasion, dismissed from the presence of her employer.

To say that Paula, Comtesse de Gramont, was beautiful would be banal.   There are women whom it is impossible to dismiss as pretty or plain, ugly or beautiful —to place in a sort of well-defined class.   She was beautiful undoubtedly—one of the most lovely women

I have ever seen, if not *the* most lovely—but that was only the beginning, the least part of her. It is a big claim to make, but I veritably believe that even if she had been as ugly as sin her devilish attraction would have been in no way impaired. Her figure was marvellous: her clothes unique, and yet exactly suitable for her. Not another woman in a thousand could have worn them: on the Comtesse nothing else was possible. And, finally, she possessed a charm of manner, and a gift of conversation which alone would have been sufficient to keep a dozen men at her side had she wished for them. She did not wish for them —apparently: wherefore the dozen who would have liked to be there grew to a hundred.

I was talking to Tony Graham in the Sporting Club the first time I saw her—and what Tony does not know about cosmopolitan European society is small. There was a general rustling and craning of heads as she entered, and it takes something to cause that in a place where some of the most beautiful women in the world are to be seen nightly. She was dressed in plain black, and a single diamond ornament blazed on her breast. But it was her carriage that made me look at her particularly, and ask the question that a score of other people asked simultaneously. It was completely natural, and yet utterly regal; the walk of a woman who is absolutely sure of herself and supremely indifferent to what any onlookers may choose to say. In fact, as far as she was concerned, there were no onlookers, though there was no trace of conscious superiority on her face. In short, she accomplished one of the hardest things in the world to do better than I had seen it done before.

"Who is she, Tony?" I asked when she had passed.

He chuckled and lit a cigarette.

"Paula, Comtesse de Gramont, my son," he an-

swered, "is her name, and that is the only positive
fact that I can tell you about her. And that is only
positive in that it is the name to which she answers,
and under which her suite at the Paris is registered.
There are people who say that she is a left-handed
descendant of the Hapsburgs: there are others who
affirm that since her father left the Milan in Paris the
cooking has deteriorated. You now perceive at her
side young Dorset, who doesn't care a damn who she
is, as long as he may have the privilege of losing more
money on her behalf, out of his already hopelessly
encumbered estate. Women, as you may guess, do
not love her: save for a dangerous-looking English
woman who is doubtless by this time safely in bed,
you'll never see one talking to her. Men, on the
contrary, talk to her just as much as she will let them
—which varies considerably and very capriciously.
She fails, as far as I can see, to conform to the generally accepted rules of her type. For instance, there
was a most delightful fellow here last year—Indian
Cavalry, on leave. I forget his name—but if you're
curious you'll see it up in the cemetery."

"What's that?" I cried, sitting up suddenly. Once
Tony gets started, no one who knows him listens very
much: you know he'll go on quite happily.

"Cemetery, I said," he continued. "He blew out
his brains. Lived in her pocket for three weeks, and
then killed himself. People said it was losses at the
tables; but the boy was hardly ever in here. And
that was what I was getting at: she doesn't conform
to type. I made inquiries afterwards, and the poor
fellow hadn't got a bean beside his pay. And two
years of that wouldn't have kept her in face-powder.
If she stuck to old Guggenheimer, the Berlin banker,
and one or two others of that kidney, I could understand it: if she even ostensibly stuck to them when

they were round about it would be easy to fathom. But she doesn't. If the spirit takes her, she'll tell them to go to the devil, and take up some man right under their noses. And they always come back, though, to do her justice, I don't think she would mind if they didn't. In fact, old man, a very remarkable woman."

"You know her, I suppose," I said perfunctorily; my interest in the Comtesse was exhausted.

"Oh! yes: I know her," he answered. "That is to say, I have talked to her occasionally, and sat next her at dinner on one occasion. And, as I said before, she is not *comme les autres*. Far from it."

For a moment or two Tony Graham's face grew serious.

"If I had a son or a dear friend," he went on quietly, "my prayer would be that he never came under her influence. You and I are old stagers, Bill, but a youngster——" He stared in front of him, frowning. "That boy in the Indian Cavalry wasn't the first —not by any means. There was an Englishman at Biarritz some time ago, and a young American in Rome. And others."

I gently touched his foot.

"Look out, Tony: she's coming over here."

He glanced up and rose to his feet as the Comtesse passed. She held out her hand with a gracious smile, and Tony brushed it with his lips.

"My luck," she murmured, "is atrocious. Be a saint, my friend, and order me an orangeade."

He gave the order, and then with a faint smile he introduced me.

"I was just telling Lord Telford that your luck is usually very good," he remarked, and for a while we talked on systems and their utter futility. Most certainly Tony was right over one thing: she was not *comme les autres.*   As well as being the best-dressed, she was easily the most *distinguée* woman in the room, and it was difficult to believe that some of the things he had told me were not exaggerated.   Round such a woman, stories would be bound to gather, and Tony was the most chronic gossiper of my acquaintance. And yet for him he had been singularly serious. . . .

Fate decrees these things, I suppose.   First my idle curiosity, then her wish for something to drink, and then young Peter Bermingham suddenly arriving.   Is it all blind chance, or is there an ordered scheme of things leading to some definite end?   If she hadn't wanted an orangeade, the probability is they would never have met, and if they hadn't . . .   Lord! but it's a funny world.

"Hullo! sir," I heard a cheery voice at my elbow. "What are you doing in these gilded haunts of vice?"

"It's you, is it, Peter," I said, looking up.   "I thought you were ski-ing down avalanches at Wengen or somewhere."

"Just come from there," he answered.   "Had the most glorious sport."

And as he spoke, his eyes were fixed on the Comtesse, who was talking to Tony Graham.

"I say, sir," he whispered, "you might introduce me, would you?"

Into my mind flashed Tony's remark, but it was impossible to refuse, more especially as at that moment she turned and spoke to me.   She acknowledged the introduction with a charming smile, and waved him to a seat beside her, into which Peter dropped with alacrity.

He was an extraordinary good-looking boy—the very best type of Englishman—and, that evening with his face tanned by the Swiss mountain air, he was just about as perfect a specimen of young manhood as one could well imagine. His father was one of my oldest friends, and young Peter himself I had known since he was born. Six months before he had been married to a girl I had never seen, and, being abroad at the time, I had not been able to attend the ceremony. But I gathered from what his father had written me that she was charming, and just the right sort for Peter.

At the moment, however, she seemed a little out of the picture, which consisted exclusively of the Comtesse. Apparently she had long wanted to try winter sports, and, short of trying them, a detailed description of their joys and difficulties by Peter was the next best substitute. She got it—for ten minutes: then she rose. To-morrow he must tell her more. Assuredly he would: there was nothing which would give him greater pleasure. And was it my imagination, or was there a strange gleam of triumph in the eyes of Paula, Comtesse de Gramont, as she left us?

"What a perfectly stunning soul," said Peter ecstatically after she had disappeared. "Who is she?"

"A collector of specimens," answered Tony Graham quietly. "You'd better be careful, young feller: too much of that lady ain't good for the soul."

"How's your wife, Peter?" I asked, as I saw him flush a little angrily. "It was a great disappointment for me that I couldn't attend your wedding."

"She's fine, sir, thank you. I was forgetting you'd never seen her. She went back a week ago from Wengen—sister getting married or something—so I thought I'd barge down here for a day or two on the way home."

"When are you going back?" I asked.

"Oh! shortly," he answered vaguely. "Depends rather. Well, I think I'll push along over to the old pub. I'm feeling a bit weary. Good night, sir. See you to-morrow."

With a nod to Tony Graham he was gone, and for a while we sat in silence. And it wasn't until we parted for the night that the subject was alluded to again.

"Get that boy away to-morrow, Bill, if you can," he said. "By the milk train at crack o' dawn, if there is such a thing."

He laughed a little mirthlessly.

"There's going to be trouble if you don't. The poor devil is hooked already."

"Rot, Tony," I said. "You've got the damn woman on the brain. The boy is only just married."

But it wasn't rot, and I knew he was right even as I was answering him. Young Peter was hooked, and he didn't even struggle. He seemed to be hypnotized by her during the next two or three days: it was pitiful to watch. He was for ever with her—lunching, walking, dining; and at length I made up my mind to have a talk to him. After all, though he was twenty-nine, he was almost like a son to me: and though it's ticklish work butting in on things of that sort, it struck me pretty forcibly that it was just a plain duty.

I cornered him one morning just before lunch at Ciro's. I guessed he was waiting for her, so the time was not propitious. But as it was the first time I'd seen him alone for two days the opportunity had to be taken.

"Look here, young fellow," I said, "how much longer is Monte Carlo going to have the pleasure of your company?"

He got a bit red in the face.

"Oh, I dunno, sir," he stammered. "Haven't really thought about it."

"Then it's about time you began," I said. And

then I let him have it straight from the shoulder. "It's not playing the game, Peter, for you to go on monkeying round with the Comtesse de Gramont, while the girl you've just married is waiting for you in England. Cut it out, boy; the woman is rotten to the core."

It wasn't till then I realized how far it had gone. He drew himself up very straight and stared at me.

"Only the fact, Lord Telford, that you are considerably older than myself and a friend of my father's prevents me hitting you in the face. So I will content myself with requesting you to go to the devil." And then he added, with a sort of suppressed fury: "How dare you say such a thing of Paula?"

Well, that didn't help much—distinctly otherwise, in fact. I talked it over with Tony Graham, and he shrugged his shoulders.

"'A rag and a bone,' Bill," he said. "The old story. And you might as well talk to her about it as to that palm tree. She's got him—she's going to keep him, and when she's finished with him she'll throw him away like the core of an eaten apple."

"I think I'll write to his father," I said. "Not that old Jim can do any good, but he'd take it hard if he thought I hadn't let him know."

So I wrote to Jim Bermingham that night, and four days later he arrived in Monte Carlo. He came straight up to my room, and I told him all the facts of the case as far as I knew them.

"It's a bad case, Jim," I said, "a real bad case. She's got him absolutely under her thumb. He's infatuated! He's mad about the woman. I've done what I can, but he cuts me now when he meets me. You see I told him what I thought of her. Honestly, it's not the boy's fault; she's enough to turn any man's brain."

"I must talk to him," he said heavily. "Get him home somehow. Poor little Ruth suspects something already. You see he hasn't written her—not a line. And when she heard I was coming here, she wanted to come too. Had the devil of a job preventing her." Suddenly he shook his fist across the sunlit bay. "Curse this foul woman."

A couple of hours after I met him on the terrace. He seemed to have aged, and I guessed what had happened.

"Useless, Bill," he almost groaned. "Absolutely useless. Told me frankly that he'd made a ghastly mistake in marrying Ruth, and that though he was frightfully sorry for her he wasn't going to make the still more ghastly mistake of going on living with her. That this cursed woman was the only woman in the world for whom he could ever care; that she was his soul mate and a lot of other truck of that sort."

He stared out to sea and his face was grey.

"Oh, God, Bill," he muttered, "that Peter should do this thing. For he'll take it hard—my boy will, when she's finished with him and he finds her out for what she really is."

"But is he intending to marry her, Jim?" I asked. "Divorce and that sort of thing. Is that his idea?"

"It's his idea right enough," he said bitterly. "But whether it is hers or not is a very different matter."

And from what I knew of the lady's past history, it certainly wasn't, though I didn't tell him so.

Three days after Jim arrived, Peter left and with him the Comtesse de Gramont. They had given no indication that they were going, and Peter had not even said good-bye to his father. In fact, it was several hours before we found out that they had left in the morning for Taormina, in Sicily.

Old Jim was distracted. He felt, I think, that while he was in the same place with them he could more or less keep an eye on the situation, which was absurd but understandable. And his first thought was to follow them immediately. It was Tony Graham who dissuaded him.

"What's the use?" he pointed out. "You can *do* nothing, my dear fellow. And it's only torturing yourself unnecessarily. Take it from me, Bermingham, there is only one cure in a case of this sort—time. When it's over, then will be the moment to try and mend things up a bit. And not at once even then. The boy will be like a wounded animal for a while: he'll want to hide himself."

And so the three of us waited on. What exactly Jim wrote to the girl I don't know, but if she'd suspected before she must have known by this time. And then suddenly one morning I saw it in the *Continental Daily Mail*. It danced in front of me, that stunning, paralysing paragraph, so that for a while I could scarcely read it:

Shocking Tragedy at Taormina.

A dreadful tragedy took place last night in the celebrated ruins of the Greek Theatre at Taormina. It seems that a young Englishman had climbed to the top of the ruins, which, on the western side, are some thirty to forty feet high, and in the darkness must have missed his footing. The drop here is sheer, and the unfortunate gentleman was killed instantly by the fall. He has been identified as Mr. Peter Bermingham.

I thought Jim would go mad when at last he'd grasped the fact. He idolized Peter, who was an only child as well as an only son. Nothing would persuade him that it was an accident; it was merely the influence of that vile woman. She'd driven his boy off his head, and in a moment of insanity he'd killed himself. And so thought Tony Graham and I, though we didn't say so.

The one thing to do was to prevent Jim making a fool of himself, and stirring up some scandal, which would make matters worse. Nothing he could do would bring the poor lad back to life again: nothing he could do would punish the woman as she deserved. It was difficult to make him see it: the poor old chap was beside himself with grief. I think if Paula, Comtesse de Gramont, had crossed his path, he'd have strangled her with his own hands—Jim who would as soon have thought of lifting his hand to a woman as he would of kicking a sick child.

But she didn't. When we arrived—he and I—at Taormina she had gone. And Jim was calmer by then. He looked twenty years older, but he did all the necessary formalities with a stiff upper lip.

They were sympathetic, were the authorities. "A terrible thing for the signor: incredible how it could have happened. But undoubtedly an accident—oh, yes, undoubtedly. In the dim light. A false step. . . . Terrible. . . ."

But one thing Jim and I did do before he took his dead back to England: we climbed to the spot where it had happened. It was a large flat bricked floor some five yards by five yards, close by the custodian's house. There were two of these spaces. No one could have *accidentally* walked off the edge, any more than one accidentally walks off a railway platform on to the line.

For a while Jim stood there looking with unseeing eyes across the town towards snow-capped Etna. And then he turned to me.

"Some day, Bill," he said, "my boy will be avenged. I don't know when, and I don't know how, but it will come."

Without another word he walked back to his hotel, and shut himself in his room. And the next day he left.

* * * * *

Three years later I came back from the East. A wanderer from birth, I was homesick for England, but my brother, who was commanding one of the battalions in Malta, persuaded me to break my journey there. The tragedy of young Peter Bermingham had faded from my mind, and it wasn't until I was dressing for dinner and saw through my window the snow peak of Etna, rising ghost-like from the sea away to the north, that it came back to me. Where, I wondered, was the Comtesse de Gramont? Had there been others who followed Peter's example, and that of the man in the Indian Cavalry? What of old Jim, and the girl whom Peter had married?

And then at mess came the amazing answer to at least one of those questions. The Second-in-command had just returned from eight days' leave at Taormina, where his mother was spending a few weeks. It was he who told me the Comtesse de Gramont was there too. Damned attractive woman: all the old dears in the hotel buzzing like a swarm of bees whenever they saw her. A trifle chutney, he opined, but extraordinarily good-looking. Did I know her by any chance? Yes—slightly, and the conversation dropped.

What a staggering coincidence, I thought, as I undressed that night. And then and there I decided to alter my plans. Instead of going on to Marseilles, I, too, would go and stop at Taormina. There was a boat next day to Syracuse, and when I announced my intention of catching it, a twinkle appeared in the eyes of the Second-in-command.

"A charming place," he said thoughtfully. "You know it—er—slightly, don't you, sir?"

"Wrong, Johnny," I answered. "Quite wrong. But have it your own way."

And so I met the Comtesse de Gramont for the second time. She was dining at a table not far from mine, and she had her back to me. With her was a much younger woman—quite pretty, but simply dressed. One of those people whom you dismiss as a nonentity, but quite a nice little thing in her way. A new companion I decided: presumably Miss Muggleston had been replaced.

And now as I went through my solitary dinner, I began to wonder what had really brought me there. Idle curiosity—the coincidence—what? And if she recognized me as she probably would, what was I to say? How should I meet her?

To be friendly with her was out of the question—and yet one must preserve the conventionalities. Peter's death had been accepted as an accident: on the surface the matter was closed. To reopen it would be a stupid solecism, and could lead to nothing except unpleasantness. Whatever one may think, the world demands a certain measure of acting. . . .

Out of the corner of my eye, I saw the Comtesse push back her chair, and as she passed my table I became engrossed in the dangerous task of eating spaghetti in a manner suitable for public view. And so, somewhat naturally, she failed to recognize me, which was what I wanted. I was still doubtful what line to take when we did meet.

In fact, the more I thought of it the more did it seem to me that my sudden whim to come there had been a foolish one. I decided I would catch the Rome express the next day, and until then keep out of her way.

And so after dinner I lit a cigar and went for a stroll. Almost unconsciously my steps led me through the narrow paved main street towards the ruins of the Greek theatre. The last time I had walked that street had been with Jim, and my mind was full of him as I climbed the steps towards the ruins. Poor old chap! Broken up, I supposed, completely. And that dear wife of his! God! it's a cruel thing to lose your all as they had done. And in such a rotten way, too.

I sat down on a big smooth boulder to finish my cigar. Below me the lights of Giardini twinkled round the shore of the bay; in front—on the top of Etna— a faint glow of pink showed up against the night. From the village close by came the sounds of a flute and a woman singing, and I wondered if it was just such a night three years ago when Peter had thrown in his hand. Black and sharp-cut above me to my left I could see the theatre. They liked tragedy— the Greeks: but had they ever staged a grimmer one in their theatre when it stood, than that which had been enacted in its ruins?

And even as the thought flashed through my mind it happened. To this day it staggers me as I think of it. There was one terrified agonizing scream, and something fell from the top of the theatre. Then a dull crash—not twenty yards from where I sat—and silence.

For a moment I sat stupefied; then I got up and rushed to where the thing lay. I could see it sprawling on the white stone—motionless. It was a woman, and before I got to her some premonition told me the truth.

"I don't know when, I don't know how, but it will come."

It had. Paula, Comtesse de Gramont, lay dead at my feet on the same spot that Peter Bermingham had died three years before.

A terrified girl appeared from inside the theatre

suddenly. I looked at her, and it was the companion I had noticed at dinner.

"Mon Dieu! Monsieur," she cried, "what has happened? Is she dead?"

"She is dead," I answered gravely. "You are her companion?"

"Yes," she nodded. "But how terrible. The Comtesse was standing on the edge watching the view, and suddenly she seemed to sway. And before I could get to her she gave a dreadful scream and disappeared."

I pacified her as best I could, and told her I would inform the police.

"Your evidence will be wanted," I said, "but don't worry yourself. It will only be a formality."

It was only a formality, but during the next few days I wondered mightily. I am not a superstitious man, and yet there are more things in heaven and in earth . . . The old tag. Had some strange power come out of the darkness to force that woman to her doom? Did she see, as she stood there, Peter beckoning to her, or standing at her side compelling her to do even as she had made him do?

Jim had no doubts upon it.

"I told you so," he said gravely, as I sat with him after dinner a fortnight later, at his place in Sussex. "I don't profess to account for it, but it must be more than a mere coincidence, Bill. The same place exactly: the same death. Remorse, perhaps; if such a devil as that woman was could feel such a thing. But nothing will ever convince me that some power outside our ken was not at work to cause her death."

For a while we talked, and it seemed to me he must be right. He'd aged dreadfully had the dear fellow: things didn't seem worth while any longer. In fact, all he and his wife had left now was Ruth—Peter's widow—and that wasn't the same thing.

"She's a sweet girl, Bill," he said. "You've never seen her, but she's coming home to-morrow."

"Has she been living here ever since it happened?" I asked.

"No," he answered, "she's been away for a year. She wanted to travel, and both Nell and I thought it would do her good. Of course, we'll lose her some day—we can't be selfish, but we've made her feel that this is her home as long as she wants it."

"And has she any idea of what happened?" I asked.

"Good heavens! No, old man," he cried emphatically. "She thinks it was just an accident. Why, I don't suppose that Ruth has any idea that women like that woman even exist. She's very far from being one of these modern products. I wouldn't have her know the truth for the world. She was suspicious at first, of course, but I succeeded in setting her mind at rest. A dear girl: I'm glad you're going to meet her at last."

And the next day I met Ruth Bermingham—but it wasn't a case of at last. She came across the garden towards me, and for a space we stared at one another in silence. For Ruth Bermingham was the terrified girl who had rushed out from the ruins of the old Greek theatre in Taormina, just after the Comtesse de Gramont had fallen from the top: Ruth Bermingham was the companion who had replaced Miss Muggleston.

"It was stupid of me not to realize," she said steadily, "that the Lord Telford of Taormina was the Bill Telford Dad so often talks about. But it didn't occur to me somehow."

"Good God! my dear child," I cried, "explain. I'm completely dazed."

"And yet it's very easy," she said quietly. "But I will explain, and when you've heard my explanation,

you must take what steps you think fit. You were
with Dad, weren't you, when Peter killed himself?"

I started slightly, but said nothing.

"Of course, those two old dears think that I thought
it was an accident. They didn't know that I had a
letter from Peter, written the day he did it. I burnt
that letter months afterwards, but I know it by heart.
It was a ghastly letter—smudged and incoherent. It
was a terrible letter written from the depths of Peter's
tortured soul. He admitted everything to me: he hid
nothing, he pleaded no excuse. He merely said that
a power stronger than his own had taken possession
of him, and that unless she would marry him he was
going to kill himself. And then there was something
about my divorcing him."

She stared across the garden towards the old house.

"I was furious at first," she went on. "It seemed
so despicably weak. To sacrifice all this for what
seemed to me to be merely a passing passion. And
I was hurt—bitterly hurt. I dried up—something inside me was killed. And then as time went on the
anger left me; the pitiful side of that letter grew uppermost in my mind. And with pity for him there grew
a deadly, overmastering hatred for that woman. At
first it was purposeless. I just hated her. And then
little by little it crystallized into the determination to
make her suffer, even as she had made Peter. How
I was to do it I hadn't an idea, but sooner or later I
was going to do it.

"It was about this time last year that the opportunity came. The Comtesse de Gramont was advertising for a companion. She was in London, and it
seemed to me that here was my chance. I answered
the advertisement in person, and my luck held. She
engaged me under another name, and I told them here
that I was going to travel."

Once again she paused, and I didn't interrupt her.

"I don't think, Lord Telford," she went on after a while, "that it would be possible for me to explain to you the manner of woman she was. Before men she kept up a certain restraint: before me she kept up none. It was partly my fault, because, at times, I used to apparently sympathize with her in order to be quite, quite sure. She was the cruellest devil that the mind of a novelist has ever conceived of, in fact, if you put that woman's character as I knew it in a book no one would believe you. She wasn't particularly immoral in the accepted sense of the word, her one passion in life was to get men raving mad about her and then turn them down with the shrug of a shoulder and a bored sneer. I tell you, Lord Telford," she cried passionately, "there have been times when I have had to exercise all my self-restraint not to smother her face with vitriol. She was a fiend— without heart, without pity, without remorse.

"But I waited. There was no hurry, and I had made up my mind what to do. I dropped out hints about my longing to see Sicily; I said I'd heard of the wonderful beauty of Taormina. And one day she suddenly decided to go there.

"'A beautiful place, my little one,' she remarked. 'And one day, when we are there, I will take you to the Greek theatre and tell you a story that will amuse you.'

"My heart was thumping so that I thought she must hear it, but I merely smiled and thanked her. And so we come to the night that it happened. We went out after dinner, and walked to the ruins. I knew what was coming, but now that the moment had actually arrived I felt quite calm.

"'That story you promised to tell me, Comtesse, I reminded her. 'I am full of curiosity.'

"She laughed. Have you ever heard her laugh, Lord Telford, when she was being natural? It was the essence of refined cruelty expressed in a sound. And thus did she laugh that night high up in the old Greek theatre.

" 'A story, my dear,' she said, 'but not a new one. Merely a man—and a rather stupid man. But then they are all that. This one was rather good-looking, but a dreadful bore. Peter something or other—I've forgotten his name. And he wearied me. He was so dreadfully serious. He had some absurd wife in England, I think—and would you believe it, he wanted me to run away with him and marry him. He was most insistent about it. In fact, it was on this very spot that he went down on his knees and became positively crude. Of course I mentioned the dear non-existent Comte—my devoted husband—and pointed out that as we were Roman Catholics, divorce was out of the question.

" 'He grew very white, and then the really thrilling thing happened. He said he'd throw himself off the top here unless I came away with him—divorce or no divorce. It was better than a play, and to help him on I laughed in his face. My dear, he did it: right in front of my eyes. Was killed instantly. Luckily there was no one about, and so I got back to my hotel without anyone knowing I'd been here all the time. Bermingham—that was his name. I remember now. It must have been quite a shock to the absurd wife.'

" 'It was,' I said. 'So she became a companion to you, Comtesse, and now she laughs in your face.'

"She was standing near the edge, Lord Telford, when I seized her. And she gave one scream. Then she disappeared—and the rest you know. I acted, of course. I had to. But it was all cut and dried in

my mind.   And if it hadn't—by some strange freak
of fate—been you . . ."

She broke off and sat staring at me.

"You two made friends?"   Jim's voice hailed us from
across the lawn.   "Mum wants to talk to you, Ruth,
and hear about your travels."

Without a word Ruth Bermingham rose and went
indoors, and Jim took her vacant chair.

"Good girl, isn't she, Bill," he said.   "By the way,
I wouldn't mention the fact of that woman's death.
The coincidence of the place might bring things back
to her."

"Precisely," I murmured.   "I won't."

x   THE PORTERHOUSE STEAK

NO one would have noticed him particularly as he
walked along Piccadilly.   He had on a blue
lounge suit; his collar was spotlessly white.   And he
walked with a curious, slow deliberation which betokened the man in no hurry.   In the midst of the
hurrying, jostling crowd he was just an inconspicuous
unit.

Had anyone working in one of the offices high above
the street taken the trouble to follow this particular unit's
movements he would have come to the conclusion that
he was one of the band of leisured idlers who have
nothing better to do than to stroll along the streets when
the spirit moves them and look at the shops.   More
than likely this hard-working spectator would have
envied him as he returned to his books and ledgers.

For this inconspicuous unit was undoubtedly a most
pronounced shop-looker.   Every twenty yards or so he
would pause and, leaning a little forward on his stick,

stare into a window. Tobacconists, hosiers, Cook's office, all came alike to him; his tastes were evidently catholic. But there was one thing which the watcher from his distant point of observation would have been unable to see; a little thing—and yet such a big one. This idle lounger had a strange method of examining the goods so temptingly displayed. His eyes were tight shut.

For ten or perhaps twenty seconds he would stand there while the midday traffic of London rolled unceasingly by; then, opening his eyes again, he would resume his stroll. Grey eyes they were—steady and indomitable, with a wonderful glint of humour behind them. His face was clean-shaven and good to look at, though to a doctor it might have seemed altogether too thin and fine-drawn.

He passed the Piccadilly Hotel, and once more became apparently engrossed in a shop window. This time it was a jeweller's, but the man was quite unaware of the fact. All he was aware of was that the roar of the motor-buses appeared to be coming from a great way off, and that everything seemed strangely unreal. There was a buzzing in his head, as if wheels were spinning round, and his knees felt weak. With an effort he pulled himself together; he'd never fainted in his life before, and it wouldn't do to start now. Somehow or other he'd got to get as far as King Street in Covent Garden.

He walked on, his head thrown back and a faint smile round his lips. As usual there was a block at Piccadilly Circus, and he paused for a moment by an open Rolls-Royce. A girl was driving, and by her side sat a man whose back seemed vaguely familiar. And it was just as he got abreast of the man that someone jostled him, and he stumbled and nearly fell. He lurched up against the side of the car, but recovered himself at once with a word of apology, only to see the man lean forward with a positive shout of joy.

"Bill Carruthers, by all that's holy! Bill—you old blighter, how are you? My sister Joyce."

The man on the pavement took off his hat, and the girl looked at him with a friendly smile.

"I've heard such a lot about you from Tom, Mr. Carruthers, that I feel I know you already."

But Tom Caldwell was speaking again.

"Lunch, Bill; you must! Look here, we must get on; we're blocking the traffic. Where are you going now?"

"To a place in King Street," answered the other.

"Hop in the back; we'll take you there. And then —lunch. I insist."

He opened the door and half-forced the other man in, and the next moment the car was gliding towards Leicester Square. And again the sense of unreality came over Bill Carruthers. Subconsciously he realized that the girl drove with the sure touch of an expert, but his brain was foggy and dull at one moment and full of freakish fancies the next. Like fever dreams; only Carruthers had no fever.

"What number, old man?" Tom's voice roused him, and he sat up with a jerk. Of course; he'd come to King Street in Tom Caldwell's car. Really—this would never do; the luxury of wool-gathering would never do for him. He fumbled in his waistcoat pocket and produced a slip of paper.

"430 D. It's a warehouse of sorts."

Joyce Caldwell drove slowly along and stopped before the door.

"Hurry up, old man," said Tom. "And then we'll go off and make an oyster or two wilt."

Brother and sister watched him cross the pavement and go through the swing doors.

"Dear old Bill! Fancy running into him like that."
Tom lit a cigarette. "The last time I saw him was at
the Divisional dinner three years ago."

"What is he doing now?" asked his sister.

"The Lord knows. Clever chap; probably making
a fortune."

"For a man who is making a fortune," said the girl
quietly, "his clothes are a bit shabby."

"What damned rot!" cried her brother indignantly.
"His clothes are perfectly all right. What's the matter
with them? And anyway—even if they were threadbare—what's that got to do with it? Bill's one of the
salt of the earth; apart altogether from the trifling fact
that he saved my life." He looked at the girl with
growing wrath. "If you don't want to lunch with us
because his clothes aren't all you fancy, he and I will
lunch alone."

She turned her head and looked at him. And it was
only when a man saw Joyce Caldwell full face that he
could realize her unique and wonderful charm. It lay
in her expression rather than in any particular beauty of
feature, and as she looked at her brother he understood,
not for the first time, the cause of the relays of men who
always surrounded her.

Just now that expression reminded him of a mother
tolerantly reproving her young and foolish offspring.

"You were always a fool, Tom," she said calmly.
"And lately I have noticed symptoms of your becoming
a damned fool."

Then she leaned forward on the steering wheel and
stared down the street, while her brother made explosive
noises in his throat beside her.

"Well, anyway," he said at length, "will you lunch
or will you not?"

"Of course I shall lunch," she answered. And then
she added, with apparent irrelevance, "I think he's got

the bravest eyes of any man I've ever met—and the proudest."

The swing door opened again, and Bill Carruthers came across the pavement.

"Finished, old man?" cried Tom.

"Quite," said the other, with a grave smile. "The interview was most decisive."

"Splendid! Then pop in again and we'll tackle this matter of lunch. Where shall we go?"

"The Milan grill," said his sister quietly, and let in the clutch.

Tom raised his eyebrows.

"I thought you loathed the bally place. The last time you went there you said you'd never seen so many gluttonous human beings in your life."

She swung the car into the Strand.

"Perhaps they will be better to-day. And, by the way, Tom, don't order any cocktails before lunch."

"Not have a cocktail?" he gasped. "When I've only just met Bill? But—why not?"

"Because they're not at all good for anybody in Lent," she answered. "Don't ask questions, old man; do what I say. We'll leave the car in Waterloo Place."

A few minutes later they entered the Milan grill.

"Go and get a table, Tom," said the girl. "And hurry up about it; I'm most frightfully hungry. A nice corner one, where we can talk." She sat down as her brother departed and smiled at Carruthers. "I am so glad to meet you. Tom used almost to bore Dad and me with his panegyrics on a man we didn't know."

"A dreadful exaggerator is Tom," answered Carruthers.

"When a man saves another man's life a little exaggeration is allowable."

"It was nothing," said Carruthers simply. "Had the positions been reversed, he would have done the same for me."

He swayed suddenly in his chair, and gripped the table in front of him. His eyes were closed, and the buzzing in his head grew louder. Then it passed and he glanced quickly at the girl. But she had noticed nothing and he heaved a sigh of relief. To be asked if he was ill or anything like that would be more than he could stand. This utterly adorable girl—dear old Tom—it was out of the question that they should ever know. And though few people pray in the Milan grill—yet a strange prayer went up at that moment. . . .

"Dear God! let me eat like a gentleman."

And the man who prayed was Bill Carruthers.

"I've got a table, old thing," came Tom's voice. "And I've ordered lunch."

"What have you ordered?" said his sister.

"A few oysters; a bird; some pêches Melba, and a bottle of bubbly."

"Well, as far as I'm concerned, Tom, go and cancel it," remarked the girl. "I want a full-size porterhouse steak, with fried potatoes and all sorts of vegetables. And before that, to get on with at once, an omelette. You and Mr. Carruthers can please yourselves. I'm hungry."

"Hungry!" gasped Tom. "Why, great heavens, my dear woman, you must be up the pole. It takes three men to lift one of their porterhouse steaks."

"Splendid!" said the girl. "That's just what I feel like. What about you, Mr. Carruthers?"

"Well, really, I feel rather like it myself," answered Carruthers, forcing a smile.

"Then there you are, Tom," said his sister. "Two full-size porterhouse steaks, and two omelettes. And you can have your oysters and your bird. And let us know as soon as the omelette is ready."

Slightly dazed, her brother retired again to the grill-room, to countermand his original order, leaving the other two outside. And suddenly the girl gave an annoyed exclamation. She was peering into the inner recesses of one of those mysterious feminine bags, and then she looked up at her companion.

"How aggravating!" she cried. "I've left all my change at home. Could you give me some silver for a ten-shilling note?"

A dull red stained Carruthers' cheeks, and he fumbled in his pockets.

"I—er——" he began, but the girl had opened a new compartment with an air of relief.

"It's all right," she said. "My mistake. It was here all the time."

She wasn't looking at him, and the red died slowly down, leaving him whiter than ever. What an escape! What a merciful escape!

He made some humorous remark concerning the intricacies of these indispensable abominations, but it seemed to fall flat. At any rate, she made no answer—only went on fumbling with her bag.

"You fool," ran her thoughts, "you stupid fool! Didn't you know already without that? Oh! won't that idiot Tom ever come?"

He did at last, wearing a slightly aggrieved expression, and his sister rose at once to her feet.

"Come on," she cried. "I'm simply famishing."

"Well, if you eat that steak, you'll have to hire a crane to lift you out of your chair," said Tom, waxing sarcastic. Events somehow were not turning out quite as he anticipated. No cocktail, no nice lunch, porterhouse steaks—— And Joyce—what the devil was the matter

with her? She seemed so quiet, so different to usual.
Before Bill, too, of all people.

He dug a fork into an oyster with an air of peevish-
ness; no accounting for girls. And then suddenly he
happened to glance across the table at Bill, and the suspicion of a frown appeared on his face. He banished it
instantly; he was loyal was Tom. But Bill's coat-sleeve
had slipped back a little, revealing his shirt-cuff. Well,
apart from the fact that the shirt was flannel—after all,
fellows did wear grey flannel shirts with single button
cuffs presumably, or no one would make the beastly
things—apart from that, it struck him that the cuff was
not too clean.

He started in heavily on plays. His best friend
couldn't call Tom a brilliant conversationalist, but he
had one invaluable asset. What he lacked in quality,
he made up in quantity. He burbled serenely on, and
his audience could listen or not as they pleased. It
made not the slightest difference to them or to Tom.

And on this occasion a vague feeling that all was not
quite as it should be spurred him on to dizzy heights.
He launched into a completely pointless story which had
something to do with a girl and a mashie niblick and the
pond hole at Worplesdon. In fact, the only merit in
the story was that it was interminable. It lasted well
into the porterhouse steak. And at the crucial moment,
just as the *bonne bouche* was coming, Joyce interrupted
him.

"Tell the waiter to give us some champagne, Tom."

Tom spluttered out like a motor running short of
petrol.

"Good Lord! haven't you had any?"

"Not yet," said his sister calmly. "But I'd like some
now, and so would Mr. Carruthers."

"My dear old Bill," cried Tom, "forgive me. I
apologize; I abase myself."

He signed furiously to the waiter, and then looked quickly at Bill. The old boy looked different, somehow; more like his old self. Coming to think of it, he hadn't looked too fit before lunch; bit washed out and cheap. Morning after the night before sort of business.

"How's the old porterhouse steak, people? Great heavens! old thing"—he gazed at his sister's plate— "you don't mean to say you've lowered it?"

"Very nearly all," she answered.

"Judging by your conversational efforts you must have been pretty busy," said Tom brightly, "and old Bill's going strong still. Remember those bully stews in France, old man? Gad! how they used to go down. But then one really was hungry."

Bill smiled slightly.

"Extraordinary condition to have been in, wasn't it, Tom?"

"Good old days in some ways and all that," said his host profoundly. "But it seems to me I've been doing most of the talking. How's yourself, Bill? Haven't been working too hard, have you? Struck me you weren't looking so frightfully fit, don't you know? Doesn't do to overdo it, old man. Why don't you come down and spend a week-end with us? The governor would love to meet you."

Into the grey eyes there came a sudden glint of laughter. Courage had come back, and God alone knew that it had been only just in time. What sudden Heaven-sent whim had caused that glorious girl to decide on a porterhouse steak was beside the point; perhaps it was true that there was a Power who tried a man thus far and no farther. But he couldn't go and spend a week-end for the very good reason that he'd pawned his evening-clothes two months ago.

"It's very good of you, Tom," he said gravely.

"But I'm too busy at the moment.   Later on, perhaps."

"Can't you manage one afternoon away from the office?" asked the girl.   "It's such a glorious day, and we could run down there in the car.   Then back after dinner."

Bill Carruthers almost laughed.   Into his mind there flashed his recent interview with an oleaginous Jew in King Street, and that gentleman's last remark:

"Get out of my offith, before I kick you out.   I've nothing for you."

Kick him out!   The little swine—the miserable little swine.   He glanced at the girl, and she was looking at him with a strange, grave smile that made his heart miss a beat and then race for two or three.   Take a pull, Bill Carruthers; this won't do.   Penniless down-and-outers don't count in the social scheme.   But she'd never know, and Tom would never know—and, oh, God!—to forget for one day.

"I think I can manage that," he said quietly.   "It's very good of you to suggest it, Miss Caldwell."

"Then let's go at once," she cried.   "Pay the bill, Tom; Mr. Carruthers and I will be in the car."

He sat beside her on the way down, with Tom in the back.   She didn't speak much, and, leaning back in his corner, he studied her profile.   Once, as if realizing his occupation, she turned and looked at him with the same grave little smile on her lips.

"I'm glad you could come, Mr. Carruthers," she said. "I don't think you can realize how much Tom means to Dad, and but for you——"

She left her sentence unfinished, and once more stared at the road in front.   And the man by her side lay back in his seat breathing in the peace of the country in spring. He felt like a swimmer who had been battling in heavy seas, and had come at last to calm water.   Outside the breakers still seethed and roared; to-morrow he would have to start the weary fight all over again. But to-day was his; just one day of make-believe.

The car swung through two iron gates, and up a long drive towards a big house screened by huge trees. Velvety lawns stretched down to a lake on which two stately swans sailed majestically. It was just a bit of old England—untouched, unspoiled. And there are not many left.

There was no house-party, for which fact Bill Carruthers heaved a sigh of relief. And all through the long, lazy afternoon—warm, by some kindly dispensation, as a day in July—the four of them sat and talked on the terrace overlooking the lake. Make-believe it might be—this courteous, charming, grateful old man; Joyce—he called her that in his mind just because it was make-believe; dear old Tom—but how utterly wonderful! And the minutes flew and the shadows lengthened until a sudden chill little breeze warned them that it was still early spring. So they went indoors and Tom took him upstairs to wash.

"Ten minutes, old man," he said, as he left him. "And the governor is routing out the vintage port."

He shut the door to find Joyce beckoning to him.

"Come into Dad's study," she said. "I want to talk to you both."

A little surprised, he followed her into the room where his father was already standing in front of the fireplace.

"What's the mystery?" he inquired, lighting a cigarette.

"During the war," said his sister quietly, "you may remember that I drove an ambulance in Serbia. And there was one particular thing I saw a good deal of. That thing was starvation. There's no mistaking it."

The two men exchanged a surprised glance; what on earth was Joyce driving at?

"To-day, Tom—I saw it again." She gave a little twisted smile, and turned her back on both of them. "Why do you suppose I told you not to have cocktails? Why do you think I ordered that awful porterhouse steak? Why, just because he was faint for food: starving. I don't believe he's tasted anything for days."

Tom's honest face slowly turned a deep magenta.

"Rot! bunkum!" he stammered.

"My dear, surely you're mistaken!" said her father mildly.

"I tell you I'm not mistaken," said the girl, with a little stamp of her foot. "I've seen it too often to be mistaken. I saw it when Tom spoke to him in Piccadilly; I saw it again when he left the car in King Street. Didn't you see the way he walked, Tom? But I wasn't quite sure how bad he was till you were ordering lunch. He nearly fainted outside in the lounge." She swung round facing them. "Starving, Dad, starving; without a copper in his pockets. Don't ask me how I know; I do. And he saved Tom's life. What are we going to do about it?"

"My dear," said her father helplessly, "I quite agree. What are we going to do about it?"

"Look here, Joyce," said her brother, "are you sure about this?"

"Absolutely," answered the girl.

"But you talked about his leaving the office and all that sort of thing."

"Because you've only got to look in his eyes for one second to realize that he's as proud as Lucifer. If he thought I'd guessed the condition he was in he'd never have come for this run."

"Then it boils down to this: we've got to find him a job, and a good one," said Tom decisively. "And until we've done that he's got to stop on in this house. Good heavens!" he went on. "I can't believe it. Bill starving! Why didn't he let me know?"

"Just because of that pride of his, of course. Why did he say he couldn't get away for a week-end on account of work? Because he wasn't going to tell us that he had no clothes to wear. And if he thinks we are offering him a job out of charity, he'll throw it back in our faces."

"Merridew asked me to-day whether I had taken any steps to find a successor for him," interposed her father.

"By Jove, governor—the very thing!" cried Tom. "Don't you think so, Joyce?"

"Well, there's just one point, my dear boy. Does he know anything at all about land agent's work?"

"Does it matter, Dad?" Joyce slipped her hand through her father's arm. "Does anything matter except that the man who saved Tom's life out in France is penniless and starving? We're both rather fond of Tom, you know."

The old man smiled.

"I suppose we are. All right; I'll ask him if he'd care to take it on. Even if he doesn't know anything about it, he can learn. And he struck me as being exactly the type of man I'd like to have for the job."

"He's one of the best," said Tom simply.

"Do you mind, Dad, if you'd let me lead up to it?" said Joyce. "You can come in—you and Tom—at the last moment; but I think I can do the preliminary part better."

"My dear—I shall be only too delighted," cried her father.

"And, of course, he'll stop here to-night, anyway. As it wasn't arranged, Tom can easily suggest lending him anything he wants. There's the gong. Now, don't forget—not a word, not a hint, of what I've told you."

With a final warning glance at both men she went out into the hall as Bill Carruthers came down the stairs.

"Mr. Carruthers," she said, "would you mind frightfully if we didn't go back to town to-night?   I find there are one or two things I must do here, and Tom can fix you up for the night."

"Of course I can, old boy," said Tom.   "Anything you want."

Into Bill Carruthers' mind there flashed a picture of his bed that night if they did go back to town—a seat on the Embankment.   Truly Fate was being kind to him for this one day—even if it was make-believe.

"I am in your hands, Miss Caldwell," he said.   And then his mouth twitched with an irresistible smile.   "I don't think the business will suffer in my absence."

It was dangerous, he knew, but all through dinner he let his thoughts centre on the girl who sat so gracefully facing her father.   It comes quickly to a man sometimes, that blinding certainty that he has met the one woman who matters or ever will matter.   And it had come to Bill Carruthers that day.   What matter the sheer futility of it?   Nothing and no one could take from him his dreams.

He hardly heard some remark she made to her father; he was watching a little tendril of hair that had escaped just by her ear.   And when she turned to him he had to pull himself together with an effort.

"I beg your pardon," he murmured.   "For the moment I was thinking of other things."

"I was wondering if you knew of anyone, Mr. Carruthers, who could take the place of Mr. Merridew—Dad's estate agent?"

"Merridew is getting on in years," said her father

"and I've got to find a successor somewhere. Six hundred a year and a house."

Six hundred a year and a house! The words rang in Carruthers' brain. Six hundred a year and a house!

"Would the work be very difficult?" he heard himself saying.

"Nothing that a moderately intelligent man can't pick up in a year," said his host. "Of course, he must like an outdoor life and be a gentleman."

"Pity old Bill can't take it on himself," said Tom, cracking a nut. "He loves an outdoor life. Honestly, old man, with your tastes I don't know how you stick the City."

And now temptation was hammering at him. Why not? A job; a country job; a house. And Joyce. To see her sometimes. . . . To speak to her. . . .

"It is hardly likely that such an idea would appeal to Carruthers," said the old man, but he looked at his guest a little questioningly. "Of course, if it should, I need hardly say that there is no man living I would sooner have in the job than the very gallant gentleman who saved Tom's life."

He raised his glass with old-fashioned courtesy towards the man who sat so silently staring in front of him. So it wasn't a make-believe day after all; he wouldn't have to start that awful, weary round again to-morrow. All he had to do was to accept, and put the past out of his mind for ever. After all, he had done nothing to be ashamed of; it hadn't been his fault—these last few months of hell. So why not?

He glanced at the girl, and she was looking at him with a curious intentness. He looked at Tom, and he was lighting a cigarette. He knew the thing was his for the asking; he knew he could do the work. And still he hesitated.

"Accept, you fool," rang a voice in his brains. "Ac-

cept at once, and later on you can allude jokingly to the
fact that it was a very fortunate offer for you. Don't
give yourself away; don't humiliate yourself needlessly."

Came the answer quiet and insistent: "You're taking
a job under false pretences. They think you a successful man. Would they have offered you this thing if they
knew you'd even pawned your underclothes?"

And suddenly he hesitated no longer. He turned to
his host, and when he spoke his voice was steady.

"You have made me a very wonderful offer, Mr. Caldwell—how wonderful it is you can have no idea. Unfortunately, your offer has been made without a full
knowledge of the facts. When Tom and Miss Caldwell saw me in Piccadilly this morning I was on my way
to answer an advertisement for a job as a night porter.
When I got to the place I found that the post had already
been filled; to be exact I was the twenty-fifth unsuccessful applicant. And the Jew I interviewed removed any
lingering hope I had that he desired to look at me any
longer. Other Jews and employers of labour have been
doing the same thing now for five months.

"I'm afraid I was rather at the end of my tether.
Until lunch to-day my only food during the last few
days has been a bit of bread and the outside rind of an
old onion given me on the Embankment some nights
ago by a drunken woman. That is why I accepted
Tom's offer of lunch. But during lunch I let it be
understood by him and your daughter that I was doing
well in the City. That was a lie; but it never dawned
on me that it would have any consequences. Now, of
course, things are different. Believing that I was what
I said I was, you have tentatively suggested that I should
become your estate agent. That has made it necessary
for me to tell you the truth. I apologize for not having
done so before; but"—for a moment his voice faltered—
"I was looking on this as a day of make-believe. It has

given me new hope and strength to carry on. There is only one other thing I'd like to say—it was stupidity and not dishonesty that brought me to my present position. I was swindled out of what money I had."

"You silly old fool—you silly, damned old fool!" broke in Tom gruffly. "What the devil do you want to tell us that for, when it's obvious to anyone who knew you? I take it hard, Bill. Why didn't you let me know?"

"I don't like charity, Tom," said the other, smiling. His eyes came round to the girl, but she had left her chair and was standing by the open window staring out into the garden.

And then the old man spoke.

"I take it hard, too, dear fellow," he said. "Have I no rights at all as Tom's father? Because you've had bad luck, what has that got to do with the offer I have made you?"

"But you made it," stammered Carruthers, "thinking that—thinking that I was—what I said I was."

"No, he didn't," began Tom eagerly—and then stopped short. Willingly would he have bitten his tongue out—but it was too late. The mischief was done.

"So you knew?" said Carruthers quietly. He rose to his feet, and the grey lines had settled on his face again. "I see; I ought to have guessed. Charity: for saving Tom's life."

"That is unjust and unfair, Mr. Carruthers," said a quiet voice at his elbow. It was Joyce: Joyce with her head thrown back and a wonderful light in her eyes. "It is true that my father knew—I told him. I saw the condition you were in: I've seen starvation too often in Serbia during the war not to recognize it. But to state that Dad has made you this offer out of charity is belittling you and belittling us. You've been to these

other men—strangers—asking for work. Had they
offered it, would you have said it was charity? They
knew the condition you were in; men like you don't ask
for jobs as night porters for preference. And yet when
my father offers you a job you turn it contemptuously
down. Presumably you regard it as such a poor one
that it's beneath you to accept it."

From behind him came the sound of a closing door,
but he was barely conscious of it.

"Great heavens! Miss Caldwell—you can't think I
meant it that way." He stretched out an imploring
hand. "You can't think that I'm such an unspeakable
cad as to view your father's wonderful offer like that."

"I'm really not very interested in what you think,"
she said coolly. "All I know is that my father has
made you a certain suggestion, and that you regard it as
charity. If that isn't what you think, all I can say is
that you've expressed yourself very badly."

And suddenly something snapped in Bill Carruthers'
brain. A continued course of starvation wears the
human mechanism out to snapping point, and that point
had come to him. He broke down and cried like a
child—his face buried in his hands. And with infinite
tenderness in her eyes she watched him even as she had
watched other men cry just because they had dropped a
knife on the floor or something equally trivial.

Tom's face appeared for a moment at the window,
and she signed to him imperatively to go away. Then
she waited, being the manner of a girl who has learned
many things in the book of life. And after a while the
shaking shoulders grew still, and he looked up at her.

"So that was why you ordered a porterhouse steak?"

"Of course," she answered, with a smile. "And a
jolly good steak it was!"

He stood up, facing her.

"I'm not going to apologize for making a fool of myself," he said quietly. "I would to most people—but not to you. I think you're the most wonderful girl I've ever met. And because you're that, you'll understand what I'm going to say. It's not due to weakness; and, believe me, it's not impertinence. It is a statement of fact, as unalterably true as the fact that we are together in this room. Six hours can sometimes mean as much —aye, more—than six years. In these six hours— nine, to be accurate—since I first met you, I have learned the meaning of the word love. There will never be another woman in my life except you. And that is the real reason why I cannot accept your father's offer, though naturally that is not the reason I shall give him. I shall tell him that I don't know enough of the work to feel justified in accepting. But I want you to know the truth. And above all I want to thank you for doing what no other girl in the world could have done for me to-day—saved me from cracking, when the end was very near."

She had stood very still as he spoke, and her eyes had never wavered from his.

"Then you intend to return to London to-morrow?" she said, as he finished.

"If you'll be good enough to take me in the car," he answered. "I'm afraid my finances do not allow of a train fare."

"Nor, presumably, of my doctor's bill."

He stared at her uncomprehendingly.

"My dear man," she remarked, "if I've got to spend the next few weeks eating porterhouse steaks with you, I shall have to go into a home. In fact, I refuse to do it. So I'll just tell Dad you're sorry you were a fool— and you can start with old Merridew to-morrow."

And then, for the first time, her voice shook a little.

"You silly old ass; you dear, silly old ass! Don't you realize that I was never nearer making a fool of myself in my life than when I saw the look on your face after I asked you for change while we were waiting for lunch?"

She went to the door, leaving him staring after her.

"Dad," she called, "Bill's going to take on the job— er—for a time."

"Splendid!" answered her father. "Till he gets something better."

"I rather think that's the way he looks at it," she remarked demurely. And then she looked at Bill. "Isn't it?"

X I   THE OLD DINING-ROOM

I

I DON'T pretend to account for it; I am merely giving the plain unvarnished tale of what took place to my certain knowledge at Jack Drage's house in Kent during the week-end which finished so disastrously. Doubtless there is an explanation: maybe there are several. The believers in spiritualism and things psychic will probably say that the tragedy was due to the action of a powerful influence which had remained intact throughout the centuries; the materialists will probably say it was due to indigestion. I hold no brief for either side: as the mere narrator, the facts are good enough for me. And, anyway, the extremists of both schools of thought are quite irreconcilable.

There were six of us there, counting Jack Drage and his wife. Bill Sibton in the Indian Civil, Armytage in the Gunners, and I—Marshall by name, and a scribbler of sorts—were the men: little Joan Neilson— Armytage's fiancée—supported Phyllis Drage. Ostensibly we were there to shoot a few pheasants, but it was more than a mere shooting party. It was a re-union after long years of us four men who had been known at school as the Inseparables. Bill had been in India for twelve years, save for the inevitable gap in Mesopotamia; Dick Armytage had soldiered all over the place ever since he'd left the Shop. And though I'd seen Jack off and on since our school-days, I'd lost touch with him since he'd married. Wives play the deuce with bachelor friends though they indignantly deny it—God bless 'em. At least, mine always does.

It was the first time any of us had been inside Jack's house, and undoubtedly he had the most delightful little property. The house itself was old, but comfortably modernized by an expert, so that the charm of it still remained. In fact, the only room which had been left absolutely intact was the dining-room. And to have touched that would have been sheer vandalism. The sole thing that had been done to it was to instal centra heating, and that had been carried out so skilfully that no trace of the work could be seen.

It was a room by itself, standing apart from the rest of the house, with a lofty vaulted roof in which one could just see the smoky old oak beams by the light of the candles on the dinner-table. A huge open fireplace jutted out from one of the longer walls; while on the opposite side a door led into the garden. And then, at one end, approached by the original staircase at least six centuries old, was the musicians' gallery.

A wonderful room—a room in which it seemed almost sacrilege to eat and smoke and discuss present-day affairs —a room in which one felt that history had been made. Nothing softened the severe plainness of the walls save a few mediæval pikes and battle-axes. In fact, two old muskets of the Waterloo era were the most modern implements of the collection. Of pictures there was only one—a very fine painting of a man dressed in the fashion of the Tudor period—which hung facing the musicians' gallery.

It was that that caught my eye as we sat down to dinner, and I turned to Jack.

"An early Drage?" I asked.

"As a matter of fact—no relation at all," he answered. "But a strong relation to this room.   That's why I hang him there."

"Any story attached thereto?"

"There is; though I can't really do it justice.   The parson here is the only man who knows the whole yarn. —By the way, old dear," he spoke to his wife across the table, "the reverend bird takes tea with us to-morrow. But he is the only man who has the thing at his finger-tips.   The previous owner was a bit vague himself, but having a sense of the fitness of things, he gave me a chance of buying the picture.   Apparently it's a painting of one Sir James Wrothley who lived round about the time of Henry VIII.   He was either a rabid Protestant or a rabid Roman Catholic—I told you I was a bit vague over details—and he used this identical room as a secret meeting-place for himself and his pals to hatch plots against his enemies."

"Jack *is* so illuminating, isn't he?" laughed his wife.

"Well, I bet you can't tell it any better yourself," he retorted with a grin.   "I admit my history is weak. But anyway, about that time, if the jolly old Protestants weren't burning the R.C.'s, the R.C.'s were burning the Protestants.   A period calling for great tact, I've always thought.   Well, at any rate, this Sir James Wrothley—when his party was being officially burned —came here and hatched dark schemes to reverse the procedure.   And then, apparently, one day somebody blew the gaff, and the whole bunch of conspirators in here were absolutely caught in the act by the other crowd, who put 'em all to death on the spot. Which is all I can tell you about it."

"I must ask the padre to-morrow," I said to his wife. "I'd rather like to hear the whole story. I felt when I first came into this room there was history connected with it."

She looked at me rather strangely for a moment; then she gave a little forced laugh.

"Do you know, Tom," she said slowly, "at times I almost hate this room. All my friends gnash their teeth with envy over it—but sometimes, when Jack's been away, and I've dined in here by myself—it's terrified me. I feel as if—I wasn't alone: as if—there were people all round me—watching me. Of course, it's absurd, I know. But I can't help it. And yet I'm not a nervy sort of person."

"I don't think it's at all absurd," I assured her. "I believe I should feel the same myself. A room of this size, which, of necessity, is dimly lighted in the corners, and which is full of historical associations, must cause an impression on the least imaginative person."

"We used it once for a dance," she laughed; "with a ragtime band in the gallery."

"And a great show it was, too," broke in her husband. "The trouble was that one of the musicians got gay with a bottle of whisky, and very nearly fell clean through that balustrade effect on to the floor below. I haven't had that touched—and the wood is rotten."

"I pray you be seated, gentlemen." A sudden silence fell on the table, and everybody stared at Bill Sibton.

"Is it a game, Bill?" asked Jack Drage. "I rather thought we were. And what about the ladies?"

With a puzzled frown Bill Sibton looked at him. "Did I speak out loud, then?" he asked slowly.

"And so early in the evening too!" Joan Neilson laughed merrily.

"I must have been day-dreaming, I suppose. But that yarn of yours has rather got me, Jack; though in the course of a long and evil career I've never heard one told worse. I was thinking of that meeting—all of them sitting here. And then suddenly that door bursting open." He was staring fixedly at the door, and again a silence fell on us all.

"The thunder of the butts of their muskets on the woodwork." He swung round and faced the door leading to the garden. "And on that one, too. Can't you hear them? No escape—none. Caught like rats in a trap." His voice died away to a whisper, and Joan Neilson gave a little nervous laugh.

"You're the most realistic person, Mr. Sibton. I think I prefer hearing about the dance."

I glanced at my hostess—and it seemed to me that there was fear in her eyes as she looked at Bill. Sometimes now I wonder if she had some vague premonition of impending disaster: something too intangible to take hold of—something the more terrifying on that very account.

It was after dinner that Jack Drage switched on the solitary electric light of which the room boasted. It was so placed as to show up the painting of Sir James Wrothley, and in silence we all gathered round to look at it. A pair of piercing eyes set in a stern aquiline face stared down at us from under the brim of a hat adorned with sweeping plumes; his hand rested on the jewelled hilt of his sword. It was a fine picture in a splendid state of preservation, well worthy of its place of honour on the walls of such a room, and we joined in a general chorus of admiration. Only Bill Sibton was silent, and he seemed fascinated—unable to tear his eyes away from the painting.

"As a matter of fact, Bill," said Dick Armytage, studying the portrait critically, "he might well be an

ancestor of yours.   Wash out your moustache, and give
you a fancy-dress hat, and you'd look very much like
the old bean."

He was quite right: there was a distinct resemblance,
and it rather surprised me that I had not noticed it
myself.   There were the same deep-set piercing eyes,
the same strong, slightly hatchet face, the same broad
forehead.   Even the colouring was similar: a mere
coincidence that, probably—but one which increased
the likeness.   In fact, the longer I looked the more
pronounced did the resemblance become, till it was
almost uncanny.

"Well, he can't be, anyway," said Bill abruptly. "I've
never heard of any Wrothley in the family."   He looked
away from the picture almost with an effort and lit a
cigarette.   "It's a most extraordinary thing, Jack," he
went on after a moment, "but ever since we came into
this room I've had a feeling that I've been here before."

"Good Lord, man, that's common enough in all conscience.   One often gets that idea."

"I know one does," answered Bill.   "I've had it
before myself; but never one-tenth as strongly as I feel
it here.   Besides, that feeling generally dies—after a
few minutes: it's growing stronger and stronger with me
every moment I stop in here."

"Then let's go into the drawing-room," said our
hostess.   "I've had the card-table put in there."

We followed her and Joan Neilson into the main part
of the house; and since neither of the ladies played, for
the next two hours we four men bridged.   And then,
seeing that it was a special occasion, we sat yarning over
half-forgotten incidents till the room grew thick with
smoke and the two women fled to bed before they died
of asphyxiation.

Bill, I remember, waxed eloquent on the subject of
politicians, with a six-weeks' experience of India, butting

in on things they knew less than nothing about; Dick
Armytage grew melancholy on the subject of the block
in promotion.   And then the reminiscences grew more
personal, and the whisky sank lower and lower in the
tantalus as one yarn succeeded another.

At last Jack Drage rose with a yawn and knocked the
ashes out of his pipe.

"Two o'clock, boys.   What about bed?"

"Lord! is it really?"   Dick Armytage stretched himself.   "However, no shooting to-morrow, or, rather,
to-day.   We might spend the Sabbath dressing Bill up
as his nibs in the next room."

A shadow crossed Bill's face.

"I'd forgotten that room," he said, frowning.   "Damn
you, Dick!"

"My dear old boy," laughed Armytage, "you surely
don't mind resembling the worthy Sir James!   He's a
deuced sight better-looking fellow than you are."

Bill shook his head irritably.

"It isn't that at all," he said.   "I wasn't thinking of
the picture."   He seemed to be on the point of saying
something else—then he changed his mind.   "Well—
bed for master."

We all trooped upstairs, and Jack came round to each
of us to see that we were all right.

"Breakfast provisionally nine," he remarked.   "Night-
night, old boy."

The door closed behind him, and his steps died away
down the passage as he went to his own room.

*   *   *   *   *

By all known rules I should have been asleep almost
as my head touched the pillow.   A day's rough shooting, followed by bed at two in the morning should produce that result if anything can, but in my case that
night it didn't.   Whether I had smoked too much, or

what it was, I know not, but at half-past three I gave up the attempt and switched on my light. Then I went over, and pulling up an armchair, I sat down by the open window. There was no moon, and the night was warm for the time of year. Outlined against the sky the big dining-room stretched out from the house, and, as I lit a cigarette, Jack Drage's vague story returned to my mind. The conspirators, meeting by stealth to hatch some sinister plot; the sudden alarm as they found themselves surrounded; the desperate fight against overwhelming odds—and then, the end. There should be a story in it, I reflected; I'd get the parson to tell me the whole thing accurately next day. The local colour seemed more appropriate when one looked at the room from the outside, with an occasional cloud scudding by over the big trees beyond. Savoured more of conspiracy and death than when dining inside, with reminiscences of a jazz band in the musicians' gallery.

And at that moment a dim light suddenly filtered out through the windows. It was so dim that at first I thought I had imagined it; so dim that I switched off my own light in order to make sure. There was no doubt about it: faint but unmistakable the reflection showed up on the ground outside. A light had been lit in the old dining-room: therefore someone must be in there. At four o'clock in the morning!

For a moment or two I hesitated: should I go along and rouse Jack? Someone might have got in through the garden door, and I failed to see why I should fight another man's burglar in his own house. And then it struck me it would only alarm his wife—I'd get Bill, whose room was opposite mine.

I put on some slippers and crossed the landing to rouse him. And then I stopped abruptly. His door was open; his room was empty. Surely it couldn't be he who had turned on the light below?

As noiselessly as possible I went downstairs, and turned along the passage to the dining-room. Sure enough the door into the main part of the house was ajar, and the light was shining through the opening. I tiptoed up to it and looked through the crack by the hinges.

At first I could see nothing save the solitary electric light over the portrait of Sir James. And then in the gloom beyond I saw a tall figure standing motionless by the old oak dining-table. It was Bill—even in the dim light I recognized that clean-cut profile; Bill clad in his pyjamas only, with one hand stretched out in front of him, pointing. And then, suddenly, he spoke.

"You lie, Sir Henry!—you lie!"

Nothing more—just that one remark; his hand still pointing inexorably across the table. Then after a moment he turned so that the light fell full on his face, and I realized what was the matter. Bill Sibton was walking in his sleep.

Slowly he came towards the door behind which I stood, and passed through it—so close that he almost touched me as I shrank back against the wall. Then he went up the stairs, and as soon as I heard him reach the landing above, I quickly turned out the light in the dining-room and followed him. His bedroom door was closed: there was no sound from inside.

There was nothing more for me to do: my burglar had developed into a harmless somnambulist. Moreover, it suddenly struck me that I had become most infernally sleepy myself. So I did not curse Bill mentally as much as I might have done. I turned in, and my nine o'clock next morning was very provisional.

So was Bill Sibton's: we arrived together for breakfast at a quarter to ten. He looked haggard and ill, like a man who has not slept, and his first remark was to curse Dick Armytage.

"I had the most infernal dreams last night," he grumbled. "Entirely through Dick reminding me of this room. I dreamed the whole show that took place in here in that old bird's time."

He pointed to the portrait of Sir James.

"Did you?" I remarked, pouring out some coffee. "Must have been quite interesting."

"I know I wasn't at all popular with the crowd," he said. "I don't set any store by dreams myself—but last night it was really extraordinarily vivid." He stirred his tea thoughtfully.

"I can quite imagine that, Bill. Do you ever walk in your sleep?"

"Walk in my sleep? No." He stared at me surprised. "Why?"

"You did last night. I found you down here at four o'clock in your pyjamas. You were standing just where I'm sitting now, pointing with your hand across the table. And as I stood outside the door you suddenly said, 'You lie, Sir Henry!—you lie!'"

"Part of my dream," he muttered. "Sir Henry Brayton was the name of the man—and he was the leader. They were all furious with me about something. We quarrelled—and after that there seemed to be a closed door. It was opening slowly, and instinctively I knew there was something dreadful behind it. You know the terror of a dream; the primordial terror of the mind that cannot reason against something hideous—unknown——" I glanced at him: his forehead was wet with sweat. "And then the dream passed. The door didn't open."

"Undoubtedly, my lad," I remarked lightly, "you had one whisky too many last night."

"Don't be an ass, Tom," he said irritably. "I tell you—though you needn't repeat it—I'm in a putrid funk of this room. Absurd, I know: ridiculous. But

I can't help it.   And if there was a train on this branch
line on Sunday, I'd leave to-day."

"But, good Lord, Bill," I began—and then I went on
with my breakfast.   There was a look on his face which
it is not good to see on the face of a man.   It was
terror: an abject, dreadful terror.

II

He and Jack Drage were out for a long walk when
the parson came to tea that afternoon—a walk of which
Bill had been the instigator.   He had dragged Jack
forth, vigorously protesting, after lunch, and we had
cheered them on their way.   Bill had to get out of the
house—I could see that.   Then Dick and the girl had
disappeared, in the way that people in their condition
do disappear, just before Mr. Williams arrived.   And
so only Phyllis Drage was there, presiding at the tea-
table, when I broached the subject of the history of the
dining-room.

"He spoils paper, Mr. Williams," laughed my
hostess, "and he scents copy.   Jack tried to tell the
story last night, and got it hopelessly wrong."

The clergyman smiled gravely.

"You'll have to alter the setting, Mr. Marshall," he
remarked, "because the story is quite well known round
here.   In my library at the vicarage I have an old manuscript copy of the legend.   And, indeed, I have no reason
to believe that it is a legend: certainly the main points
have been historically authenticated.   Sir James Wrothley, whose portrait hangs in the dining-room, lived in
this house.   He was a staunch Protestant—bigoted to
a degree; and he fell very foul of Cardinal Wolsey, who
you may remember was plotting for the Papacy at the
time.   So bitter did the animosity become, and so high
did religious intoleration run in those days, that Sir
James started counter-plotting against the Cardinal;

which was a dangerous thing to do. Moreover, he and his friends used the dining-room here as their meeting-place."

The reverend gentleman sipped his tea; if there was one thing he loved it was the telling of this story, which reflected so magnificently on the staunch no-Popery record of his parish.

"So much is historical certainty; the rest is not so indisputably authentic. The times of the meetings were, of course, kept secret—until the fatal night occurred. Then, apparently, someone turned traitor. And, why I cannot tell you, Sir James himself was accused by the others—especially Sir Henry Brayton. Did you say anything, Mr. Marshall?"

"Nothing," I remarked quietly. "The name surprised me for a moment. Please go on."

"Sir Henry Brayton was Sir James's next-door neighbour, almost equally intolerant of anything savouring of Rome. And even while, so the story goes, Wolsey's men were hammering on the doors, he and Sir Henry had this dreadful quarrel. Why Sir James should have been suspected, whether the suspicions were justified or not I cannot say. Certainly, in view of what we know of Sir James's character, it seems hard to believe that he could have been guilty of such infamous treachery. But that the case must have appeared exceedingly black against him is certain from the last and most tragic part of the story."

Once again Mr. Williams paused to sip his tea; he had now reached that point of the narrative where royalty itself would have failed to hurry him.

"In those days, Mrs. Drage, there was a door leading into the musicians' gallery from one of the rooms of the house. It provided no avenue of escape if the house was surrounded—but its existence was unknown to the men before whose blows the other doors were already beginning to splinter.   And suddenly through this door appeared Lady Wrothley.   She had only recently married Sir James: in fact, her first baby was then on its way.   Sir James saw her, and at once ceased his quarrel with Sir Henry.   With dignity he mounted the stairs and approached his girl-wife—and in her horror-struck eyes he saw that she, too, suspected him of being the traitor.   He raised her hand to his lips; and then as the doors burst open simultaneously and Wolsey's men rushed in—he dived head-foremost on to the floor below, breaking his neck and dying instantly.

"The story goes on to say," continued Mr. Williams, with a diffident cough, "that even while the butchery began in the room below—for most of the Protestants were unarmed—the poor girl collapsed in the gallery, and shortly afterwards the child was born.   A girl baby, who survived, though the mother died.   One likes to think that if she had indeed misjudged her husband, it was a merciful action the part of the Almighty to let her join him so soon.   Thank you, I will have another cup of tea.   One lump, please."

"A most fascinating story, Mr. Williams," said Phyllis. "Thank you so much for having told us.   Can you make anything out of it, Tom?"

I laughed.

"The criminal reserves his defence.   But it's most interesting, Padre, most interesting, as Mrs. Drage says. If I may, I'd like to come and see that manuscript."

"I shall be only too delighted," he murmured with old-fashioned courtesy.   "Whenever you like."

And then the conversation turned on things parochial until he rose to go.   The others had still not returned, and for a while we two sat on talking as the spirit moved us in the darkening room.   At last the servants appeared to draw the curtains, and it was then that we heard Jack and Bill in the hall.

I don't know what made me make the remark; it seemed to come without my volition.

"If I were you, Phyllis," I said, "I don't think I'd tell the story of the dining-room to Bill."

She looked at me curiously.

"Why not?"

"I don't know—but I wouldn't." In the brightly lit room his fears of the morning seemed ridiculous; yet, as I say, I don't know what made me make the remark.

"All right; I won't," she said gravely. "Do you think——"

But further conversation was cut short by the entrance of Bill and her husband.

"Twelve miles if an inch," growled Drage, throwing himself into a chair. "You awful fellow."

Sibton laughed.

"Do you good, you lazy devil. He's getting too fat, Phyllis, isn't he?"

I glanced at him as he, too, sat down: in his eyes there remained no trace of the terror of the morning.

III

And now I come to that part of my story which I find most difficult to write. From the story-teller's point of view pure and simple, it is the easiest; from the human point of view I have never tackled anything harder. Because, though the events I am describing took place months ago—and the first shock is long since past—I still cannot rid myself of a feeling that I was largely to blame. By the cold light of reason I can exonerate myself; but one does not habitually have one's being in that exalted atmosphere. Jack blames himself; but in view of what happened the night before—in view of the look in Bill's eyes that Sunday morning—I feel that I ought to have realized that there were influences at work which lay beyond my ken—influences which at present lie not within the light of reason.   And then at other times I wonder if it was not just a strange coincidence and an— accident.   God knows: frankly, I don't.

We spent that evening just as we had spent the preceding one, save that in view of shooting on Monday morning we went to bed at midnight.   This time I fell asleep at once—only to be roused by someone shaking my arm.   I sat up blinking: it was Jack Drage.

"Wake up, Tom," he whispered.   "There's a light in the dining-room, and we're going down to investigate. Dick is getting Bill."

In an instant I was out of bed.

"It's probably Bill himself," I said.   "I found him down there last night walking in his sleep."

"The devil you did!" muttered Jack, and at that moment Dick Armytage came in.

"Bill's room is empty," he announced; and I nodded.

"It's Bill right enough," I said.   "He went back quite quietly last night.   And, for Heaven's sake, you fellows, don't wake him.   It's very dangerous."

Just as before the dining-room door was open, and the light filtered through into the passage as we tiptoed along it.   Just as before we saw Bill standing by the table—his hand outstretched.

Then came the same words as I had heard last night.

"You lie, Sir Henry!—you lie!"

"What the devil——" muttered Jack; but I held up my finger to ensure silence.

"He'll come to bed now," I whispered.   "Keep quite still."

But this time Bill Sibton did not come to bed; instead, he turned and stared into the shadows of the musicians' gallery.   Then, very slowly, he walked away from us and commenced to mount the stairs.   And still the danger did not strike us.

Dimly we saw the tall figure reach the top and walk

along the gallery, as if he saw someone at the end—and at that moment the peril came to the three of us.

To Dick and Jack the rottenness of the balustrade; to me—*the end of the vicar's story.* What they thought I know not; but to my dying day I shall never forget my own agony of mind. In that corner of the musicians' gallery—though we could see her not—stood Lady Wrothley; to the man walking slowly towards her the door was opening slowly—the door which had remained shut the night before—the door behind which lay the terror.

And then it all happened very quickly. In a frenzy we raced across the room to get at him—but we weren't in time. There was a rending of wood—a dreadful crash—a sprawling figure on the floor below. To me it seemed as if he had hurled himself against the balustrade, had literally dived downwards. The others did not notice it—so they told me later. But I did.

And then we were kneeling beside him on the floor.

"Dear God!" I heard Drage say in a hoarse whisper. "He's dead; he's broken his neck."

*   *   *   *   *

Such is my story. Jack Drage blames himself for the rottenness of the woodwork, but I feel it was my fault. Yes—it was my fault. I ought to have known, ought to have done something. Even if we'd only locked the dining-room door.

And the last link in the chain I haven't mentioned yet. The vicar supplied that—though to him it was merely a strange coincidence.

The baby-girl—born in the gallery—a strange, imaginative child, so run the archives, subject to fits of awful depression and, at other times, hallucinations— married. She married in 1551, on the 30th day of

October, Henry, only son of Frank Sibton and Mary his wife.

God knows: I don't.   It may have been an accident.

XII   WHEN GREEK MEETS GREEK

I

"BUT, Bill, I don't understand.   How much did you borrow from this man?"

Sybil Hamilton looked at her brother, sitting huddled up in his chair, with a little frown.

"I borrowed a thousand," he answered sulkily. "And like a fool I didn't read the thing he made me sign—at least, not carefully.   Hang it, I've only had the money six months, and now he's saying that I owe him over two.   I saw something about twenty-five per cent., and now I find it was twenty-five per cent. a month.   And the swine is pressing for payment unless——" He broke off and stared into the fire shamefacedly.

"Unless what?" demanded his sister.

"Well, you see, it's this way."   The boy stammered a little, and refused to look at her.   "I was jolly well up the spout when this blighter told me what I owed him, and I suppose I must have showed it pretty clearly.   Anyway, I was propping up the bar at the ·Cri., getting a cocktail, when a fellow standing next me started gassing.   Not a bad sort of cove at all; knows you very well by sight."

"Knows me?" said the girl, bewildered.   "Who was he?"

"I'm coming to that later," went on her brother. " Well, we had a couple more and then he suggested tearing a chop together.   And I don't know—he seemed so decent and all that—that I told him I was in the soup. Told him the whole yarn and asked his advice sort of business. Well, as I say, he was bally sporting about it all, and finally asked me who the bird was who had tied up the boodle. I told him, and here's the lucky part of the whole show—this fellow Perrison knew him. Perrison was the man I was lunching with."

He paused and lit a cigarette, while the girl stared at him gravely.

"Well," she said at length, "go on."

"It was after lunch that he got busy. He said to me: 'Look here, Hamilton, you've made a bally fool of yourself, but you're not the first. I'll write a note to Messrs. Smith and Co.'—those are the warriors who gave me the money—' and try and persuade them to give you more time, or even possibly reduce the rate of interest.' Of course, I was all on this, and I arranged to lunch with him again next day, after Smith and Co. had had time to function. And sure enough they did. Wrote a letter in which they were all over me; any friend of Mr. Perrison's was entitled to special treatment, and so on and so forth. Naturally I was as bucked as a dog with two tails, and asked Perrison if I couldn't do something more material than just thank him. And—er—he—I mean it was then he told me he knew you by sight."

He glanced at his sister, and then quickly looked away again.

"He suggested—er—that perhaps I could arrange to introduce him to you; that it would be an honour he would greatly appreciate, and all that sort of rot."

The girl was sitting very still. "Yes," she said quietly, "and you—agreed."

"Well, of course I did. Hang it, he's quite a decent fellow. Bit Cityish to look at, and I shouldn't

think he knows which end of a horse goes first. But
he's got me out of the devil of a hole, Sybil, and the
least you can do is to be moderately decent to the bird.
I mean it's not asking much, is it? I left the governor
looking at him in the hall as if he was just going to
tread on his face, and that long slab—your pal—is
gazing at him through his eyeglasses as if he was mad."

"He's not my pal, Bill." Sybil Hamilton's colour
heightened a little.

"Well, you asked him here, anyway," grunted the
boy. Then with a sudden change of tone he turned
to her appealingly. "Syb, old girl—for the Lord's
sake play the game. You know what the governor is,
and if he hears about this show—especially as it's—
as it's not the first time—there'll be the deuce to pay.
You know he said last time that if it happened again
he'd turn me out of the house. And the old man is
as stubborn as a mule. I only want you to be a bit
decent to Perrison."

She looked at him with a grave smile. "If Mr.
Perrison is satisfied with my being decent to him, as
you put it, I'm perfectly prepared to play the game.
But——" She frowned and rose abruptly. "Come
on, and I'll have a look at him."

In silence they went downstairs. Tea had just been
brought in, and the house-party was slowly drifting
into the hall. But Sybil barely noticed them; her eyes
were fixed on the man talking to her father. Or rather,
at the moment, her father was talking to the man, and
his remark was painfully audible.

"There is a very good train back to London at seven-
thirty, Mr.—ah—Mr.——"

Her brother stepped forward. "But I say, Dad,"
he said nervously, "I asked Perrison to stop the night.
I've just asked Sybil, and she says she can fix him up
somewhere."

"How do you do, Mr. Perrison?" With a charming smile she held out her hand. "Of course you must stop the night."

Then she moved away to the tea-table, feeling agreeably relieved; it was better than she had expected. The man was well-dressed; perhaps, to her critical eye, a little too well-dressed—but still quite presentable.

"You averted a catastrophe, Miss Hamilton." A lazy voice beside her interrupted her thoughts, and with a smile she turned to the speaker.

"Dad is most pestilentially rude at times, isn't he? And Bill told me he left *you* staring at the poor man as if he was an insect."

Archie Longworth laughed.

"He'd just contradicted your father flatly as you came downstairs. And on a matter concerning horses. However—the breeze has passed. But, tell me," he stared at her gravely, "why the sudden invasion?"

Her eyebrows went up a little. "May I ask why not?" she said coldly. "Surely my brother can invite a friend to the house if he wishes."

"I stand corrected," answered Longworth quietly. "Has he known him long?"

"I haven't an idea," said the girl. "And after all, Mr. Longworth, I hadn't known you very long when I asked you."

And then, because she realized that there was a possibility of construing rather more into her words than she had intended, she turned abruptly to speak to another guest. So she failed to see the sudden inscrutable look that came into Archie Longworth's keen blue eyes—the quick clenching of his powerful fists. But when a few minutes later she again turned to him, he was just his usual lazy self.

"Do you think your logic is very good?" he demanded. "You might have made a mistake as well."

"You mean that you think my brother has?" she said quickly.

"It is visible on the surface to the expert eye," he returned gravely. "But, in addition, I happen to have inside information."

"Do you know Mr. Perrison, then?"

He nodded. "Yes, I have—er—met him before."

"But he doesn't know you," cried the girl.

"No—at least—er—we'll leave it at that. And I would be obliged, Miss Hamilton, in case you happen to be speaking to him, if you would refrain from mentioning the fact that I know him." He stared at her gravely.

"You're very mysterious, Mr. Longworth," said the girl, with an attempt at lightness.

"And if I may I will prolong my visit until our friend departs," continued Longworth.

"Why, of course," she said, bending over the tea-tray. "You weren't thinking of going—going yet, were you?"

"I was thinking after lunch that I should have to go to-morrow," he said, putting down his tea-cup.

"But why so soon?" she asked, and her voice was low. "Aren't you enjoying yourself?"

"In the course of a life that has taken me into every corner of the globe," he answered slowly, "I have never dreamed that I could be so utterly and perfectly happy as I have been here. It has opened my mind to a vista of the Things that Might Be—if the Things that Had Been were different. But as you grow older, Sybil, you will learn one bitter truth: no human being can ever be exactly what he seems. Masks? just masks! And underneath—God and that being alone know."

He rose abruptly, and she watched him bending over Lady Granton with his habitual lazy grace. The indolent smile was round his lips—the irrepressible twinkle was in his eyes. But for the first time he had called her Sybil; for the first time—she *knew*. The vague forebodings conjured up by his words were swamped by that one outstanding fact; she *knew*. And nothing else mattered.

II

It was not until Perrison joined her in the conservatory after dinner that she found herself called on to play the part set her by her brother.

She had gone there—though nothing would have induced her to admit the fact—in the hope that someone else would follow: the man with the lazy blue eyes and the eyeglass. And then instead of him had come Perrison, with a shade too much deference in his manner, and a shade too little control of the smirk on his face. With a sudden sick feeling she realized at that moment exactly where she stood. Under a debt of obligation to this man—under the necessity of a *tête-à-tête* with him, one, moreover, when, if she was to help Bill, she must endeavour to be extra nice.

For a while the conversation was commonplace, while she feverishly longed for someone to come in and relieve the tension. But Bridge was in progress, and there was Snooker in the billiard-room, and at length she resigned herself to the inevitable. Presumably she would have to thank him for his kindness to Bill; after all he undoubtedly had been very good to her brother.

"Bill has told me, Mr. Perrison, how kind you've been in the way you've helped him in this—this unfortunate affair." She plunged valiantly, and gave a sigh of relief as she cleared the first fence.

Perrison waved a deprecating hand. "Don't mention it, Miss Hamilton, don't mention it. But—er—

of course, something will have to be done, and—well, there's no good mincing matters—done very soon."

The girl's face grew a little white, but her voice was quite steady.

"But he told me that you had arranged things with these people. Please smoke, if you want to."

Perrison bowed his thanks and carefully selected a cigarette. The moment for which he had been playing had now arrived, in circumstances even more favourable than he had dared to hope.

"Up to a point that is quite true," he remarked quietly. "Messrs. Smith and Co. have many ramifications of business—money-lending being only one of the irons they have in the fire. And because I have had many dealings with the firm professionally—over the sale of precious stones, I may say, which is my own particular line of work—they were disposed to take a lenient view about the question of the loan. Not press for payment, and perhaps—though I can't promise this—even be content with a little less interest. But —er—Miss Hamilton, it's the other thing where the trouble is going to occur."

The girl stared at him with dilated eyes. "What other thing, Mr. Perrison?"

"Hasn't your brother told you?" said Perrison, surprised. "Oh, well, perhaps I—er—shouldn't have mentioned it."

"Go on, please." Her voice was low. "What is this other thing?"

For a moment he hesitated—a well-simulated hesitation. Then he shrugged his shoulders slightly.

"Well—if you insist. As a matter of fact, your brother didn't tell me about it, and I only found it out in the course of my conversation with one of the Smith partners. Apparently some weeks ago he bought some distinctly valuable jewellery—a pearl necklace, to be exact—from a certain firm. At least, when I say he bought it—he did not pay for it. He gave your father's name as a reference, and the firm considered it satisfactory. It was worth about eight hundred pounds, this necklace, and your very stupid brother, instead of giving it to the lady whom, presumably, he had got it for, became worse than stupid. He became criminal."

"What do you mean?" The girl was looking at him terrified.

"He pawned this necklace which he hadn't paid for, Miss Hamilton, which is, I regret to say, a criminal offence. And the trouble of the situation is that the firm he bought the pearls from has just found it out. He pawned it at a place which is one of the ramifications of Smith and Co., who gave him, I believe, a very good price for it—over five hundred pounds. The firm, in the course of business, two or three days ago—and this is the incredibly unfortunate part of it—happened to show this self-same necklace, while they were selling other things, to the man it had originally come from. Of course, being pawned, it wasn't for sale—but the man recognized it at once. And then the fat was in the fire."

"Do you mean to say," whispered the girl, "that—that they might send him to prison?"

"Unless something is done very quickly, Miss Hamilton, the matter will certainly come into the law courts. Messrs. Gross and Sons"—a faint noise from the darkness at the end of the conservatory made him swing round suddenly, but everything was silent again —"Messrs. Gross and Sons are very difficult people in many ways. They are the people it came from originally, I may tell you. And firms, somewhat naturally, differ, like human beings. Some are disposed to be lenient—others are not. I'm sorry to say Gross and Sons are one of those who are not."

"But couldn't you see them, or something, and explain?"

"My dear Miss Hamilton," said Perrison gently, "I must ask you to be reasonable. What can I explain? Your brother wanted money, and he adopted a criminal method of getting it. That, I am afraid— ugly as it sounds—is all there is to it."

"Then, Mr. Perrison—can nothing be done?" She bent forward eagerly, her hands clasped, her lips slightly parted; and once again came that faint noise from the end of the conservatory.

But Mr. Perrison was too engrossed to heed it this time; the nearness, the appeal of this girl, who from the time he had first seen her six months previously at a theatre had dominated his life, was making his senses swim. And with it the veneer began to drop; the hairy heel began to show, though he made a tremendous endeavour to keep himself in check.

"There is one thing," he said hoarsely. "And I hope you will understand that I should not have been so precipitate—except for the urgency of your brother's case. If I go to Messrs. Gross and say to them that a prosecution by them would affect me personally, I think I could persuade them to take no further steps."

Wonder was beginning to dawn in the girl's eyes. "Affect you personally?" she repeated.

"If, for instance, I could tell them that for family reasons—urgent, strong family reasons—they would be doing me a great service by letting matters drop, I think they would do it."

She rose suddenly—wonder replaced by horror. She had just realized his full meaning.

"What on earth are you talking about, Mr. Perrison?" she said haughtily.

And then the heel appeared in all its hairiness. "If I may tell them," he leered, "that I am going to marry into the family I'll guarantee they will do nothing more."

"Marry you?" The biting scorn in her tone changed the leer to a snarl.

"Yes—marry me, or see your brother jugged. Money won't save him—so there's no good going to your father. Money will square up the Smith show —it won't square the other." And then his tone changed. "Why not, little girl? I'm mad about you; have been ever since I saw you at a theatre six months ago. I'm pretty well off even for these days, and———" He came towards her, his arms outstretched, while she backed away from him, white as a sheet. Her hands were clenched, and it was just as she had retreated as far as she could, and the man was almost on her, that she saw red. One hand went up; hit him—hit the brute—was her only coherent thought. And the man, realizing it, paused—an ugly look in his eyes.

Then occurred the interruption. A strangled snort, as of a sleeper awakening, came from behind some palms, followed by the creaking of a chair. With a stifled curse Perrison fell back and the girl's hand dropped to her side as the branches parted and Archie Longworth, rubbing his eyes, stepped into the light.

"Lord save us, Miss Hamilton, I've been asleep," he said, stifling a yawn. "I knew I oughtn't to have had a third glass of port. Deuced bad for the liver, but very pleasant for all that, isn't it, Mr.—Mr. Perrison?"

He smiled engagingly at the scowling Perrison, and adjusted his eyeglass.

"You sleep very silently, Mr. Longworth," snarled that worthy.

"Yes—used to win prizes for it at an infant school. Most valuable asset in class. If one snores it disconcerts the lecturer."

Perrison swung round on his heel. "I would like an answer to my suggestion by to-morrow, Miss Hamilton," he said softly. "Perhaps I might have the pleasure of a walk where people don't sleep off the effects of dinner."

With a slight bow he left the conservatory, and the girl sat down weakly.

"Pleasant type of bird, isn't he?" drawled Longworth, watching Perrison's retreating back.

"He's a brute—an utter brute," whispered the girl shakily.

"I thought the interview would leave you with that impression," agreed the man.

She sat up quickly. "Did you hear what was said?"

"Every word. That's why I was there." He smiled at her calmly.

"Then why didn't you come out sooner?" she cried indignantly.

"I wanted to hear what he had to say, and at the same time I didn't want you to biff him on the jaw—which from your attitude I gathered you were on the point of doing."

"Why not? I'd have given anything to have smacked his face."

"I know. I'd have given anything to have seen you do it. But—not yet. In fact, to-morrow you've got to go for a walk with him."

"I flatly refuse!" cried Sybil Hamilton.

"More than that," continued Longworth calmly, "you've got to keep him on the hook. Play with him; let him think he's got a chance."

"But why?" she demanded. "I loathe him."

"Because it is absolutely essential that he should remain here until the day after to-morrow at the earliest."

"I don't understand." She looked at him with a puzzled frown.

"You will in good time." It seemed to her his voice was just a little weary. "Just now it is better that you shouldn't. Do you trust me enough to do that, Sybil?"

"I trust you absolutely," and she saw him wince.

"Then keep him here till I come back."

"Are you going away, Archie?" Impulsively she laid her hand on his arm.

"To-morrow, first thing. I shall come back as soon as possible."

For a moment or two they stood in silence, then, with a gesture strangely foreign to one so typically British, he raised her hand to his lips. And the next instant she was alone.

A little later she saw him talking earnestly to her brother in a corner; then someone suggested billiard-fives. An admirable game, but not one in which it is wise to place one's hand on the edge of the table with the fingers over the cushion. Especially if the owner of the hand is not paying attention to the game. It was Perrison's hand, and the agony of being hit on the fingers by a full-sized billiard ball travelling fast must be experienced to be believed. Of course it was an accident: Longworth was most apologetic. But in the middle of the hideous scene that followed she caught his lazy blue eye and beat a hasty retreat to the hall. Unrestrained mirth in such circumstances is not regarded as the essence of tact.

III

It was about ten o'clock on the morning of the next day but one that a sharp-looking, flashily dressed individual presented himself at the door of Messrs. Gross and Sons. He was of the type that may be seen by the score any day of the week propping up the West End bars and discoursing on racing form in a hoarse whisper.

"Mornin'," he remarked. "Mr. Johnson here yet?"

"What do you want to see him about?" demanded the assistant.

"To tell him that your hair wants cutting," snapped the other. "Hop along, young fellah; as an ornament you're a misfit. Tell Mr. Johnson that I've a message from Mr. Perrison."

The youth faded away, to return in a minute or two with a request that the visitor would follow him.

"Message from Perrison? What's up?" Mr. Johnson rose from his chair as the door closed behind the assistant.

The flashy individual laughed and pulled out his cigarette-case.

"He's pulled it off," he chuckled. "At the present moment our one and only Joe is clasping the beauteous girl to his bosom."

"Strike me pink—he hasn't, has he?" Mr. Johnson slapped his leg resoundingly and shook with merriment.

"That's why I've come round," continued the other. "From Smith, I am. Joe wants to give her a little present on account." He grinned again, and felt in his pocket. "Here it is—and he wants a receipt signed by you—acknowledging the return of the necklace which was sent out—on approval." He winked heavily. "He's infernally deep, is Joe." He watched the other man as he picked up the pearls, and for a moment his blue eyes seemed a little strained. "He wants to give that receipt to the girl—so as to clinch the bargain."

"Why the dickens didn't he 'phone me direct?" demanded Johnson, and once again the other grinned broadly.

"Strewth!" he said, "I laughed fit to burst this

morning. The 'phone at his girl's place is in the hall, as far as I could make out, and Joe was whispering down it like an old woman with lumbago. 'Take 'em round to Johnson,' he said. 'Approval—approval— you fool.' And then he turned away and I heard him say—'Good morning, Lady Jemima.' Then back he turns and starts whispering again. 'Do you get me, Bob?' 'Yes,' I says, 'I get you. You want me to take round the pearls to Johnson and get a receipt from him. And what about the other thing—you know, the money the young boob borrowed?' 'Put it in an envelope and send it to me here, with the receipt,' he says. 'I'm going out walking this morning.' Then he rings off, and that's that. Lord! think of Joe walking."

The grin developed into a cackling laugh, in which Mr. Johnson joined.

"He's deep—you're right," he said admiringly. "Uncommonly deep. I never thought he'd pull it off. Though personally, mark you, I think he's a fool. They'll fight like cat and dog." He rang a bell on his desk, then opening a drawer he dropped the necklace inside.

"Bring me a formal receipt form," he said to the assistant. "Have you got the other paper?" he asked, as he affixed the firm's signature to the receipt, and the flashy individual produced it from his pocket.

"Here it is," he announced. "Put 'em both in an envelope together and address it to Joe. I'm going along; I'll post it."

"Will you have a small tiddley before you go?" Mr. Johnson opened a formidable-looking safe, disclosing all the necessary-looking ingredients for the manufacture of small tiddleys.

"I don't mind if I do," conceded the other. "Here's the best—and to the future Mrs. Joe."

A moment or two later he passed through the outer office and was swallowed up in the crowd. And it was not till after lunch that day that Mr. Johnson got the shock of his life—when he opened one of the early evening papers.

"DARING ROBBERY IN WELL-KNOWN CITY FIRM

"*A most daring outrage was carried out last night at the office of Messrs. Smith and Co., the well-known financial and insurance brokers. At a late hour this morning, some time after work was commenced, the night watchman was discovered bound and securely gagged in a room at the top of the premises. Further investigation revealed that the safe had been opened—evidently by a master hand—and the contents rifled. The extent of the loss is at present unknown, but the police are believed to possess several clues.*"

And at the same time that Mr. Johnson was staring with a glassy stare at this astounding piece of news, a tall, spare man with lazy blue eyes, stretched out comfortably in the corner of a first-class carriage, was also perusing it.

"Several clues," he murmured. "I wonder! But it was a very creditable job, though I say it myself."

Which seemed a strange soliloquy for a well-dressed man in a first-class carriage. And what might have seemed almost stranger, had there been any way of knowing such a recondite fact, was that in one of the mail bags reposing in the back of the train, a mysterious transformation had taken place. For a letter which had originally contained two documents and had been addressed to J. Perrison, Esq., now contained three and was consigned to Miss Sybil Hamilton. Which merely goes to show how careful one should be over posting letters.

IV

"Good evening, Mr. Perrison. All well, and taking nourishment, so to speak?"

Archie Longworth lounged into the hall, almost colliding with the other man.

"You look pensive," he continued, staring at him blandly. "*Agitato, fortissimo.* Has aught occurred to disturb your masterly composure?"

But Mr. Perrison was in no mood for fooling: a message he had just received over the telephone had very considerably disturbed his composure.

"Let me have a look at that paper," he snapped, making a grab at it.

"Tush! Tush!" murmured Archie. "Manners, laddie, manners! You've forgotten that little word."

And then at the far end of the hall he saw the girl, and caught his breath. For the last two days he had almost forgotten her in the stress of other things; now the bitterness of what had to come rose suddenly in his throat and choked him.

"There is the paper. Run away and play in a corner."

Then he went forward to meet her with his usual lazy smile.

"What's happened?" she cried a little breathlessly.

"Heaps of things," he said gently. "Heaps of things. The principal one being that a very worthless sinner loves a very beautiful girl—as he never believed it could be given to man to love." His voice broke and faltered: then he went on steadily. "And the next one—which is really even more important—is that the very beautiful girl will receive a letter in a long envelope by to-night's mail. The address will be typed,

the postmark Strand.   I do not want the beautiful girl
to open it except in my presence.   You understand?"

"I understand," she whispered, and her eyes were
shining.

"Have you seen this?"   Perrison's voice—shaking
with rage—made Longworth swing round.

"Seen what, dear lad?" he murmured, taking the
paper.   "Robbery in City—is that what you mean?
Dear, dear—what dastardly outrages do go unpunished
these days!   Messrs. Smith and Co.   Really!   Watchman bound and gagged.   Safe rifled.   Work of a
master hand.   Still, though I quite understand your
horror as a law-abiding citizen at such a thing, why
this thusness?   I mean—altruism is wonderful, laddie;
but it seems to me that it's jolly old Smith and Co.
who are up the pole."

He burbled on genially, serenely unconscious of the
furious face of the other man.

"I'm trying to think where I've met you before,
Mr. Longworth," snarled Perrison.

"Never, surely," murmured the other.   "Those
classic features, I feel sure, would have been indelibly
printed on my mind.   Perhaps in some mission, Mr.
Perrison—some evangelical revival meeting.   Who
knows?   And there, if I mistake not, is the mail."

He glanced at the girl, and she was staring at him
wonderingly.   Just for one moment did he show her
what she wanted to know—just for one moment did
she give him back the answer which was to him the
sweetest and at the same time the most bitter in the
world.   Then he crossed the hall and picked up the
letters.

"A business one for you, Miss Hamilton," he murmured mildly.   "Better open it at once, and get our
business expert's advice.   Mr. Perrison is a wonderful
fellah for advice."

With trembling fingers she opened the envelope, and, as he saw the contents, Perrison, with a snarl of ungovernable fury, made as if to snatch them out of her hand. The next moment he felt as if his arm was broken, and the blue eyes boring into his brain were no longer lazy.

"You forgot yourself, Mr. Perrison," said Archie Longworth gently. "Don't do that again."

"But I don't understand," cried the girl, bewildered. "What are these papers?"

"May I see?" Longworth held out his hand, and she gave them to him at once.

"They're stolen." Perrison's face was livid. "Give them to me, curse you."

"Control yourself, you horrible blighter," said Longworth icily. "This," he continued calmly, "would appear to be a receipt from Messrs. Gross and Sons for the return of a pearl necklace—sent out to Mr. Hamilton on approval."

"But you said he'd bought it and pawned it." She turned furiously on Perrison.

"So he did," snarled that gentleman. "That's a forgery."

"Is it?" said Longworth. "That strikes me as being Johnson's signature. Firm's official paper. And—er—he has the necklace, I—er—assume."

"Yes—he has the necklace. Stolen last night by —by——" His eyes were fixed venomously on Longworth.

"Go on," murmured the other. "You're being most entertaining."

But a sudden change had come over Perrison's face —a dawning recognition. "By God!" he muttered, "you're—you're——"

"Yes. I'm—who? It'll come in time, laddie—if you give it a chance. And in the meantime we might

examine these other papers.   Now, this appears to my
inexperienced eye to be a transaction entered into on
the one part by Messrs. Smith and Co. and on the
other by William Hamilton.   And it concerns filthy
lucre.   Dear, dear.   Twenty-five per cent. per month.
Three hundred per cent.   Positive usury, Mr. Perrison.   Don't you agree with me?   A rapacious blood-
sucker is Mr. Smith."

But the other man was not listening: full recollection had come to him, and with a cold look of triumph
he put his hands into his pockets and laughed.

"Very pretty," he remarked.   "Very pretty indeed.
And how, in your vernacular, do you propose to get
away with the swag, Mr. Flash Pete?   I rather think
the police—whom I propose to call up on the 'phone
in one minute—will be delighted to see such an old
and elusive friend."

He glanced at the girl, and laughed again at the look
on her face.

"What's he mean, Archie?" she cried wildly.
"What's he mean?"

"I mean," Perrison sneered, "that Mr. Archie Longworth is what is generally described as a swell crook
with a reputation in certain unsavoury circles extending
over two or three continents.   And the police, whom
I propose to ring up, will welcome him as a long-lost
child."

He walked towards the telephone, and with a little
gasp of fear the girl turned to Archie.

"Say it's not true, dear—say it's not true."

For a moment he looked at her with a whimsical
smile; then he sat down on the high fender round the
open fire.

"I think, Mr. Perrison," he murmured gently,
"that if I were you I would not be too precipitate over
ringing up the police.   The engaging warrior who sent

this letter to Miss Hamilton put in yet one more enclosure."

Perrison turned round: then he stood very still.

"A most peculiar document," continued the man by the fire, in the same gentle voice, "which proves very conclusively that amongst their other activities Messrs. Smith and Co. are not only the receivers of stolen goods, but are mixed up with illicit diamond buying."

In dead silence the two men stared at one another; then Longworth spoke again.

"I shall keep these three documents, Mr. Perrison, as a safeguard for your future good behaviour. Mr. Hamilton can pay a certain fair sum or not as he likes —that is his business: and I shall make a point of explaining exactly to him who and what you are—and Smith—and Gross. But should you be disposed to make any trouble over the necklace—or should the idea get abroad that Flash Pete was responsible for the burglary last night—it will be most unfortunate for you—most. This document would interest Scotland Yard immensely."

Perrison's face had grown more and more livid as he listened, and when the quiet voice ceased, unmindful of the girl standing by, he began to curse foully and hideously. The next moment he cowered back, as two iron hands gripped his shoulders and shook him till his teeth rattled.

"Stop, you filthy swine," snarled Longworth, "or I'll break every bone in your body. Quite a number of men are blackguards, Perrison—but you're a particularly creeping and repugnant specimen. Now— get out—and do it quickly. The nine-thirty will do you nicely. And don't forget what I've just said: because, as there's a God above, I mean it."

"I'll be even with you for this some day, Flash

Pete," said the other venomously over his shoulder. "And then——"

"And then," said Longworth contemptuously, "we will resume this discussion. Just now—get out."

v

"Yes: it is quite true." She had known it was—and yet, womanlike, she had clung to the hope that there was some mistake—some explanation. And now, alone with the man she had grown to love, the faint hope died. With his lazy smile, he stared down at her—a smile so full of sorrow and pain that she could not bear to see it.

"I'm Flash Pete—with an unsavoury reputation, as our friend so kindly told you, in three continents. It was I who broke open the safe at Smith's last night, I who got the receipt from Gross. You see, I spotted the whole trick from the beginning; as I said, I had inside information. And Perrison is Smith and Co.; moreover he's very largely Gross as well—and half a dozen other rotten things in addition. The whole thing was worked with one end in view right from the beginning: the girl your brother originally bought the pearls for was in it; it was she who suggested the pawning. Bill told me that the night before last." He sighed and paced two or three times up and down the dim-lit conservatory. And after a while he stopped in front of her again, and his blue eyes were very tender.

"Just a common sneak-thief—just a common, worthless sinner. And he's very, very glad that he has been privileged to help the most beautiful girl in all the world. Don't cry, my dear, don't cry: there's nothing about that sinner that's worth a single tear of yours. You must forget his wild presumption in falling in love with that beautiful girl: his only excuse is that he couldn't help it.   And maybe, in the days to come, the girl will think kindly every now and then of a man known to some as Archie Longworth—known to others as Flash Pete—known to himself as—well, we won't bother about that."

He bent quickly and raised her hand to his lips; then he was gone almost before she had realized it. And if he heard her little gasping cry—" Archie, my man, come back—I love you so!"—he gave no sign.

For in his own peculiar code a very worthless sinner must remain a very worthless sinner to the end—and he must run the course alone.

XIII   JIMMY LETHBRIDGE'S TEMPTATION

I

"WHAT a queer little place, Jimmy!"   The girl glanced round the tiny restaurant with frank interest, and the man looked up from the menu he was studying with a grin.

"Don't let François hear you say that, or you'll be asked to leave."   The head-waiter was already bearing down on them, his face wreathed in an expansive smile of welcome.   "To him it is the only restaurant in London."

"Ah, m'sieur! it is long days since you were here." The little Frenchman rubbed his hands together delightedly.   "And, mam'selle—it is your first visit to Les Coquelins, n'est-ce-pas?"

"But not the last, I hope, François," said the girl with a gentle smile.

"Ah, mais non!"   Outraged horror at such an impossible idea shone all over the head-waiter's face.   "My guests, mam'selle, they come here once to see what it is like—and they return because they know what it is like."

Jimmy Lethbridge laughed.

"There you are, Molly," he cried. "Now you know what's expected of you. Nothing less than once a week —eh, François?"

"*Mais oui, m'sieur.* There are some who come every night." He produced his pencil and stood waiting. "A few oysters," he murmured. "They are good *ce soir*: real Whitstables. And a bird, M'sieur Lethbridge —with an *omelette aux fines herbes*——"

"Sounds excellent, François," laughed the man. "Anyway, I know that once you have decided—argument is futile."

"It is my work," answered the waiter, shrugging his shoulders. "And a bottle of Corton—with the chill just off. *Toute de suite.*"

François bustled away, and the girl looked across the table with a faintly amused smile in her big grey eyes.

"He fits the place, Jimmy. You must bring me here again."

"Just as often as you like, Molly," answered the man quietly, and after a moment the girl turned away. "You know," he went on steadily, "how much sooner I'd bring you to a spot like this, than go to the Ritz or one of those big places. Only I was afraid it might bore you. I love it: it's so much more intimate."

"Why should you think it would bore me?" she asked, drawing off her gloves and resting her hands on the table in front of her. They were beautiful hands, ringless save for one plain signet ring on the little finger of her left hand. And, almost against his will, the man found himself staring at it as he answered:

"Because I can't trust myself, dear; I can't trust myself to amuse you," he answered slowly. "I can't trust myself not to make love to you—and it's so much easier here than in the middle of a crowd whom one knows."

The girl sighed a little sadly.

"Oh, Jimmy, I wish I could! You've been such an absolute dear. Give me a little longer, old man, and then—perhaps——"

"My dear," said the man hoarsely, "I don't want to hurry you. I'm willing to wait years for you—years. At least"—he smiled whimsically—"I'm not a little bit willing to wait years—really. But if it's that or nothing —then, believe me, I'm more than willing."

"I've argued it out with myself, Jimmy." And now she was staring at the signet ring on her finger. "And when I've finished the argument, I know that I'm not a bit further on. You can't argue over things like that. I've told myself times out of number that it isn't fair to you——"

He started to speak, but she stopped him with a smile.

"No, dear man, it is not fair to you—whatever you like to say. It isn't fair to you even though you may agree to go on waiting. No one has a right to ask another person to wait indefinitely, though I'm thinking that is exactly what I've been doing. Which is rather like a woman," and once again she smiled half sadly.

"But I'm willing to wait, dear," he repeated gently. "And then I'm willing to take just as much as you care to give. I won't worry you, Molly; I won't ask you for anything you don't feel like granting me. You see, I know now that Peter must always come first. I had hoped that you'd forget him; I still hope, dear, that in time you will——"

She shook her head, and the man bit his lip.

"Well, even if you don't, Molly," he went on steadily, "is it fair to yourself to go on when you know it's hopeless? There can be no doubt now that he's dead; you know it yourself—you've taken off your engagement ring—and is it fair to—you? Don't worry about me for the moment—but what is the use? Isn't it better to face facts?"

The girl gave a little laugh that was half a sob.

"Of course it is, Jimmy. Much better. I always tell myself that in my arguments." Then she looked at him steadily across the table. "You'd be content, Jimmy—would you?—with friendship at first."

"Yes," he answered quietly. "I would be content with friendship."

"And you wouldn't bother me—ah, no! forgive me, I know you wouldn't. Because, Jimmy, I don't want there to be any mistake. People think I've got over it because I go about; in some ways I have. But I seem to have lost something—some part of me. I don't think I shall ever be able to *love* a man again. I like you, Jimmy—like you most frightfully—but I don't know whether I'll ever be able to love you in the way I loved Peter."

"I know that," muttered the man. "And I'll risk it."

"You dear!" said the girl—and her eyes were shining. "That's where the unfairness comes in. You're worth the very best—and I can't promise to give it to you."

"You are the very best, whatever you give me," answered the man quietly. "I'd sooner have anything from you than everything from another woman. Oh, my dear!" he burst out, "I didn't mean to worry you to-night—though I knew this damned restaurant would be dangerous—but can't you say yes? I swear you'll never regret it, dear—and I—I'll be quite content to know that you care just a bit."

For a while the girl was silent; then with a faint smile she looked at him across the table.

"All right, Jimmy," she said.

"You mean you will, Molly?" he cried, a little breathlessly.

And the girl nodded.

"Yes, old man," she answered steadily. "I mean I will."

*   *   *   *   *

It was two hours later when Molly Nicholls went slowly upstairs to her room and shut the door. Jimmy Lethbridge had just gone; she had just kissed him. And the echo of his last whispered words—"My dear! my very dear girl!"—was still sounding in her ears.

For a while she stood by the fireplace smiling a little sadly. Then she crossed the room and switched on a special light. It was so placed that it shone directly on the photograph of an officer in the full dress of the 9th Hussars. And at length she knelt down in front of the table on which the photograph stood, so that the light fell on her own face also—glinting through the red-gold of her hair, glistening in the mistiness of her eyes. For maybe five minutes she knelt there, till it seemed to her as if a smile twitched round the lips of the officer—a human smile, an understanding smile.

"Oh, Peter!" she whispered, "he was your pal. Forgive me, my love—forgive me. He's been such a dear."

And once again the photograph seemed to smile at her tenderly.

"It's only you, Peter, till Journey's End—but I must give him the next best, mustn't I? It's only fair, isn't it?—and you hated unfairness. But, dear God! it's hard."

Slowly she stretched out her left hand, so that the signet ring touched the big silver frame.

"Your ring, Peter," she whispered, "your dear ring."   .

And with a sudden little choking gasp she raised it to her lips.

II

It was in a side-street close to High Street, Kensington, that it happened—the unbelievable thing. Fate decided to give Jimmy two months of happiness; cynically allowed him to come within a fortnight of his wedding, and then——

For a few seconds he couldn't believe his eyes; he stood staring like a man bereft of his senses. There on the opposite side of the road, playing a barrel-organ, was Peter himself—Peter, who had been reported "Missing, believed killed," three years before. Peter, whom a sergeant had categorically said he had seen killed with his own eyes. And there he was playing a barrel-organ in the streets of London.

Like a man partially dazed Jimmy Lethbridge went over towards him. As he approached the player smiled genially, and touched his cap with his free hand. Then after a while the smile faded, and he stared at Jimmy suspiciously.

"My God, Peter!" Lethbridge heard himself say, "what are you doing this for?"

And as he spoke he saw a girl approaching—a girl who placed herself aggressively beside Peter.

"Why shouldn't I?" demanded the player. "And who the hell are you calling Peter?"

"But," stammered Jimmy, "don't you know me, old man?"

"No!" returned the other truculently. "And I don't want to, neither."

"A ruddy torf, 'e is, Bill," chimed in the girl.

"Good God!" muttered Lethbridge, even then failing to understand the situation. "You playing a barrel-organ!"

"Look here, 'op it, guv'nor." Peter spoke with dangerous calmness. "I don't want no blinking scenes 'ere. The police ain't too friendly as it is, and this is my best pitch."

"But why didn't you let your pals know you were back, old man?" said Jimmy feebly. "Your governor, and all of us?"

"See 'ere, mister," the girl stepped forward, "'e ain't got no pals—only me. Ain't that so, Billy?" she turned to the man, who nodded.

"I looks after him, I do, d'yer see?" went on the girl. "And I don't want no one coming butting their ugly heads in. It worries 'im, it does."

"But do you mean to say——" began Jimmy dazedly, and then he broke off. At last he understood, something if not all. In some miraculous way Peter had not been killed; Peter was there in front of him—but a new Peter; a Peter whose memory of the past had completely gone, whose mind was as blank as a clean-washed slate.

"How long have you been doing this?" he asked quietly.

"Never you mind," said the girl sharply. "He ain't nothing to you. I looks after 'im, I do."

Not for a second did Jimmy hesitate, though deep down inside him there came a voice that whispered—"Don't be a fool! Pretend it's a mistake. Clear off! Molly will never know." And if for a moment his hands clenched with the strength of the sudden hideous temptation, his voice was calm and quiet as he spoke.

"That's where you're wrong." He looked at her gently. "He is something to me—my greatest friend, whom I thought was dead."

And now Peter was staring at him fixedly, forgetting even to turn the handle of the machine.

"I don't remember yer, guv'nor," he said, and Jimmy flinched at the appalling accent. "I've kind o' lost my memory, yer see, and Lizzie 'ere looks after me."

"I know she does," continued Jimmy quietly.
"Thank you, Lizzie, thank you a thousand times. But
I want you both to come to this house to-night." He
scribbled the address of his rooms on a slip of paper.
"We must think what is best to be done. You see,
Lizzie, it's not quite fair to him, is it? I want to get
a good doctor to see him."

"I'm quite 'appy as I am, sir," said Peter. "I don't
want no doctors messing about with me."

"Yer'd better go, Bill." The girl turned to him.
"The gentleman seems kind. But"—she swung round
on Jimmy fiercely—"you ain't going to take 'im away
from me, guv'nor? 'E's mine, yer see—mine——"

"I want you to come with him to-night, Lizzie," said
Lethbridge gravely. "I'm not going to try and take
him away from you. I promise that. But will you
promise to come? It's for his sake I ask you to bring
him."

For a while she looked at him half-fearfully; then she
glanced at Peter, who had apparently lost interest in the
matter. And at last she muttered under her breath:
"Orl right—I'll bring him. But 'e's mine—mine.
An' don't yer go forgetting it."

And Jimmy, walking slowly into the main street,
carried with him the remembrance of a small determined
face with the look on it of a mother fighting for her
young. That and Peter; poor, dazed, memory-lost Peter
—his greatest pal.

At first, as he turned towards Piccadilly, he grasped
nothing save the one stupendous fact that Peter was not
dead. Then, as he walked on, gradually the realization
of what it meant to him personally came to his mind.
And with that realization there returned with redoubled
force the insidious tempting voice that had first whispered: "Molly will never know." She would never
know—could never know—unless he told her. And

Peter was happy; he'd said so.   And the girl was happy
—Lizzie.   And perhaps—in fact most likely—Peter
would never recover his memory.   So what was the
use?   Why say anything about it?   Why not say it was
a mistake when they came that evening?   And Jimmy
put his hand to his forehead and found it was wet with
sweat.

After all, if Peter didn't recover, it would only mean
fearful unhappiness for everyone.   He wouldn't know
Molly, and it would break her heart, and the girl's, and
—but, of course, *he* didn't count.   It was the others he
was thinking of—not himself.

He turned into the Park opposite the Albert Hall,
and passers-by eyed him strangely, though he was
supremely unaware of the fact.   But when all the
demons of hell are fighting inside a man, his face is apt
to look grey and haggard.   And as he walked slowly
towards Hyde Park Corner, Jimmy Lethbridge went
through his Gethsemane.   They thronged him; pressing in on him from all sides, and he cursed the devils out
loud.   But still they came back, again and again, and
the worst and most devilish of them all was the insidious
temptation that by keeping silent he would be doing the
greatest good for the greatest number.   Everyone was
happy now—why run the risk of altering things?

And then, because it is not good that man should be
tempted till he breaks, the Fate that had led him to
Peter, led him gently out of the Grim Garden into Peace
once more.   He gave a short hard laugh which was
almost a sob, and turning into Knightsbridge he hailed
a taxi.   It was as it drew up at the door of Molly's house
that he laughed again—a laugh that had lost its hardness.
And the driver thought his fare's "Thank you" was
addressed to him.   Perhaps it was.   Perhaps it was the
first time Jimmy had prayed for ten years.

"Why, Jimmy, old man—you're early; I'm not

dressed yet." Molly met him in the hall, and he smiled at her gravely.

"Do you mind, dear," he said, "if I cry off to-night? I've got a very important engagement—even more important than taking you out to dinner, if possible."

The smile grew whimsical, and he put both his hands on her shoulders.

"It concerns my wedding present for you," he added.

"From the bridegroom to the bride?" she laughed.

"Something like that," he said, turning away abruptly.

"Of course, dear," she answered. "As a matter of fact, I've got a bit of a head. Though what present you can be getting at this time of day, I can't think."

"You mustn't try to," said Jimmy. "It's a surprise, Molly—a surprise. Pray God you like it, and that it will be a success!"

He spoke low under his breath, and the girl looked at him curiously.

"What's the matter, dear?" she cried. "Has something happened?"

Jimmy Lethbridge pulled himself together; he didn't want her to suspect anything yet.

"Good heavens, no!" he laughed. "What should have? But I want to borrow something from you, Molly dear, and I don't want you to ask any questions. I want you to lend me that photograph of Peter that you've got—the one in full dress."

And now she was staring at him wonderingly.

"Jimmy," she said breathlessly, "does it concern the present?"

"Yes; it concerns the present."

"You're going to have a picture of him painted for me?"

"Something like that," he answered quietly.

"Oh, you dear!" she whispered, "you dear! I've been thinking about it for months. I'll get it for you."

She went upstairs, and the man stood still in the hall staring after her.   And he was still standing motionless as she came down again, the precious frame clasped in her hands.

"You'll take care of it, Jimmy?" she said, and he nodded.

Then for a moment she laid her hand on his arm.

"I don't think, old man," she said quietly, "that you'll have to wait very long with friendship only."

The next moment she was alone with the slam of the front door echoing in her ears.   It was like Fate to reserve its most deadly arrow for the end.

III

"You say he has completely lost his memory?"

Mainwaring, one of the most brilliant of London's younger surgeons, leaned back in his chair and looked thoughtfully at his host.

"Well, he didn't know me, and I was his greatest friend," said Lethbridge.

The two men were in Jimmy's rooms, waiting for the arrival of Peter and the girl.

"He looked at me without a trace of recognition," continued Lethbridge.   "And he's developed a typical lower-class Cockney accent."

"Interesting, very," murmured the surgeon, getting up and examining the photograph on the table.   "This is new, isn't it, old boy; I've never seen it before?"

"I borrowed it this afternoon," said Jimmy briefly.

"From his people, I suppose?   Do they know?"

"No one knows at present, Mainwaring—except you and me.   That photograph I got this afternoon from Miss Nicholls."

Something in his tone made the surgeon swing round.

"You mean your fiancée?" he said slowly.

"Yes—my fiancée.   You see, she was—she was

engaged to Peter.   And she thinks he's dead.   That is the only reason she got engaged to me."

For a moment there was silence, while Mainwaring stared at the other.   A look of wonder had come into the doctor's eyes—wonder mixed with a dawning admiration.

"But, my God! old man," he muttered at length, "if the operation is successful——"

"Can you think of a better wedding present to give a girl than the man she loves?" said Jimmy slowly, and the doctor turned away.   There are times when it is not good to look on another man's face.

"And if it isn't successful?" he said quietly.

"God knows, Bill.   I haven't got as far as that—yet."

And it was at that moment that there came a ring at the front-door bell.   There was a brief altercation; then Jimmy's man appeared.

"Two—er—persons say you told them——" he began, when Lethbridge cut him short.

"Show them in at once," he said briefly, and his man went out again.

"You've got to remember, Bill," said Jimmy as they waited, "that Peter Staunton is literally, at the moment, a low-class Cockney."

Mainwaring nodded, and drew back a little as Peter and the girl came into the room.   He wanted to leave the talking to Jimmy, while he watched.

"Good evening, Lizzie."   Lethbridge smiled at the girl reassuringly.   "I'm glad you came."

"Who's that cove?" demanded the girl suspiciously, staring at Mainwaring.

"A doctor," said Jimmy.   "I want him to have a look at Peter later on."

"His name ain't Peter," muttered the girl sullenly. "It's Bill."

"Well, at Bill, then. Don't be frightened, Lizzie; come farther into the room. I want you to see a photograph I've got here."

Like a dog who wonders whether it is safe to go to a stranger, she advanced slowly, one step at a time; while Peter, twirling his cap awkwardly in his hands, kept beside her. Once or twice he glanced uneasily round the room, but otherwise his eyes were fixed on Lizzie as a child looks at its mother when it's scared.

"My God, Jimmy!" whispered the doctor, "there's going to be as big a sufferer as you if we're successful."

And he was looking as he spoke at the girl, who, with a sudden instinctive feeling of protection, had put out her hand and taken Peter's.

Like a pair of frightened children they crept on until they came to the photograph; then they stopped in front of it. And the two men came a little closer. It was the girl who spoke first, in a low voice of wondering awe:

"Gawd! it's you, Bill—that there bloke in the frame. You were a blinking orficer."

With a look of pathetic pride on her face, she stared first at the photograph and then at the man beside her. "An orficer! Bill—an orficer! What was 'is regiment, mister?" The girl swung round on Jimmy. "Was 'e in the Guards?"

"No, Lizzie," said Lethbridge. "Not the Guards. He was in the cavalry. The 9th Hussars," and the man, who was holding the frame foolishly in his hands, suddenly looked up. "The Devil's Own, Peter," went on Lethbridge quietly. "C Squadron of the Devil's Own."

But the look had faded; Peter's face was blank again.

"I don't remember, guv'nor," he muttered. "And it's making me 'ead ache—this."

With a little cry the girl caught his arm, and faced Lethbridge fiercely.

"Wot's the good of all this?" she cried. "All this muckin' abaht? Why the 'ell can't you leave 'im alone, guv'nor? 'E's going to 'ave one of 'is 'eads now—'e nearly goes mad, 'e does, when 'e gets 'em."

"I think, Lizzie, that perhaps I can cure those heads of his."

It was Mainwaring speaking, and the girl, still holding Peter's arm protectingly, looked from Lethbridge to the doctor.

"And I want to examine him, in another room where the light is a little better. Just quite alone, where he won't be distracted."

But instantly the girl was up in arms.

"You're taking 'im away from me—that's wot yer doing. And I won't 'ave it. Yer don't want to go, Bill, do yer? Yer don't want to leave yer Liz?"

And Jimmy Lethbridge bit his lip; Mainwaring had been right.

"I'm not going to take him away, Lizzie," said the doctor gently. "I promise you that. You shall see him the very instant I've made my examination. But if you're there, you see, you'll distract his attention."

She took a step forward, staring at the doctor as if she would read his very soul. And in the infinite pathos of the scene, Jimmy Lethbridge for the moment forgot his own suffering. Lizzie—the little slum girl—fighting for her man against something she couldn't understand; wondering if she should trust these two strangers. Caught in a net that frightened her; fearful that they were going to harm Bill. And at the bottom of everything the wild, inarticulate terror that she was going to lose him.

"You swear it?" she muttered. "I can see 'im after yer've looked at 'im."

"I swear it," said Mainwaring gravely.

She gave a little sob. "Orl right, I believe yer on the level. You go with 'im, Bill. Perhaps 'e'll do yer 'ead good."

"'E's queer sometimes at night," said Lizzie, as the door closed behind Mainwaring. "Seems all dazed like."

"Is he?" said Jimmy. "How did you find him, Lizzie?"

"'E was wandering round—didn't know nuthing about 'imself," she answered. "And I took 'im in—and looked after 'im, I did. Saved and pinched a bit, 'ere and there —and then we've the barrel-organ. And we've been so 'appy, mister—so 'appy. Course 'e's a bit queer, and 'e don't remember nuthing—but 'e's orl right if 'e don't get 'is 'eadaches. And when 'e does, I gets rid of them. I jest puts 'is 'ead on me lap and strokes 'is forehead— and they goes after a while. Sometimes 'e goes to sleep when I'm doing it—and I stops there till 'e wakes again with the 'ead gone. Yer see, I understands 'im. 'E's 'appy with me."

She was staring at the photograph—a pathetic little figure in her tawdry finery—and for a moment Jimmy couldn't speak. It had to be done; he had to do it— but it felt rather like killing a wounded bird with a sledge-hammer—except that it wouldn't be so quick.

"He's a great brain surgeon, Lizzie—the gentleman with Bill," he said at length, and the girl turned round and watched him gravely. "And he thinks that an operation might cure him and give him back his memory."

"So that 'e'd know 'e was an officer?" whispered the girl.

"So that he'd know he was an officer," said Jimmy. "So that he'd remember all his past life. You see,

Lizzie, your Bill is really Sir Peter Staunton—whom we all thought had been killed in the war."

"Sir Peter Staunton!" she repeated dazedly. "Gawd!"

"He was engaged, Lizzie," he went on quietly, and he heard her breath come quick—"engaged to that lady." He pointed to a picture of Molly on the mantelpiece.

"No one wouldn't look at me with 'er about," said the girl thoughtfully.

"She loved him very dearly, Lizzie—even as he loved her. I don't think I've ever known two people who loved one another quite so much. And——" for a moment Jimmy faltered, then he went on steadily: "I ought to know in this case, because I'm engaged to her now."

And because the Cockney brain is quick, she saw—and understood.

"So if yer doctor friend succeeds," she said, "she'll give yer the chuck?"

"Yes, Lizzie," answered Jimmy gravely, "she'll give me the chuck."

"And yer love 'er? Orl right, old sport. I can see it in yer face. Strikes me"—and she gave a little laugh that was sadder than any tears—"strikes me you 'anded out the dirty end of the stick to both of us when you come round that street to-day."

"Strikes me I did, Lizzie," he agreed. "But, you see, I've told you this because I want you to understand that we're both of us in it—we've both of us got to play the game."

"Play the game!" she muttered. "Wot d'yer want me to do?"

"The doctor doesn't want him excited, Lizzie," explained Lethbridge. "But he wants him to stop here to-night, so that he can operate to-morrow. Will you tell him that you want him to stop here?—and stay here with him if you like."

"And to-morrer she'll tike 'im." The girl was staring at Molly's photograph. "'E won't look at me—
when 'e knows. Gawd! why did yer find 'im—why
did yer find 'im? We was 'appy, I tells yer—'appy?"

She was crying now—crying as a child cries, weakly
and pitifully, and Lethbridge stood watching her in
silence.

"Poor kid!" he said at length. "Poor little kid!"

"I don't want yer pity," she flared up. "I want my
man." And then, as she saw Jimmy looking at the
photograph on the mantelpiece, in an instant she was
beside him. "Sorry, old sport," she whispered impulsively. "Reckon you've backed a ruddy loser yourself.
I'll do it. Shake 'ands. I guess I knew all along that
Bill wasn't really my style. And I've 'ad my year."

"You're lucky, Lizzie," said Jimmy gravely, still
holding her hand. "Very, very lucky."

"I've 'ad my year," she went on, and for a moment her
thoughts seemed far away. "A 'ole year—and——"
She pulled herself together and started patting her hair.

"And what, Lizzie?" said Jimmy quietly.

"Never you mind, mister," she answered. "That's
my blooming business."

And then the door opened and Mainwaring came
in.

"Does Lizzie agree?" he asked eagerly.

"Yes, Bill—she agrees," said Jimmy. "What do
you think of him?"

"As far as I can see there is every hope that an operation will be completely successful. There is evidently
pressure on the right side of the skull which can be removed. I'll operate early to-morrow morning. Keep
him quiet to-night—and make him sleep, Lizzie, if you
can."

"What d'yer think, mister?" she said scornfully.
"Ain't I done it fer a year?"

Without another word she left the room, and the two men stood staring at one another.

"Will she play the game, Jimmy!" Mainwaring was lighting a cigarette.

"Yes—she'll play the game," answered Lethbridge slowly. "She'll play the game—poor little kid!"

"What terms are they on—those two?" The doctor looked at him curiously.

"I think," said Lethbridge, even more slowly, "that that is a question we had better not inquire into too closely."

IV

It was successful—brilliantly successful—the operation. Lizzie made it so; at any rate she helped considerably. It was she who held his hand as he went under the anæsthetic; it was she who cheered him up in the morning, when he awoke dazed and frightened in a strange room. And then she slipped away and disappeared from the house. It was only later that Lethbridge found a scrawled pencil note, strangely smudged, on his desk:

"Let me no wot appens.—LIZZIE."

He didn't know her address, so he couldn't write and tell her that her Bill had come to consciousness again, completely recovered except for one thing. There was another blank in his mind now—the last three years. One of his first questions had been to ask how the fight had gone, and whether we'd broken through properly.

And then for a day or two Lizzie was forgotten; he had to make his own renunciation.

Molly came, a little surprised at his unusual invitation, and he left the door open so that she could see Peter in bed from one part of his sitting-room.

"Where have you buried yourself, Jimmy?" she cried.

"I've been——" And then her face grew deathly white as she looked into the bedroom. Her lips moved, though no sound came from them; her hands were clenching and unclenching.

"But I'm mad," he heard her whisper at length, "quite mad. I'm seeing things, Jimmy—seeing things. Why—dear God! it's Peter!"

She took a step or two forward, and Peter saw her.

"Molly," he cried weakly, "Molly, my darling——"

And Jimmy Lethbridge saw her walk forward slowly and uncertainly to the man who had come back. With a shaking little cry of pure joy she fell on her knees beside the bed, and Peter put a trembling hand on her hair. Then Jimmy shut the door, and stared blankly in front of him.

It was Lizzie who roused him—Lizzie coming shyly into the room from the hall.

"I seed her come in," she whispered. "She looked orl right. 'Ow is 'e?"

"He's got his memory back, Lizzie," he said gently. "But he's forgotten the last three years."

"Forgotten me, as 'e?" Her lips quivered.

"Yes, Lizzie. Forgotten everything—barrel-organ and all. He thinks he's on sick leave from the war."

"And she's wiv 'im now, is she?"

"Yes—she's with him, Lizzie."

She took a deep breath—then she walked to the glass and arranged her hat—a dreadful hat with feathers in it.

"Well, I reckons I'd better be going. I don't want to see 'im. It would break me 'eart. And I said good-bye to 'im that last night before the operation. So long, mister. I've 'ad me year—she can't tike that away from me."

And then she was gone. He watched her from the window walking along the pavement, with the feathers nodding at every step.   Once she stopped and looked back—and the feathers seemed to wilt and die.   Then she went on again—and this time she didn't stop.   She'd "'ad 'er year," had Lizzie; maybe the remembrance of it helped her gallant little soul when she returned the barrel-organ—the useless barrel-organ.

*   *   *   *   *

"So this was your present, Jimmy."   Molly was speaking just behind him, and her eyes were very bright.

"Yes, Molly," he smiled.   "Do you like it?"

"I don't understand what's happened," she said slowly.   "I don't understand anything except the one big fact that Peter has come back."

"Isn't that enough?" he asked gently.   "Isn't that enough, my dear?   Peter's come back—funny old Peter. The rest will keep."

And then he took her left hand and drew off the engagement ring he had given her.

"Not on that finger now—Molly; though I'd like you to keep it now if you will."

For a while she stared at him wonderingly.

"Jimmy, but you're big!" she whispered at length. "I'm so sorry!"   She turned away as Peter's voice, weak and tremulous, came from the other room.

"Come in with me, old man," she said.   "Come in and talk to him."

But Jimmy shook his head.

"He doesn't want me, dear; I'm just—just going out for a bit——"

Abruptly he left the room—they didn't want him: any more than they wanted Lizzie.

Only she had had her year.

XIV   THE MAN WHO COULD NOT GET DRUNK

"YES; she's a beautiful woman.   There's no doubt about that.   What did you say her name was?"

"I haven't mentioned her name," I returned.   "But there's no secret about it.   She is Lady Sylvia Clavering."

"Ah!   Sylvia.   Of course, I remember now."

He drained his glass of brandy and sat back in his chair, while his eyes followed one of the most beautiful women in London as she threaded her way through the tables towards the entrance of the restaurant.   An obsequious head-waiter bent almost double as she passed; her exit, as usual, befitted one of the most be-photographed women of Society.   And it was not until the doors had swung to behind her and her escort that the man I had been dining with spoke again.

"I guess that little bow she gave as she passed here was yours, not mine," he said, with the suspicion of a smile.

"Presumably," I answered a little curtly.   "Unless you happen to know her.   I have that privilege."

His smile grew a trifle more pronounced, though his eyes were set and steady.   "Know her?"   He beckoned to the waiter for more brandy.   "No, I can't say I know her.   In fact, my sole claim to acquaintanceship is that I carried her for three miles in the dark one night, slung over my shoulder like a sack of potatoes.   But I don't know her."

"You did what?" I cried, staring at him in amazement.

"Sounds a bit over the odds, I admit."   He was carefully cutting the end off his cigar.   "Nevertheless it stands."

Now when any man states that he has carried a

woman for three miles, whether it be in the dark or not, and has followed up such an introduction so indifferently that the woman fails even to recognize him afterwards, there would seem to be the promise of a story. But when the woman is one of the Lady Sylvia Claverings of this world, and the man is of the type of my dinner companion, the promise resolves itself into a certainty.

Merton was one of those indefinable characters who defy placing. You felt that if you landed in Yokohama, and he was with you, you would instinctively rely on him for information as to the best thing to do and the best way to do it. There seemed to be no part of the globe, from the South Sea Islands going westward to Alaska, with which he was not as well acquainted as the ordinary man is with his native village. At the time I did not know him well. The dinner was only our third meeting, and during the meal we confined ourselves to the business which had been the original cause of our running across one another at all. But even in that short time I had realized that Billy Merton was a white man. And not only was he straight, but he was essentially a useful person to have at one's side in a tight corner.

"Are you disposed to elaborate your somewhat amazing statement?" I asked, after a pause.

For a moment or two he hesitated, and his eyes became thoughtful.

"I don't suppose there's any reason why I shouldn't," he answered slowly. "It's ancient history now—ten years or so."

"That was just about the time she was married," I remarked.

He nodded. "She was on her honeymoon when it happened. Well, if you want to hear the yarn, come round to my club."

"Why, certainly," I said, beckoning for the bill. "Let's get on at once; I'm curious."

"Do you know Africa at all?" he asked me, as we pulled our chairs up to the fire. We had the room almost to ourselves; a gentle snoring from the other fireplace betokened the only other occupant.

"Egypt," I answered. "Parts of South Africa. The usual thing: nothing out of the ordinary."

He nodded. "It was up the West Coast that it happened," he began, after his pipe was going to his satisfaction. "And though I've been in many God-forsaken spots in my life, I've never yet struck anything to compare with that place. Nwambi it was called—just a few shacks stretching in from the sea along a straggling, dusty street—one so-called shop and a bar. It called itself an hotel, but Lord help the person who tried to put up there. It was a bar pure and simple, though no one could call the liquor that. Luke-warm gin, some vile substitute for whisky, the usual short drinks, and some local poisons formed the stock; I ought to know—I was the bar-tender.

"For about three miles inland there stretched a belt of stinking swamp—one vast malaria hot-bed—and over this belt the straggling street meandered towards the low foot-hills beyond. At times it almost lost itself: but if you didn't give up hope, or expire from the stench, and cast about you'd generally find it again leading you on to where you felt you might get a breath of God's fresh air in the hills. As a matter of fact you didn't; the utmost one can say is that it wasn't quite so appalling as in the swamp itself. Mosquitoes! Heavens! they had to be seen to be believed. I've watched 'em there literally like a grey cloud."

Merton smiled reminiscently.

"That—and the eternal boom of the sea on the bar half a mile out, made up Nwambi. How any white man ever got through alive if he had to stop there any length of time is beyond me; to be accurate, very few did. It was a grave, that place, and only the down-and-outers went there. At the time I was one myself.

"The sole reason for its existence at all was that the water alongside the quay was deep enough for good-sized boats to come in, and most of the native produce from the district inland found its way down to Nwambi for shipment. Once over the belt of swamp and a few miles into the hills the climate was much better, and half a dozen traders in a biggish way had bungalows there. They were Dagos, most of them—it wasn't a British part of the West Coast—and I frankly admit that my love for the Dago has never been very great. But there was one Scotchman, Mactavish, amongst them—and he was the first fellow who came into the bar after I'd taken over the job. He was down for the night about some question of freight.

"'You're new,' he remarked, leaning against the counter. 'What's happened to the other fellow? Is he dead?'

"'Probably,' I returned. 'What do you want?'

"'Gin—double tot. What's your name?'

"I told him, and he pondered the matter while he finished his drink.

"'Well,' he said at length, 'I warned your predecessor, and I'll warn you. Don't fall foul of my manager down here. Name of Rotherhill—I do *not* think. Don't give him advice about keeping off the drink, or he'll kill you. He's killing himself, but that's his business. I'm tough—you look tough, but he's got us beat to a frazzle. And take cover if he ever gets mixed up with any of the Dagos—the place isn't healthy.'

"It was just at that moment that the door swung

open and a tall, lean fellow lounged in. He'd got an eyeglass screwed into one eye, and a pair of perfectly fitting polo boots with some immaculate white breeches encased his legs. His shirt was silk, his sun-helmet spotless; in fact, he looked like the typical English dude of fiction.

" 'My manager, Rotherhill,' said Mactavish, by way of introduction.

"Rotherhill stared at me for a moment or two— then he shrugged his shoulders.

" 'You look sane; however, if you come here you can't be. Double gin—and one for yourself.'

"He spoke with a faint, almost affected drawl, and as I poured out the drinks I watched him covertly. When he first came in I had thought him a young man; now I wasn't so sure. It was his eyes that made one wonder as to his age—they were so utterly tired. If he was indeed drinking himself to death, there were no traces of it as yet on his face, and his hand as he lifted his glass was perfectly steady. But those eyes of his—I can see them now. The cynical bitterness, the concentrated weariness of all Hell was in them. And it's not good for any man to look like that; certainly not a man of thirty-five, as I afterwards discovered his age to be."

Merton paused and sipped his whisky-and-soda, while from the other side of the room came indications that the sleeper still slept.

"I never found out what his real name was," he continued thoughtfully. "Incidentally, it doesn't much matter. We knew him as Rotherhill, and the J. which preceded it in his signature was assumed to stand for James or Jimmy. Anyway, he answered to it, which was the main point. As far as I know, he never received a letter and he never read a paper, and I guess I got to know him better than anyone else in that hole.

Every morning, punctual to the second at eleven
o'clock, he'd stroll into the bar and have three double-
gins.   Sometimes he'd talk in his faint, rather pleasant
drawl; more often he'd sit silently at one of the rickety
tables, staring out to sea, with his long legs stretched
out in front of him.   But whichever he did—whatever
morning it was—you could always see your face in his
boots.

"I remember once after I'd been there about a
month, I started to pull his leg about those boots of
his.

" 'Take the devil of a long time cleaning them in
the morning, don't you, Jimmy?' I said, as he lounged
up to the bar for his third gin.

" 'Yes,' he answered, leaning over the counter so
that his face was close to mine.   'Got anything further
to say about my appearance?'

" 'Jimmy,' I replied, 'your appearance doesn't signify one continental damn to me.   But as the only
two regular British *habitués* of this first-class American
bar, don't let's quarrel.'

"He grinned—a sort of slow, lazy grin.

" 'Think not?' he said.   'Might amuse one.   However, perhaps you're right.'

"And so it went on—one sweltering day after another, until one could have gone mad with the hideous
boredom of it.   I used to stand behind the bar there
sometimes and curse weakly and foolishly like a child,
but I never heard Rotherhill do it.   What happened
during those steamy nights in the privacy of his own
room, when he—like the rest of us—was fighting for
sleep, is another matter.   During the day he never
varied.   Cold, cynical, immaculate, he seemed a being
apart—above our little worries and utterly contemptuous of them.   Maybe he was right—maybe the thing
that had downed him was too big for foolish cursing.

Knowing what I do now, a good many things are clear which one didn't realize at the time.

"Only once, I think, did I ever get in the slightest degree intimate with him. It was latish one evening, and the bar was empty save for us two. I'd been railing against the fate that had landed me penniless in such an accursed spot, and after a while he chipped in, in his lazy drawl:

" 'Would a thousand be any good to you?'

"I looked at him speechless. 'A thousand pounds?' I stammered.

" 'Yes; I think I can raise that for you.' He was staring in front of him as he spoke. 'And yet I don't know. I've got more or less used to you and you'll have to stop a bit longer. Then we'll see about it.'

" 'But, good Heavens! man,' I almost shouted, 'do you mean to say that you stop here when you can lay your hand on a thousand pounds?'

" 'It appears so, doesn't it?' He rose and stalked over to the bar. 'It doesn't much matter where you stop, Merton, when you can't be in the one place where you'd sell your hopes of Heaven to be. And it's best, perhaps, to choose a place where the end will come quickly.'

"With that he turned on his heel, and I watched him with a sort of dazed amazement as he sauntered down the dusty road, white in the tropical moon, towards his own shack. A thousand pounds! The thought of it rang in my head all through the night. A thousand pounds! A fortune! And because, out in death-spots like that, men are apt to think strange thoughts—thoughts that look ugly by the light of day—I found myself wondering how long he could last at the rate he was going. Two—sometimes three—bottles of gin a day: it couldn't be long. And then—who knew? It would be quick, the break-up; all the quicker because there was not a trace of it now. And perhaps when it came he'd remember about that thousand. Or I could remind him."

Merton laughed grimly.

"Yes, we're pretty average swine, even the best of us, when we're up against it, and I lay no claims to be a plaster saint. But Fate had decreed that Jimmy Rotherhill was to find the end which he craved for quicker than he had anticipated. Moreover—and that's what I've always been glad about—it had decreed that he was to find it before drink had rotted that iron constitution of his; while his boots still shone and his silk shirts remained spotless. It had decreed that he was to find it in the way of all others that he would have chosen, had such a wild improbability ever suggested itself. Which is going ahead a bit fast with the yarn—but no matter.

"It was after I'd been there about three months that the incident happened which was destined to be the indirect cause of his death. I told you, didn't I, that there were several Dago traders who lived up in the foot-hills, and on the night in question three of them had come down to Nwambi on business of some sort—amongst them one Pedro Salvas, who was as unpleasant a specimen of humanity as I have ever met. A crafty, orange-skinned brute, who indulged, according to common knowledge, in every known form of vice, and a good many unknown ones too. The three of them were sitting at a table near the door when Rotherhill lounged in—and Mactavish's words came back to me. The Dagos had been drinking; Jimmy looked in his most uncompromising mood. He paused at the door, and stared at each of them in turn through his eyeglass; then he turned his back on them and came over to me.

"I glanced over his shoulder at the three men, and

realized there was trouble coming. They'd been whispering and muttering together the whole evening,
though at the time I had paid no attention. But now
Pedro Salvas, with an ugly flush on his ugly face, had
risen and was coming towards the bar.

"'If one so utterly unworthy as I,' he snarled, 'may
venture to speak to the so very exclusive Englishman,
I would suggest that he does not throw pictures of his
lady-loves about the streets.'

"He was holding something in his hand, and Jimmy
swung round like a panther. His hand went to his
breast pocket; then I saw what the Dago was holding
out. It was the miniature of a girl. And after that
I didn't see much more; I didn't even have time to
take cover. It seemed to me that the lightning movement of Jimmy's left hand as he grabbed the miniature, and the terrific upper-cut with his right, were
simultaneous. Anyway, the next second he was putting the picture back in his breast pocket, and the
Dago, snarling like a mad dog, was picking himself
out of a medley of broken bottles. That was phase
one. Phase two was equally rapid, and left me blinking. There was the crack of a revolver, and at the
same moment a knife stuck out quivering in the wall
behind my head. Then there was a silence, and I
collected my scattered wits.

"The revolver, still smoking, was in Jimmy's hand:
Salvas, his right arm dripping with blood, was standing
by the door, while his two pals were crouching behind
the table, looking for all the world like wild beasts
waiting to spring.

"'Next time,' said Jimmy, 'I shoot to kill.'

"And he meant it. He was a bit white round the
nostrils, which is a darned dangerous sign in a man,
especially if he's got a gun and you're looking down
the business end of it. And no one knew it better

than those three Dagos. They went on snarling, but not one of them moved an eyelid.

"'Put your knives on that table, you scum,' ordered Jimmy.

"The other two obeyed, and he laughed contemptuously.

"'Now clear out. You pollute the air.'

"For a moment or two they hesitated: then Salvas, with a prodigious effort, regained his self-control.

"'You are brave, Señor Rotherhill, when you have a revolver and we are unarmed,' he said, with a sneer.

"In two strides Jimmy was at the table where the knives were lying. He picked one up, threw me his gun, and pointed to the other knife.

"'I'll fight you now, Salvas,' he answered quietly. 'Knife to knife, and to a finish.'

"But the Dago wasn't taking any, and 'pon my soul I hardly blamed him. For if ever a man was mad, Jimmy Rotherhill was mad that night: mad with the madness that knows no fear and is absolutely blind to consequences.

"'I do not brawl in bars with drunken Englishmen,' remarked Salvas, turning on his heel.

"A magnificent utterance, but ill-advised with Jimmy as he was. He gave a short laugh and took a running kick, and Don Pedro Salvas disappeared abruptly into the night. And the other two followed with celerity.

"'You'll be getting into trouble, old man,' I said, as he came back to the bar, 'if you start that sort of game with the Dagos.'

"'The bigger the trouble the more I'll like it,' he answered shortly. 'Give me another drink. Don't you understand yet, Merton, that I'm beyond caring?'

"And thinking it over since, I've come to the conclusion that he spoke the literal truth. It's a phrase often used, and very rarely meant; in his case it was the plain, unvarnished truth.   Rightly or wrongly he had got into such a condition that he cared not one fig whether he lived or died; if anything he preferred the latter.   And falling foul of the Dago colony was a better way than most of obtaining his preference.

"Of course, the episode that night had shown me one thing: it was a woman who was at the bottom of it all.   I didn't ask any questions; he wasn't a man who took kindly to cross-examination.   But I realized pretty forcibly that if the mere handling of her picture by a Dago had produced such a result, the matter must be serious.   Who she was I hadn't any idea, or what was the trouble between them—and, as I say, I didn't ask.

"And then one day a few weeks later I got the answer to the first question.   Someone left a month-old *Tatler* in the bar, and I was glancing through it when Rotherhill came in.   I reached up for the gin bottle to give him his usual drink, and when I turned round to hand it to him he was staring at one of the pictures with the look of a dead man on his face.   I can see him now with his knuckles gleaming white through the sunburn of his hands, and his great power-ful chest showing under his shirt.   He stood like that maybe for five minutes—motionless; then, without a word, he swung round and left the bar.   And I picked up the paper."

Merton paused and drained his glass.

"Lady Sylvia's wedding?" I asked unnecessarily, and he nodded.

"So the first part of the riddle was solved," he con-tinued quietly.   "And when two days passed by with-out a sign of Rotherhill, I began to be afraid that he had solved his own riddle in his own way.   But he hadn't; he came into the bar at ten o'clock at night, and leaned up against the counter in his usual way.

" 'What have you been doing with yourself?' I said lightly.

" 'I've been trying to get drunk,' he answered slowly, letting one of his hands fall on my arm with a grip like steel. 'And, dear God! I can't.'

"It doesn't sound much—told like this in the smoking-room of a London club. But though I've seen and heard many things in my life that have impressed me—horrible, dreadful things that I shall never forget —the moment of all others that is most indelibly stamped on my brain is that moment when, leaning across the bar, I looked into the depths of tae soul of the man who called himself Jimmy Rotherhill—the man who could not get drunk."

Once again he paused, and this time I did not interrupt him. He was back in that steaming night, with the smell of stale spirits in his nostrils and the sight of strange things in his eyes. And I felt that I, too, could visualize that tall, immaculate Englishman leaning against the counter—the man who was beyond caring.

"But I must get on with it," continued Merton after a while. "The club will be filling up soon and I've only got the finish to tell you now. And by one of those extraordinary coincidences which happen far more frequently in life than people will allow, the finish proved a worthy one.

"It was about two days later. I was in the bar polishing the glasses when the door swung open and two men came in. They were obviously English, and both of them were dressed as if they were going to a garden-party.

" 'Thank heavens! Tommy, here's a bar, at any rate,' said one of them. 'I say, barman, what have you got?'

"Well, I had a bit of a liver, and I disliked being called barman.

" 'Several bottles of poison,' I answered, 'and the hell of a temper.'

"The second one laughed, and after a moment or two the other joined in.

" 'I don't wonder at the latter commodity,' he said. 'This is a ghastly hole.'

" 'I wouldn't deny it,' I answered. 'What, if I may ask, has brought you here?'

" 'Oh, we've had a small breakdown, and the skipper came in here to repair it. We've just come ashore to have a look round.'

"I glanced through the window, and noticed for the first time that a steam-yacht was lying off the shore. She was a real beauty—looked about a thousand tons —and I gave a sigh of envy.

" 'You're not in want of a barman, by any chance, are you?' I said. 'If so, I'll swim out and chance the sharks.'

" ''Fraid we've got everything in that line,' he answered. 'But select the least deadly of your poisons, and join us.'

"And it was as I was pulling down the gin and vermouth that Jimmy Rotherhill came into the bar. He got about half-way across the floor and then he stopped dead in his tracks. And I guess during the next two seconds you could have heard a pin drop.

" 'So this is where you've hidden yourself,' said the smaller of the two men—the one who had done most of the talking. 'I don't think we'll trouble you for those drinks, barman.'

"Without another word he walked out of the place —and after a moment or two the other man started to follow him. He hesitated as he got abreast of Jimmy, and then for the first time Rotherhill spoke :

" 'Is she here?'

" 'Yes,' answered the other. 'On board the yacht. There's a whole party of us.'

"And with that he stepped into the street and joined his pal. With a perfectly inscrutable look on his face Jimmy watched them as they walked through the glaring sun and got into the small motor-boat that was waiting alongside the quay. Then he came up to the bar.

" 'An artistic touch, doubtless, on the part of Fate,' he remarked quietly. 'But a little unnecessary.'

"And I guess I metaphorically took off my hat to him at that moment. What he'd done, why he was there, I neither knew nor cared; all that mattered to me was the way he took that last rotten twist of the surgeon's knife. Not by the quiver of an eyelid would you have known that anything unusual had happened: he drank his three double-gins at exactly the same rate as every other morning. And then he too swung out of the bar, and went back to his office in Mactavish's warehouse, leaving me to lie down on my bed and sweat under the mosquito curtains, while I wondered at the inscrutable working out of things. Was it blind, the Fate that moved the pieces; or was there some definite pattern beyond our ken? At the moment it seemed pretty blind and senseless; later on—well, you'll be able to form your own opinion.

"You know how quickly darkness falls in those latitudes. And it was just before sunset that I saw a boat shoot away from the side of the yacht and come full speed for the shore. I remember I wondered casually who was the mug who would leave a comfortable yacht for Nwambi, especially after the report of it that must have been given by our two morning visitors. And then it struck me that, whoever it might be, he was evidently in the deuce of a hurry. Almost before the boat came alongside a man sprang out and scrambled up the steps. Then at a rapid double he came sprinting towards me as I stood at the door of the bar. It was the smaller of the two men who had been ashore that morning, and something was evidently very much amiss.

"'Where is she?' he shouted, as soon as he came within earshot. 'Where's my wife, you damned scoundrel?'

"Seeing that he was quite beside himself with worry and alarm, I let the remark go by.

"'Steady!' I said, as he came gasping up to me. 'I haven't got your wife; I haven't even seen her.'

"'It's that card-sharper!' he cried. 'By God! I'll shoot him like a dog, if he's tried any monkey-tricks!'

"'Dry up, and pull yourself together,' I said angrily. 'If you're alluding to Jimmy Rotherhill——'

"And at that moment Jimmy himself stepped out of his office and strolled across the road.

"'You swine, you cursed card-cheat—where's Sylvia?'

"'What the devil are you talking about?' said Jimmy, and his voice was tense.

"'She came ashore this afternoon, saying she would return in an hour,' said the other man. 'I didn't know it at the time, Mr.—er—Rotherhill, I believe you call yourself. The boat came back for her, and she was not there. That was four hours ago. Where is she?'

"He was covering Jimmy with his revolver as he spoke.

"'Four hours ago, Clavering? Good heavens! man —put down your gun. This isn't a time for amateur theatricals.' He brushed past him as if he was non-existent and came up to me. 'Did you see Lady Clavering?'

"'Not a trace,' I answered, and the same fear was in both of us.

"'Did she say what she was coming on shore for?' He swung round on the husband.

"'To have a look round,' answered Clavering, and

his voice had altered. No longer was he the outraged husband; he was a frightened man relying instinctively on a bigger personality than himself.

" 'If she's not about here, she must have gone inland,' said Jimmy, staring at me. 'And it'll be dark in five minutes.'

" 'My God!' cried Clavering, 'what are we to do? She can't be left alone for the night. Lost—in this cursed country! She may have hurt herself—sprained her ankle.'

"For a moment neither of us answered him. Even more than he did we realize the hideous danger of a white woman alone in the bush inland. There were worse dangers than snakes and wild animals to be feared. And it was as we were standing there staring at one another, and afraid to voice our thoughts, that one of Mactavish's native boys came down the street. He was running and out of breath; and the instant he saw Jimmy he rushed up to him and started gabbling in the local patois. He spoke too fast for me to follow him, and Clavering, of course, couldn't understand a word. But we both guessed instinctively what he was talking about and we both watched Jimmy's face. And as we watched it I heard Clavering catch his breath sharply.

"At last the boy finished, and Jimmy turned and looked at me. On his face was a look of such cold, malignant fury that the question which was trembling on my lips died away, and I stared at him speechlessly.

" 'The Dagos have got her,' he said very softly. 'Don Pedro Salvas is, I fear, a foolish man.'

"Clavering gave a sort of hoarse cry, and Jimmy's face softened.

" 'Poor devil,' he said. 'Your job is going to be harder than mine. Go back to your yacht—get all your men on shore that you can spare—and if I'm not back in four hours, wait for dawn and then strike inland over the swamp. Find Pedro Salvas's house—and hang him on the highest tree you can find.'

"Without another word he swung on his heel and went up the street at a long, steady lope. Twice Clavering called after him, but he never turned his head or altered his stride—and then he started to follow himself. It was I who stopped him, and he cursed me like a child—almost weeping.

" 'Do what he told you,' I said. 'You'd never find your way; you'd be worse than useless. I'll go with him: you get back and bring your men ashore.'

"And with that I followed Jimmy. At times I could see him, a faint white figure in the darkness, as he dodged through that fever-laden swamp; at times I found myself marvelling at the condition of the man, bearing in mind his method of living. Steadily, tirelessly, he forged ahead, and when he came to the foothills I hadn't gained a yard on him.

"And then I began wondering what was going to happen when he reached Salvas's bungalow, and by what strange mischance the girl had met the owner. That it was revenge I was certain; he had recognized her from the picture, and I remember thinking how bitter must have been his hatred of Rotherhill to have induced him to run such an appalling risk. For the risk was appalling, even in that country of strange happenings.

"I don't think that Jimmy troubled his head over any such speculations. In his mind there was room for only one thought—an all-sufficient thought—to get his hands on Pedro Salvas. I don't think he even knew that I was behind him, until after it was over and the curtain was falling on the play. And then he had no time for me."

Merton gave a short laugh that had in it a touch of sadness.

"A good curtain it was, too," he continued quietly. "I remember I made a frantic endeavour to overtake him as he raced up to the house, and then, because I just couldn't help myself, I stopped and watched—fascinated. The window of the big living-room was open, and the light blazed out. I suppose they had never anticipated pursuit that night. Leaning up against the wall was the girl, with a look of frozen horror on her face, while seated at the table were Pedro Salvas and three of his pals. And they were drinking.

"It all happened very quickly. For one second I saw Jimmy Rotherhill framed in the window—then he began shooting. I don't think I've mentioned that he could shoot the pip out of the ace of diamonds nine times out of ten at twenty yards, and his madness did not interfere with his aim. And that night he was stark, staring mad. I heard three shots—so close together that only an artist could have fired them out of the same revolver and taken aim; I saw the three friends of Pedro Salvas collapse limply in their chairs. And then there was a pause; I think Jimmy wanted to get at *him* with his hands.

"But it was not to be. Just for a moment the owner of the bungalow had been so stupefied at the sudden appearance of the man he hated that he had simply sat still, staring; but only for a moment. The movement of his arm was so quick that I hardly saw it; I only noticed what seemed to be a streak of light which shot across the room. And then I heard Jimmy's revolver again—the tenth, the hundredth of a second too late. He'd drilled Pedro Salvas through the heart all right—I watched the swine crumple and fall with the snarl still on his face—but this time the knife wasn't sticking in the wall.

"She got to him first," went on Merton thoughtfully. "His knees were sagging just as I got to the window, and she was trying to hold him up in her arms. And then between us we laid him down, and I saw that the end was very near. There was nothing I could do; the knife was clean into his chest. The finish of the journey had come to the man who could not get drunk. And so I left them together, while I mounted guard by the window with a gun in each hand. It wasn't a house to take risks in.

"He lived, I think, for five minutes, and of those five minutes I would rather not speak. There are things which a man may tell, and things which he may not. Sufficient be it to say that he may have cheated at cards or he may not—she loved him. If, indeed, he had committed the unforgivable sin amongst gentlemen all the world over, he atoned for it. And she loved him. Let us leave it at that.

"And when it was over, and the strange, bitter spirit of the man who called himself Jimmy Rotherhill had gone out on the unknown road, I touched her on the shoulder. She rose blindly and stumbled out into the darkness at my side. I don't think I spoke a word to her, beyond telling her to take my arm. And after a while she grew heavier and heavier on it, until at last she slipped down—a little unconscious heap of sobbing girlhood."

Merton paused and lit a cigarette with a smile.

"So that is how it was ordained that I should carry the Lady Sylvia Clavering, slung over my shoulder like a sack of potatoes, for three miles. I remember staggering into the village to find myself surrounded by men from the yacht. I handed her over to her distracted husband, and then I rather think I fainted myself. I know I found myself in my own bar, with people pouring whisky down my throat. And after a while they cleared off, leaving Clavering alone with me. He began to stammer out his thanks, and I cut him short.

" 'No thanks are due to me,' I said. 'They're due to another man whom you called a card-cheat—but who was a bigger man than either you or I are ever likely to be.'

" 'Was?' he said, staring at me.

" 'Yes,' I answered. 'He's dead.'

"He stood there silently for a moment or two; then with a queer look on his face he took off his hat.

" 'You're right,' he said. 'He was a bigger man than me.' "

Merton got up and pressed the bell.

"I've never seen him from that day to this," he said thoughtfully. "I never saw his wife again until to-night. And I've never filled in the gaps in the story. Moreover, I don't know that I want to."

A waiter came over to his chair.

"You'll join me? Two whiskies-and-sodas, please, waiter—large ones."

XV   THE SAVING CLAUSE

I GUESS I don't hold with missionaries.   I've been in most corners of this globe, and I reckon that the harm they do easily outweighs the good.   Stands to reason, don't it, that we can't all have the same religion, same as we can't all have the same shaped nose?   So what in thunder is the good of trying to put my nose on to your face, where it won't fit?   And it sort of riles me to see these good earnest people labouring and sweating to do to others what they would only describe as damned impertinence if those others tried to do it to them.

Yet, as I see it, there's no reason why the others shouldn't. 'Tisn't as if any particular branch had a complete corner in truth, is it?

But there are exceptions, same as to most things. And for the past twenty years whenever I've said I don't hold with missionaries, I've always added a saving clause in my mind. Care to hear what that saving clause is? Right: mine's the same as before.

It was just after the Boer War that it happened. I'd come home: got a job of sorts in London. Thought a few years of the quiet life would do me good, and an old uncle of mine wangled me into the office of a pal of his. Funny old thing my boss was, with a stomach like a balloon. And I give you my word that he was the last man in London whom you'd have expected to meet at the Empire on a Saturday night. It was sheer bad luck, though I don't suppose I could have stood that job, anyway, for long.

I'd met a pal there, you see, and I suppose we'd started to hit it a bit. Anyway, a darned great chucker-out came and intimated that he thought the moment had come when we'd better sample the cool night air of Leicester Square.

Well, I don't say I was right: strictly speaking, I suppose I should have accepted his remark in the spirit in which it was intended. But the fact remains that I didn't like his face or his frock-coat—and we had words. And finally the chucker-out sampled the cool night air —not me. The only trouble was that just as he went down the stairs, my boss was coming up with wife and family complete. And that chucker-out was a big man: I guess it was rather like being hit by a steam-roller. Anyway, the whole blessed family turned head over heels, and landed on the pavement simultaneously with the chucker-out on top.

Again strictly speaking, I suppose I should have gone

and picked them up with suitable words of regret.   But
I just couldn't do it: I was laughing too much.   In fact
I didn't stop laughing till I began to run—the police
were heaving in sight.   Still, you boys know what the
Empire was like in those days: so I'll pass on to Monday
morning.

Not that there's much to say about Monday morning,
except that it closed my connection with the firm.   The
old man had a black eye where the chucker-out had
trodden on his face, and the hell of a liver.   And he
utterly failed to see the humorous side of the episode.
As far as I could make out his wife had smashed her
false teeth in the mêlée, and was as wild as a civet cat;
and only the fact that his own firm would be involved
had prevented him giving my name to the police.   My
own private opinion was that it wasn't so much the firm
he was worrying about as himself.   Still, that's neither
here nor there: all that matters is that my job in London
terminated that morning.

Maybe you're wondering what the dickens all this
has to do with missionaries and my saving clause, but
I'm coming to that part soon.   And I want you to realize the frame of mind I was in when I found myself
propping up the Criterion bar just before lunch on that
Monday.   It may seem strange to you that a bloke like
me could ever have stomached quill-driving in a City
office, but the fact remains that at the time I was
almighty sick with myself at having got the sack.   And
as luck would have it, I hadn't been in that bar more
than five minutes when a bunch of four of the boys blew
in, whom I'd last seen in South Africa.   They were the
lads all right, I give you my word: four of the toughest
propositions you're ever likely to meet in your life.
There was Bill Hatton who had graduated in the Kimberley diamond rush: Andy Fraser who had left Australia hurriedly, and it didn't do to ask why: Tom Jerrold

with a five-inch scar on his face that he'd picked up in Chicago: and last but not least Pete O'Farrell.

Gad! he was a character, was Pete. A great big hulking fellow of about six feet three, with muscles like an ox, and a pair of blue eyes that went clean through you and came out the other side. I once saw him tackle four policemen in Sydney, and get away with it. So did one policeman who ran for his life: the other three went to hospital.

As soon as they saw me Pete let out a bellow like a bull, and led the charge.

"If it isn't old Mac," he shouted. "Gee—boy, but it's great to see you, even if your face is like a wet street. What's stung you?"

"I've lost my job, Pete," I said. "Upset the boss and all his belongings into Leicester Square on Saturday night and got the boot."

"You mean you're at a loose end," he said, and he looked at the other three. "What about it, boys?"

"Sure thing," said Andy, "if he'll come."

"Of course he'll come," cried Pete. "Bring your poison into this corner, Mac, and we'll put you wise."

So we went and sat down in a corner, and they told me the scheme. It doesn't much matter what it was: it's got nothing to do with the yarn. But it appeared they were sailing for South America the following Friday, and they wanted to know if I'd go with them. Something to do with a revolution in some bally little state, and Pete swore we'd all make our fortunes.

Well, I guess if I hadn't been feeling so sick with myself I shouldn't have gone. I ain't no lizard lounger myself, but from past experience I knew that hunting with that bunch meant a pretty fast pace. Particularly Pete. He was a darned good fellow, but if he got a bit of liquor inside him, it was well not to contradict him.

I will say, to do him justice, it took more than a bottle of whisky to get him into that condition, but whisky was only four bob in those days.

At any rate I did go. And on Friday morning we sailed in a tin-can sort of effect from Liverpool. She was really a cargo-boat that took a few passengers, and she just suited our pockets. Moreover she was going to call at some obscure spot, where none of the big lines touched, and which, according to Pete, was the exact place from which we could best start our operations.

We ran into bad weather right away, and by Jove! that old tub could roll.

Mercifully we were all good sailors, and it wasn't until we went below for dinner that we realized there was another passenger. She only accommodated six, and up till then we had thought we were one short. But there were six places laid at the table, with a seat at the end for the skipper, who was on the bridge and had sent down word for us to start without him.

The cabins led off the dining-saloon, and suddenly during a slight lull in the ship's movement, Pete began to laugh.

"Holy Smoke! boys," he cried, "listen. Steward, who is the occupant of the sixth seat, whom I hear enjoying himself in his cabin?"

The steward grinned.

"Gent by the name of Todmarsh, sir," he answered. "Ain't never been to sea before. 'E's in a hawful condition."

"Well, I hope he doesn't make that row all night," said Pete. "I'm in the next cabin. Good evening, skipper. We've taken you at your word and started."

"Quite right," said the captain, hanging up his oil-skin. "We're in for a bad forty-eight hours, I'm afraid."

"You've got the brass band all complete, anyway," grinned Andy. "Who is Mr. Todmarsh, skipper?"

For a moment or two he didn't answer. From under a pair of great bushy eyebrows he took us all in: then he chuckled.

"Well, gentlemen," he said, "I've had some pretty strangely assorted bunches in this saloon during my time but I'll stake my oath that mixing you five and Mr. Todmarsh will constitute a record."

It was Andy Fraser who turned pale.

"Don't say," he gasped, "that he's a parson."

"That's just what I do say," howled the skipper delightedly. "At least he's a missionary."

"Steward—a double whisky," said Pete feebly. "Skipper—it ain't fair. You ought to have had a notice hung over the side. Where's he going to?"

"Same place as you," answered the other. "Then he's going up into the interior. So you'll be able to look after him when he lands. It's the first time he's left England."

Well, gentlemen, I don't want to tread on anybody's corns. I have always had the highest respect for the Church myself, but I think you'll agree with me that what the skipper said about ill-assorted bunches was right. The trouble was that the ship was so small—at least the passenger part of it—that you couldn't get away from one another. And the prospect of three weeks cooped up with a devil-dodger was a bit of a staggerer.

It was three days before we saw him, and then the staggerer became a knock-out. I found Pete and Andy holding one another's heads on the deck, and asked 'em what the trouble was. Personally I hadn't seen him yet, and it was just as they began to sob in unison that Mr. Todmarsh appeared from below. Gosh! I've never thought of such an extraordinary-looking little bird in

my life.   Boys—that man had to be seen to be believed.
Making all due allowances for the fact that he had been
sick for three days without cessation, Todmarsh won the
freak stakes in a canter.

His face was pasty, and his eyes behind his spectacles
were weak and watery.   He can't have stood more than
five feet three, and his physique was that of a stunted
child.

"Good morning, Mr. Todmarsh," said Pete gravely.
"Hope you're feeling better."

"I thank you, yes," he answered, and at that moment
Bill Hatton and Tom Jerrold hove in sight.   Then they
disappeared again quickly and I saw 'em a minute or
two later with their foreheads pressed against something
cold.

It was Pete who called a council of war, which was
duly held in the saloon over the forenoon bracer.   Todmarsh, enveloped in a rug, was up on deck, and we
knew we shouldn't be disturbed.

"Look here, boys," said Pete, "that little guy is worse
than anything I could have believed possible.   I reckon
that the temptation to pull his leg is going to be almost
more than we can bear.   But it seems to me that since
there are five of us and only one of him, it's up to us to
give the poor beggar a sporting chance.   He must have
a certain amount of guts presumably to start off on his
own, when he's made that way.   So I votes we play the
game by him and treat him square.   Anyway, no
monkeying about with religion—that's his affair, not
ours."

Well, we did our best.   Pete only blasphemed twice
at lunch, and Andy darned near choked in biting off
a story half-way through, that he'd suddenly remembered was unprintable.   But that guy was difficult.   He
didn't *say* anything on the subject of alcohol—but he
looked a lot.   Still, we could have stood that, and the

general cramped style of the conversation, if he hadn't come butting in after dinner.

We were playing poker, when in he comes from a stroll on deck. I'll admit his arrival coincided with Pete's remarks on the subject of a full house aces while Tom had fours, and for a moment or two we didn't see him. But the next instant, blowed if he hadn't advanced to the table and snatched up the pack of cards.

Well, I suppose, looking back on it now, that it showed a certain amount of pluck. But at the moment it struck us as an unwarrantable piece of impertinence.

"Look here, little man," said Pete ominously, "if that's your idea of fun and laughter it isn't mine. Put back those cards on the table."

"Never," cried Mr. Todmarsh. "These are the devil's counters!"

"Devil's grandmother," said Pete, getting up and putting his hand on the little man's shoulder. "See here, Mr. Todmarsh—you're a missionary. I and my pals are not: it takes all sorts to make a world, you know. But there's no reason why we shouldn't all live quite happily together on board this ship, if you'll mind your business same as we're going to mind ours."

"This *is* my business," answered the other. "To play cards for money is one step down the road to Hell."

"Well, I'm afraid we're too darned near the bottom of the hill to worry about that," said Pete quietly. "Put back those cards on the table."

"I will not," said Todmarsh defiantly.

For just a moment I thought Pete was going to lose his temper, and Heaven alone knows what would have happened to the little blighter if Pete had hit him. He'd have burst. However he didn't: he took both Mr. Todmarsh's wrists in one of his hands and took the pack out of his pocket with the other.

"Don't do it again," he said gently.   "You're a stupid little man, and you've got a lot to learn.   But now you've lodged your complaint, and salved your conscience: so, all I say to you is——don't do it again.   Next time I might hurt you."

And it wasn't until we were having our final nightcap that anyone alluded to it again.

"You know," said Andy as he put down his glass, "he's mad and all that, but for a thing of that size to do what he did to five fellows like us——well, it's not too bad."

And that, I think, is what we all felt until the following day, when a thing happened that changed the whole atmosphere.   In the bucketing we'd had, a lot of the cargo had got shifted, and the men were straightening things up under the first officer.   As a matter of fact Pete and I for want of a bit of exercise were lending a hand ourselves, and the job was almost done when a heavy case suddenly toppled over and caught one of the sailors underneath.

My God! but it was a nasty sight.   The poor devil had the lower part of his body pretty well squashed flat: the mess was something frightful.   There he was screaming fit to beat the band, though it was obvious to all of us that he was a goner.   As I say——still, I'll draw a veil over the details.

"Get the missionary, Mac," shouted Pete to me.

I raced off, and found him on deck.

"Accident, Mr. Todmarsh," I said.   "Man dying. No hope."

I'd got him by the arm and was hurrying him along.

"You can say a prayer or something, can't you?   It's a matter of seconds."

It was: the poor chap's groans were getting feebler. A bunch of his pals were round him, while Pete was holding up his head. They made room for us as we came, and I heard Pete mutter—"Hurry: hurry."

And then I looked round: there was no missionary. He was being sick in the corner: he was still being sick when the groans ceased. And it was left to Pete to say —"God rest your soul, old chap."

Then he got up, and I can't say I blame him. He lifted Mr. Todmarsh some five feet in the air with his boot, and left him where he lay.

"And if the little swab complains to the captain, Mac," he said to me grimly, "I'll do it again."

But he didn't complain: he shut himself into his cabin for twenty-four hours. He didn't even come on deck when we sewed up in some canvas what was left of the poor devil who had been crushed and buried him overboard.

"Ashamed to show his face," remarked Pete. "And that's the wretched little coward who had the gall to speak about devil's counters."

It was about three o'clock next afternoon that he suddenly appeared again. We were lounging about on deck—it was beginning to get almighty hot—and he went straight up to Pete.

"I want to thank you, Mr. O'Farrell," he said, "for kicking me."

Pete stared at him.

"Are you trying to be sarcastic?" he said curtly.

"Far from it," answered the other. "The fact that you did what you did is as nothing to the mental torture I've been suffering since it happened. I failed that poor chap, and my only prayer is that I may have a chance of atoning. It's no excuse to say that it was the first time I'd ever seen an accident, and that the sight of it made me physically sick. I failed him, and there's no more to be said. I realize that I was just a rotten coward. And that's why I'm glad you kicked me, because it's

part of my punishment that I should realize the contempt you rightly feel for me."

With that he was gone, leaving Pete staring after him
speechlessly.

"Well, I'm damned," he muttered at length. "I
reckon that little cove has me beat."

He filled his pipe thoughtfully, and then he looked at
me.

"What do you make of him, Mac?"

"Well, it *was* a nasty sight, Pete," I answered. "And
they say that medical students often faint at their first
operation. But for all that if you hadn't kicked him
yesterday, I should."

"I reckon I just felt wild at the moment," he said.
"But now—somehow or other—I wish I hadn't."

And for the next two or three days I often noticed a
puzzled frown on his face. He seemed to be trying to
size the little man up. He used to peer at him, when
he wasn't looking, as if he was some strange specimen,
until we started pulling his leg about it.

"Can't help it," he grinned. "The blighter sort of
fascinates me. I've never met anybody like him before.
But what for the life of me I can't make out is what good
he thinks he's going to do. I was leaning over the side
this morning talking to him. And there were a couple
of sharks in the water. So I told him a pretty lurid
story of what I'd once seen happen to a fellow bathing
at Durban, when a shark got him. I give you my word,
boys, he was the colour of putty and shaking like a leaf
when I'd finished. Well, what I want to get at is what
earthly use a freak with nerves like that is going to be.
Told me he always suffered from a vivid imagination
ever since he could remember: told me—hullo! what on
earth has bitten the skipper?"

The captain was coming along the deck towards us,
and his face was white.

"I've got the most appalling news, gentlemen," he said gravely. "There's a case of plague on board."

"Good God!" Pete sat up staring at him. "Plague!"

"Yes. I'm sorry to say there's no doubt about it whatever. We've got, as you know, no doctor on board, but I've seen plague before. And the symptoms are absolutely unmistakable."

It was then that for the first time I noticed Todmarsh. His eyes were fixed on the skipper's face, with a look in them of such terror as I have never seen before or since. His lips were moving as if he was trying to speak, but no words came.

"There is only one thing to be done," went on the captain, "and that is to try not to think about it. I shall segregate the case completely, but in a boat of this size it's very difficult. And since I've been in contact with it I shall take my meals in future by myself. But I thought it was only fair to warn you at once, gentlemen, as to what has happened. I'll get every ounce I can out of her, but we can't make land in under eleven days at the earliest."

"Plague!" Tom Jerrold got up suddenly. "I was in Canton in '94. We had a hundred thousand deaths. Hell!"

He moved over to the side as the skipper left us—and I noticed that Todmarsh had gone too.

"This is a proper lucky trip, boys," said Pete. "First a man crushed to death, and now plague. The tame freak is a mascot all right."

He laughed, but it didn't ring quite true.

"Where is the little blighter?" he went on. "This will put the wind up him."

"Probably gone below to pray," sneered Andy. "Plague! What the hell did we come in this rank tub for?"

"Go to blazes," snarled Pete. "Sorry, Andy." He

pulled himself together. "No good quarrelling. I guess we're all in the same boat, literally as well as metaphorically."

The breeze blew over, but it showed which way the wind had already begun to set. I don't know if any of you gentlemen have ever had a similar experience; if not I hope for your sake that you never will. Hot as blazes: a dead flat calm: a small cargo-boat with no doctor—and plague. Men's tempers become a bit ragged: they get apt to see insults where none are intended. And, what is worse still, you begin to watch your next-door neighbour when you think he isn't looking. You see, there's nothing to do: it's the inaction that frays one's nerves—and the fear. You can banish it for a bit: you can forget it for a while with the help of some whisky—but back it comes gnawing at you sooner or later. Are you going to be the next victim?

The first afternoon it wasn't so bad. After all there was only one case: with luck it might not spread. Besides we had something to amuse us—Todmarsh. It was Andy who discovered him, sitting in a deserted corner reading a medical book. And it was Andy who, of the whole bunch of us, took the show hardest from the very beginning. Outwardly, at least. It seemed to bring out all his worst points.

"Hullo! missionary," he said harshly, "reading about the plague, are you? You don't need to read, my lad: I'll tell you."

And he did for five minutes, till Pete growled at him to shut up, and Todmarsh sweated and shook like a man bereft of his senses.

"Don't worry, little man," said Tom Jerrold, "you'll be all right out in the open here. As long as you keep away from infection."

"Is it terribly infectious?" quavered the other.

"To blazes with you," cried Pete angrily. "You

haven't got the courage of a louse. Why don't you draw a circle round yourself, and stop inside it? We'll throw you your food."

It was the following morning that the first man died, and we had him overboard almost before the life was out of his body. And that afternoon there were two more cases. If possible it was hotter—the sea more oily. There wasn't a breath of wind: the deck was like a burning plate. And still ten days to go. But what finished us was that Todmarsh seemed to have taken Pete literally. He hadn't actually drawn a circle round himself, but when he wasn't below in his cabin he was sitting as far away from us as possible. He used to eat his grub on deck, and after he'd finished it he'd disappear for hours on end.

And we baited him—baited him brutally. I make no excuses for it: I was as bad as the others. We used to form a ring round him, and rag him cruel. This second exhibition of cowardice had put the tin-hat on. We were none of us too happy ourselves: only, you see, you don't show that sort of thing.

But it had no effect: he just stood there and sweated, and backed away if any of us came close to him. It was the day that three men went down with it, I remember, that Andy suddenly lost control of himself. He made a sudden dart for the little man and shook him like a rat. And Todmarsh screamed like a wounded hare.

"Stand away! Don't touch me!"

We pulled Andy off: he was mad for the moment and in another instant he'd have flung him over the side.

"Quit it, Andy," growled Pete. "Leave the little swab to his own devices."

And then came the worst thing of the lot: the saloon steward, William, got it. That was when there were still five days to go, and he was the tenth case. We

found him groaning in the pantry when we went down
for lunch.   And I guess it didn't improve our appetites.
Poor devil—his was a pretty rapid case: he was dead
next morning.

And so we went on through that dead calm sea.   Save
for the fact that we were now short-handed, even a gale
would have been welcome—except that it would have
meant less speed.   We never saw the skipper: he regarded himself as being in quarantine.   And there was
nothing we could do to help him.   Pete and I shouted
to him once—he was up on the bridge—to know if we
could assist.   But he shook his head.

"I've got all the help I want," he answered.   "And
there have been no fresh cases for two days—so perhaps
we're through."

It was in the middle of that night that Pete came into
my cabin and woke me up.

"Mac," he said gravely, "the missionary is ill.
Listen."

Through the open door you could hear him groaning,
and we looked at one another with the same thought
in each of our minds.   Illness in that ship meant only
one thing.

"We'll have to go to him, Pete," I said.

So we went.

"Don't come near me," he croaked at us as soon as
we appeared.   "I'm not feeling well."

"Look here, Todmarsh," said Pete, staring at him,
"there's no good beating about the bush.   I'm afraid
your isolation tactics haven't succeeded.   You've got
it."

"I know I have," he said hoarsely, and turned his
face away.

He was delirious in a couple of hours, and all through
another interminable day we could hear him shouting
about atonement and cowardice.   And there was noth-

ing to be done except to listen and to wait for the end.

"I'm sorry for the poor little devil," said Andy. "I'm sorry I baited and ragged him. But, by Jove! you fellows, if ever there was a case of cold feet getting punished this is it." Which is, I think, what we all felt.

He only spoke one coherent word before he died, and that was to Pete and me.

"I have atoned, haven't I?"

"Of course you have, my dear fellow," said Pete awkwardly. "And we're deuced sorry and . . ."

He shrugged his shoulders hopelessly: the missionary was rambling again. He was back once more in his childhood, and for a while we listened to hopes and aspirations which sounded too pathetic for words coming as they did from such a miserable specimen of humanity. To do something big and great—that was his ambition: to be a leader of lost causes—a man whom men would follow. This little undeveloped, undersized creature.

And then suddenly he spoke one intelligent sentence.

"It will be all right, William. Quite all right on the other side."

For a moment he sat bolt upright, and his eyes behind his spectacles were shining with a strange look of exaltation. Then he fell back: the eleventh case had gone the way of the others.

"A gallant little gentleman," said a voice behind us. The skipper was standing in the door. "I don't know what I'd have done without him."

We both stared at him speechlessly.

"And I'm glad you were with him to help him over the barrier, as he has helped all the others."

"What's that?" stammered Pete.

"You knew, surely?" said the skipper, looking at him in surprise. " 'It will be all right, William. Quite all

right on the other side.'   And he's said that to every
one of them.   He told me he was keeping away from
you for fear of infecting you."

And for the one and only time that he's ever done
such a thing in his life I should imagine, Pete O'Farrell
broke down and sobbed like a child.

Well—that's my saving clause.   I don't hold with missionaries, always excepting little Todmarsh.   Another?
Well—talking is dry work.

XVI   THE   RUBBER   STRAP

DO you know that game called "Are you there?"
You may find it being played in mess on guest
night after dinner, and you will assuredly find it included in any sports that may be held on an ocean-
going liner.   Its rules are simple: its charm immense
—to the onlookers.   You lie down on the deck facing
your opponent, grasping his left hand with your own.
Each of you in his right hand holds a rolled-up copy
of an illustrated weekly, or some similar weapon.   A
pillow cover is then placed over each of your heads to
blindfold you.   At the word go, one of you says: "Are
you there?"   The other answers "Yes," at the same
time moving his head into a position of safety.   Any
position may be chosen so long as his left elbow remains on the deck, and his left hand remains in yours.
You then lift your right hand and aim a heavy blow
with the weapon it contains at the place where you
imagine his head to be.   If you hit it you count one
and then it's his turn.   You go on till one or other
of you is stunned.   In fact, a great game—for the
onlookers.

And my reason for this brief dissertation on one

pastime of the idle rich, is that it was directly responsible for my hearing a very strange yarn. I am aware that when a teller of stories prefaces one of them with the remark that it is true, the sophisticated reader prepares himself resignedly for a worse lie than usual. And so I won't say that this is true, but merely that it was told me by an American who claims to be a direct descendant of George Washington.

The game was over: the corpses had been laid out on the deck to cool. Personally I had not competed: nor had the American. On the subject of being butchered for a Roman holiday our ideas coincided remarkably. On other points too, there seemed no great divergence in our opinions.

"I've some fruit syrup in my cabin," he remarked, thoughtfully watching one of the corpses arise and stagger aft to die. "Also some vermouth."

"I can supply gin and a shaker," I put in hopefully.

"Good," he said. "Are we there? Yes."

He mixed two of the best, and then he pulled out his cabin trunk and started rummaging through the contents.

"See that?" he said. "What do you think of it?"

It was a piece of black india-rubber about fifteen inches long, an inch wide and half an inch thick.

"A rather good weapon for 'Are you there,'" I answered.

"I thought you'd say that," he grinned. "And used for just one blow at a time it would be. Used another way. . . . See here. Put your leg up on that bunk."

I did so, and he raised the rubber thong in his hand.

"I'm not going to hit you hard," he said. "But just see how long you can stand it."

He started above my knee, and worked gradually up

my thigh: then back again.   And he didn't hit hard.
He hit no harder than the smack you would give a
naughty child, and a small child at that.   Tap; tap;
tap—that rubber thong wound itself round my leg in
a different place each time.   No one blow could even
be said to hurt, and yet I only stood twenty-five of
them.   There's no good suffering agony for nothing.
After about the tenth hit every single muscle and sinew
in my leg started shrieking at the same moment: after
the twenty-fifth I should have begun to shriek myself
if I hadn't given in.

He smiled and mixed me another cocktail.

"A souvenir," he said, "of a very strange affair.
That game this afternoon put me in mind of it."

"Having half-killed me," I said, "the talking is on
you.   Fire ahead."

"It took place in Paris after the war," he began.
"Everything, including discipline, was a bit lax—same
as it was in England.   But the war was over and
nobody minded very much as long as things were kept
within reasonable bounds.   I'd been in our Intelligence myself, and when my division went back over-
seas I got leave to stop on in France for a while.

"I was sitting in my hotel one morning, when in
walked a man I knew fairly intimately.   His name was
John Thripley, and he was in charge of one of our big
military stores.   Not ordnance, but commissariat:
tobacco, ham, tinned beef, all that sort of stuff.   I'd
been over it once while the fighting was on, and there
was enough there to have fed all the belligerent armies
for a year.

"I gave him a hail, and he came over and sat
down.

"'Morning, John,' I said.   'You look worried.
Mice been at the cheese?'

"'In a manner of speaking,' he answered.   'Only

they're damned large mice. I'm floored, Bill, and that's straight: and it's a pretty serious business.'

" 'What's up,' I said. 'Can I help?'

"He shook his head doubtfully.

" 'I'll tell you what it is, but I don't want it to go any further. You know I'm in charge of "A" dump, don't you? Well, about two months ago a bunch of indents were presented in the ordinary way for stuff. I think there were about half a million cigarettes, and some boots and two or three hundredweights of ham. Everything was perfectly in order—I've examined the vouchers myself—and so the stuff was loaded on to the lorry that had come for it, and the lorry was driven away.

" 'Naturally I thought no more about it, until the next morning produced another batch of similar indents from the same people. The storekeeper brought it to me—by mere luck it happened to be the same man who had handled the vouchers the previous day —and asked me what he was to do. Well, there was only one thing to be done. I got on the telephone to the people who wanted the stuff, and asked 'em what under the sun they wanted with two such big demands on consecutive days.

" 'The guy at the other end of the wire began to splutter and asked me what the devil I was talking about. He hadn't sent in two indents: he'd only sent in one. A lorry had left that morning for the stuff, driven by a man named Wilson. And sure enough Wilson was there right enough cursing good and strong at the delay. So there was nothing for it but to load up the lorry and let him go. Whatever mistake had occurred was nothing to do with him.

" 'Back I went to the office and hauled out yesterday's indents. Not a flaw to be found in 'em: they were, on the face of things, absolutely genuine. So

then I got on the telephone all the way round.   I rang
up everyone I could think of, and asked them the same
question.   Had a lorry—and I gave 'em the type of
bus it was—turned up for them with the following
stores on board—and I gave 'em a detailed list of the
stores.   No—it hadn't: same answer everywhere.   But
in case it did arrive they'd ring me up.

" 'Well—I never got deafened with that telephone-
bell.   Not only the stores but the whole blamed lorry
were never heard of again.   About seventy-five thousand dollars' worth of stuff completely vanished.

" 'There was always the possibility of accident, of
course, and so I promptly reported the matter to the
police.   But as the days went by and no news came
in, I had to come to the conclusion that we'd been had
all right, and that a bare-faced robbery had been committed right under our noses.'

" 'Just a moment, John,' I put in.   'Did no one
recognize the driver?'

" 'I thought of that,' he answered, 'but it's a blank.
The driver and his mate had on goggles, and the other
fellow who helped to load was just an ordinary sort
of bloke—quite inconspicuous.   My storeman says he
might remember him, but he wouldn't swear to it.
Don't forget, Bill, we get 'em in by the score daily
and if a bunch are out on a game like that they're not
going to employ a man with a wooden leg and a strawberry mark on his face.

" 'Now that was the beginning of it.   Four days
later, Anston who runs "C" store loaded up two thousand pairs of boots, two thousand cardigans, and two
thousand suits of underclothes on another lorry.   And
damn it, that disappeared into the blue also.   Over I
went as soon as I heard of it to see Anston, and we compared those indents.   Not a trace of resemblance in
the writing—not a clue.   His, to all appearances, were

just as genuine as mine, and there we were stung again good and hard. It was obvious what had happened : it was obvious that the stolen stuff had been sold to the French, or was being kept in some secret place for disposal to them in due course. It was also obvious that we were up against a thoroughly daring gang, of whom at any rate some must be our own people.

" 'So that very morning we called a general meeting of all the fellows who were running stores to discuss what was to be done. They'd done it twice now with success, and we felt pretty sure they wouldn't be able to resist the temptation of trying it again. The point was how to catch 'em. They weren't fools, and they must know that the loss had been discovered. Recognition was wellnigh impossible. We had six big depots lying some distance apart, and granted that they only tried one robbery at each they'd be fairly safe in using the same men each time. But since it was more than likely that there was a biggish gang of them, there was nothing to prevent 'em changing round. So at last we decided that the only thing to do, in the event of a big indent coming in, was to ring up the formation making the demand and get it confirmed before issue.

" 'By Jove! Bill. We got some pretty blasphemous confirmation down the telephone. What the hell, etc., etc.? Wasn't the indent there staring us in the face? Were we trying to be funny? You see we weren't over-communicative as to why we were doing it. No one likes to admit he's been soaked properly.

" 'For a fortnight nothing happened. Then in comes Payton one morning to see me, gibbering at the mouth with rage.

" ' "They've stung me, John. Three days ago. Jam, ham, tinned beef—every darned thing you can think of. Best part of fifty thousand dollars' worth. My telephone was out of action that morning, and I was infernally busy. The indent was signed by Jack Cooper: I'd swear to his signature in a thousand. If I've seen it once, I've seen it a hundred times. It was a forgery."

" 'He lit a cigarette, and ramped up and down the office.

" 'I took it out to him, and damn it! it even deceived him. It wasn't until we found there was no carbon duplicate in his office that he was quite sure he hadn't signed it himself and forgotten about it.

" 'Well that made three of us who had taken it in the neck and we were getting sorer than Hell. Cartwright of "D" store, and the other two, Mason and Digby, who hadn't been caught were kind of tolerant about it—the implication being that we'd better come along to them and learn our job. At least that was the idea until Cartwright loaded up a lorry with a hundred thousand dollars' worth of stuff which was wanted urgently. He verified everything : had the driver brought into his office to have his photograph taken from about forty different angles, and generally read the riot act all round. That lorry broke down thirty miles out of Paris. The men had stopped at an inn to have their lunch, and no power on earth would start the engine after. I'm no motorist but I gather something had gone in the magneto.

" 'Well luckily another lorry—an empty one—passed shortly after, going the same way. So they changed the stuff over, and that was that. Cartwright swelled our numbers to four, though he swears it wasn't his fault. Anyway, none of the stuff was ever seen again.

" 'And that left Mason and Digby. Mason started the ball rolling in fine style. It seems one morning that he got suspicious of a driver who turned up, and there being no flies on Jake Mason he was hit with a brilliant idea.   So he got himself nailed up in a packing-case reputed to contain tinned meat, and was loaded up with the rest of the stuff.   As far as I can make out he was put in upside down and had a sixty-mile drive, so he must have had a real fine morning.   Still, he didn't care so long as he could run them to ground. He'd got two guns with him, and he wasn't going to hesitate about using them.

" 'Of course, as I said to him, it might have been a darned good show if the lorry hadn't been a perfectly genuine one.   But when they unpacked Jake, the scene was a trying one.   They first of all thought he was trying to be funny: then they insisted he was mad. And when poor old Jake tried to explain it wasn't a success.   They had indented for tinned meat, and Jake as a substitute left them cold.   However, he pacified them after a while, and went back to Paris by train, to find the line in his office darned near fused with the blasphemy coming over it from another quarter.   What had happened to the lorry that had started off that morning for Beauvais?

" 'At the time Jake had been packed up in his box, so he sent for his quarter-master.   Yes—perfectly true. A lorry had started right enough, and the quarter-master had not only rung up to find out that it was all right, but in addition he knew the driver personally. They came from the same town in the States.

" 'And here, Bill, the matter becomes even more serious than before.   Up to date there had been no violence: this time there was.   The driver was found more dead than alive in a ditch: his mate is still in hospital unconscious, and the lorry has never been seen again.'

"John Thripley lit a cigarette, and intimated that he was thirsty.

" 'That's a very strange story, John,' I remarked.

'For five lorries to disappear like that beats cock-fighting.'

" 'Five lorries worth a quarter of a million dollars at a conservative estimate,' he grunted. 'But it's not the money I mind so much—it's not mine. What gets my goat is being stung like that. And the point is, Bill, there is still the sixth lorry to go. Your criminal, and mark you this is no ordinary man, is a darned conceited fellow. And I'm open to a bet that he won't be happy till he's done in Digby. There's another thing, too: he's getting to the end of his tether or he wouldn't have taken to violence. Highway robbery in broad daylight on a main road is a pretty dangerous operation.'

" 'They probably stopped the lorry and asked for a lift,' I said. 'And then laid out the driver and his mate at a suitable opportunity. Have you got no suspicions at all?'

" 'Not the faintest vestige,' he answered. 'And the police seem as floored as we are. They take up the line, and I hardly blame 'em for it, that the criminals are our own people, and that we ought to be able to look after our own affairs. Of course they don't actually say that—but they imply it.'

"The door swung open at that moment, and an officer came in. I didn't know him, but John Thripley did, and I heard him whistle under his breath.

" 'It's Digby,' he said. 'And something has happened.'

"Just then the new-comer saw John, and came over to our table.

" 'By God! Thripley,' he said grimly, 'I don't rest until I've caught those swine. Have you heard what happened last night? It's murder—cold-blooded murder this time.'

" 'The devil it is,' said John. 'You can speak

out: I've just been telling my friend here all about it.'

" 'I was sitting in my office the night before last about five o'clock,' said Digby, 'when one of my sergeants came in.'

" 'Look here, Captain,' he said to me, 'I reckon I've got a line on those crooks.'

" 'Good man,' I cried. 'Who are they?'

" 'I'd sooner not say, sir,' he said, 'for I may be wrong.'

" 'How did you get the line,' I asked him.

" 'Well,' he said with a bit of a grin, 'there's a little cabaret called the *Petit Souris* where I go sometimes to have a drink and a dance. And there's a girl there —Marie is her name—who seems to like dancing with me. I was sitting at a table with her last night, and I found I'd run out of cigarettes. So she pulls out a paper packet of Fatimas and offers it to me.

" ' "Hullo! Marie," I said, "where did you get these from? You're becoming a proper little American."

" 'She laughed and told me that all the girls had them now as they were so easy to get.

" ' "Is that so," I answered. "I didn't know you found it any easier to get 'em now than before. Do the boys give 'em to you?"

" 'She shook her head, and then suddenly she sat up in her chair and laid her hand on my arm.

" ' "Do you see that man who has just come in?"

" 'I looked over at the door, and saw an American soldier standing there with a girl on each arm. He'd got the face of a Chicago tough, but in about ten seconds you couldn't see him for girls. They were round him like bees round honey.

" ' "He seems popular," I said.

" ' "Because he gives away so many presents," said

Marie. "Cigarettes, and jam, and meat, and a pair of boots to Lisette's father, and . . ."

" 'But I guess I wasn't listening, Captain: I was just staring at her and then at him.

" ' "Where does he get them from, Marie?" I said.

" 'She shrugged her shoulders: she wasn't interested in that.

" ' "But I don't like him," she went on. "He is a *cochon*."

"Digby chewed savagely at his cigar.

" 'There's no good my repeating the whole conversation,' he went on. 'All that matters is that my sergeant was pretty well convinced in his own mind that this fellow knew a good deal more than was healthy about these robberies. I don't know whether he gave himself away or not—he must have: but the fact remains that I've just been to the mortuary to identify his dead body. He'd been plugged through the heart at close range. You could see the mark of the scorch on his coat.'

" 'When did it happen?' I asked.

" 'Some time last night,' he answered. 'And I don't quit Paris till I've caught the guy who did it.'

"Which was a very fine sentiment, but easier to say than to carry out. The sergeant had not mentioned the man's name: in fact, Digby couldn't say if he even knew it. All that we had to go on was that he looked like a Chicago tough, and had been in this cabaret place two nights previously. Also—and in this, so it seemed to me, lay our trump card—that he was well-known and popular with the little ladies of the quarter.

"Quite obviously the *Petit Souris* was our jumping-off ground, but at once there cropped up a difficulty. If this man was the man or one of the men we wanted, he was pretty well certain to know both Digby and Thripley by sight. And the instant he saw them in such an unexpected haunt he'd be bound to smell a rat. Now we hadn't an atom of proof to go on, and the one essential thing was not to scare our bird if we were to have a hope of bringing it home to him.

" 'There's only one thing to do,' I said. 'Let me go to this place alone. I've got plain clothes here, and he won't know me. I'll get in touch with this girl Marie if I can, and if I see this fellow I'll remember his face and that will put us a step forward, anyway. Once he's known, it oughtn't to be difficult to get enough proof to convict him.'

"So that evening I went off to the *Petit Souris*. I got there about nine, and found it the usual sort of place. There were some twenty girls there, a few Frenchmen and two or three Britishers. But there was no sign of any American soldier.

" 'Tell me,' I said to the waiter who brought my drink, 'is there any girl here of the name of Marie?'

" '*Mon Dieu!* m'sieur,' he cried, 'half a dozen at least.'

" 'I guessed that,' I answered. 'But throw your memory back, my lad, three nights ago. Do you remember an American *sous officier* who was in here sitting at a table with one of those six Maries?'

"He gave me a quick look of suspicion, and I knew I'd started one hare. His face assumed a look of bovine imbecility and he shook his head. So many people came in that he had completely forgotten the incident. He regretted it deeply, but he couldn't assist me.

" 'You may keep the change,' I remarked, showing him a twenty-franc note, 'if your memory improves. But it must be the right Marie.'

"He hesitated: cupidity struggling with fear. Then suddenly he leant forward on the pretence of drying the table with a napkin.

" 'This is not a good place for Americans, sir,' he whispered. 'I would go if I was you.'

" 'Well you're not me,' I said. 'And I'm not going. Now then—has your memory come back?'

"He shrugged his shoulders.

" 'As m'sieur wishes. The girl you want is the one in green sitting by herself three tables away.'

" 'Good for you,' I said. 'There's the note.'

"He bustled away, and after a moment or two I glanced casually at the girl. She was a pretty little thing, and I noticed she kept looking at the door as if she was expecting someone. And very soon I noticed another thing, too. All the other girls—at least all those who hadn't got men with them—were looking at her surreptitiously and whispering amongst themselves. Evidently there was some secret which concerned her, and of which, so it struck me, she was in ignorance.

"Further, it seemed to me that I was the object of a considerable amount of interest. At first I thought it was simply because I was a stranger, but after a while I began to realize that it was something more than that. It's hard to explain exactly what I mean, but it struck me that in some way my presence was being connected with this girl Marie. It wasn't the waiter because I'd noticed it before I spoke to him. It couldn't be me personally for I'd never been to the place before, and no one there knew me. So it boiled down to the fact that it must be because I was an American.

"Well there was no good wasting time. I was there to see Marie, and get what I could out of her. So when I'd finished my drink I got up and strolled over to her table, conscious that every girl in the room was watching me.

" 'Will you give me the pleasure of a dance, mam'-selle,' I asked.

"She stared at me for a while without speaking.

" 'I am not dancing to-night,' she said quietly.

" 'Too bad,' I answered, sitting down beside her. 'I've been watching you, and it seems to me you're waiting for somebody. I wonder if I can guess who it is.'

" 'Are you an American officer?' she asked.

" 'I am,' I said. 'Why do you ask?'

" 'Then, m'sieur—go away. This place is not safe for you. It is not safe for any American. *Mon Dieu!* if I only knew what had happened . . .'

"She broke off, and sat there twisting her handkerchief between her fingers.

" 'Happened to whom,' I asked her.

" 'M'sieur—do you know a Sergeant Franklin?'

"Now that was the name of Digby's murdered sergeant: I'd asked him.

" 'What do you know of Sergeant Franklin,' I said cautiously.

" 'Listen, m'sieur—he was my friend. He promised that he would be here last night—but he never came. And I must see him. I must warn him.'

"I took the bull by both horns.

" 'Marie,' I said: 'Sergeant Franklin was murdered last night.'

"For a moment I thought she was going to faint. Her face turned the colour of the tablecloth, and her breath came in little gasps.

" 'Take a pull at yourself, my dear,' I went on. 'It's because of that that I'm sitting here talking to you. Do you know who it was who killed him?'

"But she hardly seemed to hear the question.

" 'So that's what all the mystery is,' she whispered savagely. 'They knew—these pigs.'

"She sat up suddenly and stared at the door.

" '*Mon Dieu!* he is early to-night. M'sieur, don't

look round. For God's sake don't look round. Do you want me to help you to find the man who murdered Sergeant Franklin?'

" 'Sure thing, Marie,' I said. 'But will you be all right. I don't want to get you into trouble.'

"She laughed a little harshly.

" 'What does it matter about me,' she cried impatiently. 'Don't you understand that I loved him. And that brute—that devil killed him. Because of what I said. Do you suppose I mind—now—if they kill me. As they will.'

"She added those last three words under her breath.

" 'Will you promise to do exactly what I say?'

" 'I promise.' I saw there was no time for argument.

" 'First—give me your address.'

"I told her the name of my hotel.

" 'Good. To-morrow morning I will ring you up there. Then come to the address I shall give you, and bring with you some friends. But now to-night there is not much time. In a few seconds a man will come up to this table. He will insult you: I, too, shall seem to agree with him. Say nothing: answer nothing— just go.'

"She sat back in her chair, laughing, and snapped her fingers in my face. It was done so suddenly: her change of expression was so abrupt that for a moment I was nonplussed. Then, as a coarse voice spoke from behind my shoulder, I understood.

" 'And who under the sun may you be?'

"I turned round to find an American private regarding me offensively, and for a moment my temper almost got the better of me. I'd forgotten that I was in plain clothes and that he couldn't know I was an officer. He was a villainous-looking swine—one of the type it's better to avoid unless you're asking for trouble—

and I guessed at once that this was the Chicago tough of whom Sergeant Franklin had spoken to Digby.

" 'Get out,' he snarled. 'Beat it while the going's good, or you may find yourself leaving feet first.'

"The girl laughed as I rose to my feet, and got rid of a choice bit of Parisian *argot* at my expense. And then for an instant the man turned away to shout to the waiter and her eyes rested on his back. By Jove! I've never seen such a depth of concentrated hatred on anyone's face before or since. It was diabolical—devilish. But when I got to the door he was sitting beside her with his arm round her waist, and she was pointing a derisive finger at me. Evidently the game had commenced. The point that worried the others was whether it was genuine—or not.

"They were all round in my hotel early the next morning, to say nothing of the Provost Marshal, and we discussed it while we waited. Personally, I felt sure that the girl was on our side, but they weren't so certain. They hadn't seen that look in her eyes, and were sceptical about the whole thing.

" 'On her own showing,' as Digby said, 'this fellow has been giving things away lavishly. Granted that it's the same man, didn't she tell that poor devil Franklin so? So is she likely to split on him?'

"And at that very moment the telephone bell rang. I picked up the receiver and from the other end came her voice.

" 'Come at once to 15, Rue de St. Gare!'

"It was tense, that voice of hers—tense and quivering with excitement, and her mood communicated itself to me.

" 'Come on, you fellows,' I cried. 'The Kid has done what she said.'

"We tumbled into a couple of taxis, each of us with a gun in his pocket. There was always the possibility of a trap, and we were taking no chances. And in ten minutes we arrived at her house. She came down to meet us at the door, and her face was white, with dark rings under her eyes.

" 'Good morning, Marie,' I said, holding out my hand. 'What has happened?'

" 'Come and see,' she answered briefly, and led the way upstairs.

"We crowded into the room after her to find a strange sight confronting us. Lashed hand and foot to a chair was the man I had met the night before, and he was unconscious.

" 'You want the truth,' she said quietly. 'All right: you're going to have it. Go in there.'

" 'Look here, Marie,' I said nervously. 'What are you going to do?'

"With a girl of that type you never can tell, and I had visions of vitriol and other choice devices.

" 'Don't be afraid,' she said contemptuously. 'I'll leave the brute for you just as he is.'

"It was her bedroom we went into, and it was behind the chair where the man sat bound so that he couldn't see us though we could see him.

" 'Don't make a sound,' she said to us. 'I'm going to wake him.'

"She picked up a jug of cold water and flung it in his face, and after a moment or two he gave a spluttering cough and his head moved.

" 'What the hell has happened?' he muttered stupidly.

"Then he stared at the girl who was facing him across the table.

" 'I'll kill you for this,' he snarled, and she laughed and picked up that india-rubber strap.

" 'What are you going to do with that,' he shouted, and there was terror in his voice.

" 'Get the truth, you devil,' she answered.

"You could see the man's great muscles heaving and straining at the ropes that held him, but she'd lashed him in too well, had Marie.

" 'What's the good of the truth,' he screamed. 'I'll deny it after, and there will be no proof.'

" 'I'll chance that,' she said quietly, and started in on him with the strap.

"Up one leg—down the other; up one arm—down the other; again and again and again, while we watched, fascinated. At the beginning of the third circuit he gave an awful groan, and she paused.

" 'Who killed Sergeant Franklin?' she asked.

"A flood of abuse was the only answer.

"At the beginning of the fifth she repeated the question, and by this time the sweat had come clean through his clothes, and he was dripping like a sponge. But he still stuck it.

"At the beginning of the seventh he gave in.

" 'I did,' he croaked.

" 'Why did you kill him?' she demanded.

" 'Because he knew too much,' he muttered.

" 'About you stealing the lorries?' she went on.

" 'Of course,' he cried. 'What else? Let me get up, you devil; let me get up.'

" 'Not yet. I want the names of the men who have been helping you.'

"He gave 'em—half a dozen in all, and six men in the back room jotted down those names as he said them.

" 'Now let me up, you she-cat,' he snarled. 'And may God help you when I get my hands on you.'

"But Marie had slipped suddenly to the floor, and when we got to her we found she'd fainted."

The American paused, fingering the rubber strap thoughtfully.

"What was the end?" I asked.

"The chair in America for him," he answered grimly. "Our methods of examination are a little more drastic than yours, and we got the truth pretty effectively out of his confederates. They were deserters—the lot of 'em—and O'Brien, the leader, was an expert forger to boot. Moreover he was wanted for murder on our side as well: so, as there was a prejudice against killing an American in France, they did the good deed in America."

"And Marie?" I asked.

"They got her all right, though I don't know how. Someone gave her away I suppose. Personally, I never saw her again. But once—just before I left Paris I was walking through the cemetery where Franklin was buried. And there was a little bunch of cheap flowers on his grave. They were old and faded, and I turned to an attendant near by:

" 'Who put these here?' I asked.

"He shrugged his shoulders.

" 'A girl, m'sieur,' he answered. 'And I have let them remain. They are dead—but then so is she.'

" 'What's that?' I cried. 'Marie dead.'

" 'M'sieur knew her,' he said indifferently. 'But yes—she is dead. She was stabbed in the heart not a hundred yards from the cemetery gates the same evening that she put those flowers on the grave. Who by? M'sieur, who knows? *C'est la guerre, n'est-ce-pas*—or very nearly.' "

XVII   ROUT OF THE OLIVER SAMUELSONS

IT is not advisable, when you speculate, to put your money into a tin mine that contains no tin. Further, it is not advisable, when you speculate, to put *all* your money into anything. But if you combine the two, and put all your money into a tin mine that contains no tin, you are asking for the trouble that Major Jack Delmont asked for—and got. And with him in the getting were his wife and his daughter, Molly.

She was twenty-one when it happened, was Molly, and a combination of the astounding good looks of both her parents. And since it was a catastrophe impossible to conceal, she was present at the council of war which was held in the Delmont household.

Her father—utterly penitent—invited them both to walk on his face and roast him over a slow fire; her mother, after one "Oh! Jack, *dear*, how could you?" went to her man and kissed him. Molly went for a walk.

She returned with her mind made up, and the next morning, having bought a third return to London, she departed for the day.

"I am," she announced on her return, "going to do something terribly original. I am going to be a governess."

"Ye gods!" said her father.

"Darling child," said her mother.

"Angels both," said Molly. "If Daddy will make a fool of himself, it's up to me to show that there are still some brains in the family. So I have taken a post to-day."

"You don't mean you've done it already?" cried her father.

"Who with, dear?" asked her mother.

"Mrs. Oliver Samuelson," said the girl. "Who says that's nothing?"

"Who the deuce is Mrs. Oliver Samuelson?" demanded her father.

"The world's worst horror," laughed Molly. "Told me she didn't allow followers in the house. Joking apart, she's pretty grim, Daddy. Rolls in boodle. The woman in the office, who seemed quite a human sort of soul, told me about her. They've rented Ladbroke Towers."

"Ladbroke Towers!" cried her father. "Why, I used to shoot there with the old man. He died about a year ago. It's a wonderful house, Kiddie."

"So I gathered from Mrs. Oliver Samuelson," said the girl gravely. "She expatiated at length on its charms, and her great friendship with the present Earl, and the social life that she led, and so on and so forth. Naturally, I was suitably impressed."

"I hate it, my dear," said her father gloomily. "What a blithering idiot I was!"

"Dry up, my pet," laughed Molly. "It's no good going into all that again."

"What's the family, Molly?" put in her mother.

"I gather my principal charge is one Oswald, aged nine. A child who requires careful handling. Also, I am to help Mrs. Oliver Samuelson in her correspondence."

"I hate it," repeated her father, and Molly promptly kissed him on the top of his head.

"It won't be as bad as it sounds," she said, with a show of confidence she was far from feeling. "And if it is, I can always chuck it."

Which was not a good prophecy. For, six months later, she found that it was immeasurably worse than it had sounded, and she hadn't chucked it. Times out of number she had been on the point of doing so, and then the knowledge that the two people she loved most in the world could just get on on the pension, if she wasn't there, restrained her.

The Oliver Samuelsons were an altogether beastly family. And, let it be clearly understood, beastly is the *mot juste*. The family consisted of five members: father, mother, daughter and two sons, and it is a doubtful point as to which of the five was the most unpleasant. In fact, the generally accepted theory was that it was whichever you happened to be with last.

But they rolled in money—positively wallowed in it. Detach the Oliver, and the reason is clear. Who has not heard of Samuelson's Certain Cure for Chilblains, of Samuelson's Excellent Eradicator of Eczema, of Samuelson's Perfect Paralyser of Pimples? Well—these were the people.

Now far be it from me to suggest that there is any reason why the vendor of patent medicines should not be quite as charming a person as anyone else. There is nothing inherently debasing about paralysing pimples. There is, further, no earthly reason, as far as I can see, why a man should not reap a large reward for performing such a meritorious act. The cause of their beastliness was not that: it was simply them. If Mr. Samuelson had been the Archbishop of Canterbury, or a stockbroker, or even an author, he would still have been beastly. And the same applies to the rest of them.

It was the successful manipulation of a hundred thousand pounds during the rubber boom that caused the trouble. Before that they had been content to be beastly in comparative obscurity, but when Mrs. Samuelson had at last grasped the fact that they were millionaires, her social aspirations, always there, though hitherto suppressed, soared to dizzy heights. Such things have happened before: such things will happen again. It matters not whether one likes it or doesn't like it—the thing is inevitable. And, after all—why not?

The man who makes a million pounds may be, and very often is, a nicer fellow than the heir to several thousand acres and a castle badly in need of repair. And had that been so in the case of the Oliver Samuelsons, these words would never have been written. At the risk of repeating myself, I wish that to be clear. What I am about to relate happened not because they were *nouveaux riches*, or patent-medicine vendors, but simply because they were beastly. Had Mr. Oliver Samuelson been an author, as I said before, it would still have happened. I can't make it clearer than that.

Why their social aspirations should have been settled on a country place I do not profess to say. They none of them rode, shot or fished: they were all of them profoundly bored anywhere except in London. But since the motives inspiring the Oliver Samuelsons are, I am glad to say, a sealed book to me, I can only record the fact that they decided to obtain a country house—I beg your pardon, seat.

Now it so happened that, some three months previous to their momentous decision, the Earl of Ladbroke had consumed his last glass of port and been gathered to his forbears, leaving Ladbroke Towers sadly encumbered. His wife was dead: his only son was prospecting somewhere in the back of beyond. And the family lawyer was deteriorating badly at golf through worry over death duties. If only he could let the house, all might yet be well; but would the new Earl agree? And if he did, could he find a tenant?

To him, then, there came one day, like a direct answer to prayer, Mr. Oliver Samuelson. It was true that, dire though the necessity was, there were moments when the lawyer wondered if the price was not too great —moments when the full horror of his visitor sank into his soul. But, being a man of stern determination and a vigilant custodian of the Ladbroke interests, he banished these vacillating thoughts. He explained politely that to sell was out of the question, but that he had his lordship's authorization to let for five years. And he then mentioned a figure the size of which staggered even him.

Mr. Oliver Samuelson didn't turn a hair. He ejected from his mouth a considerable portion of chewed cigar; ground it into the carpet with his foot, and announced that a few odd thousand this way or that made no difference to him. And a month later the family was in residence.

Now, as all the world knows, Ladbroke Towers is situated in the centre of the most cliquish county in England. And, as the months went by, the fact gradually penetrated into the brain of Mrs. Oliver Samuelson that, though money will obtain a country seat, money will not fill it. Not, at least, with the people whom she was desirous of knowing. Business friends of her husband were delighted to come and stay: acquaintances of her son and daughter were only too ready to drink her champagne and play poker till three in the morning. But the county families remained icily aloof.

A few called—once, and there the matter ended. Invitations to shoot and to dine were declined; the large ball given at Christmas was exclusively attended by people from London. And there, but for one or two things, the matter would have ended.

The first concerned the matter of the head keeper, a man whose father and grandfather had been head keepers there before him. Annoyed by the smallness of the bags, and refusing to realize that it was entirely due to the badness of the shooting, Mr. Oliver Samuelson sacked him on the spot. The fact that his wife was going to have a baby and that there was no other cottage for him to go to, was nothing to do with Mr. Samuelson.

"Get out, and get out quick. You're useless."

The second concerned a girl in the village and the heir to the Samuelson fortune. An unpleasant case without a redeeming feature.

There were other things, too—things which revealed them in their true colours; things which caused a letter to be penned by a gentleman who signed himself Bimbo. It breathed a certain despair, that letter; the writer realized that nothing could be done, since he was fully aware that the state of the recipient's finances was even more hopeless than usual. And the recipient, a vast young man with a large mouth and a jink in his nose, mopped his forehead in the stifling heat and grinned gently to himself. Then he sat down and answered Bimbo's letter. And the envelope of the answer was addressed to His Grace the Duke of Ledmonton. Moreover, its contents made that worthy nobleman sit up with a gasp and hurriedly seek his wife.

"Impossible," she said. "Out of the question. Tiny has got 'em again."

It was some two months later that an extremely pretty girl, leading a singularly unpleasant-looking little boy by the hand, walked through one of the many copses which surround Ladbroke Towers. On her face was an expression of utter weariness; in her free hand she carried a book.

Molly Delmont was very near breaking-point. If only that beast of a man would leave her alone she could go on sticking it, but she knew his character far too well by now not to realize the futility of any such hope. Mr. Oliver Samuelson, junior—her present charge's brother —was of the brand that regards a pretty governess as fair game. It was his mother she was afraid of. Only too well did she know that once that lady got an inkling of what was going on she'd be kicked out of the house within an hour. And what on earth was she to do then?

She sat down in a leafy glade, and opening the book at random she began to read mechanically. And it wasn't until she'd finished that a little twisted smile crossed her lips as she realized what she had been reading.

"There are no Prince Charmings to-day, dear. It's only a fairy story."

"What an exceedingly reprehensible statement to make to the young!"

With a little gasp of surprise she swung round—only to gasp again at what she saw. Standing on his head in a clearing in the bushes was one of the largest young men she had ever seen in her life.

"Most reprehensible," he repeated. "I'm surprised at you."

"What's that man doing that for?" demanded Oswald.

"I really don't know, dear," said the girl, sternly repressing a strong desire to laugh. "Do you know you are trespassing?"

"That's why I'm standing on my head."

"But what on earth has that got to do with it?" she cried helplessly.

"Absolutely nothing," he agreed. "Do go on reading."

"But I can't go on reading with you standing on your head. It's ridiculous."

"There I must beg to disagree," he remarked. "I take up no more room this way than any other; I don't spoil the acoustics of the wood; in fact, my position here doesn't affect the situation in the slightest."

"For goodness' sake," cried the girl, beginning to laugh helplessly, "do get the right way up."

"As you will," said the large young man resignedly. In his normal position, he seemed even vaster than before. He was wearing an old shooting-coat and a pair of grey flannel trousers of great antiquity, and as he rose to his feet he picked up a large ash-plant stick. He was without a hat, and the sun striking through the trees glinted on fair, crisp hair. His mouth was big; his nose had a jink in it—but all the girl could notice were his eyes. Big, brown eyes they were, steady and clear, and just at the moment bubbling over with laughter.

"Who on earth are you?" she said at length.

"Prince Charming," he retorted gravely, to see her flush a little and bite her lip.

"That," she said quietly, "is rather impertinent. As I said before, you're trespassing; so do you mind going?"

"Strongly," he answered, sitting down on the grass. "In the first place, I should hate you to think that I meant to be impertinent; in the second, I want to talk to you."

"But I don't know you," she cried.

"I rather anticipated you might say that," he agreed. "Hence my method of introducing myself.   The ordinary common dictates of humanity require that you should satisfy yourself that I'm not insane.   And that will take you a long time.   May I smoke?"

He held out his case to her, but she shook her head.

"Oswald," she called out.   "Don't go too far away."

"His name is Oswald, is it?" said the large young man, lighting a cigarette.   "May I be pardoned for stating that he seems to me a singularly unpleasant child?"

"He's the most abominable little beast I've ever met," answered the girl, and he saw that her eyes had suddenly filled with tears.   "He's———"

She broke off abruptly and rose.

"You must really go away," she said.   "You don't understand."

"That's why I'm not going away," he answered.   "I want to understand."

"He'll sneak to his mother about this—sneak in a beastly sort of way."

"Are you his———"

"I'm his governess," she broke in defiantly. "And if it wasn't that I've got to, I'd sooner beg in the streets than have anything to do with these horrors."

"I like the way you said 'horrors,' " he said, with a smile. "I must make their acquaintance. The Oliver Samuelsons, aren't they?"

"Yes. You know this part of the country, do you?"

"Slightly," he answered gravely. "This is Lord Ladbroke's place, isn't it?"

"Yes. He's abroad. And he let Ladbroke Towers to them for five years. They've been here a year now."

"I gather from your tone that you think that a year too long."

She shrugged her shoulders.

"It's nothing to do with me. They'd be equally horrible wherever they were. But it makes me wild to think of a wonderful old place like this being let to such people."

"Miss Delmont, may I ask for an explanation?"

They both turned round to find a short, stout woman regarding them through lorgnettes.

"Where is Oswald? And who is this person?"

"He was here a moment ago, Mrs. Samuelson," said the girl, flushing, and wondering if her last remark had been heard. "He can't be far away."

"How often have I told you, Miss Delmont, about his getting lost?"

"Not much danger of that," said the large young man gravely. "Anyone finding him would return him at once."

For one moment the lorgnettes quivered. Was it conceivable that this unknown and badly dressed young man intended anything by that remark? But no; she dismissed the idea.

"What are you doing here?" she demanded.

"At the moment, just standing on my feet," he answered. "But I can quite easily stand on my head, if you like. In fact, I prefer it."

"You must be mad," she gasped, as the large young man promptly proceeded to do so.

"Far from it," he answered happily. "Why don't you try it yourself?"

A choking sound came from Molly Delmont, instantly suppressed as the voice she dreaded most in the world came from behind her shoulder.

"Hullo! What's all this? What's that fool doing there?"

The large young man resumed his normal position, and stared at the new-comer. That sudden stiffening of the girl had not escaped his notice, and the reason thereof did not seem hard to find. With eyes in which there was no longer laughter, he took in every detail of the man confronting him—the coarse neck, the hairy hands, the sensual mouth—and what he saw was not good.

"Thought that would bring you to your senses," sneered the other. "You don't mind frightening women, but when a man comes along———" He shrugged his shoulders contemptuously. "Get off this land, or I'll have you run off."

The large young man smiled.

"I'm going. And you're quite right—it was entirely your appearance that brought me this way up. I could see your legs far too well before."

"What the devil do you mean?" snarled the other thickly.

"Your tailor ought to know better," said the large young man placidly. "To send you out in plus-fours is an outrage on public decency, and a probable cause of civil riot."

The next moment he was gone.

"Doubtless somewhat rude," he murmured to himself as he strolled along towards the road. "But how pleasant. Great Heavens! the half of these people hath not been told me."

And then, somehow or other, the Oliver Samuelsons faded from his mind, and the picture of a girl with blue-grey eyes that were filled with tears replaced them.

"So there are no Prince Charmings to-day, aren't there?" He apostrophized a squirrel that was regarding him from a tree. And then he thought of the face he contemplated every morning when shaving. "True, O Queen! I suppose you're right."

He stepped out on to the road, and stood a moment thinking. There remained to be seen the father and daughter, and the large young man was cogitating on the best method of bolting that particular badger when he saw a car come out of the lodge gates some four hundred yards away.

It came rapidly towards him, raising a cloud of dust behind it, and his keen eyes saw at once that a man was sitting beside the driver. It might be or it might not, he reflected, and since from earliest infancy he had always believed in taking a chance, he stepped without further ado into the centre of the road and stood there waving his hands. There came a harsh scraping of brakes and the car pulled up. Whereupon the large young man leant upon the bonnet and realized that the chance had come off. Seated beside the chauffeur was the head of the family of Oliver Samuelsons.

"You were exceeding the speed limit," said the large young man accusingly.

Mr. Oliver Samuelson turned a deep magenta.

"What the——? Who the——?" he spluttered. "Are you in the police?"

"No," conceded the other. "I am not in the police. But, as a law-abiding citizen, I felt impelled to reason

with you.   Once start on the downward path of sin, and
you'd be setting fire to churches next.   It's a fearful
thing to set fire to a church, you know."

"Do you mean to say," howled the infuriated owner
of the car, "that you had the confounded impertinence
to stand in the middle of the road and wave your
arms merely to tell me that I was exceeding the speed
limit?"

"Far from it," said the large young man.   "But this
is my only suiting, and you were making such an infernal
dust.   Besides, I wanted to meet you."

"You wanted to meet me?" spluttered the other.

"And now that I have, I don't ever want to do so
again."

The large young man came round and stood by the
door of the car, and his face was very close to that of Mr.
Oliver Samuelson.

"You miserable medicine-monger," he said grimly,
"how dared you sack Rodgers?   You, who couldn't hit
a sitting cat at five yards."

Then he stepped back.

"Don't let me detain you any more.   If you're catching a train, I hope you've missed it."

He watched the car drive off, and after a while he
strolled on slowly in the same direction.

"I have now seen eighty per cent. of the family," he
murmured thoughtfully.   "I will take the daughter on
trust."

"Well, Tiny—was I right?"

The large young man finished his whisky and soda
and placed the empty glass on the table beside him with
some deliberation.

"My dear old Bimbo," he remarked, "unless with
mine own eyes I had seen them, I would not have believed them possible.   But—and this is the point—if

it was only that, I wouldn't feel justified in taking any
further steps. After all, they cannot help their appearance, and old Samuelson had a perfect right to refuse
to cancel the lease and quit."

"You've heard from your lawyer definitely on that
point?"

"I was in London when the answer arrived," said the
other. "Bimbo—they must go. Alexa, you tell me,
was rude enough to say that I'd got 'em again when you
read her my letter. Well—it's cut and dried: I heard
two days ago. There's gold where I've been, and
workable tin—and it's mine. Even if I'm not a millionaire, I've got ample to keep the place going. And, as
I said before—the Oliver Samuelsons must go."

The Duke of Ledmonton thoughtfully lit a cigarette.

"How do you propose to do it?"

"That, old boy, shall be revealed in due course. But
there's one thing I can tell you now. Alexa and you
will have to assist."

The large young man turned round as he got to the
door.

"Have you seen the perfectly glorious girl with blue-
grey eyes, whose job in life is to look after Oswald?"

"Who on earth is Oswald?" spluttered the other.

But he spoke to an empty room: the large young man
had already departed on his more or less lawful occasions. Not that it mattered much to him whether they
were lawful or not: all that he cared about was that they
should be secret. And so it was with a distinct appearance of stealth that, as dusk was falling, he approached
a certain building hidden in the woods some quarter of
a mile from Ladbroke Towers. It was an old chapel,
which, owing to lack of money, had been allowed to fall
into disrepair.

It was a gloomy spot, and as he opened the door the
air inside struck dank on his face. But the large young

man never hesitated; closing the door carefully behind him, he disappeared into the gloom beside the altar. And then there came a sudden click, and the chapel was empty.

Half an hour later another click might have been heard, as the large young man, with a faint smile on his face, stepped back into the chapel. And then with startling abruptness the smile faded and was replaced by something very different.

"You brute; you brute—let me go!"

"Not much, my dear," came in a coarse, triumphant voice. "You're altogether too pretty. I'm going to have a kiss."

Which, unfortunately for the heir of the Oliver Samuelsons, was where he was wrong. What he did have was a vague sort of feeling that a thing like a steam-hammer had met his face; a further vague sort of feeling that the back of his head was being used as a pile-driver on a stone floor—and then oblivion.

"Good Heavens! You haven't killed him, have you?"

Molly Delmont gazed at the motionless figure on the floor, and then looked up, a little shyly, at the man who stood beside her.

"I fear not," said her companion gravely. "I think his jaw is broken, but that's all."

"Where did you come from?" cried the girl.

"I told you this morning that fairy tales were not extinct," said the large young man with a smile. "I just appeared because you wanted me."

For a moment or two he stared straight into her eyes —stared until hers, misty and shining in the dim light, fell before his.

"I don't understand," she said a little nervously. "What are you doing here?"

"What are you?" he countered.

"I often come here," she answered. "And this evening that brute followed me. What are we going to do about him?"

"Leave him where he is to cool," he said calmly. He took her by the arm and gently forced her towards the door. "I don't particularly want him to recognize me when he comes to—so let's go."

"But who are you?" she insisted.

"Well, you didn't like Prince Charming," he answered gravely. "So shall we cite another fairy story—Beauty and the Beast?"

"Don't be ridiculous," she said, and the large young man saw the colour rise in her cheeks. "I do wish you'd tell me what you were doing in there."

"I will, if you promise not to pass it on."

"Of course I promise," she said eagerly.

"I was seeking a method of ridding the locality of the Oliver Samuelsons."

"In that chapel?" she said incredulously, and the large young man nodded.

"In that chapel," he repeated.

"Well, you'll never do it," answered the girl. "They got a letter only the other day from some lawyer in London asking them if they would cancel the lease, and they were furious. The old man is as stubborn as a mule. And, anyway"—she added curiously—"what on earth has it got to do with you?"

"What do you bet I don't do it?" he said, ignoring her last question.

"Anything you like."

"I shall hold you to that," he said quickly. "And now I'm going. But don't forget one thing. If that swine in there gives you any more trouble, or if you want me at any time, drop me a line to—to——"

He hesitated for a moment or two.

"To Ely View Cottage," he concluded. "It's on the

Duke of Ledmonton's place. Address it care of Mr. Rodgers."

"Is that the man Mr. Samuelson sacked?" she said.

"It is. The Duke let him have a spare cottage on his place."

"You know Mr. Rodgers?"

"Very well indeed," said the large young man.

"And that's why you're doing this. To pay out the Samuelsons." With a sudden little nervous movement she put her hand on his arm. "Do be careful. I'd like to see them paid out; they deserve it. But they're vindictive—and if they find out—— Oh! you see they've got money, and you haven't—— And it's money that counts."

"Not in fairy stories," he interrupted gravely. "Then —it's only love."

And before she could think of anything further to say, he was gone.

Exactly how the fact that the Duke and Duchess of Ledmonton would accept an invitation to dinner, should one be received from the Samuelson family, became known to Mrs. Samuelson is one of life's little mysteries. Perhaps it was due to a conversation between the large young man and little Mrs. Carlton, which caused that charming lady to laugh immoderately and then go and call at Ladbroke Towers. Certain it is that some three weeks after the use of Mr. Samuelson junior's head as a pile-driver, invitations had gone forth far and wide requesting the county to dine, and, to Molly Delmont's stunned surprise, they had all been accepted.

"It's amazing," she said to the large young man, whom she had happened to meet—not, strangely enough, for the first time—in the ruined chapel. "The whole bunch are coming to-night."

"It should be an amusing evening," he remarked gravely. "How is our friend's jaw?"

"He's been in London ever since you hit him," she said happily. "But I have no doubt he'll be back this afternoon. And, incidentally, what about your bet now? This dinner will be the culminating moment of their lives. They have arrived. The only way to get rid of them after this will be to burn down the house."

"You have got the most angelic dimple," said the large young man earnestly. "But apart from that, I shall be there."

"You'll be there? What do you mean?"

"Fairy story again," he answered. "The invisible man."

And certainly there was no sign of him that evening when the guests had assembled in the hall, which was hardly surprising in view of the fact that Molly had written out the invitations herself. But he was such an amazing individual that she half-expected suddenly to see him standing on his head at the top of the stairs, or popping up through the table at dinner.

He intrigued her so vastly, did that large young man. Rodgers' nephew, so the worthy gamekeeper had told her, but still—— Of all the perfect dears she had ever met——!

What made her feel so nervous was the fear that he would do something rash. He was just the type who wouldn't care, and she'd hate it if anything happened to him. And it was as she reached that stage in her reflections that a loud, raucous laugh came from somewhere up in the ceiling. A sudden silence settled on the table, and everyone peered up into the dimness of the lofty dining-room.

"Good evening, Duchess," came in a harsh, metallic voice. "How are the corns to-night? Samuelson's Certain Cure works wonders. Soak the feet in hot water, at the same time consuming one of Samuelson's Perfect Pink Powders.''

Molly stole an aghast look at the Duchess, to find to her amazement that she was apparently shaking with uncontrollable laughter.

"I would like to take this opportunity," continued the voice, "of bringing to the notice of this august company all my wonderful medicines. As a family we admit frankly that our habits are awful and our appearance vile. That, however, does not alter the fact that we can eradicate eczema, intimidate itch, and paralyse pimples. In proof of this, ladies and gentlemen, a small box of my omnipotent ointment will be presented free, gratis, and for nothing, to each of you on your departure to-night. I thank you for your kind attention."

"Good evening, Duchess. How are the corns?"

"Good God!" howled Mr. Samuelson. "It's starting again."

The next day every servant was sacked: that evening at dinner, when only the family were present, the most lurid revelations descended upon their heads from the ceiling.

The following day an army of workmen appeared with orders to discover the accursed thing or perish in the attempt. Hardly were their ladders in position when the family lawyer, whose golf still maintained its erstwhile brilliance, was announced.

"You will bear in mind, Mr. Samuelson," he said suavely, "that I cannot allow any tearing down of walls. I should regard that as a structural alteration, which would automatically cancel your lease."

The day after, the workmen having departed, Mr. Oliver Samuelson locked the dining-room door, and ordained that they should feed elsewhere. That afternoon, from far and near, came callers in ones and twos, in threes and fours, demanding with oaths and curses, with prayers and blandishments, to be allowed to hear the ghost. And even as they paused outside the door came the voice, muffled, it is true, but quite distinct: "Have you tried my purple pills?"

Then the papers got hold of it, and reporters descended in hordes. A prominent member of the Society for Psychical Research gave it as his considered opinion that it was Mr. Samuelson's ectoplasm giving tongue from the roof—or words to that effect.

And finally, Mrs. Samuelson's nerve broke. She flatly refused to remain one day longer in the house. And her progeny backed her. It was the end. Beaten all along the line, the Oliver Samuelsons returned to their pristine obscurity, and with their departure silence came to the dining-room. No more could one hear the merits of the omnipotent ointment extolled: no·longer were the habits of the Samuelson family pointedly discussed.

The prominent member of the Society for Psychical Research claimed that it proved his point: the reporters denounced the whole thing as an advertising stunt that had misfired: the county breathed freely again: and the vast young man emerged one morning from the ruined chapel bearing in his arms a gramophone and several records.

"There used," he explained to Molly Delmont, who was waiting for him outside, "to be a musicians' gallery in the dining-room, from which a secret passage ran to the chapel. The gallery has been removed, but the passage still remains. And that's that."

"But how did you know?" she asked.

"I was sort of brought up on the place, you see," he said gravely. "But don't let's worry about that. All that matters is that I've won my bet. And, you remember, don't you, what the wager was for?"

"No, I don't," she said, looking away.

"Anything I liked," he answered softly.

And suddenly she found both her hands in his.

"Molly, you know what I want."

"But, my dear," she cried, "it's madness. I haven't got a penny. What should we live on?"

"Don't be basely utilitarian," he laughed. "I love you. That's all that matters in a fairy story. Except one thing. You've got to love me."

"Idiot," she whispered.

"Do you, darling, do you?"

"Of course, we're both qualifying for an asylum," she said helplessly. "But I do: I can't help it. I take back what I said about there being no Prince Charmings."

And still he looked at her gravely, but with a wonderful light in his eyes.

"You darling," he said. "You darling. Molly—haven't you guessed? I'm not Rodgers' nephew. And it wasn't for his sake that I drove those people into outer darkness, but for yours and mine. We must have somewhere to live. And I thought the old place would do."

"So you're Lord Ladbroke," she said, slowly.

"Terrible thing to have to admit," he answered. "But I am. Moreover, we have a custom in our family. Every Ladbroke carries his bride through the front door when she first arrives—and kisses her. I've just invented a new one. In future, every Ladbroke will carry the girl he is going to marry through the chapel door—and kiss her. The custom starts now."

"But, my dear," she whispered. "I don't even know your name."

"Just Beauty and the Beast, darling. Though most people call me Tiny."

Half an hour later the new custom was still being rehearsed.

XVIII CYNTHIA DELMORTON'S MISTAKE

CYNTHIA DELMORTON was a singularly beautiful girl, and for all I know is so still. Her
figure was perfect: her face almost flawless. There
were critics who said that her nose was a trifle too long:
there were others, on the contrary, who denied the fact
with oaths and curses. But seeing that she had been
painted by three of London's leading artists who one
and all declared that she was the most perfect thing they
had ever seen, the nose question cannot have been very
serious.

Her origin was a little obscure. She lived in a
charming house in South Audley Street with an elderly
lady who rejoiced in the name of Aunt Hester. Moreover, she undoubtedly had money—lots of it. There
was a rumour that the late Mr. Delmorton had really
been Smithson and Co., Ltd.—one of those charitable
firms whose aim in life is to ease other people's financial
troubles by lending them money on note of hand alone.
And if such a base rumour over the lovely Cynthia could
possibly be true, she had certainly possessed the most
notorious blood-sucker in London as her father—a
man without a tinge of mercy or a thought of com-
passion.

The fact however remained, that she was extremely
wealthy. Which was a far more important matter than
the method by which the money had been obtained.
And the result had been that divers men of all ages and
positions had laid their hands and hearts at her disposal.
Some of them had been genuinely infatuated by her
beauty: others by her bank balance. But one and all
of them, when their offer was turned down, thanked
almighty Heaven for their escape. Except one poor
boob, who blew out his brains. . . . For the beautiful

Cynthia had one very unpleasant trait, which never manifested itself until the last moment. She would lead a man on until he was wellnigh crazy—and then laugh in his face.

Of course when the man she did decide to marry appeared, there would be no laughter. At least if there was it would be carefully concealed. But so far that lucky being had not arrived. And when he did he would have to be something pretty special. Cynthia Delmorton was essentially not one of those who—to paraphrase the well-known line—had danced with Princes and kept the common touch. Nothing under an Earl would be good enough for her final choice—and not a modern creation at that. But until that blissful day arrived, she saw no reason why good-looking men should not go wild about her, and throng her charming drawing-room.

And then one spring that complete disrespecter of persons, influenza, descended upon the house. Within an hour so did Sir William Harbottle, London's most fashionable and futile doctor. He consumed a glass of port and ate a biscuit, and with deadly accuracy diagnosed the disease. He continued to descend at ten guineas a time, more port and more biscuits, and finally pronounced his lovely patient convalescent.

"But, my dear young lady," he announced as he stroked her arm, "we require setting up. We are a little run down."

The "we," needless to state, was a pleasing conceit of Sir William's: no one regarding his ample presence need have panicked unduly.

"We will take a sea voyage."

"Dear Sir William," she murmured. "A sea voyage?"

"Where the bracing ozone will set us up again. Restore our wasted tissues: remove our lassitude. And then we shall return fresh and invigorated for the ardours of June in London."

And the more she thought of the idea the more she liked it. Up to date her sea voyages had consisted of occupying a cabin whilst crossing the Channel: this was going to be something quite different. Some new frocks: a flirtation or two—there was bound to be some man on board who would fill the bill: and a real rest cure.

Aunt Hester proved the first obstacle. For that usually malleable woman, having heard of Cynthia's decision, stuck in her toes and jibbed definitely. Nothing would induce her to go on the sea. She loathed it and detested it: she was always seasick—and, in short, rather than do so she would resign her position as Cynthia's companion.

"If you must have someone with you, my dear," she said, "why not ask Marjorie. She's a nice girl: she won't get in your way and you'll be doing her a real kindness as well."

Cynthia cogitated. Yes: Marjorie Blackton would do. Better perhaps than Aunt Hester. Her idea of a companion was what most people would describe as an unpaid maid, and if her Aunt was continually seasick she would be more nuisance than she was worth.

"Write and ask her," she said thoughtfully. "Tell her that as far as clothes are concerned, she can send any reasonable bill in to me."

Marjorie Blackton was an old school friend of hers. At least she was the only girl at the very expensive place at which Cynthia had been "finished" whom she did not actually dislike. For even at that age she neither loved nor was loved by her own sex. But for some strange reason Marjorie bestowed on her one of those peculiar adorations which arise and flourish in girls' schools.

Strange, because it would have been impossible to find two more totally dissimilar characters. Marjorie was everything that her idol was not. Unselfish, utterly lovable, frank and open, she was the exact antithesis of Cynthia. And the latter, though slightly flattered for a time, soon took advantage of the state of affairs. She practically made the younger girl her fag. It was "Marjorie, do this" and "Marjorie, fetch that," from the beginning of term till the end. And the same relationship had continued after they left school, though necessarily not to the same extent.

Then quite suddenly Mr. Blackton lost most of his money, and for a while Cynthia had debated whether to ask Marjorie to come as her companion. As far as she was capable of affection for anybody she was fond of her, but having given the matter due consideration she had come to the conclusion that an older woman would be more suitable from every point of view. And so she dismissed Marjorie from her scheme of things, as was her custom when a person was no longer of use to her. Now she proposed to bring her back temporarily into that scheme: a proposal which met with the other girl's delighted approval as soon as she heard of it.

And so, some three weeks later the two of them stepped into the boat-train at Waterloo bound for Southampton. The most luxurious cabin in the S.S. *Ortolan*, 12,000 tons, of the Union Steamship Line had been engaged: a number of immaculately clothed young men, who had pleaded in vain to be allowed to accompany them as far as the ship, clustered round the carriage door.

"Now you must all promise to be good while I am away," said Cynthia impartially. "And when I come back in June . . ."

It was at that moment that the train began to move, but she managed that every member of the group should think that her unfinished sentence was addressed to him personally.

"Thank God that's over, my dear," she said languidly. "What a bore they are. Do give me my rug, will you?"

She looked up with a sudden frown: a man was standing in the door leading into the corridor. Moreover, he seemed to be on the point of depositing a weather-beaten suit-case on one of the spare seats.

"This carriage is engaged," she remarked haughtily.

The man turned round with a smile.

"Am I to understand," he said, "that you are the proud possessor of six tickets? I'm really very sorry but this is the only compartment in the train that isn't full."

"I gave orders that I required a carriage to myself," she said with her most freezing look.

"Dear me," he answered politely. "If it wasn't for the fact that you can't give orders for anything of the sort, I should say that someone had blundered. However, what would you like me to do? Stand in the corridor, or go into the guard's van?"

"If you persist in intruding," she said icily, "I would prefer that you do so in silence."

"Why—sure," he remarked genially. "Doubtless we shall have lots of time for conversation before we get to the Cape."

He buried himself behind a newspaper, leaving Cynthia gasping. The Cape? Was this odious mortal going to the Cape with her? True he was young, and of pleasing appearance, but he must clearly be put in his place and punished. And she was an adept at doing both.

It was at that moment that she got her second shock. Marjorie was undoubtedly smiling at the man behind her magazine; the man was grinning at Marjorie behind his paper. She knew it: she had done it so often herself with other men.

But what she could do was one thing: what Marjorie could do was quite another. For her companion and a strange man to indulge in mutual smiles at her expense was a state of affairs not to be tolerated for an instant. And the small fact that she was completely wrong—that all that had happened was, that Marjorie suddenly seeing him grinning at her had involuntarily smiled back just because it was good to be alive—cut no ice. She wouldn't have believed it anyhow; but then Cynthia Delmorton's joy in living lay, not in just life but merely in what she could get out of it.

They were running through Eastleigh when the man spoke again. Five times during the journey had Marjorie got up to do something for Cynthia—and three out of the five times she could far more easily have done it for herself. And five times during the journey had an amused and faintly contemptuous glint come into the man's eyes. But he remained buried behind his paper until the train began to slacken, when he folded it up.

"Would you care to sit at my table?" he asked gravely. "I'm the second officer, and I generally manage to collect a cheery bunch."

For a moment Cynthia stared at him speechlessly; the second officer. . . .

"Surprised at my not being on board, I suppose," he went on cheerfully. "Pretty exceptional, I agree. But the old man is a sportsman, and my business was sudden and urgent. However, would you like me to fix it up about the table?"

"I think it would be very nice," said Cynthia quietly, and Marjorie glanced at her in some trepidation. She knew that tone of old—knew what it portended. She knew that before the end of the voyage this poor young man was going to wish he had never been born. And it was a shame. . . .

But she couldn't warn him, and he rushed into the trap.

"Splendid. I'll arrange it. But I warn you from what I hear we're going to have it a bit choppy as far as Madeira."

They did: and Marjorie for the first time began to see Cynthia in her true light. She was loyal clean through: she tried to make excuses—but the plain fact emerged that for selfishness her employer was in a class by herself. True, she was ill—slightly, for a couple of days; but until they anchored off Funchal Cynthia treated her and the stewardess like a couple of slaves. Then she was graciously pleased to emerge from her cabin, and show herself for the first time to the admiring gaze of her fellow-passengers.

"Well, well, how are you?"

A cheerful voice hailed the lovely invalid, and she looked up from her deck-chair to see their travelling companion. He looked different in uniform; in fact honesty compelled her to admit that he looked extremely nice in uniform. So she gave him one of her most bewitching smiles, and confessed that she felt a little better.

"Good," he cried. "We shall be dancing to-night, and you must play a bit of deck-tennis. Miss Blackton is a nailer at it."

He moved off and she watched him cursing four Portuguese lace vendors for blocking the gangway—watched him through narrowed eyes. How that young man was going to suffer before she'd finished with him! And what a lucky thing it was that he was really quite presentable; it made things so much pleasanter for her.

"My dear! that is Cynthia Delmorton. You must have seen her pictures in the *Tatler* and *Sketch*."

The words carried to her during a sudden lull in the raucous babel around her, and a sense of pleasant well-being stole over her. Yes; she was Cynthia Delmorton. . . . And the sun was shining, and the water was blue, and the brown-skinned boys diving off the deck for threepenny bits thrown into the water amused her. Also there was an extremely bumptious and conceited young man to punish. She smiled slightly to herself. . . . Fancy wasting her time on an officer in the Merchant Service. Still, she would do it quickly, and then turn to worthier game.

"Mr. Fraser," she called gently as he passed—Marjorie had found out his name—"won't you come and cheer me up? Besides, I want to apologize. I'm afraid I was rather rude to you in the train."

"Rude!" he laughed. "Not a bit. You were just natural. Sorry I can't stop now, but I've got to see a man about a dog in the smoking-room. You shall apologize at lunch . . . You're sitting next to me."

And with that he was gone, leaving Cynthia Delmorton utterly speechless. Never in the course of her life had any man spoken to her like that before. "See a man about a dog in the smoking-room." When she had invited him to sit by her . . . "Not rude: only natural." Was the man mad?

He certainly showed no signs of insanity at lunch. He included her breezily in the conversation; chaffed Marjorie Blackton, who had been ashore and done the time-honoured toboggan trip over the cobbles from Terreiro da Lucta, and finally challenged her to a game of deck-quoits later on.

"When you're a little stronger," he remarked, "you must play tennis."

And there was a twinkle in his eyes as he spoke, the sort of twinkle a parent might have when dealing with a fractious child.

And so it went on. The trouble about the man was that he seemed impervious to snubs. He had a hide like a rhinoceros; delicate satire flew off him like water off a duck's back. Of course he missed the point of it all—that was the reason. Completely lacking in breeding, he was unable to understand her subtle irony.

And Marjorie, who understood it only too well, felt her heart grow sick within her. At last her final delusions about Cynthia were gone. Coming out to Madeira they had began to totter; by the time they were crossing the line the crash was complete. Thank Heavens! Jim Fraser didn't appreciate the position of affairs: that was her only compensation.

And then one evening something occurred which brought her up with a start. She was sitting out by herself on the boat-deck, in the shadow of one of the funnels, when two people passed her. They didn't see her, but she recognized them at once. . . . They paused between two of the boats, not three yards away from her, and she heard Cynthia's voice.

"You really are the most attractive man, Jim."

Marjorie could have screamed. It was too cruel. Surely, surely she needn't carry her vindictiveness to such a point as that. The poor devil had done her no harm: she cared not the snap of a finger about him. But just to gratify her petty spite, she was going to lead him on—and then shake with laughter in his face. Marjorie half rose; then with a little gasp that was half a sob she crouched back again. For Cynthia was in his arms.

With a sick numbness she watched him kiss her: heard Cynthia's low triumphant laugh: heard her whispered "Darling."

Then she was gone, leaving him standing by the boats. For a second she paused by the top of the companion, and her words floated back—"There is always to-morrow."

For a little while he stood there; then suddenly with a little start he saw Marjorie. He came over to her slowly, and sat down beside her.

"You saw," he said quietly. "I'm sorry."

"So am I," she answered gravely. "Very sorry. Oh! Mr. Fraser," she went on impulsively, "don't think me impertinent and foolish. But I—oh! it's so difficult to say."

He was staring at her steadily, and she went stumbling on bravely.

"You see—I know Cynthia. And I don't want to be disloyal to her—after all, she's paying everything for me. But please, please be careful. She's—she's different to most girls. She's been spoilt, I suppose—and she doesn't mean to be cruel."

"No," he agreed quietly. "It's just natural."

But she hardly heard.

"She just plays with men. . . . And then she turns them down without a thought. Can't you see—oh! can't you see? I don't want to hurt your feelings, but you must realize that she has the world at her feet, and . . . and . . ."

"And therefore is hardly likely to pay serious attention to the second officer of the good ship *Ortolan*," he said, lighting a cigarette.

She looked at him surprised: he seemed singularly calm about it.

"That's why I am so sorry you saw," he concluded.

"But I don't want you to be hurt," she cried. "And you will be."

"Why don't you want me to be hurt?" he said gently.

"Oh! because . . . Of course, I don't. I hate to see anybody hurt."

"You dear ! You dear girl." And now she was

staring at him in genuine amazement, and dimly realizing that both her hands were in his. "I'm only sorry you saw it, Marjorie, because I can't now do what I would like to. At least not at this moment."

And then he too was gone, and after a while Marjorie got up a little stiffly and went below. What on earth had he meant?

"My dear," said Cynthia, "too humorous! Our worthy pachyderm has kissed me. Up on the boat-deck."

"I saw you," she answered dully. "Oh! Cynthia—can't you leave him alone?"

"What on earth do you mean?" cried the other. And then she suddenly burst into a peal of laughter. "Why, I believe you're in love with him yourself."

"I am," said Marjorie gravely, and started to undress.

Of course this was too much of a scream altogether: it really added relish to the jest. That Marjorie—demure little Marjorie—should have fallen in love with the second officer was too exquisite.

"My dear," she cried, "but this is Romance with a capital R. Does he reciprocate your feelings?"

"Of course he doesn't," answered the other, flushing. "And, Cynthia—you won't say anything, will you?"

"My dear—trust me. Perish the thought that I should spoil love's young dream. But I must insist on being allowed to deal with the dear man just once. I'll let him down mildly, I promise you, but he has been exceedingly rude to me—and he's got to take his gruel like a good boy."

"But I'm sure he didn't mean it, Cynthia," said Marjorie miserably.

"Then he's got to learn. And anyway, my dear," she went on with a smile, "you have the remedy in your own hands. Get him to take *you* up on the boat-deck to-morrow night."

"You know I don't stand a chance if you're about,"
said Marjorie simply. "Anyway, I'm nothing to him.
But I don't think you're playing the game. He's—
he's not the type of man . . . It's not fair to a man like
him, Cynthia: it's not fair."

"Then he had better not go and see people about
dogs, my dear, when I've asked him to come and talk
to me," said the other softly. "I don't like men who
do that. Besides, he must be trained—if you're going
to marry him."

She got into her bunk and opened a book, and with
a little shiver, though the night was tropical, Marjorie
followed her example. And when at last she did fall
asleep, she got no rest. For she dreamed without cessation—dreams in which she saw Cynthia, gloating and
devilish, and a white-faced sobbing man—a man she
tried to comfort, but who always turned away from
her.

It was the day after that a piece of information arrived
in the Wireless Bulletin, which for nearly six hours
annoyed Cynthia thoroughly. Marjorie saw it first,
just as she was going in to breakfast, and thought no
more about it. The news that the Earl of Axminster
had been killed in a motor accident, interested her but
little more than the fact that the French exchange was
129.47. It was otherwise with Cynthia. Not that the
death of that well-known and sporting nobleman at the
early age of fifty-six distressed her in the slightest, but
merely because it made her wish that she had acted
otherwise. And it is annoying when one cannot rectify
a mistake. She might now have been the Countess of
Axminster. And she wasn't. Which was a distressing thought—most distressing. Had not Hedderton
—his eldest son—sat in her pocket for a complete season? In fact she had almost—but not quite—become
Viscountess Hedderton. And if she had, Hedderton

would not have gone his fool journey to Central Africa, picked up some horrible tropical disease and died. Undoubtedly most annoying.

She recalled that last evening perfectly. She had known he was coming for her answer, and during the afternoon she had finally made up her mind—balancing the points for and against. And the result had been against. Hedderton's father, she had decided, was more than likely to live another thirty years, and that was too long to wait even for one of the oldest titles in England. The fact that he was utterly infatuated with her was his misfortune and not her fault. And so without the smallest tinge of compunction she turned him down. She could see him now—white-faced and stammering . . . He couldn't quite understand: he'd been so sure . . . He had kissed her so often . . . And she had laughed softly.

"My dear man," she had said, "if I married all the men who have kissed me, I'd want an hotel to stow them in."

And he had failed to see the cheapness of the remark because, poor devil, he was still infatuated. Instead he had gone off to Africa and died. Not four months previously . . . Most annoying . . . In fact when she went in to lunch she was feeling thoroughly irritable.

Jim Fraser was already there, and he bowed to her gravely. He was looking strained about the eyes, she noticed: all through lunch he hardly spoke. Hooked already: hardly worth powder and shot. Still in her present mood she felt like making someone suffer, so she gave him her sweetest and most alluring smile.

"I'm feeling terribly depressed," she murmured. "Poor Lord Axminster is dead. Such a charming man."

A woman opposite looked at her with interest.

"Of course you knew him well, Miss Delmorton."

"Naturally," remarked Cynthia languidly. "You see, Hedderton and I were very great friends."

Marjorie squirmed, and when Jim Fraser leaned forward with a puzzled frown she could have screamed. She guessed what was coming.

"Hedderton," he said. "I don't quite follow."

"Viscount Hedderton," she explained politely. "Axminster's son. They have different names, you know."

"I see," he answered. "I suppose that is done to make it harder."

She smiled, and glanced round the table.

"What funny ideas you have, Mr. Fraser. Yes—Hedderton died in Africa."

"And who is the heir?" asked someone.

"I really don't know," she answered. "He had no brothers. There was a cousin of sorts, I believe."

She relapsed suddenly into silence; what was it Hedderton had said on that point? It was a cousin—a very charming fellow, but a rolling stone. Unmarried. Of course he might be impossible, but it was worth while bearing in mind against her return to London. She would write Aunt Hester a letter from Cape Town telling her to make inquiries. . . . It would be funny if, after all, she did pull it off. The thought of it put her in quite a good temper again.

"Don't forget you promised to show me the Southern Cross to-night, Mr. Fraser," she said as he rose from his seat.

"Am I likely to," he answered fervently.

And across the table her eyes met Marjorie's mockingly. Really life wasn't so bad after all: it had its humorous side.

But it was a side that was taxed to the uttermost that evening. The pachyderm was so terribly intense and gauche. And he would persist in harking back to Lord Axminster's death.

"It must be wonderful," he said humbly, "to know all those people who are just names to us, as intimately as you do."

He was holding her hand at the time, and gazing at her adoringly.

"I very nearly married Hedderton," she said softly. "But I'm glad I didn't—now."

"And if you had," he puzzled it out, "you would be the—the Earless of Axminster."

She gave a delighted gurgle of laughter.

"Countess," she corrected him. "But then, you see —the poor fellow is dead."

"But I'm sure he wouldn't have gone to Africa if you had married him," he said gravely.

"Well, if he hadn't and was alive, and I had married him—then I should be the Earless of Axminster. You delicious person."

"And instead of that," he cried eagerly, "you're going to be . . ."

Really, she'd die of suppressed laughter in a second. The pachyderm was on the verge of proposing: she looked round to see if by any chance Marjorie was about. This was going to be a thing too good to be missed.

"What am I going to be?" she whispered.

"Cynthia—wouldn't you rather be my wife than the Countess of Axminster?"

That finished it: self-control could stand it no longer. She burst into a peal of laughter: then she pulled herself together. The thing had become a bore; so she'd punish the pachyderm now and finish with it.

"This," she said, as soon as she had recovered herself sufficiently to speak, "is the funniest thing that has ever occurred to me. My poor dear young man, are you mad? Do you really imagine, even for one second, that I should marry you?" Laughter again overcame her.

"But you deserved a little lesson, you know. As a matter of fact I intended to give you a longer one, but I couldn't help laughing. You were so supremely ridiculous."

Once more she began to shake.

"No, Mr. Fraser, I am afraid that I must decline the riotous future you offer me. I feel it would be too much for my nerves. But as a reward for having made me laugh, I'll tell you a secret. Put the excellent alternative you gave me before Marjorie. . . . Not that the poor dear is ever likely to be Countess of anything, but still . . ."

She rose with a smile—a smile which suddenly faded from her face. For this uncouth boor was lying back in his deck-chair, literally holding his sides.

"Rich," he almost sobbed. "Not to say ripe and fruity. You're quite right, my dear woman; we've hurried matters. This jest would have stood another three days."

"What on earth do you mean?" she said.

And then he, too, rose to his feet, and stood facing her.

"Listen to me, Cynthia Delmorton," he said quietly. "In the course of my wanderings round the globe I've met some pretty rotten women. You're just about the rottenest."

"How dare you!"

In her stunned rage she could hardly get the words out.

"You're going to hear one or two home truths now," he went on calmly. "You're a calculating, mercenary snob—and you killed Hedderton as surely as if you'd shot him yourself. Only no jury, unfortunately, could convict you. I happened to see him the night before he left for Africa, poor devil."

"Will you kindly take me straight to the captain?" she said icily. "I can only conclude that you're drunk, and I wish to make a complaint."

"Certainly," he answered. "What are you going to tell him? That I was drunk last night, too—when I kissed you?"

For a moment or two she stared at him white and rigid with rage. He had got her, and she knew it: this common man had beaten her at her own game. Why he had done it was beyond her: her brain was still too dazed at the sudden turning of the tables to think clearly.

"You set out to teach me a lesson." He was speaking again. "I fully intended that you should. Your only miscalculation was that I had already determined to teach you one—one that you richly deserved. But I admit that I never even dreamed that the lesson would prove quite so subtly successful until this morning. And I'm profoundly sorry it has. I was very fond of my uncle."

"Your uncle," she stammered. "What do you mean?"

"There was a cousin of sorts, I believe," he said gravely. "There was, and—is. And he happens to be the second officer of the *Ortolan*."

"You mean," she almost screamed, "that you're Lord Axminster?"

"Precisely," he answered. "And since you have mercifully refused my invitation to become my Earless, I think we might conclude the interview. You see, I want to follow your advice and put the alternative I gave you in front of Marjorie . . . Er—good night. Oh! and the captain's cabin is the fourth from this end . . . It's the big one . . . And incidentally—one other small point. Had I not been perfectly certain that you didn't know who I was, I should never have risked proposing. The danger of your acceptance would have been too great. Still, it was kind of you to explain about us having different names."

A moment later he was alone: Cynthia Delmorton still retained sufficient thinking capacity to realize that, if she was going to have hysterics, her cabin was the most suitable place. For a while he stood looking after her: then half-consciously he turned and stared over the water towards Africa.

"Yes, old man," he muttered, "she killed you. And I loved you. Life's a funny thing."

Then with a faint smile on his lips, he strolled down to the main deck. They were dancing, and he stood in the smoking-room door watching. Life, indeed, was a funny thing. And then he saw her, coming towards him with a startled look on her face.

"What on earth has happened to Cynthia?" she cried. "She's in the most extraordinary condition."

"Biting the bedclothes," he said lazily. "Splendid. I asked her a question, you see, and she got the answer wrong. I asked her if she would sooner be my wife or Countess of Axminster."

"Jim—you proposed. But I don't understand. Did she refuse you?"

"My dear," he cried, "you don't suppose I'd be as pleased as I am if she'd accepted me. And now I want to ask you the same question. . . ."

And then suddenly he grew serious.

"Marjorie—Marjorie, darling, come up on the boat-deck. I don't make a hobby of this, my dear—and there's a lot you don't understand. But I haven't got time to explain it to you now—not until you've answered that question. Will you marry me?"

"Jim—you're mad," she whispered. "And you can't propose in the smoking-room."

"Can't I? I've just done it. But come up above and I'll do it again."

And she went. And she stayed. And an hour later he still hadn't explained; explanations are tedious things. In fact it wasn't until the following morning that she thought about the explanation, and then for a while she couldn't grasp it.

For Jim wasn't at breakfast, and a note lay on her plate. She tore open the envelope, and read the contents.

"Second Officer Jim Fraser presents his compliments to the future Countess of Axminster, and trusts that the beautiful Miss Delmorton is not still biting the bed-clothes. He further solicits her company at the eleven o'clock issue of beef tea.

"P.S. You're an adorable darling. JIM."

XIX   THE ELEVENT H   H O U R

"DANGEROUS things—Primo Packs," remarked the nondescript man to me with a faint smile.

I was focussing my camera for that oft-taken photograph of the Castle of Chillon with the Dents du Midi in the background, and I stared at him in mild surprise.

"What on earth do you mean?" I said. "Why— dangerous?"

"Take your photo," he answered. "The light is just right. And then, if you have the time and would care to listen I'll tell you how the use of a Primo Pack very nearly cost an innocent man his life."

It sounded good to me, and I told him so. A casual hotel acquaintance, he had strolled with me along the shore of the Lake of Geneva that morning. Quite a nice fellow, though a little dull, was the impression he had given me; and I remember I wondered as I lit my pipe whether he belonged to that portion of humanity that can tell a story or the other.

"They were a comparatively new innovation at the time when it happened," he began. "The ordinary rolls, of course, were well known, and the plate—so cumbrous and heavy for the average amateur—was the only alternative for most people. I mention that fact, because to-day there would be but little possibility of a similar tragedy occurring. The mechanism of the film pack is common property.

"With which preamble I'll get down to it. The first character I will introduce to you is Sir John Brayling fifteenth baronet. In many ways he was quite a decent fellow, and yet he was never popular. Partially, perhaps, because, though he lived in the centre of a sporting county, he didn't care about sport. An occasional day with a gun was his limit! the rest of his time he devoted to photography. In addition he was apt to be a bit morose; if he gave a dinner-party at Brayling House it was even money that he would sit in almost unbroken silence all through the meal. Which cannot be said to make for the gaiety of nations.

"I have mentioned photography as being his obsession: he had another—his wife. And small blame to him. Hester Brayling was the most gloriously attractive woman. She was considerably younger than he was—fifteen years to be exact, and she possessed every quality that he lacked. She rode magnificently, and played tennis and golf better than most. Also she was brimming over with *joie de vivre*.

"In her way she was undoubtedly very fond of her husband, but her affection was not comparable with his. He simply idolized the ground she walked on, and the great grief of his life was that there were no children. And as they had been married seven years it rather looked as if there never would be.

"It was when she was twenty-nine that Ronald Vane came on the scene. He was a man in the early thirties —good-looking, wealthy and a bachelor. He had taken a neighbouring house, and every mother of daughters for miles around sat up and took notice. Quite legitimately, too: Ronald Vane was one of the most delightful men I have ever met."

The nondescript man smiled as he lit a cigarette.

"Quite right," he said. "They did. I was down there a good deal at the time, and I watched the affair developing under my nose. Vane sat in her pocket out hunting: used to motor her over to play golf: danced with her just as often as the dictates of society would allow. But—and I want to make this clear—that was all. Vane was as straight a man as ever lived: so was she—if I may be pardoned the Irishism.

"Now it happened that I was a fairly privileged person. I'd known Hester since she was a child, and one day I seized a suitable opportunity to talk to her. Foolish, perhaps, but I was afraid of what was going to be the result. So I tackled her point blank on the subject.

"She looked at me quite steadily and shrugged her shoulders.

" 'What am I to do, Bill?' she said. 'I'm in love with Ronald: he's in love with me. One can't help a thing like that: it just happens. But there's nothing more to it than that I can assure you.'

" 'That's all right, my dear,' I answered, 'but how long is that state of affairs going to continue? I don't want to appear an interfering busybody, but, situated as you two are, only a miracle from Heaven can prevent John finding out sooner or later. Don't forget that every mother around here has already visualized Ronald as a prospective son-in-law. And it isn't going to be long before one of them finds it her duty to acquaint John.'

"She stared out of the window in silence for a while. Then—'What do you advise?'

"I laughed.

" 'My dear,' I said, 'I may be a fool, but I'm not a damned fool. I'd sooner keep my breath. But as a plain statement of fact from a partially sane onlooker I would offer you two suggestions. Either cut the painter and go away with him, or else suggest to him that he should give up the remainder of his lease and go big-game shooting for a couple of years or so. I admit that the novelty of my remarks almost staggers me, but at this stage of the world's history it is hardly likely that anyone will discover a new way out of your present situation. It is not exactly the first time it has happened."

" 'I wonder what John would say,' she said thoughtfully. 'I should hate to hurt him.'

" 'You'll hurt him even more,' I answered, 'if he finds out by roundabout means. And, Hester, this I do say with certainty: he's bound to do so. If you were in London it might be different—but down here it's hopeless. You and Ronald are both far too well known.'

" 'I'll think it over, Bill,' she said. 'I suppose Ronald and I, like most people in similar circumstances, have imagined that no one guessed. We've let things drift. But if you've spotted it—so have other people. I'll think it over.'

"At that I left it, and two days later I went back to London. She had taken my remarks exactly as I expected she would: she wasn't the type to be offended or annoyed. But I confess that during the next few weeks I continually found myself wondering as to whether they were going to bear any fruit."

The nondescript man paused and stared at a passing steamer.

"It's funny when one looks back on things," he continued after a while, "and tries to trace cause and effect. Would the tragedy have happened but for what I had said to her? Heaven knows. All I do know is that some two months after that conversation, in the middle of the month of July, I returned to my rooms for lunch to find a telegram awaiting me. It was short and to the point and ran as follows: 'Come at once. Hester.' So I threw some things into a suit-case and caught the afternoon train.

"I was met at the station by a man whose face was vaguely familiar, and who was in a state of considerable agitation.

" 'You probably don't remember me,' he said. 'I'm John's brother.'

"I placed him then: I'd met him once some years before staying at Brayling House. His name was Richard, and in character, appearance and everything he was the exact opposite of John. Save for a slight family likeness it was almost impossible to believe they were brothers. Richard was fair where John was dark: Richard was one of those men who can go on talking by the hour in quite an amusing way, and he was fond of sport. In fact—John's antithesis.

" 'What's the trouble?' I said as we shook hands.

" 'John has been murdered,' he answered. 'And Ronald Vane has been arrested for doing it.'

"I don't know how long I stood there staring at him foolishly: the thing was so completely unexpected.

" 'Hester wants to see you as soon as possible,' he went on. 'I've got the car.'

"All the way up to the house I bombarded him with questions, but it will make it clearer for you if I go on

a few hours and tell you the story as I pieced it together
after having heard everyone.

"It appeared then, that after my departure some two
months previously, Ronald Vane himself had gone away
for six weeks.   And during that six weeks Hester had
somewhat naturally let things drift.   On Vane's return
he and she had had things out, with the result that they
decided that the only fair and straight thing to do was
to tell her husband.

"Accordingly, one morning Vane came over to Brayling House with the definite intention of tackling Sir
John.   That was the day before the tragedy took place.
It was not a pleasant undertaking, as you can imagine,
but Vane was not the man to shirk it.

"Well, to put it tersely, the interview was not a success.   At first Sir John had been so flabbergasted that
he could hardly take it in.   But as soon as he had
grasped that this unbelievable thing had happened, that
here standing in his house was a man who was calmly
informing him that he proposed in the near future to
run away with his wife, his rage became ungovernable.
No one will deny that there was a good deal of excuse
for him: but he seemed totally unable to grasp the fact
that Vane was really doing the straight thing in telling
him the state of affairs, instead of leaving him to discover
it as a *fait accompli*.

"To cut it short, however, he went for Vane with a
hunting-crop, and Vane, who was considerably the
more powerful man, had some difficulty in wresting
it away without hurting him.   Which was the last
thing he wanted to do: he felt so desperately sorry for
him.

"In the middle of what was practically a hand-to-hand
fight a table was knocked over, and the noise brought in
the butler.   He stood in the doorway aghast at what he
saw, and a moment later Vane having got possession of

the crop managed to half-push, half-throw Sir John
away from him.

" 'Show this blackguard to the door,' Sir John panted
to the servant. 'And never let him inside this house
again or I'll sack you.'

"Well—Vane went. He got back to his house and
rang up Hester, asking her to come to him at once.
But now a further complication had arisen. Sir John,
whose mood of ungovernable fury had been succeeded
by one of sullen rage, flatly refused to even consider the
question of divorce.

" 'I can't lock you up,' he said to his wife. 'I can't
prevent you going to him. But I can prevent you
marrying him, and I will.'

"That, then, was the situation on the following morning—the morning of the tragedy: a situation which, as
you can well imagine, was common property in the servants' hall. Moreover, it was a situation which in view
of what was to come was just about as damning as it
could well be.

"At nine o'clock Sir John went out armed with his
camera. There was one particular bit of wood some
half-mile from the house that he apparently wanted to
get. At a quarter past nine one of the gardeners saw
him focussing his camera: at half-past ten he was discovered by another gardener with his head battered in
lying on the ground in front of his camera. Not much,
you say, up to date to incriminate Vane. Wait. At
half-past nine two children, belonging to one of the
keepers, passed close to the glade. They were on their
way to the village to do some shopping for their mother,
and when they came back they told her what they'd
seen.

"First they had heard two men shouting at one
another. They'd crept up behind some bushes to see
Sir John and Ronald Vane having a furious quarrel.

Mark you, there was no doubt about the identification: they knew Vane—everybody did, and, of course, they knew Sir John. They watched for a little and then, getting frightened, they ran away.

"Pretty black now you'll admit—but worse was to come. Vane himself admitted that he had met Sir John that morning, and had had a terrible row with him. He stated that he was on his way to Brayling House. It was a short cut that he frequently used. Quite unexpectedly he saw Sir John in front of him, and since it was he whom he was going to see he stopped and spoke to him. He refused to say what the quarrel was about: all he would say was that he had been unsuccessful in his request and after, he thought, about ten minutes, he left Sir John and returned to his own house, which he reached at ten-fifteen. Moreover, he utterly and flatly denied that he had killed Sir John.

"But now even worse was to come. Vane had in his possession a very heavy stick—almost a club. What strange freak of fate had induced him to take it out with him that morning he couldn't say. He admitted that he had done so: he further admitted that he lost his temper so completely with Sir John that he flung the thing at his head. It missed him, and fell in some bushes where Vane left it. It was found in the bushes right enough, but with its top covered with blood. In short, it was obviously the weapon with which Sir John had been murdered.

"I suppose," went on my companion with a short laugh, "that if you deliberately went out of your way in a work of fiction to surround your hero with every damning circumstance you could think of, it would be impossible to weave a tighter web than that which hemmed in Ronald Vane. Motive, weapon, opportunity, witnesses—everything combined to make his case hopeless from the start. In fact, on two or three

occasions when I went to see him he admitted as much
to me.

"'That I didn't do it I know,' he said.   'But were I
in the position of the jury I should find myself guilty.'

"A further trouble was his inevitable unpopularity.
To the man in the street who believed in his guilt he
was merely a scoundrel who not only had fallen in love
with another man's wife, but had murdered her husband.

"I won't bore you with an account of the trial.   From
the start the result was a foregone conclusion.   Ronald
Vane could bring no witnesses, but he insisted on giving
evidence himself.   It was useless.   The jury only retired for a quarter of an hour.

"And then came the end, and the episode that lingers
most in my mind.   Asked by the Judge if he had anything to say, I can still see Ronald Vane, his arms folded,
his face grave and a little stern.

"'Nothing, my Lord,' he said, and his voice was
quite steady.   'You have awarded me a perfectly fair
trial.   It is not your fault—nor is it mine that you have
come to the conclusion that you have.   It is the fault
of a set of utterly unprecedented circumstances.   I cannot but believe that in time some fact will come to light
which will prove my innocence.   And if it is too late'—
for the fraction of a second his voice shook—'do not
reproach yourselves too bitterly.   On the evidence as it
is I quite understand that your verdict is the only one
possible.'

"And I don't believe there was a person in court
whose conviction of his guilt was not a little shaken.
He was a big man, Vane—big in every way—and there
was something about him as he stood there that was
great.   No recrimination: no bitterness: almost, if I
may be allowed the analogy, was it a repetition of two
thousand years ago.

" 'Father forgive them for they know not what they do.'

"And then he disappeared from sight, and I led a white-faced woman back to her hotel.

"I suppose you're wondering," he went on after a while, "as to when I'm going to justify my original remark about Primo Packs. I'm coming to it now. Hester had gone back to Brayling House: her brother-in-law had insisted on that. And the days ticked on: days during which I wandered aimlessly about, racking my brains for some clue, some possibility that might have been overlooked. Nothing: it was a blank wall. Sometimes I even began to wonder if he hadn't done it: gone mad for a moment and killed Sir John without being aware of the fact.

"And then one morning I was in a chemist's shop getting some aspirin. There was only one attendant and he was explaining to a customer the working of a Primo Pack. I listened idly—I'm not interested in photography—until a sudden sentence caught my ear.

" 'As each film is taken one of these pieces of black paper is pulled out and torn off. That has the effect of moving the taken film to the back of the pack, leaving the next one in front.'

"Even then the possibility did not strike me: I just bought my aspirin and walked out. And it was only as I sat down to lunch at my club that a thought—a wild possibility—dawned on me. Wild though it was —wellnigh crazy—it was sufficient to send me dashing and lunchless to Scotland Yard.

" 'Where,' I demanded of the first official I saw, 'are the various exhibits in the Ronald Vane case?'

"He stared at me as if I was mad, and I realized I must take a pull at myself. Anyway, I finally convinced him that I was a respectable person, and he became quite helpful. You see, Sir John had been using a

Primo Pack of which one film had been taken. Ronald Vane, in the course of his evidence, had stated that he had waited while Sir John had taken it: waited for him to enter up the details in his pocket-book. That film had been taken at 9.15, and the wild idea had occurred to me that possibly another film had been taken too— one of which we knew nothing, because it was still in the front of the pack."

"Great Scott!" I cried. "I get you. Only one piece of black paper had been torn off."

"Two to be exact," he replied. "The covering and the one marked 1. Both those pieces had been found. So that number 2 film was in position for exposure. Had any photograph been taken on it?

"Jove! I don't think I'll ever forget that afternoon. I chased round various departments trying not to be buoyed up by such a wildly fantastic hope. A dozen times I solemnly adjured myself not to be a fool: a dozen times I forced myself to remember that even if a photograph had been taken the chances were a hundred to one against it being of any use to us.

"However, at last we ran the man to ground who had developed number 1, and to him I explained my idea. At first he was politely sceptical, but after a time he began to share my enthusiasm.

" 'We'll go and try,' he said. 'The pack is in my dark room.'

"I don't think I'd got a dry thing on me by the time he started. He was one of those maddeningly deliberate individuals, and in the state I then was I felt I could have drowned him in a bath of his own developer. He insisted on lecturing me on chemicals till I forgot my manners and cursed him foolishly. And then he showed himself human and apologized.

"The agony of the moment when he put the film in the dish! Subconsciously I realized that it was the last chance: that if nothing happened Ronald would die in two days.   I closed my eyes: I couldn't bear to look.

" 'My God!' I heard his tense whisper.   'There's something coming out.'

"Wiping the sweat from my eyes I peered over his shoulder.   And now he was as keen as I was: almost without breathing we watched a picture form and materialize on the yellow film.

" 'Now we'll fix it,' he cried, 'and then we'll know.'

"His hand was shaking as he put the negative into a bath of hypo, and then we both sat there and waited. It was an eternity, so it seemed to me, before he took it out and opened the door.   He held it up to the light, and then he turned and looked at me gravely.

" 'If anything was wanting,' he said, 'to prove Ronald Vane's guilt, this film supplies the deficiency.   If you will wait a moment I'll give you a print of it.'

"He disappeared, and I think I cried.   I had only vaguely glanced at the negative; I had no idea as to what had caused his words.   All I could feel was the sickening reaction after hope that had risen to a dizzy height.

"And then I began to think.   If what he said was right, Ronald Vane *had* done it.   And he hadn't: I felt he hadn't: I knew he hadn't.

" 'An astounding photograph: quite astounding.'

"His voice cut into my thoughts, and I got up and bent over the dish he had placed on the table.   He was right: it was an astounding photograph.   Occupying half of it was Sir John's face.   He was staring towards the camera and above it, and in his eyes was a look of dreadful terror.   He was looking at someone who stood behind the camera—someone whose shadow fell on the ground, someone with arm upraised to strike.   He was looking at his murderer.

" 'Evidently adjusting his stop,' said the chemist.

'He looked up suddenly: saw Vane coming for him and unconsciously pressed the bulb.'

" 'Why should you assume it was Vane?' I said dully.

"He shrugged his shoulders, and turned away.

" 'I apologize,' he said. 'But I fear, sir, that this photograph is not going to help you to clear your friend.'

" 'I suppose it won't,' I muttered. 'May I take it with me?'

"I spoke without thought: the thing was no good to me.

" 'Certainly,' he answered courteously. 'And if you like I'll give you a copy of the other one—the print of number 1 film.'

"I thanked him mechanically, and a few minutes after I left. So it was no use: I began to wish I'd never overheard that chemist in the morning. To have hoped so much and then suffer such a disappointment was the refinement of cruelty.

"For hours that evening I sat staring at the two photos. The first was just a clear-cut print of the glade with light and shade exquisitely defined: it was the second that fascinated me. That monstrous distorted shadow of the murderer: that ashen face of terror: the rest of it the glade as in the first. Astounding as he had said: unique. No such photograph had ever been taken before. And I found myself cursing childishly because it couldn't speak when I shouted at it—'Whose is that shadow?' Almost I tore it up, and then—suddenly . . ."

The nondescript man paused and lit another cigarette.

"Confound you, sir," I cried, laughing. "I understand your feelings towards the chemist."

"Are you a mathematician?" he went on irrelevantly.

"I am. And if you are you will appreciate the feeling of almost frozen calm that comes to the brain when the step of some intricate problem that has eluded you for hours, reveals itself. Such became my condition suddenly—in the twinkling of an eye. I have said that the second photograph showed one half of the glade, and that had been the part of it at which I'd scarcely glanced. Now with every sense alert I riveted my attention on it. Then, realizing I'd missed the last train, I rung up and ordered a motor-car.

"It was dawn when I reached Brayling House, and I ordered the car to wait for me in the road. It would be four hours at least before I could prove my theory, but I was too excited to think of food. The one essential thing—a cloudless sky—was present, and going to the glade I sat down and waited.

"It was two months later in the year, and so I knew that times would be different. That didn't matter. The actual directions of the shadows would be different. And that didn't matter. The essential thing would be the same.

"And it was. I dashed from the wood into the car, and drove to Brayling House.

"'Hester,' I howled from the hall. 'It's all right. We'll save him.'

"I had a dim vision of a woman's white face with hope too marvellous for words dawning on it: then I was back in the car driving full speed for London. Only the Home Secretary would do for me, and I caught him as he was dressing for dinner.

"'What on earth,' he began, as I burst past the butler into his room.

"'Sorry,' I gasped, 'I'm not an anarchist. Look at these two photos. Ronald Vane case.'

"'Two,' he cried, 'I've only seen one.'

"I handed them to him in silence, and for a while he stared at them.

"'Well,' he said. 'What of it? I don't know how

this second one was obtained, but it doesn't seem to me to alter matters. That presumably is Ronald Vane's shadow.'

" 'It isn't,' I cried. 'It can't be. If Vane committed the murder, what time was it done? It is a proven fact that he was back in his own house at 9.45. Therefore the latest at which it was done—if he did it—was 9.30. And if that is so those two photographs were taken within a quarter of an hour of one another. Which is impossible.'

" 'Why is it impossible?' he snapped.

" 'Take number 1,' I cried. 'Do you see the end of the shadow of that pointed tree on the ground? Now take number 2. Do you see where it is in that one?

" 'Now, sir, the sun cannot lie. I went down there this morning and measured things, and do you know how long it takes for that shadow to move that distance? One hour and five minutes. That second photograph was taken at twenty minutes past ten, when Ronald Vane can be proved to have been in his own house. The other shadow is the murderer all right, but it's not Ronald Vane.'

" 'Good God!' he said. 'Good God!'

"A narrow shave I think you'll agree," went on the speaker after a moment. "And a shave which—given a roll of films—would never have been necessary. Someone with due time at his disposal would certainly have spotted it, had the two photos been developed simultaneously. But the result was all right: Ronald Vane did not go to the gallows, and in due course he married his Hester."

"But," I cried, "who did it? Was that ever found out? Whose was the shadow?"

For a while he stared over the lake without speaking.

"No," he said at length, "it was never found out.

The generally accepted theory is that it was some tramp who meant to stun him for his money, and then, realizing what he'd done, fled in a panic.   Maybe that's right: maybe not."

"You have a theory of your own," I demanded.

He smiled.

"About time we got back for lunch, isn't it?   Or do you want to take some more photographs?   No.   Then let's stroll.   Only I've often wondered what Sir John did between 9.30 and 10.15.   Obviously he took no photographs.   Was he raging about the glade in a distracted way by himself, or was he talking to someone else?   If so, whom would he be likely to talk to for such a long period?   You remember I told you he was inclined to be morose.   Was someone lying up, hidden in the bushes, who desired his death and seized such a golden opportunity for throwing suspicion on another man?

"His brother Richard," he continued irrelevantly, "suffered like so many younger sons from a champagne taste with a gin income.   He has since inheriting the property demolished all that part of the wood.   Both very natural things to do—but I wonder."

XX   THREE   OF   A   KIND

HENRY PARTINGTON was a jovial-looking man of about fifty.   His hair was turning distinctly grey, but his face had that cheerful ruddiness of colouring which made him appear several years younger.   A permanent twinkle in his clear brown eyes, and a pleasant, infectious laugh completed the picture of a carefree, middle-aged man who found life good, and who wanted other people to find it good also.

Being clean-shaven, the first impression he generally gave was that he was a retired naval officer, and his intimate knowledge of various odd corners of the globe helped the illusion. Other people, on the contrary, were wont to put him down as one of that fine, but alas! diminishing band of landed gentry whose principal occupations are riding to hounds, shooting and fishing. And only one or two shrewd, hard-faced men put him down for what he really was—a rascal who lived by his wits.

But such a pleasant rascal! In fact it was his delightful charm of manner that had made him a rascal in the first place. If he had been a morose and forbidding individual, it is more than likely that he would have become a bank manager of unimpeachable morals and intense dullness. He had started life as a bank clerk, and it was the daily contemplation of incomes so immeasurably larger than his own ever could be, that had led him to formulate the simple rule that had been his through life. And the rule was that any large difference between his own worldly possessions and the other person's should be adjusted as far as lay in his power and as soon as possible. Simultaneously with arriving at this resolve he ceased to be a bank clerk, which was just as well for all concerned.

He was what would be described professionally as a first-class confidence man. He stole with the victim's full knowledge and approval. And he stole so charmingly that the victim never had an inkling that the operation was in progress. Frequently, in fact, the poor fish returned for more. Investments, real estate, transactions over jewellery, anything and everything came equally easily to Henry Partington, provided a large wad of the money that passed remained in his pocket. As a side line he counted on bridge for a thousand a year, and billiards kept him in cigars. Even golf, with a handicap of sixteen, paid for itself, and golf afforded the exercise necessary for his figure.

It was just before he had reached the age of thirty that in a moment of mental aberration he had taken unto himself a wife. Whether it was to try and make amends for having swindled the poor girl's father out of five thousand of the best, or whether he really loved her, was a point Henry Partington had frequently debated in his own mind since. But it was an academic debate since she died a year later when presenting him with Joan, his daughter. And Joan, during the early part of her life, was a sad worry to her father. As a small girl, and later as a long-legged flapper, there was no evident niche for her in Henry Partington's scheme of things. True, she lent an air of respectability—allusions to my poor dear wife and motherless child always impressed the ladies—but in her early days she was undoubtedly more trouble than she was worth.

Until one day he woke with a slight start to the knowledge that his daughter was a singularly pretty girl. He was smoking his after-luncheon cigar at a fashionable hotel on the South coast, and his glance rested casually on the tennis courts. And there he perceived his daughter holding a court. No less than seven young men were around her, and the crowd seemed to be increasing. For a moment or two his eyes narrowed: the train of thought that the spectacle had suggested to his astute brain was not very pleasant. No: a thousand times—no.

But though he banished the idea from his mind at the moment, it had returned. After all, she need never know: she could act in all innocence. The more innocent she was, in fact, the better she would act. And one day, a few months later, he finally threw his scruples overboard.

"There's a young fellow here, my darling," he murmured, "young Teffington, to be exact, whom I'd rather like you to be nice to. He's a good boy, and he's a bit worried over some of his investments. I thought I'd try and help him: a little private dinner in our sitting-room, don't you know? If you give him one or two of your angelic smiles, it will make the lad more at his ease."

So Lord Teffington got his smiles, and they cost him, at a conservative estimate, a thousand pounds apiece.

It was rapid then: he didn't even try to fight against it. Joan became bait, and the game went merrily on. And if at times the remnant of a conscience pricked him for using his daughter in such a cause, he assuaged it by assuring himself that as she had no idea what she was doing, no blame could be attached to her. Which admirable piece of casuistry might have had something to be said for it: if it had not been built on a fundamental error.

Exactly when Joan began to have her suspicions, it is difficult to say. They grew gradually in her mind, though she fought against them indignantly at first. But she was no fool, and by the time she was nineteen the polite myth of her father being something in the City was finally exploded. She knew that he wasn't anything of the sort, and though she was still far from realizing what a confounded old scamp he really was, she had a pretty shrewd idea that his method of livelihood would not stand a close scrutiny. In fiction, of course, she would have broken away from him in righteous horror at this point, and earned her own living as a governess; in practice she did nothing of the sort. In the first place, she knew nothing about teaching; in the second, no female parent would have employed her—she was far too pretty; thirdly, and

most important of all, such a proceeding would have
bored her to death.

And so she did what many people have done before
her—she drifted. She was genuinely fond of her
father, and, in spite of herself, his free and easy philosophy of life made her laugh. For, after a while,
though the matter had never been definitely mentioned
between them, that astute gentleman had sensed that
she was not quite so ignorant as he thought. And
imperceptibly the mask had dropped off when they
were alone, until, at the age of twenty, Joan had but
few illusions left with regard to her father's ideas on
the subject of *meum* and *tuum*. Which was all very
reprehensible, and might have ended Heaven knows
how unless Bill Swinburn had appeared on the scene.

Bill was something completely different to anybody
she had ever met before. In her wanderings around
hotels with her father the average man Joan had encountered had been cast in a mould. It was, doubtless, a good mould, but honesty compels the admission that it was a dull one. They were all very nice
boys, who played tennis and golf quite well and danced
quite passably: but sooner or later they all stammered
and became hot in the hand as a preliminary to blurting
out their undying passion. And there was another
mould—not a good mould—of elderly men who also
grew hot in the hand. They made her sick.

And then, one August, when she and her father
were staying at the Grand Hotel at Westbourne, Bill
Swinburn arrived. It was tea-time, and from behind
her table she watched him covertly as he got out of
the bus. And as he disappeared into the hotel, he
left her with a vivid impression of clear blue eyes set
in a keen, tanned face; of physical fitness and intense
virility; of well-fitting clothes on a perfect figure. A
bag crammed with golf-clubs followed him, together

with several suit-cases plastered with the fancy labels of foreign hotels and steamship companies.

"An undoubted lamb," she reflected in the vernacular. "Him for little Joan."

"A soldier, I should imagine," remarked her father thoughtfully. "Probably penniless, but they sometimes think they can play poker."

"Can't you ever get away from it, Dad," she cried irritably. "One of these days you'll strike a man who *can* play, and get bitten good and hard."

"Don't mock your poor old parent, my darling," he answered amiably. "I have often struck such scoundrels in the past, and I always develop a headache when I've lost a fiver."

She didn't see the stranger again till dinner, and then, as luck would have it, he had been placed at a table directly facing her. And it was over the fish that their eyes met and held for a second. Quite accidental, of course—but a second is a deuced long time—on certain occasions. Quite long enough to establish very pleasant hopes for the future—or to completely annihilate them.

He really was astoundingly pleasant to look at. And unconsciously Joan found herself building fancy pictures in her mind about him. A soldier probably, as her father had said: a clean-cut, straight-living man, with hard, cut-and-dried ideas on honour and the thing to do. And what would he think of her if he knew? A wave of bitterness against her father passed over her: she felt a sudden intense envy for the red-cheeked dowdy girl at the next table eating her second large helping of apple-tart. She would break away: she would. Go and typewrite or something: at any rate be honest.

Still silent and distraite she followed her father into the lounge. Out of the corner of her eye she saw

the stranger's tall, spare figure standing by an open
window, and then she resolutely tried to banish him
from her thoughts.   Which, if she'd stopped to think
of it, was a very dangerous sign. . . .

She started talking to a dull and worthy woman
next to her—one of her father's many smaller irons
in the fire.   And then the band struck up in the ball-
room—the signal for an immediate rush of callow
youths to her side.   But as she went to dance with the
first her heart gave a sudden little pound of excitement: her father was talking to the stranger in the
window.

He didn't come up to her till near the end, and then
her father introduced him.   And there was a glint in
Henry Partington's eyes which his daughter interpreted perfectly.   It filled her with a sick hopelessness:
it meant that something was doing.   And Joan knew
what that something was.   She wouldn't help him
over this: she'd tell him later that this stranger *must*
be left alone.   Because—oh! because. . . .

"You dance divinely, Miss Partington."

The band had stopped; the cool, grave voice in her
ear pulled her together.   She looked up at him to find
his steady eyes fixed on hers with a strange, baffling
expression in them.

"Are you staying long?" she asked lightly, as they
left the room.

"My plans are always a little vague," he answered.
"Are you?"

"About another month, I expect."

"That is my own present intention," he said gravely.
"I hope we shall have some more dances."

For about a quarter of an hour he stayed with her,
talking, and all the time she was conscious of that
inscrutable look in his eyes.   It defeated her: she
couldn't interpret it.   It seemed at times so utterly

impersonal—almost as if she was a specimen under examination; and then, quite suddenly, it would alter, and give her the intensely personal message which she had received so often from men before and never wanted till now.

For she made no bones about it to herself when she went to bed. She had only seen him for a few hours and spoken to him for a few minutes, but this man Bill Swinburn could not be dismissed as all the others had been. He was going to mean something in her life, and the question was, how big a thing he was going to be. And her last coherent thought before she fell asleep was that she would insist on her father leaving him alone. On that point she was absolutely determined. . . .

But it is one thing to be determined about a thing: it is another to carry that determination into effect. During the days that followed, Bill Swinburn seemed to deliberately lay himself out to play straight into her father's hands. He started off the very next morning by announcing casually that he had a few thousands lying idle and that he was wondering what to do with them. And Joan all but heard her father's mental snort of pure joy, like a thirsty war-horse scenting water in the distance.

So that she wasn't in the least surprised when Henry Partington casually suggested some three days later that they should ask him to dinner in their sitting-room.

"A little business talk, my pet," he remarked casually. "A very nice fellow—young Swinburn: plays a rattling good game of golf. But the old man with his strokes managed to beat him all right."

"I wish you'd leave him alone, father," she said quietly. "You know perfectly well why you want him to dinner. And so do I."

"My darling," he cried, "you misunderstand me this time, I assure you. It is true that in the past certain schemes in which I have interested myself have gone wrong, but I give you my word that on this occasion I'm on a cast-iron certainty. Our fortune, my pet, will be made. And I want that nice young fellow in on the ground floor with me."

She gave a short laugh and left the room. It wasn't the first time she had heard similar sentiments from her father, and she knew exactly what they were worth. And as she went to her room to change—she was playing golf with Swinburn in a few minutes—she came to a sudden resolve. Without giving her father away—she was too loyal for that—she would try and persuade him not to part with his money. It would be difficult, but that couldn't be helped: it just had to be done.

They had played nine holes before she broached the subject, and the half-round had opened her eyes to another aspect of the case—an aspect which made her heart beat a little quicker, but which also made her resolve the more imperative. Bill Swinburn was a class golfer; anyone could see that with half an eye. And not in a hundred years would her father beat him, even with twice his allowance of strokes. Why, therefore, had Bill lost? He *must* have done it deliberately. And if so—why?

There could be only one answer. Joan was no fool: she knew she attracted him even as he attracted her. And he'd lost merely to ingratiate himself with her father. Which didn't matter much over a game of golf, but was a totally different thing when it came to business.

"Were you playing very badly against my father, Mr. Swinburn?" she asked, as she watched him hit a screamer from the tenth tee.

"Couldn't get the putts down," he answered gravely, after she'd driven. "Good shot."

She shook her head.

"I don't believe you," she said quietly. "Do you mind if we sit down for a little. I want to talk to you."

"There is an excellent seat by the eleventh tee," he remarked. "Let us smoke a cigarette there, and look at the sea."

"Mr. Swinburn," she said, when the caddies had been dismissed to a suitable distance. "Daddy has asked you to dinner to-night, hasn't he?"

"An invitation greedily accepted," answered the man.

"Well, I want you to regard what I'm going to say in the strictest confidence," she went on quietly. "Daddy is a dear, but—but he's got one failing. He thinks he's a financial genius. He's always putting his money into the most wonderful schemes, which invariably go bust. And he's always persuading his friends to do likewise. He means it for the—for the best, but that's not much comfort when you lose your money. So I want you to promise me that whatever he says to you to-night you won't part with any of your money. I'm—I'm sure you'll only lose it."

She caught her breath a little quickly, and glanced at the man beside her. He was staring out to sea, and the knuckles of the hand which grasped the arm of the seat were gleaming white. And then he suddenly relaxed and looked at her, with the look that no woman can mistake.

"You darling," he said under his breath. "You darling."

For a moment or two she was so amazed that she could only stare at him blankly; then the warm colour flooded her cheeks, and her eyes fell.

"What do you mean?" she whispered faintly.

"Only that I adore you," he answered. "And what you've just said to me has made me the happiest man in the world."

"But why? I don't understand." And she was staring at him blankly again.

"I don't expect you do," he said, with a little smile. "And maybe you never will. Anyway, it doesn't matter. Nothing matters except one thing. Can you guess what it is?"

"No," she answered, very low.

"You angelic little liar," he laughed. "You care, Joan?"

For a while she stared at the ground: then she raised her eyes to his.

"Like hell, Bill. But oh!—it's impossible. Let's go on playing."

For the moment there was no one in sight, and she felt his arm like a steel bar round her waist. Gasping, half-suffocated, she raised her lips to his; then he let her go.

"Nothing is impossible, my beloved," he cried triumphantly. "Absolutely nothing. Come along and finish the round. I have an irresistible longing to drive into the back of the gent in plus-fours with the strawberry fair isle."

II

"My dear," remarked Henry Partington complacently, "I am glad to say that my brokers see their way to letting young Swinburn have five thousand founder's shares in that new company I am interested in. The one I talked to him about at dinner that night."

It was three days later, and Joan and her father were sitting on the front listening to the band.

"He returns, I believe, this evening," he went on,

"and to-morrow morning I will tell him the good news. Let us hope he won the cup; he is undoubtedly a very good golfer."

With a little frown the girl contemplated her shoe: she felt out of her depth. For Bill Swinburn had come to dinner as arranged, and instead of doing as she expected him to do—turn down her father firmly but politely—he had opened his mouth for the hook wider than ever. And here he was—caught.

True, when Henry Partington had left them alone for a few minutes while he went to look for a prospectus, Bill had taken her in his arms and kissed her till she was breathless and exhausted—but that was nothing to do with it. And the next day he had gone off to Portsdown to play for the Autumn Gold Cup.

What did it mean; what could it mean, except that he didn't believe the warning she had given him? And she couldn't let him be swindled by her father. Not Bill. She'd have to stop it even if it meant telling him the truth. And if she told him the truth, what would he think? What would he think of her?

"Dad, I beg of you—don't do it," she cried suddenly. "I beseech of you, don't take Bill's money."

"My dear child," he answered pompously, "as I've told you before, you're mistaken this time. This really is the goods: on my word of honour, I assure you. I'm putting him into a gold-mine."

With a little sigh of utter weariness, she rose.

"I'm going back to the hotel," she said. "I've got a bit of a headache."

There was nothing for it: she'd have to tell him herself. And if it meant the end, well—it was only fair that she should pay. It was the price for being her father's daughter, and for acquiescing in his mode of life. But until now she had never realized how terribly big it was going to be.

She didn't see him until dinner-time, and then he came over to their table with the usual lazy smile on his lips, and a special private message in his eyes for Joan.

"Did you win?" said Henry Partington.

"By two strokes," answered Bill Swinburn. "Everything went well: in fact, a most successful trip. And how is Miss Joan?"

"The same as before," she said, forcing a smile. "You must tell me about the game after dinner."

She would do it then; she'd get him alone and tell him the truth. Tell him that she'd lied to him on the golf-links when she'd implied what she had about her father; tell him that they were just a pair of crooks and swindlers, and that this wonderful scheme was just another of the same old ramps. She could picture him now as he realized the truth; see the light die out of those dear blue eyes of his; the contempt and scorn on his face as he looked at her. But it had to be done; yes—it had to be done. You can't kiss a man as she'd kissed Bill, and swindle him.

And so, with her mind made up, she left the dining-room to find that her father appeared to have made up his mind also. Henry Partington had not lived the life he had for thirty years for nothing, and that evening he remained glued to her side. Whether his astute mind suspected something of the truth or whether it was pure chance, she didn't know, but the fact remained that her father gave her no opportunity for even the shortest of private talks with Bill. And bedtime came without her having said a word.

She went up to her room, leaving the two men together, and slowly undressed. She must get at him somehow: to-morrow morning might be too late. They were probably talking business now, and Bill was believing everything her father told him. People always did: he was so terribly plausible. And Bill would put down what she had told him on the links as just a girl's ignorance.

She was in bed before the idea struck her, and she realized the only thing to do. For a moment or two she hesitated as she glanced at her watch. After midnight. . . . Then, with sudden, quick decision, as if she was afraid of changing her mind, she got up and slipped on a wrap. She opened her door and looked out; the passage was empty. And, without any further hesitation, she walked along it in the direction of Bill's room.

She had seen the number in the visitors' book, and with her heart beating in great thumps she stopped outside the door of 213. For a moment she hesitated and almost fled back to her own room: then she knocked.

There was a short pause during which she heard what sounded like the rattle of golf-clubs; then the door was opened and Bill stood looking at her.

"Joan," he whispered. "What do you want? Come in, my dear."

He closed the door behind her, but made no movement to touch her. He had evidently been polishing his clubs, for a mashie was lying across the chair and some sandpaper was on the floor. And having cleared his golf-bag away from the easy chair, he stood watching her with that same baffling expression in his eyes that she had noticed the first time they met.

"Bill," she said steadily, "I've got something to say to you. I wanted to say it after dinner to-night, but Daddy never gave me a chance. Are you going to put any money into this scheme of his?"

"I think so," he answered. "It seems a very good opportunity."

She wouldn't meet his eye, and so she didn't see the tender look on his face.

"Bill, you mustn't," she stammered. "Oh! but it's difficult. Bill—I lied to you on the links, don't you understand? I let you think that Daddy was just an ass who always lost his own money as well as other people's. I hoped that would be enough to put you off, but it evidently hasn't. Bill, we're—we're crooks."

Once again she failed to see the sudden smile that glinted on the man's face.

"That's how we live, Bill: by swindling people. You'll never see a penny of your money again if you give father that five thousand."

She stared miserably into the empty grate, only to give a sudden little gasp as his arms went round her and she felt his cheek against hers.

"And why, girl of mine," he whispered, "are you telling *me* all this? You didn't tell the others."

She twisted in his grasp so that she faced him.

"Because I love you," she said simply. "And I didn't love the others."

"You darling," he breathed. "You darling. That's all I wanted to hear."

His lips met hers, her arms stole round his neck. And then she pushed him away.

"Bill, we're mad. Don't you see that what I've told you makes—everything—impossible."

He stood up, and his smile was twisted.

"That's for you to say, my sweetheart. For I've got something to tell you . . . My God! who's that?"

On the door had come a quick, imperative knock.

"Quick, Joan," he whispered. "Through there, and into the bathroom. And not a sound, darling; not a sound. Lock the door."

Bill Swinburn cast one rapid glance round the room and straightened his tie. Then he strolled over to the door and opened it. Two men were standing outside, with the assistant manager hovering nervously in the background.

"Good evening, Bill," said the larger of the two men. "I presume you know why we're here."

"You can presume anything you like," said Swinburn pleasantly. "But there's no need to do it in the passage."

The large man smiled.

"Then we'll come inside. Now, Bill, where are they?"

"Where are what?" asked Swinburn, lighting a cigarette.

"Lady Gallader's diamonds," said the large man wearily. "We've got you this time, Bill, and as we all want to go to bed it will save a lot of trouble if you fork 'em out at once. Because if you don't I warn you I'm going to find 'em if I have to rip up every floor-board in the room."

"Most interesting," drawled Bill. "At the moment, however, the connection seems a little obscure. I gather Lady Gallader has lost her diamonds; but why this vicious animosity towards my harmless apartment."

"Look here, Bill," said the large man patiently, "in order that things may be quite clear to you I'll tell you one or two small points that you don't know. Last night at Portsdown Lady Gallader's house was broken into, and her diamonds were stolen. Don't look bored: I haven't come to the points you don't know yet. This morning at four o'clock, Greystone —you remember Inspector Greystone—was out for a very early walk. A pure fluke I admit, Bill; and bad luck for you. And he happened to see a very old friend having a morning walk also. This friend was coming from the direction of Lady Gallader's house.

Been paying a call, Bill, had you? So Greystone hid behind a hayrick and wondered. Of course he knew nothing about the burglary, but he did know a good deal about the other early walker. So he followed him back to his hotel, and from then till now, Bill, you've never been out of our sight. As soon as Greystone heard about the burglary, he 'phoned me. Then he followed you in another car; I got a warrant to search you and here we are. Bill, those stones are on you, or they're in this room. We know you haven't got rid of 'em to-day. And we're going to have 'em, if it takes us a week. You've done us every time up to date, but we've got you at last."

"Most interesting," said Bill languidly. "But to my uninitiated eye the evidence seems a trifle flimsy. Is our one and only Greystone the only man who is allowed to take an early-morning walk?"

"What were you doing down there, anyway," snapped the detective.

"Oh! ephemeral fame," sighed Bill. "Let me show you the morning paper, MacAndrew. There—W. Swinburn $72+73=145$. And Lord Gallader himself presented me with a lovely medal. One over fours, my boy—for two rounds."

MacAndrew snorted.

"I'm not denying you can play golf. Maybe you'll want a bit of practice after a few years' rest, though. Now then—where are they?"

"My dear Mac, I haven't got 'em. You've made a boss shot this time, believe you me. As, I may say, you always have on other occasions. In fact, I regard myself as a most hardly used individual. This atmosphere of harsh suspicion in which I live is not conducive to good putting."

"Cut it out," snarled MacAndrew. "If you won't tell us, we've got to do it ourselves. But I can promise you, Swinburn, you'll regret it. Take that end of the room, Thurlow, and start with the bed."

It was three o'clock before they had finished, and if Inspector MacAndrew had not actually fulfilled his threat of ripping up the floor-boards he had done everything short of doing so. And he had drawn absolutely blank.

"Damn you, Swinburn," he cried angrily. "I know you've got 'em."

He was standing in the centre of the room regarding Bill Swinburn balefully. And Bill, who was carefully cleaning his niblick, looked up with a pleasant smile.

"Sorry for your disappointment, Mac," he murmured, "but I told you you'd made a howling error. And now, if you don't mind, I'd like to turn in. There's a big open competition at Le Touquet in three days, and late nights are the devil for one's golf."

And then suddenly his eyes narrowed: MacAndrew was looking at the bathroom door.

"What is through there, Bill?" he asked.

"My bathroom," answered Swinburn, getting up and strolling over to the door.

"Then I think we'll just search your bathroom, Bill," said MacAndrew quietly.

"And I think you won't," replied Swinburn equally quietly.

A gleam of triumph had come into the Inspector's eyes.

"Getting hot, are we," he remarked grimly. "Swinburn, I order you to stand on one side."

"MacAndrew," said Swinburn, and his face was set and strained, "I give you my most solemn word of honour that there is nothing in the bathroom that will interest you."

"That is a point I prefer to settle myself," answered

the detective. "Once again I order you to stand aside."

And Bill Swinburn's forehead was wet.

"Look here, MacAndrew," he cried desperately, "if I tell you . . ."

And at that moment the bathroom door opened, and Joan stepped into the room.

"My dear," cried Bill in agony. "Oh! my dear."

But Joan took no notice of him.

"Search the bathroom," said Joan scornfully to the Inspector. "And then go."

For a while there was absolute silence in the room: then the Inspector turned to Bill.

"You didn't want that door opened, Swinburn—quite naturally. To prevent it you were just going to tell me—what? 'If I tell you'—you said."

"The great secret, MacAndrew. The thing I've never told a soul. But I'd have told you to prevent this happening." His hands were clenched: his face was stern. "Keep your eye on the ball, and your head still, and in a year or two you'll win one of the monthly spoons."

A soft gurgle of laughter from Joan broke the oppressive tension, and even the manager's face twitched into a smile.

"MacAndrew," went on Bill quietly, "you've made a mistake. It's true I was out early this morning, I don't deny it. I couldn't sleep and I went for a walk. But I don't even know where Lady Gallader's house is."

"I've not made a mistake, Swinburn," answered the other through his clenched teeth. "That was your work last night. But, as usual, you've left no trace. Never mind, my friend: it's only a question of time before I prove it."

"Well, laddie," said Bill wearily, "it's a question

of half-past three now. And as you said yourself, we all want to go to bed. Could we postpone the proof till to-morrow, or rather till later to-day."

"We cannot," snarled MacAndrew. "You were going to tell me where you'd hidden those stones, Swinburn. And unless you do—now, this instant, I shall make it my business to see that this young lady's presence in your room—in that rig—is duly known to her father."

"You ineffable swine," said Bill tensely. "You supreme cur."

He was crouching a little, and his eyes, hard and merciless, were fixed on the Inspector's face. And then, just as he was going to spring, Joan's hand was laid on his arm.

"You will be a little late, Inspector," she said quietly. "I propose to tell my father to-morrow morning first thing that I came round to my fiancé's room to-night to talk a certain matter over with him, when you interrupted us."

She felt the muscles in Bill's arm relax, and not till then did her hand drop to her side.

"Would you now be good enough to search the bathroom, and then go?"

But MacAndrew had had enough: and with a stifled curse he swung on his heel and crossed to the door.

"Sooner or later, Swinburn: sooner or later I'll catch you. And as for you, Miss, I wish you joy of your choice. You've got the smartest jewel-thief in Europe to-day."

But Bill Swinburn was taking no notice: he was staring at the girl by his side.

"Did you mean it, Joan?" he said a little hoarsely. "When you said—'my fiancé.'"

The detectives had gone: the two of them were alone.

"If you want me, Bill," she answered.

"If I want you," he almost shouted. "Why, I'm mad for you."

And then his hands dropped to his sides.

"But, my dear—it's the truth: what MacAndrew said."

"I guessed that," she said quietly. "And you were going to tell him where the diamonds were, rather than that he should open that door?"

"Why, yes, dear, I was," said Bill gravely. "Listen, my darling. That was the thing I had to tell you. I've done it for years. It's I who am the sinner—not you. I spotted your father for what he was within five minutes. And I wondered about you. Did you know, or did you not? On the golf-links I was nearly sure: to-night you told me."

Half-unconsciously he had picked up one of his brassies and was balancing it in his hand.

"Joan, I'm sick of it. MacAndrew is right: sooner or later he'll catch me. I want to marry and settle down. And you—oh! my darling—it was first sight as far as I was concerned. But before I asked you I had to make sure. So I played into your father's hands, and found out what I wanted to know. And then when you came out of the bathroom and saved the situation—why, Joan, dear, the world just stopped for a moment. Crooks, my darling, both of us: you such a tiny little one—me pretty black. But if we run straight, Joan . . ."

"Why, yes, Bill, we'll do that."

His arms were round her: his face close to hers.

"We'll run straight, boy: and we'll run together."

And then a sudden thought struck her and she smiled.

"Where are the diamonds?"

"Where everything has always been," grinned Bill.

He took a screwdriver out of his pocket, and picked up a brassie.

"You pulled my leg once about the excessive number of my wooden clubs. But I don't play with them all."

The brass plate was off the bottom of the club, and Joan saw that the head was hollow. And in the cavity was something carefully wrapped in cotton-wool.

"They're all there, and in three of the other clubs," he said.

"But, Bill," she cried, "this is Daddy's precious pearl and diamond tie-pin that he values so much."

"I know, my angel," he admitted. "I was going to give it back to him to-morrow morning as a sort of solatium for not getting my five thousand and for losing his daughter."

XXI   THE FINGER OF FATE

THE funny thing about it was that I did not know George Barstow at all well. Had he been an intimate personal friend of mine, the affair might have seemed more natural. But he wasn't: he was just a club acquaintance with whom I was on ordinary club terms. We met sometimes in the bridge-room: occasionally we had an after-lunch brandy together. And that was all.

He had obviously a good deal of money. Something in the City, but a something that did not demand an extravagant amount of his time. His week-ends were of the Friday to Tuesday variety, and I gathered that he was on the border-line of golfers who are eligible to compete in the Amateur Championship.

In appearance he was almost aggressively English.

Clean-shaven, and ruddy of face, his natural position was with his legs apart on the hearth-rug and his back to the fire.   Probably a whisky-and-soda in his hand, or a tankard of beer.   Essentially a man's man, and yet one who by no means disliked the pleasures of the occasional night-club party.   But one realized they must only be occasional.

He was, I suppose, about thirty-seven, though he was one of those men whose age is difficult to tell. He might quite easily have been in the early forties. His appearance was healthy rather than good looking: his physical strength was distinctly above the average. And to finish off this brief outline of the man, he had oined up in the earliest days of the war and finally risen to the command of a battalion.

I recognized him when he was a hundred yards away from the inn.   He was coming towards me down the road, his hands in his pockets, his head sunk.   But the walk was unmistakable.

"Great Scott! Barstow!" I said as he came abreast of me, "what brings you here at this time of year?"

"Here" was a little village not far from Innsbruck.

He glanced up with a start, and I was shocked to see the change in his face.   He looked positively haggard.

"Hullo! Staunton," he said moodily.   Then he gave a sheepish little laugh.   "I suppose it is a bit out of my beaten track."

"Come and have a spot of this," I remarked.   "I've tasted much worse."

He came across the road and sat down, whilst I studied him covertly.   Quite obviously something was wrong—seriously wrong; but in view of the slightness of our acquaintanceship it was up to him to make the first move if he wanted to.

"August and Austria hardly seem a usual combination for you," I said lightly. "I thought Scotland was your habitual programme."

"Habitual programmes have a way of being upset," he answered shortly. "Here's how."

He put his glass down on the table, and pulled out his tobacco-pouch.

"Personally, I think this is a damnable country," he exploded suddenly.

"Then," I said mildly, "is there any essential reason why you should remain?"

He didn't answer, and I noticed he was staring down the road through narrowed eyes.

"The essential reason," he said at length, "will shortly pass this inn. No, don't look round," he went on, as I turned in my chair. "You will see all there is to be seen in a moment."

From behind me I heard the jingling of bells, and the noise of some horse-drawn vehicle approaching at a rapid rate. And a few seconds after, an almost mediaevally magnificent equipage drew up at the door. I use the word "equipage" advisedly, because it was like no English carriage that I have ever seen, and I have no idea as to the correct local name for it.

The coachman was in scarlet: all the horses' trappings were scarlet also. But after a brief glance at the setting, my eyes fixed themselves on the man contained in it. Seldom, I think, have I seen a more arrogant and unpleasant-looking face. And yet it was the face of an aristocrat. Thin-lipped, nose slightly hooked, he was typical of the class of man who, in days gone by in France, would have ordered his servants to drive over a peasant in his way, rather than be delayed.

He waited without movement till a footman, also in scarlet, had dashed to the door and opened it. Then he stepped out, and held out his sleeve for an imaginary

speck of dust to be removed. And for an instant the
wild thought came to my mind that the man was
acting for the films. The whole thing seemed unreal.

The next moment the landlord appeared bent nearly
double. And my fascination increased. I'd forgotten
Barstow's words about the essential reason in my
intense interest. He advanced slowly towards a table,
the landlord backing in front of him, and sat down.
At the same time the footman, who had been delving
under one of the seats of the carriage, came up to his
table and put a leather case in front of him. He
opened it, and I gave an involuntary start. Inside
were two revolvers.

"Good God!" I muttered and glanced at George
Barstow. There was nothing mediaeval about those
guns.

But he seemed to be taking no interest in the performance whatever. With his legs stretched in front
of him he was puffing calmly at his pipe, apparently
utterly indifferent to the whole thing.

But now even stranger doings were to take place.
With great solemnity the footman advanced to a tree,
and proceeded to fix an ordinary playing-card to the
trunk with a drawing-pin. It was the five of hearts.
Then he withdrew.

The man at the table took one of the revolvers from
the case, and balanced it for a moment in his hand.
Then he raised it and fired four times.

By this time I was beyond surprise. The whole
thing was so incredibly bizarre that I could only sit
there gaping. If the man had now proceeded to
stand on his head, and drink a glass of wine in that
position, I should have regarded it as quite in keeping. But apparently the performance was not yet
over. Once again did the footman solemnly advance
to the tree. He removed the card, and pinned up

another—the five of spades. And the man at the table picked up the other revolver. Once again did four shots ring out, and then the marksman, with great deliberation, leaned back in his chair after drawing a handkerchief delicately across his nostrils.

He accepted from the almost kneeling landlord a glass of wine: then he extended a languid hand for the two targets which the footman was holding out, and examined them with an air of bored indifference. Apparently the result of the inspection was favourable: he threw the two cards on the table and continued his wine.

Now I cannot say at what moment exactly a strong desire on my part to laugh was replaced by a curious pricking sensation at the back of my scalp. But it was the way George Barstow was behaving more than the theatrical display of the other man that caused the change. From first to last he had never moved, and it wasn't natural. No man can sit calmly in a chair while someone looses off eight shots behind his back. Unless, that is to say, it was an ordinary proceeding, which had lost its interest through constant repetition. Even then, surely, he would have made some remark about it: told me what to expect. But he hadn't: from the moment the man had stepped out of his carriage he had remained sunk in silence.

A movement from the other table made me look up. The stranger had finished his wine, and was standing up preparatory to going. He made a little gesture with his hand; the footman picked up the two cards. And then to my utter amazement he came over and threw them on the table between us, in a gratuitously offensive way.

"What the devil!" I began angrily, but I spoke to empty air. The man was already clambering up to his seat at the back of the carriage. And it wasn't until the jingle of the bells had died away in the distance that I turned to Barstow.

"What on earth is the meaning of that pantomime," I demanded. "Does he often do it?"

George Barstow removed his pipe, and knocked it out on his heel.

"To-day is the sixth time," he said quietly.

"But what's the great idea?" I cried.

"Not very great," he answered. "In fact, perfectly simple. His wife and I are in love with one another and he has found out."

"Good God!" I said blankly.

And then for the first time I looked closely at the two cards. The four outside pips had been shot out of each: only the centre one remained.

And once again I muttered: "Good God!" Farce had departed: what looked very like grim tragedy had replaced it. With George Barstow of all people. If one had searched the length and breadth of Europe it would have been impossible to find a human being less likely to find himself in such a position. Mechanically I lit a cigarette: something would have to be done. The trouble was what. But one thing was perfectly clear. A state of affairs which caused a performance such as I had just witnessed could not continue. The next move in the game would probably be to substitute Barstow for the playing-card. And no one could be under any delusion as to the gentleman's ability to shoot.

"Look here, Staunton," said Barstow suddenly. "I'd like your advice. Not that there's the slightest chance of my taking it," he added with a faint smile, "because I know perfectly well what it's going to be. It will be exactly the same advice as I should give myself to another man in my position. Still—if it won't bore you. . . ."

THE FINGER OF FATE 381

"Fire right ahead," I answered. "And let's have another flagon of this stuff."

"It started in Paris three months ago," he began. "A luncheon-party at Delmonico's. There were eight of us, and I found myself sitting next the Baroness von Talrein. Our friend of this morning is the Baron. Well, you'll probably see the Baroness before you've done—so I won't waste time in trying to describe her. Anyway, I couldn't. I can give a man a mental description of a golf hole, but not of a woman. I'll merely say that as far as I am concerned, she is the only woman in the world.

"She is half English, half French. Speaks both languages like a native. And to cut the cackle, I was a goner from the first moment I set eyes on her. I don't pretend to be a moralist: I'm not. I've been what I called in love with other men's wives before, but I'd always survived the experience without much difficulty. This was something totally and utterly different."

He paused for a moment and stared over the fields.

"Totally and utterly different," he repeated. "But, except for one thing, it would have ended as other affairs of that sort have ended in the past and will in the future."

He pulled thoughtfully at his pipe.

"One doesn't mention such things as a general rule," he went on, "but the circumstances in this case are a little unusual. You're a fellow-countryman: we know one another and so on. And as I say, but for this other thing you would not have been treated to the performance this morning. I found out she was in love with me. Doesn't matter how: it was motoring back latish one night from Versailles. Well, that fact put a totally different complexion on the matter."

"Interrupting you for one moment," I said, "had you met the Baron when you found this out?"

"No—not then. He arrived about three days later. She was stopping with friends in the Bois de Boulogne. And during those three days we were never out of one another's pockets. Foolish, I suppose—but there you are. We're dealing with what is, not what might have been.

"Then that specimen arrived, that you've seen to-day. And Eloise insisted that we must be terribly careful. She was frightened to death of the man— it had been one of those damnable arranged marriages. And I suppose I was in the condition where care was impossible. I mean affairs of that sort are given away by an intercepted glance, or something equally trivial. Or perhaps it was that the woman in whose flat Eloise was staying gave us away: I never trusted her an inch. Anyway, the Baron had not been in Paris two days before he came round to see me at the Majestic.

"He was ushered into my sitting-room just before lunch, and I knew at once that he had found out. He stood by the door staring at me, and going through his usual elaborate ritual with his lace handkerchief. And at last he spoke.

"'In my country, Mr. Barstow,' he said, 'it is the custom for a husband to choose his wife's friends. From now on you are not included in that category.'

"'And in my country, Baron,' I answered, 'we recognize no such archaic rules. When the Baroness confirms your statement I shall at once comply. In the meantime . . .'

"'Yes,' he said softly, 'in the meantime.'

"'Lunch is preferable to your company.'

"And so matters came to a head. I suppose I might have been a bit more tactful, but I didn't feel like being tactful. He got my goat from the very first, apart altogether from the question of his wife. And that afternoon I decided to stake everything. I asked her to come away with me.

"I suppose," he went on after a little pause, "that you think I'm a fool. If I were in your place I certainly should. But I want you to realize one thing, Staunton. I am not a callow boy, suffering from calf-love; I'm an old and fairly hardened man of the world. And I did it with my eyes open weighing the consequences."

"What did the Baroness say?" I asked.

"She agreed," he answered simply. "After considerable hesitation. But the hesitation was on my account—not hers. She was afraid of what he would do—not to her, but to me. The man is a swine, you see, of the first order of merit. And he sort of obsesses her mental outlook. You've seen him: you can judge for yourself. Fancy being condemned to live with that for the rest of your life. However, I soothed her as best I could: pointed out to her that we lived in a civilized country in the twentieth century, and that there was nothing he could do. And finally we agreed to bolt next day. There was to be no hole-and-corner work about it: I was going to write him a letter as soon as we had gone.

"Well—she never turned up. A pitiful little scrawl came, written evidently in frantic haste. Whether he had found out, or merely suspected our intentions, I don't know. But he had left Paris early in the morning, taking her with him. Back here."

Barstow waved a hand at a big château half-hidden by trees that lay in front of us dominating the whole countryside.

"At first, I was furious. Why hadn't she refused to go? You can't compel a human being to do what they don't want to. But after a time the anger died.

I met a friend of hers——a woman, and it was she who told me things I didn't know about this menage. Things about his treatment of her: things, Staunton, that made me see red.   And then and there I made up my mind.   I, too, would come here.   That was a week ago."

George Barstow fell silent, and stared at his shoes.

"Have you seen her?" I said.

"No.   The first day I arrived I went up to call. Rather putting one's head in the lion's mouth——but I'm beyond trifles of that sort.   He must have known I was coming: as you saw by the landlord's behaviour he is God Almighty in these parts.   Anyway, I was met at the door by the major-domo, with three damned great Alsatians on leads.   The Baroness was not at home, and it would be well if I remembered that the next time I came the Alsatians would not be on leads. Then he slammed the door in my face.

"The next morning the performance you saw to-day took place.   It has been repeated daily since.   And that's the position.   What do you think about it?"

"Well, old man," I remarked, "you started off by saying that you wouldn't take my advice.   And so there's not much good my giving it to you.   What I think about it is that you should pack, put your stuff in the back of my car——and hop it.   My dear fellow," I went on a little irritably, "the position is impossible. Forgive my cold logic and apparent lack of sympathy ——but you must see that it is yourself.   After all——she is his wife.   And it seems to me that you have the alternative of a sticky five minutes with three savage Alsatians, or finding yourself in the position of acting as one of these cards.   I quite agree with your estimate of the gentleman——but facts are facts.   And it seems to me you haven't got a leg to stand on."

"I don't care a damn," he said obstinately.   "I'm

not going. Good God! man, don't you understand that I love her?"

I shrugged my shoulders.

"I don't see that sitting in that inn for the rest of your life is going to help much," I answered. "Look here, Barstow, this isn't England. They have codes of their own in this country. On your own showing that fellow is the great Pooh Bah here. What are you going to do if he challenges you to a duel? I don't know what you are like with a revolver."

"Hopeless. Perfectly hopeless."

"Well, I believe you'd have the choice of weapons. Are you any good at fencing?"

"Far, far worse than with a revolver. I've never had a foil in my hand in my life."

"Then," I cried, "you'd find yourself in the enviable position of either running away or being killed for a certainty. My dear old man, really—really, it isn't good enough. I'm extremely sorry for you and all that, but you must see that the situation is untenable. The man would kill you without the slighest compunction, and with the utmost ease. And here it would simply be put down as an affair of honour. All the sympathy would be with him."

He shook his head wearily.

"Everything that you say is right. Doubly distilled right. And yet, Staunton, I can't go. I feel that anyway here, I am near her. Sorry to have bored you with all my troubles, but I felt I had to."

"You haven't bored me in the slightest," I said. "Only frankly it makes me angry, Barstow, to see a fellow like you making such a fool of himself. You've got nothing to gain and everything to lose."

"If only I could get her out of this country," he said again and again. "He ill-treats her, Staunton. I've seen the marks of his hand on her arms."

I sighed and finished the wine. He was beyond aid. And then suddenly he sat up with a jerk: he was staring at a peasant girl who was making peculiar signs at us from behind a tree some fifty yards away. And suddenly he rose and walked swiftly towards her. I saw her hand him a note, and then dodge rapidly away. And as he came back towards me, I realized that I might as well have been talking to a brick wall. His whole face had changed: he had forgotten my existence.

"A letter from her," he said as he sat down.

"You surprise me," I murmured cynically. "From your demeanour I imagined it was the grocer's bill."

And then I stopped—a little ashamed of the cheap sarcasm. For George Barstow's hand—phlegmatic, undemonstrative Englishman that he was—was shaking like a leaf. I turned away as he opened the envelope, wondering what new complication was going to be introduced. And I wasn't left in ignorance for long. He positively jibbered at me, so great was his excitement. Unknown to her husband she had managed to get out of the house that morning, and she was hiding in the house of her maid's people in the next village.

I suppose it was foolish of me, but I think most men would have done the same. And to do him justice George Barstow didn't ask in so many words. He just looked, and his words came back to me— "If only I could get her out of the country"—I had a car: the Swiss frontier was sixty miles away.

"Get to it, Barstow," I said. "Pack your bag, and we'll hump it."

"Damn my bag!" he cried. "Staunton, you're a sportsman."

"On the contrary I'm a drivelling idiot," I answered.

"And I wash my hands of you once we're in the Engadine."

"You can," he said happily. "Jove! But this is great."

"Is it," I remarked grimly, as I let her into gear. "It strikes me, my friend, that your lady fair's absence is no longer unknown to her husband."

Galloping down the side road that led from the château was the same barouche as we had seen that morning. You could spot the scarlet-coated coachman a mile off. But the main road was good, and a Bentley is a Bentley. We passed the turn when the Baron was still a quarter of a mile away. And then I trod on the gas and we moved.

"It's a race, my boy," I said. "He'll get a car as soon as he can. And if we get a puncture . . ."

"Don't croak," he answered. "We shan't."

We roared into the village, and there, standing in the middle of the road waiting for us, was the most adorable creature I've ever seen. There was no time for rhapsodies: every second counted. But I did say to Barstow, "By Jove! old man—I don't blame you." Then we were off again. And as we left the village, Barstow, who was sitting in the back with his girl, shouted to me: "He's just come in sight."

Luckily I am one of those people who never forget a road. And in one hour and three-quarters the Austrian douane hove in sight. My triptyque was in order: the authorities were pleased to be genial. And a quarter of an hour later we were across the frontier.

"You might now introduce me," I murmured gently. "This is the first time in my life that I've assisted at an entertainment of this description, and I feel it ought to be celebrated."

And for a while we behaved like three foolish children. I know I was almost as excited as they were.

The fact that half my kit and all George Barstow's was gone for good seemed too trifling to worry about. All that mattered was that the bus had gone like a scalded cat, and that somewhere on the road, miles back, a hook-nosed blighter was cursing like blazes in an elderly tin Lizzie.

It was the girl who pulled herself together first.

"We're not out of the wood yet, George," she said. "He'll follow us all over Europe. Let's get on."

And so we got on—a rather soberer party. George and his girl doubtless had compensations in the back seat, but now that the excitement of the dash was over I began to weigh up the situation calmly. And the more I weighed it up the less I liked it. It's all very well to do a mad thing on the spur of the moment, but the time of reckoning comes. And the cold hard fact remained, that but for me George Barstow would not have been able to kidnap another man's wife. For that's what it came to, when shorn of its romance.

It was as we drove into Samaden that George leaned over and spoke to me.

"Look here, old man," he said gravely. "Eloise and I want you to leave us in St. Moritz and clear out. It isn't fair that you should be mixed up in this."

Exactly what I had been thinking myself, which was naturally sufficient to cause a complete revulsion.

"Go to blazes!" I cried. "Anyway, we can't discuss anything till we've had lunch. It's all hopelessly foolish and reprehensible, but I've enjoyed myself thoroughly. So we'll crack a bottle, and I will drink your very good health."

It was stupid, of course, leaving the car outside the hotel. And yet, as things turned out, it was for the best. The meeting had to take place some time: it was as well that I should be there when it did. It was also as well that we were late for luncheon: the room was empty.

We'd all forgotten the Baron for the moment—and then, suddenly, there he was standing in the doorway. George Barstow saw him first, and instinctively he took the girl's hand. Then I turned round, but the Baron had eyes for no one but Barstow. His face was like a frozen mask, but you could sense the seething hatred in his mind. Quite slowly he walked over to our table, still staring at George Barstow, who rose as he approached. Then he picked up a glass of wine and flung the contents in George's face. The next moment George's fist caught him on the point of the jaw, and the Baron disappeared from view.

But he rose to his feet at once, still outwardly calm.

"I shall kill you for that," he remarked quietly.

"Possibly," said Barstow, equally quietly.

"I challenge you to a duel," said the Baron.

"And I accept your challenge," answered Barstow.

I heard the girl give a gasp of terror, and I gazed at him in blank astonishment.

"Good God! man!" I cried, "what are you saying? Surely the matter is capable of settlement without that?"

But George was speaking again.

"I shall not return to your country, Monsieur le Baron," he said. "We will find some neutral *venue* for the affair."

"As you please," said the Baron icily, but I saw the triumph that gleamed in his eyes.

"And before," went on George, "leaving the details to be settled by our seconds, it would be well to have one or two matters made clear. I love your wife: she loves me. The only reason—I admit an important one—that brings you into the affair is that you happen to be her husband. Otherwise you are beneath contempt. Your treatment of her has been such as to place you outside the pale. Nevertheless you are her husband. I wish to be. There is not room for both of us. So one of us will die."

"Precisely," agreed the other with a slight laugh. "One of us will die. I presume this gentleman will act as your second."

Without waiting for my answer he stalked out of the room.

"Barstow," I almost shouted at him, "are you mad? You haven't a hope."

And the girl turned to him in an agony of fear.

"Darling," she cried, "you mustn't. You can't."

"Darling," he said gravely, "I must. And I can."

"It's murder," I said dully. "I absolutely refuse to have anything to do with it."

But on Barstow's face there flickered a faint smile.

"Or bluff," he remarked cryptically. "Though I admit it's a bluff to the limit of my hand."

And not a word more would he say.

"I'll tell you everything when the time comes, old man," was the utmost I could get out of him.

*   *   *   *   *

Now various rumours have, I know, got abroad concerning this affair. Whether my name has been connected with it or not I neither know nor care. But it is in the firm belief that nothing but good can come from a plain statement of the truth, that I am writing this.

I suppose, strictly speaking, Barstow could have refused to fight. Duelling is forbidden by the laws of England. But he was an obstinate fellow, and he certainly did not lack pluck. Moreover he felt, and it was a feeling one couldn't help admiring, that he owed it to the Baron to meet him.

The girl, poor child, was almost frantic with fear. And for some strange reason he wouldn't tell her what was in his mind. He adopted the line with her that he was no bad shot himself, and I followed his lead.

And it wasn't until he had said good-bye to her, and we were in the train, bound for Dalmatia, that he told me.

(A certain uninhabited island off the Dalmatian coast was to be the scene of the duel.)

He had, of course, the choice of weapons, and when he first told me the terms on which he intended to fight I felt a momentary feeling of relief. But that feeling evaporated quickly. For what he proposed was *certain* death for one of them.

They were to fight with revolvers at a range of three feet. *But only one revolver was to be loaded.*

"I see it this way," he said to me. "I can't say that I *want* to risk my life on the spin of a coin. I can't say I want to fight this duel at all. But I've got to. I'm damned if I, an Englishman, am going to be found wanting in courage by any foreigner. If he refuses to fight on such terms, my responsibility ends. It will be he who is the coward."

"And if he doesn't refuse," I remarked.

"Then, old man, I'm going through with it," he said calmly. "One does a lot of funny things without thinking, Staunton. And though I should do just the same again over bolting with Eloise, I've got to face the music now."

Involuntarily I smiled at this repetition of my own thoughts.

"He is her husband, and there's not room for the two of us. But if he refuses to fight, then, in his own parlance, honour is satisfied as far as I am concerned. Only one proviso do I make under those circumstances: he must swear to divorce Eloise."

And so I will come to the morning of the duel. The Marquis del Vittore was the Baron's second—an Italian who spoke English perfectly.   We rowed out from the mainland in separate boats.   Barstow and I arrived first and climbed a steep path up the cliff to a small level space on top.   Then the others arrived, and I remember noticing at the time, subconsciously, a strange blueness round the Baron's lips, and his laboured breathing.   But I was too excited to pay much attention to it.

Barstow was seated on a rock staring out to sea and smoking a cigarette, when I approached del Vittore.

"My first condition," I said, "is that your principal should swear on his honour to divorce his wife in the event of his refusing to fight."

The Marquis stared at me in amazement.

"Refusing to fight!" he said.   "But that is what we've come here for."

"Nevertheless I must insist," I remarked.

He shrugged his shoulders and went over to the Baron, who also stared in amazement.   And then he began to laugh—a nasty laugh.   Barstow gazed at him quite unmoved.

"If I refuse to fight," sneered the Baron, "I will certainly swear to divorce my wife."

"Good," said George laconically, and once more looked out to sea.

"Then shall we discuss conditions, Monsieur," said del Vittore.

"The conditions have been settled by my principal," I remarked, "as he is entitled to do, being the challenged party.   The duel will be fought with revolvers, at a range of three feet, and only one revolver will be loaded."

The Marquis stared at me in silence: the Baron, every vestige of colour leaving his face, rose to his feet.

"Impossible," he said harshly. "It would be murder."

"Murder with the dice loaded equally," I remarked quietly.

And for a space there was silence. George had swung round and was staring at the Baron. He was outwardly calm, but I could see a pulse throbbing in his throat.

"These are the most extraordinary conditions," said the Italian.

"Possibly," I answered. "But in England, as you may know, we do not fight duels. My principal has no proficiency at all with a revolver. He fails therefore to see why he should do a thing which must result in his certain death: though he is quite prepared to run an even chance. His proposal gives no advantage to either side."

"I utterly refuse," cried the Baron harshly.

"Splendid!" said George. "Then the matter is ended. You have refused to fight, and I shall be obliged if you will start divorce proceedings as soon as possible."

And then occurred one of those little things that are so little and do so much. He smiled at me, an "I told you so" smile. And the Baron saw it.

"I have changed my mind," he said. "I will fight on those conditions."

And once again there was silence. George Barstow stood very still; I could feel my own heart going in great sickening thumps. And looking back on it now, I sometimes try to get the psychology of the thing. Did the Baron think he was calling a bluff: or did he simply accept the conditions in a moment of un-controllable rage induced by that smile? What did Barstow himself think? For though he had never said so to me in so many words, I know that he had never anticipated that the Baron would fight. Hence the importance he had attached to his first con-dition.

And then suddenly the whole thing was changed. Impossible, now, for anyone or anything to intervene. Barstow's conditions had been accepted: no man call-ing himself a man could back out. The Marquis drew me on one side.

"Can nothing be done?" he said. "This is not duelling: it is murder."

"So would the other have been," I answered.

And yet it seemed too utterly preposterous—a ghastly nightmare. In a minute, one of those two men would be dead. George, a little pale, but per-fectly calm, was finishing his cigarette: the Baron, his face white as chalk, was walking up and down with stiff little steps. And suddenly I realized that it could not be—must not be.

Del Vittore, his hands shaking, took out the two revolvers. He handed me a round of ammunition, and then looked away.

"I don't even wish to know which revolver it is," he said. "Hand them both to me when you've fin-ished."

I handed them to him, and then turned round.

"I will spin a coin," I said. "The Baron will call."

"Heads," he muttered.

"It's tails," I remarked. "Barstow, will you have the revolver in the Marquis's right hand or in his left?"

He flung away his cigarette.

"Right," he said laconically.

I handed it to him, and del Vittore gave the other to the Baron. Then we placed the two men facing one another.

And suddenly del Vittore lost his nerve.

"Get it over!" he shouted. "For God's sake get it over!"

There came a click: the Baron had fired. His revolver was not the loaded one. For a moment he stood there, while the full realization of what it meant came to him. Then he gave a strangled scream of fear, and his hand went to his heart. His knees sagged suddenly and he collapsed and lay still.

"What's the matter with him?" muttered Barstow. "I haven't fired."

"He's dead," said del Vittore stupidly. "His heart—— Weak . . ."

George Barstow flung his revolver away.

"Thank God! I didn't fire," he said hoarsely.

And silence fell on us save for the discordant screaming of the gulls.

"The result of the exertion of climbing," said del Vittore after a while. "That's what we must say. And we must unload that revolver."

"There's no need," I said slowly. "It was never loaded. Neither of them were."

XXII   THE DIAMOND HAIR-SLIDE

"PITY one can't turn 'em on to fight it out like a couple of dogs." The doctor looked thoughtfully across the smoking-room.

"It won't be necessary to do much turning if this heat continues," I said. "As a matter of fact I thought they were going for one another last night."

As usual there was a woman at the bottom of it, and in this particular case it was aggravated by what appeared to be an instinctive dislike at first sight. Funnily enough I had happened to be a witness of their introduction to one another.

It was our first night out from England and I was having a gin and vermouth before dinner when one of them came in. A biggish red-faced man—the type who might have been in cattle in Australia. Mark Jefferson by name, and after he'd ordered a drink himself we started chatting. The usual desultory stuff: bad weather till we get to Gib—hot in the Red Sea, and so on.

Quite a decent fellow I thought—but the sort of man I'd sooner have as a friend than an enemy. Powerful great devil, with a fist like a leg of mutton.

We'd just ordered the rest of the half-section when the second of them appeared. Completely different stamp of man, but just as tough a nut. Tougher if anything. Hatchet-faced without much colour, but with an eye like a gimlet. His name was Stanton Blake, and at first sight you'd have thought him far the less powerful of the two. At second you'd have realized that there wasn't much in it. Different sort of strength, that's all. The sinewy power of the thin steel rope as against the massive strength of the big rope cable.

However—to get on with it. The ship gave a roll, and Blake lurched into Jefferson. And Jefferson spilt his drink on his trousers. A thing that might happen to anyone. But I've always believed myself that there is such a thing as instinctive antipathy between two people. I mean the sort of dislike that isn't dependent on any specification or spoken word. And it was present in this case. The spilling of the drink was merely the spark that brought it to life.

Blake said, "Sorry."   That I swear.

Jefferson growled something about "Clumsy devil" and turned his back.   Which he had no right to do.

My own belief, in view of what I've seen since of Jefferson's alcoholic consumption, is that those two cocktails were not exactly his first that day.   Not that he was in the slightest degree drunk; I've never seen any man on whom liquor had less obvious effect.   But when a man who is quick-tempered by nature has had a few . . .   Well, you know what I mean.

Be that as it may—the fat was in the fire.   Blake controlled himself—he didn't say anything.   But I saw the look that flashed into his eyes as he stared at the back of Jefferson's head.   And there was no mistaking it.   I remember it crossed my mind at the time that it would be better for all concerned if they weren't at the same table.

As a matter of fact they were at opposite ends of the saloon, but there was always the smoking-room as a common meeting-ground.   And as they were both good sailors the foul passage we had as far as Gibraltar didn't affect them.   But it affected most other people, which was a pity.   For after dinner that night there were only five of us who were taking an interest in things and one of those didn't play Bridge.

I confess that I very nearly refused to play myself. I am accounted a good player: I love the game.   But I play it for pleasure.   And after the little episode before dinner it struck me as problematical if much pleasure would be gained from a table which contained Jefferson and Blake.

I was right: the trouble started at once.   I sat with Blake, against Jefferson and a man called Murgatroyd. Tea in Ceylon—he was.   And the first thing naturally was how much we played for.   I said, "Half a crown" straight away, and Murgatroyd agreed.   But that wouldn't do for Jefferson. He looked at Blake and suggested a ten-pound corner. And Blake shrugged his shoulders and agreed.

"Provided," he said, "we always have it through the trip, Mr. Jefferson."

The point of which remark became obvious as the evening went on. Jefferson was a player above the average: but Stanton Blake was easily the best Bridge player I have ever sat down to a rubber with. His card sense was simply uncanny. And just once or twice the faintest suspicion of a smile would twitch round his lips —one hand, for instance, when Jefferson did quite obviously throw away a trick he should have made.

It wasn't until the last rubber that they cut together, and by then Blake was thirty pounds up on Jefferson apart from ordinary stake money. And it was during this last rubber that the buttons really came off the foils. Bridge, as we all know, can cease to be a pleasant pastime and become the vehicle of more concentrated rudeness and unpleasant back-chat than almost any other game. And though there was no actual rudeness on this occasion Blake got a thrust in that for sheer malignant venom was hard to beat.

Jefferson again made a mistake: I forget exactly what it was. He placed the king on his left when quite obviously it lay on his right, or something of that sort. And when the hand was over Blake picked out the trick containing the king in question. He spread it out on the table in front of him, and then he spoke.

"I suppose you wouldn't care to make our little arrangement a twenty-pound corner, Mr. Jefferson?"

Jefferson's face went purple.

"Thirty if you like," he said thickly.

"The limit is in your hands, Mr. Jefferson," said Blake. "However, thirty will suit me admirably."

You see—that was the trouble. From the very first

those two men loathed one another: long before the girl came in to complicate the question. She turned the feeling between them into bitter, dangerous hatred—the hatred out of which murder arises. The night when the doctor spoke to me there was murder in the air.

But to go back again a bit. The girl was sitting at my table, and she appeared for breakfast next morning. And though it is only the very young who can work up much enthusiasm over the opposite sex in the early hours, I confess that she gave my elderly heart a very pleasant kick. Her name was Beryl Langton, and she was one of the most adorably pretty creatures I've ever seen. And since we were the sole performers at our table it was only natural that we should start talking.

The rougher it was the more she liked it, she told me —and proceeded to lower two sausages and some fat bacon. She was going to Shanghai—an uncle and aunt were there who had asked her to stay.

"It's simply too wonderful, all this," she said. "Of course it's stale to you, but I've never done a longer sea trip than from Weymouth to Jersey."

Her enthusiasm was positively infectious. As far as I am concerned a sea voyage is a necessary evil to be suffered as best one can. But as we staggered up and down the deck that morning—she was doing a sort of corkscrew lurch—I found myself actually looking forward to the present one. I told her stories about the East, and she clung on to my arm and looked up into my face with eyes that shone with excitement.

"I think it's glorious," she said. "The sea is glorious, and life is glorious, and all the things I'm going to see are glorious."

"You might change your mind about the sea," I laughed, "if you were on board a boat like that."

An aged tramp was wallowing past with the waves breaking clean over her, so that she looked like a half-submerged submarine.

" 'The Liner she's a lady,' " she quoted, her eyes fixed on the other boat.   "But it's fine, you know—fine. That life. . . .   Clean and fine."

And for a moment there was a strange expression on her face.

"What about a dish of soup?" I said, and she clapped her hands.

"Splendid," she cried.   "I'm beginning to feel positively ashamed of my appetite."

We battled our way to the saloon and sat down. Two or three rather wan-looking individuals looked up in an aggrieved way as we entered, and the girl's thoroughly audible remark—"Good Lord! what an unholy frowst!" was received without enthusiasm.   Then the soup came, and she concentrated on that.   In fact she was concentrating on the second cup when a man's voice hailed me through the open port-hole behind us.

"Care to make up a rubber?"

Somewhat naturally the girl glanced round to see who it was.   It was Jefferson, and for a moment I saw his eyes fixed on her face with that sudden gleam which is unmistakable.

"No thanks," I said curtly.   "I don't care about playing in the forenoon."

"Pity," he said, but made no movement to go.   "This sea seems to have defeated nearly everybody."

He was including us both in the conversation, and I felt a quick unreasonable annoyance.   I knew, of course, that it was quite impossible to prevent him making the girl's acquaintance if he wished to: you can get to know anybody on board ship.   Besides, it was most certainly no affair of mine.   At the same time—though I had nothing against him—he wasn't the type of man I'd have chosen for my daughter, had I possessed one, to have much to do with.

Then the matter was taken out of my hands.

"I simply adore it," she said to him. "Don't you?"

"I wouldn't go so far as to say that," he smiled. "Having to hold on by one's eyebrows whenever one moves gets a bit monotonous after a time. But luckily it doesn't affect me otherwise. You look very comfy in there. May I come and join you?"

And so the second phase started. Jefferson sat with us till lunch, and it was obvious to the meanest capacity that he was immensely attracted by her. I didn't blame the man—I was attracted myself. And in his full-blooded, boisterous way he wasn't a bad fellow I decided after a while.

Then ten minutes before the bugle went, the first danger rock suddenly showed its head above water. Stanton Blake came in, and nodded good morning to me. And as he did so he saw the girl and paused close by us. Jefferson beckoned the steward, pointedly ordered "*Three* cocktails," and continued his story to Miss Langton. A more blatant request to move on could hardly have been given, and I saw Blake's face as he did so.

Of course it was only the first point in a long game. Jefferson couldn't sit permanently in the girl's pocket, even had she evinced the smallest desire that he should. And that very afternoon, happening to glance out of the smoking-room, I saw Blake and her walking up and down the deck. Jefferson saw them too, and I noticed *his* face as he did so.

From then on the situation developed rapidly. There was nothing novel about it, and had the circumstances been ordinary doubtless one would have watched with a certain amount of amusement. But Mark Jefferson and Stanton Blake were not ordinary, and from the very first there was a substratum of fear in my mind as to how it was going to end.

The girl seemed supremely unconscious of what was happening, though being a woman I don't suppose she was so in reality. But she certainly did not seem to realize that there was any difference between them and half a dozen others of us who saw a good deal of her. Moreover she never showed—openly at any rate—the smallest preference for one man over the other. She went ashore at Gib with Jefferson: it was Blake who took her up to Citra Vecchia when we anchored at Malta. And in the intervals she played deck games, and danced, and laughed, and won everybody's heart— while the strain in the smoking-room whenever those two were there at the same time grew almost unbearable. In fact there was only one point on which they agreed, and that was too trifling to ease matters.

There are I suppose on board every ship a certain number of women who prefer the smoking-room to the other saloons. And we had two of them. They appeared first just before we reached Gib with a nondescript sort of man in tow.

One of them was a harmless little thing who continually giggled: the other—well, the other I should imagine was not quite so harmless. Her name as shown on the ship's list was Delmorton—Mrs. Delmorton. She was invariably most beautifully dressed: she was an extremely good-looking woman: but—that terrible but to the man who has lived much abroad—there was an undoubted touch of the tar-brush. That she had pots of money was obvious: her jewellery was simply magnificent. But she was undoubtedly one of those women into whose past it is inadvisable to inquire too closely.

From the very first she was obviously attracted by Mark Jefferson. Their total dissimilarity of appearance probably accounted for it.   And from the very first Jefferson was equally obviously not attracted by her. Which brings me to the one point on which the two men agreed.

They were playing Bridge as usual—I had cut out for that rubber—and Mrs. Delmorton was standing behind Jefferson.   At last she turned and left the room, and quite deliberately Jefferson addressed the players in a low voice:

"If that —— nigger stands behind me any more I shall play Bridge in my cabin."

And the epithet I regret to state was one which is more applicable to underdone roast beef.

"I agree," said Stanton Blake quietly, and tears came into the eyes of all who heard.   Blake and Jefferson had agreed.

I tottered to a corner with the purser: such a moment had to be commemorated.   And it was only after a solemn two minutes' silence that I asked him about the woman.

It seemed that she'd travelled in the boat before, and always haunted the smoking-room.

"Who or what Mr. Delmorton is, I don't know," said the purser.   "I don't even know if there is one. But he must have been a pretty wealthy gentleman."

"Marvellous pearls she has," I said idly.

"They are," he agreed.   "But by far her most marvellous piece of jewellery is a thing you haven't seen. She'll wear it before the voyage is out—probably on the night of the fancy-dress ball.   Made that way, you know: black blood, I suppose.   Loves barbaric display."

"What kind of a thing is it?"

"It's a sort of hair-slide effect," he answered.   "Diamonds and emeralds.   Personally I think it's appallingly vulgar—but its value must be enormous.   I keep all her stuff, of course, locked up, and she sends for it as she wants it.   And I examined the thing the other day.   In fact I showed it to one of the passengers who happened to be in my office, who is a bit of an expert. He valued it at forty thousand pounds.   She'll show it to you if you ask her.   She adores parading the things."

But I did not trouble Mrs. Delmorton: I continued to avoid the lady like the plague.   Any interest that the voyage held for me lay in the human drama—not jewels. And the human drama continued to develop in a way that nobody liked.   I even noticed the skipper who had happened to come into the smoking-room one night, staring at them a bit hard.   Because—though I've said it before, I'll repeat it again—there were times when there was murder abroad in that ship.   And murder it might have come to on the night of the fancy-dress ball, but for Mrs. Delmorton's diamond and emerald hair-slide.

As the purser had prophesied, she wore it.   She came in some Oriental costume, and I must admit she looked magnificent in it.   And it was the hair-slide that put the finishing touch on it.   It was such a magnificent piece of jewellery, in fact, that I overcame my dislike of the lady and asked her to allow me to examine it.   There was no doubt about it—if anything, forty thousand was an underestimate.   Beryl Langton was with me at the time, and she gave a little gasp of awed envy.   A dozen or more large flawless diamonds: the same number of magnificent emeralds, and a quantity of smaller stones in an old-fashioned setting.   Barbaric: probably at one time it had belonged to some Eastern potentate.   And the net result was that I fully agreed with the purser, though naturally I did not tell the lady so.   The final effect was vulgar, unless it was worn with some fancy costume such as she had on that night.

Beryl Langton agreed with me.

"If that belonged to me," she said, in a sort of ecstatic whisper, "I'd have the whole thing reset into a dozen different pieces. Brooches, rings—and imagine a bracelet made of those smaller stones."

Then she laughed. "And to think that when I went to the purser to-day to get my poor little pearl necklace she was getting *that* out at the same time."

And we are not concerned in any way with the fatuous answer I made. Three pink gins before dinner can be responsible for a lot. . . . We are merely concerned with the extraordinary happenings in the smoking-room which took place after dinner that night. And though for reasons that will appear later it is now two years since the events I am about to describe took place, I think my memory is fairly clear on the matter. At any rate I have forgotten nothing of importance.

It was about ten o'clock when I went in there, and a glance at the card-table indicated trouble. Blake and Jefferson were partners, and the sneer on Blake's face was ugly. Mrs. Delmorton and the lady who giggled were there, and about half a dozen others.

Just as I came in the rubber ended, and Blake leaned across the table.

"Why in God's name, Mr. Jefferson," he snarled, "don't you have lessons in the game? Or else stick to snap with the curate?"

Jefferson half-rose in his seat—the back of his neck a dull purple.

"Steady," said Murgatroyd, who was playing. "Ladies present."

"I tell you what I will do, Mr. Blake," said Jefferson thickly. "I'll play you one hand of show poker for a monkey."

"A monkey." Blake seemed a bit taken aback.

"Afraid of a real gamble," sneered Jefferson.

And suddenly a grim smile flickered round Blake's lips.

"I agree," he said.

We drew round and watched with bated breath. Everyone seemed to realize that there was more than a monkey at stake.

They cut and Jefferson won.   Being show poker he dealt the cards face upwards from a new pack.   And when they each had four cards in front of them Blake had a pair of sevens, and Jefferson wanted a nine for a straight.

I looked at the two men, and Blake's fingers were twitching.   But Jefferson was absolutely calm.   He flicked the card across the table to Blake—another seven. Three—and a little gasp ran round the circle of onlookers.

"It would seem that I want a nine," he said quietly.

He held up the card with its back towards him, so that Blake could see.   And Blake's face turned livid.

"It would seem from your appearance that I've got one," he added.

He had: it was the nine of clubs.

"A monkey, I believe, Mr. Blake, was the bet," he remarked suavely.

And once again Blake smiled sardonically.

"I'll get it," he said abruptly and left the room.

"What the devil does he mean?" said Jefferson, staring after him.   "Get it?   Get what?"

"I'm so glad you won, Mr. Jefferson," said Mrs. Delmorton, leaning over him.

"Thanks," said Jefferson abruptly, his eyes still fixed on the door.

And the next moment I thought the man was going to have an apoplectic fit.   Moreover, I didn't blame him.   Stanton Blake re-entered the smoking-room carrying in his arms a live monkey.

"What's this damned foolery?" said Jefferson thickly.

"We were playing for a monkey, I believe," remarked Blake calmly. "Here it is—and a very nice one, too."

"You . . . you . . . blasted sharper!" roared Jefferson. "I suppose if we'd been playing for a pony you'd have given me a cab-horse. We were playing for five hundred pounds—and you know it."

"We were playing for a monkey," repeated Blake. "I presume I am allowed to put my own interpretation on the word."

It was at that moment that Jefferson picked up the heavy water-bottle that stood on the table, and lifted it above his head. Somebody—the first officer, I think—shouted—"Steady, for God's sake . . ."—*and all the lights went out.*

"You swine—you . . ."

Jefferson's voice came out of the darkness—and the lady who giggled gave a scream. Then after an interval the lights went on again, and we saw that Jefferson had got Blake by the throat. Mrs. Delmorton was cowering back against a chair: the monkey was gibbering in the open porthole.

"Get the skipper," shouted the first officer, and flung himself on Jefferson, with three more of us to help. And it took us all we could do to pull him off.

The skipper came rushing in, and he was in a towering rage.

"If you two men give any further trouble," he roared, "I'll clap you both in irons."

Jefferson was still struggling furiously, when there came the diversion. Mrs. Delmorton raised her hands to her hair, and gave one horrified scream.

"My slide. It's gone."

An instant silence settled on the room.

"Gone," said the skipper. "What do you mean—gone?"

"It was in my hair. You saw it, didn't you?" She turned to me.

"I certainly saw it before dinner," I said. "I can't say I've noticed it since."

"Close the doors," ordered the skipper curtly. "No one is to leave the room. Now let's get at the bottom of all this. You, sir,"—he turned to me—"will you kindly tell me what happened?"

I told him, while Blake and Jefferson sat in opposite corners glaring at one another.

"Who turned off the lights?" he said curtly as I finished.

And no one spoke.

"Did you?" He turned to the steward.

"No, sir. The switch is over there by the door. And I was the other side of the room."

"Please," came a frightened little voice through the porthole, "I did."

We all looked up: Beryl Langton—her face as white as a sheet—was looking in.

"Come in, Miss Langton," said the skipper more gently. "We'd like to know why you did it."

She came in, casting frightened glances at the two men.

"I was passing the door," she stammered, "and I saw Mr. Jefferson with a water-bottle in his hand. And I thought he was going to kill Stanton—Mr. Blake, I mean. And without thinking I switched out the light. Was it terribly wrong?"

"The point is this, Miss Langton," said the skipper gravely. "Mrs. Delmorton has lost her diamond and emerald hair-slide."

"Lost it!" cried the girl. "But I thought you'd

taken it off, Mrs. Delmorton——and put it in your cabin or something . . ."

"Taken it off!" echoed the other. "Nothing of the sort."

"Why did you think Mrs. Delmorton had taken it off?" asked the skipper.

"Because when I passed you twenty minutes or so ago——you were dancing with Mr. Norris, I think——I'm sure you hadn't got it in your hair then. I looked specially to see."

"When was the last occasion, Mrs. Delmorton," said the skipper, "that you definitely remember feeling that the slide was there?"

And that was exactly what Mrs. Delmorton could not say. In fact, when pressed, the last time that she could remember with certainty was at dinner, when I gave it back to her.

"Does anybody here remember seeing it before Miss Langton turned the lights out?" asked Murgatroyd.

And once again no one could say with certainty: we had all been far too occupied with the quarrel between the two men.

"Well, Mrs. Delmorton," said the skipper, "unless it's fallen overboard it must be on board the ship. And if it's on board the ship we'll find it for you."

"My goodness! Captain Brownlow," she almost wailed. "I've suddenly remembered too that I did lean over the rail for quite a time. . . ."

"You'd have probably noticed if it had fallen off then," he said reassuringly. "We'll find it, Mrs. Delmorton. First we'll start with this room."

We were all of us searched, and naturally no one objected. Every seat was minutely examined——even the spittoons were inspected. And there was no trace of that slide. One thing at any rate was certain: it was not in the smoking-room.

At last the skipper gave it up: even Mrs. Delmorton was satisfied. But as he left he turned once more to Jefferson and Blake.

"And as for you two gentlemen," he continued, "I meant what I said. If you can't behave yourselves I'll put you both in irons."

But the kick seemed to have gone out of them. In fact they seemed thoroughly ashamed of themselves.

"Confound it, Jefferson," said Blake, "it was only a jest. I'll write you out a cheque in the morning. . . ."

"Sorry if I was a bit hasty," said the other sheepishly. "Look here, we'd better go and join in this search. Why the cursed woman wants to wear valuable jewels in her head at all for I don't know! What's it look like, anyway?"

They went out together, Blake with the monkey on his shoulder.

"Do *you* think it was a jest?" said Murgatroyd to me as we followed them.

"I'm not a thought-reader," I laughed. "Ask me another."

Well, that ship was searched with a fine tooth-comb, but no trace of Mrs. Delmorton's hair-slide was ever discovered. And after a while the excitement died down. It was insured, anyway, so she would suffer no financial loss. And the finally accepted verdict was that it had probably fallen overboard when she was leaning over the rail.

In fact, after three days the incident was almost forgotten. And the only effect of it that remained was on Jefferson and Blake. It seemed to have sobered them up, and though by no stretch of fancy could it be said that they were friendly, one at any rate no longer feared violence when they met.

Indeed, I was told that the night before Jefferson got

off at Colombo, Blake stood him a drink. I didn't see this amazing occurrence, but that the rumour of such a thing could have been received without derisive laughter showed the change of affairs.

Blake went on to Singapore, and mindful of Beryl Langton's slip when she had called him Stanton, I watched them fairly closely. I should have been very sorry if anything had come of it: Blake wasn't the type of man for her. But nothing happened: obviously it had just been a mild board ship flirtation.

And finally, in the fullness of time, I saw her off at Shanghai. Moreover, up on the boat-deck the night before we got in, I—well . . . However, that is altogether another story. . . .

*   *   *   *   *

It is at this point that I can imagine the intelligent reader saying with a bewildered air—"What the deuce is all this about? What's the point of it?"

Sir, you are justified in your query. And if it hadn't been that my doctor ordered me to Carlsbad a week ago, I should not have wasted my own time and yours in writing it down. But he did, and the first night I was there I noticed an elderly man of unprepossessing appearance around whom the staff buzzed like blue-bottles. It was Guggenheimer—the German million-aire.

I was watching him idly, when suddenly a flutter of excitement ran through the lounge. And the cause of it was a girl with a monkey perched on her shoulder. I gazed at her speechlessly—a perfectly gowned, *soigné*, cosmopolitan woman. I gazed at her speechlessly—Guggenheimer's latest. I gazed at her speechlessly—Beryl Langton. And as she passed close to me I noticed she was wearing a lovely diamond and emerald bracelet.

But so dense can the human brain be at times that even when a biggish red-faced man came up and spoke to Guggenheimer I didn't realize anything was amiss. In fact I didn't realize it until I saw the German introduce him to the girl.

Then the brain did begin to function.   For why it was necessary to introduce Mark Jefferson to Beryl Langton was a thing no feller could understand. . . .

My mind went back to that voyage out East, and from a totally new angle I set out to consider the things that had happened.

That Mark Jefferson and Beryl Langton could have forgotten one another was obviously absurd: therefore they were playing a game: therefore they were in collusion.

If they were in collusion now, there was no inherent reason why they shouldn't have been in collusion then. With Stanton Blake as the third member of the gang.

And if that was so the three of them had fooled us all from the very first.

I lit a cigar: the thing wanted thought.   They had fooled us with only one idea—to lead up to that culminating moment in the smoking-room when they stole Mrs. Delmorton's hair-slide.

I ran over things from the beginning.   They knew Mrs. Delmorton would be travelling by the boat: they knew her habits—and they laid their plans accordingly. And then when the two men of the gang had got the attention of everyone in the smoking-room riveted on themselves, the girl switched off the lights.

One of them—Blake probably: he had the touch of a conjurer—had whipped it out of her head in the darkness.   But the point was—what the deuce had he done with it?   It hadn't been on him or in that room when the search took place.   That I could swear to.

And then suddenly it dawned on me, in all its rich genius. The monkey. The whole bet about the monkey became pointless if they were members of the same gang, unless the object was to introduce the animal into the room in a perfectly natural way.

It was the monkey that had passed the slide to the girl through the open port-hole—it had been sitting there chattering when the lights went on. And if the lights had gone on the fraction of a second too soon, it would merely have been taken as a mischievous trick.

Clever—you know: deuced clever. Of course, I may be wrong: possibly that slide is at the bottom of the Indian Ocean.

But Beryl Langton, who now calls herself Louise van Dyck, cannot have completely forgotten Mark Jefferson, who now calls himself John P. Mellon, in two years. And she does wear a lovely diamond and emerald bracelet. And she did give a start of unfeigned amazement when we found ourselves drinking the water at neighbouring tables. And she did look a bit nonplussed when I asked her about Stanton Blake and her uncle in Shanghai.

Of course, I suppose I ought by rights to warn the police or old Guggenheimer.

But I shan't. He's an unpleasant-looking man. And she *was* perfectly adorable on the boat-deck that night. Moreover, I may be wrong, but I have a sort of idea that she might . . .

No—damn it! I came here to drink the waters.

I

WHEN Jack Tennant got engaged to Mary Darnley, their world at large decided that it was good.   And it would have been difficult to decide otherwise.   Jack was one of the dearest fellows imaginable: Mary was a darling.   They each had looks: and —a detail which cannot be ignored in these prosaic days—there was a sufficiency of money on both sides to ensure comfort.

They both came from the same part of the county, so that their friends were mutual.   So, too, were their tastes.   They both went well to hounds—in fact, there was a considerable section of the hunt who would have liked to see Jack as Master: they both played tennis and golf above the average.   So that, in a nutshell, the world's decision in their case could be pronounced correct.

We had all seen the drift of affairs during the hunting season, but it was not till May that the engagement was definitely announced.   And, funnily enough, the man who actually told me was Laurence Trent. Which necessitates another peep into our little corner of England.   It had been common knowledge for two or three years that nothing would have pleased him better than that Mary should take the name of Trent, and when he told me the news I glanced at him curiously to see if he was at all upset.   But not a bit of it.

"Of course," he said, as he stuffed tobacco into his pipe, "it would be idle to pretend that I wouldn't have preferred Mary to choose someone else, but since she hasn't there is no one I'd sooner see her married to than old Jack.   They ought to make a thundering good pair."

I agreed, and felt pleasantly surprised. Not that Trent wasn't a very good fellow: he was. But somehow I didn't expect him to take it *quite* so well. I'd always felt that there was something about him, something I couldn't define, which just spoiled an otherwise first-class sportsman. Perhaps it was that he didn't lose very well at games. True, he rarely lost at all—he was easily the best tennis-player round about. But if by chance he did, though he kept himself under perfect control, and to all outward appearances took his defeat quite pleasantly, I'd seen a glint in his eyes that seemed to prove the old tag about appearances being deceptive. However, here he was taking his loss in the biggest game of all as well as Jack Tennant would have taken it himself.

"When are they going to be married?" I asked.

"Fairly shortly, I gather," he answered. "There can't be anything to wait for."

And sure enough when the announcement appeared two or three days later in *The Times*, it stated that "a marriage had been arranged and would shortly take place."

They were inundated, of course, with congratulations. And I, being old enough to be their father, felt specially honoured when they both came to dine with me quietly.

"A dull evening, my children," I said. "It was good of you to come."

"Go to blazes, Bill," said Jack. "It was damned sporting of you as a confirmed old bachelor to run the risk of asking us. You are probably proposing to retire to your study after dinner, on the pretence of writing letters, and then herald your return with a coughing fit in the hall. I warn you that if you do we shall come too, and bonnet you with your own paper-basket."

"It is true," I murmured guiltily, "that some such idea had entered my brain, but in view of your threat it shall be abandoned."

And, by Jove! they stopped till one. Just once or twice his hand would touch her arm: just once or twice a look would pass between them that made even a confirmed old bachelor wonder if he wasn't really a confirmed old fool. They were two of the best, and it did one's eyes good to see them together. Certainly if any couple ever seemed to have been smiled on by Fate, it was this one. Which made the tragedy all the more dreadful when it occurred.

However, I will take things in their proper sequence. It was on the 15th of June, so I see from my diary, that a party of us went for a picnic. Jack and his girl were there, and Laurence Trent, and several others whose names are immaterial. We went in three cars, starting after lunch, and our destination was an old ruined Priory some forty miles away which was reputed to be haunted. The ghost was said to be the black-cowled figure of a monk, and if it came to a man it meant death. There was a good deal of ragging and chaff, and one of the men, I remember, covered himself with a tablecloth and stalked about amongst the ruins. In fact the whole atmosphere of the party was what you would have expected when a bunch of healthy normal people find themselves in such a locality in broad daylight.

Laurence Trent was particularly scathing on things ghostly, and roared with laughter at the usual stories of people's aunts who had woken up in the middle of the night to feel a spectral hand clutching the bed-clothes.

"It's always somebody's aunt," he jeered. "What I want to know is if any one of you personally have ever felt this clutching hand. It's rot——the whole thing. Due to indigestion. For all that I'm glad we came, because it's a beautiful old place. I'm going to take some photographs."

He set up his camera—photography was his great hobby—and took several exposures from different angles.

"Perhaps we'll see the black monk in one of them," he laughed. "Come on, Jack—I've got one film left. You and Mary go and pose in the foreground."

Now I was standing at his side at the moment, and the rest of the party were fooling about behind us.

"That's right," he said, with his hand on the bulb. And even as I heard the click of the shutter, he muttered "My God!" under his breath. I glanced at him: his face was as white as a sheet, and he was staring with dilated eyes in front of him. Jack and Mary had turned away: no one had seen his agitation except myself.

"What's the matter, Trent?" I asked quickly.

"Nothing," he said at length, "nothing."

The colour was coming back to his cheeks, though his hands shook a little as he dismantled his camera.

"You didn't see anything, did you, Mercer? Standing by Jack?"

"Nothing at all," I said brusquely. "Did you?"

"I thought," he began, and then he shook himself suddenly. "Of course not," he laughed. "A trick of the light."

But it seemed to me that his laughter didn't ring quite true, and I watched him curiously.

"Did you think you saw the black monk?" I said jocularly.

"Go to Hell," he snapped. And then, "Sorry, Mercer. But it's best not to chaff about these things."

Which coming from the person who had chaffed

about them more than anyone else struck me as a little
cool. However, I thought no more about it. We
drove home in different cars, and when, two or three
mornings later, I saw him walking up my drive I had
completely dismissed the matter from my mind. In
fact I merely wondered what had brought him: Trent
was not a frequent visitor of mine.

"Can you give me a few minutes, Mercer?" he said
gravely, and I wondered still more at his tone of voice.
"I want to ask your advice."

"Of course," I said. "Come indoors."

I led the way, and he followed in silence.

"You remember our picnic at the old Priory," he
remarked when I had closed the study door.

"Perfectly," I answered, suddenly recalling his
strange agitation.

"You remember that when I took a photograph of
Jack and Mary, you pulled my leg and asked me if
I thought I'd seen the black monk?"

"I do," I said. "You seemed so upset."

"I was," he answered quietly. "Because that is
exactly what I had seen."

"My dear Trent," I laughed. "You! The most
scathing cynic of us all!"

But he wasn't to be drawn.

"I admit it," he said gravely. "I admit that up
to that moment I regarded anything of that sort as
old women's foolishness. All the way home in the
car: all that night I endeavoured to persuade myself
that what I had seen was a trick of the light as I said
to you. And I almost succeeded. Now I know it
wasn't!"

"You know it wasn't!" I echoed incredulously.
"But how?"

"You may remember that I took the photograph,"
he said. "And, Mercer, the camera cannot lie."

He was taking a print out of his pocket as he spoke, and I stared at him wonderingly. In silence he handed it across to me, and as I looked at it the hair at the back of my scalp began to prick. In the background stood the ruins of the Priory: in front were Jack and Mary. But it was not at them that I was looking. Standing by Jack was a black-cowled figure, with one arm outstretched towards him. The face was concealed: the hand could not be seen. But the whole effect was so incredibly menacing that I felt my throat go dry.

"A defect in the film," I stammered after a while.

"Then it's a very peculiar one," he said gravely. "I tried to think it was that, Mercer, but it was no good. That's not a defect. You see"—he paused a minute—"I saw it myself."

"Then why didn't I?" I demanded.

"God knows," he said, and for a while we fell silent.

"But this is impossible," I said at length. "Things like that don't happen."

"Exactly what I've been saying to myself," he remarked. "Things like that don't happen. And in your hands you hold the proof that in this case it has. And to me of all people. I, who have always ridiculed anything of the sort. I've heard—who hasn't?—of spirit photographs, and I've always regarded them as a not very clever type of fraud."

"You've got the film?" I said.

"No," he answered. "I haven't. I made two prints of it, and then I got into a sort of panic. Damned foolish of me, but 'pon my soul, Mercer, I've hardly been able to think straight since I developed that roll. Anyway, I put a match to it and burnt it. However, that's not the point, is it? The point is, what are we going to do?"

"Do," I repeated stupidly. "What can we do?"

"Well, ought we to warn Jack? You know the legend. Heaven knows I do. No one jeered at it as much as I did, and now I can't get it out of my mind. If the black monk goes to a man it means death. And that afternoon it went to Jack."

"Confound it, Trent," I cried irritably, "this is the twentieth century. We're talking drivel."

"Go on," he said wearily. "Say again all the things I've said already to myself. Say we're two grown men, and not hysterical children. Say that the whole thing is absurd. Say everything you darned well please. I have—several times. And then, Mercer, look at the photograph you hold in your hand."

He got up and began pacing up and down the room.

"I tell you," he went on, "I've thought of this thing from every angle. And the more I've thought of it the more utterly nonplussed have I become."

"Even granted," I said slowly, "that this—this thing was there that afternoon . . ."

"Damn it," he almost shouted, "is there any doubt about it?"

"Very well then," I said, "I'll put it a different way. Although this thing was there that afternoon, it doesn't follow that the rest of the legend is correct. That it means—death."

"I know it doesn't," he cried eagerly. "That's the one straw at which I'm clutching."

"And most emphatically," I went on, "nothing must be said about it to Jack. If—Great Scott! you know, it seems too ridiculous to be even discussing it in the broad light of day—if it does portend death, then death will come whatever we do. And if it doesn't—if there's nothing in it—there's no earthly use making Jack's life a burden to him. Wondering what's going to happen. Why, he might even break off the engagement."

He nodded two or three times.

"You're right," he said. "Perhaps I ought to have torn up the whole thing and said nothing about it. But to tell you the truth it's given me such an appalling shock that I felt I simply must talk to somebody about it. And as you were with me when it happened, I naturally thought of you. I wish to Heavens I'd never suggested going to the beastly place."

"Was it your suggestion?" I said. "I thought it was Lady Taunton's."

"I suggested it to her," he said moodily. "Anyway, it's done now, and we went. Look here, Mercer, don't think me an ass. And I shall quite understand if you would rather not. But I'd be most awfully grateful to you if you'd keep that print. Lock it away in your safe. I sort of feel," he went on apologetically, "that it would help me considerably if I could know that there was somebody else—— You know. . . ."

"Morbid," I said. "Let's tear it up, and try and forget it."

"Isn't that tantamount to confessing that we're frightened?" he said. "You can tear it up easily enough, but that isn't going to wipe it off our minds. However, I leave it to you: do as you like."

He nodded abruptly, and stepped through the open window.

"So long," he grunted, and for a while I watched him striding down the drive. Then I went back to my desk and again picked up the print. The whole thing seemed so utterly incredible that my brain felt dazed. The average Englishman who leads an outdoor life doesn't worry his head as a general rule about the so-called supernatural, and I had certainly been no exception to the rule. If I had been asked to sum up my ideas on the subject, I suppose I should have said that though I was quite prepared to believe that strange things happened outside our ken, I had never come across them and I didn't want to. And here I found myself confronted with this astounding photograph. Back and forth, this way and that, did I argue it out in my mind. And I got no farther forward. If it was a defect in the film, then in view of what Trent had seen, it was the most amazing coincidence that had ever happened. And if it wasn't . . .

The lunch-gong roused me, and for a moment or two I hesitated. My hand went out towards a box of matches: should I burn it? And then Trent's remark came back to me—"Isn't it tantamount to confessing that we're frightened?" I went to my safe and opened it. I thrust the print far into the back. Time would tell. And as the days passed, and the weeks, gradually the thing faded from my mind. When I thought of it at all, I regarded it as one of those strange inexplicable things which are insoluble.

II

The wedding was fixed for the end of September. On the 31st of August Jack Tennant was killed. To this day I remember the blank feeling of numbed shock I experienced when I heard the news. I had almost forgotten the photograph, and I just sat staring speechlessly at my butler as he told me.

It appeared that he had fallen over the edge of Draxton Quarry, and had broken his neck on the rocks below. I knew the place as well as I knew my own garden—but so did Jack Tennant. It was an old disused chalk quarry, and for years people had been agitating to have railings put round the top. And because it was everybody's business, no one had attended to it. To a stranger it was a dangerous place, but it was extraordinary that a man who knew the quarry as well as he did should have ventured so near the edge. As always when the soil is small landslips were frequent.

"It was Mr. Trent who found him, sir," concluded my butler, and instantly my thoughts reverted to the photograph. So the legend of the black monk had not proved false.

I ordered my car, and went round to see Trent. He was in a terrible state of distress, and it appeared that not only had he found Jack's body but he had seen the whole thing happen.

"I was walking back from Oxshott Farm," he said, "and when I got level with the quarry, I saw old Jack away to the left close by the top. So I started to stroll towards him. I hadn't gone more than about twenty yards, when he suddenly threw up his arms, gave a great shout and disappeared. The ground had crumbled under his feet, but what I can't understand is why he should have been standing so close to the edge. I got down to the bottom as quickly as I could, but the poor old chap was stone dead."

"What a ghastly thing," I muttered.

We looked at one another, the same thought in both our minds.

"Did you tear up that photograph?" he said at length.

"No, I kept it. It is in my pocket now. Have you got yours?"

He nodded. "Yes, I have. Look here, Mercer, what are we going to do about them?"

"I don't see that there's anything to be done," I said. "The poor old chap is dead, and nothing can alter the fact."

"I know that," he answered. "But there will be an inquest, and of course I shall be called. In fact, as far as I know, I'm the only witness: the place was absolutely deserted when it happened.   Oughtn't I to say something about it?"

"What on earth is the use?" I cried.   "As the thing stands at the moment it is merely a ghastly accident. There's nothing to tickle the public fancy over it, and it will be dismissed by the Press in a few lines.   But if you mention those photographs, you will immediately start a first-class sensation.   You'll have every reporter in England buzzing round, and it will be most unpleasant for all of us."

"I suppose you're right," he said slowly.   "And yet—I don't know.   It's all so extraordinary, isn't it? I almost feel as if I was suppressing a piece of vitally important evidence."

A shadow fell across the room, and I looked up quickly.   A man was standing in the open window —a man who bore a marked resemblance to Jack Tennant.

"Forgive my intrusion," he said gravely, "but I heard that Mr. Trent was on the lawn and . . ."   He paused, looking from one to the other of us. . . .

"That's me," said Trent, and the other bowed. "And this is Mercer."

"I'm Jack's brother," he remarked.   "I gather it was you who found him."

"Not only that, but I saw the whole thing," said Trent.   "I've just been telling Mercer about it."

Once again he told the story, and the other listened in silence.

"Is that all?" he said when Trent had finished.

"Everything.   Why?"

"Because I could not help overhearing, as I came in, a remark you made to Mr. Mercer.   You said you felt as if you were suppressing a piece of vitally important evidence."

Trent glanced at me, question in his eyes.

"I think," I said at length, "that Mr. Tennant at any rate should be told. And then he, as Jack's brother, had better decide."

And so Trent told him the other story too, whilst Tennant listened with ever-growing amazement on his face.

"You feel," said Trent, "just as I felt: just as Mercer felt when I first told him. I don't believe there was a man in England more profoundly sceptical on psychic matters than I was. But there you are: look at it."

He took his copy from his pocket and handed it to the other.

"The film I destroyed, and have never ceased regretting that I did so. But I am as convinced in my own mind that poor old Jack was under sentence of death from that day, as I am that we three are in this room. We talked it over, Mercer and I, and rightly or wrongly we came to the conclusion that it would be worse than useless to tell him. If there was nothing in it we should only be upsetting him needlessly: if the reverse then it would do no good."

"Most extraordinary," said Tennant. "A pity you destroyed the film. You have kept your copy, Mr. Mercer?"

"As a matter of fact, I have it on me now," I said, taking it from my pocket.

"They are exactly the same," cried Trent. "Two prints of the same film. Good Lord! I'm sorry. How infernally clumsy of me."

A stream of ink had shot across his desk, soaking one of the prints that Tennant was examining side by side.

"My dear sir——ten thousand apologies." He dashed round with blotting-paper. "It's not on your clothes, is it?"

"Luckily not," said Tennant. "But I'm afraid one of your prints is ruined."

"That doesn't matter. Anyway, one is all right. And that brings us to the point we've got to decide —whether or not anything shall be said about this at the inquest. Mercer thinks it will bring a swarm of journalists about our heads, and he is probably right. I, on the other hand—well, you overheard my remark. Ought we to suppress it?"

"It's certainly most strange," said Tennant thoughtfully. "You say, Mr. Trent, that you actually saw this apparition?"

"I did. And it shook me badly at the moment, as Mercer will tell you."

The other rose and went to the window, where he stood looking down the drive.

"And you didn't see it, Mr. Mercer?"

"No," I said, "I didn't. But I can vouch for Trent's agitation."

"Which was quite understandable," agreed Jack's brother. "However, the point on which you apparently want my advice is whether or not this photograph should be produced at the inquest. I unhesitatingly agree with Mr. Mercer. To produce it can do no good, and will inevitably throw us all into the limelight."

"Very good," said Trent, "I will say nothing about it."

He picked up his copy and replaced it in his pocket.

"Not much good keeping yours, Mercer, I'm afraid."

"I don't want it," I said. "Tear it up and throw it away."

"Well then, it's understood," he said as he dropped the pieces in his waste-paper basket, "that nothing should be said about this. On second thoughts I think you're right."

He paused for a moment, and then turned to Tennant.

"May I tender you my sincere sympathy in your great loss?"

"Thank you," said the other. "Jack was a dear boy. Well, Mr. Mercer, if that is your car outside I wonder if you would give me a lift back. I'm staying at the Boar's Head."

"Of course," I cried, and Trent followed us through the hall.

"Will you be at the inquest?" he said as we got in.

"I certainly shall," said Tennant, and with that we drove off.

"How is Mary taking it?" I said, as we turned into the road.

Instead of answering he made a remark which seemed to be in the most questionable taste.

"I believe I'm right in thinking that Mr. Trent was —shall we say—a runner up for Mary?"

"Really, Mr. Tennant," I said stiffly, "I am not in his confidence to that extent. And, anyway, this is hardly the time to discuss it."

"I think I remember Jack mentioning the fact to me in a letter last winter. They were getting up some amateur theatricals, and Trent was acting."

"He is a very good actor," I remarked. "In fact I believe for a while he was on the stage in London. Before he came into money."

"I thought he must be," was his somewhat surprising reply. "It's strange that a man who is presumably neat with his fingers should be so clumsy with his hands."

"I don't know that I should have called Trent particularly neat with his fingers," I said.

"That makes it even stranger," he remarked.
"People who are not neat with their fingers—men
especially—generally dislike sewing."

For a moment or two I stared at him blankly, but
his face was expressionless.

"What on earth . . .?" I began.

"Though, of course," he continued, "occupation of
some sort is a great help if one is upset. But sewing
a button on a coat is hardly one I should have expected a man to select. You didn't notice that?
Well—it's not surprising.   Like the majority of people
you see—but you don't observe.   Now on Mr. Trent's
desk was a reel of black cotton and a needle—a sufficiently unusual thing to find on a man's desk to make
one wonder why it was there. When one further
notices that the bottom leather button of his shooting-
coat is sewn on very crudely with black cotton the
connection becomes obvious."

I confess I found myself disliking the man intensely.
Within a few hours of his brother's death, that he
should callously discuss little deductions and inferences
struck me as absolutely indecent.

"Of course I may be wrong," I said coldly.   "But
the death of a boy who was almost like a son to me,
seems of more importance to my mind than the sewing
on of fifty buttons."

He turned to me with a sudden very charming smile
—a smile that brought back Jack irresistibly.

"Forgive me, Mr. Mercer," he said.   "Believe me,
I am not as callous as you think."

And with that he relapsed into a silence that continued till we reached the Boar's Head.

III

The inquest revealed nothing that we did not know
already. The jury returned a verdict of Accidental

Death, tendered their sympathy to the deceased man's family, and added a rider to the effect that steps should be taken immediately to erect a suitable fence round the top of Draxton Quarry. Trent gave his evidence with considerable emotion—as the jury well knew he and Tennant had been friends—and true to what we had arranged he said nothing about the black monk. It was therefore with some surprise that when I went into the Boar's Head for luncheon I was at once tackled on the subject by the landlord.

"It's all over the place, Mr. Mercer," he said. "Not as how I holds with that sort of stuff, but you know what folks be round here."

I made some non-committal reply and sought out Tennant.

"Are you surprised?" he said quietly. "I'm not."

"But who started it?" I cried. "You say you've said nothing, and it wasn't me."

"Which narrows the field somewhat—doesn't it?"

And at that moment Trent came in, and I tackled him.

"Good Heavens!" he muttered, "it's spread as quick as that, has it? It was my gross carelessness. Like a fool last night, I forgot to take the papers out of the pocket of my coat when I changed for dinner. And my man must have seen it. Damn the fellow! I'll sack him."

He went out fuming angrily, and I turned a little curiously to Tennant.

"Why did you say you weren't surprised?" I said.

He smiled enigmatically.

"Those sort of things have a way of coming out," he remarked. "Shall we lunch together?"

And as we were going in a page brought him a telegram. He opened it and gave a grunt of satisfaction as he read the contents.   Then he turned to me.

"Would you be good enough to ask me to dinner to-night?   And a friend of mine, too—a lady."

I stared at him blankly.

"I am aware it sounds a little strange, and my next request will sound stranger still.   Does Trent know your family intimately?   Your relations, I mean."

"Far from it," I said.

"So you could quite easily invent a niece, shall we say, without him suspecting anything."

"What the devil are you driving at, Tennant?" I cried.

"Because I would like this friend of mine to be your niece.   And I shall meet her for the first time at your house.   And so will Trent, who I want you to ask to dinner also.   Incidentally, here he is.   Ask him now, please,"—his voice was low and urgent—"and mention your niece."

There was something compelling about the man, and I found myself doing as he said.

"Dine," said Trent.   "Thanks, Mercer, I'd like to. Eight, I suppose."

"There will be a niece of mine there," I remarked. "I don't think you've ever met her.   I suppose you wouldn't care to come, Tennant."

"Will it be quite quiet?" he said doubtfully.

"Just us," I answered.   "And my niece."

"Thanks very much," he said, "I'll come."

At that moment I happened to glance at Trent, and it seemed to me that he gave a tiny frown.   It was gone in an instant, but the impression that he wasn't too well pleased at my inviting Tennant, lingered in my mind.   And it was still there when Tennant and the lady arrived at a quarter to eight.   All the afternoon I'd been racking my brains trying to think what all the mystery was about, and the instant they came I turned eagerly to Tennant.

He cut short my questions immediately.

"Listen, Mr. Mercer," he said curtly, "we haven't got too much time. This is Miss Greyson. You will call her Monica. You are her uncle: so she will call you uncle—what?"

"Most people call me Bill," I said.

"Very good. She will call you Uncle Bill. She is staying in the house: but that fact must not be alluded to in front of the servants, or they may give it away."

"But," I cried, "what is it all about?"

"With luck you'll know before the evening is out," he said gravely. "Take your cues from us, and if it's urgent—for God's sake jump to it, or it may be too late."

"What may be too late?" I said blankly.

"Monica is taking her life in her hands to-night," was his astounding reply. "Perhaps we all are. Above all—don't forget—*not a word to Trent.*"

And at that moment Trent was announced. In a sort of dream I heard a voice introducing him to Miss Greyson—and realized the voice was my own. In a sort of dream I went in to dinner, and found myself eating what was put in front of me mechanically. Taking her life in her hands. Was I mad—or was he?

After a while I pulled myself together—as host I had to make some pretence at talking—and found they were discussing the photograph.

"If I were you, Trent," Tennant was saying, "I would send that photograph to the Society for Psychical Research."

"Dash it, man," answered Trent, "I couldn't. I've cursed my man's head off for speaking about it at all, and I don't want any more publicity. I mean Mary

is in the photo, too, as well as poor old Jack. It's
incredible how it's spread all over the place so quickly."

"It is without exception the most wonderful spirit
photograph I have ever seen," said Tennant. "And
it's a thing I'm extremely interested in."

"Are you?" said Trent in surprise. "Somehow I
should never have thought it of you."

"Only, of course, as an amateur." He glanced
across at the girl. "Forgive the impertinence, Miss
Greyson, but surely you are clairvoyante?"

She looked at me with a smile.

"I don't know what Uncle Bill will say about it,"
she said, "but you're quite right, Mr. Tennant. Only
I don't want it talked about in the family, Uncle
Bill."

"My dear, I'll say nothing," I said.

"How did you know?" asked Trent curiously.

"My dear fellow," said Tennant, "when you've
dabbled in it even as little as I have, you'll recognize
it at a glance. There is something in the face—something indefinable and yet quite obvious. I should
imagine that Miss Greyson was possessed of remarkable powers."

The girl laughed.

"That, I'm afraid, I don't know. I've not done
much of it, and, of course, when one is in a trance one
knows nothing."

"It would be interesting to try to-night," said Tennant. "That is to say if Miss Greyson doesn't mind."

Trent fidgeted in his chair.

"I don't know that I'm particularly keen," he muttered. "The black monk is enough for me—at any
rate for the present."

And then for one moment, Tennant stared straight
at me, and the unspoken message might have been
shouted aloud, so clear was it.

"I think it might be quite amusing," I said. "But, of course, Monica must decide."

"I don't mind," cried the girl. "If Mr. Trent would sooner not . . ."

"Oh! I don't mind," he said sullenly.

"I can't guarantee anything," went on the girl. "Sometimes I'm told I simply talk gibberish."

"Naturally," said Tennant quietly. "No medium can ever be certain of getting results."

For a while we stopped on at the dinner-table, but the atmosphere was not congenial. Trent sat in moody silence, looking every now and then from under his eyebrows at the girl. And at length Tennant gave me an almost imperceptible movement of the head.

"Shall we go into the other room?" I said. "And then Monica shall take charge."

"Mind you," she repeated with a smile, "I don't guarantee anything."

"I suppose we put out the lights?" I said.

"It's always better," she answered. "Now if you three just sit down, anywhere you like, and keep quite still I'll see what I can do."

And the last thing I noticed as I switched off the lights was Trent's sullen, scowling face. For a while we sat in silence, and I know that my nerves were far from being as steady as I would have liked. That one remark of Tennant's kept ringing in my head— taking her life in her hands. But how? And why the secrecy over Trent?

Suddenly a long shuddering sigh came from the girl, and I sat up tensely.

"She's under," said Tennant in a low voice. "Be careful."

Again silence—and then a man's loud voice— "Peter."

"Good God!" I muttered, "it's Jack."

I could hear Trent's breath come in a quick hiss.
"Peter! Peter!"
"Is that you, Jack?" said Tennant quietly.
"Peter! The button. Proof from the button."
"What button, Jack?"
"Proof. Proof." The voice was far away. "He came down to get it."
"Jack, come back, Jack. How are you, old chap?"
"Proof. Peter—no accident. That devil—that devil . . ."
"Who, Jack—who. Did someone murder you?"
"That devil—that devil—Laurence . . ."
There came a shrill piercing scream, and a dreadful worrying noise.
"Lights," roared Tennant, and I dashed for the switch. In the room behind, a voice I didn't recognize was muttering harshly again and again:
"Yes—damn you, I did it. I did it, you swine."
On her back, on the floor, was Monica Greyson, and kneeling over her with his hands clutching her throat was Trent. His face was distorted with fury: there was murder in every line of it. And even as I watched, fascinated with horror, Tennant and another man hurled themselves on him.
"Sand-bag him, Simpson," shouted Tennant. "He'll kill her."
And the next instant Trent lay still, and Tennant with his arms round the girl was calling for brandy.
"Good enough, Simpson, I think," he said curtly, and the other nodded. "By the way, Mercer—this is Inspector Simpson of Scotland Yard."
"But what does it all mean," I said feebly.
"That that devil murdered Jack in cold blood," he said grimly. "And he's going to swing for it."
Trent, handcuffed by now, had come to, and lay glaring at the speaker.

"You wouldn't have got me but for that cursed girl," he snarled. "A man can't compete against that."

And Tennant laughed.

"It may interest you to know, Laurence Trent, that the whole thing to-night has been a fake from beginning to end. Just as your photograph of the black monk was a fake."

IV

"Has it ever occurred to you, Mercer, that by far the best way of stopping people talking about a thing, is to present them with a ready-made solution which accounts for that thing? If in addition that solution can be substantiated by an unbiased witness its value is greatly increased."

Trent had gone in the custody of Inspector Simpson, and Tennant and I and the girl—little the worse now for her rough handling—were sitting in my study.

"There is nothing so fatal," he continued calmly, "to arriving at the truth as to start with a preconceived theory. And a ready-made solution in nine cases out of ten causes just such a start. If a man is perfectly satisfied with his solution he has no incentive to try and find another.

"The preconceived theory in this case was that Jack had met his death accidentally. I was perfectly prepared to believe it: at the same time I was equally prepared to disbelieve it. And when I arrived here, I endeavoured to make my mind a blank except for three facts, none of which were conclusive and all of which were perfectly consistent with the accident theory.

"The first was that it was strange that Jack should have been standing so near the edge. Not impossible —but strange.

"The second was that it was Laurence Trent who found him.

"And the third was—that *if* it wasn't an accident—Trent is, as far as I know, the only man who had any motive for killing Jack—namely Mary.

"That was my state of mind when I first saw Trent. I had no proof whatever that it wasn't an accident: but I had no proof that it was. And then I noticed the button. To you it conveyed nothing: to me it was a most significant thing. To a man who was in the condition of agitation that he was in to set to work to sew a button on his coat struck me as most peculiar. Unless he was afraid of such a thing as finger-marks: unless, perhaps—it was still only perhaps—there had been a struggle, a button had been wrenched off his coat, and he had decided to sew it on to prevent questions.

"Then you started the black-monk question. Well, Mercer, I frankly admit I'm sceptical. But I am old enough now to realize that just because I don't happen to believe in a thing, that that is no proof of its falseness. Men of brains, men of intellect have assured me that they have indisputable proof that spirit photographs have been taken. And when Trent showed me his copy I was still prepared to believe in the possibility of its being genuine. Until you showed me yours. Did you ever see the two prints side by side?"

"Never," I said.

"And Trent never intended that anyone should. It was his one great mistake. In your copy the outstretched arm of the black monk just reached a corner of the priory behind it: in his copy there was at least the sixteenth of an inch overlap. Which proved instantly that it was merely an ordinary fake done by superimposing one film on another. It also proved instantly that we were dealing with a singularly dangerous man—and a singularly clever one."

"For the life of me I don't quite see the object," I said.

"You go to the theatre, don't you, Mercer? And you know the effect of concentrating the limelight on one figure. The audience doesn't worry about the others. Now if you were to walk into any public-house within a radius of five miles at this moment, you would find that the black monk is the sole topic of conversation. The sceptical ones will say it's co-incidence, and the superstitious that it's fate. But it would have served its purpose with both parties—and that was to occupy the front of the stage, leaving the rest in darkness.

"You were there to give an air of truth to the whole thing. Why—you believed it yourself: you vouched for his agitation when he took the photo."

"I can hardly believe that the man had planned the whole thing then," I said. "It seems too mons-trous."

Tennant shrugged his shoulders.

"Who knows? Perhaps it was a whim of the moment: perhaps he really did think some trick of the light was the black monk. And then the idea grew until it obsessed him. He was committed to nothing: all he had to do was to wait his chance. But the point is that when I left with you in the car I knew Trent had murdered Jack. Which is a totally different thing to proving it. He had destroyed the main evidence by tipping the ink over it: and even if the police arrested him—which was most unlikely—there wasn't a hope of his being convicted on the evidence I had."

He mixed himself a drink.

"Theatrical, perhaps. And yet I don't know. On the face of it it seemed so theatrical that it must be true. Wherein lay his cleverness. However, Monica proved to-night that other people could act, too."

And then came the strangest thing of that strange night.

"I suppose you realize, Peter, don't you," she said quietly, "that I was completely off?"

He stared at her blankly.

"You were what?" he stammered. "You say you were—off. Good God!"

XXIV   .   THE   HIDDEN   WITNESS

I DON'T know exactly when it was that I first realized that Miles Standish was in love with Mary Somerville. As a general rule men are very unobservant on such matters, and I suppose I was no exception. All I know is that when I mentioned the matter guardedly to Phyllis Dankerton she observed brightly that the next great discovery I should make was that the earth was round. So I suppose it must have been fairly obvious.

Anyway, it doesn't much matter, except that I'd like to get it accurate. The house-party was all there when I arrived. To take them in order there were, first of all, our host and hostess—John Somerville and his wife. He was a wealthy man—something in cotton —who had reached such a position of affluence at a comparatively early age that he could, had he wanted to, have given up business altogether. But he preferred to have something to do, and now, at the age of forty-five, he still went up to London five days a week. A smallish man, thin and spare, with shrewd thoughtful eyes that missed very little that went on around him.

It was through Mary, his wife, that I had got to know him. She was fifteen years his junior, and if ever there was a case of wondering why two people had got married, this was it. She was one of the most lovely creatures I have ever seen—the sort of girl who could have married literally anyone she chose. And then quite suddenly, five years ago, she had married John.

Personally I have always thought that money had a good deal to do with it. Not that John wasn't quite a decent fellow, but having said that you'd said all. By no possible stretch of imagination could he be regarded as the sort of man to inspire romance in a girl's heart. He was far too self-centred: far too much the business man to the exclusion of everything else. And yet Mary, with numerous men at her feet, had selected him.

My own impression was that she had begun to regret it. They got on very well together, but it was a very restrained relationship. She liked him and he was inordinately proud of her—and that was the end of it. So much for our host and hostess.

There was a married couple—Peter Dankerton and his wife. He was a Bridge fiend with the tongue of an adder—but distinctly good-looking and very amusing company.

The younger element consisted of Tony Wootton, a subaltern in the Gunners, and a jolly little kid called Marjorie Stanway, who spent most of their time practising new steps in the hall to a gramophone.

And finally there was a man called Miles Standish, who was the only one I had never met before. He was a planter of sorts out in the F.M.S. About thirty years old, he seemed to have been everywhere and done everything. He had rather a lazy, pleasant voice, and a trick of raising his eyebrows when he spoke that made the most ordinary remark seem amusing: and little Marjorie, to the fury of young Wootton, adored him openly. In fact, the outstanding personality of the party, Mary always excepted.

She introduced me to him as soon as I arrived.

"The only one you don't know, Bill," she said. "Miles—this is Bill Canford, who is almost a fixture about the house."

"A very pleasant occupation," he remarked lightly, and I got the impression that his eyes were very observant. "If I could afford to become a fixture, I should choose an English country house to do it in."

We talked on casually for a while, and he was certainly a most interesting man. And an efficient one. His knowledge, obviously acquired on the spot, of rubber and its future showed him as a man who could observe and think for himself.

"And where," I said, after a while, "is our worthy host?"

"My dear Bill," laughed Mary, looking up from the tea-table, "John has got a new toy. His present secretary's face is so frightful that he can't bear her in the same room with him. So he has got a sort of phonograph machine—a super-dictaphone I think he calls it—and he dictates his letters into it. You don't have to talk into a trumpet like you do with most of them. It stands in a corner, and looks just like an ordinary box. Then each morning she comes and takes off the records and writes down what he has said."

"It might almost have been worth while to change his secretary," said Standish lazily. "Still he is doubtless very happy."

He leant over to light her cigarette, and I was struck by the atmosphere of physical fitness that seemed to radiate from the man. Hard as nails: without an ounce of superfluous flesh on him. In fact a pretty tough customer in a rough house.

I suppose a woman would have spotted the lie of the land that night after dinner. In the light of subsequent events I now realize that the tension was already there, though I didn't get it personally. It was just a little thing—a casual scrap of conversation between two rubbers. Standish was shuffling the cards, and Phyllis Dankerton, who had been his partner, made some remark about the excellence of his Bridge not having been impaired by his living in the back of beyond.

He grinned and said, "We're not all savages, Mrs. Dankerton. Even though there aren't no Ten Commandments, and a man can raise a thirst."

"At the moment," remarked John Somerville quietly, "we don't happen to be East of Suez."

The faintest of smiles flickered for an instant round Phyllis Dankerton's lips. Then—

"How marvellously Kipling gets human nature, doesn't he?" she murmured. "You and I, Bill—and an original no trumper of mine is open to the gravest suspicion."

Yes—the tension had begun. To what extent it had grown I don't know: but it was there. As I say, I realized that afterwards. John Somerville suspected his wife and Standish. Not that he said anything, or even hinted at anything that night, with the exception of that one remark. As always he was the courteous perfect host—at least so it seemed to me. Though when, a couple of days, later I was discussing things with Phyllis Dankerton she regarded me pityingly when I said so.

"My dear man," she said, "you must be partially wanting. There is an atmosphere in this house you could cut with a knife. Our worthy John is watching those two like a cat watches a mouse. It's all excessively amusing."

"Do you think Mary is in love with Standish?" I said.

"Wasn't it Maugham who said in one of his plays that a lot of unnecessary fuss is made about the word love? Quite obviously she is immensely attracted by him—who wouldn't be? I'm crazy about him myself. And, my dear Bill, I might be eighty-one with false teeth for all the notice he takes of me. It's cruel hard on a deserving girl. There's poor old Peter who wouldn't notice the Alps unless they were covered with Stock Exchange quotations, and yet I throw myself at that brute's head in vain."

"I wonder how Mary met him," I said.

"Really, Bill," she cried impatiently, "you're intolerably dull to-day. She met him in the same way that everybody does meet people presumably. Anyway, what does it matter? The beginning has nothing to do with it: it's the end that interests me."

"You really think that it's serious," I said.

She shrugged her shoulders.

"With a woman like Mary, you never know. I don't believe she would ever have a real affair with a man if she was still living in her husband's house. But she's quite capable of bolting for good and all if she loved the man sufficiently. Cheer up, Bill," she laughed, "it's not your palaver. By the look on your face Mary might be *your* wife."

"I'm very fond of Mary," I said stiffly. "We've known one another since we were kids."

And at that moment young Wootton came in and the conversation dropped. But I couldn't get it out of my mind. That there should be even the bare possibility of Mary running away with another man seemed to knock the bottom out of my universe. And soon I found myself watching them too, and trying to gauge the state of the affair. Was Mary in love with him? That was the question I asked myself a dozen times a day. That he should be in love with her was only natural. But was the converse true? I studied her expression when she didn't know I was looking at her, and I had to admit that there was a change. For a few moments, perhaps, she would sit sunk in her thoughts, and then she would make an effort to pull herself together and be laughing and bright as she always used to be. But it was forced, and I knew it: she couldn't deceive me. And sometimes when she came out of her reverie, if Standish was in the room, her eyes would rest on him for a second, as if she was trying to find the answer to some unspoken question.

Then I started to watch him. But there wasn't much to be got from Miles Standish's face. Years of poker playing had turned it into an expressionless mask when he wished to make it so. But I managed to catch him unawares once or twice. After lunch one day, for instance. He was holding a match for her cigarette, and over the flame their eyes had met. And in his was a look of such concentrated love and passion as I have never seen before. Then, in an instant, it was gone, and he made some commonplace remark. But to me it seemed as if the truth had been proclaimed through a megaphone.

And another time it was even more obvious. Without thinking I went into the billiard-room, and they were alone there. They were standing very close together by the fireplace talking earnestly, and as I opened the door they moved apart quickly. In fact it was so obvious that I almost committed the appalling solecism of apologizing for intruding. Standish picked up a paper; Mary smiled and said, "Why don't you two men have a game?" But once again the truth had been shouted to high Heaven: these two were in love with one another. What was going to be the end of it? Was Mary going to bolt with him, or would the whole thing die a natural death when he went out East again?

I believe it might have been the latter, had John Somerville not brought matters to a head. It was after dinner, on the same day, that I had surprised them in the billiard-room.

"By the way, Standish," he said as we were beginning to form up for Bridge, "when are you going back again?"

"I haven't quite decided yet," said Standish, lighting a cigarette. "Not for some little while, I think."

"Want to pay a round of visits, I suppose, and see all your friends. I've just remembered, my dear,"—he turned to his wife—"Henry Longstaffe is very anxious to come for a few days, as soon as we can put him up. He and I have a rather considerable business deal to discuss."

I glanced at Phyllis Dankerton: a smile was hovering on her lips.

I glanced at Miles Standish: his face was expressionless. I glanced at Mary: she was staring at her husband. Because all three of them knew, as I knew, that there was no spare room in the house. If Henry Longstaffe came to stay, somebody had to go.

"I'm afraid I shall have to fold up my tent and fade away very soon," said Standish easily. "Would the day after to-morrow do for Mr. Longstaffe, or would you sooner he came to-morrow?"

"The day after to-morrow will do perfectly," said Somerville. "Sorry you can't stop longer."

And then we sat down to Bridge in an atmosphere, as Phyllis Dankerton afterwards described it, which would have frozen a furnace. Nothing more, of course, was said—but words were unnecessary. The gloves were off, and everyone knew it. Miles Standish had been kicked out of the house as blatantly as if he had been shown the door. Moreover, it had been done in the presence of all of us, which made the matter worse.

"I think John is a fool," said Phyllis Dankerton to me just before we went to bed. "And a vulgar fool at that. One doesn't do that sort of thing in front of other people. If I was Mary I'd give him such a telling off as he would never forget."

"He's an extremely angry man," I remarked. "And that accounts for it."

"Then it oughtn't to," she retorted. "It simply isn't done. To have said it to him privately would have been a very different matter. And you mark my words, Bill. Unless I'm much mistaken friend John will have achieved the exact opposite to what he intended. He has simply forced their hands."

"You think she'll run away with him?" I said.

"I think she is far more likely to now than she was before. And if she does John will be very largely to blame. To-morrow is going to be the crucial day, while he is in London. The great decision will be made then."

She gave a little bitter laugh and her eyes were very sad.

"God! what fools women are," she said under her breath. "What damned fools!"

Then she went to bed, leaving me to a final night-cap. And when I had followed her example, and lay tossing and turning, unable to sleep, there was one picture I couldn't get out of my mind. It was the picture of Mary and Miles Standish together, lean-ing over the stern of an East-bound liner. And at last they turn and look at one another, as man and woman look at one another when they love. Then they go below.

*   *   *   *   *

I must get the events of the next day straight in my mind. Phyllis Dankerton was right: it was the crucial day. But somehow or other things seem a little blurred in my head. I'm not quite certain of the order in which they happened.

First of all there came the interview between Mary and Miles Standish. I overheard part of it—deliberately. They were in the billiard-room once more, and I happened to stroll past the little window, at one end of the room, which is high up in the wall. It was open, and I could hear what they said distinctly, though they couldn't see me.

"My dear," Standish was saying, "it's a big decision that will alter your life completely and irrevocably. It's a decision that cannot be come to lightly. Divorce and that sort of thing seem a comparatively small matter when applied to other people. But when it's applied to oneself it doesn't seem quite so small. Wait, my darling, wait: let me have my say first. You are going to be the one who has to make the big sacrifice. It's not going to affect me: it never does affect the man. And in my case even less so than usual. My home is out East: it doesn't matter the snap of a finger what I do. But with you it's different. You're giving up all this: you're running away with a man who is considerably poorer than your husband. You are coming to a strange life, amid strange surroundings—a life you may not like. But a life, which, if you do leave your husband, you will have to stick to."

Yes: he put it very fairly, did Miles Standish.

There was no trace of pleading or emotion in his voice: he seemed to be at pains to keep everything matter of fact. And because of that the force of the appeal was doubled.

"We are neither of us children, Mary." The quiet, measured words went on. "We know enough to disregard catch phrases like the world being well lost for love. It isn't, and nobody but a fool would think it was. And if you come with me it won't be—it will be changed, that's all. But it's going to be a big change: that's what I want you to get into your head."

And then, at last, Mary spoke.

"I realize that it's going to be a big change, Miles. Do you really think that matters? I realize that life out there will be different to this. Do you really think I care? My dear, it's not any material alteration in surroundings that has made me hesitate—it's been something far more important and fundamental. I'm not going to mince words: you attracted me from the first time we met. But my great problem was—was it only attraction? If so, I'd have been a fool to go. It is a big decision as you say—an irrevocable one, and to take it because of a passing whim would be folly. Last night—when John said what he did to you—I knew with absolute certainty. Every single instinct and thought of mine ranged themselves on your side. I've never loved John: now I positively dislike him."

"That's not quite enough, Mary," said Standish gravely. "I don't want you to come with me because you dislike John: I want you to come with me because you love me."

"Miles—my darling."

I scarcely heard the words, so softly were they spoken. And then came silence. In my mind I could see them there staring into one another's eyes:

staring down the unknown path that they were to take together.   A little blindly I turned and walked away.   The matter was decided: the choice had been made.   For good or ill Mary was going with Miles Standish.

"Bill, what is the matter with you?   Are you ill?"

With an effort I pulled myself together: Phyllis Dankerton was looking at me with amazement on her face.

"Not a bit," I answered.   "Why should I be?"

"My dear man," she said lightly, "I am partially responsible for Peter's tummy, but I hold no brief for yours.   I don't know why you should be ill, but you certainly look it.   Incidentally, I saw our two turtle-doves making tracks for the billiard-room.   I wonder if the momentous decision has yet been reached."

I said nothing: I felt I couldn't stand the worry any more.   Phyllis Dankerton is all right in small doses, but there are times when she drives one positively insane.   So I made some fatuous remark and left her, vaguely conscious that the surprised look had returned to her face.   What the devil did it matter? What did anything matter except that Mary was going with Miles Standish?

Nothing could alter that fact now: they were neither of them the type of people who change their mind once it is made up.   And at dinner that night I found myself watching them curiously.   They were both more silent than usual, which was hardly to be wondered at.   And John Somerville, who obviously had not yet been told, kept glancing from one to the other.

That he would be told I felt sure.   The idea of bolting on the sly would not appeal to either Mary or Standish: they weren't that sort.   But would it be done after dinner, or postponed to the following day?

Or would Standish go in the ordinary course of events, leaving Mary to break the news to John?

The point was settled after dinner. John Somerville had gone to his room to write some letters, and suddenly I saw Standish glance at Mary significantly. Then with a quick little nod he left the room.

"What about a stroll, Canford?" said young Wootton, and automatically I got up. Why not?

"It strikes me," he remarked confidentially when we were out of earshot, "that there's a bit of an air of gloom and despondency brooding over the old ancestral hall. Somerville's face at dinner was enough to turn the butter rancid. And Standish seems quite different these last few days."

"When a man," I remarked, "is in love with another man's wife and the other man finds it out, it doesn't make for conviviality in the house."

He stopped dead and stared at me.

"Good Lord!" he muttered, "that's the worry, is it? Well, I'm damned. I never spotted it. But I jolly well know which of the two I'd choose. Mine host, even though I'm eating his salt, is not much to my liking."

"Perhaps not," I said curtly. "But he happens to be your hostess's husband."

"You mean to say," he began, and then suddenly he gripped my arm.

"My God! Canford—look there."

We were about a hundred yards from the house. From one of the downstair rooms the light was streaming out through the open French windows. And the room was John Somerville's study. He was standing up with his back to the desk facing Miles Standish, and it was evident that a bitter quarrel was in progress. We could hear no actual words, but the attitude of the two men told its own tale.

"Damn it—let's clear out," muttered Wootton. "Rather rotten, don't you think? Seems like spying on them. I'm going back to the house, anyway."

He strolled off, and I watched the glow of his cigarette fading away in the darkness. Then once again I riveted my eyes on the study window: on that grim, fierce, age-old struggle of two males for a female: the struggle that brings murder into the air.

And when ten minutes later I went back into the drawing-room the atmosphere was not much better. Mary glanced up quickly as I came through the window, and her face fell when she saw who it was. Wootton made a grimace at me, and Phyllis Dankerton went on playing patience religiously. Even little Marjorie Stanway seemed to feel there was something the matter, and was fidgeting about the room.

Then, suddenly, it happened. The door was flung open and Somerville's secretary dashed into the room. Her face was ashen white, and she was gasping for breath.

"Mrs. Somerville," she almost screamed, "he's dead. There's a knife in his back. He's been stabbed."

For a moment no one spoke. Then Dankerton said a little dazedly: "Who is dead?"

"Mr. Somerville," sobbed the woman. "At his desk."

And again, for what seemed an eternity, there was silence. Mary, her face as white as a sheet, was staring at the secretary, as if she couldn't grasp what had happened: young Wootton was saying "Good God!" under his breath over and over again and watching me. And at last I heard a voice say: "We must get the police." It was my own.

"Don't you think that we ought to go and make certain?" muttered Dankerton. "He may not be dead. Not the women, of course."

And then, at last, Mary spoke.

"Where is Miles?"

It was hardly more than a whisper, but it sounded as if it had been shouted through a megaphone in the deathly silence. And at that moment he appeared in the window. For a second or two he stood there looking from one to the other of us: then he spoke.

"What on earth is the matter?"

It was Dankerton who answered him.

"Somerville has been stabbed in the back," he said gravely. "His secretary says he is dead. We were just going along to see."

"Stabbed in the back!" cried Standish in amazement. "But who by?"

"We don't know," I said, and once again Wootton's eye met mine. "Let's go and see if there is anything to be done."

But there wasn't: that was obvious at the first glance. He lay there huddled over his desk, his eyes glazed and staring. And thrust into his back up to the hilt was a knife I had often seen lying on the mantelpiece. For a long while no one spoke: then Dankerton pulled himself together.

"Look here, you fellows, this is a pretty ghastly business. We must get the police at once. I'll tell the butler to ring up."

"Yes," agreed Standish quietly. "We must get the police."

His eyes were riveted on the knife: then with an effort he turned and looked at us each in turn.

"He and I had a frightful row to-night." He spoke with intense deliberation, and once again Wootton looked at me. "A frightful row."

"My dear fellow," muttered Dankerton awkwardly. "Look here, I'll see about the police."

He bustled out of the room, and suddenly Wootton took the bull by the horns.

"This is a pretty grim affair, Standish. You see Canford and I were outside there, and we saw you having words with—with him."

"Then you must have seen who did this," said Standish eagerly.

"Unfortunately I didn't," said Wootton. "It seemed to me to be a private affair, and I went back to the drawing-room."

"And I followed shortly after," I remarked.

Once more silence fell, while Standish stared at the dead man.

"I had a frightful row," he repeated mechanically, "and then I went out into the garden through the window. Damn it," he exploded suddenly, "you don't think I did it, do you?"

"Of course not, my dear chap," I cried. "Of course not."

He walked a little stiffly out of the room, and I turned to Wootton.

"What's your opinion?" I said at length.

"What's yours?" he answered. "Damn it, Canford, if he didn't do it somebody else did. And if it was anybody in the garden we'd have seen him."

"We might not," I said; "if he was hiding."

"In the back, too," he muttered. "A dirty business. God! I wish the police would come."

And in about half an hour they did. An Inspector and a sergeant arrived and with them the doctor. The cause of death was clear: the knife had penetrated the heart. Somerville had died instantaneously. Then came the turn of the police, and it soon became evident in what direction their suspicions lay. Standish made no attempt to hide the fact of his quarrel with the dead man: incidentally it would have been futile

in view of the fact that Wootton and I had seen it.
But he flatly refused to say what it was about, and he
denied absolutely that he was the man who had done it.

"Nobody said you were, sir," said the Inspector
sternly. "You go too fast!"

"Rot," said Standish curtly. "I'm not a damned
fool. If I have a violent row with a man, and a few
minutes later he is found dead, there's no good telling
me that suspicion doesn't fall on me. Of course it
does."

And the next day suspicion became certainty. A
finger-print expert arrived from Scotland Yard, and
the marks of Standish's fingers were found on the hilt
of the knife. It was proof irrefutable, and the only
explanation he could give was that in the heat of the
argument he had snatched up the knife from the
mantelpiece. But he still denied that it was he who
had struck the blow.

"Then how comes it that yours are the *only* prints
on the knife?" said the Inspector quietly.

I think the only person who believed in his innocence through the days that followed was Mary. To
us it was painfully, terribly clear. As I said to Wootton
the night before the trial it was the most obvious case,
short of having an eye-witness, that could be put before
a jury. And he agreed. He and I, of course, were
two of the principal witnesses for the prosecution, but
our evidence was really unnecessary. Standish had
never denied the fact that he and the murdered man
had had a bitter quarrel. And that and the finger-
prints on the knife formed the evidence against him.

He still refused to say what the quarrel was about,
though we all of us knew it concerned Mary. And
from the point of view of his innocence or guilt it
didn't really matter. He and the murdered man had
quarrelled over something, and in a fit of ungovern-

able rage Standish had picked up the knife and stabbed him.   That was all there was to it.

And that was all there was to it when Counsel for the Crown had finished his final speech.   The members of the jury had obviously made up their minds already: it was difficult to see how they could have done otherwise.   And Sir John Gordon—Standish's Counsel—was just rising to commence his hopeless task, when there occurred an amazing interruption. A strange, distraught-looking woman carrying a big brown box forced her way into court and shouted out: "Wait. Wait. Don't go on."   Her face seemed vaguely familiar to me, and suddenly I placed her. She was John Somerville's secretary.

Everybody was so astounded that she had reached Sir John before anyone could stop her.   And by the time ushers and attendants had rushed up to her, she had said enough to Sir John to cause him to wave them away.

"My Lord," he said, "this woman has just made a most important statement to me.   In spite of the irregularity of the proceedings I propose to put her in the witness-box."

And so Emily Turner was duly sworn, and made her statement.   And when she had finished you could have heard a pin drop in the court.

"I understand," said the Judge, "that the position is as follows.   The box in front of Sir John is the instrument which the murdered man used for dictating his letters into.   This morning, not having thought of it since the night of the tragedy, you opened the box.   And you found that a record had been made. You thereupon played that record, if that is the correct phrase, and you discovered that the conversation between prisoner at the bar and the murdered man was what was recorded.   Is that correct?"

"Yes, my Lord."

And then came a harsh voice from the dock, "Smash the thing, I tell you. Smash it."

"Silence," said the Judge sternly, and Miles Standish faced him steadily.

"My Lord," he remarked, "I give you my solemn word of honour that my conversation with Somerville that night had nothing to do with it. Moreover it affects a third person. Therefore need that record be given?"

"It must certainly be given," said the Judge. "If what this witness says is correct, a vital piece of evidence has just come to light. Turn on the machine."

I can still see that scene. Miles Standish, impassive and erect: the jury tense and expectant: the public craning forward in their seats. And the centre of everything—that plain little woman bending over the box.

There came a faint scraping like a gramophone: then it started.

"Sir. With reference to your last quotation, I beg to state——"

John Somerville's voice: God! it was uncanny. Things began to blur a bit before my eyes. John Somerville dictating a letter.

"May I have a few words with you, Somerville?"

A gasp ran through the court—instantly quelled. Miles Standish had spoken. The living and the dead —reproduced before us.

"Certainly, Standish."

"There is not much good beating about the bush, Somerville. Your wife and I are in love with one another."

"How excessively interesting."

How well I knew that cold sneering tone of Somerville's. I could see now the slight rise of his upper lip. I could see the man himself again, as I hadn't seen him since that night: as I'd never expected to see him. He was dead, damn it, dead: and that cursed instrument had brought him to life again. What was he saying now?

"I certainly can't prevent my wife going away with you, Standish. But it's going to be a little awkward for you both. Divorce proceedings bore me, and I hate being bored."

"You mean you won't divorce her, Somerville?"

"You damned swine. You utterly damned swine."

There came a pause, then Somerville's voice with fear in it.

"Put down that knife, you fool. Put down that knife."

I hadn't told them that: I'd kept that dark. I'd seen Standish pick up the knife—seen it myself. Just as he said.

"And now clear out, blast you."

Somerville's voice again—icy, contemptuous. How I'd hated his voice, the thin-lipped swine. . . . And it was then I remembered.

"Stop it," I screamed. "Stop it."

People stared at me in amazement, and suddenly I felt icy calm. The machine scraped on, then, "Hullo! Canford. What do you want? I'm busy."

Somerville's voice: he'd said it to me as I entered the room.

"What the devil—Oh! my God!"

Followed a little sobbing grunt: then silence. The record was over.

*   *   *   *   *

Yes: I did it. I'd always loathed him, and I loathed Standish worse. Because Mary loved Standish, and I loved Mary. And when Standish rushed out past me into the night I saw my chance to get them both. I wrapped a handkerchief round the hilt of the knife to prevent finger-prints: I'd thought of everything.

Everything except that cursed machine.

XXV   WILL YOU WALK INTO MY PARLOUR?

JIMMY SEFTON sat outside the Angler's Rest at Drayminster with a puzzled look on his good-natured freckled face. On the table by his side was a tankard of ale, and an opened packet of Virginian cigarettes. It was five o'clock in the afternoon, and save for him the place was deserted. Soon it would fill up, when the mystic hour arrived which allowed unfortunate mortals who were not staying in the house to get a drink, but until then he would have the place to himself—a fact for which he was thankful. He wanted to think.

No one would have called Jimmy a brainy young man, but he had a certain shrewd common sense which often serves better than a quicker and cleverer brain. He might take longer in arriving at a conclusion, but when he did get there he was generally fairly near the mark. And now he once again proceeded to run over the chain of events that was directly responsible for his presence in Drayminster.

The first had been a dinner at the "Cheshire Cheese" some three weeks previously. At it were present Teddie Morgan and Bob Durrant, two journalistic pals of his, though Teddie Morgan, to be correct, was more than a pal. He and Jimmy had been at school together, and they had joined the staff of the *Daily Leader* at the same time. And that was five years ago—five years during which acquaintanceship had grown into real friendship. The fourth member of the party was a man called Spencer, who was more or less the stranger at the board. He, too, was a writing man, but his speciality was crime. And the principal interest he had for the other three was an intimate knowledge of Scotland Yard, an institution with which they had only a bowing acquaintance.

He could recall quite clearly the gist of Spencer's remarks. Dinner was over, coffee and port were on the table. And he could still see Spencer's thin aquiline features through the thick haze of tobacco smoke, as he recounted some of the cases he had had first-hand knowledge of.

"You may take it from me," he said, "that there is not much wrong with our police system. It is the custom of lots of people to deride them as men of small brains and large feet, but nothing is farther from the truth. The local village constable may not be a particularly bright specimen, but for the matter of that the local French gendarme is not a second Newton as a general rule. And there's another thing too which lots of people are apt to forget—the difference between our legal code and those of other countries. With us the onus of proving a man guilty lies on the police: in France, for instance, the onus lies on the man proving himself *not* guilty. And the difference is enormous. There are half a dozen men at large in London to-day whom the police *know* to be criminals. But they can't arrest them because they can't *prove* it. In France they would be under lock and key in no time, and it would be up to them to prove that they weren't."

Spencer had talked on in this strain for some time, and then had come the information which had proved the first link in the chain of events that had since taken place.

"But they are up against it at the moment," he had

said thoughtfully, "up against it good and strong. And have been for some weeks. Forged notes—on a scale never hitherto attempted."

His audience had pricked up their ears: this was something better than vague generalizations about police methods.

"They're not very chatty about it at the Yard, but I have my own channels of information," he had continued. "And this is the biggest thing of its kind they have struck yet. The headquarters of the gang are in this country, but they are not dealing with English notes. Which makes it so very much harder to track them. French and Belgian notes of fairly large denomination: American five and ten dollar notes are what they are making. And that is where the complication occurs. You see the usual method of running the headquarters of a gang of this sort to earth is by getting on the line of the men who pass the notes. A fiver, let us say, comes into a bank. That fiver is never again issued, but is destroyed. The bank people find it is a forgery. Scotland Yard then sets to work to trace the movements of that fiver back to the first person who handled it. And thus, if there are several, in time the man who originally passed it is found. From him, they go still farther back, because it is not the passer they want but the utterer—the forger himself. Now in this case there is a very grave difficulty. The forger is in this country: the men who are passing the notes work in other countries. And not only that, they are mixing up the currencies. They are getting rid of American notes in Belgium, we'll say, and French notes in Italy."

"How long has it been going on for?" someone had asked.

"The Yard has been down to it for about six months now," was the answer. "And though they won't admit the fact they are no nearer the solution now than when they started. As I said it is a very big thing. Two or three of the smaller fry have been caught abroad, and though they have been subjected to foreign methods of examination nothing has been found out. Probably because they none of them knew anything to pass on. The only vague clue, which may not even be a clue at all, is that two of these men bought their forged notes in Brighton, and the other at Bognor."

"Bought!" Teddie Morgan had cried.

"That is the usual method," Spencer had explained. "A thousand-franc French note is worth roughly eight pounds. The man buys it—say for five. If he passes it he is three pounds to the good: if he doesn't he is jugged. But whichever happens the big man is a fiver in pocket. But to go back. The fact that Brighton and Bognor were selected as rendezvous for the transactions points to the possibility of the headquarters being in Sussex. But it is only a possibility."

And then Teddie Morgan had laughed.

"I will attend to the matter," he had said. "To-morrow I leave for a well-earned fortnight's holiday. The earth is mine to roam in: I shall select Sussex. And if anyone offers to sell me thousand-franc notes for a fiver, I shall dot him one with a beer mug and summon the police."

Thus the first link in the chain. The party had broken up shortly after, and no one had thought any more about it. In fact until three days previously Jimmy Sefton had not known that Morgan had even gone to Sussex. And then had come the second link. It consisted of a picture post card showing the village of Drayminster. It contained the pointed information that that village had been classified fifth in order of beauty in England. It also contained the following message written in Morgan's sprawling handwriting:

"Tell Spencer that there is many a true word spoken in jest."

Jimmy had been busy at the time, and having put the card in his pocket had forgotten all about it, until that very morning, when the third grim link appeared in the form of a paragraph in the paper. He took it out of his pocket-book now as he sat at his table and re-read it for the twentieth time.

"The body of a well-dressed young man was found in the river Dray yesterday afternoon by two farm labourers. It was discovered in the weeds some three miles from the picturesque old country village of Drayminster, one of the famous beauty spots of England. An empty fishing creel was slung round his shoulder. It is assumed that the unfortunate gentleman, who has been identified as Mr. Edward Morgan, a well-known London journalist, and who was staying at the Angler's Rest, must have slipped in one of the deep and treacherous pools of the river and been drowned. The current then carried the body to the spot where it was found. No trace of his rod has been discovered. The inquest will be held to-day."

And Jimmy Sefton had just returned from that very inquest. No difficulty about identifying the body; it was poor old Teddie right enough. From the medical evidence he had been dead about two days, and the verdict was a foregone conclusion. The landlord of the Angler's Rest, who had done the identification, had been asked by the Coroner as to whether he had not been a little alarmed when the days had passed by with no sign of his guest.

"No, sir," he had answered. "Mr. Morgan took the room for a week, and he told me that he might frequently sleep out. He was very fond of walking, and, as the weather was fine, he would very likely get a shake-down in a barn or under a hayrick."

Jimmy Sefton, who had explained to the coroner that he was a brother journalist on the same paper, and who was sitting at the back of the room, had listened to this piece of evidence in silent amazement. Not that he disbelieved the landlord—for a more transparently honest and upright man he had seldom seen—but for a very different reason. If there was one form of exercise which Teddie loathed with a superlative loathing, it was walking. He would take a bus to go half the length of Fleet Street rather than walk the distance. So that for some reason or other Teddie had deliberately lied to the worthy man whose naturally cheerful voice could even now be heard, suitably lowered for the occasion, recounting the details of the tragedy for every new arrival at the bar. Why had he lied?

Then Mr. Purley, who sold rods and flies and all the other paraphernalia of the angler's craft, had identified the deceased as the gentleman who had come to his shop to be completely fitted out four days previously—on Tuesday last. He had admitted he did not know much about it, but having been told of the marvellous trout-fishing which could be got in the river Dray he had determined to try his hand at it. To this evidence also, Jimmy Sefton had listened in some surprise. Not, it is true, with that utter bewilderment which the landlord's story had produced in his mind, but still with considerable doubt. He could not picture Teddie being suddenly seized with a desire to become an angler. He knew his tastes—none better. He had loved all games, but except for an occasional ride he had never gone in for what are known as the sports. Shooting and fishing he had had no opportunity to try his hand at. So why this sudden craving to become a fisherman?

Jimmy Sefton called for another pint of ale.

"Do you remember," he asked, "when it was that Mr. Morgan told you he might be going on a walking tour?"

The landlord scratched his head.

"Let me see, sir," he said. "To-day is Saturday. He was out, I remember, last Sunday night, but took his meals here Monday. And Monday night he was out too. And after that I never saw him again. Perhaps a week ago he told me."

"I see," said Jimmy. "Thank you."

The landlord returned to the bar, and Jimmy lit a cigarette. According to Mr. Purley it was Tuesday when Teddie had bought his tackle. It was also on Tuesday that he had sent the post card to Jimmy. So that presumably either on Monday night or on Tuesday morning he had discovered something which had caused him to alter the blind of a walking tour to that of becoming a fisherman. What was it that he had discovered? And where? Was it really as his post card suggested, that he had by some extraordinary stroke of chance stumbled on the headquarters of the forgers? And if that was so—Jimmy Sefton's jaw tightened a little at this point in his reflections—if that was so, was the verdict of "Accidentally drowned" correct? Or had Teddie Morgan been murdered?

Jimmy was not at all an imaginative young man, and his first impulse was to call himself several sorts of an ass. Murders and gangs of forgers, he told himself, were part of the stock in trade of the sensational novelist. In fact he used every single argument he could think of to prove to himself that he was wrong. But it was no use: try as he would his mind kept reverting to that one big question. Had Teddie Morgan found out too much and been murdered?

After a while he made a sort of mental table of points for and against.

For.

Number One. Teddie's remark to the landlord concerning a walking tour was so obviously a lie that it was clear he had been doing something which he did not wish to talk about.

Number Two. If there was any meaning at all in his post card, and it was highly improbable he would send a card without any reason, that something had to do with the gang of forgers.

Number Three. If he had discovered them, was it likely that a gang of such a formidable nature would allow the life of a stray journalist to stand in its way? They would undoubtedly murder him, and dispose of the body in such a way as to make it appear an accident.

Against.

Jimmy scratched his head: he could think of no point against which could be summarized as tersely as his three points for. In fact the only other alternative to his theory was that Teddie had thought at one time that he had stumbled on traces of the gang, *vide* the fact of his post card and his absence from the hotel on two nights. Then he had decided not to go on with it, had genuinely decided to try his hand at fishing, and had, as the verdict said, been accidentally drowned.

Jimmy finished his beer in a gulp, and stood up abruptly. The frown on his face had gone: his mind was made up. Because he knew the great fallacy that underlay his alternative theory. Teddie was not the type of man to decide not to go on with a thing. Once he had his jaws into a job nothing could shake him off: it had been a characteristic of his ever since he was a boy. Therefore Teddie was still on it when he was posing as a fisherman. So that even if the verdict was right, and he had been drowned, the accident had not occurred because of his devotion to fishing, but because he was following up some trail. And once that was settled the next step was obvious. Mr. Purley would receive a second order for a fishing outfit complete: Jimmy Sefton was going to take over from his pal. And the first thing to do was to get on the 'phone to his editor, because he had intended returning to London that night. He knew there would be no difficulty, especially if he gave a hint over the wire that he was on a scoop. So he went into the hotel to find the instrument. It was situated, as is so frequently the case in small hotels, in the office, which rendered any private conversation impossible. However he knew the editor sufficiently well to realize that the merest veiled hint would be all that was required. He put through the number and sat down to wait in the hall. Opposite him were a man and woman drinking a cocktail, and he glanced at them idly. They were both well dressed, and the woman, who was little more than a girl, was extremely pretty. And Jimmy, who was no more and no less susceptible than the average young man of his age, found his glance ceasing to be idle as far as she was concerned. Once she looked up and caught his eye, and it seemed to him there was just that perceptible addition of time before she looked away, that would constitute grounds for hope. Then the telephone-bell rang, and he took the call.

"*Daily Leader?*" he said. "Put me through to the Editor. Sefton speaking."

With his elbow on the table, and the receiver in his hand, he was staring out of the window. Suddenly his eyes narrowed. The lower part of the window was shut, and served sufficiently well as a mirror for him to see that the man had risen abruptly, and was now standing close to the door of the office, studying the announcement of a local cattle show. There was, he reflected, nothing inherently suspicious in such an action, but he was in the mood when the most commonplace thing took on a certain significance. Was it interest in the cattle show, or the mention of the *Daily Leader*, that had inspired the sudden movement? Then he heard the Editor's voice at the other end of the wire.

"Hullo! Is that Mr. Jameson? Look here, sir: it is urgent that I should stop at Drayminster for two or three days. Things to arrange about poor old Morgan. Yes; urgent. I can't be more explicit: this machine is specially placed for the maximum of publicity. Right —thank—you, sir."

He put back the receiver, and for a moment or two he stood there motionless. The man had returned to his seat as abruptly as he had left it. And his return had coincided with the end of the call. Once again it was not impossible that that had been the exact time necessary to allow him to study the details of the show. Not impossible: but . . . And Jimmy was thinking of all that lay behind that "but" as he turned to the girl in the office and made inquiries about a room. There proved to be no difficulty, and having fixed the details, he returned to his seat. He, too, would have a cocktail, and during its consumption he would continue the good work of finding out if his grounds for hope were justi-fied. Also he might find out other things.

After a moment or two, the man rose and, picking up his hat, left the hotel.

"I'll be back in about twenty minutes," he said, as he stepped into the road.

"Don't hurry," answered the girl. "I shan't be dull."

She picked up a copy of the *Tatler*, and Jimmy lit a cigarette and waited. Had he made a complete boss shot, or had he, by a most astounding bit of luck, stumbled on a clue? In either case, he reflected, he was perfectly safe in carrying out his plan. Further, he would soon know. If his suspicions were correct, within the next twenty minutes the girl would start a conversation with him. As he read it, that was the reason of the man's departure. And he wondered by which of the time-honoured methods she would dispense with the formality of an introduction.

She was displaying a considerable amount of extremely attractive leg—a spectacle to which he took no exception. And it was with almost a start that he averted his eyes from it to realize that the method to be used was the well-known old favourite of no matches.

"Allow me," he murmured, as she looked round despairingly.

"Thank you so much," she said with a charming smile. "I ought to have a box chained to me; I lose them so invariably."

They fell into a light conversation, and he studied her covertly. From a closer range he saw that she was older than he had at first thought, saw, too, with the discerning eye of a man who in the course of his trade has rubbed shoulders with all the types that go to make up a world, that indefinable something in her face that no art can conceal. It lies principally in the eyes and in the mouth, and it spells danger. This girl was as hard as nails. But no trace of his thoughts showed in his face: no one could act the part of a guileless youth better than he, as many people he had interviewed had discovered in the past.

The man he gathered was her Uncle Arthur and she was motoring with him on a tour. Jimmy, whose face had brightened at the first piece of news, became perceptibly depressed at the second.

"I'd hoped you were staying here," he said gloomily.

"Are you stopping in the hotel?" she asked.

"For a few days," he answered. "A great pal of mine has just been drowned here, poor old chap."

"How dreadful," she said sympathetically. "I heard something about it this afternoon."

"The inquest was this morning," he went on. "Verdict of accidentally drowned. But I wonder."

For the fraction of a second the mask slipped. Had he not been looking for it he would have missed it, so instantaneously was it replaced. But in that moment of time he saw what confirmed his suspicions—he saw fear.

"How do you mean, you wonder?" she asked, and her voice was quite normal. "Is there any doubt about it?"

"Not in the Coroner's mind," he answered mysteriously. "But there is in mine. I believe"—he lowered his voice, and glanced round the hall—"I believe he was murdered."

"Good Heavens!" she cried. "But who by? You sound so deliciously mysterious."

"I am going to let you into a great secret," he said. "And I am the only person in the world who knows it. Promise you won't say anything to a soul."

"Fingers crossed," she answered.

Jimmy leaned even closer to her.

"I believe," he said, "that Teddie Morgan was murdered by a gang of forgers whose headquarters are near here. I believe that somehow or other he did what the police so far have been unable to do—he located this gang. He wrote me a letter, in which he hinted at it, and from one or two things I've heard since I've been here I'm sure he was on their track. Now I'm a journalist," he went on with engaging candour, "and it will be a tremendous scoop for me if I can nab them."

"But how will you set about it?" she asked. "Because if what you suspect is true they might kill you."

Jimmy looked at her knowingly.

"I'm going to become a fisherman also," he said. "That's where the clue lies—near the river. Only I shall be more careful than he was. And when I've found these people I shall give the information to the police. But it will be a *Daily Leader* sensation, and I shall have the writing up of it."

"How splendid!" she cried. "Here is my uncle returning, but I'm thrilled to death. I shall simply be dying to know how you get on. When I get back to Town I must ring you up at your office, and you must come and tell me all about it."

"I'd love to," said Jimmy fervently. "But you must promise you won't say a word to a soul."

"It's our secret," she whispered softly. "I do hope you succeed."

She rose, and giving him a delicious little smile, joined her uncle in the car. One little wave of the hand, eagerly returned by Jimmy, and then they disappeared down the road.

"Do you know who those people were who have just left?" he asked the girl in the office.

"Never seen either of them before," she told him, and Jimmy returned to his chair. Three points in all, he reflected, to go on. The sudden movement of the man, the reflecting expression on the woman's face, and lastly the fact that people who tour in motor-cars generally carry luggage. On the one that had just driven off there had been none. In fact, he felt convinced that the arrow he had drawn at a venture had hit the mark. Those two people had something to do with it; he knew it. But, as Spencer had said, between knowing and proving there was a great gulf fixed.

He had acted deliberately in talking as he had. No harm was done if she was innocent: if on the contrary he was right, the next move would have to come from their side. Obviously they could not leave matters as they were. Though he had impressed on the girl that he wanted the whole thing kept a secret, he felt that in their position they could not bank on his doing so. They would feel that at any moment he might tell the police. And so it seemed to him that there were only two alternatives open to them. The first was to pack up and go: the second was to deal with him as they had dealt with Teddie Morgan. And of the two the second seemed the more probable.

For another ten minutes or so he sat on thinking: then a grin slowly appeared on his face. For a very amazing plan had suddenly dawned in Jimmy Sefton's brain—a plan which seemed to him quite unique in its simplicity. He looked at it this way and that, and in it he could see no flaw. A little acting: a little luck, and then, as he had quite truthfully said to the woman, the scoop of the year. And possibly some damned swine swinging for Teddie. Humming gently to himself he rose and left the hotel bound for Mr. Purley's shop. What the tune was is immaterial, but the words he had put to it had a certain significance.

" 'Will you walk into my parlour?' said the spider to the fly!"

The invitation of the spider came earlier than he had expected; to be exact, at ten o'clock the following morning. The previous night he had been acutely aware of two men who had sat drinking in the bar until the hotel shut, and who had seemed to betray a more than passing interest in his movements. So much more than passing, in fact, that Jimmy Sefton had done a thing which he could never remember having done before: he had slept with his window bolted and his door locked. But nothing had happened, and, as he came down the stairs encased in his newly acquired fishing outfit, it came as almost a relief to realize that the game was starting in earnest. For the girl herself was sitting in the hall.

"Hullo!" he cried joyfully. "This is an unexpected bit of luck."

"I oughtn't to be here," she confessed. "But Uncle Arthur found a wire waiting for him at Worthing, and had to go up to London. And I had nothing to do. Please let me come with you. As I told you I'm just thrilled to death."

She clasped her hands together, and looked at him appealingly.

"I promise not to get in the way, and I'd just adore to see what you are going to do."

"I don't know myself," he admitted. "You see, I haven't a notion where the gang is."

"Look here," she said after thinking deeply for a moment, "I've got an idea. You know where your poor friend's body was found, don't you?"

"I do," said Jimmy.

"Well, if you are right, and he was murdered, the brutes probably threw him into the water above that spot, and the river carried him down."

"By Jove! that's quick," said Jimmy admiringly.

"So let us get into my car and go by road to where he was found, and then explore the river upstream from there."

"You're a marvel," cried Jimmy, giving her a soulful glance. "An absolute fizzer. Let's start."

He deposited his creel and rod in the back of the car, and climbed in beside her. Up to date, he reflected, the fly was playing its part very creditably; moreover that intelligent little insect was becoming increasingly anxious to see the parlour the owner of which chattered unceasingly as they drove along.

"There's the spot," said Jimmy suddenly, and she gave a little shudder.

"Poor fellow," she whispered. "However, what do we do now?"

But it seemed that the fly's brain was unequal to the task of deciding, and after a while the spider had another idea.

"About a mile farther on," she said, "is one of Lord Cragmouth's places—Denton Hall. He is away, but I know him—and I know his butler. What about going there and asking the man whether he knows of any strangers who have arrived in these parts lately?"

For a moment Jimmy's brain spun round. What a headquarters—Denton Hall: one of the historic places of England. That it was the parlour at last he had no doubt, but for a second or two he was lost in admiration at the calm audacity of renting such a place for such a purpose.

"A marvellous idea," he said humbly. "What I should have done without you . . ."

His hand went to his forehead suddenly.

"Good God!" he muttered. "I'm going to faint. Could you—a little water—from the river. . . ."

She sprang out solicitously and hurried down to the stream. But when she came back he had so far recovered as to be standing by the back of the car.

"I'm so sorry," he said. "I'm better now. Damned silly of me."

"Are you sure?" she cried. "Why not rest a little? Or if we go on to Denton Hall, I'm sure the butler would give you some brandy."

"That sounds good to me," he said. "But really I'm quite all right now."

He got in beside her again, and a few minutes later the car swung right handed past an old lodge into the huge grounds of Denton Hall. In the distance was the house with its broad terraces running down to the big ornamental lake, with its celebrated pagoda on the little island in the middle. Farther on a line of weeping willows marked the banks of the river Dray, which passed right through the property.

The car drew up at the front door, and Jimmy's heart began to beat a trifle quicker. A glance at the butler did not inspire him with confidence. And as the door closed behind him he understood the feelings of the fly.

He looked up as three men came down the stairs, and the centre one was Uncle Arthur.

"Here he is," laughed the girl. "It was almost too easy."

"My God!" stammered Jimmy. "I don't understand . . . I . . . This is a trap."

The girl had lit a cigarette and was laughing softly to herself, but the three men had stood looking at him in silence.

"You are a very foolish young man," said Uncle Arthur at length.

"Let us come in here." He led the way into what was evidently the smoking-room.

"You are going to murder me, are you?" said Jimmy. "Like you murdered Teddie Morgan. But awkward, won't it be——having dead journalists lying about all over the place?"

"They are a tribe who can well be thinned out," answered the other genially. "Yes, Mr. Sefton, owing to your reprehensible curiosity, you are, as they say, for it. You see, you left us with no alternative."

He lit a cigarette.

"I assure you I have given the matter deep and earnest thought," he continued. "I don't want to kill you, any more than I wanted to kill that other young ass. But I have to weigh in the balance your life against my future peace of mind. I should hate to think that at any moment I might meet you, and you might say—'That charming well-dressed gentleman is a forger.'"

"And murderer," said Jimmy, lighting a cigarette in his turn.

"Have it your own way," conceded the other. "But you see my difficulty. Supposing I let you continue your hunt for my poor person—for the headquarters of the gang, as you so realistically put it. In the course of a week you might have stumbled on something—just as your friend Morgan did. Will you believe it, what put him on to us was the fact that he happened to see my butler's face one day as he passed the lodge gates?"

"Any judge would convict on that alone," agreed Jimmy affably.

"We have not all got your classical beauty of features, Mr. Sefton. Still, the point is a small one: the result was what mattered. He became most intrusive: he even trespassed on my property. In fact we actually discovered him concealed by the edge of the lake watching that charming pagoda through field-glasses. He pretended he was fishing, Mr. Sefton—even as I gather you were going to do. Yet his rod was not put together, and his basket was empty."

Jimmy strolled over to the window and looked out.

"And so you propose to kill me!" he said thoughtfully. "Will it be done with your own fair hands, dear Uncle Arthur?"

He swung round, and suddenly the room grew strangely silent. For there was a look on his face that none of them could understand.

"Admirable things—windows, aren't they," he continued. "Without curtains you can see through them: with curtains you can't. Then they act as mirrors, uncle dear. Are you going to the cattle show you were studying the notice of when I was telephoning?"

Jimmy began to laugh softly.

"And you, my dear lady, should really learn to control your face. And you shouldn't say you are touring when you haven't any luggage."

With a sudden movement he flung open the window, and waved his hand.

"My God! It is the police." Uncle Arthur had sprung to his side. "The young swine has fooled us. There are a dozen of them. Quick—bolt."

"Not this time," said a deep voice at the door, and Jimmy recognized the speaker as Superintendent Naylor of the Yard, with Spencer, and half a dozen men behind him. "So it's you, is it, Verriker? There have been times when I suspected it must be. Where's the plant?"

"I should think a visit to the pagoda might help," said Jimmy mildly, and Verriker began to curse.

"Good work, Sefton," cried Spencer. "But it gave us a bit of a shock when we got the address."

"So it did me," said Jimmy. "In fact I almost fainted in the car."

Verriker ceased cursing and stared at him.

"Do you mean to say you only found out where you were coming when you were in the car?" he said.

"Sure thing," answered Jimmy. "My dear Uncle Arthur, we have been playing a little game of the spider and the fly. And knowing the usual fate of the fly, this one decided to take a few precautions. The only trouble was that he hadn't any idea as to where the parlour was. That he was going to be invited in he felt sure, but he felt a little dubious as to the hospitality that would be extended to him there. So he invited down a few friends"—he waved his hand at the police— "to remain at hand, in case they were wanted. He thought it better that they shouldn't follow him, in case they were seen, and the spider should leave the parlour hurriedly. Besides, he wanted the spider to tell him

all that was in his heart.   And then when he had found
out his destination—he pretended to throw a faint.
And being left alone for half a minute, he wrote a little
message.   And he put the message in a little tube.
And he fastened the tube to a little leg."

"What the devil do you mean?" snarled Verriker.

"Why, just that this particular fly had taken your
advice in advance about empty fishing baskets.   You
see—his wasn't empty.   Inside it was a carrier pigeon."

X X V I   A   H O P E L E S S   C A S E

I

THROUGH the open window came the ceaseless
noise of the tree beetles.   Occasionally it would
be drowned by the coughing grunt of a lion in the
distance, or the shrill scream of some animal near by
—a scream that showed that death was, as ever, abroad
in the land outside.   But these were only interludes;
life to the man who sat at the table seemed to consist
of that eternal, damnable noise.

He was not a very pleasant sight—the sole occupant of the room.   His chin required the attentions
of a razor; his shirt, which was opened at the neck,
would have done with a wash.   His riding-breeches
were threadbare; his boots caked in mud.   And yet
for anyone with eyes to see one fact would have struck
home.   Those breeches and boots bore the unmistakable stamp of the West End.

The room was in confusion.   Dust lay thick in the
corners; a few odd letters littered the table.   The
lamp had smoked, and half the funnel was black with
soot.   Against one wall a cupboard minus its doors
leaned drunkenly—a cupboard in which unwashed

plates and an old teapot without a handle were jumbled together. And, ranged in rows along the opposite wall, empty bottles.

A full one stood on the table by his side, and after a while he picked it up and half-filled his glass with whisky. Then he resumed his study of the book that lay in front of him. A strange book to find in such surroundings, and yet one which helped to explain the riddle of the riding-breeches. It was a book of snapshots and odd cuttings from newspapers. A few groups cut from the *Tatler* and the *Sketch* were pasted in and it was at one of these that he was staring.

Bridesmaids; bride and bridegroom; best man— particularly the best man. He was in the uniform of the 10th Lancers, and for a long while the man sat there motionless, studying the face on the paper. Good-looking, with clear-cut features; a magnificent specimen of manhood, showing off the gorgeous uniform of the regiment to perfection. Then very deliberately he got up and crossed the room to the broken bit of mirror that served as a shaving glass. Dispassionately he studied his own face, not sparing himself in the examination. And at length he turned away.

"Great God!" he said, very slowly. "How did it happen?"

And the line of bottles gave answer.

He went back to the table, and started turning over the pages of the book. The regiment on parade; a stately home set in wonderful trees; groups on the moors with keepers and dogs; groups with the women he had known. . . . And at last a simple snapshot of two people—himself and a girl. Pat and self—thus ran the inscription underneath it, and for perhaps a quarter of an hour he sat there motionless, staring at it. Some big insect fussed angrily against the mosquito netting, trying to get at the light; ceaselessly

the beetles droned on—but the man at the table heard
nothing.   He was back in the might-have-been; back
at Henley—three years before the war.

Pat!   What was she doing now?   She'd stuck to
him loyally; stuck to him as only a woman can stick
to the thing she loves.   For it had started even then.
The curse was on him: the soul-rotting, hellish curse
that had brought him to this.   But at last it had had
to end: the thing had become impossible.

He had fought.   God! how he'd fought!   But it
had beaten him.   No excuse, of course: to be beaten
is no excuse for a man.   And he could still hear Pat's
voice that last time—could still see her sweet face with
the tears pouring down it.

"Jim—if you can beat it—come back to me."

And that was after he had had to send in his papers.

He hadn't beaten it; it had beaten him.   And now
Pat was married; two children—or was it three?   And
he—what was he?   His family said he was farming in
Africa.   A pleasant fiction which deceived no one.
Least of all himself.   He was not farming in Africa;
he was a drunken remittance man living on a farm in
Africa.

He closed the book, and stared with haggard eyes
into the darkness.   Why had this girl come to stop
at Merrick's farm, and opened all these old wounds?
Why had he seen her that afternoon?

She'd reminded him of Pat a little.   Cool and
dressed in white—riding Merrick's chestnut cob in a
way that showed she was used to horses.   What the
devil did she want to bring all that back to him for?
Girls and horses were all part of the life he'd lived a
hundred years ago.

"Yes, a trooper of the forces, who has owned his
own six horses. . . ."

And he wasn't even that.   Just a drunken down-

and-outer, with a father in the House of Lords who
paid him five hundred a year on condition that he
never set foot in England again.

Cool and dressed in white!   Lord! but it was something to see a girl of his own class again.   She'd stared
at him in faint surprise when he'd spoken; drink doesn't
kill a man's accent.   And by now she'd know all about
him: the Merricks would see to that.

They didn't know who he was: he'd given his name
out here as Brown.   But they did know *what* he was,
and that was all that mattered.

"A drunkard, my dear; a hopeless case."

He could hear Mrs. Merrick saying it.   Not that
she was a bad sort; quite the reverse, in fact.   But
she was the wife of a settler who had made good, and
she loathed weakness.   At first she had tried to pull
him round—to make him take an interest in his property.   For months she had persevered, and it wasn't
until she found out that he wouldn't help himself that
she gave up trying.   Contemptuously.

And he deserved it: he was under no delusions.
But now—— He stood up suddenly, and instinctively his shoulders squared.   Supposing he took a
pull at himself; it wasn't too late.   Supposing he, too,
made good.   Supposing that girl dressed in white——

And suddenly he laughed a little bitterly.   Girls
dressed in white were outside his scheme of things
altogether.   Quite deliberately he reached out for the
bottle, and tipped what was left into his glass.   Then
he performed his nightly rite.   With meticulous attention to dressing he placed it in line with the others;
called the squadron to attention, and then dismissed
them.

And ten minutes later the man who called himself
Jim Brown, having kicked off his boots, lay sleeping
heavily on his bed.

II

He'd shaved when he next saw the girl, and his shirt was clean. She was riding, as before, and he stood waiting for her to come up.

"Good morning," she said cheerily. "What a heavenly day!"

"The one compensation of this God-forsaken country," he remarked, "is that the days generally are heavenly."

She looked at him steadily.

"Why do you stay if you don't like it?"

"Entirely my duty towards my neighbour," he answered. "Think of all the grief and sorrow I should cause if I departed."

"Is that your bungalow up there?" she said suddenly.

"It is," he remarked. "And dilapidated though it looks from the outside, I can assure you the interior is much worse."

"That's good," she cried. "And as I can hardly believe it possible, I'm coming up to see."

For a moment he hesitated.

"It really isn't in a fit condition——" he began.

"Bunkum," she answered. "Do you suppose I've never seen an untidy room before?"

"It isn't altogether that," he said slowly.

Then he gave a short laugh.

"Right-ho!" he cried. "Your sins be upon your own head."

He led the way in silence, and having tethered her horse flung open the door.

"Behold the ancestral hall," he announced gravely.

Her eyes travelled round the room, resting for a moment on the array of bottles, while he watched her with a faint smile. What was she going to say?

"Get out," she remarked. "This is going to be no place for a man for the next hour or two."

It was so completely unexpected that for a moment or two he could only stare at her.

"Go on—get out," she repeated, peeling off her gloves. "You'll only be in the way."

"You topper," he said under his breath. "You absolute topper."

Then he swung on his heel and left her, not knowing if she'd heard what he'd said—and not caring.

Two hours later he returned to find her sitting on the table smoking a cigarette. And the first thing he noticed was that the empty bottles had disappeared.

"I see you've removed my squadron," he said. "It was very nearly full strength except for the officers."

"You mean those dirty old bottles," she remarked. "I've buried them outside."

"Didn't you admire their perfect dressing on parade?" he asked. "I used to call them to attention every time a new recruit joined."

She stared at him through the smoke of her cigarette.

"I've been looking at this scrap-book of yours," she said calmly. "I hope you don't mind."

"Not at all. I fear my library is somewhat deficient. But I need hardly perhaps say that Brown still remains a very good name."

He glanced round the room; everything was spotless. The shelves of the cupboard were adorned with paper; the plates were washed and neatly stacked; even the teapot seemed to have taken on a new dignity.

"You seem to have been most thorough," he said gravely. "Thank you."

"So you won the Grand Military, did you?" she remarked.

"I believe that in some former existence of mine I had that honour. Incidentally speaking," he continued, "I trust that you haven't buried the quick and the dead together."

"There are a dozen full bottles in there," she said, pointing to his bedroom. "I thought they would be more convenient for you if you woke in the night."

He stood motionless, staring at her. His face was expressionless; her eyes met his calmly and frankly.

"I deserve that," he said in a low voice.

"My dear man," she remarked. "I don't think you *deserve* anything at all. It's the wrong word. It's not for me to judge. All I say is that I think it's a pity that being who you are you should be what you are. It seems such a ghastly waste."

"Some such idea occurred to me when I took the name of Brown," he answered thoughtfully.

She shook herself a little impatiently.

"How you can have that book here—be reminded day in, day out, of everything that might be yours—and not go mad, absolutely beats me."

"Sometimes it beats me, too," he said quietly.

"Good God! man," she cried, "can't you try?"

"Good God! girl," he answered, "do you suppose I haven't?"

And for a space they were silent, staring at one another. At last she slipped from the table and went up to him.

"Sorry," she said gently, "I shouldn't have said that. Look here—can I help? Julia Merrick told me she had done her best—but Julia is married and busy. I'm neither. Shall we have a dip at it together? No slop and slush about it. If you want a drink, have one. I shan't look at you reprovingly. But if we pull together we might be able to keep whisky as a drink—not as a permanent diet."

He turned suddenly and walked over to the open window. And she being a girl of much understanding lit another cigarette and waited. In her eyes was a look of wonderful pity, but she didn't want him to see it. Something told her that she had started on the right note: that any trace of sentimentality would be fatal. For perhaps five minutes he stood there with his back to her, and only the pawing of the pony on the ground outside broke the silence. Then he swung round.

"Damned sporting offer," he said curtly. "Afraid you'll find it a bit boring, though."

"I'll chance it," she said. "Come over and dine to-night."

III

And so the man who called himself Brown began to fight again. For hours he would sit in his bungalow sweating with the agony of it, and with every nerve in his body screaming for the stuff. And sometimes the girl would sit opposite him, holding his two hands across the table and watching him with cool, steady eyes.

His face was haggard; his hands shook uncontrollably when she released them. But he fought on with every gun and rifle he possessed, and the girl fought at his side.

It happened unexpectedly as such things will—in his bungalow one evening. For three hours the girl had been with him, and that particular crisis had passed. They were sitting side by side on the stoep, watching the sun go down behind the distant Drakensburg, and without thought she put her hand on his knee.

"Jim," she whispered. "How utterly marvellous!"

And his hand closed over hers in the way there is no mistaking. She turned slowly and stared at him, and then caught her breath at the look in his eyes.

She knew instantly what was coming: knew there was
no way of stopping it.   He was down on his knees
beside her, his arms flung round her waist, his face
buried in her lap.   And for a space he went mad.

Hardly hearing—almost numbed with the suddenness of this new complication—she sat listening to the
wild dreams of the man who called himself Brown.
He was cured—with her help he had fought and
won.

"For God's sake, don't leave me, Beryl!" he said
again and again.   "Listen, dear—we'll get married.
And now that I'm all right, we'll go back to England
under my proper name.   I'll get a job—I've got influence.   And when they know I'm cured there won't
be any difficulty."

He raised his face, and with blinding clearness she
saw him for what he was.   Before he had just been
a case—a mission; now he was very much a man.   A
man grown old before his time, with the ineffaceable
ravages of drink plain to see; a man with bloodshot,
puffy eyes and trembling limbs; a travesty.

And yet, ghastly in its mercilessness though the
picture was, in some strange way she seemed to see
another one.   Shining through this terrible mask she
saw the man as he had been—clear-eyed, firm-lipped,
with the pride of youth in every line of his body.
And a pity that was almost divine took hold of her.
She leaned forward and put her hand on his hair—
and it was the hair of the man who had been that
she touched.   She kissed him on the forehead, and
it was the forehead of the man in uniform—the man
who had won the Grand Military—that she kissed.

And then he, with a little gasp of wonder, seized
her hungrily and kissed her on the mouth.   And
Beryl Kingswood sat rigid: the dream had gone—
reality had come back.   The man who had kissed her

lips was the man who called himself Jim Brown—the
drunkard.

He was mad—incoherent with joy. He couldn't
believe it: he went on pacing up and down the veranda,
painting wild dreams of the future. And every now
and then he would stop and kiss the back of her neck
—and touch her arm almost humbly.

"Stop and have dinner with me, dear," he said, "on
this wonderful night of nights. I'll take you back
afterwards."

And because she was incapable of clear thought—
because she was dazed by the result of what she had
done in that one instant—she stayed to dinner. What
was she going to do? How was she ever going to tell
him? And gradually as the hours passed the thing
began to get clearer. Dinner was over—a meal at
which he had proudly drunk orange-juice and water.
And now, sitting once again on the stoep in the darkness, her hand in his, it didn't seem so very terrible.
She would go through with it; she would marry him,
and bring him back to what he had been. She had
put her hand to the plough—she would not turn back.

"We'll make good, my dear," she whispered impulsively. "We'll make good between us."

Very tenderly and reverently he bent and kissed her
hand.

"You utterly marvellous girl," he said.

And for a space there was silence, broken only by
the ceaseless noise of the tree beetles.

IV

Thus did the man who called himself Brown struggle
to the foot-hills from which a glimpse of Heaven may
be got. And Fate ordained that he should remain
there for just one week—a week during which only
one person mattered, the wonderful girl who had pro-

mised to marry him. He got a tablecloth from the neighbouring store, and carefully mended the broken teapot handle with seccotine, so as to be able to give her tea when she came over to see him. He laid in stocks of grub, and got bowls in which he arranged flowers for her benefit. And, perhaps, greatest wonder of all, the twelve full bottles under his bed remained full.

Of the other side of the case he knew nothing— how should he? He had not been in the Merricks' bedroom on the night they had learned what had happened—the night he had walked over with Beryl after she had dined with him. He had not seen Julia Merrick positively seize her husband as he came in, and almost shake him in her excitement.

"Tom—it's too horrible!"

"It's pretty grim, I admit," he remarked. "Still, I don't see what's to be done about it. She seems to have made up her mind."

"It isn't as if she loved him even."

"What's that?" said her husband. "Doesn't she love him?"

"Of course she doesn't. How could she?"

"I dunno. Women do some damned funny things at times. Has she told you she doesn't?"

"Don't be an absolute idiot," cried Julia Merrick. "Do you suppose another woman wants to be told a thing like that? You've only got to see them together. Why, he—he almost repels her."

Tom Merrick yawned hugely.

"Well, my dear—it's beyond me. If he repels her, why the deuce has she gone and got engaged to him?"

"Because she's sorry for him. Because she thinks it her job. Because she thinks she's cured him. Because—oh! a thousand reasons—and not one of them the right one.   And from what I know of Beryl, she'll carry the thing through."

Her husband turned over sleepily.

"We'd better talk it over, my dear.   In the morning," he added hopefully.

"There's nothing to talk over," said his wife. "The thing's unnatural.   It's—it's ghastly.   Are you asleep?"

"More or less, my dear."

"Well, become a little less for a moment.   Do you honestly and conscientiously believe that that man is cured?"

"Difficult to say," he grunted.   "Personally, I wouldn't trust him a yard.   Think he's a hopeless case.   Still, you never can tell."

"Tom, if Beryl were your daughter—would you allow it?"

"Good God! no!" he cried.   "What an idea!"

"All right," said his wife quietly.   "You can go to sleep now."

And lay awake herself staring into the darkness. Dimly she had feared during the past few weeks that some such complications might occur, but never had she dreamed that Beryl would go to the length of promising to marry the man.   That he might fall in love with her she had realized was more than likely: many men did fall in love with Beryl Kingswood. But that she would accept him seemed so staggeringly outrageous that she could still hardly believe it.

What to do?   That was the problem.

And as the days passed by it became more acute. She was almost frightened of mentioning the matter to Beryl, because it seemed to make her shut up like an oyster.   Obviously she didn't want to discuss it; just as obviously her nerves were strung up to the danger point.   And Julia Merrick could have screamed with the futility of it.

Her husband was no help.

"What can I do, my dear?" he said continually. "They're both of age.   If Beryl chooses to marry the man I don't see how we can prevent her.   She's her own mistress.   She knows the danger she is running as well as we do.   He certainly seems to have kept off the drink these last few weeks."

"Couldn't you have a talk with him as man to man?" she urged.   "Say to him that it isn't fair to marry her until he is *sure*.   That he ought to give it a year at least."

"I'll have a try," he said doubtfully.   "But I tell you frankly, Julia, that fellow Brown is a queer customer to tackle.   He's got a way of looking at you which says 'Go to the devil,' plainer than any language.   Drunkard though he is, I give you my word that there are times when he makes me feel like a boy in front of a master."

"He's coming over to-night," said his wife.   "Get him alone and try."

But it wasn't necessary; as I have said.   Fate ordained that Jim Brown should stay on the foot-hills for just one week.   And that night the week was up.   Why he should have approached the Merricks' bungalow from behind instead of going to the front door is just one of those things that happen without reason.   But he did—and found himself looking into the room that Julia Merrick called the work-room.   Beryl was sitting at the table, and her name was trembling on the tip of his tongue when she looked up and he saw her face.   And it seemed as if the world stood still.

He stood there rooted to the spot, staring at hopeless, abject misery and despair.   Just for one moment he clutched at the wild hope that she had had bad news. But only for a moment; it wasn't mail day. There could be only one cause—and he knew it. Standing motionless in the darkness he watched this girl who meant salvation to him—watched her as some stranger might have watched her—impersonally. He felt conscious of only one dominant thought—to find out the truth.

Suddenly the door opened and Julia Merrick came in. He saw her pause for a moment, staring at Beryl; then he heard her speak with a sudden rush.

"My dear, now I know. You *can't* do this thing." And heard the other answer.

"I *must!*"

He crept nearer the window; he had to hear everything now.

"Why did you do it, Beryl?"

He listened to the girl's puzzled—almost halting—explanation. And because the man who called himself Jim Brown had been a person of much understanding before he became a drunkard, he understood perfectly that which only exasperated Julia Merrick.

"He must be told," said that lady decisively. "If you don't—I shall."

"If you do, Julia," said the girl, "I will never forgive you. I absolutely forbid you to tell him."

She stood up, facing the older woman squarely.

"Absolutely, you understand. I'm going through with it. I would never forgive myself if I started him off again."

"I wish to Heaven he'd have another outburst now—before it's too late," said the other. "Beryl—the risk is too ghastly. I know he's kept off it for a week or two—but he's a hopeless case. Tom says so. At least, my dear—say that you'll wait a year. Make him prove himself to that extent."

The girl shook her head.

"No, dear, I won't. I believe I can pull him through if I'm with him the whole time. And I can't be that unless I marry him. My mind is made up, Julia," she went on quietly. "I shall marry him whatever you say. And he's got to go on believing that I'm fond of him, or half my influence will be gone."

Julia Merrick shrugged her shoulders helplessly.

"So be it, Beryl. It's your choice. But I think you're making a terrible mistake."

"Perhaps I am," said the girl. "But a mistake is better than a sin. And it would be a sin to turn him down now, when he has fought so hard. Let's go, Julia; he ought to be here soon."

The light went out; the room was empty. She would be in the drawing-room by now—sitting in the chair she usually occupied. He had only to go round to the front door and walk in, and he would see her get up with that grave little smile of hers and hold out both her hands. And she would say:

"How goes it, old lad?"

And he would answer: "Quite well, my dear—quite well."

And she would say: "Well played, partner."

Yes—just go round to the front door and walk in. Wipe these last few minutes off the slate—pretend they had never been. A grave smile flickered round his lips—half-cynical, half-tender. Then, lifting his hand to the salute, the man who called himself Brown turned and walked away into the night.

v

"I'll come with you, Beryl," said Tom.

Over the girl's shoulder he glanced significantly at his wife. It was ten o'clock, and dinner was long since over—the dinner to which Jim Brown had been bidden and failed to appear.

"All right," said Beryl quietly. "Just as you like."

In silence they set out on their twenty-minute walk. The glorious African moon made it almost as light as day, and it wasn't until they came in sight of Jim Brown's bungalow that Tom Merrick spoke again.

"My dear," he said gravely, "for God's sake don't be too disappointed if—if——"

"Please don't," she said, "I'd sooner not talk."

It was as they were walking up the rise to his house that they suddenly heard his voice.

"Parade! 'Shun!"

And the girl stopped dead with a little gasp.

"Let me go first," said Tom Merrick.

"No," said Beryl firmly. "You wait outside."

She crossed the veranda and pushed open the door. In perfect dressing on the floor stood eleven empty bottles, and on the table in front of him one that was half full. And in front of the eleven was the teapot.

"That gentleman," he said, gravely indicating the latter, "is the commanding officer. Don't you think he's rather a good-looker?"

"Jim," she said steadily, "we were expecting you to dinner."

"The devil you were, my dear," he answered. "That's a bit of a break on my part."

"What are those doing there?" She pointed to the row of bottles.

"My soldiers, darling," he explained. "I took them out for an airing to-night. To spare your feelings, up to date, I've kept them in barracks under the bed, but the little chaps insisted on a field day to-night."

"You mean to say that you've been drinking all this time?"

Her voice was unutterably weary.

"Honesty, my pet, compels me to admit the fact. It was my innate politeness which made me disguise the fact in view of your well-meant efforts on my behalf. Ah! my friend, Mr. Merrick, I see. One of those honest pillars of the soil that have made our glorious Empire what it is."

"So you've lied to me," she whispered. "All this while. Oh! my God!"

And just for one brief moment did the man who had tipped eleven full bottles of whisky down the sink that night falter. Then he steadied himself and rode at the last fence.

"My dear," he said gravely, "lie is an ugly word. Shall we say—prevaricated charmingly?"

"A hopeless case, my dear," said Tom Merrick, as they neared his bungalow. "He'd gone too far."

And the hopeless case sat at his table staring with hopeless eyes into the night. The bottle in front of him was empty. At last he rose, and with meticulous attention to dressing he placed it in line with the others. He called the squadron to attention and then dismissed them.

And for a space there was silence, broken only by the ceaseless noise of the tree beetles.

XXVII   THE UNDOING OF MRS. CRANSBY

MRS. CRANSBY was a bad woman. I do not use the adjective in its strict sense: in matters of sex she was much as other women—rather less so perhaps than most. I use it in the same way as it is frequently used about a man by his fellows. And then it generally implies that the gentleman in question is a poor specimen.

Mrs. Cransby was a poor specimen, though numbers

of the opposite sex took a long time to find it out. She was amazing, in spite of the fact that her tongue was sharper than a serpent's tooth when she wanted it to be. She was always perfectly dressed, and her figure was divine. Moreover she was pretty. How she had maintained her complexion during years in the East only her maid and she knew. Though possibly her husband when footing the bill for face creams and lotions from England had a shrewd idea. Possibly also he wished her complexion was not quite so wonderful.

But her principal glory was her hair. It was in the days, be it known, before the shingle and the Eton crop, and Mrs. Cransby's hair was undoubtedly very wonderful. Personally, needless to say, I never had the opportunity of seeing it when let down: but judging as a mere male it must have reached nearly to her knees. There were masses of it, coiled about her shapely head. In colour it was exactly the right tinge of auburn: in texture it was like the finest of gossamer silk. At least so Purvis in the Gunners assured me one night in the club, when he ought to have been at home with his wife.

And perhaps because it was so very wonderful Mrs. Cransby hated to have it touched. She bit like a snapping dog if it was disturbed even accidentally. And as for anything in the nature of a caress, I understand that no man did it a second time. As a result there was never a hair out of place. At the end of a game of tennis it was still as perfectly arranged as at the beginning: at the conclusion of a dance she might just have left her coiffeur. Which is all I have to say about Mrs. Cransby's hair—a very important factor in this story.

I will come therefore to a very unimportant one— her husband. Only the fact that I have already alluded to him casually justifies the poor devil's inclusion. He was a mild little individual—something in Woods and Forests—and was always alluded to as Mrs. Cransby's husband. And his sole claim to notoriety was that he supplied the money which Mrs. Cransby spent. Of children, needless to say, there were none: Mrs. Cransby was not the type of woman to waste her time. And having got so far it occurs to me that a little more justification of my opening sentence is necessary. It shall be given in a nutshell: she was a specialist in other women's husbands. And fiancés. It was sufficient for Mrs. Cransby to know that a man was engaged to a girl for her to appropriate him on the spot. And the astounding thing was that she so frequently succeeded. I think she did it to show her power. She didn't keep him permanently—two or three months perhaps, according to the value of the specimen. Then she returned him labelled "finished with," and cast round for someone else. Which made her, of course, intensely popular with women.

In many cases no permanent damage was done: in some it was. Little Patricia Tennant for instance broke off her engagement to young Hill in the 10th Lancers because of her. She said she flatly refused to marry another woman's cast-off. And Hill, whose madness had completely passed, very nearly blew out his brains. Stanton, too, in a native Cavalry regiment, made a very complete fool of himself over her, at a time when his wife was having her first baby. Which was not at all a good thing to do, and on that occasion even Mrs. Cransby's skin was not thick enough to stand the remarks that were made. So she drifted away just before the baby arrived very much earlier than expected. And two doctors sweating through a sweltering night managed to save the mother's life.

Then there was—— But why enumerate? Mrs. Cransby was a bad woman, and this is the tale of her undoing at the hands of MacAndrew, sometime doctor and all time drunkard. And should anyone who reads these words ever meet Mrs. Cransby—she lives in London now—let him take warning, and steer clear of mentioning any name that sounds even remotely Scotch. Because she will probably start to bite the furniture, and that would be a spectacle sufficient to shake the strongest nerve.

John MacAndrew was a character. Exactly what had caused his departure from Scotland, I never inquired into. And he was not communicative. But I do know that he was one of the most brilliant students of his year, and that when he chose to, even after twenty-five years of continuous drinking, there was practically no subject on which he could not talk far more intelligently than the majority of people.

He had a small bungalow on the Irrawaddy a few hundred miles up country. There was a branch of a teak company situated there, and originally he had gone up as doctor. And somehow or other he had stayed on, though he had long since ceased to practice. Much as we all liked him, it would have been a stout-hearted man who called in MacAndrew professionally. It was there I first met him, when I was doing Assistant-Manager.

There were ten of us whites in all, though only three others come into this story. Cooper was the Manager —a capable man and a good fellow except in the early morning when he suffered from a liver like a volcano in eruption. He was a widower and his daughter Joan lived with him. And on the subject of Joan Cooper we were all of us partially demented. It wasn't because she was the only pebble on the beach either: she would have held her own anywhere. A glorious girl—absolutely unspoilt—and radiating cheeriness and affection. But no more. I think we all proposed to her in turn:

I know I did—twice. But there was nothing doing: she wouldn't dream of leaving Daddy.

Until young Jack Congleton arrived. He was a cheery youngster fresh from the Varsity, who was ultimately destined for the headquarter office in London. And he had been sent out to us to learn his job first hand.

It was after he'd been there a week, that the general drift of things became too obvious to be ignored. Even old Cooper, who as a rule saw nothing beyond matters concerning teak, sat up and took notice. Three or four times I caught him studying Jack Congleton thoughtfully in his office, when he should have been finishing important letters. But when all is said and done a prospective son-in-law is as important as any letter.

And there was nothing wrong with young Congleton. He wouldn't have won a prize in a beauty show, but he was a straight, clean, well-set-up boy. Moreover, from a financial point of view he was eminently satisfactory. He was to be taken into partnership as soon as he returned to England. And though Cooper would have murdered the man who said so, I think the advantages of having a son-in-law as partner in the firm had not escaped him. There comes a time when Burma palls and London calls. Not—to do him justice —that he would have let such an idea influence him for a moment if Congleton had been a wrong 'un. He idolized Joan far too much for that. But it was a factor that counted in young Jack's claims to eligibility.

It came to a head after he had been there three weeks. I walked into the office one morning to find a bottle of champagne on the table, and Jack somewhat sheepishly helping Cooper to lower it.

"Hear what this young scoundrel has done, Morris?" cried Cooper. "He's had the confounded impertinence to propose to Joan, and the child's brain is so weak that she's accepted him. Drink his health, my boy. This is damned bad for my liver, but it's not an everyday occurrence, thank God!"

I said the customary things, and then work went on as usual. And I don't believe any of us felt the faintest twinge of jealousy. They were such an admirably chosen pair: they were so idiotically in love with one another. Burma was so wonderful: and life was so wonderful: and each of them was so wonderful to the other.

And the most delighted of us all was John Mac-Andrew. Mac adored Joan as if she had been his daughter. And Joan adored him. Drunkard he may have been and was, but I do not believe there is a man or woman living to-day who could say of John Mac-Andrew—"That man let me down." Which is a valuation, in the big scheme of things, that is maybe of higher merit than the holding of a blue ribbon. And because Cooper was a man of understanding he had never raised any objection to his daughter knowing him.

Now it so happened that shortly after the great event of the engagement duty took me up country for over two months. And the night I got back found me sitting in my bungalow trying to polish off arrears of correspondence. There was a big batch of it and I was not too well pleased when I heard the Soldiers' Chorus from *Faust* outside, and steps ascending the veranda. It was MacAndrew's only song, and he and letter-writing did not go together.

He entered, mopping his forehead with a huge red bandana, and deposited himself in a chair. Then with great solemnity he drew from his pocket a bottle of whisky, and placed it on the table beside him.

"Are you busy, laddie?" he asked.

"Never too busy to see you, Mac," I said resignedly. "But don't drink your own whisky: try some of mine."

He shook his head.

"Not on your life, my dear boy," he answered. "My consumption is so enormous that I would not run the risk of straining our friendship to that extent. But I have no objection to your drinking your own: in fact, I shall regard such an action in the most favourable light."

"You old ass, Mac," I laughed. "Well, how is everything here?"

He filled his glass in silence, and suddenly a premonition took me that something was wrong. Now that I looked at him he seemed unusually grave for him.

"Water, Mac?" I said perfunctorily.

"Water, laddie," he cried. "Is your reason snapping?"

He finished half the glass, and then with the utmost deliberation he rolled himself a cigarette. From of old I knew there was no good trying to hurry him. He lit his cigarette, blew out a great cloud of smoke, and then looked at me from under his shaggy eyebrows.

"Do you by any chance ken a female called Cransby?" he said.

"Cransby," I cried. "Wife of the man in Woods and Forests?"

"Aye," he said.

"Yes I do. Why?"

"She's here," he answered, and finished the rest of his drink.

"Then as far as I am concerned the sooner she goes away from here the better I'll be pleased," I said. "She is a lady for whom I have no vestige or shadow of use."

He grunted, and mopped his forehead once again.

"Your opinion of her confirms my own diagnosis," he remarked. "I have no vestige or shadow of use

for her myself.   But she's here: and she's been here a
week."

"Has she been trying to make you fall in love with
her, Mac?" I chaffed.

"She has not," he answered gravely.   "But she's
been trying to make young Congleton.   And she's
succeeded."

"What?" I almost shouted.   "But what about
Joan?"

"Mon," he said, "that woman is a she-devil.   Listen
and I'll tell you what's been happening while you've
been away.   You ken what those two bairns were like,
with their billing and their cooing, and their this and
that.   You ken that each was the whole world to the
other.   One night—it was about a fortnight after you
left—the pair of them came round to see me.   And,
laddie, it was like seeing a little bit of Heaven.   Their
dreams, and their hopes—and the way they looked at
one another, and touched one another's hands, when
they thought I didn't see.

"They sat on there talking, and I let them talk and
just listened.   Maybe I dreamed myself a little; dreamed
of Scotland and the sun turning the moors from purple
to velvet black as it sets way down behind great banks of
cloud."

He paused and stared into the darkness.   And I
waited: MacAndrew was in a strange mood to-night.

"I'm talking rot," he went on abruptly.   "But I
want you to get the condition I was in that night, when
yon hell-cat appeared.   She came out of the darkness,
suddenly—and stood on the veranda smiling.   And
even then it was at young Jack that most of her smiles
were delivered.

" 'Can you tell me where Mr. Cooper's bungalow
is?' said she.   'My name is Cransby, and my husband
is seeing about the baggage.'

"The little girl got up, with that sweet look of hers, and went to her.

" 'But, Mrs. Cransby,' she said, 'we weren't expecting you and your husband for three days. I'm so sorry neither my father nor I were there to meet you. I'll take you over to the bungalow at once.'

" 'That's sweet of you,' says the woman. 'I thought my husband had written: I'm *so* sorry if we've inconvenienced you.'

"I heard her voice dying away in the distance, and then I glanced at young Jack. And he had a funny sort of half-smile, half-smirk on his face.

" 'What a damned attractive woman,' he remarked.

" 'Tastes differ,' I said, and at that we left it.

"To start with, I admit, I didn't think much of it. It appeared that the husband, and maybe you know him, he looks rather like a newt with pince-nez—was here on Government business. And he was going up country."

"Good Lord," I interrupted. "I did hear there was a Government man of sorts cruising round. But I never thought it was Cransby."

"It was and is," said Mac. "He's still cruising. And his wife is still here. Cooper told her, as he naturally had to do, that she was to use his bungalow till her husband's return."

"She can't have done much damage in a week," I said, but my tone carried no conviction. Mrs. Cransby could play the devil in a day.

"I would not have thought so either," he agreed, "until last night. At first there was nothing much to lay hold of—just a look here, and a glance there. But I saw from the little girl's face that she had spotted. She didn't say anything about it—she's proud is that bairn. But there was all the misery of the ages in her dear eyes when she thought no one was looking. And even now I don't know if she realizes how far it has gone."

"What do you mean, Mac?" I said anxiously. "She doesn't generally go to any extreme lengths."

"I was walking down by the big plantation," he went on, "about six o'clock last night. And suddenly I heard voices. It was young Congleton speaking, and I stood there almost unable to believe my ears. 'Darling,' he was saying, 'she's only a girl—but you're the most wonderful woman in the world. Irene—my beloved.' And she answered, 'Dear, dear boy. But you mustn't forget you're engaged to her, and that I'm a married woman.' I took a step forward, and there she was stroking his face. Losh ! man. I was very near sick with disgust. 'Shame on you,' I said to young Congleton, 'you miserable pup. What for are you allowing yon harpy to stroke your face, with your girl sitting at home waiting for you?'"

I grinned happily: for Mrs. Cransby to be called a harpy to her face sounded almost too good to be true.

"What happened?" I cried.

"Mon," he said, "there was a terrible scene. I'm not saying that I didn't enjoy it, for I just revelled in it. The woman got to her feet, and came towards me. Her face was set like a mask, and if she'd had the power she'd have struck me dead at her feet. 'I am not in the habit,' says she, 'of being called a harpy by people—least of all by a drunken old wastrel.' 'And I,' I said, 'am not in the habit of calling a spade anything but a spade. Good God! woman, you're old enough to be his mother.'"

"Mac," I shouted delightedly, "you didn't? Why, man, there must be three score women roaming this world to-day who would give half their worldly possessions to have heard that remark."

"I'm not denying it didn't give me a certain amount

of satisfaction," he said. "But, laddie, it's serious. The boy is fairly besotted. He called round to see me this morning and asked me how I dared to say such a thing to the most perfect and wonderful woman in the world. He said that if I wasn't a drunken old swine he'd have thrashed me to within an inch of my life. Didn't I understand that it wasn't her fault that he had fallen in love with her: that she was a loyal and devoted wife and had told him all along that his duty lay with Joan? And so on. I didn't interrupt him: I let him have his say out. And then I just put my hand on his shoulder and I said, 'Boy, in a moment of anger I told Mrs. Cransby she was old enough to be your mother. I'm sorry. But, anyway, I'm old enough to be your father. And I like you. And I'm just sick to see you making such a damned fool of yourself.' "

"The rag, and the bone, and the hank of hair," I quoted without thinking. But MacAndrew looked at me intently.

"The hank of hair," he repeated. "It's curious—the hair of that woman."

"In what way," I said. "I know she is inordinately proud of it. And if you want to disillusionize young Congleton, get him to ruffle it. She'll go for him like a Billingsgate fish wife."

"It's curious," he repeated. "Verra curious."

He lapsed into silence, sunk in a train of thought of his own. And I, too, sat thinking. What wretched freak of fate had brought the woman here? Not often did she accompany her husband to such out-of-the-way places. But now that she had come, the march of events was as inexorable as day following night. Only too well did I recognize the Mrs. Cransby touch. "Dear, dear boy. Don't you realize that I'm married."

Always the same. A kiss perhaps—just now and then: the pressure of a hand: the wonderful look implying how different things would have been if she wasn't married. And then the calm tossing aside like a worn-out glove. Stale to her: she'd done it so often before. But like a drug: she could no more resist doing it than stop breathing.

Only I felt furious with young Congleton. Within two months of having got engaged to a girl like Joan. . . . The only excuse was that he *was* very young, and that other much warier game had fallen to the same gun. Anyway, his punishment was coming: the pathetic thing was that another would have to share in that punishment.

"I'm afraid there's nothing to be done, Mac," I said at length. "You can't stop a man making a congenital idiot of himself if he's set on it. Mrs. Cransby is the only person who could do it, and you might as well ask a tiger to leave its kill."

"Verra curious," he said, "that hair of hers."

"What the devil has her hair got to do with it," I cried irritably. I thought the old boy was getting fuddled.

"Always the same," he went on. "Verra curious."

And then quite suddenly he sat up and stared into a corner of the room.

"Mon," he cried, "look at yonder rat. As big as a rabbit."

I swung round in my chair: there was nothing in the corner at all.

"Steady, old man," I said. "I don't see any rat."

"There—running across the room." He followed its course with his finger. "Lord sakes! it's vanished into the wall."

"Look here, Mac," I said gravely, "you'd better take a pull at yourself. There wasn't any rat there at all. You're imagining things."

"No rat," he muttered. "Are you sure, Bill?"

"Perfectly sure," I answered.   "You'd better go on the water-wagon for a bit."

"Aye—perhaps you're right," he said.   "That's what yon woman told me."

He got heavily to his feet, and put back the bottle in his pocket.

"No rat, you say.   And that hair of hers.   Verra curious.   Well, good night, Bill.   Maybe it will all turn out for the best.   But it's curious—curious."

And as he stumbled down the veranda steps, I heard him still muttering that it was verra curious.

The old chap breaking up, I reflected—and then my mind came back to the far more important problem of young Congleton.   Because the boy was worth saving —I felt it in my very bones.   And if what MacAndrew had told me was right, he was evidently in a bad way. Of course, I could tell him what I knew of Mrs. Cransby, and that he was only one of a large procession. But would he believe me—would it do the slightest good?   Or I could appeal to her, an even more fatuous proceeding.

"Confound and curse the woman," I cried out loud, and at that moment I heard MacAndrew stumbling up the steps again.   "And confound and curse the man," I muttered: I'd had enough of him for one night.

"Bill," he said, appearing in the window, "I'm sorry to interrupt you again.   But I've been thinking.   And it's occurred to me that I may have been imagining things.   That rat—for instance.   You say there was no rat?"

"Of course there was no rat," I cried.   "You haven't come all the way back to ask me that, have you?"

"Not exactly," he answered.   "But if I thought I saw a rat, and there was no rat—maybe I did yon woman an injustice when I said she was stroking the boy's face.   Maybe she wasn't."

I stared at him in amazement.

"What are you driving at?" I asked. "Even if you imagined she was stroking his face and she wasn't, you can't have imagined the interview you had with young Congleton."

"That is so," he agreed. "But if I made a false accusation such as that, it would be sufficient to make them both verra angry. They have done harm to the little girl, by my blundering foolishness."

"Well?" I said. What on earth was he driving at?

"So I'm thinking I would like to apologize," he went on.

"There's nothing to prevent you," I remarked. "Though from what I know of the lady, if she wasn't stroking his face she was either just going to or just had."

"That don't matter," he said obstinately. "I would have no woman say I had done her an injustice. And the fact that I do not like her is all the more reason that I should not be unfair. So I'm wanting you to do something for me, Bill. The night is yet young. And even if the sun has gone down on our wrath, there is no good reason why it should rise on it."

"For Heaven's sake, Mac," I cried, half-angry and half-amused, "get to the point. Or the sun will have risen on it."

"Go over to Cooper's bungalow," he said, "and get hold of Mrs. Cransby and young Congleton. Cooper is away out to-night, and I saw a light in the little girl's room—so maybe she has gone to bed. Bring them back with you here: I saw them sitting on the veranda."

"But, good Lord! man," I cried, "it's ridiculous. What on earth excuse am I to give them?"

"Give them the real reason," he said. "Say that I'm wanting to apologize for my rudeness. You know the woman yourself, and you can say that I'm just a drunken old man with delirium tremens, who has been babbling foolishly. And that you're verra angry with me."

I hesitated, and suddenly he put his hand on my arm.

"Go, Bill, I tell you. It's important."

"Why not go over and apologize to them there?" I said.

"Because the little girl might hear," he answered. "And I would not have her know more than is absolutely necessary. Go: go, at once."

"All right," I said reluctantly. "Though why the devil you can't wait till to-morrow, I don't know."

"She'd be wearing a topee," he remarked with complete irrelevance. "Just go now, Bill."

"What's the game, Mac?" I said, staring at him.

"One on which the little girl's happiness depends," he answered. "For the boy is a good boy really. Go, Bill, and don't come back without them."

And so I went. Half-way there I very nearly turned back: the whole thing seemed so preposterously foolish. But then I realized I'd never get rid of MacAndrew if I didn't get them, and I walked on. That they would come I felt tolerably certain: Mrs. Cransby would seize the opportunity with both hands of suppressing such an embarrassing piece of gossip. What I couldn't for the life of me understand was MacAndrew's attitude.

I found them alone on the veranda, and young Congleton's face did not register joy. Mrs. Cransby, on the contrary, gave me one of her sweetest smiles.

"Why, I declare it's Mr. Morris," she said, holding out her hand. "It must be quite three years since we met."

"At Poona," I answered. "Forgive my unceremonious call," I went on, "but I have a rather peculiar mission to perform. MacAndrew is over at my bungalow. . . ."

"Damn the drunken old sweep," exploded Congleton.

"Precisely," I agreed. "And he has been talking out of his turn. As you know I only returned to-day, and he came over to see me after dinner. Well, to come to the point, he told me a story about you two."

"Well," said young Congleton savagely, and Mrs. Cransby leaned forward in her chair with her eyes fixed on my face.

"In the middle of it," I went on, "he saw a non-existent rat in the corner. And it shook him badly. It suddenly seemed to penetrate to his brain that if he was seeing rats that weren't there he might have imagined he'd seen things that hadn't happened."

I heard Mrs. Cransby draw in her breath sharply.

"And so he is very anxious to apologize to you both for the unpardonably rude things he said."

"But, good Heavens. . . " began young Congleton foolishly.

"I think," interrupted Mrs. Cransby quietly, "that it is the least Mr. MacAndrew can do. I need hardly tell you, Mr. Morris, that he imagined the whole thing, and that his remarks were offensive to an insufferable degree. But I haven't lived so long in the East not to realize the devastating effect of alcohol as a permanent diet. And to learn to make excuses for the victims. We will come over with you. . . ."

Very reluctantly young Congleton rose and followed us. To him the whole thing was an absurd waste of time, which might far more profitably have been spent with his adored one. Was he not going to tell Cransby when he returned the whole state of affairs? So what did it matter what the old fool saw or didn't see? Besides—he *had* seen it: so what was the good of pretending he hadn't? And had some supernatural power told him that his adored one was already bored stiff

with him, and had fully determined to leave long before
her devoted spouse returned in order to prevent any
such embarrassing complications, he would have dismissed the suspicion with scornful laughter.   Had she
not kissed him that very evening?   And the fact that
even had she remembered such a great event, it sank
into utter insignificance beside the vital necessity of
silencing old MacAndrew's tongue, was hidden from
him.   Such things are hidden from those who fall to
the rag and the bone and the hank of hair. . . .

We found MacAndrew standing by the table in the
centre of the room, swaying slightly.   And the first
thing I noticed was a large bucket of water close beside
him, ·an article of furniture which most certainly had
not been there when I left.

"I have been cooling my head," began MacAndrew
gravely, "so that my words, Mrs. Cransby, shall be as
clear as those of an old man may ever be."

He was rolling his R's grandly, was Mac, and I
pulled forward a chair for Mrs. Cransby.

"I am glad to hear it, Mr. MacAndrew," she said
coldly.   "It is a pity you didn't think of the cure
sooner."

"Maybe it is," he agreed.   "But I'm an old man."

He broke off suddenly.   With his eyes dilated with
horror he was staring at Mrs. Cransby's head, and
instinctively she rose to her feet.

"What is it?" she cried.

"Lord's sake, don't move," he muttered hoarsely.
"An enormous tarantula."

He stretched out a vast hand, and seized Mrs.
Cransby's hair.   And he pulled Mrs. Cransby's hair.
And with a slight sucking noise Mrs. Cransby's hair
came off—every atom of it.   And it disappeared into
the bucket of water.

Now I have seen in the course of my life perfectly

bald men, but I have never seen, except on that occasion, a perfeçtly bald woman. And as a spectacle it shakes a man to the marrow. I stood gazing speechlessly at that shining cranium and conquering with the greatest difficulty a desire to burst into screams of laughter. Then I stole a look at young Congleton. His jaw had dropped: his eyes were fixed on the same target. And his face had rather the expression of a man looking down the wrong end of a loaded gun.

Only MacAndrew who was staring into the depths of the bucket seemed unmoved. He was agitating the water gently, and whistling under his breath. And at last he spoke in a hushed voice.

"Bill," he said, "you're right. No r-rat: no enorrmous tarantula. I must go on the water-wagon."

And at last Mrs. Cransby spoke—not in a hushed voice. She spoke for five minutes without repeating herself. Then she happened to see her reflection in the glass. And she ceased speaking, and left.

"A terrible thing," said MacAndrew thoughtfully. "No r-rat: no enorrmous tarantula. And I have never apologized for my unworthy suspicions."

He turned to young Congleton.

"Let this be a warning to you, laddie: keep off the strong drink. And maybe you'd take the lady's wig over with you when you go. If she hangs it out to dry it should be fit to wear in the morn."

A little dazedly young Congleton took the sodden mass: then he, too, left.

"Tell her," called MacAndrew after him, "that I will come to-morrow to apologize. And if I should see another enorrmous tarantula in her hair, I will leave it there."

He looked at me and his eyes were twinkling.

"I'm thinking, Bill, he's cured. And the little girl will perhaps be merciful to him. But Lord's sake! man, have ye ever seen such a fearsome spectacle as yonder woman with a head like a billiard ball?"   .

"But how the devil did you know, Mac?" I asked weakly.

"I didn't," he answered. "I just thought it was verra curious—that hair of hers. I thought that if I pulled hard enough, something might happen. And all I'm feared of now is that the judgment of the Lord may come upon me. It would be a terrible thing if I really did begin to see r-rats and enorrmous tarantulas, which were not there. Terrible."

He rose to his feet.

"Ah weel—I'll be away home."

"You mean to say, Mac, that the whole thing was a put-up job," I gasped. "Didn't you think you saw a tarantula in her hair? And that rat?"

"Laddie," he said majestically, "when I see rats and tarantulas there are rats and tarantulas. To hear you talk anyone might think I was addicted to strong drink. But I suppose nothing better can be expected of a mere Sassenach. I bid you good night."

XXVIII   A QUESTION OF MUD

"AND who," I asked, "is the somewhat inane-looking youth with the charming girl at whom you cracked a smile?"

Jim Featherstone grinned.

"He looks most kinds of an ass, doesn't he?" he said. "And yet, Bill, not only is there a deuced quick brain behind that vacuous face of his, but his actual pose of asininity on one occasion helped him to land that girl for his wife and get one of the most notorious crooks in Europe laid by the heels. No; you can take it from

me, Tommy Maunders is not such a blithering idiot as
he looks."

"One is almost tempted to murmur the obvious," I
remarked.   "But I'll spare you that if I'm right in
supposing that a story is attached."

Jim settled himself comfortably in his chair.

Well, it might amuse you (he said), though I'm not
much of a hand at spinning a yarn.   It happened two
years ago, on the occasion of the celebrated cricket
match between Robert's Rabbits and Dick's Duds.   I
don't suppose you'll find any account of the encounter
in Wisden's—like other great things in this world, it
blushed unseen.   Yet for keenness, my boy, that annual
match has Middlesex and Surrey beat to a frazzle.
Robert's Rabbits are a team raised each year by old
Bob Seymour for the express purpose of playing this
match against an eleven led by Sir Richard Templeton.
Heaven knows how the thing started, but to-day that
match is the event of the season for the twenty-two
warriors concerned.   It always takes place at Dick
Templeton's place in Warwickshire.   He has a nice
little cricket ground, and in the year dot was quite a
good average player.   Now he's got a tummy like a
balloon, and stops the ball with his foot—sometimes.

His house is charming and really old.   A big,
rambling sort of place where Charles I hid from the
Roundheads and all that sort of stuff.   And since Dick,
who rolls in boodle, is mercifully possessed of excellent
taste, all the improvements and additions he has made
fit in with the general scheme.   Which is just as well,
because he's almost doubled the original property.

The procedure is invariably the same.   Robert's
Rabbits arrive on the Wednesday; the match is played
on Thursday and Friday; and the party breaks up on
the Saturday or Monday according to what one's own
particular plans are.   The house is big enough to

accommodate everyone and several ladies besides, so, as you can imagine, it's a pretty jolly show.

Now, it so happened that the year before, the Duds had completely wiped the floor with the Rabbits. Defeat and utter annihilation had been our portion— I'm a Rabbit, incidentally.   To such an extent, in fact, that, as Bob Seymour and I had driven off on Monday morning, Dick Templeton had pursued us with words which ate deep into our souls.

"Try and give us a game next year, you lads," he had said kindly.   "It makes things so much more interesting."

Now an insult of that sort can be wiped out only with blood, and Bob had apparently been pondering on it all through the winter.   And the result of his cogitations was communicated to us as the train left Paddington.

"It was weakness in bowling," he announced. "Jim's combination of half-volleys and long hops wouldn't have got a girls' school out."

"Some of your lobs bounced six times," I retorted.

"Dry up," he said; "your leader speaks.   Now, Peter has not recovered from his hunting accident, so I had to find a substitute.   I have; and he bowls."

"That's all right, Bob," said Huntly, the wicket-keeper, doubtfully, "but what sort of a cove is he?"

You'll understand, Bill, that in a show of that sort, however keenly you may take the cricket, it is absolutely essential to have the right type of fellow.   One outsider, and the whole thing is spoilt.   And since for years our two elevens had been almost the same, perhaps varying by one or two at most, Huntly's question was not irrelevant.

"All right," said Bob reassuringly.   "I met him lunching with a man at the club.   And he seemed a very decent fellow. By name of Carruthers. He's left-hand medium, and, in addition, I gather, is good for a few runs."

Well, it sounded all right, and I must say when we came to vet him he looked all right. It's always a bit difficult coming into a big house-party who all know one another well, but he seemed perfectly at his ease at once. He could tell a deuced good story, and the general concensus of opinion was that if his cricket was up to the rest of his form, Bob had struck oil.

So much for that end of the stick. Let's get down to Tommy Maunders.

Tommy was one of Dick Templeton's main stand-bys. In spite of his face he was a bat distinctly above the average—which was the sole reason why he was included in the Duds. Every year did Dick's cricketing soul war with his parental soul, as to whether Tommy should be asked, and up-to-date cricket had triumphed. To be a little more explicit, when Tommy was at the wicket the sun got up to shine on him, in Dick's estimation; when he was not at the wicket the sun set with extreme rapidity. And the reason of the change was the charming girl you alluded to—Dick's daughter.

As a cricketer there was much to be said for Tommy; as the man who wanted to marry Moyra—Dick's daughter—the amount to be said for him did not give Dick throat trouble. As to what was Moyra's opinion of Tommy at the time I really can't tell you; as she has since married him, presumably it was not entirely adverse. But whatever she thought, one thing was quite certain: she had no intention of marrying him until her father gave his consent. And that Dick showed no signs of doing. He was quite nice about it, but very firm.

"My dear Tommy," he was wont to say, "you're not a bad bat, and you're a good cover-point, but there you begin and end. You're a lazy young devil, with

the brains of an unintelligent louse.   If only that fool
aunt of yours hadn't left you fifteen hundred a year
you might have been some use, because you'd have had
to work.   True, some firm little knows what it has
escaped, but that would have been their worry.   This is
mine, and as a husband for Moyra you don't fit the bill
at all.''

Dick was a widower, and Moyra, being the only
child, was the apple of his eye.   I think that was the
main reason why she wouldn't go against his wishes.
It certainly wasn't for lack of asking on Tommy's part.
At morn, at midday, at sunset and midnight Tommy
used to get it off his chest.   Once, rumour had it, he
was discovered in the act at breakfast, but that naturally
could not be tolerated.   So he was given six of the
best with a stump in the pavilion, in case the rumour
was true.   However, enough of that.   I will pass on
to the actual party of two years ago.

There were thirty of us altogether—our eleven, six
of Dick's—the rest of his team were local products—
and the remainder were women.   And with the exception of Bob's new find, Carruthers, and a girl whose
name I completely forget, I knew everyone there.   I
won't weary you with their names, because, with the
exception of one woman, they don't come into the story.
And that woman was Lady Carrington.

I don't know if you've ever met the lady.   If not,
you haven't missed much.   Why Dick always asked
her was a bit of a mystery; personally, I always regarded
her as one of the world's worst horrors.   I think Dick
and her husband had had some business dealings or
something of that sort; I know he disliked her himself.

Lady Carrington was a woman of about forty—good-
looking in a vapid sort of way, and entirely devoted to

Society.   She lived, in fact, for nothing else.   The
money she spent on clothes would have rebuilt a slum;
if her jewellery had been realized, the cash obtained
would have rebuilt a village.   And of that the *pièce de
resistance* was her pearl necklace.   I am not much of a
judge of these things, but even I could appreciate that
necklace.   It consisted of three ropes, each one graduated perfectly.   It was insured, I gathered, for seventy
thousand pounds, and I could well believe it.

On the Wednesday night she wore it for dinner.
My own personal opinion was that it was vulgarly
ostentatious to do so.   That, however, is beside the
point.   She wore it for dinner, and it was duly admired
by those of us who had seen it before and by those of us
who hadn't.   And the first class outnumbered the
second largely.   Lady Carrington was a hardy annual,
and, except for Carruthers and the girl, we'd most of
us seen those pearls before.

I happened to know, because he had told me so the
year before, that our host would infinitely have preferred her not to bring the necklace at all.   The house
was an old-fashioned one—low and rambling.   Even
a second-rate burglar would not have had the slightest
difficulty in breaking into it.   And with a necklace as
well known as this one, the first-class men were likely
to be attracted.

"I do wish you'd allow me to put it in my safe," he
said, as we stood around preparatory to going to bed.
"Your house in London is one thing, Lady Carrington,
but anyone could break in here."

However, she was obdurate.

"My dear man," she said, "I sleep in them.   There
are some eighteen good men and true in this house,
and if you hear me scream in the middle of the night
I shall expect a combined rush to my bedroom."

We all laughed, and the matter was left at that.

Personally, I don't think any of us cared a rap if the woman lost her necklace or not, but I could quite understand Dick's point of view.   If anything did happen he'd sooner it did so somewhere else.   However, there was nothing to be done about it.   Lady Carrington had brought her necklace; she was going to sleep in it, and that was that.

Now, though we called ourselves Rabbits and Duds we took our cricket very seriously.   And it was the invariable rule that on Wednesday and Thursday we had an early bed.   Afterwards nothing mattered, but on those two nights we all hit the hay before midnight. And on that night I remember there was a bit of Bridge, and Carruthers did some conjuring tricks—and did them wonderfully well.

After which we all turned in.   And the last thing I noticed before turning out my light at a quarter to twelve was that it had come on to rain.   To me the only importance in the fact lay in its possible effect on the game next day.   I little thought it was going to result in a marriage.

I suppose I fell asleep about twelve.   It was at a quarter-past four that I was awakened by the most appalling commotion in the house.   I got up, slipped on a dressing-gown, and went into the passage.   Various men were running about in different conditions of semi-sleep, and from a room at the end of the wing came Lady Carrington's agitated voice.

"What's happened?" I asked in alarm.

"The combined rush that was spoken of," was the reply.   "The bally woman has lost her pearls."

Just then I saw Tommy.   He was coming from Lady Carrington's room, talking to Dick Templeton, who appeared terribly worried.

"Of course, you must get the police at once, sir,"

I heard Tommy say, and Dick went on downstairs to telephone.

"My hat, old man!" said Tommy to me with a grin. "I've seen some fairly awe-inspiring spectacles in my life, but Lady Carrington in the light of early dawn wins in a canter."

"Has she really lost her pearls?" I said.

"Beyond a shadow of doubt," he answered. "According to her, she went to bed wearing her necklace as usual. She says she fell asleep almost at once—a most unusual thing for her to do. But last night she felt very sleepy, and so she did not have her usual read. She woke quite suddenly about ten minutes ago, and felt that there was something strange. For a moment or two she couldn't make out what it was; then she realized. Her necklace had gone. True to her promise, she let out a bellow that must have scared the rooks, and here you perceive the eighteen good men and true engaged in the combined rush. I was the first to arrive, and I regret to state that the pearls had undoubtedly gone. My tactful suggestion that she should search in the bed was unnecessary—she had already done so."

"I've 'phoned the police," said Dick, joining us. "Confound that woman," he muttered angrily. "I told her to let me lock the thing up. By Jove! you fellows, I wouldn't have had this happen for the world."

"Well, anyway," said Huntly, coming out of his room, "there's been a pretty useful trail left. Come and look out of my window."

His room was next but one to Lady Carrington's, and we all trooped in. The rain had ceased; the morning was perfect. And when Dick had peered out it seemed to me he gave a sigh of relief.

Huntly was right. The trail was more than useful —it was obvious. Lying on the ground was a ladder, and in the flower-bed under Lady Carrington's bed-

room were two distinct marks of feet.   The thief had
placed the ladder in the earth of the bed, climbed up
it, taken the pearls, laid the ladder down on the ground,
and departed.

"Was that ladder there last night?" asked someone.

"As a matter of fact, it was lying on the other side of
the house," said Dick.   "Rogers—he's one of the
gardeners—has been cutting ivy.   Huntly, old boy,
you couldn't have shown me a more welcome sight than
that.   I am very sorry she's lost her pearls, but thank
Heaven we now know how the burglar got in!   I'll
just go and tell her."

I wandered back to my room with Tommy, and lit a
cigarette.

"Why this profound relief on Dick's part?" I asked.

"Well, old boy, our Lady Carrington was talking a
little out of her turn.   I don't blame her—it's a bit
disconcerting to lose a thing like that.   But she was
insisting on everyone in the house being searched and
so on."

"But surely she didn't suspect one of us?" I cried.

He shrugged his shoulders.

"As I say, she was talking a little out of her turn,"
he said.   "Look here," he suggested suddenly, "what
about doing a bit of sleuthing?   Let's go and cast an
eye on the flower-bed."

"My dear Tommy," I laughed, "what do you
expect to find—the burglar's visiting-card?"

"You never can tell, laddie," he burbled genially.
"We might see something."

So I followed him, principally because there was
nothing else to do.   Hideous cachinnations were still
coming from the Carrington woman's room.   It seemed
that she was now blaming Dick for not having burglar
alarms fitted on all his windows.   And this, mark you,
at four-thirty in the morning, of all ungodly hours.

However, we reached the flower-bed, and inspected clues with a professional eye. The whole thing was perfectly obvious, as I had anticipated. There were the marks of the two feet of the ladder in the wet earth perfectly clear and distinct, like a plaster cast; there was the damp mould sticking to the wood of the uprights. And if any further proof were needed as to how the thief had got in, at that moment Dick leant out of Lady Carrington's window above us.

"There are marks of mud on the sill here," he said. "Don't go putting your great flat feet all over the place, Tommy—there may be footprints about there somewhere."

I glanced at Tommy, and for a moment I thought he'd gone bughouse. He was staring first at the ladder, then at the marks in the flower-bed, and his eyes looked as if they were popping out of his head.

"What's stung you?" I asked kindly. "Is the burglar a left-handed man with a stammer and a hare-lip?"

"I may be several sorts of an ass, Jim," he answered, "but, dash it all, that's deuced funny!"

"What is deuced funny?" I grunted.

"Oh, things," he said airily. "Mud and stuff like that. Yes, by Jove! It's most peculiar—what?"

I took no further notice. Tommy was himself again —more so than usual, if possible. Once again his face expressed that completely vacant look which was habitual to it; his brief moment of brightness had gone.

"I'm going to have a jolly now," he cried. "Go round and see that all these lazy sons of Belial are up, and all that. Coming, old flick? No. Right ho!"

I watched him depart with profound relief. Tommy in the early morning was above my form. And shortly after, floods of blasphemy in various male voices proclaimed that he was carrying out his threat.

It was six o'clock before the police arrived, and by that time we had scratched up a bit of breakfast and were feeling better. All, that is, except Lady Carrington, whose face was reminiscent of a gargoyle on a French cathedral.

Another infamy of the miscreant had come to light. Lying on the floor by her bed had been found a hand-kerchief smelling strongly of chloroform.

"That's rum," burbled Tommy when he heard it. "What about the jolly old tum-tum, and all that?"

"May I ask what on earth you mean, Mr. Maunders?" said Lady Carrington acidly.

"Icky-boo—or anything like that?" he persisted.

"Will no one suppress this impossible youth?" she asked resignedly. "No, Mr. Maunders, thank you. The jolly old tum-tum is not icky-boo, or anything like that."

"Deuced funny," said Tommy darkly, and then, as far as I remember, someone flung him out of the window, and he was forgotten in the police examination.

It was more or less a formal affair—the whole thing was so blatantly obvious. And the main point on which the Inspector concentrated was how the burglar could have known which room was occupied by Lady Carrington. It pointed strongly, he declared, to the presence of a confederate inside the house. But at that Dick stuck in his toes. All his servants had been with him for years, he pointed out; it was incredible to suspect one of them. And as for his guests, the mere idea was farcical.

"The matter is perfectly simple," he stated. "Lady Carrington's necklace is probably known to every crook in England. It was known that she was coming here; and as the principal lady guest it would be easy to find out which room she would have."

"What about Rogers, Sir Richard? Funny thing to do, to leave that ladder lying about."

"And he's going to get his tail twisted good and strong for doing so. But there's no more to it than that, Inspector. Rogers has been with me since he was a boy. He is absolutely trustworthy; I'll vouch for that."

And so to breakfast, with nothing further discovered. The Inspector searched everywhere for finger-marks, with no result.

Of clues, save the obvious ones which were plain for all to see, there were none. And so, perforce, it had to be left at the fact that some man unknown had climbed into Lady Carrington's bedroom, removed her pearls while she slept—probably with the help of a whiff of chloroform—and got away with them.

The Inspector was vaguely hopeful; he felt sure it was one of the big men. And probably Scotland Yard would be able to trace their movements. But when he left Dick's study it struck me that his optimism was more official than real.

"I wouldn't have had it happen for the world, Jim," said Dick, as the door closed behind him. "I know the wretched things are insured, but that's not the same thing at all. And from all I can see of it, it's the clearest get-away I've ever heard of. What the devil do you want, Tommy?"

He swung round irritably as the door opened and Tommy came in.

"Look here, sir," said Tommy quietly, "what will you say if I get those pearls back for you?"

"You get 'em back for me?" spluttered Dick. "What under the sun are you drivelling about?"

But Tommy was very serious.

"Perhaps I'm drivelling, and perhaps I'm not," he said.   "But you haven't answered my question."

"If you get 'em back," laughed Dick.   "Well, if you do, Tommy, you may marry Moyra."

"Glad it was you who suggested it," grinned Tommy. "Because that was going to be my price.   And it comes more gracefully from you.   But there's only one thing I ask.   Not a word to a soul.   You both promise?"

We both did, and Tommy went out whistling.

"What's the young fool talking about?" said Dick to me with a puzzled frown.   "He can't possibly know anything about it."

"If he doesn't, we'll be no worse off than we are at present," I answered.   "And I wonder if——"

I broke off and lit a cigarette.   I had just remembered Tommy's strange look early that morning as we had stood side by side staring at the marks in the flower-bed.   Was it possible that he had noticed something we had all missed?

However, if he had, he gave no sign of it that day. He drivelled on in his usual fatuous way until threatened with death unless he desisted.   And eleven o'clock found us all in the pavilion ready to start.   Nothing was to be gained by putting off the match, though I think the Carrington woman thought we all ought to be scouring the country in search of the burglar.

The Duds won the toss, and Tommy went in first —I forget with whom.   And he proceeded to knock up a very useful fifty, before being run out.   Well, I don't know if anyone else spotted it, but it seemed to me at the time that he could have got into his crease if he'd tried.   But he gave a sort of half-stumble, and was out by two yards.   And as he passed me on his way back to the pavilion he gave me a very deliberate wink.

"So, my young friend," I reflected, "I was right. You purposely ran yourself out. What's the game?"

That it was something to do with the pearls I was sure—but what? True to my promise, I said nothing, of course; but when we all assembled for luncheon and there was no sign of him, my curiosity increased. He arrived about ten minutes later and sat down next to me.

"Thank God! I'm out," he remarked, "so that I can eat 'earty. By Jove! Carruthers, old fish, that valet of yours is a pretty grim-looking bird. He gave me quite a turn when I met him in the passage."

"What on earth are you talking about?" said Carruthers sharply. "I haven't got a valet."

A sudden silence settled on the table. Was this some new development of the burglary?

"Not got a valet?" cried Tommy blankly. "Then who is that fellow with a face like a third-rate prize-fighter who said he was your valet? Said he hadn't been able to come with you yesterday, but had followed on to-day. Wanted to know which your room was."

"Did you tell him?" snarled Carruthers.

"Of course I did," bleated Tommy. "Hang it all! I thought he was your bird, and I couldn't stand his face lying about the house."

"You fool!" Carruthers had gone white with rage. "What the devil do you mean by sending a strange man into my room?"

He had pushed back his chair and risen.

"Will you excuse me, Sir Richard, if I go to the house? I haven't got much of value, but I don't particularly want to lose my links. And what is more to the point, I should think it very likely that this so-called valet of Maunders' imagination is last night's burglar, engaged in making a complete haul of the house."

"What's that?" shouted Dick. "If you're right, Carruthers, we'd better have a general round-up. Come on, you fellows!"

"Hold hard, Sir Richard," said Carruthers. "Wary does it, if we want to catch the bird. If he sees us all making tracks for the house he'll be off like a scalded cat. Let me go in alone, while you split into four parties. Each party to keep under cover and watch one side of the house."

"Right you are, Carruthers," cried Dick. "You bolt the badger, and we'll do the rest."

And it was then I turned and looked at Tommy. His eyes were bright, and one could see he was excited.

"Tommy," I said, "is all this part of the game?"

"I dunno, Jim," he answered. "First time I've tried my hand at this sort of job. And for all I know, I may have made the most ungodly bloomer. Anyway," he added, "I'm such an ass that nobody will be surprised."

We were standing together behind a clump of bushes watching the front door. Carruthers had disappeared into the house, and old Dick, who was hopping about from one leg to the other, could hardly contain himself.

"You're a drivelling idiot, Tommy," he kept on saying. "Why the devil you didn't get hold of Perkins or one of the footmen passes man's understanding. For all that, even if you're only partially responsible for getting those pearls back, I'll forgive you."

It was ten minutes before Carruthers emerged again, and it was obvious that he had drawn blank. We were hidden, of course, and he stood for a moment or two on the drive looking round to find us.

"What luck?" said Dick, coming out into the open.

"None at all," answered Carruthers. "I saw no sign of anything being disturbed in my room, and then I took the liberty of having a quick look into all the others. But not a trace could I see of anyone. Can't you give us a bit fuller description of the fellow, Maunders? It might enable the police to place him."

Tommy, whose eyes were riveted on the front door, hardly seemed to hear.

"What's that?" he said vaguely. "Description of him? Oh! you know——a funny-looking bloke, with a face like a foot. Looked a bit of a mess and all that sort of thing. Ah-h!"

He caught his breath sharply, and we all swung round. Stalking majestically through the front door came the butler, Perkins. In his hands he carried a tray; on the tray reposed a pair of white objects which proved, on closer inspection, to be cricket boots.

"What under the sun is Perkins doing?" said Dick feebly.

The butler continued to advance until he halted in front of Tommy.

"Mr. Carruthers' cricket boots, sir," he said majestically.

There was a moment's dead silence, and then I glanced at Carruthers. And he was staring at Tommy with a look of such concentrated fury on his face that involuntarily I took a step forward.

"You little rat-faced swab," he said tensely, and the next instant the pair of them were at it hammer and tongs.

"Sit on the blighter's head," spluttered Tommy with his mouth full of grass. "He's the blinking burglar."

"The devil he is!" cried Huntly, and dotted Carruthers good and hearty on the point of the jaw.

"In the trees, sir," remarked the unperturbed Perkins, when silence reigned again. "With a further

assortment lifted—I believe that is the correct word—
a few minutes ago."

"Will someone elucidate?" cried Dick hopelessly.
"Am I to understand that Carruthers is the burglar?"

"Of course you are," said Tommy, plucking mud out
of his teeth. "And he's a rotten bad bowler, too."

Carruthers looked at him venomously, and Huntly
flourished a stump.

"No more thick-ear work," he said curtly. "Is this
a fact, Carruthers?"

"Well, there's not much good denying it," he muttered sulkily. "Though how that rat-faced excrescence
found it out I don't know."

"Let's take him to the luncheon tent, Jim," said Dick.
"Perkins, go and ring up the police. Now, Tommy,
get it off your chest. How did you spot this swab?"

"Mud," burbled Tommy. "Just mud. Mud on
the ground; mud all over the place. And the jolly old
law of gravity."

Carruthers, very tense and silent, was watching him
intently.

"Where are they exactly, Carruthers?" he went on
quietly.

"In the trees," said the other. "Chuck them over."

We watched him breathlessly as he took the trees
out of his boots. In the hinge was a small plug, which
he proceeded to unscrew with the point of a knife.
And as soon as he'd got it out he held up the tree and
out poured Lady Carrington's pearls. Then he did the
same with the other, and out shot a variety of things,
including a valuable tie-pin of Dick's.

"Of all the gall," spluttered Dick. "I'll have to
have the spoons counted."

"Of that I assure you there is no need," said Carruthers affably. And to do the blighter justice, from

then on he took things like a sportsman.   For the time
being he'd forgotten what was coming to him, and he
was genuinely curious to find out where he'd made his
mistake.

"Where all you blokes slipped up," began Tommy,
"was over the jolly old ladder.   You assumed that
because it was lying on the ground outside Lady Carrington's window, the thief had got in that way.   Not
so, my hearties.   The ladder was a blind."

"How did you spot that?" demanded Carruthers.

"Mud, laddie, mud.   That's where you made your
one and only bloomer.   If you put a ladder into wet
earth the mud will adhere to its legs up to the depth of
the holes it makes.   Possibly not as far.   But by no
conceivable hook or crook can it climb up some six
inches above the depth of the hole.   The holes you
made were about three inches deep.   There was mud
on the legs for a good nine inches from the bottom."

A faint smile twitched round Carruthers' lips.

"Quick," he said quietly.   "I congratulate you."

"So, you see, chaps," went on Tommy, "that altered
the whole outfit.   If the ladder was a blind, then the
thief must be inside the house.   There was another
thing, too—that handkerchief with chloroform.   Lady
Carrington didn't feel sick: therefore the assumption
was it hadn't been used.   It was there in case of
necessity, or possibly as a further blind.   But if it
hadn't been used, something else must have been employed to keep her quiet—a dope of sorts.   You
remember she said she fell asleep very quickly last night,
which again pointed to someone inside the house.
And my suspicions naturally fell on Carruthers, simply
because he was the only bloke in the house who was a
stranger.

"When I went and jollied you all up this morning I
had a look at your basins.   The one in Carruthers'

room was full of brownish water where he'd washed the mud off his hands.   So that was that as far as little Willie was concerned.   I knew Carruthers had taken the pearls—but where were they?   That was the point. And it struck me that the easiest way of finding out was to make him show us.   If I was wrong, there was no damage done; if I was right, we nabbed the goods. So I invented the mythical valet, and installed our one and only Perkins in a cupboard where he could watch developments, trusting that the first thing Carruthers would do would be to see if the pearls were safe."

Jim Featherstone knocked out his pipe.
"Which I think proves my contention that Tommy is not such a fool as he looks.
"We straightened out one or two points later; but he was absolutely right all through.   Carruthers *had* doped Lady Carrington.   He'd slipped it into a whisky and soda she had drunk before going to bed.   He had specially wangled his introduction to Bob, knowing that Lady Carrington was always invited for the match. And he'd have got clean away with the pearls, and the other little trifles he'd lifted when he made a tour of the rooms, but for that little matter of mud.   As it was, he got seven years, and I had to stump up a wedding present."

XXIX   THAT BULLET HOLE HAS A HISTORY

"A WRITING gentleman are you, sir?" said the landlord, as he put a full tankard on the table in front of me.   "Well, well—it takes all sorts to make a world."
I did not dispute such a profound truth, but con-

centrated on the contents of the tankard. A walking tour in the hilly part of Devonshire is thirsty work, and the beer tasted as good as it looked.

"Not that I hold much with it," he went on after a while. "I reckon that it's better to be up and doing than sitting down and spoiling good paper."

Against such an outrageous assault as that I felt I had to defend myself, and I pointed out to him that one had to put in a bit of up and doing oneself before beginning to spoil the paper.

"Not that I should think there's much doing beyond sleep in this village," I added sarcastically.

"That's just where you're wrong," he remarked triumphantly. "Why, in that very chair you're sitting in a man was shot through the heart. Plugged as clean as a whistle, and rolled off the chair up against that table your beer is standing on, stone-dead. And that"—he paused for a moment, only to continue even more triumphantly—"is the man that did it."

He indicated a grey-haired man who was passing —a fine-looking old man who walked with a pronounced limp and leant heavily on a stick.

"Good evening, Mr. Philimore," he called.

"Evening, Sam," answered the other, pausing and coming over towards the door of the inn outside which we were sitting.

He stopped for a few moments discussing local affairs, and I studied him covertly. A man of seventy-five I guessed, with the clear eye of one who has lived in the open. His great frame showed strength beyond the average, and even now it struck me that many a younger man would have found him more than a match physically.

He finished his discussion, and then, with a courteous bow that included me, continued his walk.

"Sleep, indeed!" snorted the worthy Sam. "Thirty

years ago, sir, come next month, this village was more exciting than London."

"Look here, Sam," I said, "it strikes me that you'd better put your nose inside a pint of your excellent ale and tell me all about it."

He shouted an order through the door, and lit his pipe.

"You'll understand, sir," he began, when the pot-boy had brought the beer and he had sampled it, "that when the thing happened I was just flabbergasted. Couldn't make head nor tail of it, because I didn't know what it was all about. It was only afterwards, when I began making inquiries and talking to this person and that, that the whole thing was clear from the beginning. And that's the way I'm going to tell you the story."

"And quite the right way, too," I assured him.

"It starts nigh on fifty-five years ago, when I was a nipper of ten, and John Philimore—him as you've just seen—a man of twenty-one. You can talk of good-looking men—and I've seen a tidy few in my life—but you can take it from me he came first. The girls were fair crazy about him, and well they might be. Tall, upstanding, strong as a giant—they don't breed 'em nowadays. There wasn't a man on the countryside could touch him at any sport, or at swimming. Why, I can remember seeing him swim out with a life-line to a barque in distress in the October gales of 1868. Bit before your time, I reckon—but there's been no gales in these parts like 'em since.

"He lived up at Oastbury Farm, which had been his grandfather's and his great-grandfather's before him. Aye—and longer than that. Traced direct back from father to son for nigh on four hundred years was Oastbury with the Philimores. And John—he lived at home with his father, ready to take on when his time came.

"I've told you that all the girls were fair crazy about him, but John had eyes for only one—Mary Trevenna. And a proper match they were, too, in every way. Old Trevenna had Aldstock Farm—the place next to Oastbury—and though he wasn't as wealthy as the Philimores, he was quite comfortably off. And Mary was his only daughter, just as John was the only son, though he had a sister. Oh! it was a proper match! Just as John had eyes only for Mary, so she never looked at another man. I remember catching 'em one day when they thought no one was about, kissing and cuddling fine. And then John—he caught me, and I couldn't sit down for a week.

"Well—I must get on with it. When Mary was twenty, they were to get married. That was the arrangement, and that is what happened. John was twenty-two, and they were going to live in a small farm near Oastbury which his father had given them.

"It was a great wedding. The squire came—that's his present lordship's father—and everyone from the countryside. And after it was over they went off to Torquay for the honeymoon. Then they came back to the house where they were going to live, and things settled down normal again.

"Of course, you must remember, sir, that I was only a nipper at the time, helping my father in this very house. Them was the days before these new-fangled schemes of education, when folks held with a boy working and not filling his head with rubbish. But little pitchers have long ears as they say, and I very soon finds out from what folks said that there was a baby on the way.

"John Philimore came in less and less—not that he was ever a heavy drinker, but after a while he hardly ever came in at all; and when he did it was only for a moment or two, and then he'd hurry off home. Not that things weren't going well, but a lad is apt to be a bit dazed over his first.

"A boy it would be—of course: for generations now the eldest child born to the Philimores had been a boy. And a rare fine specimen, too—with such parents. John's mother looked out the lace christening robe and all the old fal-lals the women like fiddling round with at such times. And at last Mary's time came, and it was a girl—as fine a child, so I heard tell, as anyone would have wished for. But it was a girl.

"Well, sir—I don't profess to account for it; Lord knows there was plenty more time for them to have half a dozen boys, but it seemed to prey on Mary's mind that she should be the first for so many generations to have a girl as her first-born.

"I remember old Doctor Taggart coming into the inn here one night, and leaning across the bar for his brandy and water. He and my father were alone, and they paid no attention to me.

" 'Sam,' he said—my father was Sam, too—'Sam, that girl don't want to get well. There's nothing the matter with her; at least nothing serious. She just don't want to get well. I tell you I could shake her. Just mazed, she is, because it's a girl, and John near off his head.'

"And sure enough old Taggart was right. Ten days after the child was born, Mary Philimore died. She died in the afternoon at three o'clock, and with her death something must have snapped in John Philimore's brain.

"Never to my dying day shall I forget that evening. There was a bunch of people inside there, and naturally everyone was discussing it, when suddenly the door was flung open and John stood there swaying like a drunken man. He'd got no collar on; his eyes were blazing—and his great fists were clenching and unclenching at his sides. He stood there staring round the room, which had fallen silent at his entrance, and then he let out a great bellow of laughter.

" 'A murderer!' he roared. 'That's what I am— a murderer. Confound you all! Give me some brandy.'

" 'Shame on you, John,' said one of the men. 'With Mary not yet cold.'

"And John hit him on the point of the jaw, and as near as makes no matter broke his neck.

" 'Brandy,' he shouted, 'or, by God! I'll take it!'

"And take it he did, for there was no stopping him. He tipped half the bottle down his throat, and once again he let out a roar of laughter, as he stood there with his back to the bar. He looked at the men bending over the chap he'd hit, and laughed and laughed and laughed.

" 'What's it matter if he's dead?' he cried. 'One or two—what's it matter? I've murdered Mary: what's Peter Widgeley to her? I tell you I've murdered her —my little Mary. What did it matter if it was a boy or girl? But she thought it did—and she's dead. And if they hadn't hidden the brat it would be dead, too.'

"And then suddenly he grew strangely silent, and stared from one man to another. No one spoke: I guess they were all a bit scared. For maybe a minute you could have heard a pin drop in that room, and then John Philimore spoke again. He didn't shout this time: he spoke quite quiet. And in between his sentences he took great gulps of raw brandy.

"It's burnt on my brain, sir, what he said—and there it will remain. For on that night John Phili-more cursed his Maker with blasphemy too hideous to think of. He cursed his Maker: he cursed his child: he cursed his father and, above all, he cursed himself. And when he'd finished he laid the empty bottle on a table, strode across the room, looking neither to the right hand nor to the left, opened the door and went out into the night. And from that moment no man in this village saw him again for twenty years."

Mine host stared thoughtfully across the little harbour at two fishing-boats beating in.

"A bad sailor, Bill Dennett. Always keeps too long on that tack. However, sir, as I was saying, John Philimore disappeared. From time to time there came news of him in different corners of the earth—and it wasn't good news. With a wild set he'd got in, and he was the wildest of the lot. From South Africa, from Australia, from over in America we heard of him at intervals—but only indirectly. He never wrote to his father, or to his sister—and it fair broke his mother's heart. For John was just the apple of her eye. She kept on hoping against hope that he'd walk in some day, and when the weeks passed, and the months and the years, she just faded out herself—though she was still a young woman.

"That was seven years after John went, and they buried her along with the rest of the Philimores. And then five years later the old man got thrown from his horse out hunting—and he died, too—cursing his son on his death-bed for being the cause of his mother's death, even as John had cursed his father for being in part the cause of Mary's. A hard lot the Philimores —and always have been.

"And so for the first time Oastbury passed into the hands of a woman—John's sister, Ruth; though, of course, it was John's whenever he chose to return. If he'd been able to, the old man would have cut him out, and left it away from him—but he couldn't. But until John did return it was Ruth's, who went on living there with the innocent cause of all the trouble, who had been called Mary after her mother. She was twelve years old when her grandfather died, and even then gave promise of being as lovely as her mother. Of her father she knew nothing; she'd been told simply that he was abroad and no one could tell when he would return.

"On the death of the old man Ruth had written a letter to the last address at which her brother had been heard of, and she had caused advertisements to be put in the papers in Australia and South Africa. But after some months the letter came back to her, and there was no reply to the advertisements. In fact, there were a good many of us who began to think John Philimore was dead, and seeing how he had turned out, no bad riddance either.

"Well, the years went on, and Mary grew from a girl into a woman. And the promise as she'd given as a little 'un became a certainty. She was lovelier even than her mother had been, for there was a touch of the Philimore in her—in the way she stood, and in the way she looked at you. And in addition to her looks Mary stood to be a pretty considerable heiress. Old Trevenna—her grandfather—was ailing, and he had no kith nor kin but her. And if, as most of us thought, John Philimore was dead, then Oastbury became hers on her twenty-first birthday. For Ruth was only just in there as a guardian; Oastbury was John's till they proved him dead and then it passed to his child.

"So you'll see, sir, that Mary was due for Oastbury and Aldstock—and that in the days when farming was farming. It made her the biggest heiress round these parts, and the young fellows weren't exactly blind to the fact. Not that she weren't worth having without anything at all except her sweet self; but with them two farms chucked in like, the boys were fairly sitting up.

"But Mary wasn't going to be in any hurry. No one could say which way her fancy lay—not even her aunt; though it did seem sometimes as if it was towards young George Turnbury, whose father was a big miller in Barnstaple. Not that they were tokened, but when old Gurnet drew him in the sweepstake he stood drinks all round.

"A fine boy—young George—big and upstanding, who would come into a pretty penny of his own in time. And absolutely silly over Mary, as well he might be. And we was all beginning to think as things would be settled soon when the trouble began.

"I was standing at this very door—I'd been land-lord then for nigh on two years—when I saw a stranger coming up the street. A great big fellow, he was, with a curious sort of roll in his walk, such as you often see in men who had been a lot at sea. As soon as he seed the sign over the door he made for it like a cat for a plate of fish. And I give you my word, sir, I got a shock when I saw his face. From his left temple, right down his cheek as far as his chin, ran a vivid red scar. It was an old one and quite healed, but it must have been the most fearful wound that caused it. For the rest, his skin was dark brown, his nose was hooked and his eyes a vivid blue.

" 'Hot work,' he said as he came up. 'I guess I'll have a gargle.'

" 'Very good, sir,' I said. 'And what shall it be?'

" 'Whisky,' he answered. 'And bring the bottle.'

"And I give you my word again, sir, I got another shock. He tipped out a tumbler and drank it neat, same as I'd take a glass of cider.

" 'Help yourself,' he said, and when he saw me take a little and fill up with water, he threw back his head and laughed.

" 'Why the devil don't you drink milk?' he cried.

" 'If I was to drink what you've just drunk with every customer,' I said, short-like, 'I'd not be able to carry on my business.'

" 'Maybe you're right,' he answered, staring at me. 'No offence, anyway. But not having to carry on your business, I guess I'll have another.'

"He filled up his glass with neat whisky again, and then lay back in his chair, still staring at me with those blue eyes of his.

" 'Say, I guess you'll know,' he said after a moment. 'Is there a shack called Oastbury in this district?'

"Well, at that I pricked up my ears, for I'd placed him already as a man from foreign parts.

" 'There certainly is,' I said. 'If you go round the corner you can see Oastbury Farm upon the hill there.'

" 'I guess it will stop there,' says he, without moving. 'Good farm, is it?'

" 'It is accounted the best in these parts and one of the best in the whole West Country,' said I, and he nodded his head as if pleased with the news.

" 'May I ask, sir,' I went on, 'if you have by any chance news of John Philimore? I can see you come from foreign parts, and since you've asked about Oastbury, I thought you might know something of him.'

" 'Then your thoughts are correct,' he answered.

" 'For twenty years we've had no word of him direct,' I said, 'and there are those who say he's dead.'

" 'There are, are there?' he said, and finished his whisky. 'Well, they've backed a winner. John Philimore is dead right enough: he's been dead a year.'

" 'Good heavens!' I cried—for now that the news was confirmed it seemed a terrible thing. 'And what did he die of, sir?'

" 'An ounce of lead in a tender spot,' he answered shortly. 'Same as a good many other poor fools have died of. Say, now, there's a daughter of his alive, ain't there?'

" 'There is,' I said. 'Living at Oastbury Farm now. And if John Philimore is dead, the farm is hers. Leastways, it will be in a year, when she's twenty-one.'

" 'And what would happen, mister,' he said, 'if John had made a will leaving all he possessed to me?'

" 'It wouldn't be worth the paper it's written on,' I answered shortly. 'It's all tied up—see? John Phili-more could no more leave Oastbury away from his daughter than he could give away Buckingham Palace.'

" 'Are you sure o' that?' he said with a sort of snarl.

" 'Of course I'm sure of it,' I answered. 'Didn't John's father go into the whole question after John ran off to Australia? That's what he wanted to do —leave Oastbury to his daughter—all tied up and secure. Went to Exeter, he did, to a big lawyer there, to see about it. But it couldn't be done. From eldest child to eldest child it's got to go—be it male or female. And so whatever wickedness John Philimore has done, he can't do his daughter out of Oastbury. It's hers —and remains hers.'

"I tell you, sir, I was beginning to dislike this man, and I spoke a bit short.

" 'And supposing,' said he, very quiet-like, 'this daughter of his should die before she's twenty-one?'

" 'Then,' I said, 'it would go to her aunt—John's sister. Will you be wanting any more whisky?'

" 'Yes—leave the bottle, and if I shout you'll know I want another.'

"With that I left him and went indoors. And half an hour later he was still sitting at the table staring across the harbour. Then he gives a shout, and out I goes.

"'Can you give me a room here?' he says. 'I'll pay what you like, and give no trouble.'

"Well, business is business; and, though I didn't fancy him as a guest, I said I'd fix him up.

"'Good!' he cried. 'Then send out another bottle of whisky as a start. Oh! and by the way, is this wench married?'

"'She is not,' I answered. 'But I expect she soon will be.'

"'So do I,' he said, and laughed in a funny sort of way.

"'She's all but tokened to young George Turnbury from Barnstaple,' I told him, but that only made him laugh the more.

"With that I went in and sent him out the second bottle of whisky. And then, what with one thing and another, and the chaps coming in for their evening drink, and telling them the news of John Philimore's death, I forgot all about him for a time.

"I reckons it must have been about nine o'clock when George Turnbury came in. He'd been up at Oastbury, I knew, because he had had his lunch in this house.

"'Say, fellows,' he said, 'have any of you seen a queer-looking customer about the place? A great hook-nosed fellow with a huge red scar down his face?'

"'It's the stranger,' I cried. 'The one who told me John Philimore was dead.'

"'Dead?' cried George, staring at me. 'John Philimore dead?' For, of course, he hadn't heard the news.

"'That's so,' I said. 'A year ago.'

"'Good Lord!' he muttered, and I could see he was

a bit moved. After all, though he'd never known John, he'd been up at his daughter's all the afternoon.

" 'Well, anyway,' he went on, 'I saw this man nosing round Oastbury, and I tell you I didn't like the look of him. So I passed the word to some of the hands, and Heaven help him if he tries any tricks!'

" 'In my life I've never relied overmuch on Heaven,' said a voice from the door, and there was the stranger, with his eyes fixed on George. As you can imagine, sir, it was a bit of an awkward moment, because we didn't know how much he'd heard.

" 'I've found that I'm quite capable of looking after myself, young man,' he continued, crossing the room and standing close to George. 'And now may I ask why you don't like the look of me?'

"George Turnbury got a bit red in the face.

" 'I'm sorry you should have heard that,' he said. 'I didn't know you were in the room.'

" 'I'm still waiting for an answer to my question, young man,' said the other quietly, though there was a nasty note in his voice.

"Young George, he drew himself up, for he had the devil of a temper of his own, and he didn't like the stranger's tone.

" 'You'll get the answer in a looking-glass,' he said, and turned his back on him. 'I guess it was a powerful cat you tried petting,' he flung over his shoulder.

"The stranger put out both his hands quite gently and caught hold of George from behind, just above each elbow. Now George was a powerful lad, used to handling sacks of corn, and I shall never forget the look of blank amazement that spread over his face. It must have been a quarter of a minute they stood there without movement, and the reason was plain to us all. George couldn't move; he was as powerless as a child in that man's grasp. We could see him struggling so that the sweat broke out on his forehead, and there was hardly a tremor in that stranger's hands. And then the stranger laughed.

" 'It wasn't a cat, little boy,' he said. 'It was the slash of a cutlass. And the man who did it died as he did it. It was a much stronger man than you, little boy. But as far as you're concerned, don't be rude any more, or I might have to whip you.'

"And with that he let George go and swung round on me.

" 'Send me up a bottle of whisky,' he cried. 'I'm going to my room.'

"For a while after he left no one spoke. George —who had a proper pride in himself—was wellnigh crying with shame and mortification at having been made to look such a fool before us all. And, of course, a thing like that was bound to get around, if only as a measure indicating the stranger's strength. But as the days went on it was forgotten in the much more important affairs that were happening up at Oastbury. It had us all beat; we couldn't make head nor tail of 'em.

"For this stranger pretty well lived up there, and what Mary Philimore or her aunt could see in him was beyond us. He still kept on his room here; he still got through his two bottles of whisky a day, and sometimes three. But for the rest of the time he was at Oastbury.

"George was pretty near off his head about it all; seemed to think he'd got some hold over Mary—this man with the scar. And sure enough two or three times when I seed her, she seemed to have a terrible hunted look in her sweet eyes.

"Then a month after he'd arrived we heard the news. At first no one would believe it; but it was true right enough. Mary had tokened herself to this man with the scar, whose name we now knew was Henry Gaunt.

"I tell you, sir, it had us all knocked endwise. For Mary, that sweet girl, to marry this whisky-drinking bully, who was old enough to be her father, seemed a horrible sin. And once it was settled, what little mark of decency he had kept on to start with disappeared. He took a delight in picking quarrels and insulting people. He nearly killed poor old Dick, the policeman, one night—and only just escaped prison by the skin of his teeth.

"That sobered him up a bit, and he was more careful in future. But even then he was a devil. Chaps as had come to this house for years, and their fathers before them, stayed away, because they were afeared of Gaunt. And this was the man Mary was going to marry.

"Time went on and the wedding was due in a fortnight. And then one morning I was standing in the door there thinking things over, when again I seed a stranger coming up the street. The house was empty; Gaunt was up at Oastbury—but this stranger reminded me in a way of him. The same build—the same roll in his walk, and I thought to myself, I thought, 'Good Lord! This ain't another such as Gaunt.'

"And then as he got nearer I began to rub my eyes. I must be wrong, of course, but it surely was a staggering likeness to John Philimore.

" 'Hullo, Sam!' he sung out. 'Forgotten me, I suppose. I know it's you; you're so like your father.'

" 'Good God!' I said, all mazed-like; 'it's John Philimore!'

" 'The very same,' he answered. 'And why not?'

" 'But we was told you were dead, sir,' I cries.

" 'And who told you that?' he says, smiling.

" 'Why, Henry Gaunt,' I answers. 'Him as is staying here now.'

"The smile had left his face, and he stared at me speechless.

" 'Do you mean a man with a great red scar down his face?' he said in a terrible voice.

" 'That's the one,' I told him. 'And not only is he staying here, but he's tokened to your daughter.'

" 'What!' he roared, and I thought he was going to strike me. Then he pulled himself together. 'Come inside and tell me all about it. But——wait a moment. Where is he now?'

" 'Up at Oastbury,' I said, and I've never seen such a look of devilish rage on a man's face before or since.

"Well, I took him inside, and I told him all I knew. And when I'd finished he got up.

" 'Sam,' he said, 'I rely on you. Not a word to a soul that I'm back. Above all, not a word to that devil incarnate, Henry Gaunt.'

" 'You have my word, sir,' I said. 'And if you can get rid of him, I, for one, will be profoundly thankful.'

" 'I'll get rid of him all right,' he answered quietly. 'Usually back here at six, you say?'

" 'That's when he begins his second bottle,' I told him, and with that he left.

"Naturally, I was fair bursting with the news, but I kept my word and didn't breathe a hint to a soul. And as the afternoon wore on I got in such a condition of excitement at what was going to happen, that I gave old Downley, what always drank ginger ale, a double whisky by mistake. At a quarter to six Gaunt came in and, sitting down in the chair you're in, he ordered his usual bottle. In a foul temper he was over something or other and he sat there glowering

across the harbour.   There were two or three others
drinking over at that table, and by this time my knees
were shaking under me as six o'clock drew nearer.

"Five minutes to—and young George Turnbury
passed down the road on the way to the station.

" 'Hi, you—you young swab,' sung out Gaunt.
'Come here!'

"George, he took no notice and just walked on,
when, would you believe it, sir? that devil pulled out
a revolver and fired.   George told us afterwards that
he felt the wind of the bullet past his ear—it was so
close.

" 'Next time I'll hit you,' said Gaunt, 'unless you
stop!'

"George stopped.

" 'Now, you young cockerel, is it you who has been
closeted all the afternoon with the girl I'm going to
marry?'

" 'It was not,' said a stern voice behind him.   'It
was I.'

"And there was John Philimore standing just behind
Gaunt with the muzzle of his revolver pressed into
the devil's neck.

" 'And if you move, Gaunt; if you try any of your
foul tricks, I'll blow the top of your head off, as sure
as there's a God above.'

"Gaunt's face was a study.   He'd gone quite white,
and the scar looked like a streak of bright red paint,
while in his eyes there was the look of an animal at
bay, a sort of snarling fear.

" 'Is it you, John Philimore?' he said, moistening
his lips, for with that gun in his neck he dursn't look
round to see.

" 'Who else would it be, Gaunt?' said John.   'You
see, you didn't kill me after all, though it was touch
and go, Gaunt—touch and go.   If two prospectors

hadn't come along soon after you cleared out with what was left of the water, having shot me from behind, you would have killed me, Gaunt.'

"Young George, he started forward in a rage.

" 'You foul swine!' he shouted, but Gaunt heeded him not. There was only one thing he could think of at the moment, and that was that his sin had found him out. And ceaselessly he moistened his lips with his tongue.

" 'And then, Gaunt,' went on John Philimore in a terrible voice, 'having killed me as you thought, you came to my home. You knew all about it, for I'd told you—and you thought it would be a fine way of spending the rest of your foul life. And when you found it was entailed, and you couldn't get it by forgery—then, Gaunt, your infamous brain conceived a plan which would have done the devil himself credit. You went to my daughter, and told her that I wasn't really dead; that you'd lied when you said so—lied on purpose. You said that I was in prison for life for murder and bushranging: that I'd been guilty of unnameable crimes; that you had proof of it. And then, Gaunt, you told her the price of your silence. You knew our pride: you knew she'd do anything rather than that our name should be disgraced. And so you blackmailed her into the unthinkable sacrifice of marrying you. Can you tell me, Gaunt, of any single reason why I shouldn't kill you where you sit?'

"Gaunt laughed harshly, though his eyes roved wildly from side to side as if seeking some way of escape.

" 'One very good one,' he snarled. 'They'll hang you if you do.'

" 'True,' answered John Philimore. 'Then I'll flog you, Gaunt—flog you here and now till the blood drips off you. And to save bother I shall lash you up.

Sam,' he called out to me, 'you'll find a rhinoceros whip in my grip. Get it.'

"And then, sir, it happened—so quickly that one could scarce see. Of a sudden two shots rang out, and we saw John Philimore sink to the ground. And even as he fell on one side of the chair, Gaunt rolled off and fell on the other.

"We rushed up to them, young George Turnbury first of us all. And John, he looked up at him with a smile.

" 'Go up, young George,' he said, 'and tell Mary that the wedding can take place, but the bridegroom will be different.'

" 'Are you hurt, sir?' cried George.

" 'Not so badly as Henry Gaunt,' he answered.

"We looked at the man with the scar on his face, and he was dead. Shot through the heart—plugged clean as a whistle.

"Well, sir, that's the story. John Philimore was shot through the groin: maybe you noticed he still limps. And young George, he married Mary. But that shows you we don't always sleep in this village."

XXX   FER DE LANCE

CEASELESSLY the machine went on. It worked somewhat on the principle of a moving staircase. An endless canvas band, lying loosely over cross-pieces placed at intervals, formed a series of ever-advancing cradles, which vanished, each with its load, into the hold. Then the band, flattening out underneath for its return journey, came back for more.

Everything worked with the smoothness born of long practice. Overhead the garish spluttering arc-lights hissed, throwing crude shadows on train and boat alike. Occasionally, with the harsh clanging of a bell, the engine would move forward a few yards, in order to bring the opening of another truck opposite the loading-machine. A moment's respite while the train moved, and then down to it again. No pause, no respite: the s.s. *Barare* was loading bananas, and it was an all-night job. Stem after stem of the fruit —still green—was carried out of the truck by natives and placed each in its separate moving cradle, only to be seized by other natives inside the ship and stowed away in the hold.

Seated on a raised stand was an unshaven, bleary-eyed man. In front of him was a pad on which he checked the number of stems loaded; just as he had checked them for years—or was it centuries? Bananas: millions of stems of bananas had he recorded on paper —until the word banana drove him frantic. He loathed bananas with a loathing that passed description. On the occasions when he had *delirium tremens*—and they were not infrequent—no imaginary animals haunted him. He was denied a rat of any hue. Only bananas: bananas of all shapes and sizes and colours thronged in on his bemused brain, till the whole world seemed full of them.

He was a strange personality—this unkempt checker, and how he had held his job for nearly three years was stranger still. Perhaps the answer could only have been given by the quiet, clean-cut man who was his boss—a strange personality himself. For rumour had it that on one occasion, when a ship was loading, the boss had gone on board as usual. And as he reached the top of the companion he ran straight into a certain Austrian nobleman, who gave a startled gasp of amazement before drawing himself up and bowing punctiliously. Rumour had it also that that same nobleman, having paced the deck with him for a while, was heard to call him "Sir."

An ill-assorted pair, one would have thought—a drunken, down-and-out Englishman and a man whom an Austrian of ancient family called "Sir." And perhaps the reason lay in the fact that the epithet "down-and-out" is only relative. Once the crash has come, a bond of sympathy exists between those who crash, even though their falls are of different height.

The Englishman called himself Robinson when he was sober enough to remember. At other times he was apt to give a different name. The boss called himself Barlock, which, as a name, had certain advantages. It left one in doubt as to the nationality of its owner. And the two men had arrived at Port Limon about the same time in very different capacities. Barlock was taking over a responsible post in the Union Fruit Company, that vast American concern whose tentacles stretch into every corner of the West Indies and Central America. Robinson was merely drunk. He arrived as a deckhand in an old tramp, and, being temporarily mislaid when she sailed again, was left behind without lamentation or regret. And acquaintance between the two men started almost at once in a somewhat peculiar way.

Barlock was wandering round the big railway shed, which was to be the scene of his labours for the next few years, and as he stepped behind some barrels he walked on the other man.

"Don't apologize," remarked Robinson, getting unsteadily to his feet. "I'm used to it. Would you tell me if a bilge-laden old tub, whose name escapes me for the moment, has sailed?"

"If you mean the *Corsica*," said the other, "she sailed about six hours ago."

"It would appear, then, that I have been left behind. Not that it matters in the slightest degree. I have long given up any attempt at regularity in my habits. One small point, however, might be of interest. Where am I?"

Barlock smiled faintly: there was a certain whimsical note in the other's voice that amused him.

"This is Port Limon," he answered. "And in the event of your geography having been as much neglected as mine was, Port Limon is in Costa Rica."

"Costa Rica," said the other thoughtfully. "Its exact position on the globe is a little beyond me at the moment, but, provided it possesses a bar, it fulfils all my requirements."

He shambled off, leaving the other staring after him. A gentleman obviously: equally obviously a drunkard. And for a moment or two Barlock wondered how the mixture would be digested by the narrow strip of civilization that lies at the bottom of the densely wooded hills which make up the greater part of the republic. Then with a shrug of his shoulders he went about his lawful occasions.

For a week he saw Robinson no more. Then one night he found him standing at his elbow. A banana train had just creaked into the station, its bell clanging furiously. Natives were lethargically replacing greasy packs of cards in their pockets; Port Limon's justification for existence came to a groaning standstill. No bananas: no Port Limon.

"It is incredible," remarked Robinson, "that human stomachs can consume such inordinate quantities of vegetable matter. I am not a banana maniac myself, unless they are soaked in rum. And even then—why spoil the rum? But when one sees that train, and realizes that there are other trains in other places all carrying bananas, one takes off one's hat in silent

homage to the world's eaters.   By the way, I suppose
you haven't the price of a drink on you?"

A sudden idea struck Barlock.

"I have not," he said shortly.   "But I'll give you
a job of work.   Go and help load them.   You'll get
the same rate of pay as the natives."

For a moment the other hesitated: it was black
man's work.   Then, finding Barlock's steady eye fixed
on him, he gave a short laugh and peeled off his
coat.   And thus began his personal acquaintance with
bananas.   Began also a strange relationship between
the two men.

Friendship it could hardly be called.   Their positions were too widely separated.   Barlock was the
boss; Robinson a paid hand doing coolie work.   But
through the long nights, whilst the loading went
monotonously on, sometimes the difference between
them disappeared.   They became just two white men
amongst a crowd of blacks.   Moreover, they became
two white men of the same interests and station.
Away from the railway shed it was different.   Barlock, by reason of his job, belonged to the club, and
could enjoy what social life the place afforded; Robinson was down and out, living native fashion.   But
under the hissing arc-lights the two men met on a
common ground—bananas.

And then there occurred an incident which insen-
sibly brought them nearer to one another.   If a competition open to the world for the number of snakes
to the square yard was instituted, Costa Rica would
be very near the top of the list.   Moreover, her repre-
sentatives would not be of the harmless variety.   And
it so happens that on occasions members of the frater-
nity go to ground in the bunches of fruit as they lie
stacked beside the railway line, waiting to be picked

up by the train. The snake hides itself along the stem, and may or may not be discovered at the up-country siding. If it is, it is promptly dispatched; if it is not, it makes the journey to Port Limon. And so at that terminus the danger is an ever-present one, especially as the snake, after having jolted down the line in a stuffy truck, is not in the best of tempers on its arrival.

It all happened very quickly—some six months after Robinson's introduction to his new trade. He had just taken a big stem of fruit from the man standing in the opening of the truck, when a native beside him gave a shout. He had a momentary glimpse of a wicked yellow head curving out of the fruit in his arms: then there came the thud of a stick, and he dropped the bunch.

He looked up a little stupidly to find Barlock standing beside him, the stick still grasped in his hand. And for a few moments the two men stared at one another in silence, whilst a native completed the good work on the platform.

"*Fer de Lance*," said Barlock curtly. "Lucky I had a stick."

"Thanks," muttered Robinson, staring at the dead body of perhaps the most deadly brute in existence. "Thanks. Though I wonder if it was worth while."

"Don't talk rot," said Barlock, even more curtly, and moved away.

The incident was over; a Fer de Lance was dead. Robinson was alive. And there were still bananas to load. But when one man has saved another man's life, it is bound to make some difference in their relationship. And though nothing changed outwardly, though they still remained boss and paid hand, under the surface there was an alteration.

"Thanks once more," said Robinson, as the empty

train pulled out the next morning. He had followed Barlock to his room in the station, and was standing in the open door. "You were deuced quick with that stick."

"Not much good moving by numbers when there is a bone-tail about," said Barlock with a laugh.

"So you're of the breed, are you?" Robinson stared at the other man. "I always thought you were by the set of your shoulders. By numbers. God! how it brings things back. Do you know our immortal songster? I've got a new last line to one of his things:

'Gentlemen rankers out on the spree,
Damned from here to eternity.
God have mercy on such as we,
Ba—na—na.'

I load the damned things to the rhythm."

Barlock looked at him thoughtfully.

"What regiment?" he asked, after a moment.

"Thirteenth Lancers," said the other. "And you?"

"Austrian Cavalry of the Guard," answered Barlock.

"Of course, I knew you weren't English," said Robinson, "though you speak it perfectly. So we went through that performance on different sides. Funny life, isn't it? Look here, I don't want to be impertinent or unduly curious. The reason for me is obvious: I can't keep away from the blasted stuff. But you—you don't drink."

Barlock smiled grimly.

"Have you ever thought, my friend, of the difference it makes when the last two o's are lopped off a man's income? The gap between fifty thousand and five hundred is considerable."

"So that's it, is it?" said Robinson, and began to laugh weakly. "And our mutual life-belt is that rare and refreshing fruit the banana."

Suddenly he pulled himself together.

"By the way, there's just one thing I'd like to say. I don't suppose the situation is ever likely to arise, but it may do. There's a lot of tourist traffic passes through—and one never knows. I'm dead."

"I don't quite follow," said Barlock quietly.

"I should have thought it was easy," remarked the other. "But I'll be more explicit. Six or seven years ago a regrettable accident took place. An extremely drunken man fell over Waterloo Bridge into the River Thames, and the only thing that was ever recovered was his hat. Wherefore after prolonged search the powers decided that the owner of the hat had been drowned. The powers that be were wrong, but it would be a pity if they found out. There would be complications."

Barlock turned away abruptly; there are moments when a man may not look on another man's face.

"I see," he said, after a pause. "Your secret is safe with me."

"Complications," repeated Robinson dully. "Damnable complications. Well—I'll be pushing on. Thanks again for that snake business."

He slouched off down the platform, and for a time the Austrian stood staring at his retreating back. Damnable complications: the words rang in his brain. Then, with a little shrug of his shoulders, he closed his door. For when one's job is to unload bananas by night, it is necessary to sleep by day.

It was a year afterwards that the official belief concerning Robinson was very nearly justified. Two trains came in, were unloaded and departed again, but of Robinson there was no sign. And after the second, Barlock made inquiries. It was not the first time that Robinson had missed a train, but never before had it been more than that. And the result of Barlock's inquiries was short and to the point. A more than usually fierce drinking bout, coupled with the intense heat—it was the end of July—had just about finished him off. In fact, Barlock's native informant stated that he was, in all probability, already dead. However, if the boss wished he would lead him to the house where the sick man was.

The boss did wish, though once or twice on the way he almost repented and turned back. There are degrees of filth and stench even in the native quarters of Port Limon, and it seemed to Barlock that his destination reached the lowest abyss in the scale. Verminous dogs slunk garbaging along the refuse-strewn gutter; naked children, the flies swarming round them, stared at him with wide-open eyes as he picked his way along the road. And over everything, like a hot, wet blanket, pressed the tropical heat.

He thought with longing of the club at the other end of the town, where what breeze there was came fresh from the sea, and where a man could wallow in the water through the stifling afternoon. After all, this man meant nothing to him. What was he save a broken-down waster belonging to a nation largely responsible for his own present condition? And then he laughed a little cynically. Whatever Robinson was he knew that he was going through with it. White is white, however far down it has sunk.

At last his guide turned through a ramshackle gate, from which a short path, which was evidently the household dustbin, led to a dilapidated shanty. Seated outside the front door was a vast negress, who grinned expansively on seeing the white man. Her lodger was about the same, she told him, and would his honour walk in if he wished to see him. Barlock did so, dodging some hens that walked out simultaneously. And once again he almost chucked it. If the smell outside was bad, there at any rate it was not confined. But in the hovel he had just entered it was concentrated to such an extent that it produced a feeling of physical nausea. And then, as he stood there for a moment or two undecided, there came a hoarse voice from a room beyond.

"Steady, lads—steady! They're coming on again."

One of the breed, and they had gone through that performance on different sides. Yes—it had its humorous side, without doubt. Barlock crossed the room, and pulled aside a dirty hanging. Different sides, perhaps—but both were the same colour.

More hens scuttled out as he stood in the opening. The sick man was lying on some reeds in the corner, and as Barlock crossed to him he glanced up. His eyes showed no trace of recognition, and his visitor saw at once that matters were serious. It was a question of a doctor, and a doctor quickly.

Then his eyes caught sight of something that lay beside the sick man; he bent over him and removed it. And Robinson, delirious as he was, was not so far gone that that escaped him. He cursed foully, and tried to snatch it out of Barlock's hand, only to fall back weakly on the rushes.

"Listen, Robinson," said Barlock, speaking slowly and distinctly. "I'm going to get a doctor."

But the sick man only muttered and mouthed, and glared at his visitor with a look of venomous hatred.

"Now, you old devil," continued Barlock to the negress who had come shambling in, "if I find he has any more of this, you'll be sorry. Police after you, unless you're careful. I go get doctor."

He strode out, leaving the old woman shaking like a mountain of jelly. Then, having smashed to bits a bottle of illicit native spirit, he went in search of the one tolerable doctor the place boasted of. By luck he found him taking his siesta, and dragged him out despite his protests. And between them they saved what was left of Robinson.

Barlock did most of it. For hours on end when he was free did he sit beside the sick man, listening to his ravings—and in the course of those ravings learning the truth. And after a while a great pity for the wretched derelict took hold of him. For the first time he found out Robinson's real name, and truly the crash was greater than he had guessed. And for the first time he found out that there was a woman involved.

At last came the day when the fever died out, and the sick man opened sane eyes to the world.

"Hullo!" he said, staring at Barlock, "have I been talking out of my turn?"

"Don't worry about that," answered the other quietly. "I'm the only person who has heard. And it's safe with me."

"You know who I am?" persisted Robinson, and Barlock nodded.

"Yes—I know who you are," he answered.

"You know I'm married? Or rather"—the smile was a little pitiful—"was married."

"I gathered so," said Barlock. "Look here—we'll talk it all over when you're a bit stronger. You go to sleep now."

Robinson shut his eyes wearily.

"Damnable complications," he muttered. "That's why I'm dead. Because Ulrica has married again."

And at that it was left. A fortnight later Robinson reported for duty again, but now there was a difference. The fever had left its indelible mark: the physical labour required for that continuous carrying of heavy bunches of fruit was beyond his powers.

And so Barlock promoted him; he became assistant
checker. Seated on his raised stand, he checked on
the pad in front of him the number of stems loaded,
and he went on checking them as each ship came in.
Until in the fullness of time the s.s. *Barare* arrived,
and, as usual, it was an all-night job.

Leaning over the ship's rail, watching the scene,
was a tall, fair-haired man. He was smoking, and
every line of his figure breathed that lazy contentment
which only a good cigar can give. Occasionally a
faint smile flickered round his lips at some monkey-
like contortion of one of the niggers, but for the most
part his face was that expressionless mask which is
the hall-mark of a certain type of Englishman.

Suddenly his eyes narrowed: he leaned forward,
staring into the crowd below.

"Good God!" he muttered, "it can't be. But it is,
by Jove!"

Barlock was coming up the gangway, and the tall,
fair-haired man moved along the deck so that the two
met at the top.

"But what astounding luck!" he cried. "My dear
Baron—how are you? And what are you doing
here?"

The faintest perceptible frown showed for a moment
on Barlock's forehead.

"How are you, Lord Rankin?" he said. "But if
you don't mind—not Baron. My name here is just
Barlock."

The other stared at him in puzzled amazement.

"My dear fellow," he stammered, "I don't quite
follow."

"And yet it's fairly easy," answered Barlock.
"Financial considerations made it necessary for me to
work. So I now superintend the loading of bananas
for the Union Fruit Company. And since the job,

though honest and homely, is hardly one that I ever saw myself doing in the past, I decided, temporarily at any rate, to drop my title."

"Well, I'm damned!" said the other, a little awkwardly. "You stagger me, my dear chap. One thing, however, is perfectly clear. Whatever your name is here, to me you are Baron von Studeman, who was amazingly good to a young military attaché in Vienna. And I insist—first on your having a drink, and second on your meeting Ulrica."

"Ulrica!" said Barlock, standing of a sudden very still.

"My wife," explained the other. "I've been married seven years, old boy. Her young hopeful is below now, safely tucked up in the sheets."

But Barlock's eyes were fixed on the back of an unshaven, bleary-eyed man who was checking stems of bananas on a pad. Seven years: an uncommon name like Ulrica. Had the unexpected happened?

And then a peculiarity in the other's phrasing struck him.

"*Her* young hopeful!" he said, with a slight smile.

"Yes," answered Lord Rankin. "My wife had been married before. He was drowned, leaving her with a boy two years old."

Once again Barlock stared at the man with the pencil below.

"I see," he heard himself saying. "By the way, did you ever meet your wife's first husband?"

Lord Rankin raised his eyebrows. Loading bananas did not seem to have increased the Baron's tact.

"I did not," he said curtly, and changed the conversation.

But Barlock hardly heard what he was saying. The unexpected *had* happened. Back to his mind came the remembrance of that day when Robinson had stood in the doorway of his office. He saw once more the look on his face, heard once more those low-breathed words, "Damnable complications." And unless he did something the complications had arrived.

He tried to force himself to think clearly—to get the salient facts in his brain. There, on the dock, within fifteen yards of where he stood, was a man whose wife and child were on board the boat. At any moment Lady Rankin might appear, and what was going to happen then? For even if she did not recognize him, he would be bound to recognize her.

"Excuse me for a few minutes," he said. "There are one or two things I must see to on the quay."

"You'll come back?" cried the other, and Barlock nodded. At all costs he must speak to Robinson.

He went swiftly down the gangway, and crossed to the stand where he sat.

"Hullo, my noble boss!" said Robinson. "You seem a little agitated."

"Look here, Robinson," he said quietly, "you've got to pull yourself together. Something that you have long feared has happened."

For a moment the other stared at him uncomprehendingly; then he sat up with a jerk.

"You mean that——"

"I mean that Lord Rankin is on board."

"And Ulrica?"

"Yes, she is on board, and your son."

"My God!" Mechanically he was ticking off the bunches as they passed. "My God!"

"Don't look round," went on Barlock. "Rankin is leaning over the rail now, and Lady Rankin has just joined him."

He watched the other stiffen, till the sweat dripped off his forehead on to the paper in front of him.

"If I could only see her once again," he muttered.
"And the boy."

"But you mustn't," said Barlock quietly. "Of
course——you mustn't."

"Of course I mustn't," repeated Robinson dully.
"Why——no; you are right."

"So keep your back turned, Robinson," continued
Barlock.

"Yes, I'll keep my back turned, Barlock. But tell
me how she is looking, Barlock, and whether she still
has that quaint little trick of hers of throwing her head
sideways when she laughs. Go and talk to her, Barlock——while I go on counting bananas. And if maybe
she did drop her handkerchief, why, I don't think she'd
miss it much, would she, Barlock?"

"Hell!" grunted the other as he turned away.
"You poor devil."

"Come along," came Lord Rankin's cheery hail.
"We'll go and split a bottle."

"One thousand three hundred and twenty-one
bunches up to date," said Robinson, with a twisted
grin. "Yes——go and split a bottle, Barlock."

And with the feeling that the whole night was a
dream from which he would wake soon, the Baron
von Studeman went to split a bottle. It increased,
that sense of unreality, as the three of them sat in the
smoking-room, till he became conscious that his host
was looking at him curiously. And he realized he
was speaking at random and must pull himself together.

"All natives, I suppose?" said Rankin. "Don't you
find it damned boring? Except that fellow you were
talking to, who looked white."

"I rather think he is white," he answered slowly.
"As white as you or I."

It came unexpectedly, the sudden commotion on the

platform outside. There was a hoarse shouting from the natives, and then some excited babbling.

"Probably only a snake," said Barlock reassuringly. "They always lose their heads when one arrives in the bananas. Hullo! who is this young man?"

Standing in the open doorway was a small figure arrayed in a large dressing-gown.

"I say, mummie," remarked an enthusiastic treble voice, "I've had a priceless time. They've just walloped a snake."

"Tommy!" cried his mother. "You naughty boy! Why aren't you in bed?"

"That funny machine woke me up," answered the child. "So I put my head out to look. And then I saw all the bananas. So I thought I'd go and see what was happening. There was such a nice gentleman sitting on a stool who wanted to know if I'd shake hands with him."

Barlock rose a little abruptly and stared out into the darkness.

"What's this about a snake, young fellah?" said Lord Rankin.

"Well, daddie, just as I was talking to this gentleman, somebody suddenly gave a shout. And I looked round, and there was a yellowy-green snake on the platform close to me. And the gentleman sort of fell out of his chair, and the snake bit him in the hand."

"What's that you say, laddie?" Barlock's voice seemed to come from a distance. "The snake bit him in the hand?"

"Why, yes," said the child. "And then he was so funny. He said, 'I used to field in the slips, old man,' and then he went away ever so quickly, while the natives killed the snake."

"Well, come to bed at once now," cried his mother. "It's nearly midnight."

She bustled him out, leaving the two men alone.

"Young devil," chuckled Lord Rankin. "Not going yet, von Studeman, are you?"

"For a little," returned the other evenly. "I will come back later."

But he searched for twenty minutes before he found Robinson. A glance told him it was too late. The end was very near. He had been bitten in the wrist, and nothing could be done.

"A bonnie kid, Barlock," he said feebly. "I'm glad I saw him. Just got my hand there in time. It was one thousand seven hundred and thirty——"

The voice died away, and the man called Robinson lay still.

"A very narrow escape for the boy." It was an hour later, and the Baron von Studeman was standing with Lord Rankin on deck. "The snake was a *Fer de Lance*, one of the most deadly in the world. They generally remain in the bananas until the stem is lifted out. But this one apparently escaped in the truck; anyway, it was loose on the platform. And but for—Robinson's quickness, the kid would now be dead."

"Good God! It would have broken his mother's heart," said the other. "Where is this man Robinson? Because I must thank him."

"I don't think you quite realize what happened, Rankin," said the Baron quietly. "Robinson received the bite intended for the boy in his own wrist."

The other stared at him speechlessly.

"You don't mean——" he stammered, and the Baron nodded gravely.

"My God!" repeated the other. "This is too awful. Poor devil! Dead!"

He paced up and down in his agitation.

"Anything I could have done for him I would. You see, von Studeman, I didn't tell you before. But my wife's first husband was the most frightful waster. And it broke her up badly before he was drowned. Made her put everything into the kid. If anything had happened to him, I don't know what she'd have done. And this poor chap—dead. I can't get it somehow. Look here, I must do something. He was probably not too well off, and you could help me here. What about giving a present to his wife? He was married, I suppose?"

A queer smile flickered round the lips of the Baron von Studeman.

Below him the machine went on ceaselessly, for the s.s. *Barare* was loading bananas and it was an all-night job.

"Married?" he said. "Not that I'm aware of."

XXXI   THE MAN IN RATCATCHER

I

"'E AIN'T much ter look at, Major, but 'e's a 'andy little 'orse."

A groom, chewing the inevitable straw, gave a final polish to the saddle, and then stood at the animal's head, waiting for the tall, spare man with the bronzed, weather-beaten face, who was slowly drawing on his gloves in the yard, to mount. Idly the groom wondered if the would-be sportsman knew which side of a horse it was customary to get into the saddle from; in fact one Nimrod recently—a gentleman clothed in spotless pink—had so far excelled himself as to come to rest facing his horse's tail. But what could you expect these times, reflected the groom, when most of the men who could ride in days gone by would ride no more; and a crowd of galloping tinkers, with rank

cigars and ranker manners, had taken their places?
When he thought of the men who came now—and the
women, too—to Boddington's Livery Stable, renowned
for fifty years and with a reputation second to none, and
contrasted them with their predecessors, he was wont
to spit, mentally and literally. And the quods—
strewth! It was a fair disgrace to turn out such 'orses
from Boddington's. Only the crowd wot rode 'em
didn't know no better: the 'orses was quite good
enough—aye! too good—for the likes o' them.

"Let out that throat-lash a couple of holes."

The groom looked at the speaker dazedly for a
moment; a bloke that knew the name of a single bit of
saddlery on a horse's back was a rare customer these
days.

"And take that ironmonger's shop out of the poor
brute's mouth. I'll ride him on a snaffle."

"'E pulls a bit when 'e's fresh, Major," said the
groom dubiously.

The tall, spare man laughed. "I think I'll risk it,"
he answered. "Where did you pick him up—at a
jumble sale?"

"'E ain't much ter look at, I knows, Major," said
the groom, carrying out his instructions. "But if yer
'andle 'im easy, and nurse 'im a bit, 'e'll give yer some
sport."

"I can quite believe it," remarked the other, swinging into the saddle. "Ring the bell, will you? That
will give him his cue to start."

With a grin on his face the groom watched the
melancholy steed amble sedately out of the yard and
down the road.

Before he had gone fifty yards the horse's head had
come up a little, he was walking more collectedly—
looking as if he had regained some of the spring of
former days. For there was a *man* on his back—a man

born and bred to horses and their ways—and it would be hard to say which of the two, the groom or the animal, realized it first. Which was why the grin so quickly effaced itself. The groom's old pride in Boddington's felt outraged at having to offer such a mount to such a man. He turned as a two-seater racing car pulled up in the yard, and a young man stepped out. He nodded to the groom as he removed his coat, and the latter touched his cap.

"Grand day, Mr. Dawson," he remarked. "Scent should be good."

The new-comer grunted indifferently, and adjusted his already faultless stock, while another groom led out a magnificent blood chestnut from a loose-box.

"Who was the fellah in ratcatcher I passed, ridin' that awful old quod of yours?" he asked.

To such a sartorial exquisite a bowler hat and a short coat was almost a crime.

"I dunno, sir," said the groom. "Ain't never seen 'im before to the best of me knowledge. But you'll see 'im at the finish."

The other regarded his chestnut complacently.

"He won't live half a mile if we get goin'," he remarked. "You want a horse if hounds find in Spinner's Copse; not a prehistoric bone-bag." He glanced at the old groom's expressionless face, and gave a short laugh in which there was more than a hint of self-satisfaction. "And you can't get a horse without money these days, George, and dam' big money at that." He carefully adjusted his pink coat as he sat in the saddle. "Have the grey taken to Merton cross-roads: and you can take the car there, too," he continued, turning to the chauffeur.

Then with a final hitch at his coat, he, too, went out of the yard. For a while the old groom watched him dispassionately, until a bend in the road hid him from sight. Then he turned to one of his underlings and delivered himself of one of his usual cryptic utterances.

"'Ave yer ever seen a monkey, Joe, sittin' on the branch of a tree, 'uggin' a waxwork doll?"

"Can't say as 'ow I 'ave, Garge," returned the other, after profound cogitation.

"Well, yer don't need to. That monkey'd be the same shape 'as 'im on a 'orse."

II

The meet of the South Leicesters at Spinner's Copse generally produced a field even larger than the normal huge crowd which followed that well-known pack. It was near the centre of their country, and if Fate was kind, and the fox took the direction of Hangman's Bottom, the line was unsurpassed in any country in the world.

It was a quarter to eleven when the tall, spare man, having walked the three-quarters of a mile from Boddington's, dismounted by the side of the road, and thoughtfully lit a cigarette. His eyes took in every detail of the old familiar scene; and, in spite of himself, his mind went back to the last time he had been there. He smiled a little bitterly: he had been a fool to come and open old wounds. This game wasn't for him any more: his hunting days were over. If things had been different: if only—— He drew back as a blood chestnut, fretting and irritable under a pair of heavy hands, came dancing by, spattering mud in all directions. If only—well! he might have been riding that chestnut instead of the heated clothes-peg on his back now. He looked with a kind of weary cynicism at his own mount, mournfully nibbling grass: then he laid a kindly hand on the animal's neck.

"'Tain't your fault, old son, is it?" he muttered.

"But to think of Spinner's Copse—and you. Oh! ye gods!"

"Hounds, gentlemen, please." The man looked up quickly with a sudden gleam in his eyes as hounds came slowly past. A new second whip they'd got; he remembered now, Wilson had been killed at Givenchy. But the huntsman, Mathers, was the same—a little greyer perhaps—but still the same shrewd, kindly sportsman. He caught his eye at that moment, and looked away quickly. He felt certain no one would recognize him, but he wanted to run no risks. There weren't likely to be many of the old crowd out to-day, and he'd altered almost beyond recognition—but it was as well to be on the safe side. And Mathers, he remembered of old, had an eye like a hawk.

He pretended to fumble with his girths, turning his back on the huntsman. It was perhaps as well that he did so for his own peace of mind; for Joe Mathers, with his jaw slowly opening, was staring fascinated at the stooping figure. He was dreaming, of course; it couldn't be him—not possibly. The man whom this stranger was like was dead—killed on the Somme. Entirely imagination. But still the huntsman stared, until a sudden raising of hats all round announced the arrival of the Master.

It was the moment that the tall, quiet man, standing a little aloof on the outskirts of the crowd, had been dreading. He had told himself frequently that he had forgotten the girl who stepped out of the car with her father; he had told himself even more frequently that she had long since forgotten him. But now, as he saw once more the girl's glowing face and her slender, upright figure, showed off to perfection by her habit, he stifled a groan, and cursed himself more bitterly than ever for having been such a fool as to come. If only—— Once again those two bitter words mocked him. He had not forgotten; he never would forget; and it was not the least part of the price he had to pay for the criminal negligence of his late father.

He glanced covertly at the girl; she was talking vivaciously to the man whom he had designated as a heated clothes-peg. He noticed the youth bending towards her with an air of possession which infuriated him; then he laughed and swung himself into the saddle. What had it got to do with him?

Then on a sudden impulse he turned to a farmer next him.

"Who is that youngster talking to the Master's daughter?" he asked.

The farmer looked at him in mild surprise. "You'm a stranger to these parts, mister, evidently," he said. "That be young Mr. Dawson; and folks do say he be engaged to Miss Gollanfield."

Engaged! To that young blighter! With hands like pot-hooks, and a seat like an elephant! And then, quite suddenly, he produced his handkerchief, and proceeded most unnecessarily to blow his nose. For Mathers was talking excitedly to Sir Hubert Gollanfield and Major Dawlish, the hunt secretary; and the eyes of all three men were fixed on him.

"I thought it was before, sir, and then I saw him mount, and I know," said Mathers positively.

"It can't be. He was killed in France," answered the Master. "Wasn't he, David?"

"I've always heard so," said Dawlish. "I'll go and cap him now and have a closer look."

"Anyway, Joe, not a word at present." The Master turned to Mathers. "We'd better draw the spinney first."

Through the crowd, as it slowly moved off, the secretary threaded his way towards the vaguely familiar figure ahead. It couldn't be; it was out of the question.

And yet, as he watched him, more and more did he begin to believe that the huntsman was right. Little movements; an odd, indefinable hitch of the shoulders; the set of the stranger's head. And then, with almost a catch in his breath, he saw that the man he was following had left the crowd, and was unostentatiously edging for a certain gap, which to the uninitiated, appeared almost a cul-de-sac. Of course, it might be just chance; on the other hand, that gap was the closely guarded preserve—as far as such things may be guarded—of the chosen few who really rode; the first-flighters—the men who took their own line, and wanted that invaluable hundred yards' start to get them clear of the mob.

Slightly quickening his pace, the secretary followed his quarry. He overtook him just as he had joined the bare dozen, who with hats rammed down, sat waiting for the first whimper. They were regarding the new-comer with a certain curiosity as the secretary came up; almost with that faint hostility which is an Englishman's special prerogative on the entrance of a second person to his otherwise empty railway carriage. Who was this fellow in ratcatcher mounted on a hopeless screw? And what the devil was he doing here, anyway?

"Mornin', David." A chorus of greeting hailed the advent of the popular secretary, but, save for a brief nod and smile, he took no notice. His eyes were fixed on the stranger, who was carefully adjusting one of his leathers.

"Excuse me, sir." Major Dawlish walked his horse up to him, and then sat staring and motionless. "My God, it can't be——" He spoke under his breath, and the stranger apparently failed to hear.

"What is the cap?" he asked courteously. "A fiver this season, I believe."

"Danny!" The secretary was visibly agitated.

"You're Danny Drayton!   And we thought you were dead!"

"I fear, sir, that there is some mistake," returned the other.   "My name is John Marston."

In silence the two men looked at one another, and then Major Dawlish bowed.

"I beg your pardon, Mr. Marston," he said gravely. "But you bear a strange resemblance to a certain very dear friend of mine, whom we all believed had been killed at Flers in 1916.   He combined two outstanding qualities," continued the secretary deliberately, "did that friend of mine: quixotic chivalry to the point of idiocy, and the most wonderful horsemanship."

Once more the eyes of the two men met, and then John Marston looked away, staring over the wonderful bit of country lying below them.

"I am sorry," he remarked quietly, "that you should have lost your friend."

"Ah, but have I, Mr. Marston; have I?" interrupted David Dawlish quickly.

"You tell me he died at Flers," returned the other. "And very few mistakes were made in such matters, which have not been rectified since."

"He disappeared a year or two before the war," said the secretary, "suddenly—without leaving a trace.   We heard he had gone to New Zealand; but we could get no confirmation.   Do you ever go to the Grand National, Mr. Marston?" he continued, with apparent irrelevance.

The stranger stiffened in his saddle.   "I have been," he answered abruptly.   Merciful heavens! wouldn't some hound own to scent soon?

"Do you remember that year when a certain gentleman rider was booed on the course?" went on the secretary reminiscently.   "It was the year John Drayton and Son went smash for half a million: and it was the son who was booed."

"I don't wonder," returned the stranger. "He was a fool to ride."

"Was he, Mr. Marston? Was he? Or was it just part of that quixotic chivalry of which I have spoken? The horse was a rogue: there was no one else who could do him justice: so, rather than disappoint his friend, the owner, the son turned out."

"And very rightly got hissed for his pains," said John Marston grimly. "I remember the smash well—Drayton's smash. It ruined thousands of poor people: and only a legal quibble saved a criminal prosecution."

"True," assented the secretary. "But it was old Drayton's fault. We all knew it at the time. Danny Drayton—the son——"

"The man who died at Flers," interrupted John Marston, and the secretary looked at him quietly.

"Perhaps: perhaps not. Mistakes *have* occurred. But whether he died or whether he didn't—the son was incapable of even a mean thought. He was not to blame."

"I must beg to differ, sir," returned John Marston. "The firm was Drayton *and Son*: the son was responsible as much as the father. If one member of a firm goes wrong, the other members must make good. It is only fair to the public."

"I see," answered the secretary. "Then I wonder who the other member of the firm can have been? The father died soon after the exposure: the son died at Flers." He looked John Marston straight in the face.

"That would seem to account for the firm," returned the other indifferently.

"Except for one thing," said the secretary, "the significance of which—strangely enough—has only just struck me. There's a certain old farmer in this district, who invested one hundred pounds with Drayton—all his savings.   Along with the rest, it went smash.   A month or two ago he received one hundred and thirty-five pounds in notes, from an unknown source.   Seven years' interest at five per cent. is thirty-five pounds." And suddenly the secretary, usually one of the most unemotional of men, leaned forward in his saddle, and his voice was a little husky.   "Danny!   You damned quixotic fool!   Come back to us: we can't afford to lose a man who can go like you."

The man in ratcatcher stared fixedly in front of him—his profile set and rigid.   For a moment the temptation was wellnigh overwhelming: every account squared up—every loss made good.   Then, ringing in his ears, he heard once more the yells and cat-calls as he had cantered past the stand at Aintree.

"As I said to you before, sir," he said, facing the secretary steadily: "my name is John Marston.   You are making a mistake."

What Major Dawlish's reply would have been will never be known.   He seemed on the point of an explosion of wrath, when clear and shrill through the morning air came Joe Mathers' "Gone away."   The pack came tumbling out of covert, and everything else was forgotten.

"It's the right line," cried John Marston excitedly. "Hangman's Bottom, for a quid."

The field streamed off, everyone according to their own peculiar methods bent on getting the best they could out of a breast-high scent.   The macadam brigade left early, and set grimly about their dangerous task. The man whose horse always picked up a stone early if the run was likely to be a hot one, and arrived cursing his luck, late but quite safe, duly dismounted and fumbled with his outraged steed's perfectly sound hoof. The main body of the field streamed along in a crowd —that big section which is the backbone of every hunt, which contains every variety of individual, and in which every idiosyncrasy of character may be observed by the man who has eyes to see. And then in front of all, riding their own line—but not, as the uninitiated might imagine, deliberately selecting the most impossible parts of every jump, merely for the sport of the thing—the select few.

They had gone two miles without the suspicion of a check, before the secretary found himself near Sir Hubert. Both in their day had belonged to that select few, but now they were content to take things a little easier.

"It's Danny, Hubert," said the secretary, as they galloped side by side over a pasture field towards a stiff-looking post and rails. "Calling himself John Marston."

The Master grunted—glancing for a moment under his bushy eyebrows at the man, two or three hundred yards in front, who, despite his mount, still lived with the vanguard.

"Of course it is," he snorted. "There's no one else would be where he is, on a horse like that, with hounds running at this rate."

They steadied their pace as they came to the timber, and neither spoke again till they were half-way across the next field.

"What's his game, David? Confound you, sir,"—his voice rose to a bellow, as he turned in his saddle and glared at an impetuous youth behind—"will you kindly not ride in my pocket? Infernal young puppy! What's his game, David?"

"Quixotic tommy-rot," snorted the other. "He knows I know he's Danny: but he won't admit it."

"Has Molly seen him yet?" Sir Hubert glanced away to the left, where his daughter, on a raking black, had apparently got her hands full.

"I don't know."

The secretary, frowning slightly, followed the direction of the other's gaze.   David Dawlish was no lover of young Dawson.   He watched the girl for a moment, noting the proximity of the blood chestnut close to her: then he turned back to his old friend.   "That black is too much for Molly, Hubert," he said, a trifle uneasily. "He'll get away with her some day."

"You tell her so, and see what happens, old man," chuckled Sir Hubert.   "I tried once."   Then he reverted to the old subject.   "What are we going to do about it, David, if it is Danny?"

"There's nothing we can do," answered the other. "Officially, he's dead; the War Office have said so.   If he chooses to remain John Marston we can't stop him."

And so for the time the matter was left; the hunting-field, when the going is hot enough for the veriest glutton, is no place for idle speculation and talk.   There is time enough for that afterwards; while hounds are running it behoves a man to attend to the business in hand.

The pace by this time was beginning to tell.   The main body of the hunt now stretched over half a dozen fields; even the first-flight section was getting thinned out.   And it was as David Dawlish topped the slight rise which hid the brook at the bottom of the valley beyond—the notorious Cedar Brook—that he found himself next to Molly Gollanfield.

Streaming up the other side were hounds, with Joe Mathers safely over the water and fifty yards behind them.   Two or three others were level with him, riding wide to his flank, but the secretary's eyes were fixed on a man in ratcatcher who was just ramming an obviously tiring horse at the brook.   With a faint grin, he noted the place he had selected to jump; the spot well known to everyone familiar with the country as being

the best and firmest take-off. He watched the horse
rise—just fail to clear—stumble and peck badly; he
saw the rider literally lift it on to its legs again, and sail
on with barely a perceptible pause. And then he
glanced at Molly Gollanfield.

"Well ridden; well ridden!" The girl's impulsive
praise at a consummate piece of horsemanship made him
smile a little grimly. What would she say when she
knew the identity of the horseman? And what would
he say?

They flew the brook simultaneously, young Dawson
a few yards behind, and swept on up the other side of
the valley.

"Who is that man in front, Uncle David?" called out
the girl. "It's a treat to watch him ride."

"His name, so he tells me, is John Marston," said
the secretary quietly.

"Has he ever been out with us before?"

They breasted the hill as she spoke, to find that
the point had ended, as such a run should end—but
rarely does—with a kill in the open. The survivors of
the front brigade had already dismounted as they came
up, and for a few moments no one could think or speak
of anything but the run. And it was a Captain Malvin,
in one of the Lancer regiments, who recalled the mysterious stranger to the girl's mind.

"Who is that fellow in ratcatcher, Major?" Malvin
was standing by her as he spoke, and the girl glanced
round to find the subject of his interest.

He had dismounted twenty or thirty yards away, and
was making much of his horse, which was completely
cooked.

"Saw him in Boddington's," remarked young Dawson. "How the devil did he manage to get here on
that?"

"By a process known as riding," said Malvin

briefly. "If you mounted that man on a mule, he'd still be at the top of a hunt—eh, Miss Gollanfield?"

But Molly Gollanfield was staring fascinated at the stranger. "Who did you say it was, Uncle David?" Her voice was low and tense, and Malvin glanced at her in surprise.

"John Marston," returned the secretary slowly, "is the name he gave me."

And at that moment the man in ratcatcher looked at the girl.

"John Marston," she faltered. "Why—why—it's Danny! Danny, I thought you were dead!"

She walked her horse towards him and held out her hand, while a wonderful light dawned in her eyes.

"Danny!" she cried, "don't you remember me?"

And gradually the look of joy faded from her face, to be replaced by one of blank amazement. For the man was looking at her as if she had been a stranger.

Then, with a courteous bow, he removed his hat. "You are the second person, madam, who has made the same mistake this morning. My name is John Marston."

But the girl only stared at him in silence, and shook her head.

"I've been watching you ride, Danny," she said, at length, "and just think of it—I didn't know you. What a blind little fool I was, wasn't I?"

"I don't see how you could be expected to recognize me, madam," answered the man. "I hope you'll have as good a second run as the one we've just had. I'm afraid this poor old nag must go stablewards."

He looped the reins over his arm, and once more raised his hat as he turned away.

"But, Danny," cried the girl, a little wildly, "you can't go like this."

"Steady, Molly." Young Dawson was standing

beside her, looking a little ruffled. "I don't know who the devil Danny is or was; but this fellow says he's John Marston. You can't go throwin' your arms round a stranger's neck in the huntin'-field. It's simply not done."

"When I require your assistance on what is or is not done, Mr. Dawson, I will let you know," returned the girl coldly. "Until then kindly keep such information to yourself."

"Mr. Dawson!" The youth recoiled a pace. "Molly! what do you mean?"

But the girl was taking not the slightest notice of him; her eyes were fixed on the stranger, who was talking for a moment to David Dawlish.

"You forgot to take my cap," he said to the secretary, with a smile. "If you like I will send it along by post; or, if you prefer it, I have it on me now."

And at that moment it occurred. It was all so quick that no one could be quite sure what happened. Perhaps it was a horse barging into the black's quarters; perhaps it was the sudden flash of young Dawson's cigarette-case in the sun. Perhaps only Uncle David saw what really caused the black suddenly to give one wild convulsive buck and bolt like the wind with the girl sawing vainly at its mouth.

For a moment there was a stunned silence; then, with an agonized cry, Sir Hubert started to clamber into his saddle.

"The quarry!" His frenzied shout sent a chill into the hearts of everyone who heard, and half the hunt started to mount. Only too well did they know the danger; the black was heading straight for the old disused slate-pit.

But it was the immaculate Dawson who suffered the greatest shock. He had just got his foot into the stirrup when he felt himself picked up like a child and deposited in the mud.   And mounted on *his* chestnut was the man in ratcatcher.

"Keep back—all of you."   The tall, spare figure rose in the saddle and dominated the scene.   "It's a one-man job."   Then he swung the chestnut round, gave him one rib-binder, and followed the bolting black.

"Hi! you, sir!" spluttered Dawson, shaking a fist at the retreating figure.   "That's my horse."

But no one paid the smallest attention to the aggrieved youth; motionless and intent, they were staring at the two galloping horses.   They saw the man swinging left-handed, and for a moment they failed to realize his object.

"What's he doing?   What's he doing?"   David Dawlish was jumping up and down in his excitement. "He'll never catch her like that."

"He will," roared the cavalryman.   "Oh, lovely, lovely—look at that recovery, sir—I ask you, look at it! Don't you see his game, man?"   He turned to the secretary.   "He's coming up between her and the quarry, and he'll ride her off.   If he came up straight behind, nothing could save 'em.   It's too close."

Fascinated, the field watched the grim race—helpless, unable to do anything but sit and look on.   The man in ratcatcher had been right, and they knew it, when he had called it a one-man job.   A crowd of galloping horses would have maddened the black to frenzy.

And as for the two principal performers, they were perhaps the coolest of all.   For a few agonizing seconds, when the girl first realized that Nigger was bolting, she panicked; then, being a thoroughbred herself, she pulled herself together and tried to stop him.   But he was away with her—away with her properly; and it was just as she realized it, with a sickening feeling of helplessness, that a strong, ringing voice came clearly from behind her left shoulder.

"Drop your near rein, Molly; put both hands on your off, and pull—girl—pull! I'm coming."

She heard the thud of his horse behind her, and the black spurted again. But the chestnut crept up till it was level with her girths—till the two horses were neck and neck.

"Pull, darling, pull!" With a wild thrill she heard his voice low and tense beside her; regardless of everything, she stole one look at his steady eyes, which flashed a message of confidence back.

"Pull—pull on that off rein."

She felt the chestnut hard against her legs, boring into her as the man, exerting every ounce of his strength, started to ride her off.

The black was coming round little by little; no horse living could have resisted the combined pull of the one rein and the pressure of the consummate rider on the other side. More and more the man swung her right-handed, never relaxing his steady pressure for an instant, and, at last, with unspeakable relief, she realized that they were galloping parallel with the edge of the quarry and not towards it. It had been touch and go— another twenty yards; and then, at the same moment, they both saw it. Straight in front of them, stretching back from the top of the pit, there yawned a great gap. She had forgotten the landslip during the last summer.

She saw the man lift his crop, and give the black a heavy blow on the near side of his head; she heard his frenzied shout of "Pull—for God's sake—pull!" and then she was galloping alone. Dimly she heard a dreadful crash and clatter behind her; she had one fleeting glimpse of a chestnut horse rolling over and over, and bumping sickeningly downwards, while something else bumped downwards, too; then she was past the gap with a foot to spare. That one stunning blow with the crop had swung the amazed black through half a right-angle to safety; it had made the chestnut swerve through half a right-angle the other way to——

Ah, no! not that. Not dead—not dead. He couldn't be that—not Danny. And she knew it was Danny; had known it all along. Blowing like a steam-engine, the black had stopped exhausted, and she left him standing where he was, as she ran back to the edge of the gap.

"Danny! Danny—my man!" she called in an agony. "Speak—just a word, Danny. My God! it was all my fault!"

Feverishly she started to clamber down towards the still figure sprawling motionless below. But no answer came to her; only the thud of countless other horses, as the field came up to the scene of the disaster.

Sir Hubert, almost beside himself with emotion, was babbling incoherently; the secretary and Joe Mathers were little better.

"Only Danny could have done it," he cried over and over again. "Only Danny could have saved her. And, by Gad! sir, he has—and given his life to do it." He peered over the top, and called out anxiously to the girl below: "Careful, my darling, careful; we can get to him round by the road."

But the girl paid no heed to her father's cry: and when half a dozen men, headed by David Dawlish, rode furiously in by the old entrance to the quarry, they found her sitting on the ground with the unconscious man's head pillowed on her lap.

She lifted her face, streaming with tears, and looked at the secretary.

"He's dead, Uncle David. Danny! my Danny! And it was all my fault."

For a few moments no one spoke; then one of the men stepped forward.

"May I examine him, Miss Gollanfield?" He knelt down beside the motionless figure. "I'm not a doctor, but——" For what seemed an eternity he bent over him; then he rose quickly. "A flask at once. There is still life."

It was not until the limp body had been gently placed on an extemporized stretcher, to wait for the ambulance, that the cavalryman turned to David Dawlish.

"Danny!" he said thoughtfully. "Not Danny Drayton?"

"Himself and no other," replied the secretary. "Masquerading as John Marston."

The cavalryman whistled softly. "The last time I saw him was at Aintree, before the war. I never could get to the bottom of that matter."

"Couldn't you?" said David Dawlish. "And yet it's not very difficult. 'The sins of the fathers are visited' —you know the rest. He disappeared; and every single sufferer in that crash is being paid back."

"But why that dreadful quod to-day?" pursued the soldier.

"All he could get, most likely. Boddington's cattle are pretty indifferent these days." Dawlish glanced at the stretcher, and the corners of his mouth twitched. "The damned young fool could have had the pick of my stable if he'd asked for it," he said gruffly. "Danny —on that herring-gutted brute—at Spinner's Copse! But he was always as proud as Lucifer, was Danny: and I'm thinking no one will ever know what he's suffered since the crash." And then, with apparently unnecessary violence, the worthy secretary blew his nose. "This cursed glare makes my eyes water," he announced, when the noise had subsided.

The cavalryman regarded the dull gloom of the old pit dispassionately.

"Quite so, Major," he murmured at length. "Er—
quite so."

III

"Well, Sir Philip!" With her father and David
Dawlish, Molly was waiting in the hall to hear the
verdict. The ambulance had brought the unconscious
man straight to the Master's house: and for the last
quarter of an hour Sir Philip Westwood, the great
surgeon, who by a fortunate turn of Fate was staying
at an adjoining place, had been carrying out his examination. Now he glanced at the girl, and smiled
gravely.

"There is every hope, Miss Gollanfield," he said
cheerfully.

With a little sob the girl buried her face against Sir
Hubert's shoulder.

"As far as I can see," continued the doctor, "there
is nothing broken: only very severe bruises and a bad
concussion. In a week he should be walking again."

"Thank God!" whispered the girl, and Sir Philip
patted her shoulder.

"A great man," he said, "and a great deed. I'll
come over to-morrow and see him again."

He walked towards the front door, followed by Sir
Hubert, and the girl turned her swimming eyes on
David Dawlish.

"If he'd died, Uncle David," she said brokenly,
"I—I——"

"He's not going to, Molly," interrupted the secretary.
Then, after a pause, "Why did you put the spur into
Nigger?" he asked curiously.

"You saw, did you?" The girl stared at him miserably. "Because I was a little fool: because I was mad
with him—because I loved him, and he called himself
John Marston." She rose, and laughed a little wildly.

"And then when Nigger really did bolt I was glad—glad: and when I saw him beside me, I could have sung for joy. I knew he'd come—and he did. And now I could kill myself."

And staunch old David Dawlish—uncle by right of purchase with many sweets in years gone by, if not by blood—was still thinking it over when the door of her room banged upstairs.

"A whisky and soda, Hubert," he remarked, as the latter joined him, "is clearly indicated."

"We'll have trouble with him, David," grunted the Master. "Damned quixotic young fool. He's got no right to get killed officially: it upsets all one's plans. Probably have to pass an Act of Parliament to bring him to life again."

"Leave it to Molly, old man." The secretary measured out his tot. "Leave it all to her."

"I never do anything else," sighed Sir Hubert. "What is worrying me is young Dawson."

"There's nothing really in that, is there?" David Dawlish looked a little anxiously at his old friend: as has been said before, he was no lover of young Dawson.

"There's a blood chestnut stone-dead at the bottom of a pit," returned the other. "However——"

"Quite," assented Dawlish. "Leave it to Molly: leave it all to her."

Which, taking everything into consideration, was quite the wisest decision they could have come to; it saved such a lot of breath.

They both glanced up as a hospital nurse came down the stairs. "Miss Gollanfield asked me to tell you, Sir Hubert," she remarked, "that the patient is conscious. She is sitting with him for a few minutes."

"Oh, she is, is she?" Sir Hubert rose from his chair a little doubtfully.

"Sit down, Hubert; sit down," grinned Dawlish. "Haven't we just decided to leave it all to her?"

"Well, John Marston! Feeling better?"

The man turned his head slowly on the pillow, and stared at the girl.

"What an unholy——" he muttered. "How's the horse?"

The girl looked at him steadily. "Dead—back broken. We thought you'd done the same."

"Poor brute! A grand horse." He passed one of his hands dazedly across his forehead. "I had to take him—I couldn't have caught you on mine. I must explain things to your fiancé."

"My what?" asked the girl.

"Aren't you engaged to him?" said the man. "They told me——" The words tailed off, and he closed his eyes.

For a moment the girl looked at him with a great yearning tenderness on her face; then she bent over and laid a cool hand on his forehead.

"Go to sleep, Danny Drayton," she whispered. "Go to sleep."

But the name made him open his eyes again.

"I told you my name was John Marston," he insisted.

"Then I require an immediate explanation of why you called me darling," she answered.

He looked at her weakly; then with a little tired smile he gave in.

"Molly," he said, very low, "my little Molly. I've dreamed of you, dear; I don't think you've ever been out of my thoughts all these long years. Just for the moment—I am Danny; to-morrow I'll be John Marston again."

"Will you?" she whispered, and her face was very

close to his. "Then there will be a scandal. For I don't see how John Marston and Mrs. Danny Drayton can possibly live together. My dear, dear man!"

Thus did the man in ratcatcher fall asleep, with the feel of her lips on his, and the touch of her hand on his forehead. And thus did two men find them a few moments later, only to tiptoe silently downstairs again, after one glance from the door.

"Damn this smoke," said David Dawlish gruffly. "It's got in my eyes again."

"You're a liar, David," grunted Sir Hubert. "And a sentimental old fool besides. So am I."

XXXII THE HOUSE BY THE HEADLAND

"YOU'LL no get there, zurr. There'll be a rare storm this night. Best bide here, and be going to-morrow morning after 'tis over."

The warning of my late host, weather-wise through years of experience, rang through my brain as I reached the top of the headland, and, too late, I cursed myself for not having heeded his words. With a gasp I flung my pack down on the ground, and loosened my collar. Seven miles behind me lay the comfortable inn where I had lunched; eight miles in front the one where I proposed to dine. And midway between them was I, dripping with perspiration and panting for breath.

Not a puff of air was stirring; not a sound broke the deathlike stillness, save the sullen, lazy beat of the sea against the rocks below. Across the horizon, as far as the eye could see, stretched a mighty bank of black cloud, which was spreading slowly and relentlessly over the whole heaven. Already its edge was almost overhead, and as I felt the first big drop of rain on my forehead, I cursed myself freely once again. If only I had listened to mine host: if only I was still in his comfortable oak-beamed coffee-room, drinking his most excellent ale. . . . I felt convinced he was the type of man who would treat such trifles as regulation hours with the contempt they deserved. And, even as I tasted in imagination the bite of the grandest of all drinks on my parched tongue, and looked through the glass bottom of the tankard at the sanded floor, the second great drop of rain splashed on my face. For a moment or two I wavered. Should I go back that seven miles and confess myself a fool? or should I go on the further eight and hope that the next cellar would be as good as the last? In either case I was bound to get drenched to the skin, and at length I made up my mind. I would not turn back for any storm, and the matter of the quality of the ale must remain on the laps of the gods. And at that moment, like a solid wall of water, the rain came.

I have travelled into most corners of the world, in the course of forty years' wandering; I have been through the monsoon going south to Singapore from Japan, I have been caught on the edge of a waterspout in the South Sea Islands; but I have never known anything like the rain which came down that June evening on the south-west coast of England. In half a minute every garment I wore was soaked; the hills and the sea were blotted out, and I stumbled forward blindly, unable to see more than a yard in front of me. Then, almost as abruptly as it had started, the rain ceased. I could feel the water squelching in my boots, and trickling down my back, as I kept steadily descending into the valley beyond the headland. There was nothing for it now but to go through with it. I couldn't get any wetter than I was; so that, when I suddenly rounded a little knoll and saw in front a low-lying, rambling house, the idea of sheltering there did not at once occur to me. I glanced at it casually in the semi-darkness, and was trudging past the gate, my mind busy with other things, when a voice close behind me made me stop with a sudden start. A man was speaking, and a second before I could have sworn I was alone.

"A bad night, sir," he remarked, in a curiously deep voice, "and it will be worse soon. The thunder and lightning is nearly over. Will you not come in and shelter? I can supply you with a change of clothes if you are wet."

"You are very good, sir," I answered slowly, peering at the tall, gaunt figure beside me. "But I think I will be getting on, thank you all the same."

"As you like," he answered indifferently, and even as he spoke a vivid flash of lightning quivered and died in the thick blackness of the sky, and almost instantaneously a deafening crash of thunder seemed to come from just over our heads. "As you like," he repeated, "but I shall be glad of your company if you cared to stay the night."

It was a kind offer, though in a way the least one would expect in similar circumstances, and I hesitated. Undoubtedly there was little pleasure to be anticipated in an eight-mile tramp under such conditions, and yet there was something—something indefinable, incoherent—which said to me insistently: "Go on; don't stop. Go on."

I shook myself in annoyance, and my wet clothes clung to me clammily. Was I, at my time of life, nervous, because a man had spoken to me unexpectedly?

"I think if I may," I said, "I will change my mind and avail myself of your kind offer. It is no evening for walking for pleasure."

Without a word he led the way into the house, and

I followed. Even in the poor light I could see that the garden was badly kept, and that the path leading to the front door was covered with weeds. Bushes, wet with the rain, hung in front of our faces, dripping dismally on to the ground; and green moss filled the cracks of the two steps leading up to the door, giving the impression almost of a mosaic.

Inside, the hall was in darkness, and I waited while he opened the door into one of the rooms. I heard him fumbling for a match, and at that moment another blinding flash lit up the house as if it had been day. I had a fleeting vision of the stairs—a short, broad flight—with a window at the top; of two doors, one apparently leading to the servants' quarters, the other opposite the one my host had already opened. But most vivid of all in that quick photograph was the condition of the hall itself. Three or four feet above my head a lamp hung from the ceiling, and from it, in every direction, there seemed to be spiders' webs coated with dust and filth. They stretched to every picture; they stretched to the top of all the doors. One long festoon was almost brushing against my face, and for a moment a wave of unreasoning panic filled me. Almost did I turn and run, so powerful was it; then, with an effort, I pulled myself together. For a grown man to become nervous of a spider's web is rather too much of a good thing, and after all it was none of my business. In all probability the man was a recluse, who was absorbed in more important matters than the cleanliness of his house. Though how he could stand the smell—dank and rotten—defeated me. It came to my nostrils as I stood there, waiting for him to strike a match, and the scent of my own wet Harris tweed failed to conceal it. It was the smell of an unlived-in house, grown damp and mildewed with years of neglect, and once again I shuddered. Confound the fellow! Would he never get the lamp lit? I didn't mind his spiders' webs and the general filth of his hall, provided I could get some dry clothes on.

"Come in." I looked up to see him standing in the door. "I regret that there seems to be no oil in the lamp, but there are candles on the mantelpiece, should you care to light them."

Somewhat surprised I stepped into the room, and then his next remark made me halt in amazement.

"When my wife comes down, I must ask her about the oil. Strange of her to have forgotten."

Wife! What manner of woman could this be who allowed her house to get into such a condition of dirt and neglect? And were there no servants? However, again, it was none of my business, and I felt in my pocket for matches. Luckily they were in a watertight box, and with a laugh I struck one and lit the candles.

"It's so infernally dark," I remarked, "that the stranger within the gates requires a little light to get his bearings."

In some curiosity I glanced at my host's face in the flickering light. As yet I had had no opportunity of observing him properly, but now as unostentatiously as possible I commenced to study it. Cadaverous, almost to the point of emaciation, he had a ragged, bristly moustache, while his hair, plentifully flecked with grey, was brushed untidily back from his forehead. But dominating everything were his eyes, which glowed and smouldered from under his bushy eyebrows, till they seemed to burn into me.

More and more I found myself regretting the fact that I had accepted his offer. His whole manner was so strange that for the first time doubts as to his sanity began to creep into my mind. And to be alone with a madman in a deserted house, miles from any other habitation, with a terrific thunderstorm raging, was not a prospect which appealed to me greatly. Then I remembered his reference to his wife, and felt more reassured. . . .

"You and your wife must find it lonely here," I hazarded, when the silence had lasted some time.

"Why should my wife feel the loneliness?" he answered harshly. "She has me—her husband. . . . What more does a woman require?"

"Oh! nothing, nothing," I replied hastily, deeming discretion the better part of veracity. "Wonderful air; beautiful view. I wonder if I could have a dry coat as you so kindly suggested?"

I took off my own wet one as I spoke, and threw it over the back of a chair. Then, receiving no answer to my request, I looked at my host. His back was half towards me, and he was staring into the hall outside. He stood quite motionless, and, as apparently he had failed to hear me, I was on the point of repeating my remark when he turned and spoke to me again.

"A pleasant surprise for my wife, sir, don't you think? She was not expecting me home until to-morrow morning."

"Very," I assented. . . .

"Eight miles have I walked, in order to prevent her being alone. That should answer your remark about her feeling the loneliness."

He peered at me fixedly, and I again assented.

"Most considerate of you," I murmured, "most considerate."

But the man only chuckled by way of answer, and, swinging round, continued to stare into the gloomy, filthy hall.

Outside, the storm was increasing in fury. Flash followed flash with such rapidity that the whole sky westwards formed into a dancing sheet of flame, while the roll of the thunder seemed like the continuous roar of a bombardment with heavy guns. But I was aware of it only subconsciously; my attention was concentrated on the gaunt man standing so motionless in the centre of the room. So occupied was I with him that I never heard his wife's approach, until suddenly, looking up, I saw that by the door there stood a woman —a woman who paid no attention to me, but only stared fearfully at her husband, with a look of dreadful terror in her eyes. She was young, far younger than the man—and pretty in a homely, countrified way. And as she stared at the gaunt, cadaverous husband she seemed to be trying to speak, while ceaselessly she twisted a wisp of a pocket-handkerchief in her hands.

"I didn't expect you home so soon, Rupert," she stammered at length. "Have you had a good day?"

"Excellent," he answered, and his eyes seemed to glow more fiendishly than ever. "And now I have come home to my little wife, and her loving welcome."

She laughed a forced, unnatural laugh, and came a few steps into the room.

"There is no oil in the lamp, my dear," he continued suavely. "Have you been too busy to remember to fill it?"

"I will go and get some," she said, quickly turning towards the door.

But the man's hand shot out and caught her arm, and at his touch she shrank away, cowering.

"I think not," he cried harshly. "We will sit in the darkness, my dear, and—wait."

"How mysterious you are, Rupert!" She forced herself to speak lightly. "What are we going to wait for?"

But the man only laughed—a low, mocking chuckle —and pulled the girl nearer to him.

"Aren't you going to kiss me, Mary? It's such a long time since you kissed me—a whole twelve hours."

The girl's free hand clenched tight, but she made no other protest as her husband took her in his arms and kissed her. Only it seemed to me that her whole body was strained and rigid, as if to brace herself to meet a caress she loathed. . . . In fact the whole situation was becoming distinctly embarrassing. The man seemed to have completely forgotten my existence, and the girl so far had not even looked at me. Undoubtedly a peculiar couple, and a peculiar house. Those cobwebs: I couldn't get them out of my mind.

"Hadn't I better go and fill the lamp now?" she asked, after a time. "Those candles give a very poor light, don't they?"

"Quite enough for my purpose, my dear wife," replied the man. "Come and sit down and talk to me."

With his hand still holding her arm he drew her to a sofa, and side by side they sat down. I noticed that all the time he was watching her covertly out of the corner of his eye, while she stared straight in front of her as if she was waiting for something to happen. . . . And at that moment a door banged upstairs.

"What's that?" The girl half-rose, but the man pulled her back.

"The wind, my dear," he chuckled. "What else could it be? The house is empty save for us."

"Hadn't I better go up and see that all the windows are shut?" she said nervously. "This storm makes me feel frightened."

"That's why I hurried back to you, my love. I couldn't bear to think of you spending to-night alone." Again he chuckled horribly, and peered at the girl beside him. "I said to myself, 'She doesn't expect me back till to-morrow morning. I will surprise my

darling wife, and go back home to-night.' Wasn't it
kind of me, Mary?"

"Of course it was, Rupert," she stammered. "Very
kind of you. I think I'll just go up and put on a
jersey. I'm feeling a little cold."

She tried to rise, but her husband still held her;
and then suddenly there came on her face such a look
of pitiable terror that involuntarily I took a step forward. She was staring at the door, and her lips were
parted as if to cry out, when the man covered her
mouth with his free hand and dragged her brutally
to her feet.

"Alone, my wife—all alone," he snarled. "My
dutiful, loving wife all alone. What a good thing I
returned to keep her company!"

For a moment or two she struggled feebly; then
he half-carried, half-forced her close by me to a position behind the open door. I could have touched
them as they passed; but I seemed powerless to move.
Instinctively I knew what was going to happen; but
I could do nothing save stand and stare at the door,
while the girl, half-fainting, crouched against the wall,
and her husband stood over her motionless and terrible.
And thus we waited, while the candles guttered in their
sockets, listening to the footsteps which were coming
down the stairs. . . .

Twice I strove to call out; twice the sound died
away in my throat. I felt as one does in some awful
nightmare, when a man cries aloud and no sound
comes, or runs his fastest and yet does not move. In
it, I was yet not of it; it was as if I was the spectator
of some inexorable tragedy with no power to intervene.

The steps came nearer. They were crossing the
hall now—the cobwebby hall—and the next moment
I saw a young man standing in the open door.

"Mary, where are you, my darling?" He came

into the room and glanced around. And, as he stood there, one hand in his pocket, smiling cheerily, the man behind the door put out his arm and gripped him by the shoulder. In an instant the smile vanished, and the youngster spun round, his face set and hard.

"Here is your darling, John Trelawnay," said the husband quietly. "What do you want with her?"

"Ah!" The youngster's breath came a little faster, as he stared at the older man. "You've come back unexpectedly, have you? It's the sort of damned dirty trick you would play."

I smiled involuntarily: this was carrying the war into the enemy's camp with a vengeance.

"What are you doing in this house alone with my wife, John Trelawnay?" Into the quiet voice had crept a note of menace, and, as I glanced at the speaker and noticed the close clenching and unclenching of his powerful hands, I realized that there was going to be trouble. The old, old story again, but, rightly or wrongly, with every sympathy of mine on the side of the sinners.

"Your wife by a trick only, Rupert Carlingham," returned the other hotly. "You know she's never loved you; you know she has always loved me."

"Nevertheless—my wife. But I ask you again, what are you doing in this house while I am away?"

"Did you expect us to stand outside in the storm?" muttered the other.

For a moment the elder man's eyes blazed, and I thought he was going to strike the youngster. Then, with an effort, he controlled himself, and his voice was ominously quiet as he spoke again.

"You lie, John Trelawnay." His brooding eyes never left the other's face. "It was no storm that drove you here to-day; no thunder that made you call my wife your darling. You came because you knew

I was away; because you thought—you and your mistress—that I should not return till to-morrow."

For a while he was silent, while the girl still crouched against the wall staring at him fearfully, and the youngster, realizing the hopelessness of further denial, faced him with folded arms. In silence I watched them from the shadow beyond the fireplace, wondering what I ought to do. There is no place for any outsider in such a situation, much less a complete stranger; and had I consulted my own inclinations I would have left the house there and then and chanced the storm still raging outside. I got as far as putting on my coat again, and making a movement towards the door, when the girl looked at me with such an agony of entreaty in her eyes that I paused. Perhaps it was better that I should stop; perhaps if things got to a head, and the men started fighting, I might be of some use.

And at that moment Rupert Carlingham threw back his head and laughed. It echoed and re-echoed through the room, peal after peal of maniacal laughter, while the girl covered her face with her hands and shrank away, and the youngster, for all his pluck, retreated a few steps. The man was mad, there was no doubt about it: and the laughter of a madman is perhaps the most awful thing a human being may hear.

Quickly I stepped forward; it seemed to me that if I was to do anything at all the time had now come.

"I think, Mr. Carlingham," I said firmly, "that a little quiet discussion would be of advantage to everyone."

He ceased laughing, and stared at me in silence. Then his eyes left my face and fixed themselves again on the youngster. It was useless; he was blind to everything except his own insensate rage. And, before I could realize his intention, he sprang.

"You'd like me to divorce her, wouldn't you?" he

snarled, as his hand sought John Trelawnay's throat. "So that you could marry her. . . . But I'm not going to—no. I know a better thing than divorce."

The words were choked on his lips by the youngster's fist, which crashed again and again into his face; but the man seemed insensible to pain. They swayed backwards and forwards, while the lightning, growing fainter and fainter in the distance, quivered through the room from time to time, and the two candles supplied the rest of the illumination. Never for an instant did the madman relax his grip on the youngster's throat: never for an instant did the boy cease his sledge-hammer blows on the other's face. But he was tiring, it was obvious; no normal flesh and blood could stand the frenzied strength against him. And, suddenly, it struck me that murder was being done in front of my eyes.

With a shout I started forward—somehow they must be separated. And then I stopped motionless again: the girl had slipped past me with her face set and hard. With a strength for which I would not have given her credit she seized both her husband's legs about the knees, and lifted his feet off the ground, so that his only support was the grip of his left hand on the youngster's throat, and the girl's arms about his knees. He threw her backwards and forwards as if she had been a child, but still she clung on, and then, in an instant, it was all over. His free right hand had been forgotten. . . .

I saw the boy sway nearer in his weakness, and the sudden flash of a knife. There was a little choking gurgle, and they all crashed down together, with the youngster underneath. And when the madman rose, the boy lay still, with the shaft of the knife sticking out from his coat above his heart.

It was then that Rupert Carlingham laughed again, while his wife, mad with grief, knelt beside the dead boy, pillowing his head on her lap. For what seemed an eternity I stood watching, unable to move or speak; then the murderer bent down and swung his wife over his shoulder. And, before I realized what he was going to do, he had left the room, and I saw him passing the window outside.

The sight galvanized me into action; there was just a possibility I might avert a double tragedy. With a loud shout I dashed out of the front door and down the ill-kept drive; but when I got to the open ground he seemed to have covered an incredible distance, considering his burden. I could see him shambling over the turf, up the side of the valley which led to the headland where the rain had caught me; and, as fast as I could, I followed him, shouting as I ran. But it was no use—gain on him I could not. Steadily, with apparent ease, he carried the girl up the hill, taking no more notice of my cries than he had of my presence earlier in the evening. And, with the water squelching from my boots, I ran after him—no longer wasting my breath on shouting, but saving it all in my frenzied endeavour to catch him before it was too late. For once again I knew what was going to happen, even as I had known when I heard the footsteps coming down the stairs.

I was still fifty yards from him when he reached the top of the cliff; and for a while he paused there silhouetted against the angry sky. He seemed to be staring out to sea, and the light from the flaming red sunset, under the black of the storm, shone on his great, gaunt figure, bathing it in a wonderful splendour. The next moment he was gone. . . . I heard him give one loud cry; then he sprang into space with the girl still clasped in his arms.

And when I reached the spot and peered over, only the low booming of the sullen Atlantic three hundred feet below came to my ears. . . . That, and the mocking shrieks of a thousand gulls. Of the madman and his wife there was no sign.

At last I got up and started to walk away mechanically. I felt that somehow I was to blame for the tragedy, that I should have done something, taken a hand in that grim fight. And yet I knew that if I was called upon to witness it again, I should act in the same way. I should feel as powerless to move as I had felt in that ill-omened house, with the candles guttering on the mantelpiece, and the lightning flashing through the dirty window. Even now I seemed to be moving in a dream, and after a while I stopped and made a determined effort to pull myself together.

"You will go back," I said out loud, "to that house. And you will make sure that that boy is dead. You are a grown man, and not an hysterical woman. You will go back."

And as if in answer a seagull screamed discordantly above my head. Not for five thousand pounds would I have gone back to that house alone, and when I argued with myself and said, "You are a fool, and a coward," the gull shrieked mockingly again.

"What is there to be afraid of?" I cried. "A dead body; and you have seen many hundreds."

It was as I asked the question out loud that I came to a road and sat down beside it. It was little more than a track, but it seemed to speak of other human beings, and I wanted human companionship at the moment—wanted it more than I had ever wanted anything in my life. At any other time I would have resented sharing with strangers the glorious beauty of the moors as they stretched back to a rugged tor a mile or two away, with their wonderful colouring of violet and black, and the scent of the wet earth rising all around. But now . . .

With a shudder I rose, conscious for the first time that I was feeling chilled. I must get somewhere—talk to someone; and, as if in answer to my thoughts, a car came suddenly in sight, bumping over the track.

There was an elderly man inside, and two girls, and he pulled up at once on seeing me.

"By Jove!" he cried cheerily, "you're very wet. Can I give you a lift anywhere?"

"It is very good of you," I said. "I want to get to the police as quickly as possible."

"The police?" He stared at me surprised. "What's wrong?"

"There's been a most ghastly tragedy," I said. "A man has been murdered and the murderer has jumped over that headland, with his wife in his arms. The murderer's name was Rupert Carlingham."

I was prepared for my announcement startling them; I was not prepared for the extraordinary effect it produced. With a shriek of terror the two girls clung together, and the man's ruddy face went white.

"What name did you say?" he said at length, in a shaking voice.

"Rupert Carlingham," I answered curtly. "And the boy he murdered was called John Trelawnay. Incidentally I want to get a doctor to look at the youngster. It's possible the knife might have just missed his heart."

"Oh, daddy, drive on, drive on quick!" implored the girls, and I glanced at them in slight surprise. After all a murder is a very terrible thing, but it struck me they were becoming hysterical over it.

"It was just such an evening," said the man slowly: "just such a storm as we've had this afternoon, that it happened."

"That what happened?" I cried, a trifle irritably; but he made no answer, and only stared at me curiously.

"Do you know these parts, sir?" he said at length.

"It's the first time I've ever been here," I answered. "I'm on a walking tour."

"Ah! A walking tour. Well, I'm a doctor myself, and unless you get your clothes changed pretty quickly, I predict that your walking tour will come to an abrupt conclusion—even if it's only a temporary one. Now, put on this coat, and we'll get off to a good inn."

But, anxious as I was to fall in with his suggestion myself, I felt that that was more than I could do.

"It's very good of you, doctor," I said; "but, seeing that you are a medical man, I really must ask you to come and look at this youngster first. I'd never forgive myself if by any chance he wasn't dead. As a matter of fact, I've seen death too often not to recognize it, and the boy was stabbed clean through the heart, right in front of my eyes—but . . ."

I broke off, as one of the girls leaned forward and whispered to her father. But he only shook his head, and stared at me curiously.

"Did you make no effort to stop the murder?" he asked at length.

It was the question I had been dreading, the question I knew must come sooner or later. But, now that I was actually confronted with it, I had no answer ready. I could only shake my head and stammer out confusedly:

"It seems incredible for a man of my age and experience to confess it, doctor—but I didn't. I couldn't. . . . I was just going to try and separate them, when the girl rushed in . . . and . . ."

"What did she do?" It was one of the daughters who fired the question at me so suddenly that I looked at her in amazement. "What did Mary do?"

"She got her husband by the knees," I said, "and hung on like a bull-dog. But he'd got a grip on the boy's throat, and then—suddenly—it was all over. They came crashing down as he stabbed young Trelawnay." Once again the girls clung together shuddering, and I turned to the doctor. "I wish you'd come, doctor: it's only just a step. I can show you the house."

"I know the house, sir, very well," he answered gravely. Then he put his arms on the steering-wheel and for a long time sat motionless, staring into the gathering dusk, while I fidgeted restlessly, and the girls whispered together. What on earth was the man waiting for? I wondered: after all, it wasn't a very big thing to ask of a doctor. . . . At last he got down from the car and stood beside me on the grass.

"You've never been here before, sir?" he asked again, looking at me fixedly.

"Never," I answered, a shade brusquely. "And I'm not altogether bursting with a desire to return."

"Strange," he muttered. "Very, very strange. I will come with you."

For a moment he spoke to his daughters as if to reassure them; then together we walked over the springy turf towards the house by the headland. He seemed in no mood for conversation, and my own mind was far too busy with the tragedy for idle talk.

But he asked me one question when we were about fifty yards from the house.

"Rupert Carlingham carried his wife up to the headland, you say?"

"Slung over his shoulder," I answered, "and then . . ."

But the doctor had stopped short, and was staring at the house, while, once again, every vestige of colour had left his face.

"My God!" he muttered, "there's a light in the room. . . . A light, man; don't you see it?"

"I left the candles burning," I said impatiently.

"Really, doctor, I suppose murder doesn't often come your way, but . . ."

I walked on quickly, and he followed. Really the fuss was getting on my nerves, already distinctly ragged. The front door was open as I had left it, and I paused for a moment in the cobwebby hall. Then, pulling myself together, I stepped into the room where the body lay, to halt and stare open-mouthed at the floor. . . .

The candles still flickered on the mantelpiece; the furniture was as I had left it; but of the body of John Trelawnay there was not a trace. It had vanished utterly and completely.

"I don't understand, doctor," I muttered foolishly. "I left the body lying there."

The doctor stood at the door beside me, and suddenly I realized that his eyes were fixed on me.

"I know," he said, and his voice was grave and solemn. "With the head near that chair."

"Why, how do you know?" I cried, amazed. "Have you taken the body away?"

But he answered my question by another.

"Do you notice anything strange in this room, sir?" he asked. "On the floor?"

"Only a lot of dust," I remarked.

"Precisely," he said. "And one would expect footprints in dust. I see yours going to the mantelpiece; I see no others."

I clutched his arm, as his meaning came to me.

"My God!" I whispered. "What do you mean?"

"I mean," he said, "that Rupert Carlingham murdered John Trelawnay, and then killed himself and his wife, five years ago . . . during just such another storm as we have had this evening."

XXXIII   THE MAN WHO WOULD NOT PLAY CARDS

I

"THANKS very much, but as I told you before—
I don't play cards."

The speaker, a tall, bronzed man whose clear eye and slightly weather-beaten face proclaimed him to be no dweller in cities, paused at the smoking-room door, and stared, a little deliberately, at the man who had just accosted him.   It was the second time that day that this same gentleman had endeavoured to rope him into a game of poker—"just small stakes, you know" —and Hugh Massingham disliked being asked things twice.   Almost as much as, in this particular case, he disliked the appearance of the asker.

He paused long enough to let the stare become pointed; then he opened the door and stepped out on deck.   He hated the stuffiness of the smoking-room, with its eternal cards and whisky pegs, and with an atmosphere so thick with tobacco smoke that at times he could hardly see across it.

Away to port, like a faint smudge on the horizon, lay the North Coast of Africa, and Hugh Massingham, with a faint smile, wondered just how many times he'd seen that smudge before.   And how many times he'd see it in the future.

He leaned over the rail staring at the water thoughtfully.   It depended, of course, on Delia.   Things are apt to depend on a man's wife.   There was no necessity for him to go back to the East—no financial necessity—yet somehow he hoped Delia would like to come, at any rate, for a few years.   England, from all he heard, didn't sound much of a place to live in just now, but, of course, she'd have to decide.

Surreptitiously he put a hand into his breast pocket

and pulled out a photograph. It was the likeness of a woman—little more than a girl—with a pair of eyes that, even on the cardboard, mocked and haunted him. It was the likeness of a girl who was more than passing lovely; it was the likeness of his wife; a wife with whom he had spent his whole married life of one week. Involuntarily he smiled. A week together, out of four years. But if tactless Governments will conduct campaigns in Mesopotamia, some such result is hardly to be wondered at.

He drew in a deep breath, and once again started to stroll up and down the deck. He wondered if she'd find him much changed: a bit thinner, perhaps, but enteric tends to remove superfluous flesh. And what would she be like? Grown a little—no longer a lovely girl, but a lovely woman. The photograph was nearly five years old, and she had been nineteen then—no, nearly twenty. A week out of four years—a week!

With a faint smile still on his lips, he turned and re-entered the smoking-room. The persuasive gentleman, he noticed, had settled down to his game of poker with four youngsters, and for a moment Massingham frowned. He knew the type—knew it inside out; and whoever might lose at that quiet game of poker, there was one player who would certainly win. Not that he accused the persuasive gentleman for a moment of anything unfair; but he was of the type who had forgotten more about poker than the other four players combined were ever likely to know. With a slight shrug of his shoulders, he walked over to the bar and called for a gin and bitters. It was no business of his, and, from time immemorial, youth has had to pay for its experience.

It was about ten o'clock that night that it became increasingly evident that youth was paying with a vengeance. The persuasive gentleman had a very considerable proportion of the total number of chips beside him, to say nothing of a small library of written chits. And two of the other four players were looking worried, very worried. The thing was perfectly absurd; had they not played poker pretty consistently in the mess? Made a bit of money out of it, too, taking it in the long run. But to-night the luck was simply infernal. Hugh Massingham smiled grimly to himself. Truly, the lambs had walked docilely to the slaughter.

For a while he watched the persuasive gentleman narrowly through half-closed eyes; then, because it was still no business of his, he moved towards the door for a final stroll on deck before turning in. And it was as he was on the point of opening it that one of the youngsters rose suddenly with a muttered curse.

"I can't play any more," he said shortly. "I'm holding good cards, but they always seem to go down."

Hugh smiled once again; it isn't the man who holds bad cards who loses heavily at poker; it's the man who holds good ones when somebody else is holding a bit better. Then something in the boy's face made his hand drop to his side; quite evidently he had lost more than he could comfortably afford. And the persuasive gentleman's complacent smirk made Hugh annoyed. He disliked the persuasive gentleman.

"Have your revenge to-morrow night," he remarked with a kind of oily suavity, and with a grunt the youngster drained his whisky and soda sullenly.

"Won't someone else take his place?" As if by accident the speaker's eyes met Hugh's, and it may have been due to the procession of whiskies, or it may have been due to the fact that the dislike was reciprocal, but the persuasive gentleman allowed himself the pleasure of a very faint sneer. "You, as you have told me twice, do not play, do you?"

It wasn't the words, but it was the way they were said that decided Massingham. The persuasive gentleman should have his lesson.

"I don't mind taking this gentleman's place for half an hour," he remarked quietly. "What stakes are you playing?"

"Maximum five-pound rise, and limit of a hundred in the pool," returned the other, and Hugh's eyebrows went up. He called those small stakes, did he?

For a while the game went on normally without any hands of importance, and it was not until they had been playing about twenty minutes that the cards became interesting. And that hand they were very interesting! It was Hugh's deal, and he dealt, as usual, slowly and methodically. The three youngsters threw their hands in at once; only the persuasive gentleman remained. And Hugh noted that the little finger of his left hand twitched slightly as he glanced at his cards.

"How many?" he demanded.

"One," said the other, and his voice was oily as ever.

"I stand," said Hugh, laying his cards face downwards on the table.

Then began the betting, and the youngster whose place he had taken watched eagerly in his excitement. They mounted a fiver at a time, until the persuasive gentleman reached the limit of a hundred.

"I'll see you at a hundred," drawled Hugh.

And a little gasp of envy ran round the spectators as the originator of the quiet game laid down four aces.

"You dealt 'em to me," he remarked with a smirk, his hand already stretched out to collar the pool.

"Er—one moment," murmured Hugh, and the persuasive gentleman turned white. Four aces. Only a
straight flush could beat it. Surely——

Another gasp ran round the group. Hugh had
just turned up his hand. And the three, four, five,
six, and seven of clubs being a straight flush beats
four aces.

For a moment Hugh allowed himself the luxury of
watching the other's face. Then he spoke. "I certainly dealt you four aces, my friend; so I took the
precaution of dealing myself a straight flush. And
that is the reason why I do not play cards. Years
of boredom by myself on a plantation made me take
up card-conjuring as a hobby. And I did this simple
little trick to-night in order to demonstrate to you
boys that even a fine card-player like the gentleman
opposite may be quite helpless when playing with a
stranger. In fact, I could win money off him just as
easily as he can win money off you."

The persuasive gentleman appeared to be the least
pleased member of the group, though the fact that
after all he had not lost his money appeased him
somewhat.

"Anyone, sir," he remarked, a little thickly, "can
win money by cheating."

"Not anyone," said Hugh amicably. "But we'll
let that pass. Only I'd win money off you playing
perfectly fair. You're not a good gambler; your finger
twitches. Good night."

And he was still smiling as he turned in.

II

With fingers that fumbled over the unaccustomed
stiff shirt, Hugh Massingham was dressing for dinner.
His first dinner with his wife for four years. It was
the moment he had dreamed of through long, swelter-

ing days in Mesopotamia—and now that it had come, he was afraid.

Things were different to what he had expected; Delia was different. He could hear her now, moving about in the next room, and her voice as she spoke to her maid. Somehow, he hadn't expected that maid. He had hoped—well, it didn't much matter what he'd hoped. Anyway, it was absurd: naturally, his wife would have a maid.

It wasn't that that made him pause every now and again and stare a little blankly in front of him; it was something far bigger and more fundamental than such a triviality as a maid. And even to himself he would hardly acknowledge what it was. She was shy—naturally, any woman would be after such a long separation. And then the idea of associating shyness with his singularly self-possessed and lovely wife made him smile grimly. It was not that. No, it was simply— and Hugh Massingham took a deep breath like a man about to dive—it was simply that she had· become a stranger to him. Or, to put it more accurately, he had become a stranger to her. The kiss which she had given him had been such as a sister would give to her brother. True, there had not been much time —some people had arrived to play Bridge and had remained most of the afternoon. Delia wouldn't hear of their going away, though they had half-suggested it. And he had spent the afternoon at his club—the afternoon of which he'd dreamed through four long weary years. A stranger—he was a stranger in his own house. With a twisted apology for a smile, he put on his coat and switched out the light. Time doubtless would straighten out the situation; but there had been enough time already in their married life. There had been four years.

Dinner, perfectly served and faultlessly cooked,

merely continued the hollow mockery of his home-coming. He felt that he might have been dining with any pretty woman at any house; not with his wife in his own. In fact, except that he happened to pay for it, it wasn't his house. Everything about it was hers—except himself. He was merely the stranger within his own gates.

"A little different, Delia, to what I had imagined it," he remarked quietly, as the servant, having placed the port in front of him, left the room.

For a moment she looked at him narrowly; then she leaned back in her chair.

"In what way?" she asked calmly. "Don't you think the flat is comfortable?"

They had got to have a straight talk, anyway; per-haps it was as well, she reflected, to get it over and done with. There was no good starting on false pretences.

"Very." He rose and stood by the fireplace look-ing down at her. "It wasn't the flat I was alluding to." With ostentatious deliberation he selected a cigarette and lit it. "Do you know it's four years since we've seen one another?"

"Quite strangers, aren't we?" she agreed lightly.

"Exactly—the very word. Strangers. But through no wish of mine."

"Nor mine, either, my dear man. It's simply the inevitable result of four years' separation."

"I disagree; the result is by no manner of means inevitable. However, I won't press the point. But was it absolutely essential that those people should have stopped to Bridge this afternoon? They had the decency to suggest going."

It was not a happy way of putting it, and a red spot burned for a moment on his wife's cheek.

"And I had not the decency to let them, you

imply." She laughed a little shortly. "Well, since you've started this conversation, I suppose we may as well have it out."

Hugh's hand clenched suddenly behind his back, and he stood very still. A little dully, he wondered what was coming.

"I can only hope that you will be sensible and try and look at the matter from all points of view." She, too, lit a cigarette, and stared at him deliberately. "In the first place, I suppose I've changed—considerably. And in order to save any misunderstanding, it's just as well that we should both know where we stand."

"You mean you don't love me any more?" said her husband slowly.

"Don't be ridiculous," she cried. "I never said anything of the sort. I'm very fond of you. But"—she stirred a little restlessly in her chair—"I've never believed, as you know, in beating about the bush, and there is another man whom I'm very fond of, too."

The dull, sickening blow, which wellnigh stunned him mentally, showed not at all on Hugh Massingham's face.

"One can't help these things," continued his wife gravely, "and I think you'll agree that it is best for everybody to discuss matters as they are—rather than go on living as if they were otherwise."

"Quite," he murmured grimly. "Please go on."

"We need neither of us insult our intelligences by regarding the matter in the light that our fathers and mothers would have looked at it. The fact that a married woman falls in love with a man who is not her husband is not a thing to hold up hands of pious horror at—or so it seems to me; it is just a thing which has happened, and if one is sensible, the best course is to see the most satisfactory way out for all concerned. Don't you agree?"

"Your argument certainly has its points," concurred Hugh. Great heavens! was this conversation real, or was he dreaming?

"Jimmy Clements has kissed me—but that's all."

His wife was speaking again, and he listened dully.

"Jimmy Clements! Is that the man's name?"

He threw his cigarette, long gone out, into the grate.

"Yes—that is the man. He's been asking me for months to go away with him, but I've refused. I didn't tell him why, but I'm going to tell you now. I wouldn't go until you'd come home, and I'd seen you again, and made sure—that——" She hesitated, and the man laughed grimly.

"Made sure that you really did love Mr. Jimmy Clements more than me! Dreadful thing to make a second mistake."

"Put it that way, if you like," she answered quietly. "Though it wasn't from quite such baldly selfish motives that I refused to go with him. I tried, Hugh, to argue the thing out as best I could; I tried to be fair to him and to you. I realized that I might be wrong—that I didn't really love him——" the man by the fireplace made a quick, convulsive movement— "and, anyway, I realized that I must give you a chance if you want to have it. If, after what I've told you, you decide to let me go—well and good; we can arrange details easily. If, on the other hand, you refuse, and in the course of a month, say, I find that I was not mistaken, and that I'm fonder of Jimmy than I am of you, well, I shall have to take the law into my own hands."

Hugh Massingham laughed shortly.

"I see," he answered. "You have put things very clearly." He turned on her with an expressionless face. "I take it, then, that as matters stand at present, I am on trial."

"If you wish," she said. "I realize that you have a perfect right to refuse that trial, and tell me to go; but, after all your goodness to me, I could not do less than offer it to you."

"Your generosity touches me," he remarked grimly. "And——"

It was at that moment that the servant opened the door and announced: "Mr. Clements."

"Are you coming to Hector's, Delia?"

An immaculately clad young man entered, with his evening overcoat on his arm and a top-hat in his hand, to stop in momentary confusion on seeing Hugh.

"I beg your pardon," he muttered. "I—er——"

"This is my husband, Jimmy," said Delia composedly, and the two men bowed.

"My wife was just talking about you, Mr. Clements," said Hugh impassively, while he took in every detail of the other's face—the mouth, well-formed, but inclined to weakness; the eyes that failed to meet his own; the hands, beautifully manicured, which twitched uneasily as they played with his white scarf.

Good God! This effeminate clothes-peg! To be on trial against—this! He stifled a contemptuous laugh; there was Delia to be considered.

"Pray don't let me detain you from Hector's; though I'm not quite certain what it is."

"A night-club, Mr. Massingham," said the other nervously. "But perhaps Mrs. Massingham would prefer not to go this evening?"

"I am convinced my wife would prefer nothing of the sort," returned Hugh, and for a moment his eyes and Delia's met. Then with a faint shrug she stood up. "Four years in Mesopotamia do not improve one's dancing." He strolled to the door. "I shall

wander round to the club, my dear," he murmured.
"And, by the way, with regard to your offer, I accept
it."

"Good Lord, darling!" whispered Clements, as the
door closed. "I'd got no idea he'd come back. What
an awful break!"

But she was staring at the door, and seemed not to
hear his remark. It was only as he kissed her that
she came back to the reality of his presence.

"Let's go and dance, Jimmy," she said feverishly.
"I feel like dancing—to-night."

III

"Halloa, Hugh! Got back, have you?"

The words greeted Massingham as he strolled
through the club smoking-room in search of a seat,
and with a start he looked at the speaker. So engrossed
had he been in his own thoughts that he had failed to
notice his brother-in-law, John Ferrers, till he was right
on top of him.

"Yes, John—back," he said slowly. "Back to-day
—after four years."

Ferrers grunted and leaned over to pull up a chair.
Something wrong—quite obviously. A man doesn't
come to his club on the first evening home after four
years, under normal circumstances.

"Have a drink!" Ferrers beckoned a waiter and
gave the order. "How do you think Delia is looking?"

"Very well," said Hugh quietly. "Very well indeed. She has gone off to a place called Hector's
to-night."

Ferrers paused in the act of lighting his pipe, and
looked at him in mild amazement. "Delia gone to
Hector's to-night! What the devil has she done that
for?"

"A gentleman of the name of Clements—Jimmy

Clements—arrived in his glad rags after dinner," remarked Hugh. "She went to Hector's with him—I came here."

"Young Clements!" muttered Ferrers. "I didn't know——" He looked quickly at Hugh; then he resumed lighting his pipe. "If I were you, Hugh—of course, I know it's not my business—but if I were you I wouldn't let Delia go about too much with young Clements. He's a—well, he's a useless young puppy to begin with, and his reputation is nothing to write home about in addition."

"Ah! is that so?" Hugh lay back in his chair and stared at his brother-in-law. "I had already classed him as a puppy; but I didn't think he was big enough to have a reputation of any kind—good or bad."

"My dear fellow—he's young, he's good-looking, and he's sufficiently well off to be able to do nothing. Also I believe he dances perfectly. Whether it's those assets, or whether it's something which the vulgar masculine eye is unable to appreciate, I can't tell you. But I do know this: that three ordinary, decent, sensible young married women of my acquaintance have made the most infernal fools of themselves over that youth." John Ferrers shook his head. "I'm hanged if I know what it is. It must be the war or something. But a lot of these girls seem to have gone completely off the rails."

He sighed ponderously; he was a good-hearted individual, was John Ferrers, but anything which deviated from his idea of the normal generally called forth a mild outburst. Also, he was very fond of his sister.

And really it wasn't quite the thing to go barging off to a night-club the day your husband returned after four years. Especially with young Clements. It came back to his mind now, as he sat there pulling at his pipe, that off and on he had seen her about with the fellow; in the park, and twice at a theatre. Also having supper once at the Ritz, and two or three times at dinner. Of course, there was nothing in it, but—still —confound it! the first night after four years.

"Are you going to take Delia out East with you, old boy?"

"That depends, John, on a variety of circumstances," remarked Hugh quietly.

"I would if I were you," grunted the other. "It's been lonely for her, you know, and——" He became very interested in his pipe. "I wouldn't take too much notice of that young ass. Delia is far too sensible a girl to make a fool of herself over any man —let alone Clements. But"—and John Ferrers drained his glass decisively—"the next time I see her, I shall tell her a few home truths."

"Oh, no, John!" said Hugh, "you won't. I don't want you to allude to the matter at all. But I want you to tell me one thing. In those three cases you mentioned, did any question of divorce come up?"

"Divorce!" John Ferrers sat up in his chair abruptly. "What the deuce are you talking about?"

"The three cases you were speaking of," returned Hugh imperturbably. "What manner of man is this Clements, if things pass the dallying stage and come to a head?"

"Oh!" His brother-in-law sat back, relieved. "I can't tell you more than that Mr. James Clements does not strike me as the type who would ever face the music. While he can take his pleasure with other men's wives, I don't think he has any intention of providing himself with one of his own."

"That was my diagnosis of his character," said Hugh. "I'm glad you confirm it."

John Ferrers rose as another member came up. "Will you join us, Hugh? Snooker."

"No, thanks, old boy. Not to-night. So long."

With a faint smile he watched his worthy brother-in-law as he crossed the room. Then, having ordered another drink, he lay back in his chair and closed his eyes. And it was not till an hour later that he rose and wrote a short letter to a certain firm of shipping agents. Then he left the club, with the look on his face of a man who had made up his mind.

IV

It was Hugh himself who opened the door of the flat at two o'clock in the morning and let in his wife. Clements was standing behind her on the landing, and Hugh nodded to him.

"Had a good time?" he asked genially, standing aside to let Delia in. "Come in, Mr. Clements, and have a nightcap before you go. No? Really, I insist."

Gently but firmly he propelled his reluctant guest towards the dining-room. The last thing which Mr. James Clements wanted was a drink in his present surroundings. In fact, Mr. James Clements wanted more than words can express to retire to his lonely bachelor couch, where he could meditate at leisure on how best to extricate himself from a situation which had suddenly ceased to appeal to his somewhat peculiar sense of humour. Really he had credited Delia with a little more knowledge of the rules of the game. For months he'd been suggesting that there were possibilities by the sad sea waves at a delightful little fishing village down in Cornwall; or if that was too far afield he knew of a charming little hotel on the upper reaches of the Thames. In fact, the whole of his vast experience in such matters would have been at her disposal, and for no rhyme or reason, so far as he could see, she had continually refused his suggestion. And he was not used to being refused. Up to a point,

of course, a little coyness and hesitation was delightful; but pushed to an extreme it became tedious. And
then, to cap everything, on the very night when this
large and somewhat uncouth-looking husband had returned from the back of beyond, Delia had become
serious.

Hector's had not been a success; though he had
manfully tried to be his own bright self. But there
had been long silences—rather awkward silences—
when he had been conscious that Delia was studying
him—almost as if he was a stranger to her. And
since he had an uneasy suspicion that he had not altogether shone during his meeting with her husband, he
had found things increasingly difficult as the evening
wore on.

"Say when, Mr. Clements." Massingham was pouring some whisky into a glass, and he stepped up to the
table.

"That's enough, thanks. Yes, soda, please. And
then I must be off."

"The night is yet young," said his host, "and I
rather want to have a talk with you, Mr. Clements."

The youngster looked up quickly at the words; then
he glanced at Delia, who was staring at her husband
with a slight frown.

"Rather late, isn't it?" he murmured.

Massingham smiled genially. "Two—late! You
surprise me, Mr. Clements. I thought that was about
the time some of you people started to live." He
splashed some soda into his own glass. "It's about
my wife—about Delia. Absurd to call her anything
but Delia to you, isn't it? I mean, we three need not
stand on formality."

Clements stiffened slightly; then, because he was
painfully aware that his hands were beginning to
tremble, he put them in his pockets.

"Really, Mr. Massingham," he laughed slightly, "you're very kind." Surely to Heaven she hadn't told her husband—anything.

"Not at all," returned Hugh. "Not at all, my dear fellow. It is absurd—as you said yourself, my dear, earlier in the evening—for us to become in any way agitated or annoyed over an unfortunate but very natural occurrence. And I consider it very natural, Clements, that you should have fallen in love with my wife. I regard it in many respects as a compliment to myself."

His eyes were fixed steadily on the other's face, and a wave of contemptuous disgust surged up in him, though outwardly he gave no sign. The pitiful indecision of this king of lady-killers: the weak mouth, loose and twitching—surely Delia could see for herself what manner of thing it was. But his wife was sitting motionless, staring in front of her, and gave no sign.

"I—er, really," stammered Clements.

"Don't apologize, my dear fellow—don't apologize. As I said, it's a most natural thing, and though this discussion may seem at first sight a trifle bizarre, yet if you think it over it's much the best manner of dealing with the situation."

"Er—quite."

Clements shifted uneasily on his feet, and endeavoured feverishly to regain his self-control. Of course, the whole thing was farcical and Gilbertian; at the same time, just at the moment it appeared remarkably real. And he couldn't make up his mind how to take this large, imperturbable man.

"I told my husband, Jimmy," said Delia, speaking for the first time, "that we were in love with one another—and that you'd asked me to go away with you."

With intense amusement Hugh watched Clements'
jaw drop, though his wife, still staring in front of her,
noticed nothing.

"Most kind of you," remarked Hugh affably, and
Delia looked at him quickly. "Most flattering. But
my wife apparently decided that it wouldn't be quite
fair to me—so she waited till I came home. And
now I'm on trial—so to speak."

Clements sat down in a chair; his legs felt strangely
weak.

"The trouble is," continued Hugh, "that circumstances have arisen only to-night which prevent me
standing on trial. I found a letter waiting for me at
my club which necessitates my return to the East at
once—probably for a year."

"By Jove—really!" Clements sat up; the situation
looked a little brighter.

"Going East at once?" Delia was staring at him
puzzled.

"I'm afraid I must," returned her husband. "And
so it makes things a little awkward, doesn't it? You
see, Mr. Clements, my wife's proposal was this. If
after a few weeks of my presence she still found that
she preferred you to me, she was going to tell me so
straight out. Then—since, as I think you will agree,
a woman must always be a man's first consideration
—I would have effaced myself, gone through the
necessary formalities to allow her to divorce me, and
left her free to marry you. If, on the other hand,
she had found that after all she could not return your
devotion—well, we should then have gone on as we
are. Perhaps not exactly the Church's idea of morality
—but for all that, very fair. Don't you agree?"

Clements nodded; speech was beyond his power.

"Now," continued Hugh, lighting a cigarette, "this
sudden necessity for me to go East has upset her plan.

I can't wait for those few weeks of test, and so we are confronted with a difficulty. I feel that it is not fair to keep her from you for a year or possibly longer; on the other hand, I feel that it is rather hard luck on me to relinquish her without a struggle. You said, Mr. Clements? Sorry; I thought you spoke." He flicked the ash off his cigarette, and, crossing the room, he opened a bureau on the other side. "And so I've evolved a plan," he remarked, coming back again with a pack of cards in his hand. "A time-honoured method of settling things where there are two alternatives, and one which I suggest can be used with advantage here. We will each cut a card, Mr. Clements. If I win, Delia comes East with me—on the clear understanding, my dear, that you may leave me at any moment and return to Mr. Clements. I wouldn't like you to think for an instant that I am proposing to deprive you of your absolute free will whichever way the cards go. If I lose, on the other hand, I go East alone, and the necessary information to enable you to institute divorce proceedings will be sent you as soon as possible."

His wife rose quickly, and stood in front of him. "I'll come East with you, Hugh—anyway, for a time. It's only fair."

"Quite," agreed Clements. "It's only fair."

"Not at all," remarked Massingham decidedly. "I wouldn't dream of accepting such a sacrifice. It's a totally different matter if I win it at cards: then I shall hold you to it. Otherwise I go East alone. I have, I think, a certain say in the matter, and my mind is made up."

He turned to Clements, who was staring at him open-mouthed: then he glanced at Delia, and she, for the first time, was looking at Jimmy Clements.

"I suppose," he remarked suddenly, "that I'm not

making any mistake? You do wish to marry Delia, don't you, Mr. Clements?"

For a moment that gentleman seemed to find difficulty in speaking. Then—"Of course," he muttered. "Of course."

"Good!" said Massingham. "Then we'll cut. Ace low—low wins."

He put the pack on a small table by the other man: then he turned away.

"Cut—please."

"But, Hugh,"—his wife laid her hand on his arm—"it's impossible—it's——"

"Not at all, Delia. It's all quite simple. Have you cut?"

"I've cut the King of Hearts." Clements was standing up. "So it looks as if I lose." His voice seemed hardly to indicate that the blow had prostrated him.

Massingham turned round, while his wife's breath came sharply.

"It does—undoubtedly," he remarked. "Yes—mine's the two of clubs. So you come, Delia." He broke off abruptly, his eyes fixed on the chair in which Clements had been sitting. The next moment he stepped forward and pulled a card from the crack between the seat and the side. "The ace of diamonds," he said slowly. "What is this card doing here? I don't quite understand, Mr. Clements. Ace low—low wins—and the ace of diamonds in your chair. I didn't watch you cut—but did you not want to win?"

"I—I—don't know how it got there," stammered Clements foolishly. "I didn't put it there."

"Then one rather wonders who did," said Massingham coldly. "It makes things a little difficult."

For a moment or two there was silence: then Delia spoke.

"On the contrary," she remarked icily, "it seems

to me to make them very easy. Good night, Mr. Clements. I shall not be at home to you in future."

And when Hugh Massingham returned a few minutes later, having shown the speechless and semi-dazed Clements the front door, his wife had gone to her room.

"Undoubtedly one rather wonders who did," he murmured to himself with a faint smile. "But I think —I think, it was a good idea."

v

"It was a sort of infatuation, Hugh. I can't explain it." With her arm through his—she hadn't quite found her sea-legs yet—they were walking slowly up and down the promenade deck of the liner.

He smiled gently.

"Doesn't need any explanation, darling," he answered. "It's happened before: it will happen again. There are quite a number of Mr. James Clements at large—more's the pity."

"I know," she said. "I know that. But somehow he seemed different."

"HE always does." For a while they continued their walk in silence. "Quite cured, little girl?"

"Quite, absolutely." She squeezed his arm. "I think I was well on the way to being cured, before —before he cheated. And that finished it."

"Ah!" Hugh stopped a moment to light a cigarette.

"It simply defeats me how, after all he said, he could have done such a thing."

"I wouldn't let it worry you, sweetheart. The matter is of little importance. Halloa! What do these people want?"

"Glad to see you about again, Mrs. Massingham." An officer in the Indian Army, returning from leave, and his wife came up. "Would you and your husband care to make up a four at Bridge?"

"Would you, dear?" She turned to him, and Massingham smiled.

"You go, Delia. You'll be able to find a fourth, and you've walked enough. I never play cards, myself."

"What a refreshing individual," laughed the officer's wife. "Does it bore you?"

"Intensely," murmured Hugh. "And I'm such a bad player."

He watched his wife go away with them: then, leaning over the rail, he commenced to fill his pipe. Away to starboard, like a faint smudge on the horizon, lay the north coast of Africa: two days in front was Malta. And then—— Surreptitiously he put a hand into his breast pocket and pulled out a photograph. Yes: it had been a good idea.

XXXIV   A QUESTION OF PERSONALITY

I

THE personally conducted tour round Frenton's Steel Works paused, as usual, on reaching the show piece of the entertainment. The mighty hammer, operated with such consummate ease by the movement of a single lever, though smaller than its more celebrated brother at Woolwich Arsenal, never failed to get a round of applause from the fascinated onlookers. There was something almost frightening about the deadly precision with which it worked, and the uncanny accuracy of the man who controlled it. This time it would crash downwards delivering a blow which shook the ground: next time it would repeat the performance, only to stop just as the spectators were bracing themselves for the shock—stop with such mathematical exactitude that the glass of a watch beneath it would be cracked but the works would not be damaged.

For years now, personally conducted tours had come round Frenton's works. Old Frenton was always delighted when his friends asked him if they might take their house-parties round: he regarded it as a compliment to himself. For he had made the works, watched them grow and expand till now they were known throughout the civilized world. They were just part of him, the fruit of his brain—born of labour and hard work, and nurtured on the hard-headed business capacity of the rugged old Yorkshireman. He was a millionaire now, many times over, but he could still recall the day when sixpence extra a day had meant the difference between chronic penury and affluence. And in those far-off days there had come a second resolve into his mind to keep the first and ever present one company. That first one had been with him ever since he could remember anything—the resolve to succeed; the second one became no less deep rooted. When he did succeed he'd pay his men such wages that there would never be any question of sixpence a day making a difference. The labourer was worthy of his hire: out of the sweat of his own brow John Frenton had evolved that philosophy for himself. . . .

And right loyally he had stuck to it. When success came, and with it more and more, till waking one morning he realized that the *big* jump had been taken, and that henceforth Frenton's would be one of the powers in the steel world, he did not forget. He paid his men well—almost lavishly: all he asked was that they should work in a similar spirit. And he did more. From the memories of twenty years before he recalled the difference between the two partners for whom he had then been working. One of them had never been seen in the works save as an aloof being from another world, regarding his automatons with an uninterested but searching eye: the other had known every one of his men by name, and had treated them as his own personal friends. And yet his eye was just as searching. . . . But—what a difference: what an enormous difference!

And so John Frenton had learned and profited by the example which stared him in the face: things might perhaps be different to-day if more employers had learned that lesson, too. To him every man he employed was a personal friend: again all he asked was that they should regard him likewise. . . .

"Boys," he had said to them on one occasion, when a spirit of unrest had been abroad in the neighbouring works, "if you've got any grievance, there's only one thing I ask. Come and get it off your chests to me: don't get muttering and grousing about it in corners. If I can remedy it, I will: if I can't, I'll tell you why. Anyway, a talk will clear the air. . . ."

In such manner had John Frenton run his works: in such manner had he become a millionaire and found happiness as well. And then had come the great grief of his life. His wife had died when Marjorie, the only child, was born. Twenty years ago the sweet, kindly woman who had cheered him through the burden and heat of the day had died in giving him Marjorie. They had been married eight years, and when she knew that their hopes were going to be realized, it seemed as if nothing more could be wanting to complete their happiness. The stormy times were over: success had come. And now . . . a child.

When the doctor told John Frenton he went mad. He cursed Fate: he cursed the wretched brat that had come and taken away his woman. For weeks he refused to see it: and then Time, the Great Healer, dulled the agony. Instead of a wife—a daughter:

and on the girl he lavished all the great wealth of love of which his rugged nature was capable.   He idolized her: and she, because her nature was sweet, remained a charming, unaffected girl.   Some day she would be fabulously rich, but the fact did not concern her greatly. In fact, she barely thought of it: it would be many long days before her dearly loved dad left her.   And so it had been up to a year ago. . . .   Then she'd met the man.

It would perhaps be more correct to say that the man had met her.   The Honourable Herbert Strongley received an intimation from an aunt of his, that if he would find it convenient to abstain for a while from his normal method of living, and come and stay with her in the country, she would introduce him to a charming girl staying at a neighbouring house.   She specified who the charming girl was, and suggested that though from his birth Herbert had been a fool, he couldn't be such a damned fool as to let this slip.   She was an outspoken lady was this aunt. . . .

The Honourable Herbert made a few inquiries, and left London next day for a protracted stay with his relative.   It took him a week—he possessed a very charming manner did Herbert—before he was formally engaged to Marjorie.   The armament of nineteen has but little resisting power when exposed to the batteries of a good-looking delightful man of the world who is really bringing all his guns to bear.   And because the man was a consummate actor when he chose to be, he had but little more difficulty in getting through the defences of her father.   Marjorie seemed wonderfully happy: that was the chief thing to John Frenton. And he was getting old: carrying out his usual routine at the works was daily becoming more and more of a strain.   Why not?   He had no son—everything would go to his girl and her husband at his death.   His life-

work would be in their hands. . . . If he'd had his
way, perhaps, he'd have chosen someone with a little
more knowledge of the trade—the Honourable Herbert
didn't know the difference between mild and tool steel:
but after all a happy marriage did not depend on such
technical qualifications. As a man he seemed all that
could be desired, and that was the principal thing that
mattered. He could trust his managers for the
rest. . . .

And so his prospective son-in-law became a prospective partner. Ostensibly he was supposed to be
picking up the tricks of the trade, a performance which
afforded him no pleasure whatever. He loathed work
in any form: he regarded it as a form of partial insanity
—almost a disease. During the hours which he spent
in the office, his reason—such as it was—was only saved
by the help of *Ruff's Guide* and telephonic communica-
tion with his bookmaker. . . . But he was far too
astute a person to run any risks. He was playing for
immeasurably larger stakes than he could afford to
lose, and in addition he was quite genuinely fond of
Marjorie in his own peculiar way. He intended to
marry her, and then, when the old man was dead—
and he was visibly failing—the Honourable Herbert
had his own ideas on the subject of Frenton's Steel
Works. The only trouble was that Frenton's Steel
Works had their own ideas on the subject of the
Honourable Herbert, though that gentleman was
supremely ignorant of the fact. Without a slip he had
acted his part before John Frenton: with just the right
eagerness to learn he had played up to the managers:
but—and it was a big but—he had forgotten the men.
They had never even entered into his calculations, and
it would doubtless have amazed him to hear that he
had entered very considerably into theirs. For the
men did not like the Honourable Herbert—in fact, they

disliked him considerably: and since there was no secret regarding his future—a future which concerned them intimately—this error in the calculations was serious. They were a rough-and-ready crowd, with rough-and-ready ideas of justice and fair play. In addition they idolized Marjorie Frenton and her father to a man. It had taken them about a month to size up the new partner, and that was six months ago. Since then, slowly and inexorably—their brains did not work very quickly—the determination that they would *not* have the Honourable Herbert as John Frenton's successor had crystallized and hardened. For a while they had waited: surely the old man would see for himself that the man was useless. But the old man did not see: the Honourable Herbert still strolled yawning through the works, taking not the slightest notice of any of the hands—the man whom they in future would have to work for. Very good: if old John could not see it for himself, other steps would have to be taken to dispose of the gentleman.

They might have been peaceful steps, but for an incident which had occurred the day before the personally conducted tour already mentioned. It was conducted by the Honourable Herbert himself, and consisted of the house-party staying with John Frenton and Marjorie. The house-party noticed nothing unusual, somewhat naturally: they were bored or interested according to their natures. But as the tour progressed, a look of puzzled wonder began to dawn in Marjorie's eyes. What on earth was the matter with the men?

It was some time since she had been in the works, and the change was the more pronounced because of it. Instead of cheery smiles, sullen faces and black looks followed them wherever they went: she sensed that the whole atmosphere of the place was hostile. And after a while the uneasy suspicion began to form in her mind that the object of this hostility was her fiancé. She took advantage of the halt at the steam-hammer to draw him on one side.

"What on earth is the matter with the men, Herbert?" she demanded. "I've never seen them like this before."

The Honourable Herbert cursed under his breath. He, too, had been painfully aware of the scowls which had followed them, though he had hoped against hope that Marjorie would not notice. Moreover, he had known only too well the reason of the demonstration. And now it would come to old John's ears. . . . He cursed again, as the girl looked at him with questioning eyes.

"Lord knows, my dear," he answered abruptly. "I suppose the blighters have got some fancied grievance."

" 'Blighters! Fancied grievance!' " The girl stepped back a pace in genuine amazement. "Then why don't you have them together and ask them, like daddy used to do?"

As she spoke she glanced over his shoulder, and for a moment her eyes met those of a man standing behind him. He was looking at her deliberately and intently, and suddenly, to her surprise, he held up a twisted slip of paper in his hand. Then he pointed to the floor and turned away. It had been done so quickly that for a while she could hardly believe her eyes. One of the men, trying to pass a secret note. . . . To her. . . . What on earth *was* the matter with everybody? . . .

Once again the man looked at her with the suspicion of a smile on his face, and she frowned quickly. He was impertinent, this youngster, and she turned to her fiancé. She remembered now that the last time she had been round she had seen him working on a lathe: that

it had struck her then that he had seemed different from
the others—his hands, oily though they were: the cool
unembarrassed look in his eyes: his way of speaking.
. . . Almost as if he had been her equal. . . . And
now he was presuming on her kindness then. . . .

Her hands clenched involuntarily as she looked at
her fiancé.

"What is the name of that man with his back half
towards us, over there?" she demanded. For the
moment the "fancied grievance" was forgotten in more
personal matters.

The Honourable Herbert, thankful for the respite,
swung round. Then as he saw the subject of her
question his jaw set in an ugly line.

"John Morrison," he answered shortly. "And if I
had my way I'd sack him on the spot. A useless, argu-
mentative, insubordinate swine. . . ."

And it was as this graceful eulogy concluded that
John Morrison looked at her again. Her fiancé had
moved away, and she was standing alone. For a
moment she hesitated: then she, too, turned to join the
rest of the party. And lying on the ground where she
had been, was her handkerchief. . . .

It was done on the spur of the moment—a feminine
impulse. And the instant she had done it, she regretted
it. But there had been something in her fiancé's voice
as he spoke that had come as a shock to her: something
ugly and vicious; something new as far as she was concerned. Though what that had to do with John
Morrison passing her a note was obscure.

"You dropped your handkerchief, Miss Frenton."
A courteous, well-bred voice was speaking close behind
her, and she turned slowly to find John Morrison holding it out to her.

"Thank you," she answered. Rolled up inside it
she could feel the twisted wisp of paper, and as the

Honourable Herbert came up with an angry look on his face she hesitated.

"What do you want?" he snapped at the man.

"Miss Frenton dropped her handkerchief, sir," answered Morrison impassively.

The other grunted.

"All right. Get on with your work."

Marjorie hesitated no longer. With a sort of blinding certainty there flashed into her mind the conviction that something was wrong. She didn't stop to analyse her thoughts: she merely felt convinced that John Morrison was not an insubordinate swine, and that in the note she held in her hand lay the clue to a great deal that was puzzling her at the moment. And so with a gracious smile at the man she slipped her handkerchief into her bag. . . .

It was ten minutes before she found an opportunity of reading the note. It was in pencil, and the hand-writing was small and neat.

"It is immaterial to me what action you take on receiving this," it ran. "But if you are in any way interested in your fiancé's future, I most strongly advise you to suggest a change of air to him. Of his capabilities as a husband, you must decide for yourself: of his capabilities as the boss of Frenton's, other people have already decided, as possibly you may have noticed this morning. So get him away, and *keep him away*. You haven't got much time."

"Get him away, and keep him away." The words danced before the girl's eyes. She was conscious of no anger against John Morrison: merely of a stunned surprise. The thing was so totally unexpected. "Of his capabilities as the boss of Frenton's, other people have already decided." And even as she read and re-read the sentence, she found that she was actually asking herself the question—"Was it so totally unexpected after all?" That matters should have come to a head in such an abrupt way was a staggering shock: but . . . She crumpled the note into her bag once more, and walked slowly towards the waiting cars. A hundred little half-defined thoughts came crowding in on her memory: a hundred little things which had not struck her at the time—or was it that she hadn't allowed them to strike her?—now arrayed themselves in massed formation in front of her.

She paused with her foot on the step of the car. The Honourable Herbert was solicitously bending over a stout and boring aunt of hers, and she watched him dispassionately. "Of his capabilities as a husband, you must decide for yourself." Impertinent. . . . And yet she was not conscious of any resentment.

"Come up to lunch, Herbert," she said, as he stepped over to her. "I want to talk to you afterwards."

He raised his eyebrows slightly.

"I shall be very busy this afternoon, dear."

"I think the works will stand your absence for one afternoon," she remarked quietly, and he bit his lip.

"I'll be there, Marjorie." He fumbled with her rug. "One o'clock sharp, I suppose."

He stood back, and the cars rolled off.

"What a charming man your fiancé is, my dear!" cooed the elderly female sitting beside Marjorie. "So polite: so . . . so . . . impressive."

The girl smiled a little absently, and nodded. "Impressive. . . ." It struck her that the word exactly described Herbert. He was impressive. And then because she was loyal clean through, she started to fan herself into a furious rage at the abominable impertinence of this wretched man John Morrison. Herbert was right: he was an insubordinate swine. . . . How dare he—how *dare he*—hand her such a note! He

ought to be sacked at once. She would tell Herbert
about it after lunch, and he would explain matters. Of
course he would explain—of course. . . .

John Frenton was standing on the steps as the cars
drove up, and impulsively she went up to him.

"Herbert is coming to lunch, daddy," she cried,
putting her arm through his.

"Is he, darling," said the old man, patting her hand.
"That's all right." He turned to the rest of the party
as they came up. "Well—what do you think of my
works? None in England to beat 'em, my friends, not
if you search from John o' Groats to Land's End. And
as for a strike, it's unknown, sir, unknown. . . . My
men don't do it, whatever other firms may do."

He passed into the house talking animatedly to one
of his guests, and for a while Marjorie stood, staring
over the three miles of open country to where the high
chimneys of Frenton's Steel Works stuck up like
slender sticks against the dull background of smoke.
Then with a little sigh she, too, went up the steps into
the house.

II

"Herbert, I don't quite understand about this
morning." She was in her own sitting-room, and her
fiancé, standing in front of the fire, was lighting a
cigarette. "What is the matter at the works?"

All through lunch the Honourable Herbert, in the
intervals of being charming to the ghastly collection of
old bores—as he mentally dubbed them—who formed
the party, had been puzzling out the best line to take
at this interview. That the girl had seen that something was wrong was obvious: no one but a blind
person could have failed to notice it. And now that
the interview had actually started he was still undecided. . . .

"My dear little girl," he remarked gently, sitting down beside her and taking her hand. . . . "Why worry about it? As I told you this morning, some little grievance, I expect—which I'll inquire into. . . ."

The girl shook her head.

"It's something very much more than a grievance," she said, quietly but positively. "There's something radically wrong, Herbert. I want to know what it is."

"Good heavens! Marjorie,"—there was a hint of impatience in his voice—"haven't I told you I'll inquire into it? Do be reasonable, my dear girl."

"I'm being perfectly reasonable," she answered, still in the same quiet tone. "But I don't understand how things have got as far as they have without any steps on your part. You say you don't know what's the matter. Daddy would have known long ago—and remedied it." The Honourable Herbert's opinion of daddy, at that moment, remained unspoken. . . . "You see," went on the girl, "they're just part of daddy, are the works. He was only saying to-day that he had never had any strikes. And now, when he's getting old . . ." She stirred restlessly in her chair, and looked at the fire. "Of his capabilities as the boss of Frenton's, other people have already decided." The words danced before her in the flames, and almost passionately she turned to the man beside her. "Don't you see," she cried, "don't you realize that I feel responsible? You're there—as a partner—because you're my fiancé. That's the only reason. The works will come to me when daddy dies: I shall be responsible for them—I and my husband. . . ."

"You could always turn the thing into a Limited Company, darling," murmured the man, "if you found it too great a strain." He waited for an answer, but none came, and after a while he continued in an easy, reassuring voice. "Of course, I understand, my little Marjorie, your feelings on the matter."

"Do you?" she interrupted slowly. "I wonder."

"I'm only a beginner," he went on, and his voice was a trifle hurt. "One can't pick up all sorts of technical knowledge in a month, or even a year. . . ."

"Technical knowledge isn't wanted, Herbert—so much as human knowledge, personality. I could run those works—with the help of Mr. Thompson and the other managers. . . . Ah, dear!"—she bent forward quickly—"I don't want to hurt you. But I just can't imagine what would have happened if dad had gone round the works with us this morning. . . . I believe it would have almost killed him. . . ."

"Very well, dear, if those are your feelings there is no more to be said." With quiet dignity her fiancé rose to his feet. "If you are not satisfied with me . . ." He left the sentence unfinished.

"I am," she cried quickly. "I am, Herbert—perfectly satisfied. But . . ."

"Then don't think any more about it," he said quickly. "I'll go down, little girl, and find out what the trouble is. And then I'll put it right, and let you know. . . ."

"You'll let me know this evening, won't you?"

For a moment he hesitated.

"If possible, Marjorie. . . ."

"But of course it's possible," she cried impulsively. "At *our* works, you've only got to ask. . . . Have the men together and ask. . . ."

The Honourable Herbert's face was expressionless as he bent over and kissed her.

"Quite so, darling," he murmured. "Quite so. Don't worry about it any more. . . ."

And it was not until he was at the wheel of his car driving back to his office that he gave vent to his real feelings. "Ask the men?" He saw himself doing it. The cursed luck of the thing. But for that one episode yesterday, he could have bluffed it through, until they were married at any rate. After that he had never had an intention of carrying on a deception which bored him to extinction: there would be no need to. . . . But now. . . . The marvel to him was that they hadn't struck already. And once they did, and John Frenton came down to the works and the cause became known—good-bye to his hopes of the future. Marjorie would never forgive him. And as the realization of what that would entail struck him seriously for the first time, he swore savagely. He had been banking on the Frenton millions not only morally but actually. And if they failed to materialize. . . . Once again he cursed under his breath. . . .

It was after dinner that night that Marjorie made up her mind. She had twice rung up her fiancé with no result. The first time he had not come in: the second he had just gone out—to the local theatre, the servant believed. With a frown she hung up the receiver, and turning away walked slowly to her father's study.

"I want to see the book of addresses, daddy," she said quietly.

It was one of old Frenton's hobbies to have the address of every one of his men entered in a large book, which enabled periodical gifts to arrive if there was any illness in the family.

"It's over there, girlie," he said, with a sleepy smile. "What do you want it for?"

"Mrs. Tracy has just had a baby," she announced, turning over the leaves.

But it was not under the T's that she looked. Mendle, Morgan, Morrison . . . Morrison, John, 9,

Castle Road. . . . Thoughtfully she closed the book, and put it back in its proper place. Then she crossed the room, and kissed her father lovingly on his bald head.

"You're a dear old thing," she whispered. "Go and play billiards with the general. . . ."

A few minutes later she was driving her little runabout towards Castle Road. An onlooker, had he been able to see under the thick veil she wore, would have been struck with the likeness of the small determined face to that of old John Frenton. Like her father—once she came to a decision, she required some stopping. And since her fiancé had left after lunch she had become more and more uneasy, more and more certain that something was being kept from her—something which concerned the Honourable Herbert pretty closely. And if it concerned him, it concerned her: she, as she had told him, had brought him into the firm. . . .

Castle Road proved to be a better neighbourhood than she had expected. Most of the hands preferred to live nearer to the works, and this street struck her as being more suitable for well-to-do clerks. But she was far too preoccupied to worry overmuch with such trifles. John Morrison and the truth were what she wanted. She left the car at the end of the street, and walked to Number 9.

Yes. Mr. Morrison was at home. A disapproving sniff preceded the opening of a sitting-room door, which closed with a bang behind her. She heard the steps of the landlady going down the stairs, and then she took an uncertain pace forward.

". . . I . . ." she stammered. Undoubtedly the man in evening clothes facing her was John Morrison, but he looked so different. And whoever had heard of a factory hand getting into a smoking-jacket for dinner? . . . And the room. . . . The prints on the walls: the big roll-top desk: golf-clubs in the corner, and to cap everything—a gun-case.

"I think there must be some mistake," she said haltingly. "I must apologize. . . . I . . ." She turned as if to leave the room. . . .

"I hope not, Miss Frenton." She gave a little start: she had hoped he had not recognized her. "Won't you come and sit down by the fire and tell me what I can do for you?"

After a moment's hesitation she did as he said.

"You must admit, Mr. Morrison,"—she loosened her veil as she spoke—"that there is some excuse for my surprise."

The man glanced round the room with a slight smile.

"Yes," he murmured. "I can understand it causing you a slight shock. Had I known you were coming I would have tried to make it less—er—startling."

"What on earth are you doing in the works?" she asked curiously.

"My poor concerns will keep, Miss Frenton." A charming smile robbed the words of any offence. "I don't think it was to discuss me that you came to-night. My note, I suppose. Am I to be rebuked?"

"No," she answered slowly. "I am to be enlightened, please."

"Have you spoken to Strongley about it?" he asked, after a pause.

She raised her eyebrows.

"I asked *Mr.* Strongley what was the matter with the men, after lunch to-day."

"I stand corrected." With an expressionless face John Morrison held out a heavy silver cigarette-box to her, but she shook her head.

"No, thank you," she said curtly, and he replaced

the box on the table. "But please smoke yourself, if you want to."

"And what did Mr. Strongley say?" asked the man.

"Nothing." She stared at the fire with a little frown. "He didn't seem to know: but he said he'd find out and ring me up. He hasn't done so, and I want to know, Mr. Morrison—know the truth. There's something radically wrong down there. What is it?"

John Morrison thoughtfully lit a cigarette and leaned against the mantelpiece, staring down at her.

"May I ask you one or two questions, Miss Frenton: questions which, though they may sound impertinent, are not intended in that spirit?"

"Yes." She looked up at him steadily. "But I don't promise to answer."

"How long ago did you meet Herbert Strongley?"

"About a year."

"And how long was it before you got engaged to him?"

She shifted a little in her chair.

"Not very long," she said at length.

He did not press the point: though a faint smile hovered for a moment on his lips.

"Not very long," he repeated softly. "Are you quite sure, Miss Frenton—and this is a very important question—are you quite sure that you haven't made a mistake?"

"It may be important, but it's one I absolutely refuse to answer." She faced him angrily. "What business is it of yours?"

"Absolutely none—at the moment," he said quietly. "But you've come to me to find out what the trouble is. And if you have not made any mistake with regard to your engagement, I advise you to carry out the suggestion contained in my note. Get your fiancé away from

Frenton's, and keep him away, both before and after your marriage.   It will come, I imagine, as a blow to your father, but you can easily turn it into a company."

"You mean—that the men don't like Herbert?" She forced herself to ask the question.

"I mean," he answered deliberately, "that the men loathe and detest him, and that only the love they have for you and your father has staved off trouble up till now.   And even that love will fail to avert a crisis after—well, after the regrettable episode that happened yesterday."

"What was it?" she demanded, and her voice sounded dead to the man.

"I don't think we need bother as to what it was," he said quietly.   "Shall we leave it at the fact that however excellent a husband Strongley may make, as a boss of Frenton's he is a complete failure?"   He bit his lip as he saw the look on the girl's face.   Then he went on in the same quiet voice.   "Things like this hurt, Miss Frenton: but you are the type that appreciates frankness.   And I tell you quite openly that the men are after your fiancé.   And I don't blame them."

"You side with them, do you?"   She threw the words at him fiercely.

"Am I not one of them?" he replied gravely.

"You know you're not."   She stood up and faced him.   "You're not one of the ordinary hands.   Look at your evening clothes; look at that gun-case in the corner. . . ."   She paused as she saw the sudden look on his face.   "What is it?"

"Into this room quickly," he whispered.   "You must stop there till he goes.   Good Lord!   What a complication!"

"Who is it?" she cried, startled by his evident agitation.

"Strongley," he whispered. "Heard his voice in the hall. Absolutely unexpected."

He closed the door, and she found herself in his bedroom, just as the landlady ushered in the second visitor.

And if she had been surprised on her first entrance to John Morrison's rooms, it was evident that the Honourable Herbert was even more so.

"Good Lord, man," he spluttered. "Why the glad rags? I—er—of course, it's no business of mine, but your general appearance gave me a bit of a shock."

To the girl listening intensely on the other side of the door it seemed as if a note of relief had crept into her fiancé's voice—relief in which a certain amount of uneasiness was mingled.

"What can I do for you?" John Morrison asked gravely.

"Well—er—don't you know"—undoubtedly the visitor was not at all sure of his ground—"your rooms and that sort of thing have rather knocked me. I mean—er—I'm rather in the soup, Morrison: and I really came round to ask your advice, don't you know. I mean you saw the whole thing—yesterday: and though I'm afraid I lost my temper with you, too, yet even at that time I saw you were different. And—er—I thought . . ."

The Honourable Herbert mopped his forehead and sank into a chair.

"The mere fact that I change for dinner doesn't seem to alter the situation appreciably," said Morrison quietly.

"No, by Jove—I suppose not." The other sat up and braced himself for the plunge. "Well, what the hell am I to do? And what the devil are the men going to do? Are they going to strike?"

"No—I don't think so." Morrison smiled at the

sudden look of relief on Strongley's face. "They're too fond of Mr. Frenton and his daughter. It's you they're after."

"What are they going to do?"

"Give you a pleasant half-hour under the steam-hammer," said Morrison deliberately, and the other rose with a stifled cry. "Just to test your nerves. Let it drop to within an inch to you—then stop it. And if that doesn't expedite your departure—they'll take other steps. . . ."

"But, damn it, Morrison,"—his voice was shaking—"don't you understand I can't go? I—er—good Lord! do you suppose I want to stop here for one second longer than I must? I loathe it. Can't you stop 'em, man: tell 'em I'm clearing the instant I'm——"

"Married," said Morrison quietly.

"Well, yes," said the other. "I'll have to be frank with you—and I can see you'll understand." His eyes strayed round the room. "I admit absolutely that this isn't my line: I detest the show. But old Frenton is wrapped up in these works—and—well—he looks for a son-in-law who will carry on. After I'm married I can explain things to him, don't you know. And until then—well, we must stave off this trouble, Morrison."

"Wouldn't it be a little more straightforward to explain your views to him before the marriage?"

"Perhaps it would have been," said the other, with apparent frankness. "But it's too late now—and then there's that damned show yesterday. That's what I'm so afraid will come out." He stared at the fire. "I didn't mean to hurt the fellow," he went on querulously. "And I'm certain he dropped that spanner on my toe on purpose."

"Still, that hardly seems sufficient justification for slogging a boy, who is not quite all there, over the head with an iron bar, does it?" Almost unconsciously his eyes travelled to the bedroom door as he spoke, and then he grew suddenly rigid. For the door was open, and the girl stood between the two rooms with a look of incredulous horror on her face.

"So that's what was the matter with Jake," she said slowly, and at the sound of her voice Strongley swung round with a violent start.

"Marjorie . . ." he gasped, "what on earth . . ."

"Why didn't you tell me at the beginning?" she demanded, staring at him with level eyes. "Why lie about it? It seems so unnecessary and petty. And then—to hit Jake over the head. . . . You . . . Take it back, please." She laid her engagement ring on the table. "And I think you'd better go—at once. The fault was partially mine; and I wouldn't like them to punish you for my—for my mistake. . . ."

Without another word she turned and left the room. And it was not till the front door banged that Strongley turned his livid face on John Morrison.

"You swine," he muttered. "I believe this was a put-up job."

John Morrison laughed.

"Yes—you told me you were coming, didn't you?"

"No—I didn't tell you," said Strongley slowly, with a vicious look dawning in his eyes. "Which perhaps accounts for the fact that Miss Frenton was here. . . . In your bedroom. . . . How nice. . . . The gentleman workman and the employer's daughter. . . . A charming romance. . . . I should think Mr. Frenton will be delighted to hear it to-morrow. . . ."

Not a muscle on John Morrison's face moved.

"More than delighted, I should imagine. . . . Except that it will be a little stale. Personally, I am going up to tell him to-night." He smiled slightly. "I don't like you, Strongley; I know far too much about

you. But I *did* pass Miss Frenton a note to-day at
the works warning her to get you away. . . ."

"Your solicitude for my welfare is overwhelming,"
sneered Strongley.

"Good heavens!" laughed John Morrison. "I
didn't care a damn about you. I was afraid the men
might get into trouble. Steady! Don't get gay with
me. I'm not half-witted; and I can hit back. . . ."

III

It was in London the following spring that Marjorie
Frenton next saw John Morrison. She had not been
present at the interview with her father—was in
ignorance that it had ever taken place until the next
day. And on that next day John Morrison had
disappeared, leaving no trace. . . . For a while she
had waited, wondering whether he would write—but no
word came. After all, why should he? There was
nothing to write about. . . . It was merely curiosity on
her part—nothing more, of course. . . . A workman
in evening clothes. . . . Enough to make anybody
curious. . . .

And now there he was—three tables away, dining
with a very pretty woman. He hadn't seen her yet.
. . . Probably wouldn't remember her when he did.
. . . After all, why should he? . . . And at that
moment their eyes met. . . .

She looked away at once, and started talking to the
man next to her: but even as she spoke she knew John
Morrison had risen and was coming towards her.

"How are you, Miss Frenton?" She looked up
into his face: met the glint of a smile in the lazy blue
eyes.

"Quite well, thank you, Mr. Morrison," she answered
coldly.

"Hullo, Joe!" A woman opposite had begun to

speak, to stop with a puzzled frown at Marjorie's words. "Morrison! Why Morrison? . . . Have you been masquerading, Joe, under an assumed name?"

"I did for a while, Jane," he said calmly, "to avoid you; you know how you pursued me with eligible girls. . . . Battalions of 'em, Miss Frenton—ranged in rows. I had to disappear stealthily in the dead of night. . . ."

"Well, when are you going to get married?" demanded the woman, laughing.

"Very soon, I hope. . . . I do much better than you, Jane, in these things. The girl I've got my eye on is a girl who summoned several hundred factory hands together; and told 'em she was sorry for a mistake she'd made. And she halted a bit, and stumbled a bit—but she got through with it. . . . And then the men cheered 'emselves sick. . . ."

"Good heavens! Joe. . . . Factory hands!" gasped the woman. "What sort of a girl is she?"

"A perfect topper, Jane." Out of the corner of his eye he glanced at Marjorie, whose eyes were fixed on her plate. "By the way, Miss Frenton, has your father turned his works into a company yet?"

"Not yet," she answered, very low.

"Ah! that's good." He forced her to meet his eyes, and there was something more than a smile on his face now. "Well, I must go back to my sister. . . . And I'll come and call to-morrow if I may. . . . Jane will expose my wicked deceit doubtless. . . ."

"Mad—quite mad," remarked the woman opposite, as he went back to his interrupted dinner. "Morrison, did you say? I knew he wanted to study labour conditions first-hand—why, Heaven knows. He's got works of his own or something. . . . But all the Carlakes are mad. . . . And I'd got a splendid American girl up my sleeve for him. . . ."

"Carlake," said Marjorie, a little faintly. "Is that Lord Carlake?"

"Of course it is, my dear. That's Joe Carlake. . . . Mad as a hatter. . . . I wonder who the girl is. . . ."

XXXV   THE   UNBROKEN   LINE

I

"MY dear man, where have you been buried? You don't seem to know anybody. That's Bobby Landon, Lord Fingarton's only son. Just about to pull off *the* marriage of the season."

I accepted the rebuke meekly: a spell of three years in Africa investigating the question of sleeping-sickness does almost count as burial.

"Oh! is that Lord Landon?" I murmured, glancing across the crowded restaurant at a clean-looking youngster dining with a couple of men. "See—who is he engaged to?"

"You win the bag of nuts," laughed my fair informant. "Robert Landon, only son of Earl Fingarton of Fingarton, is about to marry Cecilie, youngest daughter of the Duke of Sussex. A fuller society announcement can be given if required, bringing out the pleasing union of two historic families in these socialistic days. . . ." She laughed again. "But, speaking the normal mother tongue, a first-class boy is marrying a topping girl, which is all that matters."

"It's all coming back to me," I said slowly. "I'm getting warm. There was another son, wasn't there, and he died."

"I believe so," she answered; "in fact, I know there was. But he died before I was born. That was the first wife's son.   Daddy would be able to tell you all about that."

"What's that, my dear?"   My host leaned across the table with a smile.

"Sir Richard was asking me about Lord Fingarton's family history, old man," she remarked brightly.   "I was telling him that I was slightly on the youthful side, and that you would elucidate the matter in your well-known breezy style. . . ."

"It doesn't require much elucidation," he said slowly.   "It was a mixture of tragedy and good fortune. . . ."

"I remember that the first son died, Bill, but . . ." I paused and waited for him to continue.

"He broke his neck in the hunting-field the day after he came of age.   And the accident broke his mother's heart.   They were absolutely wrapped up in that boy—both of 'em. . . .   Six months later she died in Scotland, at Fingarton. . . ."   He puffed thoughtfully at his cigar, and unconsciously my eyes wandered to the youngster at the neighbouring table.

"And where exactly does the good-fortune part of it come in?" I asked at length.

"This way," he answered.   "They idolized the boy, and he certainly was the first thing in their lives.   But when he died, the thing that came only one degree behind their love for him of necessity took first place. . . .   Family. . . .   While he lived, the two things were synonymous: they both centred in the boy himself. . . .   And he was a splendid boy—better even than this one."   Again he paused, and smoked for a while in silence.   "You see—Betty Fingarton was too old to have another child, when the accident took place . . . I think that fact hastened her death.   And the man who would have come into the title was an outsider of the purest water—a distant cousin of sorts.

. . . Bob used to move about like a man in a dream —dazed with the tragedy of it all. But I remember that even then, before she died, he realized that her death would—how shall I put it—help matters. Not that he ever said anything: but I knew Bob pretty well those days . . . I've lost sight of him a bit since. . . . It was a horrible position for the poor old chap. The Fingartons have kept their line direct since 1450. Family was his God . . . and he idolized Betty. Then she died; and Bob married again. . . . Quite a nice girl, and she made him a thundering good wife. . . . But he told me, the night before he married, that the price of duty could sometimes be passing high. . . . It was with him. . . ."

My host paused and sipped his brandy, while the girl at my side whispered a little breathlessly:

"I didn't know all that, daddy. Poor old Uncle Bob!"

I looked at her inquiringly, and she smiled.

"He's always been uncle to me," she explained. "Though lately I've hardly seen him at all. . . . He buries himself more and more up at Fingarton. . . ."

"And what of the present Lady Fingarton?" I inquired.

"I like her—she's a dear," answered the girl. "Though I think daddy always compares her with the first one." Her father smiled, but said nothing. "She is generally here in Town. . . . She likes to be near Bobby. . . ."

For a while we were silent, while the soft strains of the orchestra stole through the smoke-laden air above the hum of conversation. . . . It had gripped me— the picture painted by Bill Lakington, in his short, clipped sentences. The tragedy of it—and, as he had said, the good fortune, too. . . . Duty: pride of family —aye, they have their price. Mayhap Betty Fingarton was paying her share in the knowledge that the next of the line was not her son. . . . Or did she, with clearer vision, understand the workings of the Great Architect, which at first must have seemed so inscrutable? . . .

"When is the wedding?" I asked.

"In about a month," said the girl. "Everyone will be there."

"Personally," I murmured, "I shall be one of the forty or fifty odd million who won't. So you can send me an account of it."

"Where are you going, Sir Richard?"

"To a little village way up in the outskirts of Skye," I replied with a smile. "More burial, young lady— and more hard work."

"You ought to take a bit of a rest, Dick," said Bill Lakington. "You deserve it. . . ."

"After I've broken the back of the book, I shall," I answered.

"Are you writing a novel, Sir Richard?" inquired the girl.

"No such claim to immortality," I sighed. "My subject is the mode of life of Glossina palpales—with illustrations."

"And who are they when they're at home?" she asked dubiously.

"Flies—whose conduct is not above suspicion. Shall I present you with a copy?"

"Rather. As long as you don't expect me to read it. Hullo! Bob. Going to anything to-night?"

"We're staggering to Daly's, old thing. . . ." With a feeling of mild curiosity I glanced at the boy who had paused by our table on the way out: a clean-cut, good-looking youngster. No outsider, this future seventeenth earl, like the distant cousin. . . . Yes, one could see where the good fortune came in. . . .

We, too, were going to Daly's, and we all passed
out of the restaurant together.   I had a word or two
with the youngster as we waited for the car: he was
keen as mustard on hearing about Africa, and especially
Uganda. . . .

"Everybody is tottering out to the country these
days, Sir Richard, and 'pon my word, I don't blame
'em. . . ."

"If they can, no more do I.   But the head of the
family can't go, my dear boy. . . .   That's the draw-
back to responsibility."

"Do you know Fingarton?"   A gleam came into
his eyes as he spoke.

"I'm afraid I don't," I answered.   "I've never me
your father."

"Go and look him up, if you're in those parts," he
said impulsively.   "It'll do the dear old governor
good. . . .   He's burying himself too much up there,
and it's lonely for him.   I've written and written just
lately, and I can't get any answer out of him. . . .   I
want him to come South—he will for my wedding, of
course—but these last few months, if ever I do get a
line from him, it's in reply to a letter about three weeks
old. . . ."

"Come on, Sir Richard. . . ."   Molly Lakington
was calling me from the car. . . .   "We mustn't miss
the last part of the first act. . . ."

Undoubtedly not, and with a nod to the youngster
I stepped into the car.

"A good lad that, Bill," I remarked.

"Aye . . . a good lad. . . .   But not *quite* so good
as the other," he answered thoughtfully.

"He's good enough for Cecilie, anyway, old man,
and that's saying a good deal," said Molly. . . .

By the light of a passing lamp I saw Bill Lakington's face.   He was smiling quietly to himself, as a

man smiles when he has his own opinion, but refuses to argue about it. . . .

"Besides, you scarcely knew the first son," pursued Molly. "I've heard you say so yourself."

"No, my dear, but I knew the first wife," answered her father, still with the same quiet smile. Evidently, on the subject of Betty Fingarton, Bill was adamant.

And at that moment we drew up at Daly's and the conversation ceased. We were in time for the last part of the first act as the girl had demanded—though apparently one priceless song about a Bow-wow named Chow-chow had eluded us. . . . My sorrow at this failure on our part was heightened by the information that it was one of the best Fox Trots you could dance to. . . . I was very anxious to know what a Fox Trot was: in Uganda, as a form of amusement, it is in but little vogue. . . .

But we'd missed it, and though I endeavoured to bear up under the staggering blow, I found my attention wandering more and more from the stage, and centring round the story of the sixteenth Earl Fingarton and his first wife Betty.

The picture of the old man, shutting himself up more and more in his Highland castle, waiting for the time when he could be relieved of duty, and go once more to the woman he loved, came between me and the stage. . . . *His* child to carry on the line, but not *hers*. . . . But it would be carried on in direct descent—that was the great point—it would remain unbroken. The sacrifice of the father had had its reward. . . .

"There is Lady Fingarton in the box opposite," said Molly Lakington in my ear, as the lights went up at the end of the first act. . . . "Sitting next to Bobby . . . and Cecilie on the other side."

I glanced across the theatre. The youngster was just getting up to go out and smoke, and for a moment or two he bent over a lovely girl, who smiled up into his face. Then he turned to his mother, and she too smiled—a smile of perfect happiness. She was a sweet-looking woman of rising fifty, and on a sudden impulse I spoke my thoughts to Bill Lakington.

"He ought to come down, Bill: he oughtn't to bury himself. He'd like it—once he'd broken away. It's not fair to them—or himself. Why doesn't he?"

"I can't tell you, old man . . ." he answered slowly. "I know no more than you. He's happy up North: when he does come he's always hankering to get back again."

"But they go up there, I suppose?"

"Sometimes," he said, leaning back in his chair. "Sometimes. But never for long. . . . When shooting starts, and he has guests."

"I agree with Sir Richard," said Molly decidedly. "It's not fair. He's got the son he wanted, and now he sees as little of the woman who gave it him as he can. . . . He ought at any rate to pretend. . . ."

The orchestra was filing back: the smokers were returning to their seats. And as the safety-curtain rolled slowly up, I glanced once more across the theatre at Lady Fingarton. Did she feel that, too? And it seemed to me that her eyes were weary. . . . He ought at any rate to pretend. . . .

II

And so, but for a strange turn in the wheel of fate, the matter would have rested as far as I was concerned. For an evening the story of the sixteenth Earl Fingarton and his wife Betty had appealed to my imagination, then stress of work drove it from my mind. In Scotland, especially in the Highlands, the fierce pride of family and clan seems natural and right: from time immemorial that pride has been a dominant trait of those who live there.

And up in Skye, where I wandered for a while before settling down to work, the old Earl's action seemed easier to understand. . . . As a man, his heart had died with his wife Betty; as the sixteenth of his line, he had gone forth into the world, which had ceased to interest him, and taking unto himself another wife, had waited until she gave him a son. Then, his duty over, he had come back to his dead and his memories. . . . Callous, perhaps, to the living; primitive in his treatment of his second wife, as men of old were primitive in their treatment of women, regarding them as merely the bearers of their children—yet understandable. . . . Look on the glory of Glen Sligachan, and it is understandable. Country such as that in another part of the Highlands belonged to the Fingartons, and the breathless marvel of it is not to be lightly parted with. It must remain for a man's son, and his son's son . . . a sacred heritage. There must be no outsider to break the line.

Thus did it strike me as I settled down to work in the island that I loved. And then, as I have said, it gradually faded from my mind. Vast tracts of territory at present infested with sleeping-sickness could, I felt convinced, be rendered immune from that dreadful scourge if my proposals were adopted. Starting from the point at which the German Commission under Professor Koch had left off, years before the war, I had carried his investigations several steps farther. And I knew that I had been successful. So I found an undisturbed place to write, and quickly became absorbed in my task. Without undue conceit, I knew it was an important one. . . .

And then, one evening, after I had been working for about a fortnight, occurred the strange turn of the wheel which was to bring my attention back from the dark interior of Africa to things much nearer at hand. I had finished for the day, and was sitting by the open window watching the sun sink in a blaze of golden glory over the Coolin Hills, when a small urchin obtruded himself into my line of vision, and stared at me fixedly in the intervals of sucking his thumb. The inspection apparently proved satisfactory, and after a while the small urchin spoke. His language required interpretation by my landlady, but finally I gathered that the attentions of a medical man were wanted. And since the local doctor was away, he wanted to know whether I would come.

"It's for Mrs. MacDerry, sir," explained my landlady. "She's old and ailing fast."

No doctor can disregard a call of such a sort, and though I had certainly not come to Skye with the idea of attending to the local man's practice during his absence, I followed my small guide to a little house some half a mile away. He left me at the door, and after a moment's hesitation I knocked. It was opened almost at once by a somewhat stern and forbidding-looking woman, who stared at me suspiciously, and then curtly inquired what I wanted.

"Nothing," I answered, a little nettled by her tone. "But from the boy who led me here I gathered you wanted a doctor."

"It was Doctor Lee I sent him for," she snapped.

"Well, Doctor Lee is out," I replied. "But doubtless he will be back soon, so I'll go away."

I turned away, distinctly annoyed at my reception, and was on the point of passing through the little gate when the woman overtook me.

"Are you a clever doctor?" she demanded.

"I have been told so," I remarked, suppressing a smile.

"Then come inside and see what you can do for my mistress."

"Is your mistress Mrs. MacDerry?"

"Aye," she nodded. "It's herself." Without another word she turned and led the way up the narrow path, apparently taking it for granted that I would follow.

"What's the matter with your mistress?" I asked as I reached the door.

"If you're clever you'll find out for yourself," she remarked tersely, and again I suppressed a smile. An uncompromising handmaiden this. . . .

She left me alone in the room which in such houses is generally alluded to as the parlour, and while I waited I stared about me idly. And as I stared my vague curiosity gave way to acute surprise. Generally the furniture in such rooms must be seen to be believed: stuffed birds in glass domes, and beaded ornaments of incredible design meet one at every step. And should one lift one's eyes in a moment of panic to the walls, innumerable photographs of wedding groups leap at you in mute protest. But there was nothing of that sort in this room. . . .

Everything was in the most exquisite taste, from the bric-à-brac on a beautiful inlaid table, to the baby Grand standing in the corner. I glanced at some of the pictures, and my surprise changed to amazement. Three at least were genuine Corots. . . . And the next thing that caught my eye were half a dozen pieces of Sèvres. . . .

"Will you come this way, please?" The woman's harsh voice from the door interrupted my inspection, and I followed her slowly up the stairs.

I found Mrs. MacDerry propped up in bed await-

ing me. The bedroom, in the quick glance I took
around it, seemed in keeping with the room below;
then my attention centred on my patient. She was
an old lady—sweet and fragile-looking as her own
Sèvres china—and it needed but a glance to see that
the fires were burning low. For Mrs. MacDerry the
harbour was almost reached.

"It is good of you to come, doctor——" She
paused inquiringly.

"Morton is my name," I answered gently, drawing
up a chair beside the bed.

"Doctor Lee seems to be out," she continued, "and
—and . . ."

Her voice died away, and she lay back on her pillows,
while the harsh-voiced woman bent over her with a
look of such infinite love on her weather-beaten face
that I inwardly marvelled at the transformation.

"You see"—the invalid opened her eyes again as
my fingers closed round the weak, fluttering pulse—
"it's very important, Doctor Morton, that I should
see my husband. . . . He has been up in London,
and came down by the mail from Euston last night.
. . . So he should be here in a few hours, shouldn't
he?"

"He should," I answered, taking out a notebook
and pencil. "Don't talk, Mrs. MacDerry . . . just
rest."

I scribbled a few lines and handed the paper to the
maid. I knew only the simplest drugs would be available, and it was going to be a stiff fight to keep the
feeble flame alight even for a few hours.

"Either go yourself, or send the boy at once to the
nearest chemist for those drugs," I whispered.
"There's no time to be lost. . . ."

She left the room without a word, and once more
the weak voice came from the bed.

"Can you do it, doctor; can you keep me . . . till my husband comes?"

"Of course, Mrs. MacDerry, and long after he's come," I said cheerfully; but she only shook her head with a faint smile.

"You can't deceive me," she whispered. . . . "Besides, I don't want to stay on. . . . It's finished—now; only I just want to hear from his own lips that it went off well. . . . That it's not all been in vain. . . ."

And then for a while she lay very still—so still that once I thought she had gone. But she stirred again, and said a few words which I could not catch. Faintly through the open window came the ceaseless murmur of the distant sea, while from a dozen cottages on the hillside opposite little yellow beams of light shone out serenely into the darkening night. And after a while I rose and lit the lamp, shading it from the face of the woman in the bed. One swift glance I stole at her, and she was sleeping with a look of ineffable peace on her face. . . . Then once more I sat down to wait. . . .

It was an hour before the maid returned with the drugs, and the slight noise she made as she entered the room roused the sleeper. . . .

"Has he come?" she cried eagerly, only to sink back again with a tired sigh as the maid shook her head.

"He couldn't be here yet, Mrs. MacDerry," I said reassuringly. "Not for an hour or two. . . . And now I want you to drink this, please. . . ."

Without a word she did as I told her, and once again closed her eyes.

I beckoned to the maid. "Get a hot bottle. And a little brandy. . . ."

"Can you do it, doctor?" she said, gripping my arm tight. "Can you let him see her alive?"

"Yes—I think so. . . . But he will have to come to-night."

She left the room, and for a while I stood by the window staring out into the night.   Was it my imagination, or did I see the headlights of a car coming over the pass in the distance? He would have to come that way if he'd crossed from Kyle to Lochalsh. . . . But they had vanished again, and I couldn't remember if the road dipped behind a rise there or not. . . .

"Do you often go to London, Doctor Morton?" The invalid's voice was a little stronger, and I crossed to the bed.

"Very often, Mrs. MacDerry," I answered.   "In fact, except when I'm abroad, I generally live there. At the moment I've come up here to work. . . ."

"Ah!   I see." . . .   She smiled faintly.   "I haven't been to London for over twenty years.   I haven't left Skye for over twenty years. . . .   I suppose it's changed a lot. . . ."

"Yes—I think you'd find it different to twenty years ago. . . .   Motors everywhere instead of hansoms. . . ."

"I've never been in a motor-car," she said, still with the same sweet smile.   "I've been buried, doctor— just buried. . . ."

"You could not have chosen a lovelier tomb," I answered gently; and she nodded her head.

"Those are three delightful Corots you have downstairs," I continued after a moment.   "I was admiring them before I came up. . . ."

She looked at me quickly.

"You know about such things, do you?"

"I'm a collector myself in a mild way," I answered.

"They belong to my husband," she said abruptly; and once more closed her eyes.   "Tell me, doctor," she continued after a while, "what is happening in London?"

"The usual things, Mrs. MacDerry. . . . In that respect I don't think there is much change since you were there. The world dances and goes to theatres as ever. . . ."

"But is there no big event," she persisted, "in the season this year? . . . No big ball . . . or . . . or marriage?"

"Why, yes," I answered, "there's a big marriage. . . . It's just taken place. . . ." And though I saw those two fragile hands clenched tight, no suspicion dawned on me as I spoke. "Lord Fingarton's only son has just married the Duke of Sussex's youngest daughter. . . ."

"And what do they say of Lord Fingarton's only son?" she demanded. "Is he a worthy successor of his father?"

"They say that he's a good lad," I answered. "I thought so myself when I spoke to him the other night. . . ."

"You spoke to him?" she cried. "Tell me about him—everything you can. . . ."

And still I did not suspect. . . . I told her of the boy; I sketched him for her to the best of my ability, and she listened eagerly. And then when I had finished, something—I know not what—made me add one sentence for which, till my dying day, I shall be thankful.

"There is only one criticism," I said, "which I can make. And that was given by a man who knew the first Lady Fingarton well. Good though this boy is—he is not *quite* so good as the one who died. . . ."

"Who was the man who said that?" she whispered breathlessly.

"Sir William Lakington—the great heart specialist," I answered, and at that moment clear and distinct through the still night came the thrumming of a motor-car.

"Is it—my husband?" She listened tensely, and I crossed to the window. The car had stopped outside the gate, and already a man was striding up the narrow path to the front door.

"He has come, Mrs. MacDerry," I said cheerfully. . . . "Now I want you to have another drink of this. . . ."

I poured out the dose, and as I held the glass to her lips, the bedroom door gently opened and a man came in. I glanced up at him to ensure silence, and met a pair of piercing eyes, which were staring at me from under great bushy eyebrows. His huge frame seemed to fill the whole doorway; then, on tiptoe, he crept towards the bed.

I laid the glass down, and turned away. My part was over, save for a word of warning. And so I beckoned to him, and he followed me to the window.

"You have not got long, Mr. MacDerry," I whispered. "The sands are very low." It was then that I noticed a huge roll of illustrated papers under his arm. "I shall be downstairs: call me if you want me."

"Is it the end?" he whispered, and I bowed gravely.

"It is the end," I answered.

I heard him whisper, "Thank God I was in time"; and then I left them together.

For maybe half an hour I sat in the room downstairs. Once the maid came in to know if I would have anything to eat, and after that the house grew very silent. Only the murmur of a man's deep voice above broke the stillness, and at length that, too, ceased. And then suddenly I heard him calling me from the landing, and went upstairs.

One glance was enough, and he looked at my face

and understood. Mechanically I stooped and picked up one of the papers that had slipped off the bed: then I moved away . . . I could do no more for the sweet old lady: she had passed beyond all earthly aid.

I put the paper on the table within the circle of light thrown by the lamp. It was a copy of the *Tatler* open at the page of photographs taken at the big wedding. There was one of young Landon and his bride—a good photo: and then I found myself staring foolishly at one of the others. I bent forward to examine it closer; there was no mistaking the great spare frame and thick eyebrows. Why had Robert, Sixteenth Earl of Fingarton, rushed post-haste from the wedding of his son to the death-bed of Mrs. Mac-Derry? And why had she called him—husband? . . .

III

It was the following day that, closely muffled up, he came into my room as I worked.

"Do I disturb you, Sir Richard?" he asked as I rose.

So he had made inquiries about my name. . . . "Not at all," I answered gravely. "Sit down."

He took the chair I indicated, and for a while he stared at me in silence.

"It was unfortunate that Doctor Lee was out," he said at length. "And Hannah—the maid—had naturally no idea who you were. I, on the contrary, know you well by reputation. . . ."

I bowed silently.

"And you know me, Sir Richard?"

Again I bowed.

For a while he drummed with his fingers on the table, then once again he fixed his piercing eyes on me.

"I want you to listen to a short story," he said quietly. "It's very short, and"—his voice shook a little—"your reception of it is very important. I am no spinner of glib phrases: I have no tricks of speech to captivate your imagination. But I have an idea that the story I have to tell requires no assistance. Nearly fifty years ago a son was born to a certain man and his wife. He was their only child; the woman was not strong enough to have another. But that son was enough: he was the heir that was needed to an historic house. . . . And then there was an accident, and the boy broke his neck out hunting. . . ."

He broke off and stared out of the window. "The woman was too old to have another child," he went on after a while, "and so it seemed that that historic name would pass out of the direct line. And it would go to a man who had recently been expelled from his London clubs for cheating at cards. . . . He was openly boasting of his good fortune: had already started to raise money on his prospects. . . ." He paused again, his great fists clenched.

"A few months later the woman fell ill. And though she loved the man as it is given to few men to be loved, she was glad—for the sake of his family. She thought she was going to die, and then he could marry again. . . . She prayed to die, and her prayer was not heard, though maybe it was one of the most divinely unselfish prayers that a human heart has ever raised. . . . Then one night, as she was recovering, the man found her with a glass of something by her bedside. . . . And he didn't leave her till she had sworn that she would not take that way out. . . ."

He shifted restlessly in his seat. "It was about then that the plan was conceived. It was hazy at first, and the man would have none of it. . . . But after a while he began to think of it more and more. . . . And, one day, to his amazement he found that the woman had an unexpected ally in the shape of the heart specialist who was attending her."

"Who was the heart specialist?" I asked quietly.

"Sir William Lakington," he answered. "You see, Sir Richard, through a turn of fate, this man is in your hands. He has no intention of hiding anything from you. . . . That same day the prospective heir, who had married a barmaid, became the father of twin sons; and the man made up his mind. The woman died, and was buried in the family vault. . . . Such was the story that was told the world. And then, with the help of that great-hearted doctor, the woman was smuggled away. For twenty-four years she has lived by herself with only one maid—buried, scarce daring to leave the house, in case she should be recognized. Through those long years the man has visited her just now and then. . . . Not too often, again for fear of discovery, though when he did come he came disguised, save only last night, when nothing mattered but the fact that it was the end. And through those long years her only mainstay has been the knowledge that *his* son will succeed to the title—that the line is still direct. . . . Fate decreed it was not to be hers; but no word of complaint or disappointment has ever passed her lips. Maybe they did wrong—that man and that woman: maybe they sinned. But they did it for the best at the time, and when, ten years afterwards, the man who would have been the heir was confined in an inebriates' home, it seemed to them that they had been justified. And now in your hands, Sir Richard, rests the issue as to whether that sweet woman's sacrifice shall have been in vain. . . . Rests also the issue of a dreadful scandal. . . ."

The deep voice ceased, and I rose and stood by the window. The sun was glinting on the hills opposite, bathing them in a riot of purple and gold: a cart was moving lazily along the rough track below the house. . . . Maybe it had been a sin; who was I to judge?

The risk was over now, the sacrifice finished. And God knows that sacrifice had been heavy. At the time they had done it for the best: that best was good enough for me.

"You have told me a very wonderful story, Mr. MacDerry," I said, as I turned and faced him. "For a short time I foolishly confused you with Lord Fingarton: I must apologize for my mistake. May I express my deepest sympathy with you in your terrible loss, and assure you that I will attend to all the necessary formalities with regard to Mrs. MacDerry's death? . . ."

For a moment I thought he would break down: instead he took my hand and wrung it. . . . And then without a word he was gone.

*   *   *   *   *

It was a year later that I went with Bill Lakington to the christening of a man-child. They are not entertainments that I generally patronize, but this was an exception. Judging by the noise it contributed to the performance, it was a fine, lusty child: certainly its parents seemed more than usually idiotic about it.

"He's aged, Dick," said Bill to me after it was over. "Bob's aged badly."

Coming towards us down the aisle was a tall gaunt man, whose piercing eyes gleamed triumphantly from under his bushy eyebrows. He stopped as he reached us, and held out a hand to each. And so for a moment we stood in silence. . . . Then he spoke:

"The line is unbroken, old friends—the line is unbroken."

Without another word he was gone.

I

"IT depends entirely," remarked the Great Doctor, twirling an empty wine-glass in his long, sensitive fingers, "what you mean by fear. The common interpretation of the word—the method which I think you would use to portray it on the stage"—he turned to the Celebrated Actor, who was helping himself to a cigarette from a silver box on the table in front of him— "would show a nervous shrinking from doing a thing: a positive distaste to it—a probable refusal, finally, to carry out the action. And rightly or wrongly—but very naturally—that emotion is the object of universal scorn. But"—and the Great Doctor paused thoughtfully—"is there no more in fear than that?"

The Well-known Soldier drained his port. "It would be a platitude to remark," he said, "that the successful overcoming of fear is the highest form of bravery."

"That if, for instance, our young friend had overcome his fear this afternoon," said the Rising Barrister, "and had jumped in after that horrible little dog, it would have been an act of the highest bravery."

"Or the most stupid bravado," supplemented the Celebrated Actor.

"Precisely my point," exclaimed the Great Doctor. "What is the dividing line between bravado and bravery?"

The Well-known Soldier looked thoughtful. "The man," he said at length, "who exposes himself to being killed or wounded when there is no necessity, with probably—at the bottom of his mind—a desire to show off, is guilty of culpable bravado. The man who, when his battalion is faltering, exposes himself to certain death to hold them is brave."

"Two extreme cases," answered the Doctor. "Narrow it down, General. What is the dividing line?"

"I suppose," murmured the Soldier, "when the results justify the sacrifice. No man has a right to throw his life away uselessly."

"In those circumstances," said the Rising Barrister, "there can be no fixed dividing line. Every man must decide for himself; and what is bravery to you, might be bravado in me."

The Doctor nodded. "Undoubtedly," he agreed. "And with a thoughtful man that decision may be very difficult. For the fraction of a second he will hesitate —weigh up the pros and cons; and even if he decides to do it finally, it may then be too late."

"Only a fool would have gone in after that dog," said the Actor dogmatically.

"Women love fools," answered the Barrister, *à propos* of nothing in particular; and the Celebrated Actor snorted contemptuously.

"Which is why the man who is reputed to know no fear is so universally popular," said the Soldier. "If such a man exists, he is most certainly a fool."

The door opened and their hostess put her head into the room. "You men have got to come and dance," she cried. "There's no good looking at one another and hoping for Bridge: you can have that afterwards."

The strains of a gramophone came faintly from the drawing-room as they rose dutifully.

"I cannot perpetrate these new atrocities, dear lady," remarked the Soldier, "but if anybody would like to have a barn dance, I shall be happy to do my best."

"Sybil shall take you in hand, Sir John," she answered, leading the way across the hall. "By the way, young

Captain Seymour, the V.C. flying-man, has come up. Such a nice boy—so modest and unassuming."

As they entered the room a fresh one-step had just started, and for a while they stood watching. The two sons of the house, just home from Eton, were performing vigorously with two pretty girls from a neighbouring place; while Sybil, their sister, who was to take the General in hand, floated past in the arms of a keen-eyed, bronzed young man who had won the V.C. for a flying exploit that read like a fairy-tale. The other two couples were girls dancing together; while, seated on a sofa, knitting placidly, were two elderly ladies.

"And where, Lady Vera," murmured the Actor to his hostess, "is our young friend Peter?"

She frowned almost imperceptibly and looked away. "He disappeared after he left the dining-room," she remarked shortly. "I suppose, in view of what occurred this afternoon, he prefers to be by himself."

The Actor ran a delicate hand through his magnificent grey hair—it was a gesture for which he was famous—and regarded his hostess in surprise. "Even you, Lady Vera!" he remarked pensively. "I can understand these young girls blaming the boy; but for you—a woman of sense——" He shrugged his shoulders—another world-famed movement, feebly imitated by lesser lights.

"I don't think we will discuss the matter, Mr. Deering," she said, turning away a little abruptly.

It had been a somewhat unpleasant incident at the time, and the unpleasantness was still apparently far from over. Madge Saunderson, one of the girls stopping in the house, had been the owner of a small dog of rat-like appearance and propensities, to which she had been devoted. She shared this devotion with no one, the animal being of the type that secretes itself under chairs and nips the ankle of the next person who unsuspectingly sits down.   However, *De mortuis . . .* And since its violent death that afternoon, Toots— which was the animal's name—had been invested with a halo.   Its atrocious habits were forgotten: it lived in everyone's memory as poor little Toots.

It was over its death that Peter Benton had made himself unpopular.   Not far from the house there was a disused mill, past which, at certain times of the year, the water poured in a black, evil-looking torrent, emerging below into a deep pond cupped out in the rocks.   For a hundred yards before the stream came to the old mill-wheel the slope of the ground affected it to such an extent that, if much rain had fallen in the hills above, the current was dangerous.   The water swirled along, its smoothness broken only by an occasional eddy, till with ever-increasing speed it dropped sheer into the pond, twenty feet below.   Occasionally battered things were found floating in that pond— stray animals which had got caught in the stream above; and twice since the mill had closed down twenty years ago a child had been discovered, bruised and dead, in the placid pool below the wheel.   But, then, these had been small animals and children—quite unable to keep their feet.   Whereas Peter Benton was a man, and tall at that.

Into this stream, flooded more than usual with the recent rain, had fallen poor little Toots.   Being completely blind in both eyes, it had serenely waddled over the edge of the small hand-bridge which spanned the water, and had departed, struggling feebly, towards the mill-wheel seventy yards away.   At the moment of the catastrophe Peter Benton and Madge Saunderson were standing on the bridge, and her scream of horror rang out simultaneously with the splash.

The man, seeing in an instant what had happened,

raced along the bank, and overtook the dog when it had gone about half-way, at the point where the current quickened and seemed to leap ahead. And then had occurred the dreadful thing.

According to the girl, afterwards, he just stood there and watched Toots dashed to pieces. According to the man—but, incidentally, he said nothing, which proved his cowardice, as the girl remarked. He had nothing to say. Instead of going into the water and seizing the dog, he had stood on the bank and let it drown. And he had no excuse. Of course, there would have been a certain element of risk; but no man who was a man would have thought of that. Not with poor little Toots drowning before his eyes.

And his remark at the moment when she had rushed up to him, almost hysterical with grief, showed him to be—well, perhaps it would be as well not to say what she thought. Madge Saunderson had paused in her narrative at tea and consumed a sugar cake.

"What *did* he say, Madge?" asked Sybil Rackshurst.

"He said," remarked Miss Saunderson, " 'Sorry. No bon, as they say. It really wasn't worth it—not for Toots.' Can you beat it?" she stormed. " 'Not for Toots!' Poor little heart—drowning before that brute's eyes."

"Of course," said Sybil thoughtfully, "the mill-stream is very dangerous."

"My dear Sybil," answered Madge Saunderson coldly, "if you're going to take that point of view I have nothing more to say. But I'd like to know what you'd have said if it had been Ruffles."

The terrier in question regarded the speaker with an expectant eye, in which thoughts of cake shone brightly.

"What happened then?" asked one of the audience.

"We walked in silence down to the pool below," continued Madge. "And there—we found him—my

little Toots. He floated to the side, and Mr. Benton
was actually daring enough to stoop down and pull him
out of the water. It was then that he added insult to
injury," she went on, in a voice of suppressed fury.
" 'Rotten luck, Miss Saunderson,' he said; 'but in a
way it's rather a happy release for the poor little brute,
isn't it? I'm afraid only your kind heart prevented
him being put away years ago.' "

A silence had settled on the room, a silence which
was broken at length by Sybil.

"He *was* very old, wasn't he?" she murmured.

Madge Saunderson's eyes flashed ominously.
"Eighteen," she said. "And I quite fail to see that
that's any excuse. You wouldn't let an old man of
ninety drown, would you—just because he was old?
And Toots was quite as human as any old man, and far
less trouble."

Such had been the official *communiqué*, issued to a
feminine gathering at tea-time; in due course it travelled
to the rest of the house-party. And, as is the way
with such stories, it had not lost in the telling.

Daisy Johnson, for instance, had retailed it with some
gusto to the Rising Barrister.

"What a pity about Mr. Benton, isn't it?" she had
murmured before dinner, moving a little so that the
pink light from a lamp fell on her face. Pink, she
reflected, was undoubtedly the colour she would have
for all the shades when she had a house.

The Rising Barrister regarded her casually. "What
is a pity?" he asked.

"Haven't you heard?" she cried. "Why, this afternoon poor little Toots—Madge Saunderson's dog—
fell into the mill-stream."

"Thank God!" ejaculated the Barrister brutally.

"Oh, I know he wasn't an attractive dog!" she
said.

"Attractive!" he interrupted. "Why, the little beast's snorts reverberated through the house!"

"But still," she continued firmly, "I don't think Mr. Benton should have let it drown before his eyes without raising a finger to save it. He stood stock-still on the bank—hesitating; and then it was too late. Of course, I suppose it was a little dangerous." She shrugged a delightful pair of shoulders gracefully. "I don't think most men would have hesitated." She glanced at the Rising Barrister as she spoke, and if he failed to alter the "most men" to his own advantage the fault was certainly not hers. It struck him suddenly that pink gave a most attractive lighting effect.

"Er—perhaps not," he murmured. "Still, I expect he was quite right, you know. One—er—should be very careful what one says in cases of this sort."

Which was why a few minutes later he retailed the story to the Celebrated Actor, over a sherry-and-bitters.

"The faintest tinge of the yellow streak," he said confidentially. "There was something or other in France—I don't exactly recall it at this moment. I know I heard something."

But the Celebrated Actor flatly refused to agree. "I don't know anything about France," he said firmly. "I know a lot about that dog. If a suitable occasion arises, I shall publicly propose a vote of thanks to young Benton. Would you believe me, sir, only yesterday, when outlining my part in my new play to Lady Vera and one or two others, the little brute bit me in the ankle! True, I had inadvertently trodden on it, but——" He waved a careless hand, as if dismissing such a trfling cause.

From all of which it will be seen what the general feeling in the house was towards Peter Benton on the night in question. And Peter, a very discerning young man, was not slow to realize it. At first it had amused

him; after a while he had become annoyed.   More or
less a stranger in the locality, he had not known the depth
of the mill-stream; and he frankly admitted to himself
that he had hesitated to go into that black, swirling
water, not a stone's throw from the mill itself, in order
to save a dog.   He had hesitated, and in a second it
had been too late.   The dog had flashed past him, and
he had watched it disappear over the fall by the wheel.
It was only later that to him the additional reason of
the dog's extreme age and general ill-health presented
itself.   And the additional reason had not added to his
popularity with the animal's mistress.

He quite saw her point of view: he was annoyed
because no one apparently saw his.   And he was far
too proud to attempt any explanation—apart from seeing
the futility of it.   He could imagine the cold answer—
"Doubtless you were perfectly right.   Poor little Toots
is dead now.   Shall we consider the incident closed?"

Savagely he kicked the turf on the lawn outside the
window where they were dancing.   For three in suc-
cession Sybil had had Captain Seymour as her partner,
and Peter had hoped——

"Oh, hang that horrible little dog!" he muttered to
himself, striding viciously away into the garden.

A brilliant moon was shining, flooding the country
with a cold white light, in which things stood out almost
as clearly as by day.   Half a mile away an unfinished
factory chimney, still with its scaffolding round it, rose
sheer and black against the sky.   Around it new works
were being erected, and for a while Peter stood motionless, gazing at the thin column of bricks and mortar.

Only that morning he had watched men at work on
it, with almost a shudder.   They looked like so many
flies crawling over the flimsy boards, and he had waited
while one workman had peered nonchalantly over the
edge of his plank and indulged in a wordy warfare

with the man below. It seemed that unless the latter mended his ways he would shortly receive a brick on his blinking nut; but it was the complete disregard for their dizzy height that had fascinated Peter. He could imagine few professions which he would less sooner join than that of steeplejack. And yet the funny thing was that on the occasions when he had flown he had not noticed any discomfort at all.

Presumably there was some scientific reason for it— something which would account for the fact that, though he could fly at twenty times the height of St. Paul's without feeling giddy, on the occasion when he had looked over the edge of that great dome from the little platform at the top he had been overcome with a sort of dreadful nausea and had had to go back quickly.

"Why, Peter, what are you doing here all alone?" A voice behind him made him look round.

For a moment the dog episode had gone out of his mind, and, with a quick smile, he took a step towards the speaker. "Why, Sybil," he said, "how topping you look! Isn't it a glorious night?" And then suddenly he remembered, and stopped with a frown.

"Peter," said the girl quietly, "I want to hear about this afternoon from you, please."

"Haven't you heard all there is to be heard?" he answered, a little bitterly. "Miss Saunderson's dog fell into the mill-stream. I failed to pull it out: to be strictly accurate, I failed to attempt to pull it out. That's all there is to it."

They faced one another in the moonlight, and after a while the girl spoke again. "That's not like you, Peter. Why did you let it drown?"

"Because," said the man deliberately, "I did not consider I was called on to risk my life to save a dog. Even poor little Toots," he added cynically.

"Supposing it had been a child, Peter?" said the girl gravely.

"My God!" answered the man, very low. "As bad as that, is it? Oh, my God!"

"They're saying things, Peter: all these people are saying things."

The man thrust his hands into his pockets, and stared with brooding eyes at the black, lifeless chimney.

"Saying I'm a coward, are they?" He forced the words out. "What do you think, Sybil?"

The girl bit her lip, and suddenly put her hand on his arm. "Oh, Peter," she whispered, "it wasn't like you—not a bit!"

"You think," he said dispassionately, "that I should have been justified—more, that I ought to have jumped into the mill-stream in flood to save that dog?"

But the girl made no answer: she only looked miserably at the man's averted face.

"I don't know," she said at length. "I don't know. It's so—so difficult to know what to say."

Gently Peter Benton removed her hand from his arm. "That is quite a good enough answer for me, Sybil." He faced her gravely. "The thing is unfortunate, because I was going to ask you—to-night——" His jaw set and he turned away for a moment. Then he faced her again. "But never mind that now: the situation, as they say in Parliament, does not arise. I would like you, however, to know that I do not think about the matter at all. For one brief second this afternoon I did think about it; for the fraction of a minute I had made up my mind to go in after the dog. And then I realized how utterly unjustifiable such an action would be. Since that moment—as I say—I have not thought about the matter at all."

"And supposing it had been Ruffles?" asked the girl slowly.

For a while the man hesitated. Then: "My decision would have been the same," he answered, turning on his heel.

II

Inside the house the Celebrated Actor and the Rising Barrister were each proving to their own satisfaction, if not to their partners', that the modern dance held no terrors for them. The two boys were getting warmer and more energetic; Lady Vera, after chatting for a little with the Great Doctor and the Well-known Soldier, had left them to their own devices, and had joined the two elderly ladies on the sofa.

In a corner of the room sat Captain Seymour talking to Madge Saunderson, though, incidentally, she was doing most of the talking; and with them sat the two other girls. Every now and then Seymour frowned uncertainly, and shook his head: the invariable signal for all three girls to lean forward in their most beseeching manner and look adoringly up into his face.

"I wonder," remarked the Doctor, after watching the quartette for a while, "what mischief those girls are plotting?"

The Soldier adjusted his eyeglass and looked across the room. "Probably asking for his autograph," he answered cynically. "What I want to know is where my teacher has gone to—Miss Sybil."

"I saw her go out into the garden some time ago," said the Doctor. "By Gad, but I'm sorry about this afternoon!"

The Soldier pulled at his cigar. "I am not well versed in the family history," he murmured, "and the connection is a trifle obscure."

"That confounded dog!" answered the Doctor. "Those two are head over heels in love with one another."

"And you think——?"

"My dear fellow," said the Doctor, "Sybil is one of the dearest girls in the country.   I brought her into the world; in many ways she is like my own daughter. But—she is a girl.   And if I know anything about the sex, she'd find it easier to forgive him if he'd stolen."

A peal of laughter from the quartette opposite made both men look up.   Seymour was nodding his head resignedly and Madge Saunderson was clapping her hands together with glee.

"Don't forget," her voice came clearly across the room, "we'll pretend it's a bet."

It was at that moment that Sybil appeared in the window, and the Soldier let his eyes dwell on the girl approvingly.

"What a thoroughbred!" he said at length, turning to the Doctor.   "I'm not certain it isn't better—as it is."

"Hang it, man!" said the Doctor irritably.   "The boy is a thoroughbred, too.   What did you say yourself after dinner about the results having to justify the sacrifice?"

But the Soldier only grunted non-committally.   It would doubtless be an excellent thing if theory and practice never clashed.

Sybil came slowly into the room, and Madge Saunderson rose with a meaning glance at Captain Seymour.

"Syb," she cried, "we've got the finest bet on you've ever thought of!   I've betted Captain Seymour six pairs of gloves that he doesn't climb up Mill Down chimney in the moonlight, and he's betted me five hundred of his most special cigarettes that he does."

For a moment a silence settled on the room, which was broken by Lady Vera.   "But are you quite sure it's safe, my dear?" she remarked, searching for a dropped stitch.   "It might fall down or something."

Miss Saunderson laughed merrily. "Why, Aunt Vera," she cried, "there are men working on it every day. It's quite safe—only I bet he'll have cold feet, and not get to the top—V.C. and all." She flashed a smile at the flying-man. "And it's a ripping evening for a walk."

The Doctor turned to his companion. "I wonder what that young woman's game is?" he remarked thoughtfully.

"I don't know," answered the Soldier. "I suppose you've got a good head for heights, Seymour?" he called out.

"Pretty fair, sir," replied the airman, with a grin. "I don't mind twenty thousand feet, so I don't think Mill Down chimney should worry me much."

"The two things are not quite alike," said a quiet voice from the window, and everyone turned to see Peter Benton standing there, with his hands in his pockets. "I've got a shocking head for height myself, but I never noticed it when I was flying."

"I think I will chance it," answered Seymour with a slight drawl, and having recently been supplied with Madge Saunderson's version of the dog accident his tone was understandable.

"Let's all go down and see he doesn't cheat," cried one of the girls, and there was a general exodus of the younger members of the party for wraps. Only Sybil, with troubled eyes, stood motionless, staring out into the brilliant moonlight; while Peter, lighting a cigarette, picked up an illustrated paper and glanced through it. And to the Doctor, watching the scene with his shrewd grey eyes, the only person in the room who seemed ill at ease was the flying-man himself.

"What would the world be like," he remarked to the Soldier, "if woman lost her power to cause man to make a fool of himself?"

"Good Lord! my dear fellow," said the other, "it's only an after-dinner prank. That boy will do it on his head."

"I dare say he will," returned the Doctor. "But it's cheap, and he knows it." He rose. "Shall we go down and witness the feat?"

"Why not?" answered the Soldier. "It may stop Deering telling us again about his new play."

Half an hour later the whole house-party were grouped round the base of the chimney. Close to, it seemed to have grown in height, till it towered above them into the starlit sky. The girls were chattering gaily, standing around Seymour—except for Sybil, who stood a little apart; while the two Eton boys were busily engaged in deciding on the correct method of ascent. Seated on a pile of bricks sat the four men, more occupied with a never-ending political argument than the performance of climbing the chimney; while in the background, standing by himself, was Peter Benton, with a twisted, bitter smile on his face.

He was under no delusions as to why the bet had been made: just a further episode, thought out by a spiteful girl, to show his conduct that afternoon in a blacker light. On the surface, at any rate, it was more dangerous to the ordinary man to climb this chimney than to go into the mill-stream. And this was being done merely for sport—as a prank; while the other might have saved a dog's life.

With a laugh, Seymour swung himself off the ground, and started to climb. He went up swiftly, without faltering; and after a while even the political discussion ceased, and the party below stared upwards in silence. In the cold white light the climber looked like some gigantic insect creeping up the brickwork, and gradually as he neared the top the spectators moved farther

away from the base of the chimney, in order to see him
better. At length he reached the limit of the main
scaffolding; only some temporary makeshift work continued for the few feet that separated him from the
actual top. He hesitated for a moment, apparently
reconnoitring the best route; and Madge Saunderson,
cupping her mouth in her hands, shouted up to him:

"Right up, Captain Seymour, or you won't get your
cigarettes."

And Seymour looked down.

It would be hard to say the exact moment when the
watchers below realized that something was wrong—
all, that is, save Madge Saunderson and the other two
girls who had been in the quartette.

It was the Doctor who rose suddenly and said,
"Heavens! he's lost his head!"

"Don't shout!" said the Soldier imperatively.
"Leave it to me." He looked up, and his voice rang
through the night: "Captain Seymour—General Hard-
castle speaking. Don't look down. Look up—do you
hear me?—look up. At once!" But the face of the
aviator still peered down at them, and it almost seemed
as if they could see his wide, staring eyes.

"My God!" muttered the Soldier. "What are we
going to do?"

"Let's all shout together," said the Actor.

"No good," cried the General. "You'll only confuse
him."

And it was then that the quiet voice of Peter Benton
was heard. He was talking to Madge Saunderson,
who with the other two girls had been whispering
together, ignorant that he was close behind them in
the shadow.

"Do I understand you to say, Miss Saunderson, that
Captain Seymour is only pretending?"

"You had no business to hear what I said, Mr.

Benton," she answered angrily. "I wasn't talking to you."

But the Doctor appeared interested, and very few of either sex had ever hesitated for long when he became serious.

"You will kindly tell me at once whether this is a joke," he said grimly.

For a moment the girl's eyes flashed mutinously, and then she laughed—a laugh which rang a little false.

"If you wish to know, it is," she answered defiantly. "I wanted to find out if Mr. Benton would consider a human life worth saving."

She laughed again, as the four men with one accord turned their backs on her.

"Perhaps it would be as well, then," said Peter calmly, "for you to tell Captain Seymour that the charming little jest has been discovered, and that he can come down again."

She looked at him contemptuously; then, raising her voice, she shouted to the man above:

"You can come down, Captain Seymour: they've found out our little joke."

But the aviator remained motionless.

"Come down," she cried again. "Can't you hear me?" But Seymour's face, like a white patch, still peered down, and suddenly a girl started sobbing.

"It would seem," remarked Peter, "that the plot is going to be successful after all."

The next moment, before anyone realized what was happening, he was climbing steadily up towards the motionless man at the top.

There was only one remark made during that second ascent, and it came from the Doctor.

"You deserve, young woman," he said quietly to Madge Saunderson, "to be publicly whipped through the streets of London."

Then silence reigned, broken only by Peter, as he paused every now and then to shout some encouraging remark to the man above.

"I'm coming, Seymour. Absolutely all right. Can't you send for óne of your bally machines, and save us both the trouble of climbing down again?"

Between each remark he climbed steadily on, until at last he was within a few feet of the aviator.

"Look away from me, Seymour," he ordered quietly, gazing straight into the unblinking, staring eyes above. "Look at the brickwork beside you. Do as I tell you, Seymour. Look at the brickwork beside you."

For what seemed an eternity to those below the two men stayed motionless; then a great shuddering sigh broke from them—Seymour was no longer looking down.

It was only the General who spoke, and he was not conscious of doing so. "By Gad! you're right, Doctor," he muttered. "He's thoroughbred right enough— he's thoroughbred."

And the Great Doctor, whose iron nerve had earned for him the reputation of being one of the two finest operating surgeons in Europe, wiped the sweat from his forehead with a hand that shook like a leaf.

Then began the descent.

"Look at the brickwork the whole time, Seymour— and hold fast with your hands. Now give me your right foot: give me your right foot, do you hear? That's it—now the left."

Step by step, with Peter just below him, the aviator came down the chimney, and he was still thirty feet from the bottom when the onlookers saw him pause and pass a hand over his forehead. He gazed down at them, and on his face there was a look of dazed surprise—like a man waking from a dream. Then he swung himself rapidly down to the ground, where he stood facing Peter.

"You've saved my life, old man," he said a little breathlessly, with the wondering look still in his eyes. "I—don't understand quite what happened. I seemed to go all queer—when I looked down." He laughed shakily. "Dashed funny thing—er—thanks, most awfully. Good Lord! What's the matter, old boy?"

He leant over Peter, who had pitched forward unconscious at his feet.

"I think," remarked the Well-known Soldier to no one in particular, as they walked back, "that the less said about this little episode the better. It was a good deal too near a tragedy for my liking."

"A most instructive case," murmured the Great Doctor, "showing, first of all, the wonderful power of self-hypnotism. I have heard of similar cases in those old-fashioned London houses, where the light in the hall has fascinated people leaning over the banisters two or three stories above it, and caused them to want to throw themselves over."

"And what is your second observation?" murmured the Rising Barrister, who was always ready to learn.

"The influence of mind over matter," returned the Doctor briefly, "and the strain involved in the successful overcoming of intense fear. Young Benton has never, and will never, do a braver thing in his life than he did to-night."

"Ah!" murmured the Celebrated Actor, running his hand through his hair. "What a situation! Magnificent! Superb! But, I fear, unstageable."

They entered the drawing-room, to find the conversation being monopolized by a new-comer—a captain in the Coldstream. It was perhaps as well: the remainder of the party seemed singularly indisposed to talk.

"Climbin' chimneys? Might be in you flying wallahs' line—but not old Peter. D'you remember, Peter, turnin' pea-green that time we climbed half-way up Wipers Cathedral, before they flattened it?" The Guardsman laughed at the recollection. "No— swimming is his stunt," he continued to everyone at large. "How he ever had the nerve to go overboard— in the most appalling sea—and rescue that fellow, I dunno. It was a great effort that, Peter."

But the only answer was the door closing.

"A good swimmer, is he?" remarked the Great Doctor casually.

"Wonderful," answered the other. "The rougher it is the more he likes it. He got the Royal Humane Society's medal, you know, for that thing I was talking about. Leave-boat—off Boulogne."

He rattled on, but no one seemed to be paying very much attention. In fact, the only other remark of interest was made by the Rising Barrister, just as the door closed once again—this time behind Sybil.

"That was what I remember hearing about in France," he said calmly to the Great Doctor. "You remember I was mentioning it to you before dinner. I knew there was something."

"Wonderful!" murmured the Actor. "Quite wonderful!"

The Rising Barrister coughed deprecatingly, and lit a cigarette.

XXXVII "GOOD HUNTING, OLD CHAP"

I

THE Well-known Soldier leaned back in his chair, and thoughtfully held his glass up to the light.

"Personally," he remarked at length, "I would sooner be sent to prison for five years for a thing I had done than be let out after two and a half for a thing I hadn't."

"An interesting point," conceded the Celebrated Actor. "But to the casual observer, unversed in psychology, it might appear to be merely a choice between five years of hell and two and a half."

The Celebrated Actor, it may be stated, had recently been dipping into various "ologies" in the course of studying his newest and greatest part. Luckily for the sake of the public, the leaves of most of the treatises were still uncut, which ensured that his rendering of the strong, silent Napoleon of finance would not differ appreciably from his own celebrated personality. Incidentally, he had never intended that it should, but the author of the play was a serious young man, and the Actor was nothing if not tactful.

"I am inclined to disagree, General," said the Eminent Divine. "Surely the moral support of a clear conscience——"

"Quite," murmured the Actor. "Quite."

"Would cut no ice, Bishop," declared the Soldier. "Two and a half years is too long a time for such a comparatively frail support as a clear conscience. Especially a youngster's."

"Exactly," agreed the Actor. "Exactly. Two and a half years of hell for something one has not done. . . . Appalling—quite appalling." With great care he continued the delicate process of peeling a walnut.

But the Bishop was not convinced. "All the time

he would know that a mistake had been made; that sooner or later he would be cleared in the eyes of the world. Whereas if he was guilty he would know that no such chance existed, and that when he came out from prison he would be an outcast—a jail-bird."

The Soldier shook his head and drained his glass. "Right in theory, Bishop; right in practice, too, if the clearing had been quicker. But two and a half years is too long. Hope would die: a youngster would grow bitter."

"Where is he now?" demanded the Celebrated Actor, sweeping back his hair with the gesture for which he was rightly famous.

"No one knows," said the Soldier quietly. "He came out a week ago. His brother met him at the prison gates, but Hugh gave him the slip. And since then he's hidden himself. Of course, he could be traced, but his father is wise, I think, in not doing so."

The Bishop nodded. "He will find himself in time; and it's best to leave him alone till he does. A good boy, too."

For a while the three men were silent while the soft summer breeze played gently through the old-fashioned garden outside, and the wonderful scent of the laburnum came fragrant through the open windows.

"I forget exactly what happened," remarked the Actor, at length. "I was producing *King Lear* at the time, I remember, and——" He glanced inquiringly at the General.

"A fairly common story," returned the Soldier, lighting a cigarette thoughtfully. "The boy had been an ass and owed a lot of money to some bookmaker. Then he plunged on the Derby—the year Signorinetta won at a hundred to one—and went down, like most of us did. Two days afterwards a couple of thousand in cash was missing. Also the books were falsified over a long period. Everything pointed to him, and they found him guilty, though he protested his innocence all through. A month ago the real thief confessed—two and a half years too late."

The General shrugged his shoulders, and then suddenly sat motionless, staring with narrowed eyes into the darkness outside.

"Quaint how one's eyes deceive one at night." He sat back again in his chair. "For a moment I thought I saw someone moving by the edge of the lawn."

"And your niece?" pursued the Actor. "Weren't they engaged or something?"

"Yes. It almost broke Beryl's heart. You know, of course, the dog was his?"

"I did not," said the Actor. "Ah! that accounts, of course, for her terrible grief."

"If I had my way," snarled the General fiercely, "I'd flog that young swine Parker to within an inch of his worthless life. And then I'd put a trap on his own leg."

The Actor nodded. "I agree, General. Personally, I am no great dog-lover. They have a way of concealing themselves about the furniture which is most disconcerting should one inadvertently sit upon them. But a trap——"

He shuddered, and poured himself out some more port.

"If only we could get hold of the boy," mused the General, returning to his original theme. "I can guess what he's feeling, and the longer he goes on without the human touch, the harder and more bitter he'll become. He wants to be made to shake hands with reality again; to hit something, if you like—but to get it over. He's bottling it up——I know it; and it's a bad thing for a youngster to bottle up bitterness."

The Soldier rose and strolled over to the window.

For a while he leaned against the open frame, smoking quietly, and hardly conscious of the argument which had started in the room behind him. The power of the stage as a pulpit was an evergreen with the Celebrated Actor, and he felt in no mood for a discussion on the matter. The youngster, Hugh Dawnay, was filling his mind, and also Tommy, that morning.

He'd helped the vet. put the little terrier under, with a dose of prussic acid, and after it was over the two men had stared at one another, and then looked away, as is the manner of men who are feeling deeply.

"I hate it, more and more each time," said the vet. gruffly. "Poor little chap!"

"It's worse than a man," snapped the General. "A dog trusts a fellow so—so infernally. Damn that young Parker!"

With which explosion he had blown his nose loudly and stalked off for a long walk.

At length he pitched his cigarette away and turned back into the room. And at that moment, very clear and distinct from somewhere in the garden, there came a low whistle.

"Hush! you fellows, listen!" The argument ceased at his abrupt words, and the two men stared at him, as he stood motionless half-way between the table and the window. "Did you hear that whistle?"

"Personally, I did not," remarked the Actor, "but at the moment I was engrossed in other matters. A vulgar habit—whistling—but not, I regret to say, uncommon."

"There's someone in the garden," said the General. "I thought I saw something move earlier, and just then I heard a whistle most distinctly."

"My dear man," said the Actor, with a beneficent wave of his shapely hand, "are there not maidservants in the house? I fear that soldiering destroys romance."

The Soldier grunted. "Perhaps you're right. My mind was busy with other things. I think I'll take a stroll outside, too, for a bit. Give me a hail when you've finished your discussion."

He moved once more towards the window, only to pause on the threshold.

"Why, Hugh, my dear lad," he said quietly, "it's good to see you again. Come in."

And the Celebrated Actor and the Eminent Divine, looking up quickly at his words, saw a man standing outside on the path, whose face was the face of one into whose soul the iron had entered.

For a moment or two Hugh Dawnay hesitated. Then, with the faintest perceptible shrug of his shoulders, he stepped into the room. He glanced at each man in turn; then his eyes came back to the Soldier's face and rested there.

"Good evening, General." His voice was quite expressionless. "I must apologize for intruding like this."

"Apologize!" The Soldier smiled at him. "What the devil is there to apologize about? I'm just amazingly glad to see you. Do you know the Bishop of Sussex and Mr. Trayne?"

"I had the pleasure of seeing you act, Mr. Trayne, just before I was so kindly accommodated at His Majesty's expense." Hugh's voice was as expressionless as ever. "I suppose you are still charming London with your art?"

For the first time in his life the Celebrated Actor felt at a loss. Had some charming woman made the remark to him—and many had—he would have known his cue. A deprecating wave of his hands—a half-hearted denial—a delicately turned compliment; it was all too easy. But as he stared at the boy on the other side of the table—the boy with the tired face of a man

—the cloak of mannerisms which he had worn successfully for twenty years slipped off, and the soul of the great artist—and he was that, for all his artificiality—showed in his eyes. More clearly, perhaps, than either of the other two, he realized the dreadful laughter which was shaking the boy's soul; realized the bitter cynicism behind the ordinary words. More clearly than they could, he saw himself, he saw the room, he saw life through the eyes of Hugh Dawnay.

"I still strut my small part," he said gravely. "I still win a little brief applause. And if I can help those who see me to forget the bitterness and sorrow of the day, even though it be only for a while, it is enough." He rose, and laid both his hands on the boy's shoulders. "Forgive an old mummer's presumption, my lad. Don't think me an impertinent fool prating of what I do not know and cannot understand. You have been in the depths. God knows how deep and bitter they have been—God and you—unjustly, unfairly—I know that. And to you at the moment we seem typical of the smug respectability which pushed you there. Vain words of regret—empty phrases of sorrow—cannot give you back your two and a half wasted years any more than my playing alters the realities of the past. But maybe the hour or two of forgetfulness helps a man to face the realities of the future. Will you not try to forget, too?"

"And what play will you stage for me, Mr. Trayne," answered Hugh quietly, "which will help me to forget? Will you cast me for the principal part, or am I to be one of the audience?" The boy threw back his head and laughed silently. "Two and a half years of the same soul-killing monotony. Why, I became an expert at talking to the man next to me, who was a 'lifer.' They couldn't prove he'd actually intended to murder the girl, and his counsel successfully pleaded drink. A charming fellow." Once again he laughed; then, with a quick movement, he thrust his hands in his pockets and, stepping back towards the window, faced the three men for a while in silence.

"For a moment or two you must listen to me," he said, and there was a harsh commanding ring in his voice. "Each of you is old enough to be my father in years; I am older than all of you combined in reality. At least, that is how I feel just now. You, Mr. Trayne, have talked about forgetfulness; in time, perhaps, I shall forget. But there's something inside me at the present moment which is numbing me. I can't feel, I can't think, I can't hate—I'm simply apathetic. I don't want to have anything to do with men; I want to get right away from them. And I'm going—I'm going; but I'm not going alone." He swung round and faced the Soldier. "Do you know why I've come here to-night, General?"

The Soldier looked at him quietly. "To see Beryl? Because she'd like to see you, Hugh."

But Hugh Dawnay shook his head. "No, not to see Beryl. I'm not fit to see her—yet. Perhaps in a year or two—if she isn't—married by then. No, it's not to see any human being; not even her. It's to get Tommy; and take him with me out into the big spaces where, perhaps, in time, one may see things differently."

Unconscious of the effect of his words on his listeners, he had turned and was staring into the soft summer night.

"All the time that I've been in prison"—and his voice had lost its harshness—"I've thought of that little chap. I've sat on my stool in the cell, and I've felt his cold, wet muzzle thrust into my hand: I've seen his eyes—those great brown eyes—staring up at me, asking for a hunt. But there's no hunting in prison

—no rabbits: and I used to promise him that when I came out we'd go off together, just he and I—on to the moors somewhere—and be alone. He wouldn't mind even if I'd done it—even if I had stolen the money. That's the wonder of a dog: where he's so infinitely better than a man." The boy gave a little sigh, and for the first time a genuine smile flickered round his lips. "I've been all round the house, whistling and looking for him—but I expect he's in the drawing-room somewhere. With Beryl, perhaps. I wonder, General, if you'd get him for me?"

He glanced at the Soldier, and slowly his eyes dilated, as he saw the look on the older man's face. He glanced at the Bishop, who was staring at the cloth; he glanced at the Actor, who was staring at the Bishop, and suddenly he gave a little choking cry.

"My God!" he muttered brokenly, "don't tell me that! Don't say that Tommy is—dead!"

It was the Soldier who answered, and his voice was suspiciously gruff.

"The little fellow was mauled in a trap this morning, old chap: and we had—to put him out of the way."

"Mauled in a trap?" The boy's voice was dead. "Tommy mauled in a trap? Who laid the trap?"

And it was the Actor who sat up, with a sudden light in his eyes, and supplied the information.

"Young Parker, who is farming the bit of ground next to here," he said, with almost unnecessary distinctness. "You can see his house through the trees."

"Young Parker? I remember young Parker." Covertly the Celebrated Actor watched the boy's face, and what he saw there seemed to afford him satisfaction.

"Where is the little dog buried?" asked the boy quietly.

"Underneath the old yew-tree," said the General. "Beryl put a ring of stones around his grave this afternoon."

"I see," said the boy. "Thank you. I'm sorry to have troubled you."

The next instant he was gone, and it was the Actor who stopped the Soldier as he was on the point of going after him.

"The boy has got his part," he remarked cryptically. "At present he requires no prompting."

"What the deuce are you talking about?" demanded the General irritably.

But the Celebrated Actor was himself once more.

"Leave it to me, my dear fellow," he murmured magnificently, throwing back his head in another of those famous gestures which were the pride and delight of countless multitudes. "Leave it entirely to me. The stage is set: very soon the curtain will ring up." He stalked to the window, and stood for a moment on the path outside, while the other two looked at one another and shrugged their shoulders.

"Can't feel, can't think, can't hate. That boy feels and thinks and hates—hates, I tell you, at this moment."

With which Parthian shot the Celebrated Actor vanished into the night.

"What on earth is the fellow driving at?" said the Soldier peevishly.

But the answer to that question was apparently beyond the scope of the Eminent Divine, and in silence the two men listened to the scrunch of the Actor's footsteps on the gravel growing fainter and fainter in the distance.

II

Half an hour later they were still sitting at the table. The Actor had not returned: there had been no further sign of Hugh, and the inaction was getting on the Soldier's nerves. Twice had he risen and gone to the window: twice had he taken a few steps into the darkness outside, only to return and hover undecidedly by the fireplace.

"I feel I ought to go and look for the boy," he remarked for the twentieth time. "Trayne's such an ass."

And for the twentieth time the Bishop counselled patience.

"In some ways he is," he agreed: "in others he's very shrewd. He's got more imagination, General, than both of us put together, and real imagination is akin to genius. Leave him alone: he can't do any harm."

With a non-committal grunt, the Soldier sat down, only to rise again immediately as a tall, slight girl in white came in through the open window. There was a misty look in her eyes, and her lips were faintly tremulous, but she came straight up to the General and put a hand on his arm. The other hand, with a piece of paper clutched in it, she held behind her back.

"Hugh has come back, Uncle Jim," she said. "Did you know?"

"Yes, old lady, I knew. Have you seen him?"

"No, I haven't seen him. Did he—did he come for Tommy?"

The General nodded. "Yes. And I told him what had happened."

For a moment the girl's lips quivered. "Poor old Hugh!"

Very gently the Soldier stroked the girl's hair. "We must give him time, Beryl. He's—he's not quite himself yet. By the way," he added, struck by a sudden thought, "if you haven't seen him, how do you know he's come back?"

The girl's eyes filled with tears. "I went out to Tommy's grave again—I wanted to see that the little fellow was comfortable, and—and—I found this."

She held out the scrap of paper to the Soldier, and then broke down uncontrollably. And the man, having glanced at it, coughed with unnecessary violence and handed it to the Eminent Divine.

"It was just like him—just like Hugh," sobbed the girl. "And Tommy—why, what more would Tommy want?" She picked up the paper and stared at it through her tears. " 'Good hunting, old chap.— H. D.' Good hunting. He's got a soul—I know he has. He's having the most glorious chase after bunnies now—somewhere—somewhere else. Isn't he?"

She turned appealingly to the Bishop, but that eminent Pillar of the Church was engrossed in the study of a very ordinary print, and from the assiduous manner he was polishing his glasses he seemed to be having difficulties with his eyesight.

And it was thus a moment or two later that the Celebrated Actor found them.

"Successful." He barked the word grandiloquently from the window. "Utterly and completely successful. The curtain is shortly going up: it would be well if the audience took their seats as silently as possible."

"What do you mean, Mr. Trayne?" The girl was staring at him in amazement through her tears.

"A very human play, my dear young lady, is on the point of being acted. As producer, general manager, and box office combined, I beg to state that there will be only one performance. The financial receipts will be *nil*: the moral receipts will be a soul regained. And who shall say that it is not a more tangible asset?" For a while he stared magnificently at nothing, with one hand thrust carelessly out—that attitude which had long caused infatuated denizens of the pit to stand for hours in dreadful draughts lest they should fail to secure the front row. Then he returned with an effort to things mundane. "Follow me," he ordered, "and do not talk or make a noise."

"Where's the boy, Trayne?" demanded the General, almost angrily. In his own vernacular, he was feeling rattled.

"You shall see in good time. Come."

It was a strange procession which might have been seen wending its way through the darkness a little later. First came the Celebrated Actor—supremely happy, as befits the great showman who has the goods to offer. Then, a few steps behind him, was the Well-known Soldier, periodically muttering under his breath, and with the girl's hand on his arm. Behind them again trotted the Eminent Divine, unable to see very well in the dark, and continually stubbing his toes on various obstructions in the ground.

"Where is he taking us to?" whispered the girl to her uncle.

"Heaven knows, my dear!" he answered irritably. "The man's an ass, as I've said before."

"But what did he mean about the very human play?" she persisted. "And the soul regained?"

Before the Soldier could answer, the guide turned and, holding up his hand, demanded silence.

"We approach the stage," he declaimed. "Silence is essential."

He led the way between some trees, and finally halted behind a clump of low bushes.

"Personally," he whispered, "I am a man of peace, but it struck me from my rudimentary knowledge of pugilism that the clearing in front was ideally suited to that brutal form of amusement. And when I suggested it to Hugh, he quite agreed."

"You suggested it to Hugh!" said the Soldier slowly, and gradually a look of comprehension began to dawn in his eyes. "Why, Actor-man, Actor-man, I retract every thought I've had about you to-night."

He peered cautiously through the bushes, and a slow smile spread over his face.

"Tell me, Actor-man," he whispered, "how did you get the other?"

"I howled such insults as I could think of in my poor way through the window."

Then he, too, cautiously peered over the top of the bush. "What think you of my show, Soldier-man?"

"It is altogether beautiful and lovely to regard," replied the other. "Can the Church see?"

And, behold, the Church was lying on its stomach to get a better view.

The moonlight shone down, clear and bright, on the little glade in front. At the back of it, in the trees, stood young Parker's house, but young Parker himself, with an ugly sneer on his face, was engaged in removing his coat. Facing him stood Hugh Dawnay, and in the cold white light his eyes shone hard and merciless.

"So you want me to thrash you as well as stop your damned dog poaching," laughed young Parker. "All right, you bally jail-bird, come on!"

He rushed in as he spoke and his fist shot out as he closed. The fight had started, and from that moment no one of the fascinated audience spoke or moved. Parker was the heavier of the two, but the boy was the better boxer. In fact, in the strict sense of the word, the young farmer was not a boxer at all—but he was fit and he was strong. And had it not been for the two and a half years' hard manual labour which the other had gone through, the issue in all probability would have been different.

As it was they fought all out for five minutes, and then young Parker grew wild. He became flurried —tried rushing—his fists whirling like flails. And the more flurried he grew the more cool and collected became the boy. And then came the end. A right-arm jolt below his heart brought the farmer's head forward, a left upper-cut under the jaw laid him out. For a while the spectators watched him moaning on the ground, while the Church wriggled ecstatically under its sheltering bush.

"Had enough, you swine?" asked the boy quietly.

The prostrate figure mumbled something.

"Get up and swear to me that you will never again lay a trap in that part of your land. Get a move on!" he snarled.

"All right." The farmer shambled to his feet, watching him sullenly. "I swear."

"Now go down on your knees and apologize for calling me a jail-bird. Hurry up, you filthy scum! On your knees, I said."

And as young Parker went on his knees, according to order, the girl, her eyes shining like stars, clapped her hands softly together.

"Quick!" said the Celebrated Actor authoritatively. "Back to the house, you people. The play is over and my estimate of the receipts is, I think, correct."

Stealthily as it had come, the procession moved back to the house. At intervals, the Eminent Divine was observed to jolt with his right, following it up with a slashing left upper-cut into space, what time he chuckled consumedly. And even a slight error as to distance, which caused him far more pain than the tree which he unfortunately smote, failed to damp his spirits. The Soldier walked with a spring in his step, the Actor hummed gently under his breath, and it was only as they reached the open window of the dining-room that they realized that the girl had slipped away in the darkness and was not with them.

"Where is Beryl?" said the General, pausing on the path.

"Heaven help the man!" fumed the Actor, addressing space. "His past career, we understand, is comparatively distinguished from a military point of view. But"——and he turned accusingly to the Soldier——"you must have driven every woman you ever met completely off her chump."

"Chump," chuckled the Bishop, feinting with his right and gently upper-cutting the Celebrated Actor's celebrated chin. "What is chump, you old sinner?"

But the Well-known Soldier only smiled——a trifle sadly. "She's all I've got, old chap, and her happiness is mine."

"She is happy now," remarked the Actor quietly. "The boy's all right."

For a while the three men were silent, each busy with his own thoughts. And then over the General's face a grin began to spread.

"Tell me, you charmer of foolish women," he demanded, "how did you manage it?"

"Your vulgar gibe leaves me unmoved," returned the Actor calmly. "To-night is merely a proof of how brains and imagination control every situation. I hope you both appreciate my inference."

"Go on," chuckled the General. "The Church and the Army hide their diminished heads."

"What better destroyer of apathy is there than scrapping with someone, whom in less civilized and more primitive days one would have killed? I followed him. I suggested it to him——I even went so far as to assist him in his search for a suitable spot on which to do it. And then"——he paused magnificently——"I drew the badger. I bolted the fox. I extracted young Parker."

"How?" murmured the Church.

"I hit him first on the head with an over-ripe pear, which I threw through the window. A wonderful shot—not once in a hundred times would I do it again. And as he jumped up from the table where he was sitting, I spoke to him from my heart."

"Yes," grinned the Soldier. "And what did you say?"

"I said, 'You dirty louse—you maimer of little dogs —come out and fight, unless you're a coward as well as a swine.' Then," murmured the Actor, "I ran as fast as I could, for fear he might mistake his opponent and start on me."

For a space there was silence, while the Army and the Church shook hopelessly, and the Stage impressively lit a cigar. And it was as he deposited the match in an ash-tray on the table that he saw the piece of paper lying in front of him. He read what was written on it, and then he turned slowly and looked at the other two.

"So that's what he was doing under the yew-tree," he said softly. "Dear lad! Why, yes, he's a dear lad."

"Of course he is," returned the Soldier gruffly. "What the devil did you think?"

It was under the yew-tree that the boy and the girl met. She was kneeling there, her frock gleaming white in the moonlight as Hugh came through the trees, and for a time he watched her without speaking. Two and a half years—more—since he had seen her, and now it seemed to him that she was more lovely than ever. His eyes took in every detail of her, as she bent forward and laid both her hands on the little grave, and, suddenly, with a great wave of wonder, he realized that all the bitterness had gone from his soul. The past was blotted out—sponged from the slate; he was alive again, and the present— why, the present held out beckoning hands of welcome.

"Beryl," he whispered very low, but not so low that she failed to hear him.

"Why, Hugh, dear," she answered. "I was afraid you'd go away without seeing me."

"I should, if—Tommy had been alive."

He knelt beside her, and together they rearranged two or three of the stones.

"I put a bit of paper here," he said, after a moment.

"I found it," she answered. "That's how I knew you were here—first. Oh! Hugh,"—almost unconsciously she found herself in his arms—"poor little chap! And I'd been telling him all last week he'd be seeing you soon."

"You darling!" The boy's voice was husky. "He knows—Tommy knows."

And so for a while they clung together, while the scent of the summer flowers drifting idly by mingled with the scent of her hair.

"If he'd been here, Beryl, I was going to take him," he said, at last. "I was bitter—dear heavens! but I was bitter. I felt I didn't even want to see you. We were going hunting together—just he and I—out in the wilds."

"And now, boy," whispered the girl, "are you bitter any more?"

"No," he answered wonderingly. "I'm not. Because, Beryl, because I've thrashed that swine who killed him. Something seemed to snap in me as he went down and out, and I was conscious of a sort of marvellous happiness."

"I know," she said, laughing a little and crying a

little, as a girl will do. "I know, dear boy. I saw you do it."

"You saw me thrash him!" he said, amazed. "But how? I don't understand."

"We all did!" she cried: "Uncle Jim and the Bishop and Mr. Trayne and me. Mr. Trayne came back and told us to come."

"I see," said the boy slowly. "I see. I think I'll go and thank Mr. Trayne."

But there are other things in this world more important even than a debt of gratitude to the most celebrated of Actors, and half an hour later the boy and the girl were still pacing slowly up and down the lawn. There were so many things to be discussed—so many glorious plans to be made for the future—the future out of which the blackness had vanished so completely. And it was with almost a feeling of reproach that the girl suddenly turned to him.

"Why, boy!" she cried, "we've forgotten Tommy."

"Tommy!" he said. "Why, so we have." He stared at her for a while, and there was a little quizzical smile on his lips. "It's funny, isn't it?" he went on slowly, "that the greatest thing the little chap has ever done for me he has done by his death." He took her in his arms and held her very close. "If he'd lived, it might have all come right—in time; but now——"

And Hugh Dawnay finished his sentence in the only way such sentences can be finished.

"Come in, you two youngsters."

The General's voice came cheerfully from the dining-room, and arm-in-arm they walked towards the open window.

Half-way there they paused, and instinctively their eyes turned towards the old yew-tree.

"Why, there he is, boy," breathed the girl. "Don't

you see him, and the black mark on his neck and his tail wagging?"

"It's the shadows, darling," answered the boy. "The moonlight through the trees."

Maybe, maybe. Who knows?

Gently he led her on, and she passed into the room ahead of him. And from the path outside there rose once again into the soft summer night the farewell message of a friend to a friend:

"Good hunting, old chap."

XXXVIII MAN WITH HIS HAND IN HIS POCKET

"I'LL take one card."

With the expressionless face of the born gambler, the man glanced at his draw, and laid the five cards face downwards on the table in front of him. Not a muscle twitched as he leaned back in his chair, his right hand thrust deep in his trouser-pocket. So had he played all through the evening, losing with steady persistence and losing highly: losing, in fact, as only a man can lose who is holding good cards at poker when somebody else is holding a little better. And now he had drawn one card to three of a kind, and it had come off. There were four eights in the hand in front of him, and they had made their appearance just in time. For Billy Tindal knew only too well that the chips by his side represented everything that was left out of a matter of twenty thousand pounds. The play was high at the Ultima Thule Club in Bond Street.

A fat man opposite him had also taken one card, and Tindal's keen eye noticed the twitching of his fingers as he laid his cards down. A bad gambler, but having a run of the most infernal luck, this fat fellow. So much the better: he'd probably got a straight at least—possibly a full house. Fours could be ruled out: the fat man was the type who would always discard two if he held three of a kind.

They were playing without a limit, and at length Billy Tindal leaned across the table.

"My chips are finished, I'm afraid," he remarked, with a faint drawl. "Will you take paper till the end of the hand?"

"Certainly," said the fat man, in a voice which shook a little.

"Good!" With his left hand Tindal scrawled an IOU, quite regardless of the spectators who had collected at the rumour of big play which flies round with such mysterious rapidity. He might have been playing halfpenny nap for all the interest he apparently took in the game.

The fat man saw him at five thousand pounds—which was just four thousand more than Billy Tindal possessed in the world. And the fat man laid down a straight flush.

"You're lucky, sir," said Tindal, with a genial smile, lighting a cigarette with a perfectly steady hand. "I'll just cash a cheque and get you the chips."

A faint murmur of admiration passed round the on-lookers: this clean-shaven, steady-eyed man with the whimsical smile was a gambler after their own hearts. Then in a couple of minutes he was forgotten: players at the Ultima Thule are, in the main, a selfish brand of individual. Possibly had they suspected the utter hopelessness seething behind the impassive face of the man who stood by the buffet eating a caviare sandwich and drinking a glass of champagne, they might not have forgotten him so quickly. But they did not suspect: Billy Tindal saw to that. It was only as he turned to help himself to another sandwich that a look of despair came into his eyes. No one could see: the mask could slip for a moment. Ahead lay ruin and disgrace. The cheque could not be met next morning: there was no human possibility of raising the money in the time. And to the descendant of a long race of gamblers there was something peculiarly abhorrent in failing over a debt of honour.

"Bad luck—that last hand of yours, sir." A thickset, middle-aged man beside him was making a careful study of the various edibles. "Just came up in time to see the show-down."

"I have known the cards run better," answered Tindal curtly.

"I can see that you're a born gambler," continued the man, "and being one myself—though not in this particular line—one has, if one may say so, a sort of fellow-feeling." He was munching a sandwich and staring round the room as he spoke. "The nerve, sir —the nerve required to stake everything on the turn of a card—on the rise or fall of a market—by Heaven, it's the only thing in life!"

Almost against his will—for he was in no mood for talking—Billy Tindal smiled.

"Your game is the Stock Exchange, is it?"

"It is, sir—and there's no game like it in the world. Even when ruin stares you in the face, you've still got till next settling day. You've still got a chance."

"I wish the same thing applied here," said Tindal, with a hard laugh.

"As bad as that, is it?" remarked the other sympathetically. "Never mind: the luck will change. I guess there have been times when I've felt like stealing or forging or doing any other blamed thing under the sun to put my hand on some ready money."

Tindal smiled mirthlessly, and said nothing. The

point of view coincided rather too unpleasantly with his own.

"And mark you, sir," continued the stranger dogmatically. "I've got a greater respect for a man who wins through, by fair means if possible—but, if not, by foul—than for the weakling who goes down and out. The first, at any rate, is a *man*."

Again Tindal smiled. "Leaving out the ethical side of your contention, sir," he remarked, "there are one or two small practical difficulties that occur to one's mind. It is sometimes as difficult to find the foul means as it is to find the fair. Burglary and forging rank high amongst the arts, I believe, which are not taught at most of the public schools."

The other man shrugged his shoulders contemptuously. "Of course you mustn't take me too literally. But"—he thumped an enormous fist into the open palm of his other hand—"there's always a way, sir, if you've got the nerve to take it. Nerve: that's the only thing that counts in this world. Without it— why, you can go and grow tomatoes in the country! Nerve, and the capability of seizing the right moment. With those two assets you come to the top and you stay there." For a moment or two he stared fixedly at the half-averted face of the younger man; then he gave a jovial laugh. "Anyway—if you start to recoup your fortunes with journalism—you needn't give those as the opinions of Paul Harker. Not that they aren't pretty widely known, but in this world one must pretend."

Tindal glanced at the speaker. So this was the celebrated Paul Harker, was it? What the devil was it he'd overheard at the club that afternoon about him? Not knowing him, at the time it had made no impression; now he recalled it hazily. Something to do with a woman. He frowned slightly as he tried to remember; then he gave a short laugh. What on earth did it matter? What did anything matter except that cursed cheque?

"Well, I'll say good night, Mr. Harker." He put down his empty glass. "It would take a mighty big journalistic scoop to put me straight—bigger even than your ideas on life."

"Which way are you going?"

"Half-Moon Street. I've got rooms there."

"I'll stroll with you. The atmosphere of this place is fierce."

In silence the two men got their coats and strolled into Bond Street. The theatres were just over, and a stream of cars were pouring westward with their loads of well-dressed, wealthy occupants. Life—life in London—for people with money! With a cynical smile Billy Tindal lit a cigarette. It was what he had promised himself after years in the wilds.

He barely heard his companion's occasional remarks: it was just as they turned into Half-Moon Street that it struck Billy that Paul Harker had made some suggestion and was waiting for an answer.

"I beg your pardon, Mr. Harker," he said apologetically, "but I'm afraid my mind was wandering. You were saying——"

"I was suggesting that if you've got nothing better to do you should come to my house in Curzon Street. My wife has a spiritualistic séance on. Starts at midnight. Come in and see the fun."

For a moment Billy hesitated. After all, why not? Anything was better than a solitary contemplation of his own confounded foolishness.

"It's very good of you——" he began, but the other cut him short.

"Not at all. Only too pleased you can manage it."

"But won't your wife—— I mean, I'm a complete

stranger." He paused doubtfully by the door of his rooms.

"My wife won't mind," answered Paul Harker, taking him by the arm. "Do you good, my dear fellow. Take your mind off."

It was really deuced good of this fellow Harker. Sympathy of a gambler for a gambler sort of idea. He could only hope that Mrs. Harker would see eye to eye with her husband.

"Here is the house, Mr. Tindal. Come in." With a smile of welcome Paul Harker stood aside to let the younger man pass.

"I didn't know you knew my name, Mr. Harker," said Billy Tindal, as a footman relieved him of his coat.

"I asked who you were at the Ultima Thule. Come on up and meet my wife." Then, in a hoarse undertone just before they reached the room, he turned to Tindal. "I don't know whether you believe in this stuff; but, for Heaven's sake, pretend to."

He gave a heavy wink, and Billy smiled. Undoubtedly Paul Harker was quite a pleasant fellow.

II

There were six women in the room when they entered and one somewhat anæmic-looking man.

"Hope I'm not late, my dear," said Paul Harker, breezily, to a pale, delicate-looking woman who rose to meet them. "I've brought a friend who is interested in these things. Mr. Tindal—my wife."

Billy Tindal bowed, and took a chair beside her.

"We hope for some very interesting results to-night, Mr. Tindal," she remarked. "Professor Granger feels confident of getting a tangible materialization."

"Indeed!"

Mindful of his host's injunction, he nodded portentously. His ideas on what a tangible materialization was were of the vaguest: if it was anything like Professor Granger, he inwardly trusted the experiment would fail.

For a few minutes they continued to talk generalities: then Mrs. Harker rose and crossed to the Professor, leaving Tindal to his own devices. With some interest he glanced round the room. Heavy black curtains hung over the windows and the door. The furniture was reduced to a minimum, the whole of the centre of the floor being empty. Around the walls were ranged easy chairs draped in some dark material: the carpet, thick and luxurious, was dark also. In fact, the whole room was sombre—sombre and silent.

Curiously he glanced at his companions. In one corner four of the women were talking in low, restrained tones, evidently impressed with the solemnity of the occasion, and involuntarily Tindal smiled. They seemed so very earnest—and so very dull. Then he looked at the other woman who was standing by Paul Harker. She seemed of a different type—very far from being dull. Tall and perfectly proportioned, she was dressed in black, and as his eyes rested idly on the pair it struck him that his host found her far from dull also. And at that moment they both turned and looked at him.

It was the first time he had seen the woman's face, and he found himself staring foolishly at her. She was one of the most beautiful things he had ever seen —beautiful in a sensuous Eastern fashion—and Billy Tindal suddenly realized that he was gaping at her like a callow schoolboy. Abruptly he looked away, annoyed with himself at his gaucherie, to find that he was not the only person who was interested in the lady. For his hostess, though ostensibly speaking to the Professor, was watching her husband's companion with a look on her face which left no doubt as to her feelings on the subject.

"So that's how the land lies, is it?" thought Tindal; and the remark he had overheard at the club came back to him. He knew there had been a woman in it.

"Iris, I want you to meet Mr. Tindal." His host's voice made him look up quickly. "Let me introduce you to Miss Sala."

Tindal rose and bowed: on the instant the remark had returned to his memory.

"There will be a crash soon," a man had said, "with Harker and that Sala girl."

And now he was talking to the Sala girl, and deciding that if she was beautiful at a distance she was ten times more beautiful close to.

"No," he found himself saying, "I've not done much of this sort of thing in England, though I've seen a good deal of what the African native calls *ju-ju*."

"And it interests you?" Her voice was deep and very sweet.

"Very much," said Tindal. "I'm most curious to see what is going to happen to-night."

For a moment the smile seemed to ripple over the surface of her eyes: then once more they were inscrutable.

"It's rather exciting if it comes off," she remarked thoughtfully. "Everything is pitch-dark, of course, and then you hear sighs and groans, and sometimes a hand comes out and touches you."

"But do you really believe——" began Tindal incredulously.

"I don't believe—I know," said the girl calmly. "Why, at one séance I attended a jade necklace I was wearing was wrenched off my neck. The fastening was broken, and all the beads rolled about the floor.

And everyone had been bound in their chairs, Mr. Tindal, before we started."

Billy nodded discreetly; it occurred to him that he had heard stories like that before.

"You hear something moving round the room," she continued, "something you know was not there at the beginning—and won't be there at the end. And sometimes it bumps against you, and then it goes on floundering and moving about the room. It sounds like a sack of potatoes being dragged about at times, and then it changes and you hear soft footfalls."

Again Billy nodded: he was prepared to listen indefinitely to this sort of stuff when the speaker was Iris Sala.

"It sounds more than rather exciting," he said, with a grin. "Let's hope we get the jolly old flounderer to-night."

For the moment his own trouble was forgotten: he was only conscious of a pleasurable sense of excitement. Not that he really believed in what the girl had said, any more than the average normal person believes in a haunted house. But even the most pronounced sceptic is conscious of a little thrill when he turns out the light in the bedroom which is popularly reputed to be the family ghost's special hunting-ground.

"I think it's very foolish of Mrs. Harker to wear those lovely pearls of hers." The girl was speaking again, and Tindal glanced at his hostess. He had not remarked them specially before, but now he noticed that Mrs. Harker had three long ropes of large beautifully matched pearls round her neck. "My jade beads didn't matter very much—though I lost half a dozen at least. But with those pearls—why, she might mislay a dozen if the rope was broken, and be none the wiser."

A jovial chuckle made Tindal look up. Paul Harker

was standing behind them, and he had evidently heard the girl's remark.

"I'm a Philistine, Iris. Forgive me. I don't somehow anticipate much danger to Rose's pearls."

"You're wrong, Mr. Harker," she said gravely. "You've never seen a tangible materialization. I have—and I know."

"Anyway," he laughed, "there's no use attempting to ask her to take them off, because she won't. And incidentally it looks to me as if the worthy Professor was going to get busy. There's a wild look in his eye."

"Will you take your seats, please, ladies and gentlemen? The two gentlemen on opposite sides of the room. I thank you." In a mournful way he contemplated the circle from the centre of the floor. "I would point out to all of you," he continued, "that our experiment to-night is a difficult one, entailing the highest form of will-co-operation and mental effort. If we are successful, I can tell no more than you what form this materialization will take. But I must entreat of you to concentrate with all your power on the one main salient fact of producing a tangible thing: and I must beg you most earnestly not, under any circumstances, to speak while the experiment is in progress. We will now put out the lights."

And the last thing Billy Tindal was conscious of before the lights went out were Iris Sala's grey-green eyes fixed on him with an inscrutable baffling look in them. Even in the darkness he seemed to see them: languorous, mocking, a little cynical. And there was something else—some other emotion which eluded him for the moment. It wasn't sorrow, though it seemed akin to sorrow; it was—yes, it was pity. He moved slightly in his chair, and nodded his head in the darkness. Pity—that was the other message in those wonderful eyes: and the thought brought him back to the reality of his own position.

Paul Harker must have told her, of course: told her that he'd been losing heavily, and she was sorry for him. Even to a millionaire like Harker five thousand pounds on a single hand of poker would seem fairly heavy; and to him—— He gave a mirthless little laugh, which called forth an instant rebuke from the Professor.

"Perfect silence, please."

Billy Tindal lay back in his chair and closed his eyes. His brain was racing with the feverish activity of a worried man. If it had been anything else—anything but a gambling debt. Thank God! his father was dead, and would never know the disgrace of it; but there were quite a number of relations. They'd soon find out; things of that sort can't be kept dark. What a fool, what a damnable fool he'd been!

And it was at that moment that there came a soft bump on the floor, and he heard the woman in the next chair to him draw in her breath sharply.

For a while he stared rigidly into the darkness; then, with a slight frown, he let his body relax. He was in no mood for entertainments of this type: he wished now that he hadn't come. And yet it had been very decent of Harker suggesting it—very decent. Was there a possibility, he wondered—if he made a clean breast of the whole thing to his host—was there a possibility of his lending four thousand? It seemed the only hope, the bare chance of salvation. He'd ask him after this cursed séance was over. The worst that could happen would be a refusal. And supposing he didn't refuse? Supposing—— Billy drew in a deep breath at the mere thought.

Thump! thump! Perfectly clear and audible the sounds came from the centre of the room, bringing him back to the present, and he felt the back of his scalp begin to tingle. Of course, it was a trick; and yet he didn't somehow associate the Professor with a vulgar fraud. He had struck him as a well-meaning, conscientious man, who was badly in need of exercise and an outdoor life. Probably dyspeptic.

And if so—if it wasn't a trick—what was it that was now dragging itself about?

"Like a sack of potatoes." Iris Sala's words came back to him as he sat there motionless.

Suddenly he heard the Professor's voice, trembling a little with excitement:

"Who are you? Speak!"

The noise ceased at once; only a long-drawn shuddering sigh came out of the darkness. Then after a minute or two the uncanny dragging noise commenced again: bump—slither—bump. He tried to locate it, but it seemed everywhere. At one moment it was close by, at another it sounded as if it was at the other side of the room.

It was devilish, it was horrible. He put a hand to his forehead; it was wet with sweat. He felt an insane desire to get up from his chair and rush from the room: the only trouble was that he had forgotten the exact location of the door. Besides, he might bump into the Thing on the way.

A frightened cry rang out, and Billy Tindal half-rose in his chair. It was a woman's cry: probably the Thing had touched her. The bumping had ceased, he noticed: another noise had taken its place—a slight gurgling sound, accompanied by a quick beating on the floor, as if someone was drumming with their feet on the carpet. And after a while that ceased also. Silence, absolute and complete, reigned in the room for ten minutes or a quarter of an hour. The Thing had gone.

At length the Professor spoke.

"Are you still there?" There was no sound in answer. "Manifest yourself now if you are; otherwise the light will be turned up."

Still there was no sound, though the Professor waited a full minute before speaking again.

"Will you, please, turn up the light, Mr. Harker?"

"Certainly." Paul Harker's cheerful voice came from the other side of the room, as he rose to comply with the request. For a moment or two he fumbled with the switch; then the room was once more flooded with light.

"A most satisfactory manifestation," began the Professor, only to stop with a look of dawning horror on his face. Scattered around Mrs. Harker's chair were scores of wonderful pearls. Sprawling over the arm of the chair was the unfortunate woman herself.

For a moment there was a stunned silence in the room; then with a cry Paul Harker sprang forward.

"She's fainted. I'll get brandy."

He dashed from the room, as two of the women, reassured by the words, went over to Mrs. Harker.

"I knew it was risky wearing those pearls," whispered Iris Sala in Billy's ear, but he hardly heard what she said. He was staring at the limp form of his hostess through narrowed lids, and suddenly he turned to the girl beside him.

"It's a doctor that's wanted, not brandy," he said abruptly. "Where's the telephone?"

"In the hall," answered the girl.

He ran downstairs, passing Paul Harker on the way. For what seemed an eternity he stood by the instrument before he could get through. Then he returned to the room above.

"A doctor's coming at once," he announced breathlessly, and then he stopped dead—just inside the door.

Huddled together in a group at the end of the room were all the women—all save Iris Sala. She was standing by Mrs. Harker's chair, with Paul Harker on the other side.

"There is no need for a doctor, Mr. Tindal," said Harker, in a terrible voice. "My wife is dead. And my wife has been murdered!"

"Murdered!" gasped Billy mechanically.

"Murdered," repeated Harker. "Come and see."

Dazedly Billy walked towards him, to stop and stare foolishly at the woman in the chair. For they had propped her up and laid her head back, and on her throat distinct and clear were the marks of a hand. The four fingers on one side, the thumb on the other, showed up red and angry in the bright light.

"She had a weak heart, Mr. Tindal," continued Paul Harker slowly. "Any sudden shock, such as a hand grasping her throat,"—his voice shook a little—"would have been liable to kill her. And a hand *did* grasp her throat: the hand that tore off her pearls."

"My God!" muttered Billy. "It's ghastly—ghastly! Then that thing we heard must have—must have——"

"Must have murdered my wife, Mr. Tindal. The question is—what was it we heard? I fear we shall find it difficult to persuade the police on the matter of a tangible materialization. They deal in more mundane causes."

And at that moment Billy Tindal understood. The relentless voice of the man, the strange look in the grey-green eyes of the girl—it seemed to be triumph now—cleared away the fog from his brain, leaving it ice-cold. He was a man who suddenly sees a flaring notice, DANGER, and realizes that there is peril ahead, though he knows not its exact form. And with men of the Tindal stamp it is best to be careful at such moments.

"I see," he answered slowly. "You mean that, re-garded from the police point of view, the supposition will be that one of the people who were present during the séance tore the pearls from your wife's neck, and in doing so murdered her."

"Regarded from every point of view," corrected Paul Harker harshly.

"Then under those circumstances," said Tindal grimly, "the police must be sent for at once."

With his hands in his pockets he was staring at Paul Harker, while from the other end of the room came an occasional sob from some overwrought woman.

The whole thing was like some horrible nightmare —bizarre, unreal—and the sudden arrival of the doctor came as a relief to everyone. Quickly he made his examination. Then he stood up.

"How did that happen?" he asked gravely, staring at the marks on the dead woman's throat.

"That man did it!" roared Harker, unable to contain himself longer and pointing an accusing finger at Tindal. "You vile scoundrel! you blackguard! you—you——"

"Steady, Mr. Harker!" cried the doctor sharply. "Am I to understand, sir, that you did this?" He turned in amazement to Tindal.

"You are not," said Billy evenly. "It's a damnable lie."

"I don't understand," remarked the doctor. "Will somebody kindly explain?"

It was Iris Sala who answered, and as she spoke the feeling that he was dreaming grew stronger in Billy Tindal.

"We were having a séance, Doctor," she began in her deep rich voice, "trying to get a tangible materialization. The room, of course, was in pitch-darkness, and after it was over and the lights were turned up we found that Mrs. Harker was—dead!"

Her voice faltered, and Harker lifted a grief-stricken face from beside his wife's chair.

"But what happened during the séance?" asked the doctor.

"We heard something moving about. A thing that bumped and slithered over the carpet."

"Pshaw!" snapped the doctor. "What I don't understand is why this gentleman should be accused of it."

"Because," cried Harker, getting up, "he's in desperate want of money. Look at this!" He fumbled in his pocket, and to Billy's amazement produced the cheque for four thousand he had written at the Ultima Thule. "I took this cheque to-night in exchange for one of my own—because I liked the look of you. Yes —you wicked villain—I liked the look of you; and I meant to do something for you. I brought him here, never dreaming—never thinking——" His voice broke again. "He saw my wife's pearls: was actually talking about them just before the séance started—and then when the light went out he must have snatched them off her neck. And in doing so you killed her. And to think I actually heard you doing the vile deed!"

"You deny this?" asked the doctor.

"Absolutely," returned Billy grimly.

"I feel that it is partly my fault," said the girl in a broken voice. "I never dreamed, of course, that this man was in want of money. And I told him a foolish story about how some jade beads I once had were snatched from my neck during a séance like this—by the thing that came. Of course—it wasn't true. It was a joke. But I told it just to frighten him. And I suppose he believed it, and thought he would do the same." She buried her face in her hands.

"Well, are any of the pearls missing? If so, where

are they?" The doctor's question brought Paul Harker to his feet.

"I don't even know how many my dear wife had!" he cried.

"The point seems immaterial," said Billy quietly. "Since I seem to be the object of suspicion, I should be obliged if you would search me, Doctor."

With a shrug of his shoulders the doctor complied. Methodically he ran through every pocket; then he turned to Paul Harker.

"There are no pearls on this gentleman," he said curtly.

"Ah, but he left the room. He left the room to telephone for you. He might have put them in his overcoat."

"Then we'll send for the overcoat," remarked the doctor, ringing the bell. "With your permission, that is, sir." He turned to Tindal.

"By all means," said Billy. "Only I would like to state, should they be found there, that I am not the only person who has left the room since the tragedy. Mr. Harker has also been downstairs."

Paul Harker laughed wildly.

"Yes, I know. To get brandy. Before I knew ———"

He paused as a footman opened the door.

"Bring this gentleman's overcoat," ordered the doctor, "up to this room. And be careful to see that nothing falls out of the pockets."

With one horrified glance at the motionless figure in the chair, the footman fled, returning almost immediately with the coat.

"This is your coat?" asked the doctor.

"It is," said Billy.

And then in a tense silence the doctor extracted twenty large pearls from different pockets.

"You murderer!" Paul Harker's whispered words seemed to ring through the room, and with a little strangled gasp a woman fainted. The doctor's face, grim and accusing, was turned on Billy, as if demanding some explanation which he knew full well could not be given. And of all those present only Billy Tindal himself seemed cool and calm, as, with his hands still in his pockets, he faced the ring of his accusers.

"What have you to say?" said the doctor sternly.

"One thing—and one thing only," answered Billy. "I have read in fiction of diabolical plots: to-night I have met one in real life. But, as so often happens in fiction, one mistake is made, which leads to the undoing of the villain. And one mistake has been made to-night."

And now his eyes, merciless and stern, were fixed on Paul Harker, and he noticed with a certain grim amusement that a muscle in the millionaire's face was beginning to twitch.

"Mr. Harker is a man of nerve: he also believes in seizing the right moment. And to-night struck him as being the right moment."

"What are you talking about?" snarled Harker.

"For reasons best known to yourself, Mr. Harker," —he glanced from him to Iris Sala, from whose eyes the strange look of triumph had mysteriously vanished, leaving only fear—deadly, gripping fear—"you wished to get rid of your wife."

"It's a lie!" Paul Harker sprang forward, his fist raised to strike.

"You will doubtless have ample opportunity for proving it," continued Billy imperturbably. "By a happy combination of circumstances, a suitable moment —the darkness of a séance—and a suitable motive— robbery—presented themselves to your hand. Acting according to your tradition, you took them. And as far as I can see, Mr. Harker, you would have been successful had you also selected a suitable person. Therein lay your one error."

"Am I to understand," said Harker in a grating voice, "that you are accusing *me*—of murdering my wife? Why—you miserable cur——" He stopped, choking with anger.

"I make no such accusation," answered Billy. "All I state is that I didn't." He turned gravely to the doctor. "What was the cause of Mrs. Harker's death?"

"Heart failure—caused by partial strangulation with the hand."

"Which hand?"

The doctor looked at him quickly; then glanced once more at the dead woman.

"The right hand."

"You swear to that?"

"Undoubtedly I swear to it," said the doctor.

For the first time Billy Tindal withdrew his right hand from his pocket, and held it out in front of him.

"The one mistake," he said grimly.

The first, second, and third fingers were missing!

For a moment there was a deathly silence; then the doctor suddenly sprang forward.

"Stop him!" he roared.

But Paul Harker had already joined the woman he had foully killed, and in the air there hung the faint smell of burnt almonds. Prussic acid is quick.

An hour later Billy Tindal walked slowly along the deserted streets towards his rooms. The police had come and gone; everything in the room where the tragedy had taken place had duly passed before the searching eye of officialdom. Everything, that is, save one exhibit, and that reposed in Billy's pocket. And when a man has signed a cheque for four thousand pounds on a total bank balance of as many pence, his pocket is the best place for it.

XXXIX   A PAYMENT ON ACCOUNT

I

"EXCUSE me, but could you give me some idea as to where I am? I have a shrewd notion that it's Devonshire, but——"

The speaker, holding a dilapidated cap in his hand, broke off as the girl sat up and looked at him. He was a dishevelled-looking object, covered with dust, and—romance may be great, but truth is greater—it was only too obvious to the girl that he was very hot. Perspiration ran in trickles down his face, ploughing dark furrows through the thick stratum of road dust which otherwise obscured his features. His collar was open, his sleeves rolled back from his wrists, and on his back was strapped a small knapsack. An unlit pipe, which he had removed from his mouth on speaking to her, in one hand, and a long walking-stick in the other, completed the picture.

"You don't look as if you'd been flying," she remarked dispassionately. "It's Devonshire all right."

"That's a relief." She had a fleeting glimpse of a flash of white teeth as he smiled. "I had an idea it might be Kent. Or even farther. Have you ever been on a walking tour?"

"That's what you're doing, is it?"

"You know," remarked the man, "I think even Watson would regard you with scorn. And our one and only Sherlock would burst into tears." He leaned over the railings and commenced to fill his pipe. The

little garden in which the girl was sitting seemed delightfully cool and shady; the girl herself, in her muslin
frock, looking at him with an amused twinkle in her
eyes, seemed almost too good to be true. After that
interminable road, with the sun beating down from a
cloudless sky. With a sigh of relief he passed the
back of his hand across his forehead, and the girl
laughed.

"I wouldn't do it by bits if I were you. It makes
you look rather like a zebra."

"Don't mock at me," he implored, "or I shall burst
into tears. It's the very first time I've ever done anything of this sort, I promise you. I will go farther.
It's the very last as well."

"But if you don't like walking—why walk?"

"How like a woman!" He fumbled in his pocket
for a box of matches and lit his pipe. "How exactly
like! Have you never felt an irresistible temptation to
do something wild and desperate? Something which
is painted in glowing colours by some scoundrel, who
revenges himself on humanity by foully inducing
innocent people to follow his advice?"

"I once tried keeping bees," she murmured
thoughtfully.

"There you are!" exclaimed the man triumphantly.
"You see you are in no position to point the finger of
scorn at me. You were led away by fictitious rubbish
on the bee as a household pet. You expected honey:
you obtained stings. I was likewise led away by a
scoundrel who wrote on the delights of walking. He
especially roused my expectation by the number of
times he threw himself down on the soft, sweet-smelling
turf while the gentle wind played round his temples
and the lazy beat of the breakers came from the distant
Atlantic. I tried that exercise the very first day. Net
result: I landed on a thistle and winded myself."

She gurgled gently. "At any rate, I'll bet he told you that you ought to come with a map."

"Wrong again. He especially stipulated that you should have no set route. Just walk and walk; and then, I suppose, when a kindly death intervenes, your relatives can't find you, and your funeral expenses fall on the parish in which you expire."

He straightened up as the door of the house opened and a charming, grey-haired woman came slowly down the path. She glanced at him quickly—a courteous but shrewd look; then she looked at the girl.

"Sheila, dear, who——?"

"A gentleman on a walking tour, mother, who has lost his way."

"You're not far from Umberleigh," said the elder woman. "Where are you making for?"

"Nowhere in particular, as I've been explaining to your daughter, madam," smiled the man. "Finally, however, I shall take the train and arrive in London and slaughter the man who wrote the article which appeared in the paper."

"Sounds like the house that Jack built," laughed the girl. "Anyway, you'd better stop to lunch."

The man glanced at her mother, who seconded the invitation with a gracious smile.

"My name is Hewson," he remarked. "Charles Hewson." He glanced at them as he spoke, and gave a little sigh of relief: evidently the name meant nothing to them. "And I don't always look like a zebra."

He followed them slowly up the shady path, and the girl laughed again.

"Doesn't matter what you look like," she cried, "as long as you know something about postage-stamps."

"Do you collect?" he asked.

"No—but daddy does. He's partially insane on the subject."

"Sheila!" reproved her mother.

"Well, he is, darling, you know.   You always say so yourself."

For a moment the elder woman's eyes met the man's over the girl's head.   And in that momentary glance the whole story of the house and its inmates seemed to stand revealed.   The perfect love and happiness that breathed through the place; the certainty that it was the girl who was really the head of the little kingdom, with a sweet mother and an unpractical father as her adoring subjects; the glorious unworldliness of his surroundings struck the man like a blow.   The contrast was so wonderful—the contrast to his own life. If only—— Unconsciously his glance rested on the slim figure in the muslin frock.   If only—— Why not?

"I beg your pardon."   He turned apologetically to the mother.

"I only said that our name was Crossley, Mr. Hewson.   And I wondered if you would care to have a bath."

Charles Hewson looked at her gravely.   "Are you always so charming, Mrs. Crossley, to the stranger within your gates? Especially when he's a dirty-looking tramp like me."   Then he smiled quickly; it was a trick of his, that sudden, fleeting smile.   "I can think of nothing I'd like more than a bath, if I might so far trespass on your hospitality."

II

Lunch confirmed his diagnosis of the Crossley household.   The girl's father fitted in exactly with his mental picture; an utterly lovable, white-haired man of about sixty, and as unsophisticated as a child.   Time, and the stress of things worldly, seemed to have passed over the little house near Umberleigh, leaving it un-

touched and scathless. And once again the contrast
struck him, and he wondered, just a little bitterly,
whether after all it was worth it. The instant decisions,
the constant struggle, the ceaseless strain of his life—
and then, this. Country cousins, vegetating in obscurity. It struck Charles Hewson that he wouldn't
object to being a vegetable for a while. He was tired,
and he realized it for the first time. The last year had
tried even him.

It was a sudden impulse that made him suggest it,
just as luncheon was over.

"Is there a decent inn here, Mrs. Crossley, where I
could put up for a bit? I've fallen in love with this
place, and I want a rest."

"You look tired," she answered kindly. "And
this is a wonderful place for a rest cure. But I'm
afraid the inn is a long way off. If you care to"—she
paused for a moment—"we could put you up for a
few days."

"I think you're the kindest people I've ever met,"
said Hewson, and for a moment his eyes ceased to
look tired. "And I warn you I'm not going to give
you the chance of reconsidering your offer."

"You'll find it very dull," warned the girl.

He laughed as he rose from the table. "I'm open
to a small bet that you'll have to drive me away. I shall
become a fixture about the house."

He followed them into the low, old-fashioned hall,
and stood for a while drinking in the homeliness of it
all. That was what it was—homely; and in London
Charles Hewson lived in rooms and fed at his club or a
restaurant.

"I don't know if you're any judge of pewter, Mr.
Hewson," said his host, "but we've got some nice bits
here and in my study."

"One step from that to postage-stamps," laughed the

girl. "You've got to come and do a job of work in the garden later, Mr. Hewson, don't forget. I'll come and rescue you in half an hour or so."

He watched her go upstairs, then with a little sigh of pure joy he followed the old man into his study.

"Are you interested in philately, by any chance?" inquired Mr. Crossley eagerly.

Hewson shook his head. "I'm afraid I know nothing about it," he answered. "I was once commissioned by a young nephew to send him all the stamps I could find which had pretty pictures on them. You know, harbours, and mountains, and elephants. I found them in all sorts of outlandish places when I was going round the world." He gave one of his quick smiles. "But I'm afraid that is the extent of my knowledge."

"The schoolboy collection." The other waved a tolerant hand. "Now I'm sure that that would have bored him."

With reverent hands he lifted a card and handed it to Hewson. "Look at that, sir; look at that. The complete set of New Brunswick—the first issue, unused."

Hewson gazed dispassionately at ten somewhat blotchy pieces of paper, and refrained from heretical utterance. To his Philistine eye the set he had bought in Samoa or elsewhere depicting jaguars and toucans were infinitely more pleasing.

"Valuable, I suppose?" he hazarded.

The other waved a deprecating hand. "Several hundred—if I chose to sell. Mercifully," he went on after a little pause, "it wasn't necessary."

For a second Hewson's shrewd eyes were fixed on him; then he resumed his study of the rarities. Money trouble, was there?

"Now this *was* unique—this set." His host was looking regretfully at another card. "Mauritius. And then I had to dispose of the penny orange-red. Worth the better part of a thousand pounds alone." He laid down the card. "Oh! I do hope I shall be able to get it back. I sold it to a dealer in the Strand, and I told him at the time that I should want to buy it back again. That was a month ago, and I thought I should have been able to by now."

Once again Hewson's keen eyes were fixed on the other.

"Expecting a legacy?" he remarked casually.

"A legacy! Oh! no!" The old man smiled. "But I had a very wonderful chance, given me by an acquaintance, of doubling my small capital." For a moment Hewson stopped smoking: chances of doubling capital are not handed round as a rule by acquaintances. "And I seem to have done it," continued Mr. Crossley, rubbing his hands together. "I seem to have turned my five thousand pounds into ten. In a month. Isn't it wonderful?"

"Very," commented the other. "Have you got the money?"

"No: that's what I can't understand. I suppose it must be something to do with settling day—or whatever they call it." He beamed at his listener. "I'm afraid I'm very ignorant on these matters, Mr. Hewson, but it seems almost too good to be true. I wanted the extra money so much—to give my little girl a better time. It's dull for her here, though she never complains. And if only I could get it now, I could buy back that penny Mauritius, and invest the other nine thousand." In his excitement he walked up and down the room, while his listener stared fixedly at a number of blotchy pieces of paper on a card. "Do you know anything about stocks and shares, Mr. Hewson?"

"Quite a lot," said Hewson. "In my er—small way, I dabble in them."

"Ah! then perhaps you can tell me when I can expect the money." Mr. Crossley sat down at his desk, and opened a drawer. "It was a month ago that I paid five thousand pounds for shares in the Rio Lopez Mine."

"In the what?" Hewson almost shouted.

"The Rio Lopez Mine," repeated the other. "You've heard of it, of course. The shares were standing, so my friend told me, at two pounds, so I got two thousand five hundred shares. Now, yesterday I happened to buy *The Times*, and I looked up the Stock Exchange quotations. You can judge of my delight, Mr. Hewson, when I actually saw that the shares were standing at four pounds three shillings."

"Rio Lopez four pounds!" said Hewson dazedly. "May I see the paper?"

He took it and glanced at the Supplementary List.

"MINES—MISCELLANEOUS.
"Rio Lopez Deep—4/3."

The old man was still talking gaily on, but Hewson hardly heard what he said. From outside the lazy hum of a summer afternoon came softly through the open window, and after a while he laid down the paper and commenced to refill his pipe. Such colossal innocence almost staggered him. That there could be anybody in the world who did not know that the figures meant four shillings and threepence, left him bereft of speech. And then his feeling of amazement gave way to one of bitter anger against the scoundrel who had unloaded a block of shares in a wild-cat mine, at the top of an extremely shady boom, on such a man as Mr. Crossley.

"Well, when do you think I may expect the money?" The question roused him from his reverie.

"It's hard to say, Mr. Crossley," remarked Hewson

deliberately. "Different firms have different arrangements, you know."

"Of course—of course. I'm such a baby in these things. But I do want to get my penny Mauritius back before it's sold."

Hewson bent forward suddenly, ostensibly to examine his pipe. For the first time for many years he found a difficulty in speaking; there had been no room for sentiment in his career. Then he straightened up.

"I quite understand, Mr. Crossley," he said slowly. "And perhaps the best thing to do would be to put the matter in my hands. It has occurred to me since lunch that I've really got no clothes at all here. And so I thought I'd run up to Town and get a few and then return. While I'm up there I could look into things for you."

"But I really couldn't worry you, Mr. Hewson," protested the other.

"No worry at all. It's my work. I shall charge you commission." Hewson was lighting his pipe. "You have the certificate, I suppose."

"I've this paper," answered Mr. Crossley. "Is that what you mean?"

"That's it. Will you trust it to me? I can give you any reference you like, if you care to come with me as far as Barnstaple. They know me at the bank. I shall have to join the main line there."

"Well, perhaps——" The old man paused doubtfully. "You see, Mr. Ferguson told me to keep this most carefully."

"Was Mr. Ferguson the man who sold you the shares?"

"Yes. Mr. Arthur Ferguson, of 20, Plumpton Street, in the City. He was stopping down here for a few days, and he dined with us once or twice."

Hewson rose abruptly and went to the window.

He had not the pleasure of Mr. Arthur Ferguson's acquaintance, but he was already tasting the pleasures of his first—and last—interview with that engaging gentleman. Dined—had he?

"Will you come over with me to Barnstaple this afternoon?"

"Good heavens, daddy!" came a voice from outside. "What are you going to Barnstaple for? You know this heat will upset you."

Hewson swung round as the girl came in from the garden. She was wearing a floppy sun-bonnet, and it suddenly struck him that she was one of the loveliest things he had ever seen. No wonder the old chap had tried to get a bit more money with the idea of giving her a good time.

"I've got to go up to London, Miss Crossley,"— was it his imagination, or did her face fall a little?— "to get some more clothes. And there's a little matter of business I'm going to attend to for your father. The point is that he doesn't know me—none of you know me. And in the hard-headed, suspicious world in which I live, before you entrust a valuable document to another man you want to know something about him. Now, the bank manager at Barnstaple does know me, and I suggested that your father should come over and see him."

"It sounds very mysterious," laughed the girl. "But all I know is that if daddy goes to Barnstaple in this heat, he'll have the most awful head. Suppose—" she paused doubtfully—"suppose I came? Daddy could give me the document, and then when I'd seen the bank manager I could give it to you."

Hewson turned away to hide the too obvious delight he felt at the suggestion, and glanced inquiringly at his host.

"Perhaps that would be the best solution, Mr.

Crossley," he murmured. "If it isn't troubling your daughter too much."

The old man chuckled. "If she only knew what it was for, she wouldn't mind the trouble. It's a secret, don't forget, Mr. Hewson. Now, girlie, take that envelope, and when the bank manager has told you that our kind friend here isn't a burglar, or an escaped convict"—he chuckled again—"give it to him to take to London. But you're not to look inside."

She kissed him lightly, and turned to Hewson.

"We can just catch the local train," she said, a trifle abruptly. "We'll go through the short cut."

She was silent during the walk to the station, and it was not until they were in the train that she looked at him steadily and spoke.

"What is this mystery, Mr. Hewson?"

"I think your father said it was a secret, didn't he?" he answered lightly.

"Is it something to do with money?"

"It is."

She stared out of the window: then impulsively she laid a hand on his arm.

"He's such a darling," she burst out, "but he's so innocent. He doesn't know anything about money or the world."

"Do you?" asked Hewson, gently.

"That doesn't matter. A girl needn't. But I know he's just mad to get more money—not for himself—but for me. He wants to give me a good time—like other girls, he says." She paused a moment, and frowned. "There was a man here—a few weeks ago—and daddy met him. He came to dinner. I didn't trust him, Mr. Hewson; there was something—oh! I don't know. I suppose I'm very ignorant myself. But I'm certain that he persuaded daddy to do something with his money. He was always going to the bank, and sending registered letters, after the man left.   And he's been worried ever since—until yesterday—when he recovered all his old spirits."

The train was already running into Barnstaple—the quickest journey that Charles Hewson had ever made in his life.

"I don't think," he said gravely, "that I shall be letting out the secret if I tell you that my visit to London concerns that man, and some money he invested for your father.   There's a little delay in the business— and I'm going to see about it."

They walked out of the station towards the bank, the girl clasping the precious envelope tightly.

"I want to see the manager," said Hewson to the cashier.   "Hewson is my name."

With astonishing alacrity the manager appeared from his office.

"Come in, Mr. Hewson—come in."   He stepped aside as the girl, followed by Hewson, entered his sanctum.

"I am doing some business for Mr. Crossley, of Umberleigh," said Hewson quietly.   "This is his daughter, Miss Crossley.   It concerns some shares— the certificate of which I propose to take to London with me.   Would you be good enough to assure Miss Crossley that I am a fit and proper person to be entrusted with such a matter?   I happen to be a stranger to them."

The manager's face had changed through various stages of bewilderment while Hewson was speaking, but he was saved the necessity of an immediate answer by the girl.   Charles Hewson—*the* Charles Hewson —coming to him to be vouched for!

"This is the paper."   The girl handed it over to him, and a little dazedly he took the certificate from the envelope.

"A very admirable security," said Hewson deliberately, "bought by Mr. Crossley a month ago."

"Very admirable!" spluttered the manager, only to relapse into silence under the penetrating stare of Hewson's eye.

"And if you will just vouch for me to Miss Crossley, I don't think we need detain you further."

"With pleasure." Matters were completely beyond him: but, at any rate, he could do that. "You can place things in Mr. Hewson's hands with absolute confidence, Miss Crossley."

"Thank you," said the girl, and they all rose. He opened the door and she passed into the bank. For one moment the two men were alone, and Hewson seized the manager by the arm.

"Not a word," he whispered. "They don't know who I am. Father been swindled by some swine in London."

Nodding portentously, the worthy manager followed them to the door. Assuredly one of the most remarkable episodes that had come his way, during thirty years' experience. Rio Lopez! Two thousand five hundred of them! And he was still staring dazedly at a placard extolling Exchequer Bonds, which adorned his office wall, when the London train steamed slowly out of the station. Its departure had been to the casual eye quite normal: but the casual eye is, as its name implies, casual. The departure had been far from normal.

It was just as the guard was waving his flag that a man, leaning out of the window of a first-class carriage, spoke to a girl standing on the platform.

"You say you didn't trust the man, Miss Crossley. Do you—trust me?"

"Naturally," she answered demurely, "after what the bank manager said."

"It rests on the bank manager, does it?"

She blushed faintly. "No, Mr. Hewson, it doesn't.
One doesn't need a bank manager to confirm—a
certainty."

And then the fool engine-driver had started his
beastly machine. But to call it a normal departure is
obviously absurd.

III

"Good morning. Mr. Ferguson, I believe?"

Hewson entered the office at 20, Plumpton Street,
and bowed slightly to the man at the desk. As he had
expected, the type was a common one—one, incidentally,
with which he had had a good deal to do himself. Mr.
Arthur Ferguson could be placed at once in the category
of men who consider that in business everything is fair,
and that if they can get the better of another man the
funeral is his. And as an outlook on life there is
nothing much to be said against it, provided the other
man is of the same kidney.

"Yes." Ferguson indicated a chair. "What can
I do for you, Mr.——" He paused, interrogatively.

"I have come to have a short talk with you on a
little matter of business." Hewson took the proffered
chair, while Ferguson glanced at him covertly. Who
the deuce was the fellow? His face seemed vaguely
familiar.

"Delighted!" he murmured. "Have a cigar?"

"Thank you—no. I have just come from Umberleigh, in Devonshire, Mr. Ferguson."

A barely perceptible change passed over the other's
face.

"Indeed," he said easily. "I was there myself a
little while ago."

"So I understood," remarked Hewson. "A Mr.
Crossley told me that you had been good enough to

sell him some shares while you were there—a packet of
Rio Lopez, to be exact."

"I did," answered Ferguson.   "Though I hardly see
what concern it is of yours."

"All in good time," said Hewson, taking the certificate from his pocket.   "Two thousand five hundred, I
see, when they were standing at two pounds.   And,
to-day, they're a shade over four shillings—to-morrow,
quite possibly, sixpence."

"Everything is down," remarked Ferguson, with a
wave of his hand.   "Sorry for Mr. Crossley."

"So am I," said the other.   "It seems hard luck on
an innocent old man like that to be left to carry the
baby.   He apparently placed such reliance on your
judgment, Mr. Ferguson.   Moreover, I gather you
dined with him two or three times."

"Well, what if I did?"   He leaned back in his chair
impatiently.   "Might I suggest that time is money to
some of us, and that I'm rather busy this morning?
I'd be obliged if you'd get to the point."

"Certainly," said Hewson quietly.   "I have a nice
little bunch of two thousand five hundred Rio Lopez
which I shall be delighted to sell you—on behalf of Mr.
Crossley—at two pounds a share."

For a moment or two Mr. Ferguson seemed to have
difficulty in breathing.

"Buy Rio Lopez at two!" he gasped.   "Are you
insane?"

"Not at all," murmured Hewson, lighting a cigarette.
"That is my offer."

"Good morning," laughed the other.   "You know
the way out, don't you?   And another time, my dear
sir, you'd better learn a little more about the ways of
finance before you waste your own and other people's
time coming up from the wilds of Devon."   He pulled
a paper towards him and picked up his pen.   It struck

him as one of the richest things he'd ever heard—a
jest altogether after his own heart.   And it was just as
the full beauty of it was sinking in, that his eye caught
the card which his visitor had pushed along the writing-
desk.

"Mr. Charles Hewson."   Blinking slightly he stared
at it, then he put down his pen.   "Mr. Charles Hewson."

"You may know the name, Mr. Ferguson," remarked
the other quietly.   "And I can assure you that your
solicitude for my knowledge of finance touches me
deeply."

"But, I don't understand, Mr. Hewson.   I had no
idea who you were, but now that I do know it makes
your suggestion even more amazing."

"In an ordinary way of business, certainly," agreed
Hewson.   "This is not quite ordinary.   Without
mincing words, I consider that you played Mr. Crossley
an extremely dirty trick—considering that he'd opened
his house to you, and was quite obviously as ignorant of
business as a child.   Why—the poor old chap saw the
price in the paper the other day and thought they were
standing at four pounds three shillings."   He was
staring at Ferguson with level eyes as he spoke.   "I
give you the chance of returning him the money he
gave to you.   If you do—the matter is ended.   If you
don't—I shall pay it myself.   But—and this is the point,
Mr. Ferguson, which you had better consider—if I pay
that money, I shall recover it from you.   Is it worth
your while to have me for an enemy?   As surely as I'm
sitting here, by the time I've finished with you, you'll
not have lost five thousand—you'll have lost fifty."

"It wouldn't be worth your while," blustered Ferguson, though the hand which held his cigar shook a
little.

"Worth is a comparative term," said Hewson
calmly.   "Financially, I agree: you're not big enough

to worry over. But it will afford me great pleasure and amusement, Mr. Ferguson—and from that point of view it *will* be worth while." He took out his watch. "I'll give you two minutes to decide."

He got up and strolled round the room, glancing every now and then at the man sitting at the desk. In advance, he knew the answer: any man in Ferguson's place would think twice and then again before he deliberately took up such a challenge. And quite accurately he read the thoughts that were passing in the other's mind. Dare he gamble on the possibility of Hewson—as time went by—forgetting his threat, and letting the thing drop? That was the crux. It was an insignificant amount to a man like Hewson, but—was it the money that was at the bottom of it? While a man in Hewson's position might well forget five thousand pounds, there might be some other factor which would not slip his mind. It suddenly occurred to Mr. Arthur Ferguson that there was a singularly attractive girl in the Crossley household. And if she was the driving factor . . . One thing was perfectly certain; he would willingly pay five thousand to escape a relentless vendetta with Charles Hewson as his enemy. It was no idle threat on the latter's part: if he chose to he could ruin him.

"Well?" With a snap Hewson closed his watch. "What is it to be?"

By way of answer Ferguson took out his cheque-book.

"Good. Make your cheque payable to Mr. Crossley, and make it for ten thousand. I will give you a cheque for five. You can notify the company as to the transfer."

He drew his own cheque-book from his pocket.

"And another time, Mr. Ferguson, leave the Crossleys of this world alone. Good morning."

Mr. Arthur Ferguson was still staring dully out of the window when Charles Hewson entered a stamp shop in the Strand in search of a penny Mauritius.

IV

"I can hardly believe it. In just over a month. And the stamp as well. Mr. Hewson—I can never thank you sufficiently."

Back in the sunny study at Umberleigh, Mr. Crossley stared dazedly—first at his precious stamp, then at the cheque.

"Ten thousand pounds! I must write him a letter and thank him."

"I'm sure Mr. Ferguson would like that," murmured Hewson. "But if I may give you a word of advice, Mr. Crossley, I wouldn't try a gamble like that again. Mines are precarious things—very precarious."

"You mean, I might have lost my money?" said the old man nervously.

"Such things have been known to happen," said Hewson gravely. "By the way, is your daughter not at home?"

"She has gone over to Barnstaple with her mother. I'm expecting them back at any moment. Won't they be delighted?" He chuckled gleefully, and produced the precious card containing the Mauritius set. And with a quiet smile on his face Charles Hewson watched him from the depths of an arm-chair. What a child he was: what a charming, lovable child!

"There: the complete set again." In triumph he held up the card for Hewson's inspection, and at that moment Mrs. Crossley and the girl came through the window.

The good news poured out in a torrent, while Hewson stood almost forgotten in the background.

Ten thousand pounds—two thousand five hundred

shares—capital doubled in a month—and the stamp.
The old man brandished the cheque in his excitement,
and, at length, Mrs. Crossley turned to Hewson with a
smile.

"We seem to have entertained an angel unawares,"
and her eyes were a little misty. "Thank you, Mr.
Hewson."

"No need to thank me, Mrs. Crossley," he laughed.
"These things just happen."

He glanced at the girl, who had so far said nothing.
She was staring at him steadily, and there was no
answering smile on her face.

"Did you say two thousand five hundred shares,
daddy?" Her voice was quite expressionless, as she
turned to her father.

"That's it, little girl," he cried. "Sold at over four
pounds a share. Now you'll be able to have some more
frocks!"

He kissed her lovingly, and followed his wife from
the room, still chuckling and rubbing his hands together.

"Would you explain, please, Mr. Hewson?" said the
girl in a flat, dead voice as the door closed.

"Explain, Miss Crossley! How do you mean?
You father acquired some shares a little while ago—
two thousand five hundred, as he told you—which have
just been sold at rather over four pounds a share.
Hence the stamp—and a cheque for ten thousand."

"I went into the bank at Barnstaple this afternoon,"
said the girl dully, "and I happened to speak to the
cashier. He told me who you were. You're a multi-
millionaire, aren't you?"

Charles Hewson shrugged his shoulders. "I'm
afraid I am," he laughed. "Is that what you want me
to explain?"

"Don't laugh, please," said the girl quietly. "I
said that you'd been good enough to do some business

for us—something to do with Rio Lopez shares. He
said, 'Good heavens! Miss Crossley, surely Mr. Hewson hasn't put you into Rio Lopez?' I said, 'Why not
—aren't they good shares?' You see, I didn't know
what the business was you were doing. He said,
'Good! Why the blessed things aren't worth much
more than the paper they're written on. Standing
about four shillings, I think.' And now you tell me
you've sold two thousand five hundred of them at over
four pounds." Slim and erect she stood there facing
him. "I don't know anything about business: but I'm
not a fool. So will you please explain?"

If there was anything really in the absent-treatment
business, an unsuspecting and well-meaning cashier
would have fallen dead in the bank at that moment.

"Will you come into the garden, Miss Crossley?"
said Hewson gravely. "I could explain better out of
doors."

In silence she followed him, and they found two
chairs under a shady tree.

"Ferguson," he began quietly, "the man who was
down here a month ago, was a pretty smart gentleman.
He did a business deal with your father which, legally
speaking, was quite in order. He possessed two
thousand five hundred Rio Lopez, which, at that time,
were standing at two pounds. He sold these shares to
your father knowing perfectly well that they were only
standing at such a figure because of a distinctly shady
artificial boom which had been given them. He knew
they were bound to slump—that is, fall in price. So
he—finding your father supremely ignorant of finance
—unloaded those shares on to him, and left him—as
the saying goes—to carry the baby. In other words,
shares that your father paid two pounds each for, he
would only get four shillings for to-day. This morning I interviewed Mr. Ferguson in his office. And I

persuaded him—how, is immaterial—to refund your
father the money. That's all there is to it."

"I see," said the girl. "It was very good of you.
But if my father only paid two pounds for each share—
that makes five thousand. The cheque he's got is for
ten. How did he double his capital?"

Hewson bit his lip: how, indeed?

"Oh! please be frank, Mr. Hewson. Have you
given my father five thousand pounds?"

His fingers beat a tattoo on the arm of his chair.

"Yes," he said at length. "I have. The dear old
man thought the shares were standing at four pounds:
he read the four and threepence in the paper as four
pounds three shillings. And"—he turned appealingly
to the girl—"if you could only dimly guess what pleasure
it's given me, Miss Crossley."

"Oh! stop, please." With a little cry that was half
a sob she rose. "I suppose you meant it for the best:
thought you were being kind. I don't suppose you
realized your—your impertinence. Because we offer
you lunch, Mr. Hewson, it gives you no right to dare to
give my father money. And now it's going to be doubly
hard for him—when I tell him. He'll be so—so
ashamed."

She turned away, hiding her face in her hands, and
for a while there was silence in the sunny garden. And
in that moment the man knew that the quest was over,
the quest—conscious or unconscious, it matters not—
that has been man's through the ages. But no hint of
it sounded in his level voice as he spoke: the time for
that was not yet.

"And so, Miss Crossley, you propose to tell your
father?"

"What else can I possibly do?" She turned on him
indignantly.

"Of course you must decide," he continued quietly.

"I quite see how the matter looks to you: I wonder if you are being equally fair to me.   I come here: I meet your father.   I find that he has been swindled by a man in London—a moral swindle only possible because of your father's charming innocence.   I wonder if you can realize what the atmosphere of this place means to me—an atmosphere which must depend, to a large extent, on the happiness and joy of you three."

She was watching him now, and suddenly his swift smile flashed out.   "Don't you understand, Miss Crossley, that all money is relative?   I'm going to allude purposely to my disgusting wealth.   You wouldn't think much of paying five shillings for pleasure, would you?   Well, five thousand pounds means no more to me.   And I've bought myself pleasure with that money such as I don't think you can begin to conceive of." Again he smiled: then before she could reply he went on.   "So I want you to remember, when you make your decision, what you are going to sacrifice on the altar of pride.   My feelings don't matter: but are you going to deliberately prick the bubble of your father's happiness and change him in a moment from a delighted child into a broken and worried old man?"

The girl bit her lip and stared over the rambling garden with troubled eyes.   How could she let her father take the money: how could she?   And then she heard his voice again from close behind her.

"I'm going back to London," he said deliberately, "and I would ask you to keep this as *our* secret.   I hadn't intended to go back yet: but now that you have found out—perhaps it's better.   I'll leave you free to puzzle the thing out by yourself: only I want to make one condition."

"What's that?" whispered the girl.

"I want to come back for my promised visit later." Gently he swung her round and his eyes—tender and quizzical—rested on the lovely face so close to his. "And when I come back, I'm going to ask you a question, which, if you can see your way to answering with a yes, will make me your father's debtor for life. And then we could consider the five thousand as a payment on account, which would completely and finally settle the matter."

Almost against her will, a faint smile began to twitch round the girl's lips.

"Of course, I'm not much good at business, as I said, but I didn't know that anybody ever paid on account until he had, at any rate, the promise of the goods."

"In these days of competition," murmured Hewson, "one sometimes has to pay for the right of the first refusal."

The smile was twitching again. "That right is yours without payment."

"Then I'd better get it over quickly. Sheila—will you marry me?"

"Mr. Hewson—I will not. Where are you going?"

Charles Hewson turned half-way across the lawn. "Up to London. I want to find a man there, and give him the best dinner he's ever had in his life."

"What man?"

"The sportsman who wrote that article about walking tours." It was then the smile broke bounds.

"We've got some topping peaches in the garden. Couldn't you send him some of those as—a payment on account?"

"TELEPATHY? Yes, there's something in it, you know. There must be. And that strange bond of sympathy, or what is even stronger than sympathy, which exists between some people and knows not distance, is a very real thing. I remember the case of a brother and sister who idolized one another, and he was shot through the heart in one of the Egyptian wars. And when they had made the necessary adjustments for time they found that the moment he died was the same moment that his sister called his name out loud, put her hand to her heart and fainted. And she was in England."

"I know another story, too: even stranger."

The little sandy-haired man with eyes that were the most trustful things I have ever seen—and the saddest—stared thoughtfully out to sea. In the distance a band was playing: the front was crowded with people taking their evening stroll. And I felt my heart warm to the little sandy-haired man. He seemed so terribly lonely.

"There's an hour before dinner," I said encouragingly.

"They met first in one of the intermediate Union Castle boats going down the East Coast. I don't know if you've ever done the trip, but if you have you'll know that it is one where shipboard acquaintance ripens under very favourable conditions. Lots of ports of call: cargo delays: warm nights.

"She had come on board at Naples and was bound for Delagoa Bay to join her husband, who was farming up in the Letaba district: he had embarked at Alexandria, bound for the same destination.

"And from the very first it was one of those inevitable things that only immediate flight can save. And you can't fly far on a ten-thousand-ton boat.

"I think he was one of the most attractive specimens of manhood I've ever seen. Not that he was particularly good-looking: but then that doesn't matter in the least. He was so intensely alive: you could see it bubbling out of him. To look at he was just a tall, lean, bronzed man in the early thirties: it wasn't until you began to talk to him that you realized the magnetic virility that was his.

"He had quite sufficient money for his needs, and his trip to South Africa was principally one of pleasure. And also one of escape. For he was married, too, and his wife loathed travelling. In fact, she loathed anything that took her far from London. She was, I gathered, an empty-headed, frivolous little fool, and she comes into this story for one reason only, though it's a very important one. She was a devout Roman Catholic.

"So much for him: now for the woman. Everything that he was in a man found its opposite number in her. She loved life, and life looked as if it loved her. She was gloriously pretty, danced like an angel, and was utterly unspoiled. In fact, the only remarkable thing about her was why she had married her husband.

"He was such a very ordinary man was her husband. Quite nice, you know: a decent sort of humdrum fellow with no peculiar vices and no particular virtues. The sort of man, in fact, who goes through life as one of the crowd. He was desperately in love with her, of course: crazy about her—who wouldn't have been? And he was under no delusions; she had been perfectly honest with him when they became engaged. It was a case of being caught on the rebound: he knew that. A girl so vastly attractive as she, was bound to have love-affairs. And she'd had one rather

serious one just before he came on the scene.   She
didn't tell him the name of the man, and anyway the
point is immaterial.   But this man, having been everything but definitely engaged to her, had, at the eleventh
hour, folded his tent and stolen silently away to the
fold of a war profiteer who had a daughter.

"It was a jar naturally: a jar to her pride, and a
jar to other things as well, because she had been genuinely fond of the man.   And when one is young and
the wound is raw, it is cold comfort trying to realize
that one is well out of a man who can do a thing like
that.

"But she was in the mood engendered by a deliberate jilt when she accepted her husband.   Not that she
wasn't fond of him—she was.   Very fond of him indeed: but her feelings for him were never comparable
to his for her.   His were just blind adoration, and
when she presented him with a son it seemed to him
that life could hold no more.

"The boy was four years old at the time of my story,
and was with his father in Africa.   She had been on
a visit to her people at home, and never having done
the East Coast trip she decided to go back that way
instead of by the direct route.   Just Fate moving the
pieces and chuckling inwardly.   Because by the time
the boat had reached Port Sudan things had come to
a head.   The real thing had come at last to two people,
and they both knew it.

"The moralist, of course, may hold up pious hands
in horror: fortunately, or unfortunately, according to
your outlook on life, the world pays but little attention to moralists.   And Nature pays none at all.   It
came to them quite suddenly—the certain blinding
knowledge, and once again the moralist may cry out.

"It was on the boat-deck one night, and she found
herself in his arms: she found herself kissing him even

as he was kissing her with the kisses that sweep away every barrier. All very wrong, of course, but these things happen. And it's all rather cynically humorous, too, because they wouldn't be missed if they didn't happen. But once they have, they can't be ignored. If you want peace in the menagerie, you must not loose the tiger out of its cage.

"She knew that all her former love-affairs were as nothing; she knew that her marriage was as nothing if she answered to the dictates of Nature. He knew the same. And that was the position as that intermediate liner steamed on down the Red Sea.

"He said, 'I'll get off at Aden.'

"But he didn't get off at Aden.

"He said, 'I'll get off at Mombasa.'

"But he didn't get off at Mombasa.

"I don't blame him; but then I'm not a moralist. I should have done the same in his position. Heaven knows there's little enough happiness in this world for a man to throw it away when it comes to him. The future! Lord—if every man thought of the future and regulated his every act by it we should have a world peopled by automatic codfish. He gets his punishment if he doesn't, so it's quite fair. The longer you put it off the worse it is. And if he had got off at Aden—well, I shouldn't be telling you this story.

"He stuck to his original plan and got off at Delagoa Bay, and it was there that he met the husband—the plain ordinary husband. The husband had come down from his farm to meet his wife and had brought the boy with him; and they all stayed at that big hotel overlooking the sea which is possibly one of the most perfect hotels in the world. And the husband, having eyes and thoughts for nothing except his wife, was deliriously happy. He had barely noticed the man when his wife had introduced them to one another:

he had regarded him merely as a casual shipboard acquaintance. The only coherent idea in his head was that his wife had come back; and the man who loved that wife stood in the background and tried to sort things out.

"Now I don't know how far things had gone between the two of them, but the point is almost immaterial. I know it is not so accounted by the world, but we all have our own standards. And it seems to me that the main factor in the situation was the love between the man and the woman. I want to make that clear. It wasn't just an ordinary vulgar flirtation —*une affaire pour passer le temps*—it was the real thing between two real people. When you have heard what is to come you will understand why I am so very sure on that point.

"And so for a week the play went on in that luxurious hotel—the play that was destined to finish on the twisting road that leads into the valley down Magoebas Kloof. No shadow of suspicion had entered the husband's mind: his wife was to him as she had always been. I have said that he was under no delusions as to her feelings for him: he was content that she should return his adoration with a kindly feeling of regard. So he made his little jokes and chuckled over them consumedly—he was that type of man; and felt a genuine pity for all the unlucky individuals who were not as fortunate as himself.

"Off and on he talked a good deal to the man. He was frightfully keen, amongst other things, on South Africa as a country for the right type of settler, and in the man he saw an ideal one. At the time he didn't even know the man was married; and when he learned that fact he still saw in him possibilities as a developer of country.

" 'It's capital that is wanted,' he said again and

again. 'Buy some ground; install a manager and come out for a bit every year. We shall always be delighted to put you up for as long as you like.'

"They were in the bar at the time, and the stem of the man's cocktail glass broke suddenly in his hand. A flaw, obviously, in the glass; the barman was most apologetic.

" 'Come up and see for yourself now,' went on the husband when the drink had been replaced by another. 'I can give you some very fine shooting, and the district that I am in is second to none for fertility. Cotton, citrus—it's marvellous. Unlimited water; railway at the door. . . .'

"He rambled on—keyed up on his hobby. And the man heard not one word. In fact, the husband remarked to his wife later that for such a singularly attractive man he was uncommonly dull and silent.

" 'Perhaps the poor devil is unhappily married, my dear,' he said as he was tying his tie for dinner that night. 'I've asked him to come up and stay with us. . . .'

" 'What did he say?' said the woman.

"Her back was towards him as she spoke: she was choosing a frock from the wardrobe.

" 'He didn't say one way or the other,' answered her husband. 'Why don't you have a go at him after dinner! He's exactly the type of fellow this country wants. . . .'

"He rambled on once again, and the woman heard not one word. In fact, the husband remarked jokingly to her at dinner that he would have to change a shilling into pennies in order to buy all her thoughts. I've told you he made little jokes like that, haven't I?

" 'You go and tackle him,' he said as they rose from the table. 'I've got to talk to a man over there about my last consignment of packing-cases. They were rotten; and I shall have to take some steps about it.'

"He moved off grumbling, and the man and the woman had their coffee together. And I suppose it was then that they settled it. I don't blame them for their decision, though I think that if ever there was a definite stopping-point jutting obviously out, it was then. He need not have gone to stay with them; equally he might have got off at Aden. But to go and stay with them was the deliberate taking of a fence, whereas stopping on in the boat was merely conforming to an original plan. Still, I don't blame them: there are certain things which are difficult to judge by ordinary standards. And until one has been tempted as they were tempted one should not pass judgment. Only I sometimes think that now that the man had met the husband and seen the child, it was—it was . . ."

The little sandy-haired man paused and stared out to sea.

"A P. & O., I think," he remarked.

I agreed, and wondered how a man whose eyes were full of tears could see a passing liner.

"So the man came and stayed at the husband's bungalow," he continued after a while. "They were still trying to sort things out—he and the woman—but they kept their secret very well. The husband, as he took the man riding and showed him the possibilities of the place, was utterly blind to the situation that lay under his very nose. Until one day——

"Astounding, isn't it, how suddenly one's eyes can be opened; how the fraction of a second can alter one's life? Even so it was with the husband in this case. He had been out alone to an outlying part of his farm, and in crossing a drift his boots had got very wet. So that when he dismounted they picked up a lot of mud and became filthy. Which seem tiny details, but unless they had taken place he would not have taken off his boots outside on the stoep and entered his bungalow in his socks.   Noiselessly, you see. . . .

"It was in a mirror that he saw it—the thing which brought his world crashing.   The man and the woman were standing one on each side of his son's bed, and they were staring at one another across the child.   For what seemed an eternity to the husband they stood there motionless; then they moved to the head of the bed where they were hidden from the eyes of the child.   And the man took the woman in his arms and kissed her.

"There are some things which are torture too exquisite to describe.   That was one of them.   With his heart pounding in great sickening thuds, and his mouth dry and parched, the husband stood there watching. He felt rooted to the spot; his legs refused to work. And then, after what seemed an eternity, he heard the man's voice:

" 'Dear God!   If only it had been mine!'

"She gave a little choking gasp, and with it the power of movement returned to the husband.   He moved out of the line of vision, and making no sound in his stockinged feet he went into the drawing-room. In a sort of inarticulate, hazy way he felt that he had to think things out before taking any action.

"He found himself looking at his reflection in the glass.   And the face that stared back at him was the face of a stranger.   It was drawn and white and lined, and he started muttering to himself unconsciously.

" 'This won't do; you must have a drink.   Pull yourself together.'

"He had a drink, and then he fetched his boots from the stoep.   They were both in the drawing-room when he returned, and the woman gave a little cry of consternation when she saw his face.

" 'My dear,' she said, 'are you all right?   Have you got a touch of the sun?'

" 'I'm a bit tired,' answered the husband evenly— at least his voice sounded fairly even to him.   'I'll just go and have a bath and change.'

"He tried to reason it out as he lay in the water. Why, knowing what he did, had he gone and left them alone together?   Why had he said nothing?   And what was he going to do?   Things couldn't go on as if nothing had happened.

"What was he going to do?   Bluster: tell them that he had seen: order the man out of the house.   He could do all that: he *would* do all that.   At once—before dinner.   And then, insidiously mocking, stole in an-other thought.   He tried to drive it out; it refused to be driven.   He argued with himself savagely that she was his wife; it still refused to be driven away. Was his position sufficiently strong for him to adopt such a course?

"Legally it was, of course; who cares about the law? What would be the result if he did bring matters to a head?   He knew a good deal of his wife's character; he had a shrewd estimate of the man's.   And neither of them was of the type who would be intimidated.

"If those two had fallen in love with one another, nothing that he could say would alter the fact.   And by bringing matters to a head he might merely pre-cipitate a catastrophe.

"Instinctively he knew that it was a big thing.   The matter at stake was the whole future of three people and a child.   And as he dressed for dinner he realized with a sick hopelessness that the person of those four who would count least when the decision came to be made was himself.

"Perhaps he was a coward; perhaps he didn't dare risk losing her altogether.   Perhaps, on the other hand, he may have been actuated by a strange sort of feeling of fairness. If she wanted to go, was it playing the game to try and keep her? You see, he knew he counted least.

"And so he said nothing. All through dinner he acted his part, and made his little jests at which he laughed consumedly, just as he had always done in the past. Once or twice maybe he faltered when he saw the look on his wife's face as she glanced at the man, but the lapse passed unnoticed. They were far too engrossed—the other two—to pay much attention to him. And when dinner was over he made some excuse and went out of doors.

"He left them alone purposely; he wanted to know the worst. And for an hour or so—or was it a few minutes?—he walked about blindly. God knows what his thoughts were: they were just blind chaos, I think. At times he cursed himself for a fool for not having spoken; at others the grey of blank despair clogged his mind like mist round a mountain-top. But at last he felt he could stand it no longer and he went back to the house. One way or the other, he had to know.

"It wasn't intentional: he didn't mean to overhear. But knowing what he did, perhaps it was the best thing that could have happened. His wife and the man were sitting on the stoep, and as he approached the house from one side he heard their voices. And he stopped and listened.

"She said: 'It's the boy, Bill; it's the boy.'

"And after a while the man answered. He had a singularly charming voice, and every word he said carried quite clearly to the husband standing just round the corner. Foolish from a worldly point of view perhaps to run such a risk of being overheard; but I honestly believe that it would have made no difference if he'd been sitting with them. The thing at stake was too big; the man would still have said what he did.

" 'Yes, dear—for you it's the boy. For you also, it's my wife. She wouldn't divorce me; that I know. It's contrary to her religion; if a woman with an outlook on life such as hers can be said to have a religion. And I couldn't expose you to that. I know I couldn't, in spite of the fact that at the moment I can think no coherent thought save that you're the most wonderful thing in the world and that nothing matters or ever can matter except that you and I should never be parted again. That's all that is seething through my brain now; there's no room for anything else. But deep down in me—hidden at the moment, it's true— is the sure and certain knowledge that I couldn't expose you to living with me on those terms. And so, my dear, I'm going. This afternoon brought everything to a head. We drifted on board, and somehow things were different there. Now the time has come when we can drift no longer. So I'm going—tomorrow.'

" 'Oh! my God, Bill!'

"It was pitiful, that little heart-rending gasp of hers.

" 'To-morrow, woman of mine, I shall go. But there's one thing I want you to remember through the long years ahead. If ever you want me—if ever you call to me, I will come to you, though I may be at the other end of the world.'

"And the next day he went."

The little sandy-haired man fell silent for a long while and I didn't hurry him. That he was the husband, I felt sure, and though the pathos of the thing from his point of view had got me rather gripped, I was wondering what was his reason for telling the story. Up to date it was an oft-told tale.

He must have guessed what was in my mind, I

suppose, because he suddenly looked at me with an apologetic smile.

"I expect you're wondering what this is all leading up to," he said. "I'm afraid the preamble has taken a bit of a time, but I rather wanted to make the man and the woman clear to you. The husband doesn't matter, but I wanted to make those two live in your mind. Because it's wellnigh incomprehensible—the end of the story—unless you realize the relations between them. . . .

"There was no apparent change in the woman after he went away. A little more silent perhaps; a little prone to fall into long reveries—but that was all. To her husband she was just the same as ever; if anything, she was kinder and sweeter than before. He never said a word, but he had a great longing which grew in intensity that some day she would tell him. And about eight months after the man had gone away she did. She said she thought it was fairer.

"It was after dinner one night when she told him, and her face was in the shadow. The man's name had cropped up quite naturally over an account of a meeting at Brooklands. I don't think I told you, by the way, that amongst other forms of sport he went in for motor-racing.

"She told the story quietly and simply, and her husband listened in silence.

" 'I won't say I'm sorry about it, old man,' she said at the end. 'I'm not, and there is no good pretending that I am. But I felt it wasn't playing the game not to let you know. It's over; it's finished, and humanly speaking I shall never see Bill again. Will you—shake hands on it?'

" 'My dear,' he answered, 'I'm so very glad you told me. I've been hoping all these months that you would. You see—I knew!'

"She was sitting forward in her chair staring at him in amazement.

" 'You knew!' she whispered. 'But how?'

"And then he told her what he had seen and heard, and it was her turn to listen in silence. But they had it out that night, and I think that the memory of the woman that lives most clearly in her husband's mind is the sight of her by the open window just before they went to bed. She was in white, and she was staring out into the African night. For a long time she stood there motionless, and then suddenly she swung round and held out both her hands.

" 'It was rather big of you, Jack,' she said simply. 'Thank you, dear.'

"They never alluded to the subject again; all that could be said about it had been said that night. And after a while they found themselves mentioning his name quite naturally—so naturally, in fact, that the husband began to hope that she was forgetting. And to a certain extent, I suppose, she was. Time had healed the first raw edge; had the end not come it is possible that time might have healed altogether. Who knows?"

Once again the little sandy-haired man paused, whilst he idly traced a pattern on the ground with his walking-stick.

"Do you know South Africa at all?" he continued. "Cape Town, Durban, I suppose. Well, the roads are all right there for motoring, but the same cannot be said of the country districts. It was up in the Northern Transvaal that they had their farm, at a place about seventy-odd miles from Pietersburg. For a great part of the way the road was good, but for parts of the rest it was a mere track without any real foundation at all. When the weather is fine the track is hard and just as good as the road; when it has been raining the track becomes a layer of greasy slime. Even with chains I have known that seventy miles take eight hours to do.

"They had been down to Johannesburg for a week, leaving their car at Pietersburg. And as ill-luck would have it the husband had slipped playing tennis and sprained his wrist. So that it was she who had to drive back. She had driven the car often before, though she always preferred not to. It's heavy work steering over the bumps in some of those roads—too heavy for a woman.

"The first part of the run is easy, and they made good time till they came to the high ground—a spur of the Drakensburg. And there they ran into a fine Scotch mist.

"It would have been nothing in England; it would have been nothing if the road had been good. But it was just the part where you find long stretches of unmetalled track, and in half an hour the going was wellnigh impossible. Very foolishly they had forgotten to bring any chains, and the back wheels, when they got any grip at all, were skidding all over the place. But there was no danger; it didn't matter if the car did leave the track. At least it didn't matter to start with.

"At last they got to the top of Magoebas Kloof. Below them the road dropped away, corkscrewing into the valley. They couldn't see much of it; the mist was too thick. But they knew every inch of it—so that didn't matter. And then they started to descend. For a bit everything went all right, and then—it happened. And even to this day I don't know how it happened. It was at one of the turns that the car skidded suddenly. And the woman lost her head. She jammed on the brake, and turned the wheel away from the skid instead of towards it. The back of the car swung round with a lurch, and went over the edge.

For a moment or two it seemed to pause: then the whole car disappeared.

"How the husband was saved is a miracle. He had risen to his feet instinctively, and I think the door on his side must have come open. Anyway, he was flung out against a tree, and lay there half-stunned, whilst with a series of sickening crashes the car plunged on downwards. They grew fainter and fainter—and at length they ceased."

I glanced at the little man, and his forehead was wet with perspiration.

"She was dead, of course, when we got to her; crushed and unrecognizable in the twisted debris of the car. Any chance she might have had of being thrown clear was lessened by the fact that she was driving, and the steering-wheel boxed her in. And the only thing the husband could pray for was that it had been instantaneous. The doctor said he thought so, thank God!

"It broke up the husband pretty badly, as you can guess. But there was the boy to consider, and after hanging on for a few more months at his farm he decided to go back to England. For a time he wondered if he would hear from the man, and then he realized that in all probability the accident would not have been reported in the English papers. And at last he decided to write himself. He knew his club in London, and somehow or other he felt that she would appreciate it. So he wrote him a letter telling him what had happened, and the answer came back about a week before he sailed. It was from a firm of lawyers, and ran as follows:

"*Dear Sir,*
"*You are evidently unaware that Mr. William Brox-ton was killed when competing in the Grand Prix. The*

accident was a terrible one as he was travelling at over a hundred miles an hour at the time. He was hurled against a tree, and was killed on the spot.

"By what can only be described as an amazing coincidence, the accident took place on the same day as the one which cost your wife her life. Should you require any further details we shall be happy to write you more fully.

"And so, when he got back to London, he went and interviewed that firm of lawyers. There were many gaps to be filled in—points to be cleared up. Points which, when he had thought of them sometimes on the voyage home, had left him with a queer tingling at the back of his scalp.

"The lawyer told him all he knew, which was not much: the worthy man knew little, if anything, of motor-racing. Apparently the car had overturned when travelling at speed and Broxton had been crushed between it and a tree. And the mechanic had had a miraculous escape by being hurled out between two trees and landing in a ploughed field. So the husband took the mechanic's name and address and left. There was someone else he wanted to see now.

"He ran him to earth in his club—a motor maniac surrounded by other motor maniacs.

" 'Bill Broxton?' said his friend, shaking his head. 'You were out of England, of course, at the time. Poor old Bill. I don't suppose anyone will ever get to the bottom of that accident. The only man who might throw some light on the matter—Brownlow, the mechanic—at times seems to me to be holding something back. He idolized the ground that Bill walked on—always drove with him, you know.'

" 'But what the devil can there be to keep back?' chipped in one of the group.

" 'Heaven knows,' answered the other. 'He can't

have been tight, and he can't have lost his head. Sometimes I think he must have gone mad. You see'—
he turned to the husband—'what happened, as far as
can be found out from the spectators, was this: He
was taking a slight corner, when he suddenly wrenched
his steering-wheel round almost to the full lock. The
car did one frightful skid and then turned over. Brownlow was flung clear: Bill was crushed to death. I mean,
as an accident to a driver of Bill's calibre, it was about
equivalent to opening the door of an express train and
stepping on to the lines.'

" 'What time did it take place?' asked the husband.

" 'I can easily find out for you,' said his friend, and
with that the husband left.

"Only the mechanic remained to be seen, and he
was the most important of all. He took a bit of finding—he'd gone to a new address—but at last the husband got in touch with him. A decent fellow, very,
that mechanic, but singularly uncommunicative. He
repeated the story all over again, but it seemed to the
husband that what his motor friend had said was right.
He was keeping something back.

"So at last he took the bull by the horns, and told
the mechanic much that I've told you. He didn't say
he was the woman's husband, though perhaps Brownlow guessed. And when he'd finished the other man
was staring at him with dilated eyes.

" 'My God!' he muttered, 'but it's strange. I'll
tell you now, sir, what I've never told a living soul
before. It was Mr. Broxton's last words just before
it happened. I can hear 'em now ringing in my ears
as clearly as the day of the accident. And I've never
mentioned them to anyone: it seemed to me they was
his secret, though I couldn't understand them. It was
just as we came to the corner when I saw his face
change suddenly. I don't know why I was looking

at him, but I was. He half-rose in his seat and shouted out, "Pull your wheel to the left, my darling." And as he spoke he did it himself.' "

The little sandy-haired man took out his watch and glanced at it.

"Strange, wasn't it? The times were simultaneous —I verified that. And you remember he'd told the woman he'd come to her even though he was at the other end of the world if she wanted him. And I think that in some mysterious way Bill Broxton went to his woman at the end when she called him.

"For just as those last words of his go on ringing in Brownlow's brain, so do three other words go on ringing in the husband's. They rang out clear and distinct just as the car on Magoebas Kloof disappeared over the edge:

" 'Bill—save me!' "

"WONDERFUL stuff, seccotine," remarked the ship's bore. "I can assure you fellows that I've mended broken china in such a way that it defies detection."

"I can well believe it," yawned the doctor. "What about a rubber?"

"It never lets you down," pursued the other earnestly.

The fair-haired man in the corner smiled slightly.

"Let us say very rarely instead of never," he remarked in his faint, rather pleasant drawl. "I can remember a certain occasion when it let some people down rather badly."

"Then it must have been used wrongly," affirmed the seccotine supporter. "If you put it on too thick——"

"Laddie," interrupted the doctor wearily, "I believe you hold shares in the damn' stuff. Am I right in scenting a yarn?"

He turned to the fair-haired man, who shrugged his shoulders.

"It might amuse you," he said. "The night is yet young, and the deck is an unsafe place for a bachelor."

"Four long ones, steward," said the doctor firmly. "Now, sir, your reasons for mistrusting that excellent household commodity, if you please."

The fair-haired man lit a cigarette with care.

"Your sins be on your own heads," he remarked. "I warn you I'm no story-teller. However, to begin at the beginning. I'd better give it a title. I shall call it The Episode of the Kodak, the Volcano, and the Parasol with the Broken Head."

"Glass or china?" interrupted the seccotine maniac eagerly. "It makes a difference, you know."

The doctor grew profane.

"Steel," he groaned. "Tin. Asbestos. Besides, how do you know it was the parasol at all? The kodak might have been seccotined, or even the volcano."

The interrupter looked pained and subsided.

"And having given it its title," continued the fair-haired man, "we will commence the yarn."

"The first character in order of entry is the lady. We will call her Hedsdale—Mrs. Hedsdale. I noticed her the first night I arrived at Parker's Hotel in Naples. She was sitting in the lounge drinking her coffee, and she was the type of woman who took the eye. Most excessively so, in fact. I put her age at about thirty, and most of the other women in the place were staring at her as if she had an infectious disease, and surreptitiously trying to copy her frock. She was obviously English, though she was reading a French book. And she was really most extraordinarily pretty.

"The lounge was crowded, and I took one of the few vacant chairs which chanced to be opposite her. I had noted her wedding-ring, but there appeared to be no sign of a husband. There was only one cup on the tray in front of her, and she somehow gave one the impression of being alone."

The fair-haired man gazed thoughtfully at the bubbles rising in his glass.

"Well, gentlemen," he continued, "rightly or wrongly, it has always seemed to me that a pretty woman alone is one of those things that should not be. It is an unnatural state of affairs and cries aloud for rectification. And though on the one occasion that evening when I caught her eye she looked straight through me, yet I went to bed with the definite impression that in this case the rectification was not going to be very difficult. Impossible to say how these impressions arise, but . . . However, I won't labour the point. I will merely say that the following morning I was privileged to be of some small service to her. It appeared that she was unable to make a messenger from one of the shops understand what she wanted, so what more natural than that I should act as interpreter? She confessed so sweetly that she could hardly speak a word of Italian, that it was a real pleasure to help her. And the fact that I had overheard her the previous evening speaking fluent Italian to the concierge in no way, I may say, destroyed that pleasure."

"Dirty dog," chuckled the doctor.

The fair-haired man looked pained.

"The best of us lay ourselves open at times to be misconstrued," he murmured. "However, I will endeavour to bear it with fortitude. She was quite charmingly grateful to me for my small assistance, and since it transpired that she was devoted to oysters we went out and had lunch at that excellent little inn close to Lake Avernus. It appeared that the worthy Mr. Hedsdale, who answered to the name of John, was at the moment engaged in some business transaction in Rumania. It further appeared that the business transaction was likely to be of considerable duration. Dear old John was so extremely thorough in everything he did; if a thing was important he would never dream of handing it over to a subordinate. In fact, during the next week I got to have quite an affection for John. I saw his photograph—a large, somewhat placid-looking man, considerably older than his wife. Fifteen years, to be exact; he was just forty-five.

"She used to smile so sweetly when she mentioned him. His passions apparently, apart from business, were golf and photography. Every week-end, when they were at home, was devoted to these two hobbies. A little dull, perhaps, since she detested them both, but as long as dear old John was happy nothing else mattered. When business was completed in Rumania he was going to join her in Naples, and they were then going on a photographic tour through Southern Italy and Sicily preparatory to returning to London. Of course, John couldn't be too long away from his office there, but he did want a complete rest and holiday; he'd been working far too hard just lately.

"In fact, at the end of ten days, during which we did the museum, and the aquarium, and the tour to Baia, and Capri, I'd got a fairly vivid mental picture of John. I felt that he talked at breakfast and was not beyond sleeping after dinner, but was withal a tower of probity and common sense. Dear fellow! Long might he continue in Rumania. . . ."

The fair-haired man drained his glass and lit another cigarette.

"And now I must introduce Bill. I may say that from the very beginning I disliked Bill. He was one of those men whom every man and a few women spot at once as being—well, not quite all right. It wasn't that he was out of the second drawer; his birth left nothing to be desired. But there was something wrong with him: you fellows all know that indefinable thing which a man can spot at once in another man. He was very good-looking, but, in spite of his birth, he wasn't a sahib. And he was evidently an old friend of Mrs. Hedsdale's. We were sitting together in the lounge when he arrived, and I suddenly heard her call out, 'Why, it's Bill!'

"She introduced us, and during the next ten minutes I could feel him sizing me up. I noticed he called her by her Christian name—Sylvia; and for ten minutes or so we stayed there chatting. Then he got up to go and see about his room—he was staying at Bertolini's, since he couldn't get a room at Parker's—and I didn't see him again until just before dinner, when I met him in the bar. There was no one else there, and after a while he led the conversation round to Sylvia Hedsdale. Had I known her long? Did I know her husband? and questions of that sort. I told him that I had not known her long, and that I did not know her husband, and all the time I knew he was trying to find out exactly on what terms I was with the lady. He was clumsy about it, and once or twice he went over the borderline of what may be said and what may not. Of course, he got nothing out of me, and after a while he switched off the lady and started on her husband.

" 'Extraordinary fellow, John Hedsdale,' he informed me. 'Simply rolling in money. . . . Great big fat chap, always pottering round with a camera, or else foozling vilely on the golf-links. Adores her; positively eats out of her hand. The Queen can do no wrong sort of business.'

"He looked at me and grinned.

" 'Just as well—what?'

"Jove! how I disliked that man. That grin and that remark gave him away so utterly and so truthfully. You must remember we were complete strangers to one another. But in addition to giving him away as an outsider it also gave Mrs. Hedsdale away as a naughty little woman. Presumably in the past John had paid other visits to Rumania or equally convenient places, and she had not allowed the grass to grow under her feet. And as I watched them at dinner—he dined at her table—I foresaw complications. Not with dear John, but between that damned fellow Bill and myself. He seemed so extremely proprietary.

"Well, I abominate complications in an affair of that sort, and I realized that something would have to be done. I couldn't leave Naples—I was there on business —and Mrs. Hedsdale knew I couldn't. And since she was a clever little woman, I was not surprised to hear after dinner that she had just received an invitation to stop with some friends in Florence, and was leaving by the early train herself, while Bill was going on to Palermo and possibly Taormina.

"I listened with becoming politeness to their plans and even went so far as to see her off next morning in the Rome express. We duly went through the formalities of finding out when she would arrive in Florence, though I knew she had no more intention of going there than I had. And then just as she was getting into the train there occurred a trifling incident. She dropped her parasol.

"Amazing what may depend on a little thing, isn't it? A man's life hung on that."

He smiled slightly and pressed out his cigarette.

"I thought it was about time to wake you up," he continued. "I've been intolerably dull up to date, but it was unavoidable if you were to get the hang of the thing. If Sylvia Hedsdale hadn't dropped her parasol and chipped a big piece off the tail of the parrot that formed the top, I shouldn't be telling you this yarn. I picked up the broken piece and she put it in her bag. Seccotine would do the trick, and what a nuisance it was, etc., etc.

"I suppose it must have been four weeks later when the story starts again. I had practically completed the business which had brought me to Naples, and I was sitting in the bar one evening talking to two or three men when I heard a loud and jovial voice outside the door saying—'By Jove! Kitten. A bar! What about a drink?' And in walked John Hedsdale.

"I should have known him at once from his photograph, even if his wife hadn't followed him in. He was just what I had imagined him to be, and his voice exactly fitted him. For a moment or two I waited in order to get my cue from her, but the instant she saw me she bowed and smiled. So I got up at once and was introduced to John. He put out a hand like a leg of mutton, insisted that I should join them in a drink, and was immensely grateful to me for having helped his Kitten when she'd been here before.

" 'Been all over the place in Rumania,' he remarked, 'and I'm glad I didn't take her. Hotels there are positively alive. You get to be deuced agile with a cake of soap, I can tell you.'

"She shuddered.

" 'John, dear, you *don't* mean fleas?'

"He let out a bellow of laughter.

" 'But I *do* mean fleas. Battalions of 'em. Still, I've done a pretty good deal, Kitten, pretty good. And I've got my eyes on that little thing at Cartiers, my pet. You know the one you mentioned to me before we left London.'

"She smiled at him adorably and he turned to me.

" 'We're just off on a good holiday jaunt round Sicily. Are you keen on photography?'

"I told him that I didn't even know which end took the picture.

" 'A hobby, sir,' he remarked, 'and a science in itself if it is taken seriously.'

"I assured him that I could well believe it, and for ten minutes he boomed on serenely about enlargements and cloud effects, while I listened with what politeness I could. And it was only when she got up to go that he stopped.

" 'I'm really rather tired, dear,' she said. 'I think I'll have dinner in my room.'

" 'Where have you come from?' I asked, for want of something to say.

"She looked me straight in the face.

" 'From Rome to-day. We spent last night there. And from Florence the day before.'

"Then she smiled and held out her parasol.

" 'Do you remember the accident? I never got it mended till John came, and now you can hardly see the break, can you?'

" 'As good as new, Kitten. Wonderful stuff, seccotine, Mr. Straker, provided you don't use too much. I assure you that I've mended china and things with seccotine——'

" 'John, dear,' murmured his wife, 'I *am* so tired.'

"John was all solicitude, and they went out. For a moment I caught her eye, and then I joined my friends.

" 'Damned pretty woman,' said one of them, 'but that bullock of a husband seems a Number One bore.'

"And it must truthfully be conceded that dear old John was. He attached himself to us, and how I got through that evening I don't know. His wife did not appear again, and for three mortal hours I endured a monologue on her charms, fleas in Rumania, photography, and the relative merits of pitching as against running up at golf. But particularly the wonderful qualities of his Kitten, until in sheer desperation I escaped and went to bed.

"The next day it was the same. He buttonholed me in a corner of the lounge and talked without stopping for an hour. They were staying on for a week; he particularly wanted to make some camera studies of Vesuvius and Solfatara at dawn and sunset, and other appalling hours.

" 'Dear old John is so energetic, Mr. Straker,' she murmured as he bustled away to get some details out of the concierge.

" 'Do you rise at dawn and go with him?' I asked.

"The little devil looked at me and winked.

" 'So you really did go to Florence?' I pursued, a little gauchely.

" 'Of course,' she said with uplifted brows. 'Where on earth did you think I went?'

"But at that moment John returned and I was saved the necessity of replying.

" 'My dear,' he cried, 'who do you think has just arrived? I saw him getting out of the hotel bus. Young Trannock. And there he is.'

"And young Trannock was none other than Bill. He came across as soon as he saw us, and shook hands.

" 'What a pleasant surprise,' he murmured. 'I'd no idea you were here.'

" 'This is magnificent,' boomed John. 'He's a camera fiend, too, Straker. I've just been fixing up a conveyance to get me out to Solfatara to-morrow morning at dawn, Bill. Of course you'll come?'

"I must say that that one moment atoned for much. Bill's face was a perfect study. The last person he'd counted on finding in the place was me; when I'd last seen him I'd had no idea my business would take so long. And the prospect of Solfatara at dawn, leaving me in undisputed possession, so to speak, was more than he could bear. However, to give him full credit, he carried it off very well. Nothing would please him more than to go to Solfatara at three o'clock in the morning with John.

" 'No guides,' went on John. 'No one to worry one. You've been there, Straker, of course? Amazing place, isn't it? Those boiling lava pools, bubbling and smoking; the ground ringing hollow under one's feet. They tell me that they give it about another thirty years before it erupts again.'

"He babbled serenely on, completely oblivious of the situation right under his nose.

" 'Straker's no photographer, Bill. He can look after Sylvia while we enjoy ourselves.'

"He bore Bill away with him to the bar still discussing stops and speeds.

" 'How lucky that Bill likes photography,' I murmured.

" 'He loathes it,' she answered, laughing helplessly. 'But it's useful.'

" 'You know, Sylvia,' I said severely, 'you're an extremely naughty little woman. Do you usually have these—shall we say—overlaps?'

"She wasn't offended in the slightest.

" 'My dear man,' she remarked, 'it's entirely your fault. I'd no idea you were going to be here so long.'

" 'I wasn't exactly alluding to myself,' I retorted. 'I was thinking more of John.'

" 'John is very fond of Bill,' she murmured. 'In fact, I wouldn't be at all surprised if he didn't ask him to come with us on our trip. What a pity you aren't a photographer. You might have come, too.'

" 'You'd better take care, my dear,' I warned her.

'There are certain circumstances in which I would prefer to have your excellent John doing havoc with a cake of soap in the far-off Balkans.'

" 'Dear old John,' she laughed. 'I know how to manage him.'

" 'Quite obviously,' I agreed. 'But accidents will happen, and from the little I've seen of him I would prefer not to be around when one does.'

"Which was no more than the bare truth. In spite of his placid good-humour, and his unrivalled propensities as a bore, it struck me that John Hedsdale, once he was really roused, would be an ugly customer. Clearly he had not the faintest suspicion as to his wife's fidelity, and so long as she ensured that he was safely in Rumania, or some other far-removed and suitable spot, he was never likely to entertain the faintest suspicion on that score. But for Trannock to go on a trip with them seemed to be playing with fire."

The fair-haired man glanced at his watch.

"By Jove! it's late; I must be getting on with it. . . . I don't know if you gentlemen know that part of Italy; probably you do. But if you don't, Solfatara—the worthy John's destination on the following morning—is worth a little description. It is the crater of a once-active volcano which can now be walked over with safety except in certain spots. You enter by a fine avenue of acacia trees, and then, after a few hundred yards, you start over the volcano proper. If you drop a stone on the ground it rings quite hollow: in fact, you are walking over what is practically a skin a few feet thick. Below that skin is the boiling foundation, which bursts out in certain places like a witch's cauldron. There are holes here and there where the mud seethes and bubbles, and the ground is cracked and split. And it's dangerous to go too near these holes.

"A strange place; an eerie place; with little eddies of

white vapour bursting out of fissures in the hills around, and over everything the acrid smell of sulphur.   Go there when you're next in Naples, but take a guide and don't venture too near those boiling, hissing mud holes, where the temperature is more than 150 degrees Centigrade.   If the ground does give way—and it's undercut near the edge of some of the holes—it's a dreadful, frightful death.   And it's the death that Bill Trannock died on the morning that he and John Hedsdale went to Solfatara.

"It seemed that in his curiosity he approached the very edge of one of the pools.   And suddenly there was a ghastly scream as the ground collapsed under his feet.   For a few unspeakable seconds he writhed in the boiling liquid, and then it was over.

"Such was the story John Hedsdale told us on his return.   His face was grey and his eyes, set and grim, never left his wife's face.   And she, half-hysterical with the horror of it, sat and stared in front of her.

"It was an accident, of course, but it necessitated a lot of explanation with the authorities.   And since Hedsdale couldn't speak a word of Italian, it devolved on me to act as interpreter for him.

"It appeared that he was engaged in fixing his camera preparatory to taking some exposures, when he happened to turn round.   And he saw that Trannock was dangerously near the edge of one of the pools. He shouted a warning, and at that very moment it happened.   There was nothing to be done; even if he'd had a rope it would have been useless to throw it. Death in a temperature of 150 degrees Centigrade is not far off instantaneous.

"Such was the story as told by John Hedsdale, first to us and then to the authorities.   His voice never varied; his eyes still seemed to hold the horror of what he had seen.   And they seemed to hold some other look as well—a strange brooding look—a look to which I held no clue. It was a trying day, as you can imagine, and I would willingly have got out of it personally. But one can't go and leave people in the lurch.

"I hardly saw her; she had retired to her room, but he seemed to want to talk to me. Not that he talked much; but we sat together in the lounge, and I read the papers. And it was after a long silence that he suddenly got out of his chair.

" 'I'm going to develop a photograph; one I took this morning,' he said heavily. 'And to-night the plate will be dry. And after it's dry I will make a print of it, and I will develop the print. And I think it will amuse you.'

"He walked off, leaving me staring after him. After all, I hold no brief for Trannock; as I've told you, I disliked the fellow. But, dash it all, the poor devil had died the most agonizing death only that morning, and even for a photographic maniac it struck me as being a bit callous. Still, perhaps it would take his mind off the tragedy.

"I didn't see him again until after dinner, and then he came up to me in the lounge. He seemed more dazed and heavy than ever—almost as if he had been drinking. He hadn't been, but in the light of what came after I think he must have been mentally stunned. I can conceive of no other reason to account for his asking me to be present.

"He led me upstairs into his sitting-room. The electric light was burning, and on the table stood an unlit red lamp, such as is used in a dark room. Then he shut and locked the door and put the key in his pocket.

" 'I will get my wife,' he said; and I don't mind admitting, gentlemen, that I instinctively glanced round the room for a weapon of some sort. A guilty conscience makes cowards of us all, and for the first time a wild suspicion had entered my brain that somehow or other John Hedsdale had found out. But how? And, if so, could it be that the events of the morning had not been an accident?

"My thoughts were interrupted by his return with his wife through a communicating-door from the next room. And I saw at a glance that she was as bewildered as I. She was watching him a little fearfully, as if she had suddenly found a new John Hedsdale. And once when his back was turned her eyes met mine in mute inquiry. But I could only shake my head; I knew no more than she.

" 'I have a little story to tell you,' he began suddenly. 'It's about a man—a poor damned fool of a man—who married a girl just fifteen years younger than himself.'

"His wife gave a little, uncontrollable start, but she said no word.

" 'He loved this girl,' went on John Hedsdale, 'he adored her. And what is more, he trusted her—I said he was a damned fool, didn't I?'

"And now the woman on the sofa was beginning to shake and tremble.

" 'One day,' continued the inexorable voice, 'the man went to Rumania on business. He hurried through the business as quickly as possible, because he wanted to get back to the wife he adored and go on a little holiday trip they had planned together. She was going to be in Naples—that was the original idea—and he was going to meet her there. And then she changed her mind and went off to stay with a girl friend in Florence —or so she wrote to the man. And the man believed her; why shouldn't he? Did he not find her in Florence on his return from Rumania? So they travelled together back to Naples from Florence, preparatory to starting on their little trip—this damned fool and his wife.

" 'They arrived in Naples, and the day after their arrival another man came, who knew them both.   He was a friend—a great friend of the girl; this fool of a man knew that.   But that is all he knew—then.'

"For a moment the man's voice shook, and his great fists clenched at his sides.

" 'Yes—that's all the fool knew then.   And it's all he would know now but for a little accident; one of those things where the clever people slip up and the fools learn the truth.   They went to the bar—the fool and the other man—and there they found an American. And the American, who was globe-trotting, started to talk about Vesuvius and volcanoes generally.   Quite natural; quite an ordinary conversation, wasn't it, seeing that they were in Naples?   And from volcanoes they came to eruptions, and from eruptions to the big recent one of Etna.'

"I looked at the woman, and her face was the colour of putty.

" 'The other man,' continued John Hedsdale, 'had just come from Sicily, and told us of the very interesting excursion he had made from Taormina to Etna.   He had taken some photographs—did I tell you he was a photographer?   Incidentally, the fool was keen on it, too.   And the other man showed the American some photos he had taken.   One in particular to illustrate the enormous depth of the lava.   He'd had no idea until he'd seen it that it was so deep; no more had the American.   And no more had the fool.   He was staggered when he looked at the photograph; but it wasn't the lava that seemed suddenly to knock the foundation out of his life.   Dimly he heard the other two go on talking; with a hand he vainly tried to steady he held that snapshot and stared at it.   But not at the lava; at something else.   Surely he must be mistaken; surely this monstrous thing could not be?   But in his heart of hearts he knew it was so, right from the beginning.   To make quite sure, however, he went up to his wife's room, and there, having found what he sought and driven in the last nail of proof, he sat down to face things out.

" 'The fool was going to Solfatara the next morning with the other man, and gradually a plan dawned in his mind.   Not a nice plan, but when a fool realizes his folly he ceases to be nice.   And at Solfatara something happened—an accident——'

"He laughed harshly, and his wife gave a sudden little cry of terror.

" 'Ever considerate, the fool was sure the girl he adored would like a nice pretty picture—one that would make a pair with the snapshot of the lava at Etna.   So he took one, choosing his moment with care; and he developed it.   And here it is.'

"He took a plate from his pocket and adjusted it in a printing-frame.

" 'And now, with your permission, the fool will make a print of it, and develop that print in front of you.'

"With a sudden tightening round the base of the scalp, I watched his preparations.   He switched on the red lamp, turned off the other, and put in a piece of printing-paper.   Then, switching on the light again, he exposed it.   And while he exposed it I looked at his wife, and she was half-fainting.   He put the print into the dish, quite calmly and methodically; he poured the chemicals over it.

" 'Come and see,' he said.

"His wife made no movement, but I, impelled by a sort of unholy fascination, went over and stood by his side.   It came out of the paper, did that photograph—

suddenly and dramatically, as with all gaslight exposures—and, my God! gentlemen, it gave me a shock.

"There was the pool, seething and smoking, and in the centre of it—caught at the psychological moment—was the distorted, agonized face of Bill Trannock. It must have been taken from close range, literally as he died.

" 'Tear the damned thing up, man,' I shouted. 'It's horrible.'

"But he only laughed.

" 'It makes a pair,' he said harshly. 'In this the pool at Solfatara; in the other the lava at Etna. But in both something else.'

"He laid the Etna snapshot on the table, and at last I understood. There on the edge of the Etna photograph, thrown on the ground, and overlooked when the picture was taken, was the handle of a parasol. And the handle consisted of a parrot with a big bit chipped out of the tail. There in the centre of the Solfatara photo was the handle of a parasol. And the handle consisted of a parrot with a big bit chipped out of the tail.

"He dragged his wife to her feet, and forced her to the table. 'I mended it for you in Florence; I broke it again last night. And here it is.'

"He pulled the handle out of his pocket and put it between the two snapshots. And there it lay, that darned red and green bird with the broken tail, giving its mute and damning evidence. Many parasols have parrots for handles; but it is inconceivable that you should have two broken in the same place.

"And a moment later Sylvia Hedsdale gave a little moan and slipped to the floor. She had fainted, but for a while we paid no attention. We just stood there staring at one another.

" 'This morning?' I said at length.

"He looked at me heavily.

" 'Have you not told the police that it was an accident?' he said. 'Let us leave it at that.' "

The fair-haired man lit a cigarette thoughtfully.

"I've often wondered," he continued. "Wondered about that and other things. No; I'm wrong. Not about that. I am as sure that John Hedsdale murdered Trannock at Solfatara that morning as I am that we are shortly going to have a nightcap. But what I have wondered since, and what I wondered then, is whether he had any suspicions about me. In fact, I don't mind telling you that I wondered it so acutely that night that I left the next day. It struck me that this photography question might become a mania. Two were enough; a third would be quite uncalled for."

He turned to the seccotine maniac.

"You see, it does sometimes fail to stick."

The other nodded profoundly.

"Not if it's put on right. Now with china——"

The ship's doctor arose in his wrath.

"There will be a third in a minute, sir. And it will be of you, drowning in a bath of it."

XLII   A MATTER OF VOICE

"TALKING of lovely women," remarked the actor, "the most perfect, the most adorable, the most divine one I ever met had one small defect. At least most people, I suppose, would consider it a defect. She was a murderess. However, as Wilde said, the fact that a man is a poisoner has nothing to do with his prose. And in the case I'm thinking of it certainly had nothing to do with her charm.

"Of course I have no actual cast-iron proof. My

evidence would be laughed to scorn in a court of law, if one could imagine haling that glorious being into such a dreadful place. Anyway, since it all took place over thirty years ago, and, to my everlasting regret, I read in the paper only a few mornings back that she was dead, the situation does not arise.

"It was before I came to London, and I was on tour with a Number One company. For a youngster I had quite a good part. It wasn't a difficult one, but it was fairly long, and I was frightfully pleased at having got it. We were playing at one of the south coast watering-places, when I saw her first—this divine creature. She was sitting in a box and a man was with her, and whenever I glanced in their direction her eyes were fixed on me.

"Now, at twenty-five, a very soothing and pleasant sensation enwraps one when a lovely woman favours one so obviously. And when the next night found her there again, and the night after—this time alone—yours truly began to expand visibly. Being tolerably well favoured by nature in the matter of a face, I leapt, like the damned fool I was, to the obvious conclusion that this adorable being had fallen in love with me.

"The note was brought round to my dressing-room on the fourth night. To my disappointment she had not been in her usual box, but the note more than atoned. I found it lying on the table, and the man who was sharing with me started to pull my leg. However, I soon shut him up, and then found to my concealed annoyance that my hands were positively shaking with excitement. Of course he shouted with laughter, and after a while I started to laugh too.

"'Adorable man,' he jeered. 'Overcome by the beauty of your face and the marvel of your histrionic ability. . . . Go on: open it. Probably the landlady's daughter asking for an autograph!'

" 'Go to blazes,' I cried, and sat down to read it.

"It was short, but it raised me into the seventh heaven of bliss.

"*Dear Mr. Shortt* [it ran],

"*You will probably think this note a little peculiar, coming, as it does, from a complete stranger. I have watched your show for the last three nights from one of the stage-boxes, and, without wishing to flatter you in the slightest degree, there is no doubt that you stand out head and shoulders from the rest of the cast—good though all of them are.*

"*To come to the object of this letter. I have a certain request to make of you which, I trust, you will see your way to granting. As it is much too long to write, will you come and lunch with me to-morrow, at one o'clock? I shall be alone, and, since you have no matinée, we can take our time. The address you will see above.*

> "*Yours sincerely,*
> "*Violet Tarningham.*

"*P.S.—I don't think you will find the granting of the request unpleasant, so that, unless I hear from you to the contrary, I shall expect you.*

"Well, with a letter like that from a woman like that, what would you do? It merely became a question of watching the hands of the clock go round, and swearing because they didn't go faster. Of course, it could only mean one thing: she had fallen desperately in love with me. And did I blame her? No—perish the thought: far from it. It showed a very proper appreciation of a deuced fine specimen of manhood. And the only thing that worried me at all was whether she was married or not.

"I reached her hotel at one sharp, and as I walked in a man whose face was vaguely familiar passed me.

And suddenly I realized that he was the man who had been with her the first two nights in the box. Moreover, though he only glanced at me quite casually in passing, I thought I read a certain cynical amusement in his eyes.

"I frowned a little angrily, and then I forgot all about him. *She* was coming towards me with the sweetest smile and hand outstretched.

"'How nice of you to come,' she remarked, and, I give you my word, I could only stand and stare at her like the village idiot.

"Seen from the stage she had been beautiful: from close she was ten times more so. Superlatives are always dangerous; but the loveliness of that woman deserves a double-dyed superlative. And everything about her was in keeping—clothes, hands, feet. As I say, I stood there goggling like a callow boy.

"'I've ordered lunch in my private sitting-room,' she went on. 'I loathe feeding with other people, don't you? And when we've finished perhaps you can spare me half an hour or so?'

"I hastened to assure her that I could and would spare her the entire afternoon if she wanted it.

"'I mustn't monopolize you to that extent,' she laughed. 'Or I shall have hundreds of irate girls after me.'

"And so we started lunch. Half-way through I was in love with her; when the coffee came I was in a condition of blithering imbecility. She was wearing a wedding-ring, and once or twice I wondered if the man who had passed me in the hall was her husband. But there didn't seem to be any male traces in the room, such as pipes or tobacco, and after a time I ceased to worry. As I say, I was beyond human hope when the meal came to an end.

"'Tell me, Mr. Shortt,' she said, after I had obtained

her permission to smoke, 'when does your tour come to an end?'

" 'In two months,' I told her.

" 'And what will you be doing then?'

" 'I wish I could tell you, Mrs. Tarningham,' I laughed. 'But I'm afraid the futures of touring actors are not mapped out as closely as that.'

" 'You're not going to be a touring actor for long, my dear man,' she said. 'But we'll talk about that later. Two months, you say. That brings us to the end of September. Would you be free for the first few days of October?'

" 'Free as air,' I told her. 'But to do what?'

" 'To act in a little sketch with me. Of course I'm only an amateur, and you're outstanding. But—perhaps . . .'

"And then I completely lost my head. She was looking at me half sideways, with a faintly provocative smile, and the next thing I knew was that I was on my knees beside her chair and that she was in my arms.

"But—enough. Over that portion of the entertainment I will draw the veil of reticence; as your host I must consider your digestions. Sufficient to say, that the standard of her kissing was, if possible, higher than the standard of her looks.

"At last she pushed me away and pointed to a chair.

" 'Go and sit down, Mr. Man, and behave yourself,' she ordered. 'I want to discuss the play with you.'

"It appeared that she lived in Surrey; and that there was an urgent need of supplying a home for incurable dipsomaniacs, or lost cats, or something, in the village adjoining. That necessitated funds, and the idea was to get up a show. You know the sort of thing: depressing *tableaux-vivants* and a conjurer.

"Her notion was that the main item should be a

small play in which she and I should play the principal parts. My notion was that anything which enabled me to see her as often as possible was good enough for me. I hardly listened, in fact, to her explanations as to the difficulty of finding young men in the neighbourhood who could act; and how she wanted the thing to be a great success. What I did listen to was when she began to tell me as to why she had asked me.

"Heavens above! What a man will swallow when he's young and infatuated. But I will say one thing in defence of myself: she did it amazingly well. She was an absolute artist, and she would have taken in ninety-nine men out of a hundred. You see, there was no reason why my suspicions should have been aroused. Women have become infatuated with men before now, and they will undoubtedly do so again. And I merely regarded it as an astounding piece of luck on my part that the one who had honoured me was so marvellously attractive.

" 'And now I've told you far more than it's good for you to know,' she said at length. 'I want you to talk to me. No! I don't want you to make love to me; you're to sit where you are and smoke a cigarette. Tell me about your plans for the future; tell me about yourself. Because I think that perhaps I may be a little mixed up in that future. . . . Don't you. . . . No, you're to sit down and be sensible. Just talk. . . . You know, I adore your voice.'

"And so I sat and talked. She was that rare specimen—the perfect listener. She knew exactly when to put in a remark, and when to keep silent; she knew how to make a man talk his best. And she could dream your dreams and see your visions, and colour each one for you a little more vividly."

For a moment or two the actor paused and stared at the fire.

"As I told you at the beginning," he continued quietly, "it all happened thirty years ago. And yet, old and cynical as I am now and realizing as I do that I was a dupe and a cat's paw all through, I still say that, with that woman beside him a man could have reached the topmost peak.

"However, I'll get on with it. I left her that afternoon walking on air. She was going to send the sketch to me so that I could learn my part before we started rehearsing in October. And it was only as I sat down to dinner in my lodgings that it dawned on me that she'd never even mentioned the question of her husband. I wondered if he was going to take any part in the play, and what sort of a fellow he was. I felt it couldn't be the man who had been with her at the theatre, and who had passed me as I entered the hotel. No one could have behaved with such cool equanimity if he had known that his wife was proposing to spend several hours alone with another man. Guessing, too, something of the truth: realizing that she must be immensely attracted by that other man to do such a thing.

"No: it was impossible—out of the question. And yet—who was he? Was he another would-be lover whom I had beaten in the race, but who was man of the world enough to take it as he had? Did he perhaps think that I was just a passing infatuation that would die away as quickly as it had been born? Poor fool! Poor, silly fool! Though I took off my hat to him for his sportsmanship. To lose such a prize and keep a stiff upper lip was a bit of a strain on a man.

"She wasn't in the theatre that night, and after the show was over I went for a stroll along the front. It was a glorious night—warm and delightful—and after a while I sat down on the beach with my back against the wall of the esplanade. The band had long since finished, though a few couples still sat about. But it was late and most people had gone to bed, which was just what I wanted.

"I felt I had to be alone to dream over that wonderful afternoon. I was still in a completely dazed condition, and the thought of bed was an impossibility. So I sat on, seeing the most wonderful visions of the future. Only to come back to earth suddenly with a wild feeling of joy. From just above me had come her voice. And I was on the point of dashing up the steps towards her, when I realized that she couldn't be alone.

"The faint smell of a cigar was in the air—so her companion was a man. I heard his voice vaguely, and began to see red on the spot. They were just above me, leaning over the railings, and I, sitting in the darkness below, was invisible. But I could see the glow of his cigar not six feet above me: I could see the outline of her head against the sky. Who was it; who was this cursed fellow who dared to poach on my preserves? The man she had been with at the theatre? And once again I very nearly darted up the steps.

"But I didn't, and sometimes now I'm sorry I didn't. For if I had gone up those steps I shouldn't have heard the remark she made to him just before they both moved away. And I shouldn't have had my little bit of evidence which would have been laughed to scorn in a court of law. It might have made me happier; I don't know. Anyway, I sat on there in the darkness and I heard the remark.

" '*Mon ami*, it is getting a little chilly; let us go in. Of course the whole thing is a matter of careful arrangement, but on the one main point you may set your mind absolutely at rest. The similarity is simply incredible; more marked even in a room than on the stage. I tell you that I myself would not be able to tell the difference if my eyes were shut.'

"Then they moved away, and after a time I, too, got

up to go. And as might be expected, the part of the remark which boiled and seethed in my mind consisted of four short words. 'Let us go in!' It implied——— Heavens! What didn't it imply? Or was it just a conventional phrase?

"As for the rest of the remark, though I'd heard and noted every word subconsciously, it made no impression on me whatever. To me the one main point was, 'let us go in.' I couldn't get beyond that. And it was still the one main point when the tour ceased at Bristol at the end of September.

"During the whole of those two months I never saw her, and I only heard from her once. It was a short line, written from her club in London, to say she had found what she thought was a suitable sketch and that she would send it along in due course. And in the meantime I was to keep my head turned towards the dazzling goal—my own theatre in London.

"So I wrote back five pages of the most passionate adoration, and received in return—the sketch. And I confess that after I'd read the thing through I felt rather as if a bucket of cold water had been thrown over me. I had expected something a little powerful: something with some drama in it: something where she and I could let ourselves go.

"Instead of that, I waded through twenty pages of the most drivelling piffle I've ever set eyes on. I am thankful to say that I have completely forgotten its name and that of the human horror who wrote it. But I do remember that the part I had to play was that of a curate who had an impediment in his speech.

"And then, at Bristol, I got another letter from her which made it all clear. I felt a fool for not having understood before.

" 'I know it's the most ghastly rot,' she wrote, 'but you wouldn't believe the difficulties of an audience like we shall have for an amateur show. One damn, and the whole house would file out. I've read hundreds of the beastly things, and though you won't believe it there are many even worse than the one I chose. Never mind. . . . There are other things to do besides act— at any rate, act on the stage. *N'est-ce pas, mon ami?*

" 'And now a word of warning. You will of course stay with us, and you must know that my husband is a great recluse. He had a very terrible accident a few years ago which deprived him of his sight. It also disfigured him, and he is morbidly sensitive about his appearance. So don't be surprised if his manner is a little strange.

" 'Come by the nine-o'clock train, and the brougham shall meet you at the station. I can't ask you down earlier because I shall be out all day. I'm terribly busy organizing everything—but it's not the show I'm thinking of so much as . . . Well, I'll tell you that later.'

"As I say, it made everything clear. With a provincial village audience it was undoubtedly exactly the type of drivel to go down. The letter also cleared up another point: the man who had been with her in the theatre was evidently not her husband. And it was just as I was once again cogitating as to who he was that I noticed a postscript.

" 'By the way, my dear, I have had to do one thing which I know you will understand. It would be absolutely suicidal in this neighbourhood if it came out that I had met you before. Everyone would immediately leap to the worst conclusions. Even my husband might wonder, and we certainly don't want that, do we? So I have given it out that an agency in London is going to procure a suitable actor to fill the part, and that I don't even know his name. We must meet *apparently* as strangers.'

"By George!" laughed the Actor, "as I look back now I become increasingly staggered. Age cannot wither the wondrous and simple beauty of that plot in all its cold-blooded unscrupulousness. It was a work of art, and as such it must be judged. I cannot see one detail that was neglected, or one unnecessary risk that was run. It was a cast-iron certainty from the moment the tapes went up.

"However—to get on with it. I left London by the nine-o'clock train, and arrived at my destination about ten. And as I got out on to the platform a man brushed past me who was evidently going on by my train. Just for a moment the light of the solitary lamp fell on his face, and I recognized him at once. The same man again—confound the fellow! I couldn't get away from him. Moreover, he had evidently come down in the brougham, for the inside smelt strongly of smoke.

"However, I soon forgot him: was I not going to see my divinity again in a few minutes—hold her in my arms? The horses seemed to crawl: my hands were clammy: you know—all the usual symptoms. And then when I saw her I very nearly forgot the postscript instruction.

"She came across the hall towards me dressed in some grey gauzy stuff, and she was more wonderful than ever. And I gave a step forward—an uncontrollable step—before I remembered that we had never met before.

" 'Mr. Shortt, I believe,' she said, and held out her hand. 'It is very good of you to come and help us.'

" 'Not at all,' I murmured.

" 'But as the cause is very deserving perhaps you will overlook our defects,' she went on with a smile. 'Now would you like to see your room or shall we have a rehearsal at once?'

"She'd turned so that her back was towards the butler, and she gave me the suspicion of a wink. So you can be pretty certain which of the alternatives I chose.

" 'All right: I hope I'm word perfect,' she said. 'Take Mr. Shortt's things up to his room, Wilson, and see that we are not disturbed for the next half-hour or so. Don't forget, Mr. Shortt, that you must be merciful. . . . I'm only a beginner. . . .'

"She was leading the way across the hall as she spoke.

" 'Let's come in here.' She opened the door, and I followed her into a largish room. It was half smoking-room, half library, and at the opposite end was an opening in the wall across which stretched some heavy black curtains.

" 'We shan't be disturbed in here.'

"She'd shut the door behind her, and with it she'd shut out pretence. The change in her voice—I can hear it now.

" 'We shan't be disturbed in here.'

" 'Oh! my darling,' she said. 'Kiss me—kiss me—and go on kissing me. Dinner to-night was an ordeal: I thought I'd never get through it—waiting for this. These last two months have been too terrible.'

"Well, I kissed her—and kissed her—and went on kissing her, and there is no gainsaying the fact that an onlooker during the next ten minutes or so would have had his money's worth. Robert—whom I gathered was the blind husband—had gone to bed: Wilson had received orders that we were not to be disturbed, and things undoubtedly hummed.

"And then a little abruptly—I can distinctly remember a slight feeling of surprise at the abruptness—she stood up. She had been sitting in a chair facing the black curtains—I thought of that afterwards—and she suddenly pushed away my arms.

" 'Adorable man,' she said, 'I've just thought of something.   It's a little surprise for you.   I'll be back in a minute or two.'

"And the next moment she had left the room.

"I don't know how long it was before I noticed it," continued the Actor after a little pause, "—that motionless bulge in the curtains.   At first I paid no attention to it, and then the hair began to prick at the back of my scalp.   For it seemed to me that the curtains had shaken slightly.   It was close to one end, that bulge, and it was of the size and shape that would be made by a man.

"I suppose a man of action would have done something: though what was to be done God knows.   All that I did was to sit in my chair and sweat, with my tongue bone dry and the glass in my hand shaking so uncontrollably that the whisky was spilling all over the carpet.   For I realized instinctively what had happened. Robert had not gone to bed: we were caught.

"And then I heard a funny noise: it was myself trying to scream.   For a hand had appeared from behind the curtain: a hand that groped along the wall. It was tanned and sinewy, and again I heard that funny noise.   For I couldn't move: I sat there petrified with horror, even though I knew what that hand was groping for.   It was the switch, and, at last, it found what it sought.   And the next instant the room was in darkness.

"It's a confession of weakness, I suppose, but I've hated real darkness ever since.   And the darkness in that room was the most intense thing I've ever known. There wasn't a glimmer of light: just utter blackness that pressed in on one almost as if it was tangible.   And still I sat there incapable of movement.

"The glass had fallen out of my nerveless fingers, and I could feel the liquid soaking through my sock and into my shoe. And it was the physical sensation of wetness that restored some semblance of activity to my brain. Somehow or other I must get to the door—save myself and warn the girl.

"So I made a desperate effort and lurched to my feet. Then I gave a dive in the direction, as I thought, of the door. And out of the darkness there came a low laugh. I blundered on: took a table with a crash, spun round and was lost. All sense of direction was gone: I was just staggering round blindly in that inky darkness.

"Once again he laughed, and this time there was a note of triumph in his voice. I stood stock-still: a new and hideous thought had suddenly occurred to me. The husband was blind: the darkness was no handicap to him. So that my only hope lay in making no sound. If I could get to the wall, and then creep along it, sooner or later I must reach the door. I took a step back, and another and another, feeling behind me the whole time as I moved. Suddenly my hand encountered a table, and I tried desperately to visualize the room. Where had the tables been: how many were there? And I couldn't remember a darned thing.

"I ran my fingers along it trying to find the end, and at that moment I heard his breathing quite distinctly. He was close to me, and a wild, unreasoning panic seized me. I lurched back, knocked over the table, and felt a hand like a steel bar get me by the throat.

" 'Proof at last, you vile swine,' came in a voice that was half snarl, half shout of triumph. 'And I'm going to kill you.'

"I tried to scream, but his other hand was over my mouth. I tried to struggle: I was utterly powerless in his grasp. A strong man might have made some sort of a show, but I lay no claim to physical strength. And in that man's hands I felt like a baby.

"I don't know how long we fought: everything is a bit confused. I know that I heard his wild laughter through the roaring in my head, for an eternity, so it seemed to me, before the light went on. Violet was standing by the black curtains with a revolver in her hand. And even as I saw her her husband shifted one hand from my throat, whipped a long stiletto out of his pocket, and drove it with all his force into my chest.

"His grip relaxed, and I sank down. And in the last few moments before everything became blank, I heard scream after scream and the shot of a revolver. Then—oblivion."

The Actor paused and mixed himself a whisky and soda.

"Now had the knife been the eighth of an inch more to the right I should not be telling you this story to-night. The double funeral of Robert and your humble servant would have taken place simultaneously. Honestly I think that in many ways she quite liked me, and that she was glad the wound was not fatal. But from the point of view of the perfect work of art—which I maintain her plot was—the fact that I didn't die constituted the one flaw.

"I gather it was some four days before I regained consciousness to find myself in a nursing home. A doctor was standing at the foot of the bed, and seated in the window was my adored woman.

"'Splendid,' said the doctor. 'Don't move: lie quite still, Mr. Shortt. How are you feeling?'

"Violet, her dear face terribly strained, had risen and was standing beside him.

"'All right, thanks,' I said. 'A bit tied up round the chest, that's all.'

"'You're thoroughly tied up round the chest,' he laughed. 'And you've had about the closest shave of death I've ever known. Now, Mrs. Tarningham, I will give you just five minutes with him. Please see he doesn't move.'

" 'My dear,' she said brokenly after he had gone, 'if you had died.'

" 'But I didn't, sweetheart,' I answered. 'And I'm not going to. Tell me what happened.'

" 'He rushed at me,' she whispered, 'and I shot him through the heart. He's dead.'

" 'Good God!' I muttered. 'But what do people say?'

" 'I had to make up my mind on the spur of the moment,' she answered. 'The servants came rushing in, and I had to say something. And so I said he'd suddenly gone mad: that we'd been rehearsing the play, and that he had dashed out and attacked you. Then I rushed into his room and got his revolver. And when I saw him stab you and then spring at me I fired.'

" 'But do they believe it?' I cried.

" 'Yes, dear, yes. Everybody believes it: why shouldn't they? He's always been moody and morose, and just lately he's been worse. And nobody knows that we've ever met before. There we were rehearsing that silly play, and he suddenly tries to kill us both. They've found a verdict that he was a homicidal maniac. You see—I couldn't tell the truth, could I?'

"And then the doctor came back and announced that time was up, so that I hadn't time to warn her about the man whom I had seen at the station. He knew we'd met before. And she didn't come alone again: though she found a chance of whispering that it wasn't that she didn't want to. And then she went abroad: her nerves had given way.

"It was all rather beautiful, wasn't it? To the world at large it was merely a shocking tragedy in which a man had suddenly gone mad. It was cynically remarked by a few people who knew the play that such a thing was only to be expected: but to attempt to murder a complete stranger and your wife is a somewhat drastic way of showing your disapproval.

"To me it was merely the eternal triangle in which, if the man had indeed gone mad, it was not to be wondered at.   But it would have been her life or his, and, anyway, my lips were sealed.   And it wasn't until two years later that I began to wonder, and finally ceased wondering and, in my own mind, knew.

"At first my assumption had been that, after a decent interval, she would marry me.   And I'll say this for her, she disabused my mind of the notion very sweetly and gradually.   It wasn't that she wasn't fond of me, but that the whole thing had been so terrible that she wanted to try and obliterate it from her life.   And if I was with her . . .   Perhaps, in years to come we could meet again—when things might be different. . . .   But now she couldn't bear it. . . .

"And so on, and so forth.   I swallowed it whole until one night when a man came round to see me. I'd got to London then, and he came in after the show.

" 'Have you ever met Lord Raynor?' he asked after we'd talked for a bit.

" 'Not that I'm aware of,' I said.

" 'I met him out in Rapallo a few weeks ago.   I couldn't think what it was at the time that puzzled me, but I've got it now.   It's your two voices.   Every note, every inflection is exactly the same.   I mean it's positively staggering.   And you're not a bit alike to look at.   As a matter of fact, I've got a snapshot of him.'

"He handed it over, and dimly out of the distance I realized he was still talking.   For in the group was Violet, and Lord Raynor was the man who had been with her in the box and who had passed me on the platform.

"I got rid of him somehow after a while and sat there thinking.

" 'The similarity is simply incredible. . . . I tell you that I myself would not be able to tell the difference if my eyes were shut. . . .'

"By Gad! you fellows, when the damning truth first came home to me it shook my world. I got over it in time, as one gets over everything. But just at first I nearly went off my head.

"Everything from start to finish had been part of a carefully thought-out plot. Raynor was her lover: had always been her lover. And the blind husband stood in the way. Probably he suspected. 'Proof at last,' he'd said to me. Raynor had been dining there, and at the last crucial moment she substituted me.

"That poor devil when he attacked me was attacking a voice: the voice of the man he hated. She knew he was behind that curtain the whole time, and it was when she saw the curtain shake that she left the room. She knew he'd try to kill me: she hoped he'd succeed. And what greater proof of homicidal mania could be had. To kill an utter stranger for no apparent reason. . . .

"So she got her husband's money, and she got her lover—she married him a few months later—and the sole item on the debit side to be one dead mummer.

"Gorgeous, wasn't it. . . . Except for the mummer.

"For all that she was the most adorable woman I've ever known."

BIG Jim Sefton pulled himself together as his horse shied violently across the track.

"Steady, old gal," he muttered. "It's a broken branch, not a snake."

The mare, still eyeing the thing that had alarmed her, sidled warily forward, and big Jim relapsed once more into his reverie. His face, tanned to a dark mahogany, was set and a little stern: his eyes—vivid blue eyes they were, contrasting strangely with the colour of his skin—were surrounded by a network of little wrinkles that proclaimed the dweller in the open of harsh lights. And just now the look in them showed that their owner's thoughts were many miles away.

Twenty—to be exact: twenty straight ahead, at the destination to which he was riding. The burning midday sun beat down on him from a cloudless blue sky: he didn't notice it. Big Jim had sojourned under that same scorching heat for too many years now for it to worry him. Splashes of brilliant colour in the trees that flanked the track, which would have called forth the excited admiration of most people, never even caused him to turn his head. The sight of an English rose garden would have appealed to him more than all the tropical flowers in the world. He had seen them all too often: he was sick of them with a deadly nausea. To him they were typical of the soul of the country: lovely, gaudy, and—meretricious.

"It's rotten," he suddenly said aloud. "Rotten. And why the devil I stay here, God alone knows."

And then he laughed shortly: it was not the first time he had delivered himself of the same sentiment, and he was still there.

The laugh died away on his lips: once again his thoughts had gone back to the bungalow twenty miles ahead. How were the two people there faring in this land of harshness and crude contrasts? Two more unsuitable settlers it would have been hard to imagine —especially the man. And yet it was possible they had made good: in the course of his life big Jim had seen some amazingly square pegs fitting into the roundest of holes with apparent success.

It wasn't that Jack Fairbrace was a weakling—far from it. He was a good shot, and a first-class player of ball games. But he was essentially orthodox: he was part and parcel of the club life and social amenities of England. And big Jim couldn't picture him in Africa.

Enid—his wife—was different, but then a woman is always more adaptable than a man. He recalled that night at Henley four years ago when he had painted for her a description of the land he had made his own. Painted the glamour of it, and the beauty, the passion of it and the appeal. And he'd believed it—then: he invariably did when he was away, which was why he always came back. And she had listened with her lips parted and her head a little thrown back.

"Sorry, old gal," he said gruffly, as the mare fidgeted under a hand grown suddenly powerful. "For the moment I thought of other things."

For it had been on the lap of the Gods that night. The nearness of her and the scent she used had gone to his head. He could still hear the gentle lap of the water against the punt as they drifted lazily along; the faint strains of the band playing at Phyllis Court still rang in his head. And suddenly he had taken her in his arms and kissed her.

For a moment or two she had lain up against him,

her lips on his. Then, very gently, she had pushed him away.

"Jim," she had said quietly, "I ought to have told you I'm engaged. It isn't given out yet, and that's why I'm not wearing a ring."

"I see," said big Jim, and lit a cigarette with a hand that shook a little. "I'm sorry; I didn't know."

And because of a certain strict notion of honour he had gone away the next day. And she had let him go. He had said nothing more, though the Fates that govern these things alone know what would have been the result if he had. He knew that he loved her—at least he'd loved her that night; and she—well, she had wondered and waited and finally married Jack Fairbrace. Which has happened before in this world, and is likely to happen again. Moreover, she was happy with him, for Jack was a good soul and a white man. And if sometimes she thought of a big bronzed man with vivid blue eyes, and wondered where he was and what he was doing, she kept those thoughts to herself. Once or twice she had seen him before he went back to Africa, but always when other people were present. The mere fact that she had taken care that they were, may perhaps serve as a pointer.

And then one day Jim Sefton—having just finished a fifteen-months' trek in the back of beyond up Tanganyika way—arrived in Johannesburg. It was his permanent postal address, and amongst the mail that had been collecting for him he found a letter from Enid Fairbrace. It was nearly a year old and it ran as follows:

"My dear Jim,

"By the time you get this—unless you're in Johannesburg at the moment—we shall be out in Africa ourselves. A bit of a surprise, isn't it, and I can still hardly believe

that we're really going.   But things are altering so in England, and servants are so difficult, and all one's money goes on merely living.

"At any rate, we're going to try something new.   Do you remember that time you told me about the country, and how wonderful it was?   We've bought a farm, more or less in partnership with another man.   And we're coming out to make our fortunes.   So mind you come and see us if ever you happen to be in our locality.   I know it's rather like asking a man who has been in India whether he knew your cousin, but however much out of the way it is you must make a point of coming to see us—if only to tell us where we are making mistakes.   Come whenever you like; don't bother to write.

"Yours very sincerely,
"Enid Fairbrace."

He hadn't written; he had taken her at her word. It was so long now since her letter had come that he had decided it would be better to do so.   In addition, he wasn't sure exactly when he would be able to get to the address she had given: he had one or two other things to do first.   And now, those things finished, he was on his way to renew a friendship which might so easily have become something else.

It was over two years now since he had seen Enid Fairbrace, and he was conscious of a certain curious excitement at the prospect of meeting her again.   He told himself that no trace of his old feeling for her remained: that he was merely going to see the wife of a man to whom he had taken quite a liking in England.   But the curious excitement refused to vanish at this logical and cold-blooded presentation of the case, and after a while, with a little shrug of his broad shoulders, Jim Sefton admitted the truth to himself. He was in love with another man's wife: he always had been in love with her, and he'd been a silly quixotic fool to let her go without a struggle.

He glanced at the sun and realized the time was about three o'clock.

"Another three miles," he muttered to himself, and broke into a jog-trot. The track was clearly defined, and with the directions given him by the man at the railway station thirty miles back, from whom he had hired his horse, it presented no difficulties to a man like Jim Sefton. To a townsman it would probably have seemed impenetrable jungle bush: to Sefton's practised eye the route was as clearly marked as if there had been signposts.

"There's the drift, old gal," he said as the horse splashed through the shallow water. "Only another two miles to go."

And then he pulled up: a white man, with a gun under his arm, had suddenly appeared in a clearing in front of him.

"Good afternoon," said Jim Sefton. "I'm right, ain't I, for the Fairbraces' house?"

"Straight as you can go," answered the stranger, staring at him intently. "Are you a doctor by any chance?"

"I am not," said Sefton. "Why? Anybody ill?"

"Fairbrace is pretty seedy," answered the other man. "I'm Edwardes — his partner. Live with them."

"What's the matter with him?" asked Sefton. "Malaria?"

"Personally I think he's got a bad dose of tampane fever," said Edwardes. "High temperature; all the usual symptoms."

"How is Mrs. Fairbrace?" said Sefton after a pause, and once again the other man eyed him intently.

"Very fit," he answered after a little pause. "A

little uneasy, naturally, about her husband. You know them, I suppose?"

"Quite well," said Sefton. "In fact I was on my way to answer in person a year-old invitation of hers to look them up. I've been up Tanganyika way, and found the letter waiting for me two or three weeks ago in Jo'burg. Sefton is my name."

The other man nodded.

"I rather guessed you were. Heard them mention you often."

"How are they getting on?" asked Sefton. "Have you got a good show here?"

"Quite," said Edwardes briefly. "We want the railway, of course. But there's always a catch somewhere. However, you'll see for yourself. The house is on some high ground about a mile and a half ahead. And look out for snakes: there are a lot of mambas about."

"Thanks; I will," answered the other. "See you later, I take it."

With a nod he trotted on, and then, just before he got to a turn in the track, something impelled him to look back. Edwardes was still standing motionless staring after him, though the instant Sefton looked round he turned and vanished into the bush. And a slight frown showed for an instant on big Jim's forehead. Doubtless it was quite unreasonable, but he was conscious of a distinct feeling of dislike for Jack Fairbrace's partner.

The frown deepened as he rode on. He had come now to stretches of cultivated land, which he knew must belong to the people he was going to see. And though he kept a wary eye skinned for that most deadly of all snakes—the black mamba—subconsciously he took in the condition of the ground through which he was riding.

Jim Sefton was not a farmer himself, but few men in Africa had a sounder knowledge of the game. And it was soon obvious to him that this was very far from being a good show. The part he was going through was under cotton, and he could tell at a glance that the crop was poor and the weeds plentiful. In the distance there were some tired-looking orange trees chiefly remarkable for the complete absence of fruit. In fact everything showed unmistakable signs of neglect and laziness.

"Something very wrong," he reflected. "I'm glad I came."

Suddenly in the distance he saw the house, and his mare, as if sensing the end of the journey, quickened her pace. And five minutes later he was shaking hands with Enid Fairbrace whilst a boy took his horse away to the outhouse that served as a stable.

"Jim!" she cried, "but I'm glad to see you."

He smiled gravely, and studied her with his keen blue eyes.

"You're looking well, Enid," he said at length. "Awfully well. A bit worried, but I suppose that's due to Jack's fever."

"How did you know anything about that?" she asked in surprise.

"I met your partner, Edwardes, down by the drift," he answered, and if he noticed the sudden shadow that passed over her face he said nothing. "I'm sorry he's so seedy. Edwardes said something about tampane fever."

"He's got this beastly temperature which he can't shake off," she said, leading the way into the house. "I don't think it is anything serious, but it makes the poor old boy so weak and irritable. Come and see him."

He followed her into her husband's bedroom, and the sick man sat up with a smile when he saw him.

"Hallo, Jim!" he cried. "Where the deuce have
you sprung from?"

Jim Sefton sat down on the bed and laughed.

"Out of the blue, as usual, old man," he answered.
"Only got Enid's letter three weeks ago. This is a
bad affair, though, finding you down with fever. How
did you get it?"

"Out shooting the other day with Bill," said Fairbrace irritably. "That's Edwardes—my partner. Or,
to be correct, I should say I'm his. This place belonged
to him originally, and he supplies all the farming knowledge."

"He does, does he?" remarked Jim Sefton. "And
what do you supply—the capital?"

"Well, naturally I've put in a bit of cash," answered
the other. "And, by Jove! it's a pretty expensive
game. Still, as Bill says—you've got to put money
in if you want to get money out."

Jim Sefton grunted and did not pursue the topic.
He took a glance at the marks on the sick man's neck,
and felt no doubt in his own mind that Edwardes's
diagnosis was right, and that tampane fever was the
trouble. He told them so, which reassured Enid considerably, and then, having talked for a time to the
invalid, he followed her into the hall for tea. And
the first thing that struck him was the difference between the inside of the farm and what lay outside.
There were no evidences here of the laziness and neglect
which had been so obvious as he had ridden up: everything was cosy and comfortable—English chintzes, big
easy chairs, flowers prettily arranged—and with a sigh
of satisfaction he took the cup she handed him.

"You've made it charming, Enid," he said. "Perfectly charming. Jack and his partner are two singularly fortunate individuals."

And as he spoke there came the sound of a shot.

It was fairly close to, and instinctively Jim Sefton sat up in his chair.

"It's probably Mr. Edwardes," said Enid. "He's always shooting something."

"It sounded pretty near," said Sefton. "Not more than a couple of hundred yards away."

"I expect it's a snake," she answered indifferently. "There are a lot near here."

They looked round as a step came on the stoep outside, and the next moment Edwardes entered.

"Got a mamba," he cried. "A big one. Care to see it, Enid? I've got it outside."

She gave a little shudder.

"Well, please keep it there. Do you want some tea, Mr. Edwardes?"

He took the cup she handed him and sat down.

"I've really brought it up to show Jack," he remarked. "Would you believe it, Sefton, but he's never seen one all the time he's been out here."

Jim Sefton grunted his surprise and went on with his tea. At the moment he was more interested in the fact that Edwardes called his partner's wife Enid, and she, very pointedly, did not call him Bill. And during the next half-hour or so his interest did not wane. Not much ever escaped those keen eyes of his, and in this case the signs were plain to read. Edwardes was in love with Enid Fairbrace, and she was fully aware of the fact. Equally plain was the other side of the case, that she was not in love with Edwardes.

There was nothing novel in the situation, and once or twice a cynical smile twitched round his lips. When two men and a singularly attractive woman live together in the back of beyond, something of the sort is likely to occur. And the only variation that is of interest is the end, which in primitive places is frequently in keeping with its surroundings.

It was typical of the man that he should come straight to the point when he found himself alone with Enid that evening before dinner. They were strolling round the little garden she had made near the house, and suddenly he paused and waved his stick comprehensively round the ground that lay beneath them.

"What's the idea, Enid?" he remarked. "I suppose you know you're just throwing money away, going on as you are at present?"

She changed colour a little as she stared at him.

"What do you mean, Jim?" she demanded.

"My dear," he said gravely, "the work on your farm is rotten. I haven't examined it closely: I don't know whether you've got a good proposition here, granted it is worked efficiently, or not. But what I do know is that, worked as it is at present, you'll never make a penny."

"But Mr. Edwardes said it was going so well," she stammered.

"Then Mr. Edwardes is a damned liar," returned Jim Sefton. "You don't like him, do you, Enid?"

It was more of a statement than a question.

"No, I don't," she answered quietly. "I positively dislike him. But I thought he knew all about farming, and that's why——"

"You go on living in the same house with a man who is in love with you."

He lit a cigarette, and looked at her with a faint smile.

"You're pretty quick, Jim," she said.

"My dear," he answered, "I'm in love with you myself. I know it now: I've been in love with you all along. Like a fool, I let you go at the beginning, and now it's too late."

"Yes," she said very steadily, "it's too late now, Jim."

"Then it wouldn't have been too late if I'd told you before, if I . . ." For the life of him he couldn't help the tremble in his voice.

"No, my dear," she told him in a low voice. "It wouldn't have been too late. But I thought it was just a summer evening's madness."

· For a while they stood side by side in silence; then big Jim squared his shoulders.

"We can all make pretty average fools of ourselves," he said abruptly. "And I'm certainly no exception to the rule. I guess I'll have to be moving on, Enid: to stop on here is going to be a bit beyond my powers. But before I go I'd like to try and straighten up this little show of yours. There's no earthly good you two going on as you are at present."

"But what are we going to do, Jim? Jack and Mr. Edwardes drew up a sort of deed of partnership. You see, the land belonged originally to Mr. Edwardes, and the idea was that Jack's money should be used for its development."

"And a very excellent idea indeed," answered Jim dryly, "if it was being properly developed. As it is, Edwardes is not doing his side of the bargain. What has been done with the money, I don't know. If it has been put into the land, then Edwardes is hopelessly inefficient: if it hasn't, he's a scoundrel. Either way he cuts no ice, and the sooner he's told so the better. My dear," he went on after a while, "I know the brand. I've met 'em before. They generally drink too much, and they're incapable of putting their backs into an honest job of work. In this case the specimen has fallen into very pleasant quarters. He is supplied with money by Jack; he has the most charming and delightful home; and he is in love with you. And it's the last item"—his mouth tightened a little—"that gets my goat particularly."

"I hate him," said Enid under her breath. "It's the way he looks at me sometimes. Oh! Jim—if only we could get rid of him—buy him out or something—and you could come and help us."

It was out before she realized what she'd said, and Jim Sefton gave a short laugh.

"Do you think that would help, Enid?" he answered. "What about the last item?"

"I wasn't thinking, Jim," she whispered. "Forget it."

"Impossible," he smiled. "But we'll rule it out as a method of settlement."

"Anyway, you'll stop till Jack gets better, won't you, Jim?"

"Yes; I'll stop till Jack gets better. In fact, this matter can't be fixed up until he does get better. He's got to do the talking, and if he attempted to do it now it would only send his temperature up and make him worse. But I'll be here to back him up: I promise you that."

For a moment or two he stared at the sun as it sank lower and lower in the west. Then he turned to the woman at his side.

"My God! Enid—what fools we are at times; what cursed fools! You're very fond of Jack, I know; but there's something else I know too. And it was my fault, all my stupid blundering fault."

"No, dear," she answered quietly, "it wasn't. It was just one of those things that happen—why or how, one doesn't quite know when one looks back. And the only thing that is left is to play the game."

Big Jim Sefton nodded, and held out his hand.

"Right you are, partner," he said. "It's a bargain: we'll play the game."

And inside the house at that moment, whilst Jack Fairbrace tossed and muttered feverishly in his bed, his partner, with a three-finger sundowner in his hand, was perfecting the last details of his particular game.

The sudden arrival of Jim Sefton on the scene was an undoubted nuisance. He looked the type of un-compromising individual to whom explanations might prove difficult. For even as Sefton had recognized the type to which Edwardes belonged, so had Edwardes placed the new-comer with equal accuracy. And big Jim belonged to the type that the Edwardeses of this world most fear and dislike: the type that is straight as a die and yet on occasions will take the law into its own hands and administer it in a fashion distinctly illegal.

That he was bound to spot that all was not well with the farm, Edwardes knew. The marvel was that he had been able to keep it from the Fairbraces for as long as he had. But on that point he didn't feel much concern: sooner or later it would have been bound to come out. He would have preferred to have postponed it a little, until the other thing had been settled; and even now it was quite on the cards that nothing would be said until Jack got over his fever.

With a hand that suddenly shook uncontrollably Edwardes poured himself out another stiff drink. *Until* he got over his fever. . . .

It started another train of thought in his mind: the old, old train that had never been long absent ever since Enid Fairbrace had first come into his life. At first it had been vague and transitory; and then after a while it had become fixed and ugly. Once or twice he had recoiled from it—not because of some sudden interlude of decent feeling, but merely because it frightened him. Edwardes had a very wholesome re-spect for his own skin, and he was fully aware of what happened to those who broke the sixth commandment.

And even if the thing could be done so that legally there was no proof against him, that would not be sufficient for his purpose. No trace of suspicion must arise in Enid's mind that he had anything to do with it.

It had been difficult: a hundred different schemes for the removal of what he fondly believed to be the obstacle to his own happiness had suggested themselves, only to be rejected one by one. A shooting accident had held pride of place for some time, but that had at length gone the way of the others. It was true it could be staged in such a way as to make his own neck safe, but what would Enid say? To kill a man accidentally is not the surest way of gaining the widow's affection. . . .

And so it had gone the way of the others, and he had hung on, wondering and plotting, and never getting any nearer the mark until that very afternoon, when, in a flash, the master idea had come. He wondered if it was always the same: if the obvious, the only, plan invariably came suddenly like that. It was so simple, so sure. If not to-night, nor to-morrow night—then the night after. Or the one after that. He could afford to wait a few days now: he who had already waited a year.

He rose to his feet as the sound of steps outside announced the return of the others. So engrossed had he been in his scheme that he had almost forgotten Jim Sefton, and he scowled as he heard his deep laugh on the stoep. And then the scowl was replaced by a look of triumph: the second sundowner was beginning to take effect. All the more kudos to him for pulling off his plan right under the damned fellow's nose; he wasn't afraid of a dozen Seftons. His scheme was safe; absolutely and completely safe.

Throughout dinner he dominated the conversation, and the level of the whisky in the decanter fell rapidly.

He could talk well when he chose to, and if the other two were a little silent he attributed it to his own brilliance. No reference was made to the farm, and after a while he began to wonder if his fears as to Sefton's powers of observation had not been groundless. So much the better; anyway, it didn't much matter.

The meal concluded, he made some excuse and went out of doors. Sefton had declined his perfunctory suggestion that he should join him in a stroll, and stretched out in an arm-chair was watching Enid through the smoke of his cigarette. His opinion of Edwardes had been confirmed by what he had seen: he talked too much and he drank too much, which is a bad mixture in anyone, but fatal in a man whose job is the land.

And then he dismissed Edwardes from his mind. Enid was there in front of him, and thoughts were not included in playing the game. Yes: he'd been a fool—a silly quixotic fool. Or had it been, as Enid said, just one of those things that happen, one knows not why nor how?

Just once or twice their eyes met and held, and then with a sigh he rose and stretched his big frame.

"I'll go and look up the invalid," he said, "and after that I think I'll turn in pretty early."

She was doing some needlework, and just for a moment he laid his hand on her shoulder as he passed. She gave a little quiver, and his grip tightened. Then he went on into Jack's room.

For a while he stood looking down at the sick man. The fever had come back, and he was hot and restless. Outside the tree beetles kept up their everlasting chorus, and from the far distance came once the coughing grunt of a lion.

He sat down by the bed, and pulled out his cigarette-case. There was nothing to be done for Jack Fairbrace: only time would cure him. But unbidden, thrust out as soon as it was there, the thought came into his mind. Supposing he didn't pull through; supposing . . .

He shut his case with an angry snap, and a cigarette rolled out on the floor. And then things happened rapidly. At one moment he was leaning forward to pick up his cigarette: the next he was at the other side of the room with every vestige of colour out of his face. For in stooping down he had looked under the bed.

And now, silent as a cat, he again stooped down and stared. For perhaps half a minute he remained motionless: then step by step, with a puzzled frown on his face, he approached the man who still tossed and turned and muttered. He took a candle off the table and put it on the floor in order to see better, and when at length he rose to his feet his face looked as if it had been carved out of granite. For temptation—fierce, bitter temptation—had come to Jim Sefton. And it lasted—but what matter how long it lasted? Time is not the essence of the thing that put big Jim on the rack and left him sweating.

Gradually his face relaxed a little, and he shook himself like a dog. The fight was over: it almost made him laugh to think that it had ever taken place. He walked to the door and glanced out: Enid's head was still bent over her work. Then he returned to the bed, and stooping down he pulled out the thing that lay underneath. Concealing it as well as he could with his coat he crossed the hall behind Enid's back and entered Edwardes's room. And the next moment there lay under Edwardes's bed that which had caused Jim Sefton such a shock.

He re-entered the hall, and sat down opposite Enid. His expression was normal again, the hand that held

his cigarette as steady as a rock. And after a while
—it was just as his keen ear caught the sound of a
footstep outside—he spoke.

"I shall probably sit up latish with Edwardes to-
night, my dear. But don't you wait up."

She looked up at him quickly: there was a strange
new note in his voice.

"What is it, Jim? Why do you speak like that?"

But he only shook his head with a grave smile.

"Don't worry your head about anything. Just a
native superstition: that's all. Go and sit with Jack
for a bit, and then go to bed."

And as Edwardes opened the front door she rose
and went into her husband's room. Jim Sefton had
moved his chair a little so that his face was in the
shadow. And he noted the gloating look in Edwardes's
eyes as they followed her.

"Very pleasant out now," he said calmly, and
Edwardes nodded.

"Very." He sat down, so that he could watch the
door of Jack's bedroom, and Jim's eyes never left his
face. For ten minutes or a quarter of an hour they
kept up a desultory conversation, and then came the
symptom Jim Sefton had been waiting for—the thing
that proved finally what he wanted to know. Edwardes
was getting nervous, and was answering at random.

Twice he rose and walked over to the door of Jack's
room, and the second time he went in.

"Hadn't you better be careful, Enid," he said. "In
case there's a possible risk of infection and all that."

"Tampane fever isn't infectious," remarked Jim
Sefton quietly. "Still, you're looking a bit done in,
Enid: why don't you turn in?"

He was standing behind Edwardes as he spoke,
and when she saw the look in his eyes she rose at
once.

"I think I will," she said. "I'm feeling a bit sleepy. Good night."

She passed between the two men, and they waited until they heard her door close.

"You're quite right, Edwardes," said Sefton. "In this climate women can't do too much. Personally I think a little drink, and I shall follow her example."

He followed the other man back into the hall, and glanced at his watch. It was nine o'clock, and at eleven they were still sitting there. Moreover the whisky bottle that had been full was now empty.

It was when he perceived the fact that Edwardes announced his intention of going to bed. A very decent fellow, Sefton, he had decided: misjudged him badly. Bit of a fool: give no trouble, anyway. As a matter of fact, he'd meant to be in bed before; it might happen any moment now. Might have happened while they were sitting there, which would have been a bit awkward. Oughtn't to have sat up so long. Once in bed bound to be a delay, and delay fatal.

He swayed a little; his brain was most confoundedly muzzy. Damned fellow Sefton must have a head like a copper boiler. And those blue eyes of his seemed to bore into one's brain.

He staggered and pulled himself together; no doubt about it, he'd had one too many.

"Good nye, ole boy," he remarked unsteadily. "Show you round the bally farm to-morrow."

With a candle in his hand he lurched off to his room, whilst big Jim still sat motionless. Even after the door had closed he never moved, though his brain was busy. It was justice—primitive justice—if it succeeded. And if it didn't . . .

A crash from Edwardes's room announced that he had upset the water-jug. And then it came—a sudden terrible scream of mortal fear. It startled even big Jim himself, though his hand was steady as he reached for the gun beside him.

Simultaneously the doors of Edwardes's and Enid's rooms burst open. But it was on Edwardes that Jim Sefton's eyes were fixed.

"A mamba," he yelled. "I've been bitten by a mamba. Quick! Oh! my God—be quick."

"Where's the potassium permanganate?" said big Jim, and Enid darted across to a cupboard.

"It's empty," she cried in despair. "It was full this morning, I know."

And once again Jim Sefton's blue eyes were fixed on Edwardes. His face was chalky; his shaking mouth jibbered inarticulate words.

"Who emptied it?" said Jim in a terrible voice. "Who emptied it, Edwardes?"

And Edwardes cursed foully, only to begin raving once again for mercy. Into his fuddled brain had come the certainty that Jim knew; the certainty also that nothing could save him. It was he who had emptied the bottle of permanganate; it was he who had signed his own death warrant. How his plans had miscarried he had no idea—all that mattered was that they had.

A figure in pyjamas appeared in the door of Jack's room.

"What is it?" muttered the sick man weakly. "What's happened?"

But no one answered him; no one even knew he was there. For the end was close to, and Edwardes was not a pretty sight. And Enid in spite of having loathed the man was crying softly, though her brain was racing in a jumbled chaos of thought. What had Jim meant by asking who had emptied the bottle?

It was Jim who took charge when it was over. It

was Jim who went to the window of Edwardes's room
and shot the snake inside by the light of the candle
on the table.   It was Jim who put Jack back to bed,
and sat up with Enid till she fell asleep in her chair.
And he was still sitting opposite her when the dawn
came, so that the first thing she was conscious of as
she woke were those vivid blue eyes of his.

But during the days that followed he said very little,
and she asked no questions.   And it was only as he
was going a fortnight later that she could stand it no
longer.   Jack was fit; arrangements for disposing of
the farm were in train; and then they were going back
to England.

"Jim," she said, as she stood beside his horse, "there
was some mystery that night.   What was it?"

For a moment a tiny smile flickered over his lips.

"There is a native superstition, my dear," he said
gravely, "which like so many things of that sort is
founded on fact.   They say that if you kill a snake,
its mate will come to find it.   Edwardes killed a mamba
that afternoon; I killed the mate that night.   You see
the dead snake was under his bed."

"But what can have induced him to put it there?"
she cried.

"I wonder," answered big Jim Sefton.

He bent down suddenly and raised the hand lying
on his horse's neck to his lips.   Then he dug his heels
in, and without a backward glance trotted off along
the road that to a townsman's eye would have seemed
impenetrable bush.

  BLACKMAIL

I

THE letter came to me as a voice from the dead. At first the handwriting on the envelope seemed strange, and then after staring at it for a few seconds I remembered. I hadn't seen that writing for twenty years, and one is apt to forget.

The post-mark was New York, and with the letter still unopened in my hand I sat staring out of the window. So Jim Charterlands was in America—the man who at one time had been my greatest friend. We had lost touch with one another after the tragedy had happened and Jim had paid the price. I'd tried—Heaven knows—hard enough to find the dear old chap, but every time I'd come up against a blank wall.

And now here in my hand I held the answer to my search: at last Jim had broken the silence.

Unconsciously my thoughts drifted backwards to that dreadful time twenty years ago. And now that I felt instinctively that the clue to everything which had puzzled us all at the time—for there were many who loved Jim—lay here between my fingers, deliberately I refrained from opening the envelope. It had waited long years: it could wait a few more minutes while I sorted out in my mind the events as they had happened.

It had been midnight when the telephone-bell had rung in my sitting-room. I remember I had one leg of my pyjamas off and one on, and I swore at the interruption. I was sleepy and wanted to go to bed: I'd been working pretty hard on a case, and I had to be in court early the next morning. Who on earth could want me at midnight?

But the bell went on ringing insistently, and I went into the sitting-room.

"What is it?" I cried irritably into the receiver.

"Are you Mr. Pollock?" came a man's voice.

"I am. Who are you?"

"Vine Street speaking, sir. Can you come down here at once? Mr. Charterlands is here, and has asked for you as a legal adviser."

Into my mind there leapt at once the idea that Jim was tight, and wanted me to try and fix things. And my irritation did not decrease.

"What on earth does he want me for at this time?" I half-muttered, forgetting the man at the other end could hear. "I suppose the old fool has got blotto."

And from the other end came the reply:

"I'm afraid it's not that, sir: it's something infinitely more serious." And the tone of the voice even more than the words pulled me together.

"I'll come at once," I said.

All the time I dressed I wondered what Jim could have been doing: all the way down in a hansom, which I was lucky enough to pick up, I was still wondering. Wild Jim was and always had been, but there was no atom of vice in him. He had money: at least quite enough, without being actually wealthy: he had hosts of friends. So what could he have been doing?

An Inspector met me and his face was very grave. He made no attempt at beating about the bush, but came straight to the point.

"It's murder, Mr. Pollock, I'm sorry to say."

I stared at him stupidly.

"You mean that Jim—that Mr. Charterlands—is accused of murdering someone?" I said.

He nodded.

"But it's incredible," I cried angrily. "Whom is he accused of murdering?"

"A Mr. John Parsons," said the Inspector. "Perhaps you would go and see him, Mr. Pollock. He can tell you the story himself, but I am bound to admit that things look extremely black.   You see, your friend makes no attempt to deny the charge; in fact, he admits it."

"How did he do it?" I asked dully.

"He shot him with a revolver in Mr. Parsons's own study," said the Inspector.   "Will you come this way?"

II

Mechanically I followed him, until he halted before the locked door of a cell.   Jim was inside, sitting on the edge of the bed, and he got up with a cheery smile as he saw me.

"Sorry to drag you out, old man, at this ungodly hour—but as the Inspector has probably told you, I'm in a hole."

"Look here, Jim!" I cried, "there must be a mistake."

"Devil a bit, Bill," he answered.   "There's no mistake.   I've told the Inspector here everything that happened.   I went up to Hampstead to interview Mr. John Parsons after dinner.   I had a certain request to make to him, and had he seen his way to granting that request, I should not have killed him.   But as he did not see his way to doing so, I did kill him.   I warned him first, but he rather stupidly thought I was bluffing. I wasn't."

I stared at him aghast.

"But, Jim, old boy," I cried, "you don't seem to realize.   It's murder."

"On the contrary, Bill, I realize it only too well. As you say, it's murder."

"But who is this John Parsons?   I've never heard of him."

"No more had I until this morning," he answered. "But if it's of importance, and presumably it is, John Parsons is, or rather was, a foul blackmailing swine.

He was a man dead to even the twinge of a decent instinct, a loathsome brute, a slimy cur. And though I realize quite fully that legally speaking I've committed murder, from every other point of view I have merely exterminated a thing that had no right to live."

"Granted, old man," I said hopelessly. "But that's got nothing to do with it. The only point of view we're concerned with is the legal one, and legally it doesn't matter if he was all you say or an angel of light. Tell me, what was this request you went up to make and which he wouldn't grant?"

Jim smiled at me gravely, and laid his hand on my arm.

"I knew you'd ask me that, old man. It's pretty obvious, isn't it? Sticks out a yard. But I can't tell you."

"You can't tell me?" I repeated. "But why not? Presumably you've sent for me because you want me to defend you."

"If you'll be so good, Bill."

"Good be blowed, Jim!" I cried. "Of course I'll defend you. But I must know all the facts of the case."

Once again he smiled gravely and shook his head.

"You shall know all except that, Bill. Believe me, old friend, I have a very good reason."

I argued, expostulated and finally lost my temper, but it was useless. He was adamant on that one point—the most vital point in the whole case. He had gone up to interview this man Parsons, having made an appointment by telephone. The object of the interview was to demand the handing over of a certain thing. And that demand had been refused. Parsons had merely laughed at his request. So Jim had taken the revolver out of his pocket, and had warned him of his unalterable intention of killing him if the request was not complied with. And once again Parsons had laughed and, rising from his chair, had crossed to the bell.

"It was then that I shot him through the heart, Bill," said Jim quietly. "After that I locked the door, took the keys of his safe from the body, opened the safe and found what I sought. The servants were hammering on the door, but it was a stout one. I burnt the thing I had come for, and then I opened the door. And that is absolutely all there is to it."

Moreover, that had been absolutely all there was to it when he was tried. Not by even so much as a hint had Jim given away what had been the object of his visit. I warned him of the consequences, but I might have saved my breath.

"I realize all you say, old friend," he said patiently. "But it's just impossible for me to tell you. I know what it means to me, but I can't help it, whatever the result may be."

III

And so it came to the trial. The court was crammed, and the most self-possessed person there was Jim. I can see him now standing between the two warders, head thrown back a little, arms folded. And what a magnificent-looking specimen of manhood he was! He gave me a nod and a smile, but after that he looked neither to the right hand nor the left, though the court was crammed with his friends.

Quietly, inexorably, but with studied moderation, counsel for the Crown outlined the case. He made no effort to gloss over the character of the murdered man: with scrupulous fairness he went so far as to emphasize it.

"As my learned friend will doubtless tell you, gentlemen," he said, "John Parsons was that most loathsome of all things—a blackmailer. From documents discovered in his safe, no doubts can be entertained on that score. But, gentlemen, the law of England protects people against blackmail. Further, it punishes the blackmailer with the utmost severity. It is the safe-guard of a civilized community, it is the thing to which appeal must be made. And no man, under any conditions whatever, has the right to take the law into his own hands."

It was a short case. Though technically the plea was "Not guilty," there was no dispute over facts. And there was no drama to it either until I put Jim himself into the witness-box. Whether he liked it or not, I was determined to run sentiment for all it was worth. And I asked him once again the question point-blank:

"What was the request you made to John Parsons?"

He looked me straight in the face.

"I refuse to say."

"Did it concern a woman's honour?"

For a moment he hesitated; then he answered firmly:

"Yes—it did."

Of course, it was useless. Counsel for the Crown, as was his duty, pushed him hard on the point.

"Who was the woman?"

"I refuse to say."

"Will you write down the name and hand it to his Lordship?"

"I will not."

And then the Judge intervened. A little sternly he pointed out that Jim was jeopardizing his chances by his attitude, and that his consistent refusal to give any information on this point not only tended to throw doubts on the veracity of his statement, but came peril-ously near contempt of court.

Jim bowed, and I can hear now his quiet, level voice.

"My Lord, I realize what you say only too well.

May I, however, beg of you to believe that nothing is
farther from my mind than any feeling of contempt
of court.   For what it is worth, you have my word:
but I can bring you no proof, even if I wished to.   For
the proof was destroyed by me that night.   And whatever your Lordship's judgment may be on me, I thank
my God that I was able to do so."

A woman in court gave a little sob, and the Judge
frowned.

I talked to him three years after at some banquet or
other, and he told me his feelings at the moment.
Notoriously one of the most impartial men on the bench,
yet every sympathy he had was with Jim.   And he felt
that he was being stupidly quixotic.

"Are we to understand," he said, "that there is a
woman living so devoid of every decent sense that she
allows you to stand on trial for murder—a murder
perpetrated, as you say, to save her honour—without
coming forward and giving evidence?"

I saw the muscles on Jim's face tighten, and a strange
look came into his eyes.

"The woman in question is dead, my Lord."

And for a space there was absolute silence in court.

It was all over in one day.   There could only be one
end: the issue was never in doubt.   There was no
refuting the Crown's deadly arguments.   If such a pre-
cedent were allowed, where would matters end?   There
was merely prisoner's unsubstantiated word that he had
killed this man to save a dead woman's honour.   Even
if it were true, there was no justification whatever for
such an act.   And how could they possibly tell that it
was true?   The members of the jury must obliterate
from their minds all questions of sentiment.   They
must not take into account the prisoner's personality,
nor that of the dead man.   All they must concentrate

on was the fact that admittedly a man had been murdered, and that the only excuse for the act was an appeal
to sentiment which might, he allowed, be true, but
which, on the other hand, might be merely a lie put
forward as a last despairing endeavour to mitigate a
cold-blooded crime. Let them not forget that prisoner
at the bar had gone to this man's house with a loaded
revolver in his pocket. . . .

And through it all Jim listened with the same grave,
quiet attention. Never for one instant did any hint of
agitation or fear show on his face, and when the jury
left to consider their verdict, and he was removed, he
gave me one of his usual cheery smiles. They didn't
take long—ten minutes to be exact—and the verdict
was the only possible one—"Guilty."

They took a couple of sobbing women out, and they
closed the doors. And hands clenched, and knees
twitched, for it's a dreadful moment when a man's life
is declared forfeit. They asked him if he had anything to say, and because he was white clean through he
did have something to say. And it was this:

"Only one thing, my Lord. That had I been in
any other position in this court to-day, either in your
Lordship's seat, or in the jury-box, or conducting the
case for the Crown, I only hope that I should have
acted with the same scrupulous fairness towards prisoner
that has been accorded to me to-day."

And then it was over. Jim was sentenced to death,
and it seemed to me as I watched him that he was
staring at something above him—something that he
saw, and we couldn't. But then maybe my eyes were
a bit dim.

Certain it is that even to the last he never faltered.
He seemed to be sustained by some outside power; he
seemed to be curiously aloof. And all through the

days that followed he was just the same. When I told him that from every corner of the country huge petitions were arriving for his reprieve, he shrugged his shoulders and smiled a little sadly.

"Dear old Bill," he answered, "you've been just wonderful over it all. But I don't think I very much mind what happens. I'm not a particularly religious bloke, but perhaps—who knows—one might run across people over the other side."

And again he seemed to be staring through the windows of his cell at something or somebody that I couldn't see.

It was successful—the petition—and the sentence was commuted to penal servitude for life. The utter vileness of the man Parsons had a good deal to do with it, I think. And when I told Jim the news, and the two warders stood there smiling all over their faces, he wrung my hand and thanked me. But even at the time it struck me that his chief feeling was gratitude for the trouble I'd taken, rather than joy at the result.

That was the last time I ever saw him. The years rolled by, and by the law of nature his memory grew a little dim. I became increasingly busy, and Jim faded a bit from my mind. But always I had marked the date of his release: I wanted to meet him as he came out. He had earned the maximum remission of his sentence, and the Governor of the prison had promised to let me know the actual date. And then, as luck would have it, I went down with a severe attack of influenza two days before he was due to come out.

I wired to the Governor asking him to tell Jim where I was, and he told him. But Jim never came. I went to old addresses: I followed every clue I could think of, but it was useless. Jim completely disappeared, leaving no trace, and, as I have said, I gave it up, a little hurt and offended.

And now, at long last, I held in my hands a letter from him. It was a very bulky one, and I gave a start as I saw the date. It had been written two years previously, though the post-mark was recent.

"Old friend," it ran, "don't think too hardly of me. The Governor gave me your message, but fifteen years of prison changes a man. We should have been strangers, Bill, and I should have stepped back into a world I didn't know, and that didn't know me. I couldn't have borne to meet the old set again. Most of them probably are married, and to their wives, who never knew me at all, I should have been just an unknown man who'd served a life-sentence for murder. It would have been an impossible situation: I couldn't have stood it. But it was good of you to think of me—awfully good, old pal. Only I'm thankful you had 'flu, otherwise I should have had to hurt you. For I had made up my mind irrevocably to cut adrift, and I should have had a terrible job trying to make you see my point of view.

"But now, during the three years since I came out, the conviction has been growing on me that it is only fair to you to let you, who defended me so ably, know the truth. You won't get this letter until I am dead"—for a moment I stopped reading and stared out of the window—"but you'll get it then. The old lungs got touched up a bit in prison, and they tell me that I ought to go to some sanatorium. But I'm thinking it's hardly worth while. . . .

"All I ask you, Bill, is to burn this letter when you've read it, and promise me that never by word or deed will you divulge its contents to a living soul. Because it's the story of the only part of my life that counts, and the only part of the life of one other.

"I met her first at St. Moritz. She was nineteen and I was twenty-one. We were both pretty good skiers, and so she managed to get away from the two stout women who dogged her footsteps wherever she went. Because, you see, she wasn't an ordinary mortal like you and me, old man; she was a Royalty. And yet she was just an ordinary mortal like you and me, in that she loved love, and life, and most marvellous of all, she loved one, Jim Charterlands. Useless to ask how these things happen: they lie on the lap of the gods for capricious distribution. And I—great Heavens! old friend, it would be beyond my power to tell you how I loved that girl. She was more to me than life itself. We were discreet; we had to be. She was there incognito, of course, but the two Gorgons watched her like lynxes. Had they had an inkling of our feelings for one another they would have whisked her away and buried her once more in the starchy ceremony of her father's Court. For he was a King, and it should not tax your ingenuity overmuch to find out the country he reigned over.

"But there are ways of eluding even lynx-eyed Gorgons, and for four weeks we managed to do it. And for four weeks we lived in a world of our own— my girl and I. We didn't bother much over what was going to happen—the present was good enough for us. Once or twice I alluded to it, but always she put her little hand over my mouth and stopped me. So I forced myself to forget the madness of it all, and lived just for each day as it came.

"But at last there came the time when it could be ignored no longer. We were up there in the snow, eating our lunch, when she told me in her sweet, broken English:

"'To-morrow, Jim, I'm going. Going back to prison.'

"I'd known, of course, that it had to come, but that didn't make it any easier. And something snapped inside me. I caught her in my arms, and begged and implored her to sacrifice everything and marry me.

" 'You'll be happy as my wife, dear love,' I whispered. 'I've got a bit of money, and there's the whole great world in front of us.'

"Just for a little she lay in my arms with the wonder of it all in her dear eyes; and then she gave a little twisted smile.

" 'If only I could, my Jim!' she said gravely. 'If only I could! But there's something I haven't told you. Maybe I've been wicked these last few weeks, letting you kiss me and make love to me. But I couldn't help it, for I love you so, my dear. And I think I hate him.'

" 'Who?' I demanded.

" 'The man I've got to marry. It's been arranged for many years.'

"And she told me who he was. A diplomatic marriage—the usual thing: and for a while I cursed bitterly and foolishly, till the words died away in my throat and I grew silent, just staring into her dear eyes. It was to take place when she was twenty-one, so there were two years before the sacrifice.

"This isn't a love story, Bill, and, anyway, there are things of which a man does not write. And that last afternoon is one of them. Sufficient to say that we said good-bye to one another up in the white purity of the snow. And white though it was, it was no whiter than my beloved girl.

"The months went on, and I came back to London. I tried to forget in the way that men have always tried to forget, and I couldn't. Time made things no better: if anything it made them worse. The official announcement appeared in the papers full of the usual lies. How wonderful it was that the close cementing together of the two nations should be accomplished by such a

romantic love-match—you know the sort of stuff.
And I cursed the fools who wrote it, and went on all
the harder trying to forget.

"It was three months before the ceremony was due
to take place that a letter came to me at my club, and
I stood there staring at it like a man bereft of his senses.
I'd only seen her handwriting once, but I knew it in a
flash. And the post-mark was London.

"She'd sent it over by someone, of course—I'd given
her my club as an address if ever she wanted me. That
was my first thought, until I turned the envelope over.
And on the back was the name of a London hotel.

"Bill, I was shaking like a man with the palsy when
I opened that letter. I had to put it on a table before I
could get it steady enough to read. She was in London for three days, and though she felt it was madness,
she must see me again. Would I meet her that afternoon? She gave me a rendezvous, where she would
be in her car, and then we would go for a drive.

"And now I'm coming to the end, old man. Madness it may have been—the time we spent those next
three days. But it was a madness which has lived
through the long, grey years, and will live with me
till the end. She was strictly incognito: only one
girl friend was with her—a girl who loved her even
as I did. She knew, of course; she it was who came
later and told me what had happened. It was the
driver who was the traitor—God! if I could get my
hands on that man he would die even as John Parsons
died.

"But I'm jumping ahead. Why we chose Richmond
Park for our last day I don't know—though it wouldn't
have mattered much where we'd gone: the result would
have been the same. But it was there, in one of those
little copses, that I said 'Good-bye' to her for the last
time. She was leaving next day, and we sat there hand

in hand. And after a while my arms went round her, and she clung to me helplessly.

"'Always and always; for ever and ever, my man,' she said again and again.

"What's the good of labouring it? The shadows were lengthening when I kissed her for the last time, and watched her stumble a little blindly back to the waiting car. It was the end, and from that moment I have only seen her twice. Once at Victoria Station the next morning, when for a moment her eyes met mine and she smiled pitifully: once amidst the pomp and ceremony of her marriage. I watched her from the crowd, as she bowed and smiled to the cheering people. But her face was white, Bill: and it seemed to me that she was looking for someone—always looking. But maybe that was my imagination.

"Once again I came back to London and tried to forget. Now it was over, definitely finished: I told myself over and over again that I was a fool.

"'Cut it clean out, you ass: it's an episode—dead and finished.'

"But you can't cut out a part of you—a vital part, and I couldn't forget. I haven't forgotten yet: I never shall.

"It was a year later that she died. She died giving birth to a son, and a nation went into mourning. So did an obscure individual in London, but he didn't count—not until a little later. And then only he knew it and one other, and now you.

"It was the girl friend who came to me and told me what had happened. She came one morning and she had travelled over Europe without stopping. I take off my hat to that girl, Bill: she was superb—a thoroughbred clean through.

"'They're after me, Mr. Charterlands,' she said. 'But they're a day behind.'

" 'What's happened?' I asked, staring at her, bewildered.

"She made no answer, but just took an envelope from her bag and handed it to me. I took out the contents and for a few moments I could hardly believe my eyes. There were six snapshots inside, and in every one of them there appeared my girl and me. They had been taken in Richmond Park, and subconsciously I recalled an occasional click-click that I had heard that wonderful afternoon. At the time I had hardly noticed it—put it down to a cricket or something. Now I knew. Some devil had been there hidden with a camera, and this was the result.

" 'How did you get these?' I asked her.

" 'They were sent to a man at Court,' she answered quietly. 'Never mind how I got them: if you want to know, I stole them. But you know what intrigue is out there, and the man to whom they were sent is the leader of the anti-Royalist clique. For years he has been working secretly to overthrow the existing Monarchy; in the country he has a large following. He is utterly unscrupulous and he proposes, I know, to publish those photographs and circulate them. You see what people will say, Mr. Charterlands: that the late Queen had a lover. Probably they will go further and say that the boy is not the son of the King. You must stop it. I don't care about the King or his house: I do care about her reputation. You loved her: you've got a day. Do something! *You see, the films are still in existence.* And that's the man who has them. I found his name and address when I took the prints.'

"I looked at the paper she held out to me, and then I laid my hand on her arm.   •

" 'Leave it all to me,' I said, and she went away comforted.

"Old friend, the rest you know. I rang that devil

up twice on the telephone to fix an appointment. Each time he was out. So after dinner I went up to see him. He smiled when he saw me, and I had to control myself not to strike him in the face.

" 'And what can I do for you?' he asked, though he knew full well all the time.

" 'You can give me the films of those infamous pictures you took in Richmond Park,' I answered.

"He laughed again.

" 'But I value them highly,' he said. 'They've been worth a great deal of money to me, my dear boy.'

" 'You foul swine!' I cried, and he waved a deprecating hand.

" 'I regard it as a most creditable performance,' he continued. 'And really, you know, Richmond Park is a very public place for love-making. Anyone might have been there. In fact, as I followed your car and realized your destination I grew quite alarmed. But still, everything worked out very satisfactorily.'

"And at that moment the telephone-bell rang beside him. He spoke into it and his face changed suddenly. I can still see him hanging up the receiver with a cold, sneering smile.

" 'So, my young friend, you have succeeded in stealing those photographs, have you? How very interesting.'

"I realized that the pursuers had arrived in London, and that time was even shorter than I thought.

" 'Photographs for which I have been paid a very large sum,' he continued. 'And here have I got all the trouble of printing another set.'

" 'You'll never do that, you blackmailer,' I said, and he leant back in his chair still smiling.

" 'May I ask how you propose to prevent me?' he remarked. 'The negatives are in that safe, the key of which is attached to my body by a steel chain. It is possible that you are a little stronger than I am, but not much.   Anyway, there is a bell, and there are two menservants in this house who really are strong: specially engaged, in fact, for removing troublesome people.   So may I ask you again how you propose to prevent me?'

" 'By killing you,' I said, and I pulled out the revolver.

"And still he smiled.

" 'They hang people for that in England, my dear boy.   So I wouldn't if I were you.   It's a stupid bluff, you know—that revolver game.'

"Bill, sometimes now I see the look in his eyes of cringing, hideous terror when he first realized it wasn't bluff.   And I glory in it.   He gave a sort of stifled scream, and reached for the bell, just as I plugged him through the heart.

"Then I locked the door and I burnt the films, and I knew that my darling was safe.   Old friend, wouldn't you have done as I did?"

XLV   MRS.   PETER   SKEFFINGTON'S   REVENGE

THIS is the story of Mrs. Peter Skeffington.   She was a little fair-haired thing, with a pair of the most pathetic-looking blue eyes which deluded men into thinking she was helpless.   Also into desiring strongly to kiss her.   As far as I know, Mrs. Peter Skeffington did not kiss men.

The scene of this story is South Africa.   The exact locality in which it took place is neither here nor there and is immaterial.   Because South Africa is a crude country—though an almighty pleasant one—whether you regard her from the top of the Corner House at

Johannesburg or from the stoep of a back-veld farm.
And the last thing little Mrs. Peter liked was crudeness.

She had another peculiarity—she adored her husband. Now, far be it from me to say anything against
Peter Skeffington. In his way he was a very good
fellow: in his correct setting he might have done admirably. But South Africa was not that setting.

She is a crude country, but she is also a strong
country, and she demands of those who seek to live
on her that they fight and fight and go on fighting.
Skeffington gave up before the first "i" in the first
fight was dotted. In fact, the only thing that happened before he gave up fighting was that South Africa
discovered his weakness. She always does discover a
man's weakness sooner or later: she found Peter Skeffington's before he'd used his first ten-shilling book of
chits at the Rand Club, of which he'd been made an
honorary member for the duration of his stay in
Johannesburg. Of that, however, more a little later.

What exactly brought the Peter Skeffingtons to the
country is one of those little conundrums which no
logic or argument can solve. At Surbiton—let us say
—they could have lived and moved and had their being
without any harm to Surbiton or themselves. In South
Africa something had to happen. As food Peter and
his wife were thoroughly indigestible to the land of
their choice, and that entails a pain somewhere.

Why it was the land of their choice is, as I have
said, insoluble logically. Any man who knew the conditions of living would have told them that they were
totally unsuited for those conditions. He would also
have told them that out of the many land advertisements appearing so bravely in the columns of leading
London newspapers, ninety per cent. are cold-blooded,
dastardly swindles. Some day, incidentally, if I sit
next the editor of one of these papers at dinner I must

ask him why he allows these advertisements but pro-
hibits moneylenders. You do get something out of
a moneylender, anyway: it would save trouble to drop
your money in the sea in the case of the others.

To return, however, to the Peter Skeffingtons. Why
they came matters not—they came. By a great stroke
of fortune they missed the ninety per cent. already
alluded to, and stumbled into one of the seven per
cent. class which are fair to good without being very
good. The three per cent. of very good are shy,
retiring birds: they can afford to be.

They found themselves, did the Peter Skeffingtons,
in a proposition which *in time*, when God and the
Government decreed (principally the Government, in
this case: it was the usual question of irrigation), would
turn out thundering well and give them a very ample
and pleasant return for their money. In the meantime there was nothing to do but to sit down and
wait. Which is a dangerous proceeding for some
people in South Africa: especially for people with the
weakness of Peter Skeffington.

To those who know, the fact that Peter's weakness
was made manifest at the Rand Club is all that is
necessary. There are others, however, who are not
so well informed.

Of all the magnificent buildings in that marvellous
mushroom city Johannesburg, the Rand Club is one
of the most symbolical. In it you may obtain the
comforts, cellar and table, of the most exclusive London club: in it you may see—the world. Every sort
and condition of man who has been, is, or will be anything in South Africa at some time or another has
stood at the great three-sided bar. There was one
man whose boast it was that he hadn't, and he died
of drinking poisoned water.

You will see a man there who yesterday made a

hundred thousand on a rumour concerning asbestos: beside him is the man who lost a good part of it. You will see a cheerful, friendly soul surrounded by pals. The calling is on him, and why not? He only owes them half a million, and his present assets he would sell willingly for a hundred. Moreover, they know it. But in addition you will also see all the men who really count.

But one great rule is necessary for the Stranger within the Gates—learn to drink slowly. And since Peter Skeffington did not know this rule—though, seeing that his weakness was what it was, it wouldn't have much mattered if he had—South Africa had brutally probed the joint in his armour exactly one hour after he entered the bar of the Rand Club.

The trouble was threefold. First, he couldn't say No. Second, he had no head for drink. Third and worst of all, he thought he had. Which is just about as hopeless a combination as can be gathered together in a man. But had they remained in England there is no doubt in my mind that the Peter Skeffingtons would have carried on quite happily and lived to a ripe old age. In the year 1960 he would have alluded to the days when he was young and boys were boys and whisky was whisky. Because, and this is the point, Peter Skeffington was not a drunkard. He was a weak young ass who periodically drank far too much when opportunity offered. But it was the opportunity that was required—not the drink. You could have locked him up in a cellar of wine with safety for a week: you couldn't trust him in a third-rate bar for half an hour with a couple of pals. And if only someone who understood could have explained that simple fact to his wife this story would never have been written.

In the particular portion of South Africa where the

Peter Skeffingtons had settled opportunities were as blackberries on an autumn hedge. The type of opportunities, too, were of exactly the sort to prove most dangerous. In the first place he had nothing to do: in the second, most of the days in which he had to do it in were hot, dusty, arid and shadeless: in the third, there were exactly twenty-seven other men in a similar position to himself: in the fourth, there was a club placed centrally in the community where the twenty-eight met each evening for their sundowner and discussed what particular brand of nothingness they had done during the day. And discussion is dry work, especially when it concerns that ever-prevalent subject—lack of water.

The net result was obvious. Peter Skeffington returned home in varying degrees of insobriety exactly six days of the week out of seven. That was due to the fact that the Club was shut on Sundays. I was one of the twenty-eight, so I know. We didn't notice it particularly at first because he never got offensively tight, but after a while its monotony made it obvious, and several of us refused to drink with him. But it didn't do any good: there was always someone who would. Particularly Jack Dernan. . . .

Dernan was the typical product of a young country. Tall, broad-shouldered, powerful as a horse, tanned mahogany, he was a fighter from the beginning of the chapter. And if there was one thing for which he had profound contempt it was weakness in any form. Now I don't think he realized for a moment what he was doing with Peter Skeffington. Certainly not at first. He regarded him with a kind of good-natured toleration, mingled with slight wonder. He was so completely the type of man that Dernan had no use for, that he was a source of amusement. Possessed of a head that no amount of liquor ever had the slightest effect on, it was with genuine feelings of amazement that he regarded the amount necessary to render Peter Skeffington drunk.

"No well-conditioned fly could drown in it," he once remarked wonderingly. "The fellow's a damn freak."

But he didn't seem to be able to let him alone. Peter Skeffington's complete inability to absorb liquor seemed to fascinate him. He used to take mental notes of the amounts each night, and the condition arrived at. And after a time he and two or three others started private side bets on the result.

"Rather on the principle of the daily run on board ship," he explained. "Numbers from 6 to 12. 9 or 10 are good favourites, but the High Field hasn't an earthly. He'd be dead if he took more than a dozen, I should think."

"Go easy, Jack," said someone. "It can't go on like this."

"Great Scott!" cried Dernan, "I don't want to make the fellow tight. He rushes at it with his mouth open himself."

And so another of the tragedies—the square-peg and round-hole tragedies—began to gather form and shape: a tragedy which, as one traces it backwards, could have been so easily averted. If only someone could have explained things to Mrs. Peter—the real truth, instead of what she thought was the truth. If only someone could have said, "Take him away back to England, out of this country, and never let him return here save on a Cook's personally conducted tour," all would have been well. But no one did say it, and so she took him to Durban instead, to fight this insidious devil that had crept into her Peter's life—the devil of drunkenness.

She took him to Durban where they could get sea bathing, and golf and tennis, and I saw them off at the station. And there was a look in Mrs. Peter's pathetic blue eyes that I had never seen there before. It was not one of helplessness.

They stayed away three months, and the devil was conquered with surprising ease. But it was the wrong devil: the real one wasn't there to fight. There was lots to do in Durban: there was no small dusty club in Durban: and Peter, who was thoroughly ashamed of himself, behaved adorably to her in Durban. He made her all sorts of promises and vows about the future which he honestly intended to keep. And as proof of his assertions he pointed out to her the complete ease with which he had given up the stuff. Which would have meant a great deal more if they hadn't been chasing the wrong hare.

And so, the cure over, they returned triumphantly to begin all over again. For a fortnight the Club never saw him, though he drove past once or twice behind a new horse he had bought—an ugly-looking black brute with a vicious eye that no one but a Peter Skeffington would have touched with the end of a barge-pole.

And then one evening, like a bolt from the blue, came the tragedy. Peter Skeffington came into the Club, and found Jack Dernan and four or five others. That was at six. At six-thirty he was drunk, and our secretary was tearing his hair with irritation and anger.

"It's incredible," he fumed. "It's outrageous. It's indecent. Five—five drinks has that fellow had, and look at him. He's a menace to humanity. Why, damn it, a baby in arms would drink him under the table."

"But look here," I began angrily.

"*Mea culpa*, my boy," he answered, "I admit it. I said to the blighter when I saw him, 'Hullo, little stranger, have a drink?' I give you my word at the moment I'd completely forgotten all about the show. 'I will,' he answered, and then the matter passed completely out of my hands. I left him for about twenty minutes while I talked to Jackson about that mealie crop, and when I got back I found he had had four more with Jack Dernan and some others, and was tight."

He shrugged his shoulders helplessly.

"Man, you *can't* legislate for a bloke that gets tight on five whiskies and sodas."

"It's Mrs. Peter I'm thinking of," I said. "The poor little woman thinks she's saved Skeffington's soul from the curse of drink and the first time he comes into the Club he goes and does it again."

A burst of laughter came from the bar, and I went in. There were about ten of them in there, and Peter Skeffington was holding forth very solemnly on the political situation in the Union. So I got Jack Dernan on one side and put things in front of him.

"Look here, Jack," I said, "it's not playing the game to make that silly ass tight again."

"Give you my word, old man," he answered, "no one was more surprised than I was. We were playing poker dice and we'd only had four rounds when blowed if I didn't notice he was up the pole. Somebody had got the sweepstake going, and I found I'd drawn Low Field. Well, seeing that the first number is 6, I reckoned the pool was mine."

He glanced at Skeffington who was swaying gravely by the bar.

"I really am deuced sorry, but what can you do with a fellow like that?"

"Well, for Heaven's sake, stop him drinking any more," I said. "We'll lay him out to cool for a bit, and then I'll drive him home."

But Peter Skeffington had no intention whatever of being laid out to cool. He had got into the condition when he was very much on his dignity. Really, by the way we were talking, if it wasn't so perfectly ridiculous, anyone who didn't know any better might imagine that we thought he had had too much to drink. He was perfectly capable, thank you, of looking after himself, and he knew the time quite well and also that his horse and trap were waiting outside, a fact to which he trusted no one took any exception.

Jack Dernan shrugged his shoulders.

"Hopeless," he said to me. "He's worse than I've seen him. And if we go on he'll get offensive, and someone will hurt him."

It was half an hour later that Peter Skeffington descended the steps leading into the road. His eyes were slightly glazed; his speech was very precise; his legs moved stiffly. And suddenly—I know not why—an impulse came to me as I sat on the stoep watching him.

"I wish you'd let me drive you back, Skeffington. I'd rather like to feel the paces of that mare."

He regarded me solemnly.

"Another time, Tredgett, I shall be delighted," he said. "At the moment, however, the other seat is occupied with two large bags of chicken food."

"Well, for God's sake be careful with that brute to-night," said the secretary uneasily, as he saw her ears go back and the whites of her eyes show up.

"I am perfectly capable of handling her," replied Skeffington coldly, and even as he spoke he lurched against the mare, who lashed out viciously.

"Dash it," cried the secretary, half rising to his feet. "Ought we to let him go? He's not in a condition to drive."

But Skeffington was already in his seat, gathering up the reins with clumsy fingers.

"Go easy, man," cried someone, and for answer the fool slashed the animal across the quarters.

For the fraction of a second she stood stock-still at the suddenness of it: then it happened. With a spring like a thing demented the mare shot forward; there was a jerk and a crash, and the next moment she had bolted down the road with the trap swaying and bounding behind her.

"God! She's away with him."

I turned to find Jack Dernan beside me, and his face was white. We were all out in the road watching and no one else spoke. For the chicken food had been hurled out, and the reins were trailing low, and Peter Skeffington was half standing, half sitting in that crazy, tearing buggy. Once we thought it was over, but it righted itself again somehow, and then came the end. One lurch into a rut, more crazy than the others, and Skeffington was flung out. And the next moment we were all of us rushing madly down the road towards him, for it seemed to us that he had hit a tree.

It was Jack Dernan who got there first, and when we got up he was standing by the thing that lay on the ground, and his hat was off. Peter Skeffington *had* hit a tree—with his head.

In the distance a cloud of dust was disappearing as the maddened mare, now completely out of control, galloped on; whilst here at our feet was sudden, stark tragedy.

"No good doing that," said Dernan gruffly, as somebody put his hand on Peter Skeffington's heart. "Look at his head."

I did—and shuddered. His hands had hardly broken the impact at all. So we got the body back

to the Club, and there we held a council of war.   And
by common consent I was deputed to break the news
to Mrs. Peter.

"Of course," said the secretary, "you'll not mention
the fact that he was drunk."

"Of course not," I answered as I went out to start
my Ford.

But I wondered as I drove there whether she wouldn't
guess.

I found her waiting for me wild-eyed with fear.
The mare had come back twenty minutes previously.

"What's happened?" she gasped.   "What's happened to Peter?"

"Mrs. Peter," I said miserably, "you must prepare
for a shock."

"He's dead," she said quietly, and I nodded.

"How did it happen?" she said after a while.   "Don't
be afraid," she added as I glanced at her.   "I shan't
break down—yet.   I want to hear—everything."

So I told her, and when I'd finished she only asked
one question.

"Was Mr. Dernan in the Club?"

I stared at her in surprise: it was so completely
unexpected.

"Why, yes," I said.   "Jack Dernan was there."

And into her eyes there came a look to which I
had no clue.   It seemed to show a sort of savage
determination, but to what end or on what account
I could not guess.

She seemed strangely docile during the next few
days.   For instance, I had anticipated that she would
insist on seeing her husband's body, and there were
reasons why she shouldn't.   The poor devil had hit
that tree hard.   However, when I explained things to
her she made no trouble, but seemed to understand
perfectly.   And another thing that surprised us all was

the way she bore up. Even at the grave-side she retained her perfect composure, and I heard Mrs. Drage
whisper to a woman standing next her, "She's like a
woman in a dream: she'll wake up soon."

But she didn't: that was the amazing part of it.
What happened during the long nights when she was
alone only she and God knew: certain it was that during
the days that followed her husband's death I never saw
a trace of grief on Mrs. Peter's face. And I was up
there off and on a good deal; she seemed to like having
me about the place. Only that strange look—that
look of set purpose—was stamped on her features, and
it seemed to grow more quietly determined as time
went by. She wasn't going to get rid of her farm,
at any rate not yet; and I used to give her advice about
it.

And then, about two months after Peter's death,
business called me up to Rhodesia. I should be away
for six months, and I went up the afternoon before I
left to say good-bye. She gave me tea, and afterwards
I sat on talking about the farm and various things,
though I could see she was paying no attention.

And then suddenly she shot the question at me out
of the blue; at least it wasn't a question so much as
a statement.

"Of course, Peter was drunk that night." She
looked at me with a faint smile. "There's no good
denying it, Joe: your face has already given you away.
Besides—I knew."

"He undoubtedly," I began feebly, "had had something to drink."

She stopped me with a weary little gesture.

"Oh! call it that if you like," she said. "I prefer
not to mince words. He was drunk, and you know
it. You remember I took him to Durban, don't you?"

"Of course I remember," I answered.

"And you know why I took him," she went on. "He was drinking too much, at that—that damnable Club. Every night, Joe; practically every night. I cured him at Durban: never once the whole time he was there did my Peter get into that foul condition. He was cured when he got back here."

I said nothing: I didn't see that there was anything to say. Of what use to tell her that he wasn't cured at all because there was nothing to cure. Such refinements were beyond her: to her a man who got drunk was a drunkard.

"He talked to me while he was in Durban," she went on quietly, "when he was fighting against the craving."

"He told you he had a craving for it?" I asked curiously.

"But of course he must have had a craving for it," she said, staring at me as if I was a fool. "Why else should he have drunk? But he fought against it, and I helped him—and my Peter won. He was fine about it—fine."

"Quite," I agreed. "It was fine."

Once again there didn't seem anything else to say. I suppose it is finer to fight and conquer a terrible craving than to admit that one is so atrociously weak that you can't say No even when you don't want the stuff.

"Yes, he talked a lot to me during those months," went on Mrs. Peter quietly. "Particularly about Mr. Dernan."

"The devil he did!" I said, sitting up. "What had he got to say about him?"

She had turned away and I couldn't see her face.

"A great deal about his character," she answered almost carelessly. And then suddenly she swung round, and I gasped at the look in her eyes. "To my mind," she said tensely, "there is no hell deep enough, no punishment sufficiently vile for a man of that type."

"But, good God!" I stammered feebly. "I assure you, Mrs. Peter, that Jack Dernan isn't at all a bad fellow."

And the look she gave me flattened me out.

"To get hold of a man who has been fighting to conquer a craving, and who has succeeded, and tempt him and tempt him and tempt him until he falls again is your idea of a good fellow, is it? It isn't mine."

My mind went back to the night of the tragedy, and I realized the futility of any argument. To Mrs. Peter, her husband was a man who had fought and won, only to yield at last to the devilish temptation cast in his way by Jack Dernan. And was any good to be obtained by telling her the truth: telling her that, as a matter of fact, the first drink he had had that night had not been with Dernan at all? Telling her, moreover, that it would have made no odds if no such person existed in the world as Jack Dernan: that Peter Skeffington had been of the clay which, in certain conditions, was unsavable?

So I let it go, and even now, looking back with the light of what was to come behind me, I should do the same thing again under similar circumstances. For who could possibly have told that a woman of the type of Mrs. Peter could ever have done the thing she did?

I got back from Rhodesia eight months later, and one of the first men I ran into was Jack Dernan. He was in the Club as I came in, and I stopped short and stared at him in amazement.

"Good Lord, old man!" I cried. "What's the matter with you? Malaria?"

He looked ghastly: grey, with lack-lustre eyes and

a loose mouth.   He stared at me vacantly for a while,
then he spoke.

"Go to hell," he snarled, and shambled out of the
Club.

"What do you think of him?" came the secretary's
voice from behind me.

"What on earth is the matter with him?" I said as
I swung round to greet him.   "The man looks dreadful."

"Come and have a drink, Tredgett," he answered
gravely.   "I want to talk to you."

I followed him into the bar and we sat down in a
corner.   Luckily we had it to ourselves.

"You know, I suppose, that he's never out of Mrs.
Skeffington's pocket?"

"What!" I almost shouted, my drink half-way to
my lips.

"Never out of her pocket," he repeated quietly.
"I'm pretty lax myself, as you know: anybody can
do anything with reason, as far as I'm concerned: but
this has been a bit over the odds.   None of the women
here will have anything to do with her, but she doesn't
seem to care.   She's infatuated with the fellow, and he
with her.   But she's thrown the most rudimentary
social laws to the winds.   There's no reason presumably why they shouldn't get married: I've never heard
of Dernan being entangled in any way.   Instead of
that, he's up at her bungalow—alone with her until
all hours of the night.   And I'm really not surprised
that everyone has put the worst construction on it."

And in my mind was ringing a certain sentence:

"To my mind there is no hell deep enough, no
punishment sufficiently vile for a man of that type."

"But it's the change in the man himself that is so
amazing," went on the secretary.   "You remember
what he was like; you saw him a few moments ago.

And he's worse than that sometimes. His temper has become unbearable—positively unbearable. In fact, at times he's positively dangerous."

But I was hardly listening: into my mind had come a sudden ghastly suspicion.

"Has he seen a doctor?" I asked, striving to make my voice sound natural.

The secretary smiled grimly.

"Tim Murphy suggested that very thing to him," he said. "But he only did so once. Dernan flew into the most ungovernable rage, and went for him. Here in this actual bar. We had the devil of a job pulling him off, and Murphy was nearly throttled before we did. I tell you, Tredgett—the man's dangerous."

"And has no one any idea what is the matter?" I said.

The secretary shrugged his shoulders.

"He's knocking off drink considerably," he answered. "Why—I don't know. Possibly the lady has a lot to do with it. And whether it's finding him out—rawing up his nerves or something of that sort—I don't know. Anyhow, you've seen him for yourself, and can form as good an opinion as I can."

I escaped as soon as I could and went back to my bungalow. Suspicion was hammering at my brain, and I wanted to think. Could it be possible that Mrs. Peter was poisoning him? That was the ghastly thought that would not be shaken off. Of what use to tell myself that the idea was incredible: that such things don't happen outside the covers of sensational fiction? Such things *do* happen, and, though Mrs. Peter was the last woman in the world one would have deemed capable of such a thing, I couldn't forget the look on her face the last time I had seen her. And if my suspicion was right, what was going to be the upshot? Sooner or later a man in Jack Dernan's

condition of health would have to see a doctor, and
—what then?

I tried to concentrate on arrears of work, but the
figures danced before my eyes. The short dusk had
gone, and outside the African night had come down,
bringing no relief from the heat of the day. But I
felt I could stand it no longer: I must find out for
myself. Nothing would be more natural, I reflected,
than that I should go and see Mrs. Peter on my return after such a long absence. And if Dernan was
there I might be able to come to some conclusion.

I pulled out the Ford and started off. And it was
only as I approached Mrs. Peter's bungalow that I
suddenly decided to leave the car in the road and walk
up the last few hundred yards. My feet made no
sound on the earth track, and I was within twenty
yards of the house when I saw a sight which stopped
me dead in my tracks.

The light was shining out from the drawing-room
windows, and I could see every detail of the room
through the mosquito-netting. Jack Dernan was there
sitting on the sofa, and his arms were round Mrs.
Peter. His face seemed more ghastly than ever, though
she was looking up into it lovingly. And suddenly he
bent and kissed her.

"Isn't it time yet, my dearest?"

His voice, harsh and discordant, came to me through
the still night.

She reached for a little box at her side, and drew
out something that gleamed. And in my excitement
I crept closer. He was holding out his arm with the
sleeve rolled up, and I saw her taking the shining
thing in one hand whilst with the other she caught
a little roll of his skin. And then I knew: knew that
what I'd suspected was true. She was giving him an
injection from a hypodermic syringe.

For perhaps five minutes after she had done it he lay still, and you could almost watch his face change. The grey tinge disappeared; the shifty mouth grew firm; the eyes became clear.   It was the old Jack Dernan who rose to his feet—more, it was a super Jack Dernan.   He stood there—a magnificent figure of a man, with a look on his face of absolute triumph.

"My darling," he cried, "how long are you going to keep me waiting?"

His arms were stretched out to her; even I could feel the commanding presence of the man.

And Mrs. Peter lay in the corner of the sofa and laughed.

"You fool," she answered very clearly. "You damned fool!"

His arms dropped to his side and he stared at her.

"Only that I've been playing a game with you, Mr. Jack Dernan—and I've won."   She rose and crossed to the other side of the room so that the table was between them. "A game—you beast, you cur, and you never knew. You thought I was in love with you, when I hate you, loathe you, execrate you.   If it hadn't been for you, my Peter would have been alive to-night, you—you murderer.   Listen, Jack Dernan—listen now, while the dope is in you, and your brain is working clearly.   I've led you on from the very beginning, even though the touch of your hands nauseated me, and there were times when I didn't think I could go through with it.   It doesn't matter how I got hold of the stuff; it was during that time I went up to Johannesburg.   I went up there to get it, and I got it.   That's all that counts.   Then I came back here, and I made you fall in love with me. And after that I tempted you—even as you tempted Peter. Do you remember that first night, Jack Dernan? It was a bit of a job, but I did it. You were frightened at first—frightened of drugs. Even as my Peter was frightened of drink. Then you saw me use the syringe on my own arm, and that persuaded you. But there was just plain water in mine, you fool, whereas yours had the drug in it. And so it has been all the time: I've been injecting myself with water, and you with the drug. And I've acted—God! how I've acted. You've seen me, as you thought, run down, panting for it. Acting, you devil, acting."

She paused, and the man still stared at her speechless.

"It's over now. Joe Tredgett has come back from Rhodesia and he would suspect. To-night is the last night I shall ever see you; to-night finished my stock. But when the craving is on you, Jack Dernan, and every fibre of your body is shrieking for the drug it wants—think of the man you killed as surely as if you'd shot him. I've turned you into a drug maniac, and that is my revenge. Go, you brute, go."

She stood there pointing to the window, and for a space there was silence. Then, with a strange, gasping cry, Jack Dernan turned and, blundering through the mosquito-netting as if it wasn't there, disappeared into the darkness.

Two months later Mrs. Peter Skeffington sold her land and returned to England. And I don't know if she ever saw a paragraph in the Johannesburg *Star*. It ran as follows:

"A dreadful tragedy took place last night in the Germiston district, resulting in the death of four men. Two of them were well known as being engaged in the traffic of cocaine and other drugs. The third was a native, and the fourth has been identified as a man called Jack Dernan. It is thought some quarrel arose over the disposal of the stuff, and revolvers were drawn. Three of the chambers of Dernan's revolver had been discharged."

At any rate, that is the story of Mrs. Peter Skeffington. It is not a pleasant one: but it happens to be true.

XLVI   MARIE

HE was a little, wizened-up old thing, his face a network of wrinkles. Seventy I put his age at —perhaps more: though in his eyes there still dwelt something of the fire of youth, and the hand that lifted the glass of vermouth to his lips was steady. It was the choice of that drink as an *apéritif* that had started the conversation, for our own countrymen of the class to which he obviously belonged do not, as a rule, indulge in vermouth.

He was French, of course, though for the last twenty years he had lived in London, and save for a few little mannerisms of speech he might have been English. He kept a barber's shop, and every night when business was over he came to the Dubonnet for his glass of vermouth.

Georges Pitou was his name; possibly Monsieur had observed his shop in Wardour Street? I fenced delicately, but the matter was dismissed with a wave of the hand. There were two assistants.

"And Madame," I put in thoughtlessly.

"No, Monsieur," he said gravely. "I am not married."

He signed to the waiter to refill his glass.

"And Monsieur is what? I have not seen you here before."

I broke the news of my trade to him gently.

"Then," he said quickly, "you are here in search of copy?"

"Principally, Monsieur Pitou," I laughed, "I am here in search of a cheap dinner. It is one thing to write, and quite another to be read."

He nodded sympathetically.

"I know, Monsieur; sometimes one works one's very best and yet one is not appreciated. Even in my saloon I have known it to happen."

"Indeed," I murmured politely.

"Yes," he went on after a few moments, "it is an unpleasant thing not to be appreciated. Though good for a man, Monsieur, when he is young. Always there lies in front of him the goal of success, and so he is spurred on. It is when a man is old—when a man who has once been appreciated and made much of begins to lose his hold—it is then that it becomes a terrible thing. You think not, perhaps; you say that he has had his day, and that it is time he made way for someone else. Listen, Monsieur, and I will tell you a story. And you shall write it down, and send it to a magazine. Listen—for I am in the mood this evening."

He lit a cigarette and in the light of the match his face seemed even more amazingly wrinkled than before.

"Do not imagine, Monsieur," he began, "that I was always a barber. For twenty years, true, I have cut hair—and twenty years is a long time. So long that sometimes I think that I have cut hair all my life— but that is only when the black dog is about. And then I remember that there is always a bottle of wine and that life is what we make of it ourselves.

"Have you ever heard, Monsieur, of Blom's Cele- brated Circus. It was before your time, I know, and yet I thought everyone must have heard of it. For never was there a circus quite like it. In every corner of France—from Perpignan to Rheims, from the Gironde to the Vosges—Blom's Circus was a household word. To welcome it villages would hang out their flags, and towns declare a general holiday.

, "It was superb, magnificent. There was a giraffe, and a tiger in a cage; there was a pig with five feet, and a bearded woman. And, *mon Dieu!* what a woman. Never shall I forget the blow she gave me when I trimmed that beard one day in a manner that was—how do you say it?—lopsided. But I was young, Monsieur: to me it was but a jest until she hit me."

He sighed reminiscently and indicated his empty glass to the waiter.

"As you will have guessed I, too, was of the circus; I might almost say I was the circus. I can still hear those bursts of laughter, those shouts of applause as Pitou the clown darted into the ring. But it is not of myself that I would speak: merely is it necessary for Monsieur to grasp my position, and to realize that I am well qualified to tell the story by which Monsieur will make his name. For it is the story of Henri Dardot—the conjurer—and of Marie—his wife.

"It is not too much to say that the name of Henri Dardot was almost as well known as that of Pitou the clown. The amazing things he could do—with cards and rabbits and things in a hat. Once I remember there was a slight accident with regard to a top-hat he had borrowed, and in which he had promised to make an omelette. You will understand that he had in reality two top-hats, which he substituted from time to time. Behold then Henri breaking eggs gaily into the second top-hat. The omelette *aux fines herbes*—cooked to a turn—was all ready on its plate waiting to be slipped into the hat he had borrowed. He laughed and jested, and the crowd laughed too. And then suddenly the laughter froze on his lips; his face turned white under his make-up. Inadvertently he had mixed the two hats. And the hat of Monsieur le Maire, instead of containing a delicious omelette on a plate, was half full of raw eggs.

"A mistake, Monsieur—but the greatest men have made mistakes. And natural, too, at the time. For Henri was in love—in love with the most adorable girl. You have seen the field of waving corn; you have seen the scarlet poppies peeping out from between the stalks; you have seen the blue of the southern seas. Even so was the gold of her hair, and the scarlet of her lips, and the wonder of her eyes. I, too, was in love with her—we all were, but we soon saw that Henri was her choice. At the time I thought it strange, for though Henri was a superb conjurer and could juggle with soup plates, such qualifications seemed unnecessary in a husband. After all, in a happy marriage one does not make omelettes in top-hats, and the dinner service reposes on the dresser. Whereas a sunny disposition and a pretty wit, such as is vital to a clown, must be great assets in the home.

"However, it became evident that Marie had eyes for none but Henri. With her own handkerchief she wiped the inside of Monsieur le Maire's hat; with her own hands she cooked the second omelette with the eggs she had so carefully saved out of the hat and shared it with Henri. And a few days later they were married.

"Monsieur is married himself? When success comes, as it will when he writes this story, he hopes to be? I see. Well, if I tried to I can think of no better wish to offer to Monsieur than that his marriage will be as the marriage of Henri and Marie was during the first nine or ten years.

"It is incredible, but it is the truth. Never for one moment did Marie look at another man; never for one moment did Henri look at another woman. Monsieur may think now that it is not at all incredible. I can only hope that he will always be of the same opinion. And yet—who knows? There is happiness in this world too great to last; even as the happiness of those two. Fate—Nature—call it what you will, is hard and stern. It she sees us too happy, she steps in and cries 'Halt!' She keeps a book and she adds things up. And if the total is too big she gets angry. Sometimes you pay in instalments, Monsieur, and sometimes in a lump sum down. And so, though I wish you the happiness of those two during the first years of their married life, I hope at the end that the total will not be too big. Because they paid. *Mon Dieu!* how they paid!

"There was one child—a boy—and naturally his name also was Henri. And as the years passed by he became the pet of us all. He alone was allowed to pull the beard of the show lady: he alone was allowed to undo the waistcoat buttons of Monsieur Blom himself. Everywhere we went, he went with us, and sometimes, as a treat, I would make him up as a clown and he would pretend that he was the great Georges Pitou. We would watch him capering round the ring turning somersaults, and Marie would laugh and clap her hands and say that he was better than his instructor.

"And then when the boy was about nine years old, there came a day when I found Marie in tears. She was sitting upon an old packing-case, and standing by her knee was little Henri. And Henri the big—her husband—was walking up and down blowing his nose and muttering to himself.

" 'It is imbecile, Marie,' I heard him cry. 'You do not understand what the good Abbé has offered. Why, name of a name, he will make a gentleman of the boy. An *avocat*, or maybe a doctor. Does he not say that the boy has the bump of much knowledge upon his head?'

" 'But I don't want him to be a gentleman,' cried Marie. 'I want him just as he is—my little boy.'

"And the boy clutched her knees and cried too, for he loved the circus and didn't want to go away. Was not the dream of the young rascal's life to be the second Georges Pitou?

"They asked me my opinion, and I—what could I say? It was a big question to decide, Monsieur—the future of little Henri. On the one hand the convent school of the Abbé, where the boy could be educated at no great cost: on the other the circus with its free and easy life. And for two days I thought it over, while they naturally waited for my advice.

" '*Mes amis*,' I said, 'it is thus that I see it. Incredible though it may seem to us now, there may come a day when Blom's Celebrated Circus will no longer draw the public as it does at present. True—you cannot believe me: to you such a thing is inconceivable. And yet the day must come when Henri Dardot can no longer produce omelettes from top-hats. Another will take his place, you say. Perhaps so—perhaps not. But what will happen when I—Georges Pitou—wish to retire? For no man goes on for ever. What will happen then, *mes amis*?'

"The argument impressed them, M'sieur: for the idea of Blom's Celebrated Circus without Georges Pitou was frankly absurd.

" 'But that is many years away, M'sieur Pitou,' said the bearded woman.

" 'Who knows?' I said easily. 'I have my eye on a little café not far from Avignon. And when M'sieur Blom sees fit to reward me as I deserve—— But, enough. It is not of myself I would speak. It is of little Henri, and what it is best to do for the boy. What, then, will happen to him if in ten years from now the circus is no more? Ten years is a long time, and many things may take place. The good Monsieur Blom may be dead: I, Georges Pitou, may have had an accident—or I may have retired. And if that is so what will the boy do? For what training he has had will be of no use to him if there is no circus.'

"Common sense, M'sieur, you will agree. From every point of view it was better that the boy should go to a good school: from every point of view, that is, save one."

Monsieur Pitou drained his glass and stared over my shoulder into space. A strange rapt look was in his eyes, and I think he was back again at the council of war where the fate of little Henri was being discussed, with the bearded lady gazing at him with suitable reverence, and Marie holding her son tightly, fiercely, as she realized that opinion was against her.

"Yes, M'sieur, from every point of view save one— his mother's. What fools we men are—weighing up the points for and against: treating a soul as if it was a mathematical problem. For laws must conform to the soul: not the soul to laws. M'sieur perhaps may regard that as dangerous philosophy: nevertheless it is the truth. And that is why women drive men to the verge of insanity when they argue. For argument is based on law, and women know better than the law. At least they do on some things.

"Marie knew better than the law. I see it now, though at the time I didn't. Point by point I showed her the advantages that little Henri would gain by going to school. And when I'd finished, and her husband was nodding in agreement, and Alphonse, who trained the performing fleas and was always losing them—*mon Dieu!* every day, and he slept next to me: when all of us, as I say, had shown Marie clearly and logically that we were right, she just shook her head and whispered, 'You're wrong.' And then the Abbé himself interfered, and he was as big a fool as the rest of us. But he went on a different line, and so he was more successful.

"'My child,' he said to her, 'are you quite sure you are thinking of the boy and not of yourself?'

"M'sieur, it was a devilish question. Even now I can see the dawning look of terror in those wonderful blue eyes as she stared at him. For she realized she was beaten. With her woman's intuition she knew, at once, that he had penetrated her defences, and that she had lost. For she understood the hopelessness of explaining to men that if she thought of the boy she must be thinking of herself too. You can't divide a good mother and her son and treat them as two beings. A father and his child—yes: but not a mother.

"She walked away, I remember, and as she passed me I caught my breath at the look on her face. And when she'd gone we talked foolishly together, as is the way with men at such times, of the crops and politics and things that didn't matter, until Alphonse lost another of his cursed fleas, and praise be to God the Abbé went off with it. At least he swore it was on him, and he was searching for it angrily when Marie returned. She went straight up to little Henri, and picked him up, and though thirty-five years have gone by since that day, the picture she made is as clear in my mind as ever. Their two heads were together, and the little chap's arms were round her neck. And for a while she stared at the Abbé in silence, till at length he gave up the search and contented himself with an occasional scratch.

"'Monsieur l'Abbé,' she said quietly, 'take him. Take him now before I change my mind.'

"'You have decided well, my daughter,' he answered gravely, and then he muttered maledictions under his breath, for Alphonse never overfed his pets. 'You will not regret it.'

" 'I will come and see him before we leave to-morrow,' said Marie, and I saw her arms tighten round her baby. And then she started to whisper in his ear, and I—I am not ashamed to confess it—I blew my nose with violence. There are moments, M'sieur, when the strongest of us find it difficult to speak.

"Ten minutes later we stood at the door of the tent watching the little figure trotting gravely along the dusty road at the side of Monsieur l'Abbé. Was he not going to something new, where he would play with other little boys? And is not the world very good when we are nine years old, and a funny man is beside us making sudden darts at various parts of his anatomy? Is not such a performance expressly intended for the purpose of making little boys laugh? And so we watched them till a turn in the road hid them from sight.

" 'He never even waved,' whispered Marie, half to herself. 'He never even turned round once.'

"Ah! Marie, my dear, little boys don't turn round and wave when they are laughing. And little boys should always be laughing. It is the only way to balance the world's tears. They look so intently at the present—and surely an Abbé with a flea is good enough for anyone. It's not the past or the future that matters: they leave uninteresting things like that to the grown-ups. Which is why, perhaps, Marie wiped the tears from her eyes, as she thought of the last nine years, and then turned on us like a tigress.

" 'Oh, you fools!' she stormed. 'You miserable fools!'

"And there was fear as well as anger in her voice as she thought of the years to come."

The wizened-up little man drained his vermouth and lit a cigarette.

"M'sieur can perhaps picture those years," he continued after a while. "From Perpignan to Rheims,

from the Gironde to the Vosges, Blom's Celebrated
Circus continued its triumphant career. And once
every year we performed at the town where little Henri
was at school. Ah! The first of those occasions: it
was unforgettable. The excitement, and the laughing,
and the kissing that went on! Henri and all his little
friends came and sat in the front row, and cheered and
talked all through the performance; never did Georges
Pitou provoke such amusement. Never did Henri
the elder produce his omelette so superbly.

" 'That is my father,' came the proud voice of little
Henri, 'and if you're good he will give you the omelette
to eat.'

"But naturally: who else would have that honour on
such a day? And after it was over they all came and
stared at the bearded woman, and the fleas of Alphonse,
until Marie caught up her boy and carried him away
from the others. Was he happy? Were his socks
mended? *Parbleu!*—at ten years of age one is always
happy, and what is a hole in a sock, more or less?

"M'sieur—he fidgeted. Out of the corner of my
eye—was I not doing one of my tricks for the others?—
I could see that his eyes were fixed on me. He did not
want to sit with Marie in a corner and talk of his socks:
he wanted to show the others that he could jump through
a hoop. And Marie wished for nothing but that he
should sit on her knee with his arms round her neck,
and pretend that he was her baby again.

"It was the Abbé himself who came to fetch them,
and he said nothing but good of little Henri. His
father was delighted, and Monsieur Blom himself
presented the boy with a silver franc.

" 'He will make his name, that boy,' said Henri to
me that night. 'Truly we did wisely in giving him his
chance.'

"And Marie, who was sewing, said nothing, though

we didn't notice it at the time. She knew, M'sieur
—she knew even then: women are like that. And
there was nothing she could do: the matter was out of
her hands.

"It came little by little—almost imperceptibly at first,
the—how do you say it?—the crack in the violin.
And with it there came another thing, which again was
almost imperceptible at first—the waning popularity of
Blom's Celebrated Circus.

"I think it was little Henri who first put it into
words with the brutal frankness of the young. He was
twelve then, and for the last two years none of his
school friends had turned up to see the circus.

" 'It is so dull, maman,' he said. 'Always you do the
same tricks. And one gets bored with seeing the same
tricks.'

" 'But there are always new people to see them,'
cried his father. 'And an old trick is new to those
who have not seen it. What, for example, of the boy—
the new boy of whom you wrote—Jean? He has not
seen the tricks. Why did you not bring him?'

"And little Henri turned red and stammered.

" 'Jean,' he said, 'does not like circuses.'

" 'Ho, ho!' cried his father, 'and who is this strange
fellow who does not like seeing an omelette produced
from a hat?'

" 'He is the son of the Comte d'Albuise,' answered
the boy.

" '*Mon Dieu!*' chuckled his father, 'but we have
swagger friends. Tell him that if he should come
to-night, I will show him a new and wonderful card
trick.'

"And the boy turned redder than ever.

" 'He does not know that I am here, papa,' he
muttered. 'And, anyway, he would not be allowed
to come to-night: Monsieur le Comte d'Albuise is

very particular. He fears the—the measles for Jean.'

" 'And that is why you have kept silent,' cried his father. 'Good boy. Otherwise the little Jean would be jealous, *n'est-ce pas?*'

" 'Yes—he would be jealous,' repeated the boy.

" 'Considerate, you see,' cried his father when he had gone. 'A good trait which I am well pleased with. *Mais, mon Dieu,* Marie—you are crying. Was there ever such a woman? What is the matter?'

" 'Nothing, Henri, that matters,' she said quietly, but to me, later, she told the truth.

" 'It is not the measles, Georges,' she said sadly, 'that has kept him away. It is that my little Henri is ashamed of us. He does not want his friends to know that his parents are in a circus.'

"And though I told her that she was wrong, I knew that she was right. And I realized that it was what she had feared and dreaded all the time, and now it had come. To her husband she said nothing, and she made me promise that I, too, would keep silence.

" 'It is done now, Georges,' she said. 'My little boy has been taken away from me, and now we can only hinder him. But I wonder if he's really any happier than he was when he was here with us in the circus.'

" 'He had to have his chance, Marie,' I answered. 'And look how well he is doing.'

"She nodded her head a little wearily, and went on with her sewing.

" 'Georges,' she said, 'there was a time many years ago when I used to dream of the future when we had left the circus. Henri and I would have saved a little money—enough to buy a cottage somewhere and grow vegetables, and keep some hens and a pig. And in the next cottage would have been little Henri and his wife

and babies. And we would have been all together—
and so happy. But now—what is going to happen?
He would not be happy in a cottage, and the money
that we might be saving goes in his schooling and his
clothes. He must be dressed better there than if he
was still with us here, and it is terrible how much it
costs. And what is going to be the end of it all,
Georges? If only I could be sure he was going to be
happy. Nothing else would matter at all then.'

"That was all she seemed to think about, M'sieur:
was her boy going to be happy? Her own dreams had
vanished; she was trying to find others to replace them.
Sometimes when I painted for her pictures of her boy
as a great man—as a deputy, nay, as the President
himself—her eyes would sparkle and she would nod
her head and laugh. And then the joy would fade
from her face, and the life die out, until I grew almost
angry with her. But she knew, M'sieur; she knew.

"It was when the boy was eighteen that the crisis
came. For a long time we had seen it coming, but,
as is the way with true artistes, we had hoped against
hope. Business was going from bad to worse, and
Monsieur Blom grew more worried every day. No
longer did the people flock to see us: in fact, there were
performances when the only spectators were people
who had been given their seats free. And the most
worried of all of us were Henri Dardot and Marie.
The boy's expenses were increasing, and whereas the
rest of us had saved a little, they had saved nothing at
all. In fact, they were in debt. They had struggled
and struggled to make both ends meet, but you cannot
get a quart out of a pint pot. And now the last premium of their insurance was due, for when the boy had
gone to school they had insured their lives so that in
case anything happened to them his education should
not be interfered with.

"And then came the final blow.   Never shall I forget that afternoon to my dying day—the afternoon that Monsieur Blom called us all together to tell us the news. We had known things were bad, but we had not realized that they were as bad as they were.   A man was with him, a nasty-looking man smoking a large cigar.   He had on a fur coat, and Monsieur Blom seemed very much afraid of him.

" '*Mes enfants*,' he said, and his voice was trembling, 'we are in a bad way.   For twenty-five years we have been together all over France, and now——'

" 'The show is broke,' put in the man with the cigar. 'Cut the cackle, Blom.   It's not to be wondered at. It's rotten.   I watched it last night.   It's as dull as ditchwater.   You're doing the same futile tricks that you did ten years ago.   Why, I saw the conjurer— what's his name, Dardot—do that fool stunt with an omelette when I was a boy.'

"Henri Dardot's lips trembled, and Marie put her hand on his arm.

" 'It wants freshening up,' went on the man.   'And if I'm to take over the goodwill in exchange for the money you owe me, all these people will have to go. This show as it stands at present is enough to make a deaf mute sob like a child.'

"*Mon Dieu!* M'sieur—it was terrible!   We knew, as I said, that things were bad, but this news over- whelmed us.   Go—be sacked after twenty-five years! What was to become of us?   Above all—what was to become of Henri Dardot and Marie?   We, as I told you, had saved something: they had nothing at all.

"I saw them after we had left Monsieur Blom sitting together in a dark corner, and this time it was he who was crying, whilst she had her arms round his neck as in the days when they first married.

" 'My dear,' she said tenderly, 'we shall manage: somehow we shall manage.'

" 'It is little Henri,' he sobbed. 'For how are we to send him to the *avocat's* office, if we are turned away?'

"Then he got up and dashed away his tears: evidently a great idea had come to him.

" 'I will learn new tricks,' he cried magnificently. 'Now, this minute—I will think out something fresh and original.'

"And Marie clapped her hands together.

" 'I will go and tell that pig with a cigar,' she cried, 'that you are perfecting a new wonder.'

" 'Then he will not sack us. Though I wish we had the money for the insurance.'

"Monsieur—had I any alternative? You who are an artist will know how a paltry trifle like that will prevent a man from giving of his best. He is worried: he cannot concentrate. Assuredly we would show this pig in the fur coat what we could do: I, myself, had already sketched out some new turns. And Henri Dardot also.

" '*Mes amis*,' I cried. 'Do not worry about that insurance. Are we not friends, and what is mine is thine. I will pay it.'

"We embraced, M'sieur; I would brook no refusal. And then we concentrated on our new tricks. The accursed man with the cigar was persuaded at length into giving us all a week's further trial: principally, as he said, because it would take him a week to replace us. And for three days Henri Dardot thought and thought, whilst we all tried to help him. But it was hard: for undoubtedly his hand had lost its cunning.

"And then when we were almost in despair there came the great idea. M'sieur, it was a masterpiece: it was the idea of genius. At once we knew that it would make the name of Henri Dardot famous through-

out Europe, and that any thought of their being sacked
was now gone.   It would be the making of the circus,
and in my joy and excitement I told the pigdog who
smoked cigars as much.   And he laughed.

" 'We'll see,' he said.   'Anyway, it couldn't be worse
than their present show.'

"For two more days we worked out the trick, and
assuredly it was a creation of genius.   At least so it
seemed to us.   I will not weary you, M'sieur, with the
details of it: enough to say that at the great culminating
moment a box which the audience thought to be empty
was opened and revealed Marie dressed in her most
beautiful clothes standing in a blaze of light.   It was
done by electricity: little bulbs were sewn into her frock
and into her hair, and the good God alone knows how
much Henri had had to pay the local electrician to do it.
I know he had obtained his week's salary in advance,
and there was nothing of it left.   But what did it
matter: success and fame were his at last.

" 'It is true, Georges,' he said to me; 'that man is
correct, I have been lazy.   I should have used my
great skill before to perfect other masterpieces.   Then
we should not be in the position we are.   But there is
still time: this is but the first of many by which we will
save Monsieur Blom.' "

The wizened-up little man paused and lit another
cigarette.

"The circus was fuller that evening, M'sieur," he
went on after a while.   "Almost as it had been in days
gone by.   And we performed superbly.   Were we
not all worked up at the thought of Henri Dardot's
masterpiece that was to come?   And at length the
moment arrived.   I stood, M'sieur, in the wings and
I trembled with excitement.   At my side was the
accursed one with the cigar, and over and over again
I said to him: 'Now you will see, my friend—see and

understand the genius whom you thought to sack.'
And he only smiled, and dug his hands deeper in the
pockets of his coat.

"*Mon Dieu!* M'sieur, even now I can hardly bear to
think of the next few minutes. For it failed: it was a
ghastly, miserable failure. Everything went wrong.
Marie was not in the box at the right moment; the fool
of an electrician had bungled with the lights. And,
what was worse, I realized that even if it had come off
as Henri intended, it was not a masterpiece at all. It
had all seemed so different when we planned and
rehearsed it: now it was just a silly stupid thing.

"The audience giggled and somebody hissed, and I
dashed on to try and save the situation. I passed Henri
and his face was grey, whilst Marie was sobbing under
her breath. To have one's most magnificent hopes
dashed to the ground is a terrible thing, M'sieur. And
they had built so much on it.

"I darted off again as the next turn started, to find
them both talking to the man with the cigar.

" 'If possible, Dardot,' he was saying, 'your show
this evening is more utterly futile than when you
produce that damned omelette out of a hat.'

" 'But, M'sieur,' stammered Henri desperately, 'it
went wrong. To-morrow night——'

" 'There will be no to-morrow night,' answered the
other. 'You're sacked now.'

"And Henri gave a little gasping cry as if he had
been struck in the face. They were standing side by
side, he and Marie, and for a moment or two they clung
together like children: then Marie, with a sudden strange
look on her face, stepped forward.

" 'You engaged us for a week, M'sieur,' she said
quietly. 'To-morrow is the last night. Give us that
one chance.'

"For a few seconds he looked at her—did the man

with the cigar. Then he shrugged his shoulders and turned away.

" 'All right,' he said gruffly. 'But I warn you that your show is no good. And I'm not going to take you on again.'

"To Henri it was a reprieve: the next night all would be well. He slaved and worked at his trick all through the following day, and I, though my heart was heavy with misgivings, helped him. Only Marie seemed strangely silent, so much so that I tried to cheer her up. Henri was busy with the electrician, and we were standing alone. She listened to me with a little sad smile on her lips, and when I'd finished she laid her hand on my arm.

" 'Dear Georges,' she said, 'it's no good, and you know it. The trick is a failure. We're too old, Henri and I, for new things. To-night is the last night, *mon ami*,' and she seemed to be looking at something I couldn't see.

" 'Funny how the shadows play tricks, Georges,' she went on. 'I thought I saw little Henri playing with his hoop over in that corner, as he used to—years ago.'

" 'Marie,' I cried, and I was almost in tears, 'what are you going to do when you go? For you must have half of my money. I insist.'

"And then, M'sieur, she kissed me on the lips for the first and last time."

He paused—that wizened-up little man—and there was such a wonderful light in his eyes that I understood why he was not married.

"It came at last," he went on gravely, "that final performance. And Henri was trembling like a child, whilst I was no better. Only Marie was calm, with the same strange, inscrutable look in her lovely blue eyes that had been there all the day. You see, she knew,

M'sieur: all along she had known. I can't tell you how it happened—it was all so quick. The electrician swore it was no fault of his: maybe he was right. Maybe, on the other hand, it was an accident, and the fool was to blame. For suddenly, without warning, Marie—my beautiful Marie—was just a sheet of flame, and Henri's agonized cry rang through the tent. We darted to her, whilst the audience screamed in terror, but it was too late. We could do nothing; her flimsy dress had blazed too fiercely. The flames, it is true, were out, but they had done their deed.

"She never whimpered, nor cried, though she must have been in agony. Only once did she speak, and then she just whispered: 'Lift me up, my husband.'

"And Henri, who was sobbing pitifully, lifted her up. I was watching her, M'sieur, through my tears, and her poor glazing eyes turned to the corner of the tent which had been little Henri's playground. For a while she stared across at it and a faint smile crossed her lips. Then she died.

"You see, M'sieur," said the wizened-up little man gravely, "now that the premium was met the insurance money would be paid. And that was enough for her two Henris—the big and the little."

And a moment later I was alone.

XLVII   THE KING OF HEARTS

"I ASSURE you, Sir John, it's exactly what we want."

Mr. Dicker, chief Unionist agent for the constituency, rubbed his hands together, and contemplated the prospective Unionist candidate seated in a chair opposite.

"Exactly what we want," he repeated. "Mark you, Sir John,"—he lifted his hand as if to forestall any objections that might be raised—"it will have to be done with care from every point of view. Nothing could be more repugnant to a man in your position than the slightest suspicion that you were in any way boasting."

Sir John Perton nodded decisively.

"And that is precisely what we shall avoid," went on the other calmly. "Again, we must avoid giving the other side any chance of saying that we are merely drawing a red herring across the electors' track. Of course that is precisely what we are doing, but that's a detail. It will therefore have to come not in any sense as an interview with you, but in a brief account of your career and life. And young Titmarsh in the *Mercury* here is the very man to do it. He writes an 'At Random' column every week as well as his other work, and it's there we'll have the episode of cutting that pack of cards emphasized. It will appear as a detail in the account of your life; it can be magnified when it's taken out and put in the column. It's gorgeous, Sir John—gorgeous. And I wouldn't be surprised if we didn't get you in on it. Besides, it will give us all something to talk about when we go round canvassing. The man who drew the four of spades. . . . Gambling with death. . . . I'll get Titmarsh now—this instant——"

He clapped on a hat and dashed to the door: in all his movements Mr. Dicker strongly resembled a terrier after a rat.

"Just think out the story, Sir John; plenty of human interest. All that bit about the water and the pitiless sun and the natives crawling around. And then your gamble with Mr. What's-his-name on the top of the hill. Gorgeous——"

He darted from the room, and Sir John Perton rose
from his chair and crossed to the window. It looked
down on the main street of Burchester, and with his
hands in his pockets the prospective candidate watched
the sleepy midday activity below.

But it is doubtful if he saw anything; if the big
brewer's van unloading barrels opposite made any impression on his brain. For he was back in West Africa
on that cursed little show—the show that Mr. Dicker
described as gorgeous. He could feel that scorching
heat again: he could hear that terrible scream which
one of the men gave as he went mad and blew out
his brains: he could see—God! would he ever cease
to see the blazing hideous scorn in Bill Meyrick's face.
With a sudden shiver he passed his hand over his
forehead and found it wet.

He swore angrily under his breath: this would never
do. The thing was over and done with: buried beneath two years of time. Much water had flowed
under the bridge in that two years: his uncle and his
first cousin had both been killed in a motor accident
and he had come into a baronetcy which he'd never
expected. From being a comparatively impecunious
officer in a line regiment he had become owner of
River Park with an income up in the fifty thousands.
And so he'd chucked the service, and now he was
taking to politics.

He was young—still on the right side of thirty-five:
ambitious, good-looking. And the path of life is smooth
for a good-looking unmarried baronet with fifty thousand a year. People prophesy smooth things in such
cases, and, strange to say, are generally justified in so
doing. Certainly the path that stretched ahead of John
Perton seemed very much the primrose one. If only
he could forget, if only . . . His fists clenched in his
pockets: he would forget. He had forgotten till that

fool Dicker had unearthed the story from Bimbo Charteris, second-in-command of his old regiment, and now staying with him at River Park. He had forgotten: except just sometimes when Bill Meyrick's face came to him out of the darkness. . . . At night, when he couldn't sleep, he'd see it and curse it foolishly. . . .

And yet he was perfectly safe. Nothing could ever happen; the cupboard of this particular skeleton was his brain. Bill Meyrick was dead: of that there could be no doubt. Even Monica was beginning to accept it now. . . . And that reminded him—he was lunching with Monica at the hotel that day. . . .

He glanced at his watch as he heard footsteps on the stairs outside. Twelve o'clock: he'd give this reporter fellow half an hour, and then—Monica. She liked him, he knew: wasn't he Bill Meyrick's best friend? And she'd been engaged to Bill. . . . But Bill had died two years ago. . . .

"This is Mr. Titmarsh, Sir John," announced Dicker.

"Pleased to meet you, Sir John," said the reporter taking the proffered hand. "From the little Mr Dicker has told me, it seems to me we've got the goods. And if we've got the goods you can rely upon yours truly to put 'em across."

"I have explained to Mr. Titmarsh, Sir John," said Mr. Dicker a little hastily, "that it will have to be done in the most tactful way. There is nothing a soldier dislikes more than appearing to buck about what he's done."

"A proof of the article shall be sent to you, Sir John, before it's inserted in the paper," announced Titmarsh. "And if there's a word in it that offends you—strike it out."

"I am sure that won't be necessary, Mr. Titmarsh," remarked Sir John quietly. "But really, you know,

there is very little to tell. The thing was quite a
trifling little affair."

"It's good enough for us, Sir John," said Dicker
firmly. "Now if you just run over the story, Titmarsh
will make notes."

With a slight shrug of his shoulders, Sir John Perton sat down. Then a little deliberately he lit a cigarette. After all—why not? If he didn't, Charteris
would. Tell the story, and tell it well: he was quite
a good raconteur if he chose to exert himself.

"We were on detachment," he began, "half a company of the Royal Loamshires. There were three
officers and ninety men—holding a strong point. We
took up our position at midday on a Tuesday, with
the understanding that we should be relieved the following day. There was no sign of any natives when
we got there—everything seemed perfectly peaceful.
And yet by Tuesday evening we were completely surrounded. The way the natives had used the scrub as
cover was simply amazing. We never saw a sign of
them until we realized they were all around us. Even
then we didn't see them—except an isolated one here
and there. We only knew by the firing.

"You must realize that we were on a little conical
hill: the sort of position that is a death-trap if there
is any artillery about, but we knew the natives had
none. Away to the east was a range of low foot-
hills, and we knew relief would come from that direction next day. And until it came all we had to do
was to hang on, which we didn't anticipate would
prove difficult. Without artillery the natives had but
little chance of dislodging us.

"We assumed they would try and rush us that
night and they did. But we'd withdrawn all the outlying pickets and formed a sort of Cæsar's camp at
the top of the hill and we beat them off easily."

Sir John was beginning to enjoy himself: the attention of his audience flattered him.

"Wednesday came and Wednesday went with its pitiless tropical sun, and still no sign of relief. Except for a little desultory sniping the natives didn't trouble us, but they were still there. And they remained there all Wednesday night, though they didn't try to attack us again. But we were beginning to look at one another, we three officers, and wonder. There had been a good deal of ammunition expended on Tuesday night, and if something had delayed the regiment seriously—what was going to happen. . . . It was pretty obvious that the natives thought they'd got us, and they weren't going to be such fools as to lose their lives attacking us, when all they had to do was to sit tight and starve us out.

"You see that was the trouble. Food and worse still—far worse—water. Thursday night—no relief, and the situation was critical. We'd heard sounds of intermittent firing from beyond the hills, but that was all. Came Friday, and the water question had become sheer hell. We had one petrol tin left with an armed guard over it. . . .

"The Commanding Officer had taken one in the arm, and we were up against it good and proper. We had about ten rounds a man left when the ammunition was equalized out, and by Saturday morning, it was reduced to five. They very nearly got us that night. . . ."

Sir John paused for a while; undoubtedly he was telling the yarn well.

"It was about midday on Saturday that Captain Seymour who was in command came to a decision. He called Mr. Meyrick—the other officer—and me to him in a little sandy bit at the top of the hill which we'd turned into company headquarters, and he put things to us straight. Not that it was necessary: we knew already.

" 'We may be able to hold out for one more night,' he said, 'but after that it's impossible. There will be no ammunition left—and no water. If the regiment comes to-day—well and good: if it doesn't come to-morrow—it's the end. Something must have delayed them, of course, but it's possible that they don't know the desperate position we're in. I therefore propose that one of you two should undertake the forlorn hope of getting through to the regiment. They must be over there beyond the hills.'

"I remember he wouldn't look at either of us.

" 'It's the most damnable thing I've ever had to do in my life,' he went on. 'Being in command here, I cannot go myself, and I take it hard that I have to suggest to one of you two what is practically certain death. Oh! God! Listen to that.'

"It was one of the signallers who'd gone mad and was screaming for water. He blew out his brains ten minutes later.

" 'Practically certain death,' he went on. 'But I cannot disregard the fact that there is a thousand to one chance on whoever goes getting through. And it is my bounden duty not to neglect that chance. I also cannot disregard the fact that it's certain death for all of us to-morrow night if the regiment doesn't come. Therefore I must ask you to decide between yourselves which of you shall make the attempt.'

"He left it at that, and Mr. Meyrick and I drew lots. We left it till a bit later, and then we cut. It was ace high—high goes, and he drew the ten of diamonds. I drew the four of spades."

He paused for a moment and stared out of the window.

"And that's about all."

"But did Mr. Meyrick get through, Sir John?" cried Titmarsh excitedly.

Sir John Perton shook his head a little sadly.

"That's the devil of it. He was my best friend, and it's two years since it happened. He's never been heard of since. And the cruel part is that had he waited all would have been well. Just as the sun was going down and the final rays were on the foothills we'd been watching so eagerly, I saw the flash of a heliograph. It was our relief. . . ."

He got up and crossed to the window.

"They came next morning, and there were twenty of us left. Captain Seymour had been killed by a chance bullet in the night, and they'd seen no sign of Mr. Meyrick."

He swung round a little deliberately.

"You will understand, gentlemen, that in many ways it is a very personal story. And I therefore must beg of you to treat it as such. I don't want there to be any hint, for instance, that I am the source of your information. There are, of course, many people in the regiment who know the story, and from whom you might have heard it. I would be obliged if you would let it be implied that that is how you got it."

"But of course," cried Mr. Dicker. "My dear Sir John, it would lose half its value if anyone had an inkling that you were our informant."

"Of course," echoed Titmarsh. "Leave it entirely to me, Sir John."

"I will," said the prospective candidate, with a pleasant smile. "And now, if you will excuse me, I have a small luncheon-party. Good day. Back at three, Dicker."

"Gorgeous," said Titmarsh as the door closed. "You were right, Mr. Dicker. Blazing sun: thirst: ammunition running out: the man who cut the four of spades. It's a cinch, old man. Let's go and have a spot."

The two men strolled along the street and turned into the County Hotel.

"A cinch, my boy: a dead snip, Dicker—what's that line I read somewhere. . . . Thanks, Miss; a little more soda in mine. . . . By some poet . . . Kipling —no not Kipling. . . . I'll get it in a moment . . . Wait: have got. . . .

" 'Scornful men who have diced with death under the naked skies.' "

A man with a big black beard who was standing close by turned round and stared at him.

"I'll put that in next week in the column," went on Titmarsh. "And then everybody will associate the two. The man who drew the four of spades: the man who diced with death. . . . It's worth a thousand votes." He broke off suddenly and stared through the door. "Hullo! Hullo! Hullo! behold the small luncheon-party! Isn't that Miss Stratton he's with?"

Mr. Dicker nodded.

"She's helping him. And I think, my boy," he added knowingly, "I think. . . . But not a word about that. . . . Well, I must be getting on."

"I'll have a proof ready by the evening," said Titmarsh, finishing his drink.

The glass doors swung to behind them, leaving the black-bearded man alone in the bar.

"And who may those two be?" he asked the barmaid.

"The little perky one is Mr. Titmarsh who is on the *Mercury* staff," she said. "And the other is Mr. Dicker who is acting as agent for Sir John for the coming election. Sir John Perton, you know: such a nice gentleman. Always a kind word and a pleasant smile for everyone."

The black-bearded man planked some money on the counter and strode towards the door.

"Which is more than some people 'ave," she fired at his retreating back. "A beaver," she continued darkly to space as she watched him go out into the street. "And a nasty black one. What's that? Two special Martinis for Sir John? We've only got one sort in here."

She turned to the waiter who had entered the bar.

"Did you see that black beaver? A perfect 'orror. Is Sir John lunching with Miss Stratton?"

"'E is," said the waiter.

"Has she got a ring on, yet?"

"Gaw lumme!" said the waiter, "there's about ten tables in there complaining about the beef. 'Ow would I know? Give me them cocktails."

"You ain't sat on a wasp, 'ave you? There they are, and don't splash 'em over with your shaking 'and."

"Shaking foot," retorted the waiter. "With the amount you put in a glass, it wouldn't splash over in a ruddy earthquake."

He hurried away with the drinks on a tray.

"Your special ones, Sir John," he announced as he placed them on the table.

"Thank you, Charles. And we'll have lunch in five minutes."

He watched the waiter hurry away, only to stop and speak to some people by the door. He saw the people glancing at him covertly and whispering. And a faint smile of satisfaction hovered for a moment round his lips. It was good to be Sir John Perton, fourteenth baronet, prospective member of Parliament: it was good to be having lunch with Monica Stratton. And he would not have been having lunch, nor would he have been fourteenth baronet, if . . . Confound old Bimbo Charteris bringing up that yarn again. Still

it might help him. . . . Clever chap, Dicker. . . .
But Monica must never know it was he who had told
it. . . . It would undoubtedly look a bit vulgar. Besides, Bill Meyrick: even now he wasn't quite certain
how she still felt about Bill. On that subject she
always dried up.

"I say, Monica," he said as they sat down to lunch,
"there's a thing I rather want to talk to you about.
Dicker has unearthed that old chestnut, when we were
on detachment."

"You mean when you and Bill cut——" said the
girl.

He nodded.

"He's got all the details—I think a chance remark
of Bimbo's first put him on the track: and a confounded little newspaper man called Titmarsh has been
buzzing round me like a fly all the morning. Well,
the long and the short of it is that I'm very much
afraid that it will all come out in this local rag, the
Mercury. And I thought I'd tell you at once because
——" he hesitated for a moment or two—"because I
wouldn't like you to think that I had anything to do
with it. At first I flatly refused to allow it, but Dicker
pointed out how futile it was. The *Mercury* people
are backing me for all they're worth, and it's what I
gather they call a stunt. They mean to print it whatever I say. So what I've done is to stipulate that I
shall see a proof before it's printed. And I'd like
you to see one, too. I'd just hate—dash it all, Monica,
you know what I mean——to make capital out of dear
old Bill's death."

The girl smiled a little sadly.

"I know that, John. But Bill, if he knew, wouldn't
mind. And if it helps you to get in, he'd just laugh
as he always used to."

Sir John heaved an inward sigh of relief: how very

wise he'd been to tell her.   Then he looked her straight in the face.

"After I'm in, Monica—or not, as the case may be —I'm going to ask you a certain question once again."

She met his glance gravely.

"I won't promise a satisfactory answer," she said.

"Dear, is there any good hoping any longer?" he cried.   "It's two years now: we'd at any rate have heard from the old chap by this time."

"I know that," she answered.   "And you've been wonderfully patient, John.   Only . . . I don't know. I just don't know.   Don't let's talk about it now, anyway.   The important thing to be done is to get you in.   And if that story does help, Bill will be so pleased."

And it did help.   Titmarsh worked it with a skill which earned him the whole-hearted admiration of Mr. Dicker.   Of what use to issue an official statement in an interview that it was nothing?   Just ordinary duty, a thing which had no bearing on the election: a thing which the Liberal candidate would have done himself.

Of course Sir John would say that: it was his natural modesty.   And the electors could visualize him, clean-cut, good-looking, scornfully "dicing with death under the naked skies."   But by no stretch of imagination could they see his opponent, Mr. Vockins, a retired grocer, doing anything of the sort.

"Dicing with death."   Titmarsh hugged himself over the flash of genius that had recalled that line. He'd had it in for the first time in the previous day's issue, and from information received it had gone right home.   It had made the citizens of Burchester sit up and take notice.   "Dicing with death."   That's the sort of member to have.

And the county regiment, too; great thing altogether. Fine man, Sir John: fine regiment: fine fellow, Titmarsh. . . .

He looked up as the door opened and the office-boy appeared.

"A man to see you, Mr. Titmarsh. Won't give no name."

Titmarsh removed his feet from the desk as a stranger came in. He was a black-bearded man, and the sub-editor felt vaguely conscious of having seen him somewhere before.

"Good morning," said the stranger quietly. "I was reading the *Mercury* this morning, and I was much interested in your article on Sir John Perton. I think I saw you two or three days ago in the County Hotel."

Titmarsh nodded: he had recalled him now.

"May I ask you one point?" continued the stranger. "You state that on the evening of the Saturday a helio-graph was seen from the neighbouring hills—the long-looked-for message, as you so graphically put it, which announced relief. Is that statement correct?"

"Of course it's correct," said Titmarsh stiffly. "Otherwise it wouldn't be there."

"I see," murmured the black-bearded man. "And since I assume you were not there yourself, may I ask how you discovered that interesting detail?"

"From Sir John himself," said Titmarsh truculently. "He personally supplied me with one or two trifling points of that sort. Anyway, what the deuce has it got to do with you?"

The black-bearded man smiled.

"What, indeed? Good morning."

He rose from his chair, and there was a strange look in his eyes.

"Sir John himself! Well, well, Mr. Titmarsh, that is at any rate first-hand information, isn't it? Have you any use in your paper for outside contributions? Of course—nothing of mine would be up to the standard of dicing with death and naked skies. Still, I may

send something along for your consideration in due
course.   And I can promise you it will at any rate
have the virtue of being topical—and true."

With a slight nod he left the office, leaving Titmarsh
staring after him.   What the devil was the fellow getting at?   Was he out for trouble, or what?   He reached
out for the telephone: should he ring up Dicker?   And
yet—what was the use?   What could the man do?
Heliograph: that was the signalling affair on which
the sun flashed.   And Sir John had distinctly said that
just before the sun went down he'd seen it.   The final
rays on the foothills: his very words.   No use ringing
up: he'd just mention it next time he saw Dicker.

And so no telephone-bell rang, and Sir John Perton
sat down to lunch half an hour later in ignorance of
the fact that a black-bearded man who had been interested in heliographs was even then approaching
River Park.

It was a small luncheon—just the house-party con-
sisting of Bimbo Charteris, Lady Stratton and Monica.
And conversation centred round the coming election.

"I wish to heaven he'd never got hold of the yarn,"
said Sir John.   " 'Scornful men . . .'   Think of it, my
dear people.   The little blighter never told me he was
going to put that in."

"Doesn't matter, John," barked Lady Stratton.
"Anything to keep that fearful grocer out.   He's just
one of the new bunch of war profiteers.   Out of the
bottom drawer the whole lot.   Got no use for 'em.
They eat peas with a knife and talk about serviettes."

"For heaven's sake don't start mother off on that
topic," laughed Monica, "or she'll never finish her
lunch."

"Lady Stratton's quite right, old man," said Bimbo.
"You're the type of fellow we want in Parliament
to-day."

"And after all, John," put in Monica, "it was a fine show. I know you like to pretend it was nothing: Bill would do the same if the cards had gone the other way. But the fact remains that you two did dice with death, and though it may sound a bit melodramatic in cold blood at lunch or in a newspaper, it was a fine show. It catches the imagination."

"It does that all right," laughed Sir John. "If only they hadn't called me a scornful man. What is it, Jackson?"

He turned to the butler, who was standing beside him with a note on a salver.

"A gentleman has just brought this, Sir John. He would like to see you, but he wished you to have this note first."

"Will you excuse me?" Sir John took the envelope and slit it open. "Truly the worries of a prospective candidate never cease."

"Until you're in," said Lady Stratton. "Then you can sleep for years."

She paused suddenly and stared at her host. "What on earth is the matter with you, John? You look as if you were going to faint."

And assuredly Sir John Perton's face was ghastly. Every vestige of colour had left it, and he swallowed once or twice as if he were choking. The opened envelope had fluttered to the floor at his feet, and in his shaking hand he held the enclosure. It was an ordinary playing card, and Bimbo Charteris, who had involuntarily risen to his feet, glanced at it.

It was the king of hearts.

"What is it, John?" cried Monica anxiously.

"Nothing," stammered her host. "Nothing. Only, I must see this man. Will you excuse me, please?"

He pushed back his chair, and rose a little unsteadily. "Outside the front door, you say?"

And then he staggered back and leaned against the table. A black-bearded man was standing in the doorway. For perhaps the space of five seconds there was silence, and then the girl gave a little cry.

"Why, it's Bill!"

"Great Scott!" said Bimbo dazedly. "So it is!"

And once again silence settled on the room. For the man at the door said nothing: he merely stared at Sir John Perton.

"You don't seem very glad to see me, John," he said at length.

"It's a bit unexpected," stammered the other. "I thought you were dead."

"We all did, Bill, dear," said the girl, going up to him and laying her hand on his arm.

For a moment his eyes softened as he looked at her; then, with a little movement, he forced himself from her hand.

"For heaven's sake don't all stand about by the door in the middle of lunch," cried Lady Stratton. "Come and sit down, all of you. John, tell that man of yours to give me some more food, and then send him out of the room."

With shrewd old eyes that missed nothing, Lady Stratton watched her hoped-for son-in-law struggling to regain his self-control. His agitation had not been a pretty thing to see; in fact, it had been out of all proportion to what might have been expected owing to the complications that would now inevitably arise over Monica.

"What's happened?" she said in a hoarse whisper to Bimbo Charteris.

"I wish to God I knew, Lady Stratton," he answered, and his eyes were troubled.

"So you thought I was dead," said Bill Meyrick, taking the chair that Jackson had placed for him before leaving the room. "Well, as you see, I'm not. They didn't kill me: they only tortured me."

"Bill—my dear!" The girl gave a little cry.

"They tortured me day in, day out, for eighteen long months. Would you have liked to be tortured for eighteen months, John?"

Sir John Perton stared at him with haggard eyes and did not speak.

"Answer me, damn you!" snarled Meyrick.

"Steady on, Bill," said Charteris quietly. "Remember there are ladies here."

"I apologize," answered the other. "But two years of hell is apt to make one forget social amenities."

"Confound your social amenities, Bill," cried Charteris. "What's on your chest? What's all this mysterious business mean? What the dickens is this king of hearts doing?"

He bent over and picked up the card.

"You want to know the reason of the king of hearts? Why not ask John? You saw the effect it had on him."

But Sir John Perton sat motionless, with his face buried in his hands.

"There is one thing which two years' hell does for a man, Charteris. It may not be good or pretty, but it breeds a desire for revenge on the person responsible."

The girl caught her breath sharply.

"You speak strange words, Bill Meyrick," said Lady Stratton gravely. "Don't beat about the bush any more. We know what happened. You cut for it—you two—and you lost. What more is there to be said?"

"You drew the ten of diamonds, Bill," said Charteris. "And John drew the four of spades."

"Did you draw the four of spades, John?" said Meyrick quietly.

And suddenly they understood.

"Oh, my God!" said the girl, and Charteris's face was grey.

"We borrowed Private Atkinson's pack of cards, you may remember, John," went on Meyrick. "And I cut first. It was ace high——high goes. I drew the ten of diamonds. We joked about it; that put the chances definitely in your favour. And even as we joked your hands were trembling and your mouth was dry. You'd discussed your feelings pretty freely with me that afternoon——your rage and annoyance at being scuppered on a little sideshow of that description. You had a title to come and much money. It all seemed so utterly not worth while. Why the devil hadn't you chucked immediately after the big war? But on this miserable little show——who cared? Who at home even knew about it? I remember you harped on that point; it was always a failing of yours, John——your love of the limelight. You'd harped on it so much that your nerves were like fiddle-strings that day——and I knew they were like fiddle-strings. So I offered to go without cutting; but you wouldn't have that. Certainly not; appearances must be kept up. And then I cut the ten of diamonds. I saw that wild hope in your face, John, as you saw my card. Surely you wouldn't draw higher than that. For you were afraid, John; sick with fear at the thought of going. So was I."

For a while he paused, but the man at the head of the table gave no sign.

"And then someone in my platoon shouted. It was Adams; he'd been hit, but I thought it might be an attack. So I went to the edge of that little sandy plateau to see. And my back was to you, John, when you drew. What card did you draw, you cur; tell them what card you drew. You won't; what matter? They know. You drew the king of hearts, and you were trying to put it back as I turned round. With your fumbling hand you'd got out the four of spades, and for a moment you tried to bluff it off. But I got you by the wrist, John, and when I taxed you with it you broke down. Sobbed like a child. . . . I didn't blame you for that; anybody might have croaked. But to cheat a man who was your friend was not a good thing to do. . . ."

Once again he broke off, and for a long while no one spoke. And then Bimbo Charteris rose.

"Have you anything to say, Perton?"

"I haven't quite finished, Charteris," said Meyrick. "There is worse to come. What was my last word to you, John? I will refresh your memory. I said —'There's five minutes more of sunshine, John, and then the darkness will hide your shame.' And during that five minutes something happened, didn't it?"

The two women looked at him uncomprehendingly, but on Bimbo Charteris's face had come a look of scorn immeasurable. He understood.

"Oh! you cur," he muttered; "you damnable cur. You always said he'd been gone for twenty minutes or half an hour."

"But I don't follow, Bill," cried Monica. "What happened?"

"During that five minutes, Monica, John saw the helio on the hills to the east. And he never called me back. The direction I'd taken prevented me seeing it—and he never called me back though he could easily have done so. I didn't find that out till I read the interesting article in the *Mercury*, John. I have thought of you these two years merely as a cheat, and not as a would-be murderer also."

And then at long last Sir John Perton rose to his feet. His face was white and his hands trembled, though his voice was steady.

"I'm in your hands, Meyrick. I admit it all. I

cheated you, and then I let you go to your death to
keep it dark.   My only excuse is that I wasn't responsible for my actions, and that is not a man's excuse.
What are you going to do?"

Bill Meyrick stared at him thoughtfully.

" 'Scornful men who have diced with death,' " he
quoted.   "Shall I tell 'em the dice were loaded, John?
A nice article in the *Mercury*?"

Bimbo Charteris swung round.

"The regiment, Bill.   You're still one of us."

"But he's not," snapped Meyrick.

"He was when it happened."

And then Bill Meyrick felt the girl's hand on his
arm.

"Bill, dear, there's another thing you still are—
engaged to me.   Unless you want to break it off."

"Break it off!" he cried.   "Why, the worst torture
I've had has been the thought that when I did escape
I'd find you married."

The hardness had gone out of his eyes as he looked
at her.

"I'll do what you say, Monica."

"No, dear.   You'll do what you always, in the
bottom of your heart, meant to do—the big thing.
Why did you go, Bill, after you'd found he'd
cheated?"

"Because he wasn't fit to go himself."

"Because you're a bigger man than he is.   I've
always known it.   Why not let it rest at that?   He's
punished enough already."

She pushed back her chair and rose.

"Let's go, Bill.   We've two years to make up."

*   *   *   *   *

Which is the true story of why Sir John Perton,
fourteenth baronet, decided at the last moment not to

contest the constituency of Burchester, and went abroad for an indefinite period after letting River Park to his rival Mr. Vockins.

XLVIII   THE OTHER SIDE OF THE WALL

"THIS afternoon," remarked the celebrated doctor, "I have had one of the most salutary lessons of my life."

He carefully cut the end of his cigar, and his keen sensitive face seemed unduly serious.

"You've all of you at one time or another," he went on, "felt with regard to something you've just done— 'That is very good. I, personally, have done it very well. I am a big man, or, at any rate, a distinctly bigger man than my neighbour.' Of course, wild horses wouldn't drag such an admission from any of us. Should an acquaintance mention the fact of our bigness, we wave a deprecating hand. But we also regard that acquaintance as a distinctly observant fellow, whose own good points we have scarcely done justice to up to date. And we strut a little, and puff out our mental chests, while the gods above laugh. They always laugh—we're so damned comical—but very often we don't hear the laughter. This afternoon I did.

"It was two years ago almost to the day that a card was brought to me in my consulting-room. The name was unfamiliar; the man had not got an appointment, and it was after my usual hours. And for a few moments I debated as to whether I would see him or not. I was a bit tired—I'd had a ticklish operation that morning—and I was leaving London next day for a month's holiday.

"I suppose my indecision was obvious as I turned the

card over in my fingers, for my secretary suddenly spoke:

" 'I told him, Sir John,' she said apologetically, 'that I didn't think you would see him, and that you were going away to-morrow, but he seemed so terribly distressed that I hadn't the heart to refuse to bring you his card.'

" 'Show him in,' I said, and the next moment I was shaking hands with Mr. Robert Tremlin.

"He was a man of about forty—clean-shaven and dark. He was turning a bit grey over the temples, but his whole bearing and appearance proclaimed him an out-of-doors man.

" 'It's very good of you to see me, Sir John,' he said, as he sat down on the other side of my desk. 'But I really am in the most desperate trouble, and I feel I can't go on much longer. It's about my wife.

" 'I don't know if you saw in the papers a fortnight ago the account of a terrible motor accident in Devonshire. At any rate, there was one, and the car in question was mine. It contained my wife and Gerald Weymouth—a very dear friend of us both. He, poor chap, was driving when it happened, and there was no one else in the car. He was taking her over to play tennis with some friends of ours who live about ten miles away, and there is one extremely bad hill to go down. What happened no one will ever know. Gerald was an extremely good driver; moreover, he had often driven the car before. Presumably the brakes failed to act, and the car got out of control on this hill. There's a turn half-way down, with a couple of big trees beside the road, and into these two trees the car crashed. Gerald was killed instantaneously, but by some merciful act of Providence my wife was thrown clear. The car slewed sideways after the accident, and she wasn't even cut by the windscreen. She was just pitched over the door—the car was an open one—and landed on her head on the grass. And when the people from a neighbouring house came rushing up they found her there, unconscious, but otherwise apparently unhurt, save for a few bruises. The car was like scrap-iron, and poor old Gerald was dead.

" 'They carried her into their house, Sir John, and telephoned for a doctor and for me. By the time I got there he had already made his examination, and he met me at the door.

" ' "A miraculous escape, Mr. Tremlin," he said gravely. "Of course, your wife is still unconscious, but there is no need to let that alarm you. The great thing is that there is nothing broken, and when she comes to herself again, I think we shall find that beyond a severe shaking there is nothing the matter. Only, in view of the appalling nervous shock she must have had before the crash came, I consider it would be most ill-advised to tell her of Mr. Weymouth's death. She will, of course, have to know in time, but until she has fully recovered from the shock, she should be kept in ignorance of what has happened. If she asks any questions we can easily say that his leg was broken— or something of that sort—and that he has been taken to a hospital in Exeter."

" ' "Can I see her, doctor?" I asked eagerly.

" ' "Certainly," he answered. "She naturally won't know you as she is unconscious; but I repeat there is nothing to be alarmed at."

" 'So I went and saw her, and then I went out to see what remained of Gerald Weymouth. My greatest friend, Sir John; he'd been best man at my wedding; and now . . . However, I don't want to bore you with all that; sufficient to say that it must have been instantaneous, thank God!

" 'I must come to the point.'

"My visitor moistened his lips, and I pushed over a box of cigarettes.

" 'Smoke, if you care to, Mr. Tremlin,' I said. 'I shall see no one else to-night.'

"He took a cigarette and lit it, and his hand was shaking.

" 'My wife recovered consciousness the following morning, Sir John,' he went on after a while. 'I wasn't with her at the moment, but the nurse who had been sent for came and told me. We were both in the same house to which she had been taken after the accident; it belonged to friends, and the doctor didn't want her moved. I went at once to her room and found her sitting up in bed. She just stared at me blankly for a moment or two, and then turned to the nurse.

" ' "Where am I?" she said. "And who is this man? Have I been ill?"

" 'I knelt down beside her, and started to explain.

" ' "There's been an accident, darling," I told her. "You're in the Ashbys' house."

" 'But she still stared at me blankly, and after a while it became obvious that I was only distressing her by remaining. So I left the room, and waited until the doctor came.'

" 'Did she know the doctor?' I asked him.

"Mr. Tremlin shook his head.

" 'She knew no one: she knows no one now. And this is where I come to the distressing part for me personally. All through this last fortnight she has shown an ever-increasing aversion to me. I may say, Sir John, without fear of contradiction, that ours has been a wonderfully happy married life. That's what makes it so hard to understand. I adore her, and I think I can say that she feels the same for me. Or rather felt the same, until this ghastly thing took place. Now she can't bear me in the same room with her.'

" 'Have you any children?' I asked him.

" 'None,' he answered.

" 'And where is your wife now?'

" 'Still in the same house with the Ashbys.'

" 'Well, Mr. Tremlin,' I said, 'from what you tell me your wife seems to be suffering from complete loss of memory. Her aversion to you is not an uncommon feature of such cases, so you may reassure your mind on that point. A dislike to those who are nearest and dearest is a frequent symptom of brain trouble, and when memory returns the feeling is blotted off the slate and vanishes like a dream.'

" 'But when will her memory return?' he burst out. 'Sir John, this is absolutely killing me. A fortnight has passed, and there is no trace of improvement. Doctor Rodgers assures me that it is only a question of time, and that we can do nothing except wait. But though I have the greatest faith in him as an ordinary practitioner, a case of this sort is out of his beaten track. It stands to reason it must be. And that is why I've come to you. I was going to ask you to come down and see my wife, but your secretary tells me that you are going on your holiday to-morrow. Well now, I've got an idea. I don't know what plans you've made, but would it be possible for you to spend a few days with me at my house? I can give you some fishing: there are four or five horses it would be a kindness for you to exercise: and there's golf. And then perhaps you could examine my wife, and tell me what you think.'

"Well, I hadn't made any plans that couldn't be broken, and the long and short of it was that I promised to go. The poor devil was pathetically grateful, and we arranged to travel down together the next day."

The celebrated doctor blew out a cloud of smoke thoughtfully.

"So much for Mr. Robert Tremlin; now for his wife. She was an extraordinarily pretty woman about seven years younger than him, and when you met her there was absolutely nothing to indicate that anything was amiss. Tremlin motored me over to the Ashbys' house the day after I arrived—which necessitated incidentally going down the hill where the accident had occurred. The marks of the car on the trees were still plainly visible, and he showed me exactly where his wife had been pitched to. And, by Jove! you fellows, when I saw the gradient, and reconstructed the accident in my mind, it seemed inconceivable that she should have escaped death. However, that is by the way.

"Doctor Rodgers was waiting for us when we arrived, and he could only shake his head at my host's eager question.

" 'Just the same, I'm afraid, Mr. Tremlin.'

"He turned away wearily

" 'I'll wait for you in the car, Sir John,' he said.

" 'A very strange case,' said the local doctor, drawing me into a room off the hall. 'I make no pretensions to be a specialist or expert in brain matters, but I am prepared to stake my reputation on this being no case for an operation. I can find no trace of local pressure anywhere which would account for it.'

" 'A case of severe shock producing complete loss of memory,' I remarked. 'And, of course, in such cases the trouble may last for years.'

" 'Precisely,' he answered gravely. 'Though naturally I haven't told him so. It's pathetic, Sir John, quite pathetic. I think they were the most ideally happy couple I have ever met. His devotion to her was almost dog-like, and since the accident it's really been harrowing to see the way he has suffered. With his brain he understands the reason of it; with his heart he can't understand why he, of all people, should have been singled out for this acute dislike. Because it has turned to that now. To such an extent, in fact, that I have had to forbid him even to see her. And there's another thing too. . . . However, I don't think I'll mention it. I'd like to see if you notice it yourself, or whether it's my imagination. Shall we go up?'

"She was fully dressed, and as we entered the room she turned her head eagerly to look at us. As I've said she was a strikingly lovely woman, and her whole face was lit up with anticipation. And the next second the look had completely vanished: her expression was quite lifeless again. It was most noticeable, and I seized on it at once.

" 'Good morning,' I said. 'Are you expecting someone?'

" 'Yes, I am,' she answered.

" 'Who is it?' I asked.

" 'I don't know his name,' she replied wearily.

" 'Can you describe him? Because perhaps we can get hold of him for you.'

"But she seemed to have lost interest in the matter, and I could get nothing coherent out of her at all. She submitted to my examination listlessly, and after a while we went out and left her alone.

" 'There's no mistaking it, is there?' said Rodgers. 'I thought it might be my imagination, but I've never seen it so clearly. And I've never spoken about it to her as you did.'

" 'You mean that look of expectation on her face,' I said. 'If we could find out who it was and produce him, it might do the trick.'

" 'Well, it's certainly not her husband,' said he grimly. 'However, what do you make of the case?'

"I won't weary you with professional shop, beyond

saying that I concurred with him over the question of
the operation.   I could find no trace of pressure anywhere, and I told her husband so.   It was a strange
case, but by no manner of means an unique one.   We
were up, so to speak, against a blank wall.   All that
she knew and remembered was the fortnight or so of
her life that lay on this side of it: we had somehow
to get her to the other side.

" 'Is it going to be a long job, Sir John?' he asked
me.

" 'There's no good buoying you up with false hopes,'
I said.   'I can't tell you.   I don't know.   It might be
that she will waken to-morrow morning perfectly normal; it might be—years.'

" 'Oh! my God!' he muttered under his breath.

" 'Anyway, the first thing to do is to get her back to
her own house.   The familiar surroundings there may
help her to get to the other side of the wall.   And once
we've got her there we've taken an enormous step
forward.'

"So Mrs. Tremlin returned to Redlands that day,
and I watched her with the greatest curiosity.   In
fact that night I went to bed considerably more hopeful.
She had walked, for instance, out of the hall straight
into the drawing-room and sat down in the chair which,
her husband told me, she generally used.   She had
seemed, in a way, to recognize the servants; at any
rate she had accepted them.   And she had gone upstairs to her bedroom without having to be shown the
way.

"But there it ended.   Amazing though it seemed she
still failed to recognize her husband, and the poor devil
was almost distracted.   In vain to point out to him the
vagaries of the brain; he couldn't get beyond the fact
that there must be some glimmerings in her mind of
what lay on the other side of the wall, if she could find

her own way to her bedroom. And if that was the case, why was the most important thing in her life—her marriage to him—hidden from her?

"I think it was the second day after she came home, that I found her in her husband's study. I'd had to tell him to keep out of the way as much as possible, because although she no longer displayed actual aversion to him, his presence worried her. She had her meals with us, since my chief idea was that everything should proceed exactly as it had before the accident. And at table she didn't seem to mind him. It was only when he got close to her that she began to get fidgety.

"And now she was standing by his desk holding a big photograph in her hand. There was a queer excited look on her face as she turned to me, and I was instantly reminded of the first time I'd seen her.

" 'Who is this man?' she said.

"As a matter of fact the very first night I arrived Tremlin had told me.

" 'That's Gerald Weymouth,' I answered. 'Do you know him?'

" 'Where is he?' she cried, taking no notice of my question. 'I want to see him.'

" 'Is he the man you were expecting?' I said. 'The man whose name you forgot.'

" 'I think so,' she answered, passing her hand over her forehead. 'It's all so muddly. I seem to remember. . . . Gerald Weymouth. . . . Gerald.'

"Her voice died away, and I didn't press her. To excite a case of that sort is fatal, but it started me off on a new line of thought. And that night I mentioned it to her husband.

" 'It may be,' I said, 'that those few ghastly seconds, whilst the car was dashing down the hill, and she was facing what must have seemed to her to be certain death, have imprinted on her mind a recollection of him. How clear it is, I can't tell—but it's there. And if only she could see Weymouth now it might save her.'

" 'Since the poor old chap is dead and buried,' he said wearily, 'I'm afraid that doesn't advance us much, Sir John.'

" 'I know all that,' I answered. 'The point is—how clear is that recollection? Would it be possible to get a substitute?'

"He sat up with the light of hope dawning in his eyes.

" 'What do you mean?' he said.

" 'It's only a vague idea, Mr. Tremlin,' I answered. 'And I haven't even begun to think out the details. Have you ever heard the story of the man who was driving with his servant along a road he rarely used? And as they went over a rather noticeable wooden bridge, he said to his servant—"Do you like eggs?" And the servant answered, "Yes, sir." A few months later he again drove over the same bridge, not having been on that road in the interval. And as the trap got to exactly the same spot where he had put the first question, he said, "How do you like them?" And the servant answered, "Fairly hard-boiled, sir." '

"He stared at me as if I had taken leave of my senses.

" 'I assure you I'm quite serious,' I said. 'Whether the story is true or not is immaterial, but it illustrates a very well-known law—the law of Inherent Connection. The second question was put under exactly similar conditions to the first, and although there was a lapse of months between the two—for the fraction of a second that lapse was non-existent in the servant's mind. Subconsciously his surroundings recalled the first question, just as the second was put to him. Now I am wondering if we could do something of that sort in the case of your wife.'

" 'I'm afraid I must be very dense,' he said, 'but for the life of me I don't see what you're driving at.'

" 'I'm driving at this. You'll agree that for a man to ask his servant suddenly if he likes eggs and then to say no more is a peculiar thing to do. And its very peculiarity stamped itself on his servant's mind, so that when identical conditions were repeated, it immediately came to his thoughts. Moreover, it came in such a way and so naturally that his answer to the second question was quite spontaneous. Now suppose, Mr. Tremlin, we could reproduce the exact conditions which led up to the accident—let us say from the time your wife and Weymouth left the house in the car to the moment when the crash came. *Only, this time there will be no crash.*'

"He was staring at me fixedly now: he was beginning to get the idea.

" 'Understand: it's only an experiment. It may do no good; but I don't think it can do any harm. And if it's successful we shall have got your wife to the other side of the wall. She will come up to it, as she did on the day of the accident; but this time she will go through it and come out on the other side.'

" 'Man,' he cried, 'do you think there's a chance?'

" 'I certainly think there's a chance,' I said.

" 'But how can we arrange about Gerald?'

" 'There lies the principal difficulty, I admit. At the same time, I think it quite possible that a reasonable likeness will be sufficient for the purpose if all the other details are exact.'

" 'He was wearing flannels and a big white blanket coat. And he also had on a pair of motoring-goggles. By Jove! Sir John,' he almost shouted in his excitement, 'if you put on a small black moustache, I believe you could do it yourself. You're greyer, of course— but a hat conceals that; and your eyes are quite different

—which doesn't matter, either, behind goggles. You're exactly the same height and build, and your voices are much the same.'

"He was pacing feverishly up and down the room.

" 'By gad, man!—you've given me hope. Don't let's dream of failure: don't let's even mention the word. You're going to succeed: I know it.'

"And then we set to work to discuss details. The first thing was to get another Panler car—an exact replica of the one that was smashed. He wired for that in the morning. Then we had to find out as nearly as possible precisely what took place before they started. The butler could help there, for Tremlin himself had been out for lunch. So we called him in and explained the situation.

" 'I remember perfectly, sir,' he said. 'Mr. Weymouth drove the car up to the front door, which was open. He got out and entered the house, speaking to me as he passed. Mrs. Tremlin was in the drawing-room, and Mr. Weymouth went to the door and opened it. I heard him say, "Are you ready, Monica?" Then she came out, and I handed her her racket and shoes as I opened the door of the car. I said to her, "Shall I put them behind, ma'am?" and she said, "Oh! it doesn't matter: there's plenty of room here." Then they drove off.'

" 'A point to remember,' cried Tremlin. 'There was a tonneau cover over the back seats.'

" 'That is so, sir,' said the butler.

"Well, we sat far into the night discussing details, and by the time I went to bed I was as excited as he was. The whole scheme, which had started as just a vague idea, began to crystallize in my mind: I realized the possibilities. Of course, the fact that I had to play the part of Weymouth was the weak link, but during the next week, under Tremlin's direction, I managed to get his voice more or less. Also, we had two dress rehearsals for appearance. We had down a man from London who was an expert in the art of making-up, and with the help of photographs and Tremlin's criticism he turned me into a very creditable replica of Weymouth.

"And then we had to wait for the right day. I insisted on that: it must be the same sort of weather. The day of the accident had been sunny and warm; as luck would have it we had a fortnight of dull, overcast days. The car had arrived and was being kept in the local garage, from which I had driven it once or twice to get accustomed to it.

"I had left Redlands myself, and taken rooms in the local inn, as I thought it better that Mrs. Tremlin should see nothing of me. I formed no part of her pre-accident existence, and that was the atmosphere in which I wanted her steeped.

"And then at last there came the morning when her husband burst in on me at breakfast.

" 'It was just such a day as this,' he cried, and he was shaking like a man with the ague.

" 'Steady, Tremlin,' I said warningly. 'We've all got to keep cool.'

"And, truth to tell, I wasn't feeling too cool myself. Even with all our carefully arranged details there was still such a lot that must be left to chance. However, there was no question of backing out of it, and so we got on with our final preparations. Tremlin was in such a state of pitiful excitement and agitation that he was worse than useless: in spite of my warnings he was banking everything on success. And he had the hardest part, poor devil: he couldn't be there to see what happened. The butler had been carefully coached; the whole staff had been warned just to behave normally.

"The man from London started on my face in the morning, reserving the final touches till after lunch, which Tremlin had with me. But he couldn't eat anything, and it was with a feeling of relief that I saw him go after the meal. He was getting on my nerves rather badly.

"And then, at two o'clock, I left and drove up to the house. Every detail in the car was correct—side-wings, two spare wheels, tonneau cover, everything. The expert from London had done his work well, for the butler gave a positive start as he saw me.

" 'Magnificent, Sir John,' he whispered. 'You're the living image of Mr. Weymouth.'

" 'Where is she?' I asked.

" 'In the drawing-room, Sir John. I took the coffee there after lunch, as you told me.'

"So far, so good: that had been one of the many difficulties to contend with.

" 'And she has on a similar dress, Sir John: her maid managed that.'

" 'Excellent,' I said. 'You've got the racket and shoes? Then we'll get on with it.'

"Nervous, you fellows—I was as nervous as a cat. Would the whole thing, after all the trouble we'd taken, be a ghastly failure? However, there was no use hesitating, so I went to the drawing-room door and opened it.

" 'Are you ready, Monica?' I said.

"It was the crucial moment, and I saw a look of dawning amazement come into her eyes, to be replaced almost at once by an expression which defeated me. At least, it defeated me in one way only: it defeated me when I saw it on the face of a woman who was devotedly attached to her husband. Except from that point of view its meaning was too obvious.

"I stood aside, feverishly trying to think out this new and unexpected development. Then she passed me and walked quite normally towards the car. The butler was splendid: there was not a hint of hesitation in his voice as he opened the door for her.

" 'Shall I put them behind, ma'am?'

" 'Oh! it doesn't matter: there's plenty of room here.'

"And we drove off.

" 'Gerry, darling,' she said, 'I thought you were coming to lunch. You said you would.'

"Now here was the devil and all of a predicament. I had assumed that I might have to reply to an ordinary disjointed conversation on general topics; but a love-affair, and a serious one, was a different matter altogether. And I was just racking my brains as to what I should say when she spoke again.

" 'I know you couldn't help it, dear heart: but I grudge every moment you're away from me.'

"For a moment I was surprised; then I realized that once again luck was with us. She didn't require any answers from me: the answers were already there in her brain. And for the next quarter of an hour I drove in silence listening to what, to all intents and purposes, was one person speaking on a telephone.

"It wasn't pleasant, I assure you. It was obvious that Mr. Gerald Weymouth had been a pretty useful swine. Certain it was that he had eaten Mr. Tremlin's salt, and then done him the greatest injury one man may do another. Certain it was, also, that he had had no intention whatever of sacrificing his freedom and becoming involved in the meshes of the divorce court. There was no need for his answers to be spoken aloud: they were obvious without that. His career, unnecessary scandal, poor old Bob's feelings—all the old, old stunts rattled off glibly.

"And suddenly a feeling of awe came over me. Just so had this thing happened a month previously: and even as the man I represented talked of his career, death was five minutes away from him. And then my professional instincts took charge: it was so wonderfully interesting. I hardly heard some of what she said: I was so frightfully keen to see what was going to happen when we got to the hill.

" 'Why did you do it, Gerry?' Her voice suddenly arrested me. 'I used to love him so much, and now I can't bear him near me.'

"The doctor in me noted that point: the strange aversion was accounted for.

" 'Of course, I disguise it—but I can't go on. You've—you've bewitched me.'

"And now we were at the top of the hill.

" 'Gerry—be careful. Not too fast down here. . . . What's the matter—brakes gone? My God! Gerry —turn her: turn her into the bank. . . .'

"I was letting her down pretty fast, you'll understand.

" 'Turn her, Gerry.' Her voice rose to a shriek. 'Slip in a lower gear. Oh God!—you've lost your head. Bob wouldn't have . . . Bob . . .'

"Her weight fell heavily against me—she'd fainted: the car was past the two trees. I pulled up, and laid her on the grass beside the road. Then I ripped off my disguise and brought her round. Now we should see whether it was success or failure.

"She stared at me wonderingly.

" 'Who are you?' she said at length.

" 'My name is Sir John Caston,' I answered. 'I'm a doctor.'

" 'But what on earth——' she stammered in amazement.

" 'Listen, Mrs. Tremlin,' I said quietly, 'and I'll explain things. You had a very bad accident some weeks ago, and were thrown out of a car on your head. Mr. Weymouth was driving you. . . .'

" 'But he's just been driving me——'

" 'Oh, no!' I said. 'I've been driving you. Perhaps

you imagined it was Mr. Weymouth.   You had a nasty
knock on the head, you know, and that produces
delusions.'

"'But I've been talking to him to-day.'

"I smiled, and shook my head and lied.

"'You haven't said a word since you left the house,'
I remarked.   'You've had a very vivid dream—that's
all.'

"'I don't understand,' she said wearily.

"'And I don't want you to try to,' I answered.
'Don't worry your head about it at all.   Let's get on
back and see your husband.'

"'Bob! Yes—Bob wouldn't have lost his head.'

"And that was all she said.   She got into the car,
and we drove back quietly.   I talked on outside topics
and she answered quite coherently: the thing was a
success.   She had got to the other side of the wall."

The celebrated doctor rose and mixed himself a
whisky and soda; then he stood with his back to the
fire-place, looking down at us.

"An utter, complete success," he repeated.   "Little
by little we broke the truth to her, and she took it
normally and calmly—even to Gerald Weymouth's
death.   But the morning I went she asked me a question.

"'That dream, Sir John; that terrible dream, when
I thought you were Gerald.   You're sure I didn't say
anything?'

"'Perfectly sure,' I answered calmly.

"And under her breath I heard her say, 'Thank
God!'

"All that was two years ago, and at intervals I have
said to myself—'Good.   You did that very well.   No
one knows her secret, save you: you have restored her
to her normal mind, and from information received
they are still a devoted couple.   In fact, you are distinctly worthy of a pat on the back.'   And during those

two years the gods have been laughing: this afternoon I heard their mirth.

"I lunched with them both at the Ritz, and afterwards she had to go out shopping. So I sat on talking to him.

" 'Pretty satisfactory, Tremlin,' I said, full of the righteous glow of *fine champagne*.' 'I'm proud of that little experiment of ours.'

" 'Are you,' he said, with a twisted sort of smile.

" 'But, dash it, man,' I said, aggrieved. 'Aren't you?'

"He looked at me, and his eyes were weary.

" 'At any rate she called for me when she thought the end was coming.'

"I positively stuttered at him.

" 'What, under the sun, do you mean?'

" 'Only that I was hidden under the tonneau cover at the back.' "

XLIX   THE HAUNTING OF JACK BURNHAM

"IT'S an amazing story," said the doctor, "and I don't profess to account for it. Just one of those experiences which come out of the unexplored realms, and leave one utterly at a loss for any explanation. You remember Kipling's story of the man who was haunted by the ghost of the woman he'd lived with and chucked, and who went mad and died with the horror of it. Well, this might have ended the same way.

"We were at Rugby together—Jack Burnham and I. Went there the same term; were put into the same form; and were both at the same house. And there we laid the foundation of a friendship which has lasted till to-day. It was built somewhat on the law of opposites, for our characters and attainments are totally different. And the divergence was perhaps more noticeable at school than in later years. He was a magnificent athlete—a boy who stood out as a games player above the average; whereas I was always a mediocre performer. He was in the eleven and the fifteen before he was sixteen, and his physical strength was phenomenal for a boy of his age. Moreover, he was intensely matter of fact, with the temperament that enabled him to go in to bat at a crucial stage in a cricket match with the same sang-froid as he would have when batting at the nets. It's important—that point; it makes what is to come the more inexplicable.

"His father died when he was up at Oxford, leaving him quite comfortably off. I suppose Jack had four thousand a year, which relieved him of the necessity of earning his own living. It was just as well, perhaps, because I don't think the old chap would ever have set the Thames on fire by his intellectual attainments. Moreover, it enabled him to become what he'd always been at heart—a wanderer.

"If ever a man had the *wanderlust* developed in him, it was Jack Burnham. He would disappear for years at a time, leaving no address behind him—only to pop up again in London as suddenly as he'd gone. And he was one of those fellows with whom one could pick up the threads just as if they had never been broken.

"I'd been installed in Harley Street about three years when the story I'm going to tell you began. Jack had been away for eighteen months, in the North of Africa somewhere, and, strangely enough, I was thinking of him and wondering where he was when the door opened and in he walked.

"My consulting hours were over, and I got up joyfully to greet him.

" 'My dear old man,' I cried, 'this is great.'

"And then I saw his face clearly, and stopped short. There was a strained, haggard look in his eyes which I'd never seen before, and I realized at once that something was the matter.

" 'Bill,' he said abruptly as he shook hands, 'I want you to dine with me to-night. I think I'm going mad.'

" 'Is that the reason of the invitation, old boy,' I said lightly. 'You're looking a bit fine drawn. What about dining quietly with me here?'

" 'Excellent. I'd love to.'

"I went over and rang the bell, and I was watching him all the time. He kept glancing into different corners of the room, and once he swung round suddenly and stared over his shoulder. Nerves evidently like fiddle-strings, I reflected, and wondered what the devil had happened to reduce Jack Burnham, of all people, to such a condition.

"All through dinner it was the same thing. When he spoke at all his words were jerky and almost incoherent, and by the time the port was on the table I realized that something pretty serious was the matter. In fact, if I hadn't known him to be thoroughly abstemious, I should have attributed it to drink or drugs. He had to use both hands to lift his port glass, which was a bad sign.

"I didn't hurry him; it was better to let him take his fences his own way. And it wasn't until he'd lit a cigar that he took the first with a rush.

" 'Do you know anything about the occult, Bill,' he said suddenly.

" 'Just enough to leave it alone,' I answered. 'Why?'

" 'I wish to God I'd known as much as that,' he

cried despairingly. 'Bill—you've seen the condition
I'm in. My hands shaking like a man with the palsy;
my nerves screaming; my reason tottering. I tell you,
I *am* going mad—unless you can help me.'

" 'Steady, Jack,' I said. 'There's generally a cure
for most things. Tell me the yarn, old man, and take
your time over it.'

"He didn't answer for some time, and I could see
he was taking a pull at himself.

" 'See here, Bill,' he said at length, 'what I'm going
to tell you is God's truth. It's no hallucination—all
the beginning part of it; it's a cold, sober fact that I
saw with my own eyes and heard with my own ears.
Whether or not the result of what I saw and heard
is hallucination; whether or not what I'm tormented
with now, is a hideous delusion—or cold sober fact
—I'll leave you to judge. I know what I think myself.

" 'It was a year ago that the thing began. You
know I've wandered a good deal, and in the course
of my wanderings I've seen some pretty strange things
—things, that if you told 'em in a club smoking-room
would be received with smiles of derision. I've seen
black magic celebrated in age-old temples, where it
was death to stir one step outside the circle of safety;
where the blood in the great bowl placed on the floor
outside the circle swirled and heaved and monstrous
shapes rose out of it and hovered round us—waiting.
I have seen things which no man would believe second-
hand; but until a year ago I had never seen the most
dreadful thing of all—the dead restored to life.

" 'I had heard rumours of it, but I had never actually witnessed it. So that when I found myself in the
back of beyond in Morocco, as the guest of a chief-
tain for whom I had been able to do a service, and he
asked me whether I would care to see it done, I accepted
eagerly. I won't bore you with a detailed description

of what happened: anyway, no spoken word could adequately paint the horror of the scene.

" 'Picture to yourself an Arab burial-ground—just a clearing in the scrub. Around us barked the jackals, and in answer the dogs from the village a few hundred yards away gave tongue. The smoke of the camel-dung fires came acrid to the nostrils, and the cemetery looked ghoulish in the greenish light of the flares carried by some of the men.

" 'It was a woman who was going to do the thing, and while some of the men removed the earth from a recent grave, she started singing some strange incantation.

" 'At last the men uncovered the corpse, and carried it in a piece of sheeting towards the central stone of the burial-ground. Then they withdrew, leaving the woman alone. Now, mark you, Bill, that man had been dead over a fortnight. . . .'

"He passed his hand over his forehead, and it was wet with perspiration.

" 'The woman, by now, was in a state of frenzy, and the harsh wailing from the other women who were seated in a circle around her seemed to madden her still more. And suddenly she began to shine with a faint radiance; I suppose she'd rubbed phosphorus on herself. A few seconds passed and she seemed to be on fire, while the chant grew louder and louder, and then abruptly stopped as the woman advanced to the corpse.'

"Once again he paused and shook himself like a dog.

" 'I'll spare you the revolting details of the next few minutes—you wouldn't believe them if I told you; but five minutes later she withdrew and the dead man was sitting up—alive. I don't profess to explain it; I can only tell you what I saw. What power had entered that corpse to endow it with the capability of speech and movement I know not; whether it came from the woman or whether it was some disembodied spirit—possibly that of the man himself—I can't say. All I do know, is that in the ordinary accepted meaning of words, the dead lived.

" 'Now he had been an ordinary peasant in life—a man of no account; but the instant he sat up the whole circle prostrated itself around him. Grave, dread questions were asked him as to the life to come, and in every case the answer was coherent and sensible. And then my host intimated that I might ask him a question. Without thinking I said the first thing that came into my head.

" ' "What does the future hold for me?"

" 'For a while there was no reply, and, glancing up, I saw that the corpse was shaking uncontrollably. Then it spoke:

" ' "Sleeping and waking you will be haunted by horror. Day and night it will be with you until the end. Then it will pass away."

" 'That was all, and shortly after the ceremony ended. The corpse relaxed and was placed back in its grave, and I accompanied my host back to the village. He was silent and distrait, occasionally looking at me with an expression almost of fear in his deep-set eyes. But he said nothing, and as for me, my mind was far too occupied with what I had seen to want to talk. Of the answer to my question I barely thought; it seemed such an insignificant part of such an amazing whole.

" 'I left the next day, and all the leading men of the village assembled to bid me good-bye. With the morning had come an amused scepticism, though I was careful not to show it. Ventriloquism undoubtedly: my eyes tricked by the smoky light. And as for the answer to my question, I forced myself to think of that ridiculous story of Oscar Wilde's—*Lord Arthur Savile's Crime.*

" 'But there was no levity on the part of the Arabs: only a grave and dignified concern. I felt that they looked on me already as doomed and as such I was entitled to their commiseration and respect. And two months later I had forgotten all about it except as a strange and interesting experience.'

"He paused to relight his cigar, and I made no comment. In my own mind I felt tolerably certain that his morning reflections were correct and that he had been tricked, but the point was immaterial. The important part was still to come.

" 'So much is fact,' he went on after a while—'cold, hard fact. How it was done matters not. All that concerns us is that I saw and heard what I have told you. Now we come to the second chapter. I was in Biskra when it started—the thing that has gone on ever since. Never a night passes without it, Bill —so that I fight against sleep; and now hardly a day passes without it too. It's a dream at night, always the same in every detail; by day, God knows what it is.

" 'It starts with a kind of luminous cloud which swirls and dances as it retreats before me. Every moment I think I am going to catch it up—only for it to elude me always. But I know what's coming, and I wait—longing for it to happen. Out of the cloud there forms gradually a woman's face—lovely beyond the powers of description. And she beckons me to come to her. I strive madly to reach her, only to be eluded once more. I want to take her in my arms: and I swear she wants me to take her. But—never have I done so. Always just out of reach: always just beyond me. And then—sometimes very soon, sometimes after what seems hours—the horror comes. I know it's coming because I can see the look of frozen terror in her eyes, and I'm powerless to prevent it. And the horror—how shall I describe it? Something comes flapping round my head, buffeting me in the face: something that beats at me like the wing of some hideous bird till I feel smothered and choking: something that leaves behind it still the awful smell of carrion. I tell you, Bill,' he shouted, 'I smell that smell: it's still lingering with me when I wake up sweating and dripping with fear.'

"Then he pulled himself together, and went on calmly.

" 'The first time it happened I put it down as an ordinary nightmare and thought no more about it. And then two or three nights later I had precisely the same dream. That was a year ago, Bill; for the last six months I've had that dream every night. The details may vary a little, but it's always the same woman, and it's always the same ghastly horror at the end. I'm fighting for my life against that smothering, fetid terror.'

" 'Do you know the woman, Jack?' I said. 'Is she anyone you've ever seen?'

"He shook his head.

" 'No, I've never seen her: I'm certain of that.'

"And even as he spoke his face turned grey, and he stared over my head into the shadows of the room.

" 'My God!' he whispered, 'she's just behind you.'

"I swung round in my chair: there was no one there.

" 'You thought you saw her, did you?' I said quietly.

"He shook himself, and the grey look slowly left his face.

" 'That's the second part of the terror, Bill,' he muttered. 'She's gone now, but three months ago she started to come to me by day as well. I've seen her on board ship, in restaurants, in the street—always beckoning and imploring me to come to her. The first few times, so vivid was the hallucination that I thought she was really flesh and blood. I followed her—madly; to find she'd disappeared. She'd never been there at all. "Day and night it will be with you to the end." That's what that foul corpse said, and, dear heavens! it's true. It's true, Bill—I tell you: true. It's with me day and night, for even when it isn't actually there, the thought that it may come at any moment haunts me. Do you wonder I said I was going mad?'

"He leaned forward, resting his head on his hands, and I did some pretty powerful thinking. Remember I knew Jack's character, and his almost aggressive stolidity. He was the last man in the world to give way to hysterical fears: this thing that he had told me was as real to him as I was. You might call it a delusion, an hallucination—what you liked: there's no virtue in a name. To him it was reality, and as such it had to be treated. And it seemed to me that the cure would have to come largely from himself. And it would have to come soon. Otherwise, in very truth, he might go mad.

" 'Well, Bill?' he said, looking at me with haggard eyes. 'What think you?'

" 'It's difficult to say, Jack,' I answered. 'I would like a little longer to think it over. But there are a few things that seem to me to stick out as obvious. In the first place, take what you see by day. Now you *know*, you've *proved* that what you see is non-existent. *The woman is not there.* Therefore you know that she is merely a figment of your imagination. Don't misunderstand me: she seems very real. But she isn't—and with one side of your mind you know it. Now, have you tried fighting with that side of your mind? Have you tried throwing a loaf of bread at this vision: kicking it hard: telling it to go to hell: forcing yourself to believe that you see nothing? Or have you been content to acquiesce in what you imagine you see, and not help the rational side of your mind to fight? Salvation, Jack, has got to come from you yourself. I'll help to the limit of my weight: but it's you, and you alone, who have got to come to final grips with this thing!'

" 'I get you,' he said quietly. 'But what about the dream? What about that ghastly end when she has vanished?'

" 'I believe, Jack, that the first thing to tackle is the daylight manifestation. If you can get rid of that, it will strengthen your subconscious mind to fight the dream. And I think'—it was a sudden inspiration that came to me—'that I can give you an explanation of the terror at the end. The clue lies in the fetid smell you imagine. Now, in that atrocious experiment you saw carried out, didn't the same smell of carrion hang round the graveyard?'

" 'Why, yes!' he cried eagerly, 'it did.'

" 'Precisely,' I answered. 'Now, nothing will make me believe that what you described to me *really* happened that night. But you were in a state of partial hypnosis, induced by the chanting and the lighting effect, and you imagined it. And I know enough about such matters to realize your intense danger in being in such a condition in the circumstances. Your mind was a partial blank, ready to sop up impressions like blotting-paper sops up liquid. And one of the most vivid impressions that it absorbed was the fundamental one of the foul smell around you. And that impression comes back to you now each night. What the connection between it and the woman is, I don't profess to say. Don't forget that in the subconscious mind we have a jumble of disconnected thoughts, unlinked by any reason or argument. And for some strange reason the vision of this woman and this beating, suffocating stench are joined together. Get rid of one, and you'll get rid of the other.'

"He was impressed, I could see, by my purposely materialistic arguments. And when two hours later he went to bed——I insisted on his stopping with me that night——he seemed a good deal calmer. I gave him a sleeping-draught and waited until he'd gone off: then I got a book and settled myself down in his room for an all-night vigil.

"It was three-thirty when it began, and I woke with a start from a doze. And by the light of my reading-lamp I watched the terror come. Jack was sitting up in bed, his face convulsed with horror, beating with his hands at the empty air in front of him. He was croaking at it hoarsely, and his great fists were dealing savage blows at——nothing. I went over and stood beside him, and then there happened the thing which to this day I can't recall without a pricking at the back of my scalp. As distinctly as I can smell this cigar, did I smell the sickly stench of putrid carrion by his bed. And then it was gone, and Jack, wild-eyed and desperate, was staring up at me from the pillows.

" 'Again,' he said in a shaking voice——'I've just been through it again, Bill.'

" 'I know you have, old man,' I answered quietly. 'I've been with you the whole time.'

"He got up unsteadily and peeled off his pyjamas, and you could have wrung the sweat out of them on to the floor. Without a word he rubbed himself down with a bath towel; then, putting on a dressing-gown, he lit a cigarette.

" 'Every night, Bill. I can't go on. For God's sake, man, do something.'

"And that was the devil of it—what to do. I didn't tell him so, of course, but that one staggering thing— the fact that I had noticed the smell—had knocked every idea of mine to smithereens. I realized that I was up against something beyond ordinary medical skill. And—what to do. . . .

"Gad! how he fought during the next week. I kept him with me, and one night he nearly caused my butler to give notice. He bunged a glass full of whisky and soda straight at him, and then cried triumphantly, 'It went clean through her, Bill.' Unfortunately the butler was not equally transparent, and objected to receiving heavy cut glasses full of liquid in the chest.

"But the dreams went on, and at length I insisted on him seeing a brain specialist. But it was no use, and ultimately I began to despair. So did he.

" 'To the end, Bill,' he said one day. 'To the end. Pray God it comes soon.'

" 'Then it will pass away,' I reminded him. 'Don't forget that, Jack.'

"But he only shrugged his shoulders: I think he had very nearly given up hope.

"And then one night came the staggering *dénouement*. We were dining at Claridge's—just the two of us alone. I used to make him go to restaurants and theatres in the hope of taking his mind off it, and as we were finishing our fish I happened to look up. A man and a woman had just come in, and the woman was quite one of the most lovely things I've ever seen. She was dressed in pale green, and my eyes followed her as she went to the table reserved for them. Head waiters were bowing obsequiously, so they were evidently not unknown. And I began wondering who they were.

" 'Devilish good-looking woman just come in, Jack,'
I said idly. 'Three tables away on your right, in pale
green. Don't turn round for a moment: she's looking
this way.'

"I saw him glance at her a few moments later, and
the next instant I thought he'd gone mad. He was
staring at me with his eyes blazing and his face a chalky
white.

" 'You see her, Bill?' he gasped. 'She's real? You
saw her come in?'

" 'Of course I saw her come in,' I cried in amazement.

" 'She is the woman of my dream,' he said stupidly.
'The woman who haunts me.'

" 'Steady, old man,' I stammered urgently, while I
tried to grasp this vast essential fact. 'People are looking at you. You say that woman is the woman of
your dream? You're sure?'

"He laughed shortly.

" 'Don't be a damned fool. Do you think I could
make a mistake over *that*?'

" 'And you've never seen her before?'

" 'Never in my life. But one thing I'm certain of:
I'm never going to lose sight of her again. To the
end, Bill—to the end. And she and I have got to go
there together.'

"It was useless to argue, and anyway the situation
had gone beyond me. Half-dazedly I heard him send
for a head waiter, and ask who they were.

" 'Kreseltein,' he said to me slowly after the waiter
had gone. 'One of the South African diamond kings.
Returning in the *Arundel Castle* next Friday week.
To-morrow, Bill, I go to the Union Castle office in
Fenchurch Street. I also travel by the *Arundel Castle*
next Friday week.'

"He was like a man bereft of his senses for the

next ten days. The Kreselteins were staying at the Ritz, and Jack haunted the place like a detective. He lunched there, he dined there, he very nearly break-fasted there, and as the date of sailing drew nearer he grew more and more excited. And there was another strange development: from the night when he saw her first at Claridge's the dream and the daylight hallu-cinations completely ceased.

"I dined with him at the Ritz on the night before he sailed, and the Kreselteins were a few tables away. And he was his old self again.

"'It's flesh and blood, Bill, now,' he said, 'and flesh and blood I can cope with.'

"'Tell me, Jack,' I asked, 'as a matter of interest, has Mrs. Kreseltein ever seemed as if your face was familiar to her.'

"'Never,' he answered decisively. 'On the occa-sions when I've happened to catch her eye, she has always given me the blank look of a perfect stranger.'

"'I wonder who she was?' I remarked.

"'Well, I've been making a few inquiries, if you want to know,' he said. 'She's English, and she married Kreseltein when she was quite a girl. He's a German Jew, and I gather from what I've heard a pretty foul swine. He flies into the most maniacal rages if she even looks at another man. There's some story apparently about his having plugged someone in Kimberley with a revolver, who, he thought, was making love to his wife.'

"'You'd better watch it, Jack,' I said gravely.

"'My dear old Bill,' he answered, 'I'm no particular slouch with a gun myself. But even if I couldn't hit a haystack at five yards, it would make no difference. That woman is all that stands between me and in-sanity, and so I've got to go through with it. If I didn't go in the *Arundel Castle* to-morrow, as sure as I am sitting here now the dream would start again. For some strange inscrutable reason Mrs. Kreseltein is going to be mixed up in my life. Her destiny and mine are going to meet—at the end. After that— God alone knows. But it will pass away; the horror will be gone.'

"He stared at me gravely.

" 'I'm under no delusion, Bill. I've got to go through the horror in reality, and I've got to come out on the other side. Only then will its power be dead!'

"The next day I saw him off in the boat-train at Waterloo. He wrung my hand hard as he thanked me for the little I'd been able to do, and from my heart I wished him good luck. Then the train steamed out, and in almost the last carriage I saw the Kreseltein. He was deep in the morning paper; she was staring out of the window at the people on the platform. And her face was the face of a woman who was tired unto death. But lovely—Lord! how lovely —in spite of its weariness."

The Doctor paused and mixed himself a whisky and soda.

"And with that ended the first part of the story of Jack Burnham," he continued after a while. "Weeks turned into months, and I heard nothing more. Jack was always a bad letter-writer, and even this time he proved no exception. He had vanished into the blue as usual, and I had nothing for it but to bottle up my intense curiosity as well as I could.

"And then, one day came the first news, and, knowing what I did, it was grave enough in all conscience. It was in the morning paper with head-lines all complete:

" 'The disappearance of Mr. Otto Kreseltein, the well-known owner of race-horses, and one of South Africa's wealthiest millionaires, grows more mysterious daily.   It will be recalled that he left his house in Johannesburg somewhat suddenly about a fortnight ago, stating that he was going north into Rhodesia.   From that day no further news has been heard of him.   The station-master at Bulawayo states that he believes a gentleman answering to Mr. Kreseltein's description was on board the train bound for the Victoria Falls, but there were so many tourists travelling that he is unable to be certain.   In the meantime an active search is being organized.   It is thought possible that Mr. Kreseltein may be suffering from temporary loss of memory.'

"Three weeks later came another announcement.

" 'The gravest fears must now, we regret to state, be entertained concerning Mr. Otto Kreseltein.   No trace has been found of him; no word has been received for over five weeks, and in view of the fact that he was in the middle of a big scheme of amalgamation when he left Johannesburg, and told his managing director that he only proposed to be absent for four days, it is impossible to avoid fearing that something very serious has happened.'

"Once again weeks passed by, and at last it was generally assumed that he was dead.   Legally, of course, the assumption could not be entertained as yet; but from every other point of view his death was regarded as certain.   And still I had no line from Jack to assuage my curiosity.   For, inwardly, I was convinced that he could throw some light on the matter, though no mention of his name had ever been made in the papers connecting him with Kreseltein in any way.

"And then, six months later, he walked into my consulting-room.   He looked a bit pale, and fine drawn, but his eye was clear and his smile was the smile of the Jack Burnham of old.

" 'I've been to the end, Bill,' he cried.   'I've come out on the other side.   And it has passed away.'

"'Why the devil haven't you dropped me a line, Jack,' I demanded.

"'Because, old man,' he said gravely, 'there are certain things it is better not to put in writing. Have you seen the papers this morning?'

"He held out a copy of *The Times* to me, and indicated a paragraph.

"'The mystery of the disappearance of Mr. Otto Kreseltein has at last been solved. Two Englishmen, while shooting in the district north of Bulawayo, discovered the remnants of a skeleton lying behind a big rock. Vultures and other beasts of prey had long since rendered any chance of identification impossible, but some fragments of cloth and part of an envelope supplied the necessary clues. There is no doubt that the skeleton is all that remains of the unfortunate diamond magnate, whose sudden disappearance caused such a stir some months ago. What Mr. Kreseltein was doing there will probably remain an unsolved problem.'

"I put down the paper and glanced at Jack.

"'An unsolved problem,' he said with a faint smile. 'Except to me, Bill, and one other. And now to you. I shot him.'

"'The devil you did!' I said. 'Is it indiscreet to ask why?'

"'Largely because of the fact that of all the devils in human form I have ever met, Otto Kreseltein was the worst,' he answered grimly. 'He lived like a swine, and he died like one, and you can take it from me that he's no loss.'

"He flung himself into a chair and lit a cigarette.

"'I'll tell you the yarn, Bill,' he said. 'I guess you've a right to know. It was after we left Madeira that I made Joan's acquaintance—his wife, I mean. He was mad keen on Bridge, and with three others of the same kidney he spent the whole day in the smoking-room. And I talked to her. It was a case of love right from the very beginning—with both of

us, I think. Even if it hadn't been for the special
reason which actuated me; even if I'd never been
haunted by the horror, things would have come to a
head. I'm going to marry her, you know. . . . She's
in London. . . .

" 'However—to get back to it. After I'd known
her for a few days I told her everything. I felt absolutely certain that something was going to happen
some time, and I wanted her to be prepared. At first
she hardly took it seriously, but after a while I convinced her that I wasn't fooling. And I think the
thing that impressed her most was when I told her
how I'd hit your butler in the chest with a whisky
and soda.

" 'Towards the end of the voyage we grew a bit
careless, I suppose. Not to put too fine a point on
it, I was with her from after breakfast until we went
to bed. And we danced a good deal together. Off
and on in the intervals of Bridge her husband had
joined us, and I saw enough of him to fill in the gaps
left by Joan. A thin-lipped, domineering swine, Bill;
a man of the most colossal conceit—and a cad. A
clever cad, and an able cad; but once or twice when
he spoke to his wife my hands tingled to get at
him. She might have been a junior clerk getting told
off.

" 'He'd said nothing to me about being so much
with his wife, and he'd said nothing to her. So it
came as rather a surprise when, the night before we
arrived in Cape Town, he came up to me as I was
strolling up and down the deck waiting for the dinner
bugle.

" ' "I have just been—ah—speaking to my wife, Mr.
Burnham," he said softly. "And she quite understands that her acquaintanceship with you must cease
forthwith. Should you take any steps to renew it, I

shall have to deal with you in a way you may not like!"

" 'And it was the way he said it, Bill, that finished me. Foolish perhaps, but I lost my temper—badly.

" ' "When your wife tells me the same thing, Mr. Kreseltein, I shall obey immediately. Until then I would be vastly obliged if you would go to hell and remain there. Your general appearance is not conducive to an appetite for dinner."

" 'And then, Bill, the primitive man came out in him. His face was red with passion, and he shot out a great hairy hand and caught me by the wrist. He was strong—but I was stronger. I removed his hand, and I held him powerless for a few seconds.

" ' "No, Mr. Kreseltein, I win on those lines," I said. "You'd better treat your wife better in future or I may have to give you a caning."

" 'Foolish, I frankly admit—but I was seeing red, old man. And the next morning as we got off the boat it wasn't red—it was scarlet. For on Joan's arms I saw two bruises, and I realized how he had spoken to her the night before. And for a moment or two I went mad.

" ' 'I went straight up to him in the Customs, and I got his arm in a grip I knew of old. I swung him round, and he faced me livid with fury.

" ' "If I see another bruise on your wife's arm like that, you damned swine," I muttered, "I'll first break your arm—so,"—and, by Gad! Bill, as near as makes no odds I broke it then, so that he let out a squawk of pain—"and then I'll flog you till you scream for mercy."

" 'There was murder in his face when I left him, and I cursed myself for a fool. His fury was bound to be vented on Joan. And on the way up in the boat-train I made up my mind: I'd take her away.

I felt pretty certain that she'd come. And when she rang me up at the Carlton Hotel in Jo'burg I wasn't surprised.

" ' "I can't stand it, Jack," she said. "He's become a devil incarnate. He—he thrashed me last night."

" ' 'God! old man—that finished it.

" ' "Pack what you want, dear," I said, "and come to the Carlton. We leave for Durban to-night. I'm going to see your husband now."

" 'I rang off before she could say anything, and went round to his office. There was some meeting on, but I went straight into his private office. I suppose I looked a bit wild, for he rose to his feet and started opening a drawer in his desk. And I got to him just before he drew his gun.

" ' "Shall we discuss this matter with or without an audience?" I remarked.

" 'The audience settled that and left rapidly.

" ' "You thrashed your wife last night, Kreseltein," I said quietly. "We will now have a hair of the dog that bit her."

" 'Well, Bill, I broke the stick on him, and it was a stoutish weapon. And when I'd finished with him I told him I was taking her to Durban that night. He lay there huddled up in his chair with the malevolence of all hell in his eyes.

" ' "I shall not divorce her," he croaked. "And in addition to that I shall make it my business to have you followed wherever you go, so that your relationship may be known."

" 'I was on the point of starting in on him again, when he suddenly sat up and stared at me.

" ' "I admit that you are stronger than I am, Mr. Burnham," he said, "but there are other ways of settling affairs of this sort. Unless you're afraid."

" ' "Get on with it," I snapped at him.

" ' "I suggest revolvers," he remarked. "A shooting-trip in Rhodesia—from which one of us will not return."

" ' "I agree," I said instantly. "And we start at once."

" 'A sardonic smile twitched round his lips.

" ' "To-night," he answered, and with that I left him.

" 'It was Joan who interpreted that smile.

" ' "My dear," she said; "it's murder. Otto is supposed to be one of the half-dozen best revolver shots in the world."

" ' "I guessed he'd probably shot before when he suggested it," I laughed. "But, don't you see, dear heart, that it's the only way. You know I'm not a complete dud myself."

" 'And so I pacified her as best I could, though, to tell you the truth, I wasn't feeling too easy myself. I *am* a good revolver shot, but I lay no claim to being an expert.'

"He lit another cigarette, and his face was grim.

" 'We staged it well, Bill; no one suspected. And four days later we met in a belt of scrub and desert about fifty miles north of Bulawayo. We were to stand back to back at thirty paces, and at the word "Fire" we were to swing round and shoot. We tossed for who was to speak—he won. And I, like a fool, trusted him. He plugged me through the back before he spoke. I heard the report; felt the sharp, searing pain go through me, and, even as my knees gave from under me and I crashed, for the second time I cursed myself for a fool. I thought it was the end, Bill; I couldn't see clearly, though he was standing over me shaking with laughter. And then there occurred the most amazing thing. The scene seemed to fade out from my mind, and I was back again in that Arab graveyard. But this time I was the corpse. I tell you, I could see the ring of natives around me, and that dreadful woman coming at me. I could see her shining and luminous; I could hear the chanting; I could feel her as she threw herself on me. And suddenly—it's incredible, I know, but it is so—I felt strength come into my arms which had previously been numb and powerless. I felt my right arm lift, until it pointed at the woman's heart. And dimly, as if from a great distance, I heard a report. Then everything faded out, though the last act had still to come.

" 'The dream came back. I saw Joan beckoning to me, with that same dear elusive smile, and then she faded away and I knew the horror was coming. Something came flapping round my head, buffeting me in the face, and I beat at it as always. The stench of carrion was ghastly; the smothering feeling more overpowering than ever before. On and on it went, that dream, and I couldn't wake up. Until at last my eyes forced themselves open and I was awake. Vultures, Bill—dozens of them. One great brute on my chest, and others flapping around me. And a few yards away was something that lay on the ground covered with them.

" 'And then everything grew hazy again. I have a dim recollection of the filthy brutes suddenly hopping away—of seeing the thing they had left behind them—of realizing it was what was left of Kreseltein. I saw Joan's face too: imagined she was leaning over me. And Bill—she was. That wasn't a dream, as I found out later. She'd followed us, and she saved my life.

" 'Somehow she got me to a native kraal—the men carried me—and there I lay for three months. As soon as I was fit to be left she went back to Johannesburg, and there later on I joined her. For she'd been with me to the end, and the horror had passed away.

"'Can you account for it, Bill?'

"I couldn't—and to this day I can't. He married her, of course, and there has never been any return of the horror. But what was the strange power that entered the arm of a man wellnigh dead, and directed the aim of his revolver at the heart of Otto Kreseltein?"

L   THE   PROFESSOR'S   CHRISTMAS   PARTY

I

THE Professor ceased writing for a moment and stared at the window of his study. Outside the rain lashed down in typically Christmas fashion, but it was another sound that had temporarily disturbed his train of thought. At least it had seemed to him that he had heard something, though perhaps it had only been his imagination. Annoying to have one's line of argument broken. . . .

Once more he bent over his desk, reading the last sentence he had written. Then the "J" pen began to travel again across the paper.

"Before we can admit that Woman is a rational being in the same sense that the phrase may be applied to Man, we must consider, in all its aspects, the fundamental factor of Sex."

Again he raised his head: this time there was no mistake. Somebody was tapping at the window. And with a distinct frown on his face the Professor rose and pulled back the curtains, only to give a sudden startled exclamation and fling up the lower sash.

A girl was outside, huddled up against the wall, and a glance was sufficient to show that she was wet to the

skin. Her hat resembled a piece of shapeless pulp;
the sleeves of her jumper hung like sodden string to
her arms.

"Good heavens! my dear child," stammered the
Professor; "whatever are you doing out there?"

"Getting wetter and wetter," she answered. "May
I come inside?"

Without waiting for an answer she clambered over
the window-sill, producing on the Professor's best
carpet the effect of a movable shower-bath.

"It seems to be raining," remarked the Professor
brightly.

"It does," agreed the girl. "In fact, I distinctly felt
a drop."

She was crouching over the fire, warming her hands,
and it suddenly struck the Professorial eye that she was
distinctly pretty. True, she looked sufficiently be-
draggled and woebegone at the moment for the fact
almost to have escaped his notice, and yet, strangely
enough, as he redrew the curtains he was definitely
conscious that her appearance was prepossessing.

"I got lost," she announced, "and then I saw the
light in your window. I rang the bell, but nothing
happened, so I came and tapped. I hope you don't
mind."

"Of course not," he cried. "The worthy Mrs.
Clayton, who looks after me, is away for a couple of
days. That's why no one answered the bell. I say
—you *are* wet."

The girl broke into a little peal of laughter.

"My dear man, I haven't got a dry rag on my back.
So what do you propose to do about it?"

"Do about it!" The Professor started violently.
"Er—er—I'm afraid—er——"

"You see," went on the girl demurely, "I'm so afraid
I shall catch cold."

"So am I," agreed the Professor unhappily.

Assuredly this was the most ghastly complication. Supposing the girl caught pneumonia or pleurisy or something like that. Common humanity would compel him to keep her in the house, and what on earth should he say to MacEwan, who was coming down to spend a couple of days with him? MacEwan was a very clever man: he liked MacEwan. But the fact remained that MacEwan was at times almost boisterously vulgar. He was under no illusions as to what MacEwan would say on the matter: he could hear him now retailing the story with the most appalling additions of his own to the select and intimate circle to which they both belonged at the Referee Club. The Professor shuddered mentally.

"I suppose Mrs. Clayton hasn't got anything I could put on while these dry," said the girl at length.

"Good heavens!" gasped the Professor. "You've never seen Mrs. Clayton. Her bedroom floor had to be specially strengthened to support her weight. Look here,"—he swallowed audibly—"supposing I lent you a suit of my—my pyjamas."

"Angel man." The girl clapped her hands together. "The very thing. Trot along and get them."

The Professor trotted, and she heard him going upstairs.

"He's a positive pet," said the girl to herself, "and I wish I'd never come. It's a shame, and I'll tell the whole bunch so. Why, he can't be more than thirty-five, and I love his freckles."

The door opened and a hand holding pyjamas appeared.

"Here they are," came a stifled voice from the other side. "And for goodness' sake get undre—get your wet things off quickly."

The door closed abruptly, and the girl shook with

silent laughter. But she followed his advice. She had just begun to realize that it was very sound, and that she really was drenched to the skin. The jest had taken on a tinge of seriousness. If only she hadn't lost her way in the darkness and the rain between the Hall and the Professor's house it wouldn't have mattered. But she had turned a ten-minute walk into one of twenty-five, and only the thought of the jeers of the rest of the party had prevented her from going back. It was Jack Simpson who had betted her she wouldn't draw the badger.

"He's a woman hater," he had said. "He writes ghastly books, proving that women rank a little below dormice in the scheme of things. He'll probably bark at you, and then send for the police."

"Will he?" she had answered. "A thousand of my cigarettes, young fellah, that I have dinner with him to-night. Is it a bet?"

She had heard vaguely of Professor Hubert Morgan as a writer of profound and intensely dull books. Once she had been to a dinner in London where he was expected, but he had sent an excuse at the last moment and failed to turn up. And she had hazily imagined him to be an elderly man with ill-fitting clothes and spectacles. Instead she had discovered a man in the thirties, whose clever grey eyes required no artificial help. Shy, certainly, he seemed to be; but the situation was admittedly a little unconventional.

Deliberately she crossed to his desk and read what he had been writing. A bold, decisive hand she reflected, and then the sense of the words struck her. She didn't know that it was only one phrase in a long and carefully reasoned argument: if she had, being a woman, she wouldn't have cared.

"We must consider, in all its aspects, the funda-mental question of Sex."

And if Professor Hubert Morgan, who in considerable trepidation was sitting in the dining-room wondering what was going to happen next, had seen the look in Hilary Staveley's eyes at that moment, his problem would have been solved. Rain or no rain, he would have fled from the house.

"You may come in," said the girl, opening the door. "They're a little big, but that's better than their being too small, isn't it?"

She was sitting in his easy chair by the fire smoking a cigarette as he entered, and the conviction that she was pretty grew and increased in strength in the Professor's mind. She was, in fact, quite the prettiest girl he had ever seen in his life. But far from rendering the problem any easier, it only seemed to make it harder.

"My dear young lady," he remarked in his most professor-like voice, "we must really consider what is to be done."

"Do you teach much?" asked the girl.

He stared at her in surprise.

"Teach? I—ah—occasionally give lectures."

The girl nodded.

"I know. I recognize the tone of voice. Now—ah—my dear young ladies, we will just run over a list of the wives of Henry VIII. Sausage Face—that was our history master at school—used to talk like that. Tell me, Mr. Man, what do you lecture about?"

"Er—nothing, I'm afraid, that would interest you much," he answered with a faint smile. "Psychoanalysis, and things like that."

"But you must be most frightfully clever," said the girl in an awed voice. "I wonder who you are."

"My name is Morgan—Hubert Morgan."

"Not *the* Hubert Morgan?"

Feverishly the Professor sought for a firm ground.

There must surely be something to which he could anchor himself; some great and true fact—scientifically proven—to which he could cling. What was it he had written himself in *The Claims of Woman: An Analytical Study of Present Day Conditions?*

"It must never be lost sight of that Woman, being by nature the weaker vessel, is forced inexorably to deceit, flattery and even fraud in order to obtain her ends."

Like a drowning man clutching at a life-belt he clutched at his knowledge. And then rather foolishly he looked at the girl. With lips a little parted she was leaning forward in her chair staring up at him. Her great blue eyes, shining with admiration, were fixed on his. And, dash it, her ankle was most extraordinarily pretty. . . . The great and true fact—scientifically proven—began to recede.

"But I thought Professor Hubert Morgan was an elderly man and not good-looking," went on the girl, a little breathlessly. "This is *too* wonderful."

Somewhere in the Professor's brain a mental life-belt went crash. The only outward and visible sign of this unfortunate accident, was a strange stuttering noise that came from the Professor's lips, followed by a most painful and embarrassing sensation in his cheeks. In vain to reflect that the redness was due to the suspension of the action of the local vasomotor nerves: all that mattered was that the Professor blushed like an overgrown schoolboy.

"Er . . . er . . ." he stammered. And once again— "Er . . . er . . ."

Not a muscle on the girl's face twitched.

"Yes?" she said sweetly.

"We must really think—" the words poured out in a rapid torrent—"we must really think what to do."

"I leave it absolutely to you," she said gently. "I know it must be inconvenient to you to have me here, interrupting you in your work—but if I may just wait until my clothes are dry. . . ."

The Professor's local vasomotor nerves failed him again: he had followed her glance to where the clothes were drying.

"It doesn't matter about my work," he said, hurriedly averting his eyes. "It's about your—your reputation."

"But no one need ever know," she answered. "I shan't tell anybody that I came and sat here in your pyjamas. Will you?"

"Great heavens! no," gasped the Professor fervently.

"Then what does it matter? We'll have a little dinner together in pyjamas: I mean in your pyjamas—that is, my pyjamas—anyway, you know what I mean, and then my clothes will be dry, and I'll go on to the Hall."

"Are you staying there?" he inquired anxiously.

"Yes. I must have lost my way going there from the—from the station."

"But, my dear child," he cried, "they'll send out search-parties if you don't turn up. And this house is right on the road: they're certain to inquire here."

The girl shook her head.

"They won't get anxious yet. I said I mightn't be back till after dinner, and by then, my clothes will be dry. Give me another cigarette, will you?"

"Are you coming to the Hall for Christmas?" she said, as he sat down again.

"I think Lady Belmont kindly asked me," he replied guardedly. "But I'm rather busy just now, and I've got a man coming to stay with me who may stop on over Christmas."

"But you *must* come," she cried. "We're going to have the most frightful rag. Do, please. Promise you will. We're all going to dress up—just with things in the house. Nothing elaborate. And there will be a big Christmas-tree after dinner."

"I'm afraid I shan't know any of the party," he said weakly.

"You'll know me, won't you? Of course we'll have to pretend we haven't met before, but that will make it all the more fun. Or don't you—don't you want to meet me again? I really look quite nice, you know, when I haven't been out in the rain."

"I'm sure you do," agreed the Professor fervently. "And please don't think that I don't want to meet you again. I should esteem it a great—a great honour to be introduced to you—ah—formally, by Lady Belmont; and to continue, in circumstances a little more conventional, an acquaintanceship so—so strangely and, if I may say so, delightfully begun."

And Hilary Staveley, who would, had she heard such a speech from any other man she knew, undoubtedly have become hysterical from mirth, suddenly felt a queer little lump form in her throat. He was so simple, so utterly unlike anyone she'd ever met before. He was so—she searched for the right word—so trustable. And she felt more and more angry with herself for the trick she had played and was still playing. She had to go through with it now: something told her that in spite of his almost boyish gaucherie, she would prefer him not to lose his temper. But one thing she would ensure: that no one up at the Hall should split. He must always think that she had come from the station as she had told him.

At half-past seven they dined off cold beef and pickles: at nine o'clock she was still sitting by the fire wondering why a large number of the men of her acquaintance were such fools. For Hubert Morgan—his shyness overcome—had ceased to be the Professor and had proved himself a perfectly delightful companion.

And when at ten o'clock she returned to the Hall—
the rain had ceased by then—she was singularly uncommunicative. She was hailed joyously by the
assembled party, but she quite refused to be drawn.

"I'll take those cigarettes, young Jack," she remarked. "And I've quite enjoyed myself, thank you
very much."

"But what sort of a bloke is he?" demanded someone.

"Did he put you under a microscope?"

"Is his room full of dead bodies?"

"Crammed to the brim," she answered. "I sat on
his mother's corpse at dinner. But I'll tell you another
thing there is in his room—a thing which none of you
bright specimens are ever likely to have: an international
football cap."

"What ho!" said Jack Simpson as the door closed
behind her. "Our little Hilary has clicked. But
what beats me is how a fellow who has been capped can
write that sort of tripe. He's in the middle of another
book now, so somebody told me. Does anyone ever
read 'em?"

The question proved unanswerable. It was decided
that presumably somebody must, even if it was only the
wretched man who published them. But it is to be
feared that even that long-suffering gentleman would
have rebelled had the continuation of the Professor's
argument on the fundamental factor of sex been submitted to him as it was written that night. And had he
been told that four split infinitives, two flat contradic-
tions, and an obvious lie—all within the space of twenty
lines—were caused by the presence of a pair of the
author's pyjamas on his desk, he might well have
wondered if that fine brain wasn't beginning to soften.
But, then, publishers are prosaic people. . . .

II

"Of course you *must* dress up," said the girl. "Even if it's only burnt cork and a red nose."

Hilary Staveley, looking perfectly charming in a Neapolitan effect, regarded the Professor critically.

"Why didn't you come in pyjamas?" he asked with a smile.

"Haven't got any," she answered. "And I felt I didn't know you well enough to borrow yours again. I say, did I disturb you dreadfully?"

"Dreadfully," he said gravely. "But not at the time."

She looked away, acutely conscious of the message in his eyes.

"Bad thing to get into a groove, you know," she remarked lightly.

It was annoying: it was impossible: it was ridiculous. Only the second time she'd seen him, and yet . . . she was frightened of herself.

"It makes one so serious," she went on. "And nobody ought to be serious on Christmas Eve—especially after dinner."

"There are exceptions to every rule," he answered.

"Well, this isn't one of them. Now then—here's a nose. Put it on, please."

"That's your job," he answered.

It was a large, red bulbous affair secured by elastic round the head. And as she slipped it on he caught both her wrists in his hands. For a moment she let him hold them: then she drew them away.

"That wasn't playing the game," she remarked quietly. "It was almost—serious."

"I intended it to be."

And suddenly she began to shake with laughter.

"Go and look at yourself in the glass," she cried. "O

man who understands women, don't try to be serious looking like that."

"Damn the beastly thing!" exploded the Professor, but when he looked round the girl was gone. From the next room there came shouts of revelry and mirth, but he felt in no mood to join in. If he could have had his way, he would have liked to transport Hilary, with the wave of a wand, back to his own house. Just alone: in his pyjamas again.

During the last week he'd thought it over from every angle. At least, he thought he'd thought it over: he hadn't really. There was nothing to think over: it was a blatant, obvious fact. He was in love: just that and nothing more. And he'd passed through all the agonizing phases of a man in that condition. At times he blessed the moment that had made her lose her way: at others, particularly to-night, he almost cursed it. That damned fool Jack Simpson, for instance. . . . Where did he come in? He seemed so confoundedly possessive. And all the other men, who seemed to regard him as a being apart.

A bunch of them came surging through blowing whistles, and the Professor escaped to the smoking-room. He felt he must be alone to think about Hilary. He'd sat next to her at dinner, which had struck him as being a wonderful piece of luck—but it had all been different from the other time. Only natural, as he told himself—but still . . .

Of course it was only natural. That other time had been a thing apart—a mere accident. And not by word or hint must he regard it as anything but that. To presume on it in any way was out of the question: it wouldn't be playing the game. And as the phrase came into his mind he bit his lip. The very thing she'd said to him when he had imprisoned her wrists. That hadn't been playing the game: he would never have dreamed of doing such a thing had it not been for that other time. Cad unspeakable that he was to have done it! He must find her and apologize: tell her that it was just an uncontrollable impulse and that it shouldn't occur again.

He sat down in a deep arm-chair near the fire. His back was to the door, and he hardly noticed the fact that two men had come into the room and were standing by the table helping themselves to drinks. His mind was engrossed in his own problems, and he sat on motionless—so motionless that his host, who was short-sighted, and old General Laidley never saw him in the shadow.

"Damned pretty girl, that Hilary Staveley," remarked the General. "Her father and I were in Egypt together in '94. He was a wild devil if you like."

"So is the daughter, old man," returned his host with a chuckle. "Do you know what she did the other night? We've got a tame freak who lives about ten minutes from here—you've seen him to-night. One Professor Morgan: writes the most fearful trash. Well, he's a woman-hater or something or other: so our young Hilary bet that youngster, Jack Simpson— good boy that, soldier: you ought to do something for him, he's a gunner—however, she bet him a thousand cigarettes she'd not only draw the badger but dine with him. And she pulled it off. Went out from here in the pouring rain at six o'clock and got back at ten."

"How did she do it?"

"She's a bit close as to that," returned the other. "But she did it all right. Of course he hasn't an inkling that the whole thing was done for a bet. And the result, if I'm any judge of the situation, is that the poor blighter is hooked, gaffed and landed."

"Don't think I've noticed the fellow," said the

soldier. "But surely little Hilary ain't interested in landing a man of that type. I mean, there's nothing in it, is there?"

"Good Lord, no! Personally I think the modern girl wants smacking at times, but in this case it serves him darned well right. A bloke who writes his sort of stuff is riding for a fall, and I can't say I feel the slightest sympathy for him when he gets it. Kiss 'em early and kiss 'em often was our motto, Bill—and I guess it answered. . . ."

The sound of their voices died away: the room was empty again save for a man with a large, red bulbous nose who stared with unseeing eyes at the fire—eyes that looked like a dog's eyes after he's been beaten.

So that was it—was it? A joke! A bet! And everyone knew how the tame freak had been had! Everybody there that evening was roaring with laughter inwardly: Hilary was roaring with laughter. And he'd thought it was their secret.

A little unsteadily he rose to his feet, and then his jaw set as it had done that afternoon at Twickenham when he was changing into football rig and the hoarse murmur of the huge crowd came dimly to the dressing-room. There was something analogous between the two events—the two biggest of his life. His right knee had gone in that match, and he knew that never again would he be able to play in international football. And now something else had gone. . . . Never again. . . .

Stiffly he walked to the door. He must find Lady Belmont, and make his excuses for going. Pressure of work would do: that's about all they'd expect from a bloke who wrote his sort of stuff.

He passed through the room where the big Christmas-tree was standing. It was a blaze of fairy lights, and two or three children who had sneaked in against all orders were standing admiring it. But he was hardly conscious of their existence, until one of them suddenly cried out: "Oh, what a lovely nose!"

It was a little girl, in a pink filmy dress, and she was smiling up at him. He stopped for a moment and patted her head: she, at any rate, didn't realize that he was just a tame freak. And at that moment it happened. Two small boys skylarking: a sudden push: a fall.

So easy, and so quick. At one instant just a little fluffy-haired kid in her pink dress: the next a blazing mass of flames. She hadn't even time to shriek before the tame freak had picked her up and smothered her against his shirt and coat. In fact, when she started to cry out of sheer fright the flames were out. And when a terrified nurse, who had been searching everywhere for her lost charge, came running in, all she found were two scared boys, and a white-faced man with a big red nose who had little Joan on his knee. She didn't look at him even when she snatched her up: she didn't notice the beads of perspiration pouring down his forehead as, tight-lipped, he sat on in his chair. She hardly heard his reassuring remark: "She's all right, only scared," though his next— "Don't scold her, you fool woman: it's your fault"— might have made her flare up but for the sternness in the grey eyes that seemed to sweep away the ridiculous red nose. As it was, she only whimpered and left him alone, still tight-lipped and sweating.

The boys had run away, and suddenly an involuntary groan came from the chair. It was the only one: after that there was silence for a few moments till the man who had been sitting in it rose. His hands were behind his back, and he walked quite steadily towards the door. It opened just as he got there to admit Jack Simpson, who stared at him in surprise.

"Hallo!" he cried. "Feeling a bit dickey?"

"I'm not feeling frightfully fit," said the other, speaking with a sort of strained stiffness. "I think I'll go home. Would you be good enough to make my excuses to Lady Belmont for me? I don't want to cause an upheaval at the party."

He walked on, swaying a little, and Jack Simpson stared after him with a look of comprehension gradually dawning in his eyes.

"Tight, by gad!" he muttered to himself. "The freak is blotto! Holy smoke! what a supreme jape!"

He dashed off to find Hilary and impart the news.

"Tight, dear soul!" he cried. "Tight as a drum. How well I know the feeling! The room is rotating: one's every effort is concentrated on getting through the middle of the door without a cannon. Forehead bedewed with damp, hands wet and dripping, and tum-tum expostulating vociferously. Thank heavens, it generally takes me in the legs!"

She stared at him, frowning.

"Are you fooling?" she said slowly. "Do you really mean he's tight?"

"Not guard-room and boots-off business," he answered. "He's quite quiet. But solitude is indicated. So he's gone home—red nose and all."

"But where is he, Lady Belmont?" cried a woman behind them. "I want to see him and thank him."

Bella Richley's voice was penetrating, and Hilary swung round.

"Your Professor, Hilary: your Professor."

"What about him?"

"My dear! he's saved little Joan's life. The child's frock caught fire—she was playing round the Christmas-tree—and he put it out."

"Good God!" muttered Jack Simpson under his breath.

"She was blazing, and he caught her up and pressed all the flames out. And she isn't even hurt: only her frock ruined."

"I'm after him at once," cried Jack. "What a priceless fellow! And I thought . . . He's gone home, Lady Belmont: asked me to apologize and all that."

"Do, there's a good boy," said his hostess, and, turning away with the agitated mother, she didn't see a firm young hand laid on Jack Simpson's arm.

"You'll stay where you are, Jack: I'm going."

There was a look in her eyes that brooked of no argument, and in that instant the youngster knew the truth with blinding certainty. His own dreams were finished: the tame freak had won. And being a white man he spoke quite steadily.

"Of course, dear. And I apologize for what I said. He didn't want to upset the party."

"Don't tell them where I've gone, Jack."

She left him, and ten minutes later she paused by the gate leading to Hubert Morgan's house. A light was burning in his room, but the blind was down and she couldn't see in. For a moment she hesitated—should she tap on the window as she had tapped before, or ring the bell? And the window won.

She knocked, and after a pause the blind went up.

"May I come in?" she asked softly.

For a moment or two he looked at her gravely through the glass. Great heavens! couldn't she leave him alone just now? And yet, he couldn't help it: his heart had started pounding again, so that he almost forgot—the other thing. . . .

"Certainly," he remarked. "The door is open."

"But won't you open the window? Then I can come in as I did last time."

"I think you'll find the door more convenient," he answered.

With a shrug of her shoulders she turned away, and he heard her coming along the passage to his study. And when the door opened to admit her he was still standing by the window. He was facing into the room, with his hands behind his back, and he made no movement towards her.

"I hear you've been doing the young hero stunt," she said quietly, striving to read what lay behind the steady eyes that faced her. "But why run away? The mother is dying to fall on your neck."

"Then her life is in no danger," he answered, still standing motionless.

She stared at him with a little puzzled frown.

"What's the matter, Hubert?   You're so different—suddenly."

It was the first time she'd called him by his Christian name, and he winced.

"Need we keep up the jest any longer?" he said quietly.   "You've won your bet, Miss Staveley: you've hooked, gaffed and landed the tame freak—and doubtless my absence from the party will enable you to enjoy your triumph more openly than if I was there."

"So you know."

The words were hardly more than a whisper. At last she understood.

"Is that why you went away?"

"Oh, no: a trifle of that sort hardly counts. There were—other reasons."

"You call it a trifle, do you?"

"Isn't it to you? And since I prefer not to be in the picture any more, my feelings don't matter."

"And if I told you that your feelings matter everything? If I told you that it did start as a bet, but that almost as soon as I saw you I regretted it bitterly—what would you say?"

"That you are a wonderful actress," he answered stiffly.

"I deserve that," she said quietly. "But since you understand women so well, you should know we're all actresses."

She went close up to him and put her hands on his shoulders.

"But we don't always act: sometimes we're serious. I'm serious now—as you were earlier this evening. Or is it necessary for me to put on your nose again for you to recapture the mood?"

He stood there without movement, and after a while her hands fell to her sides.

"I see: you won't."

"Don't you think you'd better go?" he said through tight-set lips.

"Perhaps I had," she agreed. "Evidently you don't believe me. Good-bye; I'm sorry you found it out, and I'm still sorrier that you don't believe my explanation."

She held out her hand, but he made no effort to take it. And after a time she frowned a little angrily.

"Most of the men I know, Mr. Morgan, shake hands, at any rate, after a frank apology. I'm beginning to think that you are a tame freak—as you put it."

"Good gracious me—what's all this?"

A genial voice behind her made her turn round, and she saw the local doctor bustling in with a little bag in his hand.

"Looking after the invalid and all that? Splendid! Splendid! Now then, Morgan, let's have a look at them?"

"In one moment, doctor. Good night, Miss Staveley."

"Invalid?" stammered the girl. "What do you mean?"

The doctor looked at her in surprise.

"What's this? What's this? You said you'd burnt your hands, didn't you? At least, that's what I gathered over that infernal telephone."

With a quick movement the girl darted behind his back, and then she turned very white.

"Oh, my God!" she whispered. "Why didn't you tell me?"

Then she pulled herself together.

"I can help you, doctor: I've done a bit of Red Cross work."

They were a ghastly sight—the tame freak's hands—scorched, and burned, and blackened. Even the doctor whistled under his breath when he saw them.

"Good heavens, Morgan!" he said gravely, "you must have been in agony. Hands, of all things. How on earth did it happen?"

"Saving a kid's life," said the girl unsteadily. "That's all."

For a moment the doctor looked at her with shrewd, kindly eyes; then he bent over his task. And when, a quarter of an hour later, he was replacing the things in his bag, the twinkle returned.

"Can I offer you a lift?" he asked her. "I shall be going past the Hall."

"I think I'll just stay and see that the Professor is comfortable," she answered.

"You'll miss the Christmas-tree," said the Professor.

And the doctor swears that he distinctly heard her say: "Damn the Christmas-tree."

But he was in the hall by then and, anyway, he didn't hear any more. And if he had, he'd have heard a most unbiased criticism of the Professor's work.

"How you can have the temerity to write books about

women, beats me.   Do you mean to say that you would have let me go—not knowing about that?"

She pointed to his bandaged hands.

"I didn't want to worry you," he said feebly.

A wonderful light came into her eyes, and suddenly she was on her knees beside him.

"So I've got you hooked, gaffed and landed, have I?"

"My dear," he whispered.   "Oh, my dear! don't play the fool."

" 'We must consider, in all its aspects,' " she quoted, " 'the fundamental aspect of Sex.'   You dear idiot— don't you realize—that I'm hooked, gaffed and landed too?"

Her arms were round his neck, and for a time the fact that the blind was up escaped their attention. And it wasn't till she got up to pull it down that a profound remark emerged from Professor Hubert Morgan:

"It occurs to me, on due reflection, Miss Staveley, that I shall have to rewrite that last chapter."

L I   THE   IMPASSIVE   FOOTMAN

I

JOHN MARWOOD stirred irritably in his chair, and pulled the shawl tighter round his shoulders. On his face was the peevish, complaining look which of late years had become chronic: his whole bearing suggested the man who has a grievance against every-thing and everybody: the man who has decided that life has not given him a square deal.   It makes no difference to such a man that in the game it is often he who deals the cards: and that it is up to him to make the best of the bad hands when they come.

Far from not meeting trouble half-way, the particular breed to which John Marwood belonged anticipate it before it starts.   They seize it, they canter back with it, and they then exclaim triumphantly: "I told you so."   In fact, the only thing which seems to annoy them, and make them really aggrieved, is when they can find nothing to complain about.   It is a very rare occurrence, and mercifully for John Marwood things were not as bad as that.   One of those wretched pinpricks with which life delighted to buffet him had occurred: no one had come to give him his medicine. . . .

Out of the whole houseful of lazy, incompetent servants, not one of them could take the trouble to remember his sufferings.   He fumed angrily and muttered under his breath.   Three o'clock was the time for his tonic: it was now nearly five past.   And, of course, Grace was out—she would be.   Just when he wanted her. . . .   And the fire wanted attention. . . . Moreover, that symptom of his which he had described to her last night, that sharp stabbing pain near the right shoulder-blade, was becoming increasingly acute.   He felt convinced it was something serious, though his wife had not seemed very impressed when he had told her.   But then, she never was: she seemed to have absolutely no conception of how he suffered.

Once again he moved irritably in his chair.   Unless one of these fat brutes brought his medicine shortly he would have to get up and ring the bell.   And any walking hurt his right leg abominably.   But what did they care?   He might die at that moment, and not one of the great staff he employed would feel one single twinge of regret.   They would afterwards, of course, when they were kicked out of a soft job into the world.   Then they might begin to realize what he had done for them, and then it would be too late. He gloated over the thought for a moment or two:

he almost felt as if it would be worth while dying just to score off them. But then, he wasn't likely to die: he never had any luck. . . .

Suddenly he heard footsteps approaching the door, and the need for rapid thought arose. When had he last endeavoured to show his callous household a little of the torture he endured? Of course, it was acting in a way—but a very necessary piece of acting. . . . Only it didn't do to carry it out too often: otherwise it lost its point. . . . It was as the knock came on the door, and the handle turned, that he remembered it was at least a week since he had done it last, and that it was, therefore, quite time to do it again. . . .

With an agility remarkable considering the agony in his right leg he rose and took a couple of steps forward. Then he clutched the mantelpiece with one hand, and his right side with the other. It was as the door opened that he groaned. . . .

A man came in with a glass of medicine on a tray, and for a moment he stood watching his master with a contemptuous smile on his face. Then the mask of the good servant replaced it, and, coming forward, he placed the medicine on the table, and solicitously helped the sufferer back to his chair, where he lay with closed eyes.

"Your tonic, sir," murmured the servant, after a decent interval.

After a long pause Marwood looked wearily up at him. "How many of you are there below?"

"Four, sir." The man's eyebrows went up slightly.

"Is it too much to hope that among four of you there is one who can remember to bring me my tonic in time?"

"Very sorry, sir. The clock in the servants' hall is slow."

"Then, is it too much to hope that among four of

you there is one who can remember to put it right?"
He put out a languid hand towards the glass. "If it
is too much to hope for, I suppose I shall have to
resign myself to the agony of getting up to ring the
bell to remind you." With a profound sigh he looked
at the pink liquid. "Is this a tablespoonful?"

"Yes, sir."

With an expressionless face the man watched Marwood drain the glass: then, picking it up, he turned
to go.

"Wait." Marwood's tired voice stopped him on
his way to the door. "What sum of money do I pay
you a year?"

"Forty-eight pounds, sir."

"Forty-eight pounds." The speaker's eyes were
closed: his weariness seemed to be increasing. "Then
do you think it would be possible for you to tear yourself away from your arduous pleasures downstairs for
a sufficiently long period to attend to one or two of
the things that so very obviously want doing in this
room? I am fully aware that my comfort is a matter
of supreme indifference to the entire household; but,
in return for your forty-eight pounds a year, I hope
I am not asking too much. For instance—the fire.
It occurs to me that it might be saved from complete
extinction if you could bring yourself to place a little
coal on it."

As noiselessly as is humanly possible, the operation
was performed, and the man stood up. He had only
given his employer the opportunity for two agonized
starts of nerve-wracked anguish, which was distinctly
annoying to the invalid. Making up the fire was the
invariable occasion of some of his very choicest flights
of martyred cynicism. (And what made the servants'
hall snarl with rage was the fact that for hours on end,
when Marwood had given strict orders that he should

not be disturbed, the fire was kept up and tended by the sufferer himself. Those were the occasions when he found the strength to totter alone to the door, and hang on the outside a red board, which informed the household that his nerves were in such a condition that he required complete solitude.)

At length the man in the chair opened his eyes, and gazed at the motionless servant. Long experience had taught him that the most potent weapon in the world with what he was pleased to term "the lower orders," was a cold, malevolent sarcasm. Cursing anyone can stand—so John Marwood never cursed. He specialized in the icy sneer, and he was a fairly capable specialist. He enjoyed seeing a man writhe under his tongue: it afforded him an intense satisfaction, which can only be properly appreciated by the born bully. . . .

For a few moments the silence remained unbroken. There was no hurry, and undue precipitancy always spoilt these interviews. Each particular phase must be played to the end in order to get the full enjoyment, and the present phase was the silent interlude. It varied with the different servants, as to the length of time they could stand Marwood's eye without growing restless. And this man gave the best sport of all. In fact, on two or three occasions he had actually beaten Marwood at his own game: forced him to speak before he had intended to, before he had really prepared his remark. He stood now calmly gazing out of the window, perfectly deferential, perfectly self-composed, until Marwood could have struck him in his rage. He felt that he would willingly have given all he possessed just to see this man squirming and writhing in front of him . . . like a small boy who impales an insect on a pin. . . .

"Is there anything more you wish, sir?" Quite calmly the servant picked up the empty medicine glass.

"I suppose," said Marwood, striving to speak in his usual expressionless voice, "that you consider you have fulfilled all the obligations that can reasonably be expected of you in return for forty-eight pounds a year. Nevertheless, if it is not too much to ask, perhaps you would be kind enough to hand me that red volume from the bookshelf."

The man crossed the room and returned with the book.

"You would, of course," remarked Marwood, "give it to me upside down. And now—the evening paper . . . on that table . . ." He lay back completely exhausted. "At five o'clock—not five past or ten past—but at five, unless you are all too engrossed to think of the matter, perhaps one of you would again bring me my tonic. And until then I do not wish to be disturbed. Place the board on the door after you go out, and if it is within your power I entreat of you do not make a noise doing so."

"Very good, sir." With an inscrutable expression in his eyes the man stood watching Marwood to see if he had any further instructions. But the invalid apparently had not. He remarked "Forty-eight pounds a year. My God!" twice, in a resigned whisper, and then complete prostration supervened.

It was as the door was closing behind the servant that Marwood once more found his voice.

"It was forty-eight pounds you said," he called feebly.

"Yes, sir." Very deliberately the man held the door open, and stared at his employer's back. "In addition, however, there is a shilling a month for insurance stamps, and the usual washing bills. I will prepare a complete statement for you."

Marwood's eyes opened in speechless fury, and he sat up with a jerk. But the door had shut, and the sound of the man's footsteps had died away before he could think of a suitable answer to such a piece of gratuitous insolence. . . .

After a while he calmed down, and opened the book on his knees. As might have been expected, it was a medical treatise—one of the popular type. Couched in comprehensible language, the symptoms of every disease from housemaid's knee to consumption were set forth in its pages, and there were very few of those diseases which, at some period or other during the last six years, Marwood had not suffered from according to himself. That he had been completely unable to find any doctor who would support his diagnosis was merely a proof that all doctors were fools. Far better results could be obtained, he had come to the conclusion, by looking after oneself: and since chemists— who were also a race of fools—had a rooted objection to making up prescriptions unless they were ordered by a doctor, he had been compelled by *force majeure* to fall back on patent medicines. Of these, he consumed annually an incredible amount: and only his naturally strong constitution had enabled him to stand the strain.

This afternoon he was desirous of finding out what that sharp pain in his right shoulder-blade indicated. If he sent for one of those damned doctors, he would be told it was liver, and recommended to take exercise. . . . Exercise! Exercise!!! . . . With agonizing neuritis in his right leg.

It was no question of liver, that he knew. Heart, possibly—no, that was on the left side . . . or a tubercular growth. . . . There was a slight swelling as far as he had been able to make out the night before, by twisting round and moving a couple of looking-glasses into more favourable positions. And then the light had been wrong, and Grace had come in and laughed

at him.   She would: there wasn't a soul who cared in
the whole house—not one.   But they'd think differently . . . they'd think differently—when . . .

Rigid, motionless, Marwood stared in front of him,
gripping the arms of his chair.   Stab . . . stab . . .
stab . . . an excruciating pain had suddenly begun to
pierce him like a knife.   It started from the region
of his right shoulder and spread to his chest.   With
monotonous regularity it continued, while the flames
flickered in the grate, and fantastic shadows danced
round the darkening room.   Stab . . . stab . . . every
four or five seconds: till his whole body seemed to be
burning with the agony.

Once he raised his voice in a feeble little whining
cry.   "Liver!   They'll say it's liver."   He threw out
his hands with an impotent wail, only to put them
back on the arms of the chair again, as the pain jumped
viciously with the movement.

And then slowly it died away; the stabs became
fewer and fewer, and finally ceased altogether.   Very
carefully he lay back in his chair, and after a while
put a shaking hand to his forehead.   It was wet
with perspiration, and even at that moment he experienced a grim satisfaction at this conclusive evidence
of the agony he had suffered.   It was a pity Grace
was not there to see.   Then she wouldn't have
laughed.

He lay very silent, staring at the wall.   He was
still shaking from the effects of the bout, though the
relief from the actual pain was exquisite.   And it was
not for half an hour that the satisfaction he felt at this
proof of his sufferings was replaced by another feeling
which at first he found hard to analyse.   He shied
away from the analysis like a frightened colt; he assured
himself that it was only what he had known all along,
though none of these cursed doctors would believe him;

he proved conclusively that it only showed what he had always said—that he was a very sick man. But he proved it too conclusively; he proved it so that at last he really did believe it himself. And the feeling which replaced the satisfaction was fear-sickening, gripping fear. He who had called Wolf so often when others were about, and had raged fretfully because they had taken no notice, realized suddenly that, in truth, the Wolf had come. And John Marwood knew the conclusion of that fable.

Once again he wiped the sweat from his forehead, and, reaching out a trembling hand, he raised a glass of water to his lips. His throat felt dry and parched; the room seemed strangely hot. And then, with a sudden crash, a coal fell into the grate and lay there smoking.

With a little whimper of fear he dropped the glass and soaked himself with water.

II

You may know Tearle's Tea Shop in a certain little street off Shaftesbury Avenue; on the other hand, you may not. If you are supremely great and very beautiful, you probably patronize Rumpelmeyer's; if you aspire solely to the consumption of a good, wholesome bun, an A.B.C. is not to be despised. In fact, London's tea-shops are legion, and between them every taste from Tooting to Mayfair, and thence down again to Whitechapel is catered for. But there is only one Tearle's.

It would be hard to define the *clientèle* of Tearle's. All that one can say is that once a Tearleite always a Tearleite. The tables are sufficiently secluded to allow people to eat the mustard and cress, which is Tearle's speciality, in decency; they are not so completely hidden that it is unwise to take a step with-

out a warning cough. In short, it is Tearle's, and,
if you don't know it, go there and find out for yourself.

Grace Marwood had been sitting at her usual table
in the corner for ten minutes before Bryan Daventry
came in. He saw her as he reached the door, and, a
little abruptly, he stopped and hung up his coat and
hat. There were other pegs vacant nearer her table,
but, not for the first time, Daventry wanted those
few seconds' breathing space while he was still too
far away for her to see the expression on his face.
Because Daventry, being an ordinary decent man, to
say nothing of being a brilliantly successful doctor,
had decided some months ago that the intense, overpowering love he felt for Grace Marwood had got to
stop. Which, incidentally, is the sort of foolish thing
a man does decide.

He had never spoken about it to her. If you speak
about love, and mean it, to another man's wife, you
cannot change the conversation to easy prattle about
the weather. Something will happen one way or the
other; either you will be taken at your word, or the
lady will become peevish. And neither of these alternatives appealed to Daventry. If he had had to choose,
it would have been the first without hesitation; the
thought of making Grace angry, of cutting out these
occasional meetings, when he could sit near her, and
watch the little dark tendrils of hair curling over her
ears, could see the curve of her cheek and the soft
light in her wonderful deep blue eyes—the thought
of missing all that was inconceivable. And so he had
compromised, as has been known to happen before.
He continued to meet her, and discuss all those vague,
intimate things which mean such a big side of life to
a normal human being. But he never mentioned love,
and, of course, she had no idea of his feelings on the

matter. Which, incidentally, is the sort of foolish thing a man does think.

"You're late, *mon ami*," she said, holding out her hand as he came up.

"The ailments of the human race increase and multiply daily," he answered gravely, taking a cup of tea. "I investigated two completely fresh diseases to-day, and effectually cured both the proud proprietors."

"Bright man! Have a bun."

"I looked out the Latin for cauliflower, and told 'em they were suffering from that. Pleased as Punch —both of 'em. Then, with the help of a little Eno's, suitably coloured——" He shrugged his shoulders. "And what has Mrs. Marwood been doing to-day?"

"Existing, Bryan; just existing. John has discovered an entirely new pain."

For a moment their eyes met, and then Daventry looked away a little quickly.

"Where is the location this time?" he asked, stirring his tea.

"Oh, somewhere in his back. I found him balanced on his chest of drawers last night, with his shaving-glass in one hand, and an electric torch that wouldn't work in the other, trying to see if there was a swelling." She smiled—a fleeting, bitter smile. "Poor old John!"

"Poor old John!" echoed Daventry savagely. "My dear Grace, if poor old John took a two-mile run in the Park, wet or fine, every morning of his life for the next six months, there would be no new pains—— as I told him myself."

The girl gurgled gently. "I remember the occasion perfectly. His remarks after you had gone, on your personal appearance, your ability, your utter lack of even the remotest claim to be considered fitted to qualify as an assistant to a dresser, are indelibly stamped on my brain."

Daventry laughed with her, and for a while neither of them spoke. There was never any necessity for speech between these two; it came spontaneously when the spirit moved them; at other times they were both very content to sit and watch the pictures that dance in the flames, or twist gently upwards in the hazy blue smoke of a cigarette. His dreams were always the same, impossible of fruition, and so, maybe, the more wonderful. With her they were not so clear; they were vaguer, more rambling, less personal. She knew his feelings for her, not, perhaps, in all their intensity, but she knew he cared. And as for herself —well, only once had she really faced it. She had realized then that if she was not in love with him, it was merely because it had never been crystallized into so many words. Poor old John stood in the way, and so what was the use? For a time after that realization she had avoided Daventry, and then gradually their old intimacy returned, their old visits to Tearle's were resumed. Not one word had Bryan ever spoken to which John himself could have objected—but the knowledge was always there. Underneath, smouldering fiercely, was the flame; deliberately she ignored it. And if at times there came a faint premonition of danger, she thrust it from her. Was there not always —poor old John?

She took a cigarette from the case he was holding out to her, and waited while he lit a match.

"How goes the research, Bryan?"

For a moment his eyes gleamed with the enthusiasm of the scientist; then he grinned boyishly. And when Bryan Daventry grinned, people he was with forgot he was a brilliantly successful investigator of thirty-five; they regarded him as a schoolboy who had just been presented with half-a-crown within sight of the tuck-shop.

"It's early days, Grace, to say for certain," he answered. "But I believe honestly and candidly that I've got it. And if so——" His fist clenched on the table, and under his breath he whispered again—— "If so——"

"If so——" She looked at him with shining eyes. "Why, you'll have done what no one has done before, Bryan."

"That's so," he answered gravely. "Yes, that's so. But it's not so much that I'm thinking of: it's the suffering thousands who have died of it. Died in agony, Grace—hideous agony. It's the most awful disease—cancer. And if one can save 'em in the future —if——" Once again his eyes glowed fiercely.

"And when will you know if you are right?"

"Not for years—for certain." Quickly, incisively, his hands moved as he spoke—strong, capable hands —the hands of a great surgeon. "You see," he was talking rapidly, and the ash grew longer on her forgotten cigarette, "one operates. Apparently everything is all right; the growth is removed. But not for five, six, possibly ten years, can one be certain that it will not return. By the old method it always did —in a few months. Now, by my new way, I know it will not come back for years: I hope it will not come back at all. But it's all experiment, experiment, experiment. One must find cases; one must operate; and then one must see. Because"—his fingers drummed on the table—"there is a risk—a big risk."

"You mean that it is kill or cure?"

"More or less. At least, that's what they say." He laughed shortly. "Old Sir Henry Darlington told me so this morning. He was very nice about it; but he evidently regarded it as the enthusiasm of youth.

So do Birkett and Longhurst." He paused for a moment and stared at the girl. "I'll show 'em, Grace," he continued quietly. "I'll show 'em that it's cure—not kill. And then——" His voice rang out with a triumphant note; on his face was the look of the strong man who sees success within his reach, and already tastes the sweets of it in his mind.

The girl touched his hand with one of hers. "I know you will, Bryan," she whispered, and there was a wonderful light in her eyes. "I know it. And oh! my dear, how proud I'll be of you."

She had spoken without thinking, spoken the thing that was uppermost in her mind. And the smouldering flame seized its opportunity and burst out. The doctor had gone; it was the man who sat beside her staring into her eyes, with the unmistakable message blazing from his own. She shivered, and tried to look away, but it was too late.

"Don't say it, Bryan, don't say it. For God's sake, don't say it."

"And why not, Grace? Why shouldn't one say the truth? You've known it, my dear, all along."

He beckoned to the waitress, and paid the bill. Then, in silence, he helped her on with her coat. Once his hand brushed her neck, and with a sudden, ungovernable rush of joy he felt her shiver at his touch.

"I'm going to take you home," he said quietly. "There are one or two things I must say to you; things which should have been said before."

He beckoned a taxi and gave the driver the address. Then he got in, and the car shot out into Shaftesbury Avenue.

"You care, Grace," he said, still in the same quiet tone, and taking both her hands in his. "Thank God! I know it: I saw it in your eyes. . . . But I'd just love to hear you say it, my dear . . . once."

"Oh! Bryan. . . ." Her voice was trembling, so that he could scarcely hear the words. "What's the use, my dear . . . what's the use."

"I don't care what the use is just at the moment," he answered. "I only know that I'm a man, and you're a woman, and that I've loved you as I never believed I could have loved anyone for years." He was bending towards her as he spoke. "My dear," he whispered hoarsely. "Oh! my dear."

He caught her in his arms and kissed her; kissed her eyes, her hair, her mouth. And after a weak, little fluttering attempt to push him away, she wound her arms round his neck, and gave him back kiss for kiss.

It seemed as if they could never stop, but at length, with a little gasp, she broke away from his arms and leant back in the corner of the taxi, with closed eyes. He watched her hungrily by the light of the passing lamps, taking in every detail of the exquisite profile. For the time he was mad, past thought, past care, past everything save the unutterable wonder of the woman he had held in his arms.

"It's all wrong, Bryan," she said wearily. "Why did you do it, my dear—why?"

"As well ask a flower why it comes out in the sun," he answered gravely. "I couldn't help it, Grace; I just couldn't help it." He took one of her hands, and it lay in his, lifeless and inert. "We've been playing with fire for a long while, dear; and I've known it. But I couldn't have given up seeing you; you meant everything to me. You tried once, I know—and that ought to have warned me. But, I suppose, there are some things which are a bit too strong for us." He laughed suddenly, and drew her to him again. "What's it matter, darling, what's anything matter, except that you're you and I'm me." He was whispering close to her ear, hardly conscious of what he said. "I love you, you wonderful woman, adore you, worship you. . . . And I can't think of anything else that counts two straws—not in the whole wide world."

He tried to kiss the averted face, but this time she pushed him away, gently but inexorably.

"John matters, Bryan," she answered quietly. "That's why I don't think you must ever see me again."

"Not see you again!" With a short, amazed laugh the man looked at her. "After this! My dear, you don't love John."

"No," she said thoughtfully. "I don't . . . I don't think I ever have—not really. It's been a sort of pity all along. But I'm married to him."

"That difficulty has been got over before now," he answered grimly. "Grace! dear girl of mine—you *can't* tie yourself for life to a receptacle of patent medicines."

"I have done so; that's the trouble." She looked at him gravely; then, with a weary little laugh, she turned and stared out of the window. "Oh! Bryan, why did you do it?" The oft-repeated cry came again —came with a catch in her voice. "I did so love our friendship; our teas together; hearing about your work and life. It was the only thing that made life possible. And now—it's over."

"A man and woman like you and I want more than teas and friendship, Grace." With level eyes the man was staring at the driver's back: then they fixed themselves on the cigarette carefully placed behind his ear. "We deluded ourselves into thinking that we could cheat fate: we failed. If you like, I failed. It doesn't matter very much, does it? All that concerns us at the moment is what we are going to do now."

"What thousands of others have had to do before us," she answered wearily. "Grin and bear it, Bryan —what else?"

"What else?" he cried fiercely. "Why, everything else. Why should we do as thousands of others have done? Why should we make ourselves miserable because a lot of damned fools say it's the proper thing to do. Grace—we've only got one life. It's ours to make or mar. My dear! it's impossible for us to leave it like this—utterly, absolutely impossible. We're nearly there now: I've got no time to *make* you feel as I feel—to *make* you see the only solution." He took her hand, and held it in both of his. "Come and have tea with me to-morrow. Let's talk it over, Grace: let's see if we can't find a way out: let's be sure. . . ."

The taxi drew up at the house, and he dropped her hand. "Will you come?"

For a moment they stood together on the pavement facing one another. Then, very slowly: "I don't know, Bryan: I don't know."

"Will you ring me up?" Eagerly he pleaded with her, clinging to every second left.

"Perhaps," she answered. "But I've got to think things out—alone."

Then she left him, and the door closed behind her.

"Cold night, guv'nor." The driver's voice roused him from his thoughts.

"Very cold," he answered. "Take me to the Junior Reform, please."

And peering through the curtains of the house he had just left, stood Grace Marwood, watching the red tail-lamp of the taxi till it disappeared round a bend in the road.

III

Dinner was never a very edifying meal in the Marwood household. Grace had long given up the experiment of asking in any guests: in fact, the last time had been four years ago. The remembrance of that occasion still lingered in her memory. A certain flippant stockbroker had been present, who insisted on capping every one of his host's symptoms with those possessed by an aunt of his. In fact, the hypothetical aunt won in a canter: the finishing touch being put on when the stockbroker jovially comforted Marwood with the information that the old girl wasn't dead yet.

And to-night, as she sat opposite her husband, Grace was trying to get her bearings. In silence she had watched him hobble in between two footmen: with weary contempt she had followed the old familiar procedure. First the footstool was adjusted for the leg that had neuritis: then the cushion was put behind his back. Finally one of the men advanced with a purple liquid on a salver, which represented the last brand of patent filth that was being tried. She had grown so used to the whole programme that generally it meant nothing to her; it was part of her life, and she had accepted it as such. The thought of changing it in any way had simply never occurred to her: it was as much part of John as his face.

But now, as the meal progressed, in silence as usual —(his latest idea was that speech upset the digestion) —she was taking stock from a new standpoint. Her mind went back to the day when they were married eight years ago. She had been twenty-one—her husband ten years older: and under the influence of the inscrutable aberration which affects people at such times she had believed she loved him. She had known he was a little delicate: but he played golf and tennis, and occasionally rode to hounds. And then, a few months after their marriage, he had had a severe bout of typhoid fever. From that date things had gradually grown worse, until about three years later an aunt had died unexpectedly, leaving him all her money, thus enabling him to retire from business and become a professional invalid. Step by step she recalled the whole process; relentlessly she asked herself whether she, herself, was to blame in any way. Supposing, when she first noticed the way he was drifting, she had laughed him out of it—and gone on laughing, till for very shame he had pulled himself together! But it had all been so gradual: so impossible to say, "This ache of yours is twaddle: and if there's anything in that one, for the love of Heaven take a cold bath and go and skip in the garden." Besides, to a woman of Grace's temperament, it seemed so inconceivable that anybody could *want* to be ill. . . .

"My digestive tablet." Her husband's voice recalled her to the present, and she looked across at him.

One of the footmen was bearing a small bottle forward on a tray. He then poured out a wineglassful of warm water, and with great solemnity John Marwood consumed his pill, to frown heavily on sipping the water.

"It is, I suppose," he remarked wearily, "too much to expect that you would give me water of the right temperature. This is several degrees too hot."

And suddenly Grace laughed. "Why don't you tickle your throat, John, and slip it down like a dog? You'd get some exercise that way."

"My dear Grace,"—he stared at her in pained surprise, "are you trying to be funny?"

For a moment she seemed about to speak; then she changed her mind, and continued her dinner in silence. For the first time in their married life she saw her husband as he really was: only too clearly she realized the cause of her enlightenment. She was still undecided as to what to do when they rose from the table: her mind seemed incapable of grappling with the problem. It was so unexpected, so huge; it dazed and frightened her. Two facts alone stuck out clear above everything: she loved Bryan Daventry, and she was married to this—this receptacle of patent medicines. . . .

"If you could spare me a few minutes, Grace," he remarked, with his usual expression of studied politeness, "there is something I would like to say to you in my study."

"I will come in shortly. There is something I have to say to you, also."

She watched him totter from the room, supported by the two footmen: then she moved to the fire, and spread out her hands to the blaze. Once or twice she shivered, though the room was warm: then, turning round, she studied her reflection in the long mirror opposite. She looked at herself critically, as she would have looked at another woman: then she summed herself up.

"I am pretty, prettier than nine women out of ten. My figure is good, and so is my complexion. And I might as well be forty-eight with false teeth, as far as John is concerned. Is it worth it?"

Again she crouched over the fire, striving to read the answer in the flames. Bryan's face danced in front of her, and she pressed the back of her hand to her mouth as if she could still feel his kisses, warm and passionate, on her lips. It was impossible: she couldn't go on; she would go to him to-morrow, and tell him. . . .

"Mr. Marwood is in his study, madam."

The footman's voice at the door roused her, and she rose to her feet. And as she walked slowly down the passage to her husband's room there was a faint smile on her face.

He was in his usual chair carefully muffled up in a shawl: sudden changes of temperature were very apt to give him a chill. By his side was the inevitable red treatise on diseases, and a jug of hot water: his face bore its invariable expression of resigned misery. For a while she stood on the other side of the fireplace watching him: then she sat down.

"What is it you wish to say?" she asked.

"I can hardly anticipate that it will be of much interest to you," he remarked. "What little consideration you ever possessed for my health seems to have gone long ago. . . . But still, in case anything should happen to me, I feel it right to let you know what occurred this afternoon. Possibly you remember that stabbing pain I mentioned to you last night?"

"Yes, I do." Her voice was expressionless.

"I am honoured." He took a sip of hot water. "This afternoon when you were out, and I, as usual, was alone—it returned. For half an hour I suffered incredible agony, and I am convinced that something very serious is the matter with me." He paused impressively. "It is not that, however, which I wish to discuss with you: the matter is not likely to interest you sufficiently. It is the question of business, and money, in the event of my death. Would you be good enough to hand me that account-book?"

But Grace made no effort to rise: her eyes remained steadily fixed on her husband's face.

"How old are you, John? Forty, isn't it?"

"I hardly see the relevance of the remark: though I am flattered at your intimate knowledge."

"Forty," she continued. "And we've been married eight years. Eight years—time enough to have had two or three children."

"My dear Grace." He raised a protesting hand. "With my state of health. . . . Children. . . ."

"What do you think those eight years have meant to me, John? Living with a man the height of whose ambition is to discover a new pill."

"Really, Grace." Genuine amazement was dawning on his face. "You are talking most strangely tonight."

"Am I?" she answered. "I wonder why. The only pity is that I didn't start talking strangely, as you call it, rather sooner in our married life. I'm very much afraid it's too late now."

"Too late for what?"

"What would you say, John, if I went away and left you?" She looked at him curiously.

"Went away," he echoed. "Haven't you everything here that you want? A comfortable house—servants —money. My dear Grace, I think you're mad."

"No, John—I'm sane for the first time. During these last few years, I've watched you slowly become a useless thing. It's been so gradual—the process— that it's been difficult, at any particular moment, to put out a hand to try to stop it. . . . Besides, I don't know that I particularly wanted to. You were very happy; I, as you have just said, had a comfortable house—servants—money. You were just part of the house to me: exactly, John, as I was part of the house to you." She watched the outraged horror which was slowly overspreading her husband's face. "To-night, at dinner, for the first time I realized where we stood. I don't want a husband who is part of the house."

"And would it be indiscreet to ask what has caused this sudden illuminating discovery?"

"Not at all. I was on the point of telling you. House—servants—money: but can't you think of anything else, John, which a woman wants, besides which all those things count for nothing?"

The man swallowed twice, and leaned forward, plucking at the arms of the chair. "You mean," he muttered thickly, "that you're in love with another man?"

"Another is hardly the right word. I've never been in love with you, though, at one time, you might have made me so. But I am in love with a man."

"Who is he? What is the blackguard's name?" His voice rose to a shout, and he half-rose to his feet.

Grace looked at him unmoved. "Why should you mind, I wonder? You don't love me yourself: I'm just part of the furniture. You would infinitely sooner read about a new symptom than talk to me."

"Don't argue," he cried, "don't quibble, damn you. Who is the man?"

She gave a short laugh. "You're very nearly human to-night, John. It's the only time I've ever seen you behave like a man. But," she went on quietly, "I am not going to tell you his name: at least—not at present."

With a stupendous effort Marwood controlled himself and sat back in his chair. "Is it too much to hope," he remarked in his usual voice after a few moments, "that I shall be sufficiently honoured to be told what you propose to do?"

The girl looked at him thoughtfully. "I haven't made up my mind myself yet," she answered. "The thing has come so suddenly that I don't quite know where I am. In one way, I'm sorry: anything which completely uproots the old familiar landmarks is disturbing. But in another way, John, I'm glad—wonderfully, wonderfully glad." She stared at the fire in silence for a while, and the man watched her covertly. To all appearance he had completely recovered his self-control, but behind his mask of cynical indifference a volcano of fury and hatred was seething. She had got clean through the joints in his armour: for the first time, in so many words, she had told him that she knew his ill-health was merely a pose. And such was the manner of the man, that it was that fact which now made him boil with rage, far more than the knowledge that she was in love with somebody else. He felt an insane desire to punish her for his failure. . . .

"May I ask," he said at length, "when you made this interesting discovery?"

"A long, long while ago," she answered quietly. "But it was only this afternoon . . ."

"That things came to a head." Marwood laughed sneeringly. "And then, as befits a dutiful wife, you immediately decided to give your husband the joyful news."

"No. Oh! no, I didn't." She shook her head. "I decided to study you from the new aspect: to try and think of you as a man and not as—well, not as I have thought of you in the past. But it can't be done—not here. Your surroundings are too strong; you can't break away from them in this house. You had your digestive pill as usual, and I only just averted a discussion on the new symptom. Now, I've got an offer to make to you, John. I want to think of you as a man: I want . . . to give you a fair chance. . . . Will you come with me for two months—one month even—to Switzerland, and go in for some winter sports? Will you make an effort to break away from all this ridiculous twaddle—and live once more, as a man should live? If you'll do that, and succeed—and I know you will succeed—I'll make you—I promise you that I, on my part, will give up the—the other man. I can't promise that I won't see him again, but there shall never be anything more between us than there is now—and that is nothing." She turned to her husband. . . . "Well!"

But John Marwood made no answer. He had hardly heard the last part of her words, as with agony unspeakable, the stabbing pain of the afternoon again burned through his body. Rigid, gripping the arms

of his chair, he sat staring in front of him, while the
torture wracked him and the figure of his wife danced
before his eyes.

At last, through clenched teeth he got out two words
—"My back." Surely she must see the pain he was
in: surely even she must realize that this was no pose,
now.

But all Grace Marwood saw was the familiar spectacle
of her husband giving one of his usual performances.
That was his answer to her offer, and a bitter, contemptuous anger took possession of her.

"So that is your reply, is it?" she said slowly.
"Another dumb Crambo show. So be it: I will act
accordingly."

Without a second glance at him she turned and left
the room. As she opened the door a gasping cry
came from the man in the chair, but she took no notice:
she had heard those gasping cries before. They were
a very popular piece of business with the actor in
question.

The matter was settled: to-morrow she would go to
tea again with Bryan Daventry, and then . . . The
sight of the telephone made her pause, and after a
moment's indecision, she took the handle off the
receiver. She would ring him up now, and tell him.

"Mrs. Marwood speaking. . . . Oh! is that you?
. . . I'll come to tea to-morrow. . . . What . . . now.
. . . Oh! I couldn't; it's so late. . . ." Convention
still pulled, convention would probably have won. To
go to a man's rooms at that hour, even if it was quite
safe . . . And then one of the footmen walked past
her with a bottle of green medicine. . . . She turned to
the mouthpiece, her mind made up. "All right; in
half an hour." .

She heard the delighted cry of joy at the other end:
with a faint smile she replaced the receiver.

She paused at the foot of the stairs, as the butler came out of the dining-room. "Parkins, I want a taxi in ten minutes." Then with the smile still on her lips she went slowly up to her room.

IV

"Bryan—stop!" With a breathless little laugh she pushed him away. "You know you're really a most violent person."

"Do you wonder," he answered, taking off her cloak, "when I actually see you here, in the flesh, in my rooms? Why, you darling, I simply can't believe it. I'll be waking up in a minute and finding that it's really to-morrow morning, and that you are the elderly char-lady, who will infallibly give notice."

He pushed her gently into a huge chair by the fire, and then busied himself getting some forks out of a sideboard.

"I don't want anything to eat, Bryan."

He looked at her with a grave smile. "I don't think, somehow, you've had much dinner to-night. And"—he again busied himself with his preparations—"I have here a bird, a little caviare, and a bottle of Perrier Jouet. If I consume the whole bottle I shal be tight; if you help me and don't eat—you'll be *Voilà tout!*" He put a finishing touch to the table and then sat down opposite to her. "Has anything happened?"

"Not at all unexpected." She gave a short laugh. "I told him after dinner to-night that I'd fallen in love with someone."

"Ah! You told him that, my dear? Well?"

"I didn't tell him who it was—though he wanted to know."

"Somewhat naturally."

"But he isn't natural, Bryan. That's just the point:

there's nothing natural about him." Then, after a
little pause: "I made him an offer."

"Yes, dear." His voice was very gentle. "What
was it?"

"I told him that if he would come with me to Switzerland for two months, or even one, and take up winter
sports—if he'd show himself to be a man and not what
he is—I'd give that someone up." She heard his
breath come sharply. "I had to, Bryan; I had to give
him the chance."

"And what did he say?"

"He said nothing." She laughed at the recollection.
"He decided that that was a suitable moment to give
one of his celebrated invalid performances. I'd told
him that I'd known for years he was only posing. I
suppose he thought it was more important to try and
convince me on that point than to bother over such an
utterly insignificant thing as my being in love with
another man. So I got it all complete—including the
shuddering gasp as I opened the door and left him."
She paused, her hands locked together on her lap.
"It's finished it, Bryan. . . . If he'd gone on raving
and cursing as he did to start with, I'd have tried again.
I'd have made him come. I'd have given him some
chance even if not the one I suggested. But . . .
now . . ."

With her breast rising and falling stormily, she
stared at the fire, and for a while the man watched her
gravely. He could see the whole scene as clearly as
if he had been there himself, and as he looked at the
girl a great wonder took possession of him that any man
could be such an unutterable fool as to refuse her offer.

"So now you've come to me." He rose and sat
down on the arm of her chair.

"Yes." She looked up into his face. "Don't you
want me?"

"Want you? My dear." He bent and kissed the upturned mouth, and for a moment she clung to him.

"You do love me, Bryan—really and truly?"

"Really and truly," he answered with a little smile. "So much that . . ." He rose abruptly and stood by the fire-place with his back to her. "So much that I'm afraid. You see, I'm only a man, and not a particularly righteous specimen at that."

"Afraid! What of?"

He knew she was standing just behind him, and with a sudden gasp he swung round and caught her in his arms.

"I'm afraid because friendship isn't enough, Grace: because you know that it isn't and I know that it isn't. Because I want you immeasurably more than that; because I want everything you can give me; because I want you—all of you." He held her at arm's length and stared into the eyes which met his without flinching. "We're neither of us children; we both of us know exactly what it means. And, my dear, sooner or later, it is the woman who pays. That's what makes me afraid. It's no good hoping that we shall be exceptions to the rule; everybody has always hoped that, and found they were wrong." Gently he pushed her backwards and forwards, and though his lips were smiling, his eyes were grave and serious. As he had said, they were neither of them children, and he, at any rate, knew exactly where he stood. The trouble is that an exact knowledge of one's proximity to the top of the cliff is not of great value if there's a landslip.

"I ought not to have asked you to come round to-night, my dear," he went on slowly. "But then, we don't always do what we ought, little girl . . . not always. And I couldn't help it; I couldn't help it. When I heard your dear voice at the other end of the line—why, I just went mad." He gave a whimsical laugh, and the girl laughed too.

"Ah! but did you, my dear?" she said. "I loved your madness."

"But would you love it, Grace, if it went on?" he answered soberly. "Would there not come a time when you'd say to me, 'The madness is past; we must be sane'? And you'd find it was too late." His eyes searched her face hungrily, and suddenly he threw back his head and laughed. "What fools we are—what damned fools! Day after day, night after night, I've imagined this, Grace: thought of it—longed for it. I've seen you sitting in that chair opposite me; I've held conversations with you. And then I've woken up to reality and done some work." His hands fell to his sides, and he laughed again.

"It is reality, Bryan," said the girl with an adorable smile. "I'm here."

"Do I not know it?" he cried roughly. He seized her in his arms and rained kisses on her face—mad, passionate kisses that left her gasping and breathless. "That's why I'm such a fool. . . . You're here; I can see you, touch you. The dream has come true; and now—I'm afraid."

With a weary little sigh the girl sat down. She felt suddenly tired—tired and hopeless. She knew he was right, and yet . . .

"What are we to do, Bryan?" Helplessly she appealed to him. "I can't go back to him. It isn't as if he wanted me—he doesn't. He's just utterly selfish. And why should I?"

"For no reason at all, dear, as far as he's concerned." Even at that moment the complete change of rôle appealed to him with cynical humour. "He's absolutely unworthy of the smallest consideration. It's you I'm thinking of . . ."

"But if I'd sooner, Bryan. . . .   Surely if I'm prepared to risk it . . ."   Her hand was on his arm,
pulling him towards her.   "Don't you understand, my
dear . . . I—I love you?"

Blindly he turned towards her and held out his arms.
What did it matter? . . .   And at that moment the
telephone bell rang.

With a muttered curse, Daventry took off the
receiver.

"Speaking. . . .   Oh! it's you, Arbuthnot, is it?
. . . Where from?"   His back was towards the girl,
and she did not see the look of amazement which was
spreading over his face.   She could hear the low metallic voice of the man at the other end, punctuated occasionally by a word or two from Bryan.   The speaker
seemed to have a lot to say, and idly she wondered
who he was . . . Arbuthnot: the name conveyed nothing
to her.   And then she ceased to bother, and simply
lay back, watching the man she loved.   What a man he
was; how utterly worth the sacrifice.   After all, why
should people find out?   Why shouldn't it just be
their secret—his and hers?   And perhaps in time she
could fix up something—arrange a divorce somehow,
and . . .

"Finished your old talk?"   He had put down the
receiver, and was standing motionless, still with his
back to her.   "Then come over here at once—I'm
jealous."

After a while he turned round, and with a little cry
the girl rose.

"What is it, Bryan?   What has happened?"

"How long has your husband had this pain in his
back?"   The question was so completely unexpected
that for a moment she could only stare at him speechlessly.

"What do you mean?" she stammered at length.

"I've just been talking to Doctor Arbuthnot." His voice was devoid of all expression. "He is with your husband now. He tells me that he is suffering from a malignant cancerous growth, and suggests that I am the only man in London who can possibly save his life. He further remarks that it is an admirable opportunity for me to test my new cure."

For what seemed an eternity there was silence in the room; then, very slowly, Daventry crossed to the girl. And after a little while he spoke again with a dreadful deliberation.

"I'm going round to see your husband now. Isn't it damned funny?"

v

In the hall below Grace Marwood waited while Daventry made his examination. She felt dazed and a little stunned by the suddenness of it all; barely conscious of the presence of the servants who seemed to be ceaselessly going up and down the stairs to her husband's room on different errands. So preoccupied had she been with her thoughts that she had almost forgotten to play her necessary rôle of ignorance as Doctor Arbuthnot told her the dreadful news.

"I have telephoned for Doctor Daventry," he murmured. "A specialist, Mrs. Marwood . . . young, but extraordinarily brilliant. Should be here at any moment. . . . Until then, perhaps, it would be better if you did not see your husband. It might upset him, you know. Why not have a glass of wine and a biscuit?"

At length the worthy doctor had left her alone, only to return in a few minutes and introduce Bryan Daventry. The solemn introduction had seemed in keeping with everything; she had felt a wild desire to scream with laughter, and only Bryan's quiet, steady

eyes had pulled her together.   Then the two men had
left her alone and gone upstairs to her husband . . .

She glanced at her wrist-watch impatiently.   Half
an hour.   Surely they could have found out in half an
hour.   Cancer . . . John with cancer . . . John really
ill, in agonizing pain.   It was impossible—all imagination, as usual.   Arbuthnot was an old fool. . . .   But
why half an hour if it was only imagination?   Bryan
wouldn't take half an hour diagnosing a case of imagination. . . .   He was far too clever to be deceived, and
once he knew, he was far too straightforward not to
say what he thought. . . .   If it was imagination that
is . . .   If not . . .

Ah! if not, what then?   It altered everything at
once.   John with one of his countless little aches and
pains was one thing; John with cancer was quite another.
Dimly she tried to realize what it would mean—how it
would affect her life, but her brain would not respond.
It seemed to be whirling in a series of vicious circles,
with a jeering fate grinning at her through the centre
of each.

"You thought to escape, did you?" it mocked.
"You thought you could take matters into your own
hands?   Well, let's see what you make of this card
I've just dealt you."

Cancer!   And suddenly Grace Marwood passed her
hand over her forehead with a little cry.   After all,
he was her husband, and for the last half-hour her
thoughts had principally centred on what this thing
would mean to her—not on what it would mean to
him. . . .

She looked up as a door above opened, and her heart
began to beat a little faster.   They had decided—she
could hear their low voices—and in a moment or two
she would be told, one way or the other.   Slowly the
two doctors came down the stairs, and crossed the hall

towards her, while she peered at Bryan's inscrutable face, trying to read what was in his mind.

"Well!" Her dry lips traced the word rather than spoke it, and Bryan Daventry pulled forward a chair for her.

"Sit down, Mrs. Marwood." For a moment their eyes met; then he looked away again quickly. "I am afraid that what Doctor Arbuthnot feared is quite correct." His voice was very quiet, and he kept his face half-averted from the woman he loved. "Your husband is undoubtedly suffering from a cancerous growth, though it will be necessary for me to make another examination to-morrow."

"Is he in great pain?" she whispered.

"Very great, while it lasts, but it is intermittent," answered Daventry.

"And what—what are you going to do?" She was still staring at Bryan, but it was Doctor Arbuthnot who answered.

"You probably don't know, Mrs. Marwood," he murmured, "that Doctor Daventry has recently been engaged in the most exhaustive research work into this very disease. And it will be necessary for you and your husband to come to a decision." He glanced inquiringly at Daventry, who remained motionless, staring at the fire. After a slight pause, he turned back to Mrs. Marwood. "A decision, my dear lady, and a grave decision. As you probably are aware, science up to date has produced no certain cure for cancer. The growth can be removed with a knife, but in practically all cases it returns again. I may say in all cases when it has gone so far as I fear is the case with your husband. Consequently, speaking humanly, you have your first alternative for certain. An operation; the gradual return of the growth; a further operation. And finally the time when another operation is of no avail."

"And what is the second alternative?" Her words seemed to come from a great distance as she asked the question to which she already knew the answer.

Doctor Arbuthnot cleared his throat, and again glanced at Daventry. "The second alternative is this. Doctor Daventry in his research work believes that he has discovered a cure for this dreadful disease, which will prevent its return in the course of a few years. In other words, he believes that one operation by his process would be sufficient. But the process has not yet been put to the test of time. It may be that he is wrong, that the growth will return. . . ."

"In which case my husband would be no worse off than under the first alternative," said Grace Marwood, still in the same detached voice. She felt as if she was acting in a play.

"Yes, but there is another thing," began Doctor Arbuthnot, slowly rubbing his hands together. "Perhaps Doctor Daventry——"

At the direct request, Bryan Daventry swung round, and stared at the woman.

"The other thing, Mrs. Marwood, is this. By my method your husband might die at once." Arbuthnot had turned away and was studying an old print on the wall; for the moment he was forgotten. "He might die at once," repeated Daventry slowly.

"That is the second alternative. . . ."

Her breath coming quickly, her knuckles gleaming white on the arms of her chair, Grace Marwood stared at Bryan's face. It was the sort of situation which happened in books—impossibly unreal—grotesquely absurd. And once again the feeling that she was acting in some dreadful play came over her. Bryan's eyes were still fixed on her; the ticking of the hall clock sounded incredibly loud.

"He might die at once," she repeated foolishly.

"Perhaps it would be better—I mean——" she added hurriedly as she saw him stiffen and grow rigid—"I mean even that would be better than years of horrible suffering."

But still she stared at him fascinated, and he stared back, while the worthy Doctor Arbuthnot passed on to another print.

"Supposing my operation was successful," Bryan Daventry was speaking again—speaking mechanically, "your husband would require the most constant and unremitting attention for many years to come. He would have to leave England and live in a warmer, drier climate . . . the south of France, perhaps, or some place like that. He would, in fact, be an invalid, and an invalid in reality," he added as an afterthought.

She glanced at Doctor Arbuthnot—he was at the other end of the hall—then she stood up suddenly.

"Bryan," she whispered. "Bryan, what does it mean—to me—to you and I?"

"It means," he answered slowly, "the most devilish temptation that a human being can well be subjected to. Because—Grace," and for a moment his hand gripped her arm, "no one *can* ever find out."

"Well, have you explained everything to Mrs. Marwood?" Bryan's hand dropped to his side as Arbuthnot approached. "It is a risk, of course, my dear young lady," continued the doctor, swinging his pince-nez between his fingers, "a great risk. But as an old practitioner, who has been forced in the course of many years to see much of the dreadful agony which goes with this hideous scourge, I would venture to suggest to you that the risk is worth while. To see a dearly loved one in the throes of the most fearful pain, to realize that no medical skill can alleviate that pain, is a very terrible thing. And that, Mrs. Marwood, is what it must come to under the old methods—my methods.

Doctor Daventry is of the younger school, and, in medicine as in other things, youth will be served. Anything—anything is better than the future which I can offer your husband—even death at once." He paused, and laid a kindly hand on her arm.

"Then it is your advice, Doctor Arbuthnot," she said steadily, "that my husband should put himself in Doctor Daventry's hands?"

"Yes," answered the old doctor gravely. "That is my advice."

"I will tell him what you say." Her voice came still steady, but her eyes avoided Bryan Daventry. "Shall I go to him now?"

"Certainly. But don't over-excite him. Daventry and I will come round again to-morrow."

With a slight inclination of her head, she left the two men and passed up the stairs. And it was as they heard the door of John Marwood's room open and close that Arbuthnot turned to his companion.

"A fine girl," he remarked. "And a dreadful tragedy. But, my young friend—it's *your* chance."

"Precisely," murmured Daventry. "Precisely. It's my chance. Shall we say eleven o'clock to-morrow morning for our further examination?"

VI

Her husband was propped up in bed as Grace entered his room. For a moment she stayed close to the door, watching his profile; then she crossed to his side and stood looking down at him.

"Have they told you?" He opened his eyes as he spoke.

"Yes, John. . . . I'm sorry." Even as she said it the pitiful inadequacy of the words mocked her.

"You are more than kind," he murmured. "I trust that my trifling ailment has not interfered in any way with your plans this evening—or curtailed your enjoyment."

His wife bit her lip and turned away. It was going to be hard; everything had always been hard with John. He seemed to take a delight in making it so. But in that one brief look at his face before he had spoken the die had been cast, the decision made. She hardly realized it herself yet; the events of the past two hours were still too fresh. But one thing she did realize with an awful horror, which left her tongue-tied —for a time downstairs she had actually contemplated —murder. Not exactly that, of course. Not murder, but an accident . . . one of the alternatives. . . . And Bryan had contemplated it too. She, an ordinary normal woman, and—murder.

She shuddered a little, and as quickly as possible, so as not to disturb him, she put some coal on the fire. Murder. . . . The word danced at her out of the flames. . . . Murder. To kill her husband, or to connive at his death, so that she might be free to marry the murderer. She shuddered again, then she rose and stood at the foot of the bed. Thank God! the madness was past; the only possible course was plain to see. Whatever was best for her husband must be done; if necessary, another opinion must be taken, and . . .

"Have they told you the alternatives?" John Marwood's harsh voice broke in upon her train of thought.

"Yes, John," she answered gently. "They told me just before I came up."

"And can you detach your thoughts sufficiently from the fortunate man who has obtained your affection to give your opinion on them?" He closed his eyes wearily and lay back on his pillows.

"I want you to understand one thing quite clearly," returned his wife, still in the same gentle voice. "The fact that you have cancer completely alters everything.

Had I known earlier in the evening I should never have spoken to you about it. . . . As it is, I want you to try and forget what I said, if you can. It was—oh! I was irritated, because I thought you were shamming."

The man laughed—a little malevolent laugh. "What a dreadful shock it must have been to you when you found I wasn't. But whatever the cause, my dear Grace, of your interesting confession, the fact remains that you have confessed. And it is a source of great grief to me that we shall apparently have to leave London and go and live abroad for some years. It is dreadful to think of you being parted from him." He raised a feebly protesting hand. "Would it be asking too much of you not to shake the bed?"

"You propose, then, to let Doctor Daventry try his new cure?" she asked slowly.

"That is my intention at present," returned her husband. "What do you think about it?"

For a moment she hesitated; then: "I think we ought to get another opinion."

"May I ask why? I am fairly well conversant with the subject of cancer, and what that fool Arbuthnot says is quite correct. There is no cure known for it at present, and to continue suffering this agony for the rest of one's life is not an alluring picture. Whereas Daventry—if he is successful—will cure me of the pain, though still leaving me an invalid for some years."

"I quite understand the attraction of the idea," Grace could not forbear the thrust. "But there's another thing, John. Doctor Daventry's cure may do as you say, but it may prove—fatal, almost at once."

He raised himself on one elbow, and his face went white. "He told me there was very little fear of that, and, Grace"—the man's voice was trembling—"he said that he had every hope that it would prove successful. . . . Why—why—you see, it will be his first

case, and it's very important to him that it should
prove a cure. So he's bound to take extra care, isn't
he? I mean . . ." His voice tailed off, and he sank
back, frightened and shaking.

She watched him contemptuously. What a miserable
specimen he was. And then a wave of pity came over
her. After all, cancer might make anyone a coward.
"I'm sure he'll be successful," she said reassuringly.
"He told me this afternoon that he felt absolutely
confident that he'd discovered the cure."

It was out before she had realized what she was
saying. Had he noticed it? Had he noticed the
slip? Why, oh, why had she not said this evening?
She had only meant to comfort him, cheer him up—
and, without thinking, if he put two and two together,
she had told him the name of the man she loved.

The shaking of his hand had ceased; he was staring
at her from his pillows intently.

"You met Doctor Daventry this afternoon?" he asked
slowly.

"I did; full of his new discovery." Her tone was
light, a shade too light; and suddenly John Marwood
laughed.

"How interesting," he murmured. "How very interesting. And where did you meet Doctor Daventry?"

"At tea." She had recovered herself; at all costs
she must rid his mind of this suspicion. "Lady
Grantley had quite a crowd."

But the suspicions of a suspicious nature are not
allayed so easily, and though John Marwood said no
more, she was conscious during the remaining two
minutes she stayed with him that he was watching her
covertly the whole time. Bryan's name was not mentioned again, nor was her meeting with him alluded to;
but as she bent over her husband and kissed him—a
thing she had not done for months, and which he

suffered resignedly—her uneasiness returned in full force. She felt instinctively that he knew. Then when she reached her own room she felt inclined to laugh at her fears. After all, why on earth should he put such a construction on her words? It might be as well, however, to warn Bryan when she saw him to-morrow. . . . John had a habit of asking disconcerting questions.

He had, and he had no intention of waiting till the next day to do so. He waited just long enough to hear his wife's door close; then he reached out a languid hand and picked up the telephone by his bed. With many moans and expressions of pain, which he periodically indulged in even when alone, he rang up Lady Grantley's house.

"It is Mr. Marwood speaking," he said to the butler who answered him. "Did Mrs. Marwood leave her vanity-bag behind to-day when she had tea with her ladyship? She did not have tea, you say? Really. I must have misunderstood Doctor Daventry. He told me he thought he'd seen it there. What? Doctor Daventry was not there either? Oh, my mistake. Sorry to have disturbed you."

He replaced the telephone and lay back on his pillows. So it was Daventry, after all, was it? And they thought themselves damned clever, did they? And they didn't see that they'd played right into his hands? Oh, no. They couldn't see that they'd given him a weapon which made him safe . . . Safe . . . And if by any chance any accident did occur. . . . He chuckled horribly, almost resigned to such a thing happening, so wonderful was his dream of revenge. Only he must catch them red-handed, must have an absolute certainty to go on. Nothing less than that would be sufficient.

And as he lay gloating in anticipation, suddenly the

pain began again. Stab—stab—stab; the red-hot skewers ran through him, while he writhed and moaned, biting at the sheets in his agony.

It was half an hour later that the impassive footman, whom he hated, found him whimpering like a little child.

"Your medicine, sir," he remarked, supremely unconcerned at the spectacle. "Also the washing-bill you wished to see. And I feel sure you will be glad to hear that the kitchen clock has been put right."

Without another glance at the figure in the bed, he left the room, closing the door noiselessly. And it was only as he stood in the passage outside that his face became convulsed with a dreadful fury. But in a moment it had gone; it was just the deferential, well-drilled manservant who joined the rest of the staff in the servants' hall.

"Your call, Simpson," said his partner, lighting a cigarette from the stump of an old one.

The impassive footman glanced at his cards. "I go one heart," he remarked quietly.

" 'Ow's the old swine to-night?" demanded another player.

"Mr. Marwood seems much as usual," returned Simpson. "One heart it is. You go down, partner."

The man who had asked the question snorted, but he said nothing more. They often used to remark on the fact in the servants' hall that Simpson seemed different—somehow.

"Keeps 'isself to 'isself," as the cook had summed it up on one occasion. And so it had been allowed to remain.

VII

It was half-past eleven the following morning that Doctor Arbuthnot descended the stairs in search of

Grace Marwood. Daventry was still with her husband in his room, though the further examination had been finished some quarter of an hour previously.

"I must be going, Mrs. Marwood." The old doctor patted her hand and smiled. "Between ourselves I wasn't really wanted at all this morning. Merely professional etiquette——"

"And what have you finally decided, Doctor Arbuthnot?"

"To let Doctor Daventry operate. Your husband won't hear of anything else. Seems more cheerful this morning." He smiled at her, and once more patted her hand. "You must keep him like that, my dear young lady. Keep him cheerful and smiling. . . . Worth ten years of life to smile. . . . Well, I must be off. Daventry will tell you everything when he comes down."

The worthy man bustled away, leaving Grace in a thoughtful mood. It wasn't like John to be cheerful: since she'd known him he never had been. And, like an idiot, she had forgotten to mention anything about Lady Grantley to Bryan before he went up to her husband. For a moment or two she thought of going upstairs and interrupting them; then it struck her that seeing her in the room with Bryan might recall suspicions to her husband's mind. That for a while he had suspected, she was positive; but ever since she had left his room the preceding night she had been endeavouring, more or less successfully, to persuade herself that she had reassured his mind. And that morning, when she had gone in to see him, he had certainly seemed quite pleasant and normal—as far, that is, as John Marwood ever succeeded in being anything of the sort. He had restrained his paroxysm of silent laughter till the door had closed behind her. . . .

She looked up as a step sounded in the passage above,

and the next moment Bryan Daventry was coming towards her down the stairs.

"Has Arbuthnot gone?" He stood in front of her, looking into her eyes.

"Yes." She nodded gravely. "He said you would tell me everything. Will you come in here?"

In silence he followed her into the sitting-room and closed the door; then in silence he stood by the mantelpiece looking down at her.

"Bryan," she said abruptly, "I was mad last night."

"So was I. May I smoke?"

"Of course. Do you realize, Bryan, that for a moment—I played with the idea of—of murder?"

"So did I." He gave a short, hard laugh. "I played with it—or, rather, it played with me—all through the night."

"And now?" She breathed the question half-fearfully.

"Why now, my dear, your charming husband will have the pleasure of being my first case. And everything which medical skill and careful nursing can perform, will be devoted to prolonging his damned life, and restoring him to perfect health."

He laughed again, harshly and bitterly. "It's not entirely altruism, Grace; I don't flatter myself on that point. But there are things one can't do, I suppose. And to put it on the lowest and most selfish motive, such a foundation for our life together—afterwards—would not prove a source of abiding happiness." He took a few steps up and down the room, while the woman watched him from her chair by the fire.

"Tell me, Bryan: did he ask you anything about Lady Grantley this morning?"

He stopped in his walk. "Lady Grantley!" he echoed in surprise. "No. Why on earth should he? I hardly know the woman."

Grace Marwood gave a sigh of relief. "Thank Heavens! But don't forget if by any chance he should, you had tea there yesterday. . . . And we discussed your new cure for cancer."

Briefly she told him of her slip the night before, and he nodded comprehendingly.

"I've got it, dear," he said, as she finished. "With a nature like this you've got to be mighty careful. Though I must say he seemed positively genial this morning." He took a few steps forward and stood by her chair, while his fingers played absently with her hair. "Oh! Grace, my darling," he whispered, "what a dirty trick of Fate. What a dirty trick."

Swiftly he bent and kissed her neck, where the little soft tendrils of hair left the smooth whiteness of her skin, and she shivered under his touch.

"Will it really mean the South of France, Bryan?" she asked slowly.

"Yes, darling." His voice was grave. "Or some warm spot like that."

"And shall I never see you?"

His hands clenched by his side, and the veins stood out on his forehead.

"My God!" he muttered; "you must see me. I can't imagine life with you blotted out completely. I shall come over and see how he's getting on, every now and then—and touch your hand, Grace, and hear your voice and look into your eyes. And then I shall come back again to blankness and work; while you stay out there with blankness and him. . . . A real pukka invalid at last. . . . The goal obtained. . . . Ordered to be one by a live doctor. . . . Why, the blighter is gloating over the prospect already."

For a while they fell silent, staring at the fire; then very gently she took one of his hands in her own.

"You must write to me, Bryan; tell me how things go with you. I couldn't go on without that."

"Write." He echoed the word scornfully. "Write. Oh, yes! I'll write. Send you bits of paper with letters and words scrawled on them. . . . A wonderful substitute for you—the flesh and blood of you—your whole glorious body. What's the good of a letter when there's nothing else to follow—except another letter, and then another?"

Abruptly he dropped her hand, and strode to the window, where he stood with his back to her, staring across the street outside. Faintly the roar of distant Piccadilly came into the quiet room; the monotonous, deadening sound which forms the eternal accompaniment to London's comedies and tragedies. The human units may laugh or cry, may be born to strut their allotted span and disappear unnoticed whence they came, but the buses still run past Hyde Park Corner. . . .

"I think I'll go, Grace." Slowly he turned and faced her. "I'm not very sure of myself to-day. The operation will take place to-morrow, here. I'll make all the necessary arrangements about nurses, and Arbuthnot will give the anæsthetic. Only light food for dinner to-night, and nothing to-morrow morning."

"Very well." A little pale, but quite composed, she rose as he spoke. "There's only one thing, Bryan, I want you to know. Out of the madness last night has come sanity, but the possible alternative still remains. You have said so yourself—before we knew anything about John. Should he die, I shall know that you did everything in your power to make the operation a success. You understand that?"

"He mustn't die; he won't die." Roughly he took her in his arms. "Don't you see, Grace. I daren't let him die—I daren't."

"But you're only human, Bryan."

"I don't care—I may be. But John Marwood—
must not die. . . . Not after what we've—said, and
thought. . . ."

For a while he held her at arm's length, devouring
her hungrily with his eyes; then with a smothered cry
he drew her to him, and covered her face with kisses.
"My darling," he whispered again and again—"My
darling."

And at that moment the door opened and John
Marwood entered.

"A most entertaining spectacle," he murmured.
"Would it be indiscreet to ask if this is your normal
method of procedure, Doctor Daventry?"

He was clad in his dressing-gown and as he closed
the door with ostentatious deliberation Bryan Daventry
had a fleeting glimpse of a dark, impassive face peering
over Marwood's shoulder from the hall beyond. It
was the footman who had been at hand during his
examination that morning, and in that one brief second,
before the door closed, the thing which dominated his
mind was not the master, but the man. For there was
a strange, inscrutable look on the footman's face—a
look of mingled mockery and scorn. And it seemed
to Daventry that the object of the look was not himself,
but the malevolent hobbling figure in the dressing-gown.

"I repeat, Doctor Daventry," gasped the harsh voice,
as the sick man sank into a chair, "is this your usual
method of conducting your cases?"

With a slight frown the young doctor thrust his
hands into his pockets and stared at his patient; the
situation was undeniably awkward.

"No, Mr. Marwood," he remarked at length, "it is
not my usual procedure."

"Indeed," murmured the other. "Most gratifying!
Then might I be permitted to ask why am I thus
honoured?"

Daventry glanced at Grace; she was staring at the fire, one foot tapping ceaselessly on the fender. Then with a slight shrug of his shoulders, he turned back to Marwood.

"The reason, I should imagine, is fairly clear," he remarked gravely. "I love your wife."

"How kind of you." Marwood gave a grating chuckle. "And judging by the—shall we say—amorous position I found you in, one might almost be led to suppose that my wife loves you?"

His cold eyes searched his wife's face, and after a moment she nodded.

"I told you yesterday, John," she said quietly, "that I was in love with a man."

"Only neglecting to mention his name," he returned. "But I may say this has hardly come as a surprise after what I found out last night. After your departure, my dear Grace, I took the precaution of ringing up Lady Grantley. And, to my horror and surprise, I found that not only had you not been to tea there yesterday, but that Doctor Daventry as well had not honoured her with his presence. Wherefore, by a process of inductive reasoning, partially interrupted by a bout of intense agony, I came to the conclusion that you had lied to me. Why lie on such a matter, unless there is something to conceal? And then, remembering our interesting and harmonious chat after dinner, I put two and two together. One is glad to have such indisputable confirmation that the answer is true."

Hunched up and malignant, John Marwood sat in his chair, while his venomous eyes rested first on the doctor and then on his wife.

"You neither of you seem very loquacious," he snarled.

"You seem to be supplying that end of the business," said Daventry calmly.

"Don't talk to me like that, damn you," shrieked the other, his voice shaking with rage. "Have you got no shame whatever, you scoundrel, coming into a man's house and making love to his wife, when he is at death's door upstairs."

"If you don't stop exciting yourself, you'll have another bout of pain," said the doctor, still in the same calm voice, and the threat had the desired effect.

With a great effort John Marwood controlled himself, though the seething volcano of hatred in his mind still showed on his face.

"If I did, it would probably afford you endless amusement," he sneered.

"Endless," agreed Daventry. "And now, in view of what has occurred, it might be as well to come to the point. As a form of entertainment, this conversation bores me. I have told you I love your wife; she has told you she loves me. But I wish you to understand quite clearly, Mr. Marwood, that there has never been anything more between us than what you saw to-day."

The invalid gave a grating laugh, but Daventry continued unmoved. "In one way, I am glad you found out; it absolves me at once from the necessity of operating on you. I therefore throw up the case, and either you or I can invent some good reason to palm off on Doctor Arbuthnot."

He paused, fascinated against his will by the hideous silent laughter of the man in the chair.

"So you intend to throw up the case, Doctor Daventry, do you?" chuckled the other. "Refuse to operate, do you?"

"Somewhat naturally, I assume that you would prefer I did not," replied Daventry slowly. "And anyway, I would prefer not to."

"Do you count?" asked John Marwood suavely. "Do your wishes matter vastly?"

"They matter everything, Mr. Marwood," snapped the doctor. "On every ground I throw up the case, and refuse to operate."

"Then, Doctor Daventry," said the other slowly, "I shall institute divorce proceedings against you forthwith. There's no good laughing, because neither you nor my wife will find it a laughing matter. I don't say that I should get my divorce, but——well, you won't forget, will you, that I took the precaution of having a witness this morning. And I don't think it would do you much good professionally, Doctor Daventry; and I don't think it would do my wife much good socially, Doctor Daventry. In fact," his voice rose to a hoarse snarl, "I'll drag you both in the mud, and then I'll laugh at you."

"You won't laugh for long, Mr. Marwood," answered Daventry, his face a little white. "You'll be dead."

"I'll laugh long enough to see you hounded out of your profession. I'll laugh long enough to see everybody's door closed against my wife."

"You inhuman devil," said Daventry slowly. "Your mind is more diseased than your body."

"Perhaps it is," sneered the other. "At any rate, I don't go round to other men's houses professionally, and then seduce their wives." For a second he cowered back as if afraid Daventry would strike him; then, a little more calmly, he continued. "So you had better decide—and decide at once. Either you operate to-morrow, or the world will have another titbit of scandal to digest over its meals."

With his hands still in his pockets, Bryan Daventry walked over to the window. Once more the roar of the traffic came plainly to his ears—a contrast to the dead silence of the room behind. He heard the sudden rustle of Grace's dress as she moved, then absently he stared at a man opposite who was busy polishing the outside of a window. He was sitting on the ledge in one of the wooden flower-stands beloved of London houses, and the doctor idly wondered what would happen if the outside gave way. The earth would fall on to the pavement, but would the man? And if he did, would he still continue to whistle that damned tune from the Alhambra?

"Why are you so anxious that I should operate, Mr. Marwood, in view of what you know?" His voice sounded singularly lifeless to his ears.

"Because I consider you are the best man for the purpose."

Once again there was silence in the room. The window-polisher was standing up to his work now, and two errand-boys were staring at him enraptured.

"I suppose you have remembered what I told you," continued Daventry, "that there is a chance of my cure proving fatal?"

"I hope not, Doctor Daventry, for both our sakes —and my wife's." The voice was soft and menacing, and Daventry swung round on his heel.

"What do you mean?" he said quickly.

"Why," murmured the other, "I merely alluded to a very natural precaution on my part. Should anything happen to me—which, in the hands of a man of your skill, I do not anticipate for a moment—I shall leave a letter to be opened at my death. I shall, of course, make no accusation in it; I shall merely state—with the witness's signature attached—what I happened unfortunately to see this morning. And if people are uncharitable enough to draw their own con- clusions——"

"Stop!" thundered the doctor. "That settles it.

Under no circumstances whatever will I undertake the operation under such conditions."

"Really." John Marwood smiled gently. "Then I will tell my lawyers to institute proceedings at once."

"But, John, think." For the first time Grace Marwood intervened, and her husband with studied politeness listened to her. "Such a bargain is wicked—unfair. It's a new cure—untried; and Doctor Daventry told you last night that there was the chance of its proving fatal. The bare chance . . . against absolute recovery. You can't—you simply can't—make such a condition."

"Nevertheless, I do. Doctor Daventry need not accept it unless he wishes."

"In other words," said Bryan in a hard voice, "it's heads I win, tails you lose, Mr. Marwood."

"More or less, more or less," agreed Marwood. "With one slight modification. In the happy event of the operation being brilliantly successful, we both win, my dear Daventry—in fact, we all three win. I become completely cured; you lay the foundation of a still more brilliant reputation; Grace continues her social career in complete safety. It is," he murmured, "a form of insurance to produce, if possible, additional care—when under the anæsthetic. Accidents will happen—and they mustn't—not this time." His cold eyes fixed themselves on the young doctor. "You see, I am in a very difficult position. The one man who would benefit most by my death is the one man in whose hands I must place my life. Do you blame me for taking—er—precautions?"

For a long while Daventry stared at him in silence, and if John Marwood had expected a furious outburst at his insult he was disappointed. For Daventry's thoughts were not in the room; they were centred round a fantastic, ghastly, mental struggle waged through the sleepless hours of the past night. And it seemed to him that a Fate—inexorable but just—had confronted him. It was retribution, and only the success of his skill could wipe out his sin. The challenge was thrown down; so be it; he would accept the challenge. He could not do less.

"Very well, Mr. Marwood," he answered slowly. "I agree. I will operate to-morrow as I arranged."

Without another word he left the room, and as he closed the door, his patient's harsh, grating chuckle came to his ears.

"Your coat, sir."

He turned to find the impassive footman holding his overcoat in readiness.

"Might I ask if you are operating to-morrow, sir?"

"I am," said Daventry briefly.

"I trust you will be successful, sir."

Bryan Daventry looked at him quickly, and for a moment the eyes of the two men met. And behind the footman's steady glance there lurked the ghost of a smile.

VIII

To say that John Marwood felt pleased with himself would be totally inadequate. For the remainder of the day he literally hugged his cleverness to his bosom; he turned it over and over in his mind; he reviewed it from every conceivable angle. To have combined a subtle revenge with the maximum chance of his own complete cure struck him as being the work of a genius. The fools! The treacherous fools! And when the operation had proved successful, he wouldn't give them away publicly—that would finish things far too quickly. He'd just hold his knowledge over their heads, and every now and then he'd give

the wheel another little turn so as to keep them on
the rack. He even thought out a few of the remarks
he could say to his wife, as he sat in his invalid chair
on the sunny promenade at Nice or Cannes; biting,
sarcastic little sneers which would make her writhe.
... And at intervals her lover would come out to
examine him, and he could watch the two of them
together as a cat watches a mouse—gloatingly. Because he'd got them; *got them;* GOT THEM; and as
he realized it he shook both his fists in the air, and
the sweat glistened on his forehead with the strength
of his passion.

A faint twinge of pain sobered him down; he must
be careful—just at present—not to excite himself.
Afterwards it would be different—after he was cured.
But until then he wanted no return of that vile agony.
Besides, there was one more thing that had to be done
before the operation took place—in case anything should
happen. He refused to allow himself to consider it as
anything but the barest possibility—everybody said
Daventry was the most brilliant of the younger surgeons—but just in case of accidents it had to be done.
Besides, in every way it was the most subtle touch in
his whole scheme, and from the artistic point of view
it was inconceivable that it should be omitted. He'd
have to get that impassive brute of a footman to do
his share of it, so tact would be necessary. It was a
pity he hadn't always been quite so polite to him as
he might have been.

For a quarter of an hour the silence of the room
was only broken by the scratching of a pen on paper.
The first effort he tore up in disgust—it failed in pun-
gency; but the second proved more satisfactory, and
when he had read it through and digested it, he rang
the bell by his side.

"Ah, Simpson," he said as the door opened, "I am

sorry to have to disturb you at this unusual hour, but the circumstances are peculiar."

The footman's eyebrows went up at such an unheard-of speech, and his shoulders shook slightly. Then, with exactly the right touch of deference, he stepped to the side of the bed. "Not at all, sir," he murmured. "What can I do for you?"

"It's a terrible thing, Simpson," continued Marwood in a low, sad voice, "to have to discuss with anyone; but it is made easier in your case, because you saw the occurrence. I allude—to what happened —this morning. What we both of us saw when— when I went into the sitting-room downstairs."

"A most regrettable incident, sir," said Simpson sympathetically.

"One finds it difficult to know what to do," remarked Marwood, staring at the fire. "Very difficult. I am an invalid and, of course, Mrs. Marwood is young; but still——" He sighed heavily.

"Such an incident should not go unpunished, sir," returned Simpson firmly.

"I agree, Simpson; I agree." Apparently the fool was going to be easy. "But what can I do? My hands are tied. They made a bargain with me—me, a man with cancer. Unless I consented to their— acquaintance continuing, Doctor Daventry refused to operate. And he's the only man in London who can cure me. Simpson, I am powerless in his hands."

For a moment the footman seemed to have some difficulty in speaking. Then—"Monstrous, sir," he murmured. "Atrocious."

"Unless I condone their sin, he leaves me to a lingering death of agony. What can I do?" Weakly he stretched out his hands. "And what is worse, Simpson, is that there is a chance of the cure proving fatal ; as you may know, it's a new and untried one. Supposing it did prove fatal—and it is so easy for a mistake to occur in such matters." He looked meaningly at the footman, who inclined his head slowly. "Undoubtedly, sir," he remarked. "It is a very awkward position for you to be in."

"No one to turn to—not a soul," said John Marwood piteously. "Deserted even by my wife. It's not fair, is it? Not a square deal. And so I've written a letter, Simpson, which I want you to witness; and I shall send it to my lawyer to be opened in the event of my death." He glanced covertly at the man standing beside him, but his face was expressionless. "You don't mind doing that for me, do you?"

"Far from it, sir. I shall be delighted."

And John Marwood's fists clenched ecstatically under the bedclothes.

"I'll read you what I've written, Simpson," he continued after a moment. "It's not very long:

" 'I, John Marwood, suffering from cancer, from which terrible malady I am to be operated on to-morrow morning by Doctor Bryan Daventry, who will carry out his new cure for the first time, write these words, which will only be revealed in the event of my death. On going downstairs this morning, I discovered my wife, Grace Marwood, in the arms of Bryan Daventry, who had just concluded a professional visit to the house. They admitted their love for one another, and openly boasted to me of their misconduct in the past. Further, Doctor Daventry threatened to throw up the case and refuse to operate unless I condoned their guilty relations in the future—thereby condemning me to a lingering death or a shameful alternative. But more was to come. There is in his new cure, he admits, the possibility of a fatal result almost at once; from the expression on his face as he said it, I read the sinister intention at the back of his mind. I believe the operation will prove fatal—*in my case.*

" 'And so, standing, as I fear, at the threshold of eternity, I put these facts on paper, for people to draw their own conclusions.

" 'JOHN MARWOOD.' "

He glanced at the man beside him, but the footman's face was as impassive as ever; then he looked back at the paper in his hand.

"Under that, Simpson, I have added the following, which, if you will, and if you think it just, I will ask you to sign:

" 'I'—let me see, what is your Christian name?— 'Charles,' you say—'I, Charles Simpson, footman in the employ of John Marwood, Esq., hereby state that on the morning of November 25th, 1919, I saw Grace Marwood in the arms of Doctor Daventry, who had just concluded a professional visit to my employer.'

"If you will sign that, Simpson, I will write a covering letter to my lawyer, and then seal up that statement."

"Certainly, sir," answered Simpson. "A very just accusation."

And John Marwood might not have permitted himself the luxury of a sardonic smile had he seen the look on the footman's face as he signed. But since his back was turned away from the bed, his employer could hardly have been expected to.

"Thank you, Simpson." He glanced at the signature, and then, just before he folded the paper up, he glanced at it again.

"Your writing seems vaguely familiar to me," he remarked jovially. "And very good writing it is too. Well, there it is—with the covering letter. Will you post it for me this afternoon, Simpson?"

"Certainly, sir. Is there anything else you require, sir?"

"No, thank you. Oh! except one thing. Forty-eight, you said, I think. You're wrong, Simpson; sixty in future."

"I thank you, sir," murmured the footman from the door.

He went out, closing it without a sound. And it was only as he got to the top of the stairs that he paused and listened. For the bed in John Marwood's room was shaking as a bed will shake if the occupant is convulsed with laughter.

IX

It was in the same sitting-room in which the hideous bargain had been made the previous day that Grace Marwood waited for the result of the operation. Since Bryan had left the morning before she had only seen her husband once, and then only for a few minutes, with a nurse present the whole time.

She had remained in her own room, shunning the servants as far as possible. That the whole household knew by now she was fully aware—especially as she had never particularly liked Simpson. But as the day passed by she came to the conclusion that they must be a particularly good brand. Keenly alert though she was for the faintest trace of veiled insolence, she could detect nothing. Her maid was a little more solicitous for her comfort, perhaps, but otherwise absolutely as usual; Parkins, the butler; Mrs. Johnson, the cook—in none of them could she see the slightest difference. And after a while she ceased to worry; what did such a trifle as the opinions of servants matter compared to the other things at stake?

Whatever happened, the future seemed to hold no hope. At best—or was it at worst?—a vista of dreary years tied to a professional invalid who knew her secret and who could be trusted to remind her of the fact every day. And if not that—she drew a deep breath—if her husband did die! What then? For Bryan, professional ruin—or, at the very least, the rest of his life spent under a cloud of ominous blackness. For herself—social ruin.

Almost she wished that he had stuck to his original refusal; at any rate, that would have settled the matter definitely. And there could have been no suspicion then of the far more dreadful accusation which, however unfounded, would be bound to get about, if— there was a fatal result. Resolutely she refused to think of it; Bryan, with his genius, would succeed— must succeed.

She had had one glimpse of him as he passed through the hall an hour ago, and he had seemed to her like a man in a dream. Doctor Arbuthnot had been with him, and another doctor who, she gathered, had come more or less as a spectator. And then the door upstairs had closed, and for an hour she had been waiting. Would they never finish?

Once she had crept to the foot of the stairs to listen, but everything was silent. At that moment Bryan was operating; at that moment the wheel of Fate was turning—turning one way or the other. But which? With a shudder she went back to the sitting-room. Would they never finish?

Suddenly she stiffened and sat upright; a door above had opened, and someone was coming down the stairs. It was a man's step, and she waited tensely as he crossed the hall.

It was Doctor Arbuthnot, and he stood for a moment by the door, smiling at her.

"A most successful operation, my dear Mrs. Marwood," he announced. "Your husband has stood it wonderfully, and——"

She rose to her feet, holding to the arm of her chair for support, and suddenly the old doctor's kindly face became blurred and indistinct. There was a roaring in her ears and then a merciful oblivion. And Doctor Arbuthnot, catching her as she fell, turned as Bryan Daventry and the other doctor entered the room.

"Fainted," he said briefly. "The news proved too much. Just help me lift her on to that sofa."

For a few moments they bent over her; then, as the colour began to return to her cheeks, Bryan Daventry stepped back and stood watching her from near the fire-place.

"Just rest a little, Mrs. Marwood." Doctor Arbuthnot smiled reassuringly. "I broke the good news too abruptly, I'm afraid, and you fainted."

She slowly opened her eyes and stared round the room. What had he said—"stood it wonderfully?" So the wheel had turned; Fate had decided. And at that moment her eyes and Bryan's met and held. Then he looked away, and she lay back once more.

"A most brilliant operation, Daventry." The doctor she did not know was speaking. "You are to be congratulated. A great step in medical science."

"Thank you," answered Bryan, and his voice was dull and lifeless. "He stood it well. And in ten years or so we shall know for certain."

The woman stirred restlessly. Ten years! Oh! God—and then the others after that. . . .

"I am much obliged to you for letting me witness it," continued the other. "And it will be interesting to know from time to time how Mr. Marwood progresses."

"Most," assented Bryan. "I'll let you know, Birkett—keep you posted with the latest bulletins." He held out his hand abruptly. "Good-bye. Glad you managed to come, in spite of the short notice."

"Glad you asked me," returned the other cordially. With a slight bow to Mrs. Marwood he left the room, and Doctor Arbuthnot glanced at Bryan Daventry curiously.

"Difficult fellow to get hold of is Birkett," he said. "Usually too busy to eat."

"I made a particular point of his coming," said Daventry shortly. "Rang him up late last night. Don't you bother to wait, Arbuthnot. I'm going to have another look at the patient when he's quite out of the chloroform."

"Right." With a smile he held out his hand to Mrs. Marwood. "Don't move; lie still a bit longer. And in a short while you'll have your husband out of bed and free to travel to some nice warm climate. I envy you, my dear young lady, envy you. My old bones like an English winter less and less each year."

With a cheerful wave to Daventry he fussed out of the room, and it was not until they heard the front door close behind him that Grace Marwood sat up on the sofa and stared at Bryan dully.

"Ten years—of hell. And not over then. I don't think I can, Bryan."

"You must, my dear; and so must I." He gave a little mirthless laugh. "It's the penalty we've got to pay." Then, contemptuously—"He reminded me of the letter he had sent his lawyers this morning, before I began."

"I think that's what sticks in my throat more than anything," said the girl slowly. "He thinks he threatened you into operating—and operating successfully. And he'll never let me forget it."

"What does it matter what he thinks?" answered Daventry wearily. "At any rate, you are safe now. Of the mentality of a man who would drive such a bargain the less said the better; but that he was in a position to do so is an indisputable fact. He knew I wouldn't let you suffer—if there was the faintest possibility of avoiding it." Mechanically he lit a cigarette. "Well, I took him at his word, and he's not going to die—though I brought Birkett round in case of complications. My debt to him—our debt to him —is absolutely sponged out. As far as a human being may say such a thing, I have given him back his life. And if, Grace,"—his voice grew hard—"in the days to come he grows too vile, and you can't stand him— well, my dear, send for me, and I'll come. There is a limit to the demands one human being may make on another."

For a while he stood in front of her, watching her gravely; then, very gently, he raised her to her feet.

"My dear, dear woman," he whispered, and, bending forward, he kissed her on the lips. For a moment she clung to him, then, with a little smile, he raised both her hands to his lips. "It's a funny world," he said slowly, "damned funny. Take care of yourself, my darling."

Abruptly he turned away, and long after the door had closed behind him she stood where he had left her. Then at last, with a pitiful little moan, she sank down by the sofa and covered her face with her hands. And the inexorable turning of the wheel through the dreary future creaked mockingly through her brain.

For two hours she crouched there motionless; then with slow, lagging steps she passed through the hall and up the stairs to her husband's room.

X

It was a week before the hospital nurse could be dispensed with—a wasted week to John Marwood. Only on rare occasions had he seen his wife alone— and never the doctor. Whenever Daventry had been the nurse had remained in the room, which had necessitated his bottling up his verbal arrows, or so disguising them that they had lost half their sting.

He had tried congratulating Daventry once on the success of the operation, in a way which only just veiled the innuendo underneath, but the result had not been a success.

The cold, frozen stare which had greeted the remark on the part of the nurse, who cordially loathed her patient, and the contemptuous indifference of the doctor himself, had stung him to the boiling-point of fury. But he could wait: there was plenty of time yet to make his wife and her lover feel the lash. It was typical of the man that he always thought of Daventry as her lover, though at the bottom of his mind he knew he was not.

With his wife he had been a little more successful. He had had the satisfaction of seeing her flinch and change colour at his sneers, but she had deigned no answer, and had finally left the room in silence. But it didn't matter: there was plenty of time—years yet —to revenge himself on the guilty pair.

The nurse left in the morning, and it was in the afternoon, after a light lunch, that life began to look really good to John Marwood. That cursed, thin-lipped woman would badger him no longer; he was free: free to enjoy himself. . . . He had written the preceding day to his lawyer, requesting him to return the sealed letter, as the necessity for it no longer existed, and he was expecting to get it back by the next delivery. A wise precaution—to wait till the nurse had gone, undoubtedly: she looked the sort of woman who would read anything. . . . He hadn't quite made up his mind yet whether he would destroy it or not. There didn't seem to be much object in keeping it, and yet it was rather a pity to do away with such a literary gem, especially with Simpson's signed statement underneath. A useful document to possess: he particularly liked that phrase, "at the threshold of eternity." No: on mature consideration he would keep it. Quite possibly it would come in handy later on.

A knock came at the door, and a footman brought in the mail. Yes: there was a letter right enough from his lawyer's firm, and he picked it out and put it on one side to deal with later. Then, with a sudden change of expression, he picked it up again; it struck him that it seemed very thin to contain any enclosure. In fact, he realized at once that it didn't, and hurriedly slit open the envelope.

"DEAR SIR," [it ran] . . .
"In the absence of our Mr. Gatehouse on a short holiday we beg to say in reply to yours of yesterday's date that we are unable to find any trace of the sealed letter to which you refer."

And he had addressed it to Gatehouse, care of his firm, so that in case he was away it would be opened by them.

"Tell Simpson to come to me," he said querulously to the footman who was making up the fire.

"Very good, sir." The man departed, and John Marwood again read the brief, typewritten letter. "Unable to find any trace." What did the fool mean?

"Simpson," he cried agitatedly, as the impassive footman came into the room, "you remember that letter I gave you to send to my lawyer the day before I was operated on?"

"Perfectly, sir." A quick change came over his face, as if the question was a little unexpected, and necessitated a change of plan.

"Well, I've just had a letter saying they never had it." In his excitement he sat up in bed, and as his eyes fell on the footman his jaw dropped foolishly. "Wh—what on earth are you doing, Simpson?" he stammered.

"Locking the door, Mr. Marwood," returned Simpson imperturbably, "in order to ensure that no one will interrupt our little conversation. . . ."

"But I—I don't understand.   Who is going to interrupt us?   And, damn you, who told you to sit down?"
John Marwood was rapidly losing his temper.   If this
impertinent fellow thought he was going to presume,
he'd soon find his error.   His presence was no longer
in the least degree necessary: in fact, in many ways
it might be a good thing to get rid of him at once.
And then, with a sudden, unspeakable rage, he saw
that this impassive, insufferable servant had drawn from
his pocket the very letter which he had been told to
send to the lawyer over a week ago.   He sat there,
lolling in his chair, holding it loosely between his
fingers, and on his face there hovered a faint, mocking
smile.

"Is it too much to hope," said Marwood icily, "that
I may be honoured with some small explanation?"

"Far from it, John Marwood," returned the other.
"It is in order that you may have an explanation in
full that I have locked the door."

The invalid's eyes narrowed.   To be called John
Marwood—by one of his footmen!   What was it—
blackmail?   He became uneasily aware that some of
the statements in his death-bed accusation were, to
put it mildly, somewhat exaggerated.   But this man
couldn't know that: anyway, he couldn't prove it.

"In the first place," continued Simpson impassively,
"shall we consider this interesting effusion?   Is it too
much to say that it is an abominable tissue of vile and
malicious lies from start to finish, which by reason of
the time when it was written would have carried conviction in the event of your death?"

"You impertinent scoundrel," spluttered Marwood.
"Give me that letter at once."

Simpson laughed.   "Always ready to learn, John
Marwood, I continued to listen outside the door of the
sitting-room that day, after you had left the vantage-

point of the key-hole and gone in. And so I happen to know what really occurred. This"—he twiddled the letter between his fingers and thumb, "hardly seems to be exactly—shall we say—accurate. You seem to be finding it a little difficult to speak, so while you compose yourself—for I have a little more to say to you, John Marwood—I think I will take the precaution of removing that hand-bell from your reach. And I may say," he continued, as he resumed his seat, "that if you shout, I shall gag you."

The man in bed stared at him with dilated eyes: was he mad—or dreaming?

"In the first place," said Simpson, leaning forward and speaking in his usual dispassionate voice, "do you really think that I'm a footman by trade?"

"I—I——" stammered Marwood, "I've never thought about it."

"Do you remember, John Marwood, in the days when you had a business, a certain confidential clerk to whom, for some reason or other, you took a dislike?"

"My God!" muttered the invalid weakly. "You're . . ."

"Beginning to come back, is it? Yes—I'm Henry Firebrace: whom you sacked without a character, because in the vile meanness of your petty bullying soul you knew he despised and loathed you. You faked up a reason—anything was good enough—and you sacked him, at a time when clerks were a drug on the market, and his wife was having her first child. He tramped all over London, John Marwood, looking, begging for work—but no one wanted clerks, certainly not those without a character. And he couldn't get work." The speaker's dark eyes glowed sombrely. "No work, John Marwood—no money. And his wife was having her first child. Do you know what happened? The child was born dead, and the mother died two days later. . . ."

A log hissed and spluttered in the grate, while the man in bed stared fascinated at the speaker. Henry Firebrace! Now that he knew, he marvelled he had never recognized him before, great though the change was.

"He made one appeal to you, John Marwood, if you remember. Told you the reason of his appeal. . . . Went—down—on—his—knees. . . . And you laughed in his face, and told him that yours was a business company, and not a babies' crèche." The man in the chair swallowed twice: then in the same level voice he continued:

"For a while after his wife had died, Henry Firebrace went mad. And while he was mad he committed a burglary, and was caught by the police and sent to prison. When he came out the war had just started, and the thought of it appealed to him. So Henry Firebrace died, and Charles Simpson enlisted, and in the ordinary course of affairs was called on to kill a German every now and then. . . . And one night he started to think, John Marwood. The Germans whom he killed had never done him any harm: many of them, doubtless, were quite decent, pleasant fellows. So if he killed them, was there any logical reason why in the fullness of time he shouldn't—provided he came through all right—kill the man who had done him such grievous harm?"

"One is war: the other is murder," said Marwood thickly.

"True: but this thinker was not concerned with such niceties. All he could bother with was the thought that he would infinitely sooner put a bayonet into the stomach of the man he hated, than into that of a complete stranger, even though he was a German. So he played with the idea, John Marwood: and the more he played with it—the more he liked it." The footman's eyes, hard now and merciless, were fixed on the trembling man in bed.

"In due course he was demobilized, and having found out where you lived, he applied for a post as your footman. He heard you were an invalid, and if he had found that in truth you were—that you were, in reality, a sick man—he might even at the eleventh hour have stayed his hand, and forgone his revenge. Instead, he found that you were even viler and more utterly inhuman than you had been in the past, and that your peculiar faculty for inspiring hatred in those around you had grown with the years. So he decided to bide his time. . . ."

With a trembling hand Marwood wiped the sweat from his forehead.

"He liked to gloat over you, John Marwood, and say to himself, 'Some day I will do to him what in the past he did to me.' And not one single word you spoke, not one single act you did, ever tended to inspire in him one vestige of pity. He saw you for what you are—utterly and infinitely despicable. And then came the day when they found you had cancer." He paused and smiled slowly. "Once again he decided to give you a chance: cancer is a sufficient punishment in itself. Once again the brief twinge of mercy was killed at birth—even as his child was born dead, John Marwood—by the interview he overheard in the sitting-room. And then—this letter." He held it up in front of the other's face, and this time he laughed gently. "This letter . . . which you so trustingly gave him to post. Had you died, John Marwood, under the operation, it would have been handed direct to Doctor Daventry—even as it will be handed to him after your death—now."

With a strangled scream Marwood started up, only to be hurled back again on his pillows by the impassive footman.

"He didn't want you to die," continued Simpson. "He told Doctor Arbuthnot that he trusted the operation would be successful. And it was, John Marwood, wonderfully so. So successful that for the past week, from what he knows of your mentality, you have been gloating over the future in front of you. A revenge such as you love is yours for the asking—so you have been thinking: and in that dark, fetid mind of yours you have been planning every detail of it. . . . And now, you wretched brute, it's going to be snatched away from you." With his face blazing with implacable hatred he rose and stood over the cowering man. "For you're going to die, John Marwood, even as my wife died: and as you die just remember that your wife will be able to find happiness at last with the man she loves—and that he has been started on the road to fame by you."

His hands were on Marwood's throat, and as the terrified man's mouth opened in a plea for mercy, the footman slipped in a gag. Then he released him and stood back watching the agonized terror in the rolling eyes. After a moment he turned away and took a bottle off the shelf. He filled a wine-glass standing on the table by the bed, and then once more he bent over the other man.

"A little prussic acid, John Marwood," he murmured, and deftly holding his hand steady, he poured the contents of the glass into the other's mouth. His eyes bored into his victim's brain as he carefully caught a few drops that were spilled on his handkerchief. Then, with a quick wrench, he extracted the gag. . . .

For a moment or two he watched the writhing, convulsed man: then, as impassively as ever, he took three or four of the bottles off the shelf and placed them on the table.

And before he softly turned the key in the door and left the room, the body of John Marwood had ceased to writhe. Prussic acid is rapid in its action. . . .

XI

It was two hours later, in the middle of tea, that a violent peal on the bell of John Marwood's room disturbed the assembled servants.

"He seems to be becoming convalescent," murmured Simpson.

"Go up and see, will you?" ordered Mr. Parkins. "Our period of peace is over, I suppose."

Simpson rose and walked to the door, only to come back in a moment or two looking a little agitated.

"It's Mrs. Marwood, Mr. Parkins. I think something has happened. You'd better come."

Majestically the butler rose and followed the footman—only to pause and turn white at what he heard.

"Dead, madam?" It was Simpson who was speaking. "Impossible. Why, when I left Mr. Marwood . . ." He ran up the stairs quickly.

"Ring up Doctor Daventry at once, Parkins," said Grace Marwood. "Oh! it's dreadful. . . ." She sank into a chair, half-fainting.

"Doctor Daventry will be round at once, madam," said the butler in a shaking voice, and as he spoke Simpson came down the stairs.

"I fear, madam, there is no doubt what has happened," he murmured gently. "By some extraordinary error, Mr. Marwood must have taken a dose of prussic acid in mistake for his tonic. Both bottles are on the table by his bed: but the glass smells strongly of the poison."

The appearance of her maid cut short any further

conversations, and the butler and Simpson retired once more to the servants' hall to discuss the sudden tragedy.

"Undoubtedly prussic acid," said Simpson. "The smell is unmistakable: the effect almost instantaneous. And if he drank the whole glass it was enough to kill ten men."

"What was it doing there at all?" demanded the butler.

Simpson shrugged his shoulders. "Something to do with Doctor Daventry's treatment, I expect. It's labelled 'poison,' and marked 'for external application only.'"

"Well," declaimed Mrs. Thomson, "it don't seem right to speak ill of the dead, and 'im not cold—but for all that, I says 'Good riddance.' And I don't mind who 'ears me, neither. Lor'! Mr. Simpson, you 'ave a nerve, you 'ave. Going on with your tea, an' all. An' just seen 'im dead."

Simpson smiled. "We got used to it in France, Mrs. Thomson, you know. A little more sugar this time, please."

"What was he doing when you left him?" said the butler after a while.

"Taking his tonic—as far as I could see," remarked Simpson, helping himself to jam.

"The person I'm sorry for is that there young doctor," remarked Mr. Parkins sententiously. "After being so successful—for this to happen."

"Quite, Mr. Parkins: quite," agreed Simpson. "However, these accidents will happen."

"You're quite right, Simpson," remarked the butler reminiscently. "They will. Why, when I was with Lord Nairn . . ."

But the providential arrival of one of the footmen saved them from the remainder of the oft-told harrowing details.

"The doctor wants to see you, Simpson. Up in the bedroom."

As impassively as ever, Simpson left the room.

"I understand you saw Mr. Marwood last?" Bryan Daventry was standing at the foot of the bed as he entered.

"I did, sir—to the best of my belief." He glanced at the figure in the bed over which the bedclothes had been completely pulled.

"What was he doing?"

"Preparing to take his tonic, sir, I think. I heard the sound of bottles clinking as I left the room."

"How came this bottle of prussic acid on the table beside the bed?"

"I really couldn't say, sir. A most unfortunate tragedy." His steady, inscrutable eyes met those of the doctor, and after a while he felt in his pocket and produced a paper. "This might interest you, sir," he murmured. "I found it on the floor when I came up after Mrs. Marwood had discovered her husband's death."

Casually, Bryan Daventry glanced at it: then, as he read, his face grew black with rage. It was John Marwood's "death-bed" accusation.

"The infernal blackguard," he muttered.

"Precisely, sir," remarked the footman. "An infernal blackguard."

"Do you object if I burn that?" said the doctor slowly.

"If you don't, sir, I shall."

For a moment or two Daventry studied the paper in his hand: then he stared at the footman. "It looks as if something had been cut off at the bottom," he remarked slowly.

"Now you mention it, sir, so it does," agreed Simpson. "Shall I put it in the fire?"

In silence they watched it burn: then the footman stabbed the ashes with a poker till nothing but a fine dust was left.

"I don't quite understand you, my friend," said Daventry thoughtfully.

"Indeed, sir," murmured the footman.

"Have you always been a footman?"

"Always is a long time, sir," remarked Simpson quietly. "Might I ask if you have definitely decided on the cause of Mr. Marwood's death?"

"Yes, my friend, I have. Mr. Marwood died as the result of a dose of prussic acid administered——" he paused, and was it his imagination, or was there, indeed, the ghost of a smile lurking again behind those expressionless eyes—"administered inadvertently by himself."

"In mistake for his tonic," murmured the footman.

"In mistake for his tonic," agreed the doctor.

Simpson moved towards the door, and it was just as he was opening it that he spoke once more. And this time his voice was a little different.

"An infernal blackguard is dead, Doctor Daventry. It may be of interest to you and Mrs. Marwood to know that your secret has died with him."

He left the room: and for a long while Bryan Daventry stood frowning at the closed door. Then, with a last look at the motionless figure in the bed, he, too, went out. . . . And dimly through the window came the roar of the traffic from distant Piccadilly.

THE END

9 781473 311008